PINK

AUNT DIMITY GOES WEST

AUNT DIMITY
GOES WEST

NANCY ATHERTON

THORNDIKE
C H I V E R S

This Large Print edition is published by Thorndike Press, Waterville, Maine USA and by BBC Audiobooks Ltd, Bath, England.

Thorndike Press is an imprint of Thomson Gale, a part of The Thomson Corporation.

Thorndike is a trademark and used herein under license.

The text of this Large Print edition is unabridged.

Other aspects of the book may vary from the original edition.

Set in 16 pt. Plantin.

LIBRARY OF CONGRESS CATALOGING-IN-PUBLICATION DATA

Atherton, Nancy.
  Aunt Dimity goes West / by Nancy Atherton.
    p. cm. — (Aunt Dimity series) (Thorndike Press large print mystery)
  ISBN-13: 978-0-7862-9454-1 (alk. paper)
  ISBN-10: 0-7862-9454-X (alk. paper)
  1. Dimity, Aunt (Fictitious character) — Fiction. 2. Colorado — Fiction.
3. Large type books. I. Title.
PS3551.T426A93445 2007b
813'.54—dc22
                                   2006100920

BRITISH LIBRARY CATALOGUING-IN-PUBLICATION DATA AVAILABLE

Published in 2007 in the U.S. by arrangement with Viking,
a member of Penguin Group (USA) Inc.
Published in 2007 in the U.K. by arrangement with the author.

U.K. Hardcover: 978 1 405 64056 5 (Chivers Large Print)
U.K. Softcover: 978 1 405 64057 2 (Camden Large Print)

Printed in the United States of America on permanent paper
10 9 8 7 6 5 4 3 2 1

For
my friends in the
Colorado Mountain Club,
who've taken me to new heights

ONE

Thunder rolled and lightning stabbed the sky. Savage waves battered the cliffs, and stinging rain lashed my face as I sprawled across the stoney ground, hurt and helpless. A figure loomed above me, a dark-haired man with eyes as black and fathomless as the pits of hell. He raised a pale hand, to point at me. There was a blinding flash, a deafening explosion —

— and I woke up, heart racing. My blankets were a tangled mess, my pillows damp with sweat. With a sobbing gasp, I sat up in bed and stared into the darkness.

The night was calm and peaceful. A summer breeze wafted through the bedroom's open windows, and an early bird chirped in the back garden, as if to announce to all and sundry that it had successfully gotten the worm. I heard no thunder, no crashing waves, and the brightest light in the sky was a faint smudge of gray heralding the dawn.

I wasn't sprawled at the edge of a storm-battered cliff, at the mercy of a cold-blooded killer. I was safe at home.

My husband cleared his throat as he rolled over and propped himself up on an elbow.

"Again?" he said, caressing my back.

"Yeah," I managed shakily.

"I'll make a cup of tea for you." Bill fell back on his pillows and rubbed his tired eyes, then heaved himself out of bed and reached for his bathrobe.

"You don't have to," I said hastily. "I'm okay now, really."

"A nice cup of tea," Bill murmured sleepily. He stepped into his leather bedroom slippers and padded softly into the hallway.

Stanley, our black cat, took advantage of the open door by trotting into the bedroom and vaulting gracefully into my lap for a morning cuddle. He purred softly as I stroked the sweet spot between his ears. Calmed by his soothing rumble, I closed my eyes and released a tremulous sigh.

Six weeks had passed since an obsessed lunatic known as Abaddon had put a bullet just below my left collarbone at point-blank range, nicking an artery and shredding a ridiculous amount of muscle tissue. A host of excellent doctors had helped to heal the garish hole Abaddon had left in my body, but they'd so far failed to repair the damage he'd done to my peace of mind.

For the past month and a half, my moods had swung like a giddy pendulum, shifting from listless to restless, from cranky to weepy, without rhyme or reason, at least fifty times a day. Sleep brought no respite because with it came nightmares, except that in my case there was only *one* nightmare, the same vivid reliving of heart-chilling horror, night after night after night.

It was hardly surprising. For the past seven years, my husband and I had lived an idyllic life in a cozy, honey-colored cottage amidst the picturesque, patchwork fields of rural England. Although we were Americans, the nearby village of Finch had become our own. Our five-year-old twins had been dandled on every knee in Finch. Bill was an honored member of the darts team at the pub. I arranged flowers at the church, brought casseroles to elderly neighbors, and swapped gossip with the fluency of a native. We were a normal family engaged in commonplace activities, none of which had prepared us in the slightest for the terrifying events that had spawned my nightmare.

I'd never dreamed that an insane stalker would threaten to kill me and my family. I'd never dreamed that Bill would send me and the boys to a remote Scottish island for our own protection. I'd most assuredly never dreamed that Abaddon would find the island, kidnap the twins, and try to murder me in the midst of a Force 9 gale. It wasn't the sort of thing I could have dreamed, until it happened. But once it happened, I could dream of nothing else.

I was sick of it. Abaddon was dead and gone, killed by a providential lightning bolt that had jolted him into the roiling sea, but he lived on in my mind, a deranged squatter who ignored insistent demands for his departure. I was desperate to evict him because he was making a mess of the place and the mess was hurting everyone I loved.

My bouncing, effervescent boys had emerged unscathed from their encounter with Abaddon, but they'd taken to tiptoeing around the cottage and speaking in unnaturally hushed voices because "the bad man hurt Mummy." Annelise Sciaparelli, the boys' inestimable nanny, walked on eggshells in my presence because she never knew from one moment to the next whether I'd burst into tears, snap her head off, or lapse into a morose silence. My husband, a high-priced attorney with a well-heeled international clientele, had taken so much time off from work that half of his clients thought he'd retired or died. And I was so addled by sleep deprivation that I couldn't muster the energy to arrange flowers, visit my elderly neighbors, or contribute my fair share to the great chain of gossip that connected everyone in Finch. My world would never spin smoothly on its axis again until I rid myself of Abaddon once and for all, but I didn't know how to make him leave.

Stanley's breathy purr became a loud rumble as Bill reentered the bedroom, carrying a cup of tea on a silver salver. Stanley was, to all intents and purposes, Bill's cat. He liked it when Bill stayed at home to look after me. My ongoing incapacitation was, in many respects, the best thing that had ever happened to Stanley.

Bill placed the salver on the bedside table and rubbed his eyes again. I stared at the steaming teacup and felt guilt settle over me like a lead cape. My husband was in his midthirties, active, attractive, and extremely good at his job. He'd spent half the night in front of his computer, yet here he was, serving tea to me at dawn. It wasn't fair. He was supposed to be running the European branch of his family's venerable law firm, not playing nursemaid to an invalid wife.

"Mind if I catch another forty winks?" he asked, yawning.

"Live it up," I told him. "Catch eighty."

Bill crawled back into bed, and Stanley left my lap to curl contentedly behind Bill's knees. I drank my tea in silence, then made my way to the bathroom to prepare myself to face another day. It was bound to be a hectic one because of the parade.

The parade, as Bill called it, was the kind of thing that happened in a tight-knit community when one of its members suffered a mishap. Since my mishap had been more newsworthy than most, our parade had become a popular social event. No one wanted to be left out of a story that had made headlines in the *Times,* so once a week — on Sunday — a steady stream of neighbors appeared on our doorstep, bearing gifts and basking in reflected glory.

"And today is Sunday," I muttered, closing the bathroom door. "Bath, breakfast, church, and on with the show!"

By the time I had finished dressing, Will and Rob were up, and by the time Annelise and I had finished dressing them, Bill was up again, so we trooped down to the kitchen en masse for a hearty breakfast. We were clearing the table when the doorbell rang. Annelise quickly took the boys into the back garden — they tended to get overexcited on parade days — and Bill went to answer the front door.

"Who was it?" I asked, when he returned to the kitchen.

"Terry Edmonds," Bill replied.

I stopped loading the dishwasher and gave him a puzzled glance. Terry Edmonds wasn't a neighbor. He was a professional courier who picked up and delivered legal papers for Bill's firm.

"Since when does Terry work on Sunday?" I asked.

"Special delivery," said Bill. "I put it in the study."

"He brought it *here?*" I winced as another twinge of guilt assailed me. Bill had a high-tech office overlooking the village green in Finch, but he hadn't set foot in it since I'd been shot. "If you don't get back to work soon, Bill, you're going to have to change the address on your letterhead."

"All in good time, my love," he said.

I swung around to face him.

"Look," I said, flexing my arm gingerly. "I'm as good as new. You don't have to play Nurse Nancy anymore."

"If I didn't know better, I'd suspect that you were trying to get rid of me," Bill observed mildly.

"I *am* trying to get rid of you," I scolded. "You can't work all night and take care of

13

me all day. You'll make yourself ill and *then* where will we be? It's mid-June already, Bill, time for you to resume a normal schedule. Annelise and I can look after the boys, and I can look after myself. I don't need a babysitter anymore. I'm perfectly capable of —"

"— being on time for church," Bill inserted, "which we won't be if we don't get a move on."

I smiled grudgingly, closed the dishwasher, and called Annelise and the boys in from the back garden.

The parade began within an hour of our return from church. The doorbell rang almost nonstop for the rest of the day.

Sally Pyne, the plump and pleasantly chatty owner of the tearoom, dropped off a basket filled with her delectable Crazy Quilt Cookies, which had everything in them except coconut because Sally knew I wasn't fond of coconut. The imperious Peggy Taxman, who ruled Finch with an iron hand and a voice that could penetrate granite, gave Will and Rob bags of candy from her general store, along with a stern lecture on dental hygiene. Miranda Morrow, Finch's red-haired professional witch, bestowed an unlabeled packet of healing herbs upon us,

14

and Dick Peacock, the rotund and amiable publican, gave us three bottles of his home-made wine. Since Dick's wine was undrink-able and Miranda's herbs were quite pos-sibly illegal, Bill flushed both down the toilet after everyone had left.

Ruth and Louise Pym, the ancient and ut-terly identical twin sisters who lived up the lane from us, delivered flowers and fresh vegetables from their gardens. Mr. Malvern, the dairy farmer next door, supplied us with milk, cream, butter, and cheese. Mr. Bar-low, the local handyman, brought only his tools, but he used them to mend the sticky hinge on the back door. Lilian Bunting, the vicar's wife, filled my freezer with casseroles, stews, and soups, and the vicar brought an armload of books he found comforting in troubled times.

My favorite part of the parade occurred after the rush was over, when my best friend Emma Harris showed up to chat quietly over a cup of tea, but even she felt com-pelled to drop off a few jars of her home-made jams. No one ever left without leaving something. As a result I hadn't had to cook or bake or shop for groceries since we'd returned from Scotland.

"I'm going to bankrupt the villagers if I

don't snap out of my funk," I said gloomily.

The parade was over, as was dinner. Annelise had taken the boys upstairs for their baths. I'd offered to lend a hand, but Bill had insisted that I rest after my action-packed day, so he, Stanley, and I had retreated to the sofa in the living room to munch on Crazy Quilt Cookies, put our feet — and paws — up, and watch the fire.

"It's not a funk," said Bill. "It's posttraumatic stress and it's not something you snap out of. It's something you recover from."

"But I'm *not* recovering," I moaned. "In the past month I've tried counselors, psychiatrists, the vicar, pills, meditation, hypnotherapy —"

"— aromatherapy, massage therapy, hydrotherapy, acupuncture," Bill put in.

"And nothing's worked," I concluded.

"If I were foolish enough to risk rousing your wrath," Bill said, after a pause, "I'd point out that you haven't done anything long enough to *know* whether it was working or not. But I'm not, so I won't."

I nodded ruefully, acknowledging the hit. "Patience was never my strong suit. I don't seem to *have* any strong suits at the moment. I don't know what to try next."

"That's okay," said Bill. "I do."

He smiled mysteriously, shifted Stanley from his lap to the floor, and left the living room. He returned a moment later with one hand tucked behind his back, sidestepped his way around the couch, to keep me from seeing his hidden hand, and perched on the edge of the coffee table, facing me. His expression reminded me of the twins' when they'd accomplished a particularly ingenious bit of mischief.

"What are you up to?" I asked, eyeing him warily.

"Remember the special delivery Terry Edmonds made this morning?" he asked. "It's for you. I ordered it last night."

"It's a brain," I said promptly. "You want me to try a brain transplant."

"Wrong," he said, his eyes dancing.

"Well?" I demanded. "What is it?"

Grinning from ear to ear, Bill brought his hand around to reveal his big surprise. It was a large, white, cowboy hat. He placed it on my head.

"Saddle up, little lady," he drawled. "The Wild West is a-callin'!"

Two

"Yee-ha!" Bill cried, slapping his thigh.

Startled, Stanley bolted from the room, but I was too bewildered to move a muscle. My husband was the Harvard-educated scion of a Boston Brahmin family. He didn't drawl or slap his thigh, and the closest he'd ever come to the Wild West was a legal conference in Denver. I stared at him, dumbfounded, and wondered what on earth had come over him. Had the fumes from Dick Peacock's wine pickled his brain? Had he finally cracked under the strain of caretaking? Had I strayed into an alternate universe?

I touched the cowboy hat's crown, to make sure I wasn't hallucinating, then said, very carefully, "Bill? What are you talking about?"

"I'm talking about the one thing we haven't tried so far," he replied, beaming. "A complete change of scene, and I *do* mean complete." He swept an arm toward the cottage's bay window. "Go west, young woman! Seek your fortune in the glorious, untamed wilderness of the Colorado Rockies!"

"Are you saying that we should go to Colorado?" I asked, struggling to keep up. "As in . . . *Colorado?*"

"The one and only!" Bill exclaimed happily. "Finch isn't doing you any good. It's too familiar. You need to jump-start your batteries by plugging into a place that bears no resemblance to Finch whatsoever. And what could be more different from our too-tame English village than a log cabin in the glorious, untamed —"

"Log cabin?" I squeaked, alarmed.

"You remember Danny Auerbach, the real estate developer?" Bill registered my blank look and rushed on. "I've done a lot of work for Danny over the years. He built a cabin in the mountains a couple of years ago, and he's offered it to me a thousand times. I finally decided to take him up on his offer."

"You've bought a *log cabin?*" I said, my head spinning. "In *Colorado?*"

"I'm just borrowing it," Bill explained. "Danny likes to have friends stay there. It's near a small mountain town —"

"Aspen?" I said hopefully.

"No," said Bill, dashing my hopes. "Danny doesn't care for Aspen — he says it's over-built and overpriced — so he built his place near a mountain town called Bluebird, on a piece of land that's been in his family for ages. With Bluebird nearby you won't feel cut off from civilization, but you'll be far enough away from city lights to enjoy a feel-ing of . . ." He stretched his arms wide and stuck out his chest. *"Expansiveness."*

"Expansiveness," I echoed doubtfully.

"It's what you need, Lori," said Bill, "and it's exactly what you won't find in our cozy corner of the world."

I could do nothing for a moment but gape at him. He'd evidently forgotten how much I loved our cozy corner of the world. Finch was a sleepy backwater that scarcely merited a dot on most maps, but it pulsated with the seething passions of everyday life, and I was caught up in those passions. Would the vicar defy tradition and invite a rock band to perform at the church fête? Would Sally Pyne wear her luminous purple tracksuit to the flower show? Would the all-powerful Peggy Taxman expand her empire to include the greengrocer's shop, now that old Mr. Farnham had retired? The high drama never ceased, and the thought of missing out on a single day's worth of juicy gossip was intolerable.

Gossip deprivation aside, it just seemed wrong to leave the cottage and flee to a log cabin half a world away from Finch. The cottage was our home. To abandon it, even temporarily, would be to give in to the black-eyed demon who'd hijacked my dreams.

"I don't know, Bill," I said. "It seems like cowardice to me, like we're letting Abaddon run us out of town."

"Nonsense." Bill tossed his head dismissively. "If you go to Colorado, you'll be declaring your *independence* from Abaddon. You'll be saying, 'I'm not going to curl up in a fetal position for the rest of my life because a nutcase got the better of me. I'm going to seize the day!' " He put a hand on my knee and added earnestly, "I've seen you disagree with Peggy Taxman — *out loud* and in front of *witnesses.* You're no coward, Lori."

"What about the boys?" I said worriedly. "We'll be uprooting them, won't we? Upsetting their routine?"

"*Of course* we'll be upsetting their routine," Bill retorted. "Do you honestly think they'll mind? It's mid-June, Lori, a wonderful time of year to visit the Rockies. The boys can go hiking and trout fishing and

21

fossil hunting, and they can pan for gold in the river. If they're lucky, they'll catch their first glimpse of elk, buffalo, and bighorn sheep. There's even a ranch nearby, where they'll be able to ride with *real cowboys.*" Bill bobbed his head enthusiastically. "They'll have a tale or two to tell their friends when they start school in the fall, that's for sure."

"I don't know if Annelise —" I began, but Bill rode right over me.

"It'll be the adventure of a lifetime for Annelise," he declared. "She's been to America before, with us, but she's never traveled outside of Boston. She'll jump at the chance to see the Rockies."

I sat back on the sofa, folded my arms, and regarded Bill narrowly. He was trying much too hard to persuade me that his scheme was flawless. Wifely instinct told me that he was withholding a vital piece of information.

"Okay," I said. "What's the catch?"

"Catch?" said Bill, with an air of injured innocence. "Why do you think there's a catch?"

"Because you're chirping like a deranged cheerleader, that's why." I made a beckoning motion with my hand. "Out with it, Bill. Spill the beans. What haven't you told me?"

"Well, yes, now that you mention it, there is one small catch." Bill cleared his throat, squared his shoulders, and said, "I can't go."

"You . . . *what?*" My jaw dropped. "Are you out of your mind? Do you seriously expect me to tackle the glorious, untamed wilderness *without* you?"

"I'm sorry, Lori, but I have no choice." His shoulders drooped and he hung his head, like a defeated Little Leaguer. "As you pointed out after breakfast, I have to get back to work. Things have piled up since I've been gone, things I can't pass on to the London office. I have to see to them personally or we'll lose at least seven of our best clients. You know I'd come with you if I could, but . . ."

His words trailed off on a crestfallen sigh that cut me to the quick. Bill had devoted himself to me, day and night, for weeks on end. He'd never run out of patience or good humor, and he'd never uttered one word of complaint. He'd conceived of a marvelous journey with nothing but my well-being in mind, and all I could do was whine about him staying behind. Shame flooded through me like molten lava.

"Is this" — I ran a finger along the cowboy hat's brim — "why you were up so late last night? Were you using your computer to

23

plan the trip?"

"Yes," Bill answered, without looking at me.

"Well," I said softly, "I'll miss you like blazes, but apart from that, I think it's a brilliant plan."

Bill's head snapped up. "You do?"

"As you said, it's the only thing we haven't tried." I shrugged. "Who knows? It just might work."

"It will," said Bill, with great conviction. "I know it will."

I brushed a few stray cat hairs from the sofa. "I can't wait to tell Stanley. He'll be thrilled to have you all to himself. And you can fill me in on breaking news while I'm away."

"If Sally Pyne wears her hideous tracksuit to the flower show, you'll be the first to know," Bill said, with his hand on his heart.

He took the hat from my head and dropped it on the coffee table, then moved onto the couch and put his arms around me. I snuggled as close to him as my shoulder would allow.

"It's been a long time since I've taken a vacation in the States," I mused aloud.

"You won't have to lift a finger," Bill promised. "I've arranged everything, airline tickets, a rental car, a driver —"

"Why do we need a driver?" I asked, stiffening. It was a touchy subject. I didn't share my husband's low opinion of my driving skills.

"Your arm may feel better, but your range of motion is still limited," Bill explained gently. "You won't be able to handle mountain roads."

"Maybe not," I said, conceding the point, "but what about Annelise? She can drive."

"Annelise is English," he reminded me. "Do you really want her careering around hairpin bends on the wrong side of the road?" He shook his head. "I don't think so. I've hired the cabin's caretaker to look after you. His name is James Blackwell and he lives on the property, so he knows his way around. He'll pick you up at the airport, take you to the cabin, and act as your chauffeur while you're there. He'll be a great guide, Lori, and he'll see to it that the cabin is stocked with food, drink, and firewood."

"How long will we be away?" I asked.

"As long as you like," said Bill. "I booked open-ended airline tickets and I checked with Danny — he's not planning to use the cabin this summer and no one else has asked to borrow it."

I wondered briefly why the cabin was so unpopular, but decided not to question Bill about it. If the place turned out to be a one-room shack equipped with kerosene lanterns and an aromatic outhouse, I'd make the best of it. I'd do whatever I had to do to keep the smile on my husband's face.

"Wow," I said admiringly. "You really have thought of everything. What would you have done if I'd refused to go?"

"I would have canceled the trip and tried something else." Bill kissed the top of my head. "Like a brain transplant."

"I've always wanted to stay in a log cabin," I assured him hastily. "When do we leave?"

"The day after tomorrow," Bill replied.

I stifled an incredulous squawk and forced myself to comment benignly, "The sooner, the better. Bluebird, Colorado, here we come!"

I'd scarcely finished speaking when a chorus of earsplitting shouts came from the hallway.

"We're going!" bellowed Rob.

"We're going!" hollered Will.

Our pajama-clad sons galloped into the living room and pranced gleefully in front of the fireplace. Annelise followed at a more sedate pace, but her face was shining. I pursed my lips and looked at my husband, whose eyes were trained on the ceiling.

"You wouldn't have mentioned the trip to

26

Will, Rob, and Annelise before telling *me* about it, would you?" I asked.

"I might have let a few details slip," Bill allowed. "Inadvertently."

I transferred my gaze to Annelise. "You and the boys wouldn't have eavesdropped on our conversation, would you?"

"We might have overheard a word or two," she admitted. "Purely by accident."

"We're going to Colorado!" Rob roared. "We're going to pan for gold!"

"We're going to ride with cowboys!" Will yelled. "We're going to see buffalo!"

It sounded as though Bill had let more than a few details slip, but I didn't mind. I couldn't remember the last time the twins had made so much noise. They were hopping up and down instead of tiptoeing, and their voices were anything but hushed. Annelise's eyes were bright with anticipation and Bill was beaming like Santa Claus on Christmas Eve. Their joy was so contagious that I felt as if my troubles were at an end.

I should have known better.

THREE

We brought the evening's celebrations to a close with a marathon reading of the entire *Cowboy Sam* series, then put Rob and Will to bed. Annelise promptly retired to her room and Bill staggered into our bedroom, with Stanley at his heels, to catch up on the sleep he'd missed the night before.

I stayed with him until he nodded off, then slipped quietly out of the bedroom and went downstairs to the study. It would have been pointless for me to stay in bed. I wouldn't have been able to close my eyes if I'd missed my nightly private chat with Aunt Dimity.

A private chat was the only kind of chat I *could* have with Aunt Dimity. Don't get me wrong. I wasn't ashamed to be seen with her. She was the most intelligent, compassionate, and courageous woman I knew, but there was simply no getting around the fact that she wasn't, strictly speaking, alive.

To complicate matters further, Aunt Dimity wasn't my aunt. She was an Englishwoman named Dimity Westwood, and she'd been my late mother's closest friend. The two women had met in London while serving their respective countries during the Second World War. When the war ended and my mother returned to the States, they continued their friendship by sending hundreds of letters back and forth across the Atlantic.

Those letters meant the world to my mother. After my father's early death, she'd raised me on her own while working full time as a schoolteacher. She hadn't had an easy life, but the hard times had been softened by her correspondence with Dimity. The letters my mother sent and received became a refuge for her, a place where she could go when the twin burdens of widowhood and single motherhood became too heavy for her to bear.

My mother kept her refuge a closely held secret, even from her only child. She never whispered a word to me about her old friend or the letters that meant so much to her. As a child I knew Dimity Westwood only as Aunt Dimity, the redoubtable heroine of a series of bedtime stories invented by my mother.

I didn't learn the truth about Dimity West-wood until after she and my mother had died, when Dimity bequeathed to me a considerable fortune, the honey-colored cottage in which she'd grown up, the precious letters she and my mother had exchanged, and a curious blue leather–bound journal with blank pages. It was through the blue journal that I'd come to know Dimity not as a fictional heroine, but as a very real — some would say surreal — friend.

Whenever I opened the journal, Dimity's handwriting would appear, an old-fashioned copperplate taught in the village school at a time when little girls still dressed in pinafores. I'd nearly come unglued the first time Dimity greeted me from beyond the grave, but one mention of my mother's name had been enough to reassure me that her intentions toward me were kindly. I'd long since come to regard her as my most cherished confidante, and I hoped the day would never come when the pages of the journal remained blank.

The study was a bit messier than usual, strewn with papers that should have been filed at Bill's office. I tidied them into neat piles and placed them beside his laptop on the old oak desk beneath the ivy-covered window. Once the room was in order, I turned to say hello to a small, pink flannel rabbit named Reginald, who spent most of his time perched in a special niche on the study's bookshelves.

The sight of a grown woman conversing with a pink flannel rabbit might strike some people as odd, but to me it was as natural as breathing. Reginald had been at my side for as long as I could remember. I'd shared moments of triumph, woe, and everything in between with him for nearly forty years, and I wasn't about to stop now.

"Hey, Reg," I said, touching the faded grape-juice stain on his snout. "Ever picture yourself in a cowboy hat?"

Reginald's black button eyes glimmered in a way that seemed to say, if only to me, that he'd never in his life imagined himself wearing anything as silly as a cowboy hat, but that, if I insisted, he'd put up with it.

"Don't worry," I said. "I don't think they make them in your size."

Reginald glimmered his relief. I gave his long ears a friendly tweak, took the blue journal down from its place on the bookshelves, and curled comfortably in one of the pair of tall leather armchairs that sat before the hearth.

"Dimity?" I said, opening the journal. "Got a minute?"

I smiled as the familiar lines of elegant copperplate began to flow gracefully across the page.

I have all the minutes you need, my dear. How are you feeling today?

"Fine," I said. Then I recalled to whom I was speaking and instantly revised my answer. "Okay, so the nightmare woke me up again this morning, and I didn't have a moment's peace all day because of the parade, and my shoulder's a little achy, but other than that I'm doing pretty well." I glanced at the laptop and thought of Bill staying up half the night, planning every detail of the trip. "As a matter of fact, I'm feeling better than I have in a long time."

Splendid! To what do you owe your improvement? Acupuncture? Meditation? Hydrotherapy? Or have you decided to try something new?

"Something new," I replied. "How do you feel about log cabins, Dimity?"

I can't honestly say that I've ever felt anything about log cabins. Why? Are you planning to build one, as a form of work therapy? If so, I'd advise starting on something a bit smaller. A bird table, perhaps, or a simple bookshelf. One can never have too many bookshelves.

"I'm not going to *build* a log cabin," I said.

"I'm going to *stay* in one. In Colorado."

You've decided to leave England for America? Good heavens. Have you told Bill?

"It was Bill's idea," I told her. "It's his surefire cure for what ails me. He's convinced that a radical change of scene will exorcise Abaddon, so he's sending me, Annelise, and the twins to stay in a log cabin in Colorado, while he stays here to catch up on work. Have you ever been to Colorado?"

Never. It's mountainous, I believe.

"So I've heard. I've never been there, either. The thing is," I added, voicing for the first time a concern that had been troubling me, "I was born and raised in Chicago, Dimity. I don't really see myself as a mountain woman."

I sincerely doubt that you'll have to chop wood, haul water from a creek, or kill wild animals in order to put food on the table, if that's what's worrying you. Bill wouldn't send you to a place that wasn't equipped with a full range of modern conveniences.

"Bill's never seen the cabin," I said. "It belongs to one of his clients, a guy named Danny Auerbach, who never stays there. Danny likes to lend the cabin to friends, but not one of his friends has asked to use it this summer — not one!" I frowned anxiously. "I have a horrible feeling that there's something wrong with the place, something that scares people off."

Pull yourself together, Lori. Bill's clients are uniformly wealthy, and the wealthy do not own shabby properties. I'm sure the cabin will be lovely.

"There must be a crazy neighbor then," I insisted. "An old guy with a shotgun and a grudge against city folk."

Have you discussed your misgivings with Bill?

"No, and I'm not going to," I said quickly. "This is just between you and me, Dimity. I don't care if the cabin has a dirt floor and a trigger-happy old coot living next door — I'm not going to say a word to Bill. He needs a vacation from his lunatic wife, and I'm going to give him one."

I'm quite sure Bill doesn't see it that way, Lori.

"*I* see it that way," I declared. "Bill's been at my beck and call ever since we got back from Scotland. It's my turn to make a sacrifice, and if that means roughing it in the back of beyond for a couple of weeks, so be it."

Forgive me, Lori, but I was under the impression that you were feeling better. Did I misunderstand you?

"I *do* feel better," I insisted. "Will and Rob

are out of their minds with excitement, Annelise can't wait to leave, and Bill's been walking on air ever since I agreed to go. How could I not feel better when there's so much happiness swirling around me?" I wrinkled my nose. "I'm just a little worried, that's all."

You wouldn't be yourself if you weren't a little worried about something, dearest Lori. Nevertheless, I'm glad Bill hatched such a delightful scheme. The brisk alpine air will do you a world of good. Besides, I've never visited the Rocky Mountains, and I'd very much like to go.

"Good, because you're coming with me," I said. "So is Reginald. There are some sacrifices I'm not willing to make, and facing the vast, untamed wilderness without you and Reg is one of them."

I can't tell you how pleased I am to hear it. We will face the wilderness together, my dear, but in the meantime, the hour is growing late. Don't you think you should toddle off to bed? You'll have lots to do tomorrow.

When I thought of the work involved in packing everything the twins and I would need for an open-ended, outdoorsy sort of trip, I couldn't help but agree.

"You're right," I said. "It's toddling time. Thanks for listening, Dimity."

Thank you, Lori, for allowing me to listen. Sleep well.

"I'll try," I promised, without much hope.

When the curving lines of royal-blue ink had faded from the page, I closed the journal and looked up at Reginald.

"Well, cowpoke," I said, in my best western drawl, "I hope Buffalo Bill hasn't gotten us in over our heads. If I have to hunt for food, we're a-goin' to get *mighty* hungry."

I awoke with a gasp before dawn the next day, but I had too much on my mind to waste time shuddering, so I got up, dressed, and went downstairs to pull suitcases out of storage. I'd managed to dislodge exactly one duffel bag from its shelf in the utility room when Bill charged in after me, removed the duffel bag from my grasp, and shooed me into the kitchen to start breakfast.

It soon became apparent that Dimity and I had grossly overestimated the amount of energy I'd need to prepare for the trip. Bill had promised that I wouldn't have to lift a finger, and he saw to it that I didn't. He and Annelise allowed me to watch them pack, but if I dared to tuck so much as a sock into a suitcase, they ordered me out of the room.

Since the twins and I were clearly underfoot, I piled them into the Range Rover for a farewell tour of Finch. Our abrupt, unannounced flight to Scotland had started the rumor mills churning at breakneck speed among my neighbors, and I didn't want our Colorado trip to start another frenzy of speculation. I wanted everyone to know that the boys and I were setting out on a pleasant vacation this time, not being chased from our home by a homicidal maniac.

The villagers with whom I spoke were unanimously in favor of Bill's big idea, except when it came to his choice of destinations.

"Colorado?" said Sally Pyne, offering me a plate of fresh-baked scones. "It's a bit rough and tumble out there, isn't it? All prickly plants and vipers? Why don't you ask Bill to find you a nice B&B in Cornwall instead? The sea air would put you right in no time."

"The Rocky Mountains?" said Mr. Barlow, wiping axle grease from his hands. "I had a cousin who went there once. Collapsed on his first day. Altitude sickness. Had to be airlifted to a lower altitude. I'd book a hotel in Skegness if I were you. The sea air's like a tonic."

"America!" thundered Peggy Taxman, closing her cash register with a bang.

"Wouldn't go there if my life depended on it. Loud voices, fast food, vulgarity and violence everywhere you turn. You'd be better off in Blackpool. The twins'd love the donkey rides, and you'd be blooming after a week or two of fresh sea air."

Shy, balding, soft-spoken George Wetherhead approved of Bill's plan unreservedly, but only because he was a train enthusiast.

"The Pikes Peak Cog Railway is the highest in the world!" he exclaimed. "The views from the Royal Gorge train are breathtaking! The Cripple Creek and Victor Narrow Gauge Railroad has an 0-4-0 locomotive! Oh, how I envy you."

I didn't have the heart to tell him that a tour of historic railways was not on the agenda. Nor did I have the courage to disagree with everyone else. My neighbors were, after all, merely expressing my own doubts and misgivings.

After we'd made the rounds in Finch, I took Will and Rob to Anscombe Manor to say good-bye to Emma Harris, who owned the manor, and to the boys' ponies, who were stabled there.

Will and Rob were identical twins who bore a strong resemblance to their father. They had Bill's dark-brown hair and velvety chocolate-brown eyes, and they were, as he had been, so tall for their age that strangers couldn't believe they were only five. Like Bill, they were bright, sweet-natured, and energetic. Unlike him — and most definitely unlike me — they were completely and utterly horse-crazy.

When my sons weren't galloping over hill and dale on their ponies, Thunder and Storm, they liked to draw horses, talk about horses, sing songs about horses, and pretend to be horses. They liked to play cricket, squelch through mud puddles, and pretend to be dinosaurs, too, but they were never happier than when they were with their ponies. They couldn't leave England without saying good-bye to Thunder and Storm, and I, shaken by my neighbors' observations, couldn't face my well-meaning husband again until I'd had a calm, sensible conversation with Emma.

I found her in the stables, cleaning stalls.

"I used to think the lady of the manor had a glamorous life," I said, stepping carefully across the straw-strewn floor. "Boy, was I wrong."

Emma gave me a jaundiced look, leaned her pitchfork against the wheelbarrow, and fetched apples from a nearby basket for the boys to give to their ponies.

"Very funny," she said, wiping the sweat

from her brow as we walked into the fresh air. "Anyone who thinks living in a manor house is glamorous has never come face-to-face with an eighteenth-century drain."

"I may be able to match you on that score before the summer's out," I said, and told her about our impending journey.

"It sounds fantastic," she said, when I'd finished. "You'll have miles of trails to explore, and the mountains will be awash in wildflowers. It's a beautiful time of year to be in the Rockies."

"I'm not so sure," I said doubtfully. "Peggy's got a point, you know. America *is* loud and vulgar and violent."

"*Some* of America is nasty," Emma temporized, "but *most* of it is nice. The same could be said of England or anywhere else in the world, for that matter. And what would Peggy know about it, anyway? She's never been to America."

"But what about Mr. Barlow's cousin?" I asked. "He didn't have such a great time in the Rockies."

"He's the exception that proves the rule," Emma said firmly. "Colorado wouldn't have much of a tourist industry if visitors were falling over every five minutes from altitude sickness. You and the boys will be fine."

"What about the cabin, then?" I said.

"Don't you think there must be something wrong with it? Like bad drains?"

"The drains will be fine, Lori," said Emma. "Everything will be fine. You'll see. You'll come back from Colorado with roses in your cheeks. I wish I could come with you."

"You can!" I said, brightening.

"No, I can't," said Emma. "I've got to run the riding school and tend the garden and repair the drains and . . ." She took a deep breath, then said in a rush, "And Nell is coming home."

"*Nell's* coming home?" I cried. *"When?"*

"Tomorrow," Emma replied.

Nell was Nell Harris, Emma's eighteen-year-old stepdaughter, and the most exquisitely beautiful girl I'd ever seen or imagined. She'd been in Paris for the past year, studying at the Sorbonne.

"Does Kit know?" I asked.

"Not yet," said Emma. "I'm going to break it to him tonight, after dinner."

Kit was Kit Smith, Emma's stable master and the object of Nell's unwavering affection, an affection he tried hard not to return because he was twice Nell's age, and he thought the age difference mattered. No one else did. Nell was an extraordinarily mature eighteen-year-old.

"Good grief," I said faintly, then turned to grip Emma's wrist. "What if Kit changes his mind? What if he *proposes* to Nell? I absolutely *forbid* him to marry her until I'm back from Colorado!"

"I don't think you have much to worry about," Emma said dryly. "Kit's as stubborn as you are."

I looked toward the stables. "Lucky for Kit, so is Nell."

Once Emma had promised that she wouldn't let Kit marry anyone until I'd returned, and I had promised to bombard her with postcards, I rounded up the boys and left for home, feeling more despondent than ever.

I'd been eagerly awaiting Kit and Nell's reunion for over a year, and now it would take place without me. I didn't want to be thousands of miles away while the romance of the century was taking place. I wanted to be on hand, on the spot, if possible, when Kit's resistance melted and he gave in to the urgings of his heart. As we turned out of Anscombe Manor's curving drive, I composed a suitable message for Emma's first postcard.

"Killed bear last night," I muttered. "Skinned it this morning. If Kit and Nell elope while I'm away, I'll skin *you!*"

42

FOUR

Since Will, Rob, Annelise, and I were a seasoned team of travelers, our flight from London to Denver would have been pleasantly uneventful if only I'd been able to stay awake. Unfortunately, I dozed off somewhere over the Atlantic and nearly caused an international incident when I woke up screaming.

Annelise managed to convince the rattled cabin crew that I'd simply had a bad dream, but the other passengers watched me closely from then on, as if they were mapping out ways to subdue me if I suddenly went berserk and tried to break into the cockpit with my teeth. To avoid alarming them further — and because I don't like coffee — I kept myself awake by eating chocolate and drinking many cups of cola.

By the time we disembarked in Denver I was so hyped on sugar and caffeine I could easily have been mistaken for an amphetamine addict, so I put Annelise in charge of our passports. She got us through Customs without undue delay, and I collared a skycap to deal with our luggage. While he loaded our bags onto his cart, I put in a quick call to Bill to let him know that we'd arrived safely, carefully omitting any reference to screaming.

It wasn't hard to spot the driver Bill had hired. He was waiting for us at the end of the Arrivals barrier, holding a hand-lettered sign with my name on it; but it wasn't the sign that caught my attention, it was the man himself.

Because he wasn't a man. He was a boy: a tall, lean, broad-shouldered boy with long white-blond hair, big blue eyes, and the smooth, innocent face of a cherub. He wore a bright-red waterproof jacket, an unbuttoned flannel shirt over a T-shirt that read ROCKY MOUNTAIN HI!, and a pair of hiking trousers with zip-off legs and many, many pockets. His trousers were spattered with the same reddish mud that caked his hiking boots and stained the blue day pack that lay at his feet. He looked as though he'd hiked from Bluebird to Denver, and for a brief, hysterical moment I wondered if he expected us to hike back with him.

He'd evidently seen photographs of us

because he stuffed the sign into his day pack and gave us a friendly wave as we approached. When we passed the barrier, he ushered us and the skycap out of the main stream of passenger traffic in order to greet us properly.

"Ms. Shepherd, Ms. Sciaparelli," he said, nodding to me and Annelise in turn. "Welcome to Colorado."

"James?" I said hesitantly.

"No," he replied. "Tobias. Toby. Toby Cooper. I'm James Blackwell's replacement."

"Replacement?" I said. "My husband didn't mention a replacement."

"He probably doesn't know about it yet," Toby said. "I only found out about it yesterday." He reached into an outside pocket of the day pack and produced a flimsy sheet of fax paper. "From Mr. Auerbach. It'll explain everything."

I took the fax from him and read:

Dear Ms. Shepherd,
Welcome to Colorado! Please accept my apologies for the last-minute change in personnel. James Blackwell left my employment yesterday, rather unexpectedly, and Toby Cooper generously agreed to take his place.

Toby's father and I are old school friends. Toby's a fine young man and will do everything he can to make your stay in Colorado enjoyable. If you have any questions, please feel free to contact me.

Sincerely,
Danny Auerbach

I noted the phone number printed beneath Danny's name, then looked up to find Toby anxiously scanning my face.

"Why did James Blackwell quit?" I asked.

Toby shrugged. "I don't know. I don't know James, and Mr. Auerbach didn't give me any details when he asked me to fill in. Maybe James just decided it was time to move on."

"I see," I said. "Do you mind if I ask how old you are?"

"Twenty-one," Toby replied. "I go to college in Boulder, but I'm on summer break."

Annelise and I exchanged a glance that said, "Now we have *three* little boys to look after." Our expressions must have alarmed Toby because he began to speak at top speed.

"I know Bluebird like the back of my hand," he said. "My dad was born and raised there, and I spent every summer there with my grandparents when I was a kid. I know the hiking trails and the best fishing spots, and I can fix things, too, like a leaky pipe or a broken window — my grand-dad showed me how — so if anything goes wrong, I'll take care of it. I'm a good driver, too — no speeding tickets — and I've never been involved in an accident, not even a fender bender." A note of desperation entered his voice. "I had a summer job lined up in the administration office at school, but it fell through, so I . . . I was really glad when Mr. Auerbach offered me this one. I may be a little younger than James Black-well, but I'm a hard worker, Ms. Shepherd, and I'm very dependable. You won't be disappointed."

The eager-puppy look in his eyes was ir-resistible. I stuffed the fax into my carry-on bag and decided to go with the flow.

"I'm sure I won't," I said reassuringly. "And, please, call me Lori."

"Annelise will do for me," Annelise put in. "Sciaparelli is a bit of a mouthful for everyday use."

Rob tugged on Toby's trouser leg, and Toby squatted down to look him in the eye.

"We know a pony named Toby," Rob informed him importantly. "Do you know any ponies?"

"Are you a cowboy?" Will asked, cutting

to the chase. My sons were not known for their reticence.

"Not exactly," said Toby, "but your father told Mr. Auerbach that you like cowboys, so I've brought an essential piece of cowboy equipment for each of you." He reached into his day pack and brought forth a pair of bandanas, one red and one blue. "Which one of you is Will?"

"I am," said Will, stepping forward.

Toby promptly knotted the red bandana around Will's neck and the blue one around Rob's, thus effectively distinguishing one twin from the other. I gave him full marks for cleverness.

"Would you call a bandana equipment?" Annelise inquired.

"Absolutely," Toby replied, standing tall. "Pull a bandana over your nose and you'll breathe easier during a dust storm. Tie a damp bandana around your forehead on a hot day and you'll avoid sunstroke. If a rattlesnake strikes, a bandana makes a good tourniquet."

"Useful things, bandanas," Annelise agreed.

The boys were gazing up at Toby as if he held the keys to a kingdom of thrilling adventures, but I stared at him, aghast. What kind of vacation included dust storms, heat stroke, and deadly snakes in its itinerary? It sounded as though Bill had sent us on a survival course instead of a jolly family holiday.

"Are you all right, Lori?" Toby asked, noticing my expression.

I let out an embarrassingly high-pitched giggle, for which I immediately apologized.

"Sorry," I said. "Too much caffeine."

"You should avoid caffeine while you're here, for the first few days at least," Toby advised. He delved into the main compartment of his day pack and handed a bottle of water to each of us. "Water's your best bet. It'll help you adjust to the altitude as well as the dry air. There's lots more in the van, so drink up. And by the way," he added, straightening, "local time is seven forty-seven p.m., and yes, it's still Tuesday." The corners of his eyes crinkled charmingly as he grinned. "It's easy to lose track of time after crossing so many time zones."

"Your boots are all dirty," Will commented, peering interestedly at Toby's hiking boots.

"It's pretty muddy up in Bluebird," Toby explained. "It snowed two days ago, and we're still waiting for the last few drifts to finish melting."

"*Snow?*" I said, horrified. "In *June?*"

"We had snow in July a few years ago," Toby said cheerfully.

"But we're not dressed for snow," I protested. "And we didn't pack our winter coats."

"Yes, we did," said Annelise. "They're in the brown suitcase. Bill thought we might need them."

"Bill *knew* about the snow?" I exclaimed, rounding on her.

Toby quickly intervened. "I'm sure Mr. Auerbach told your husband to pack clothes for all seasons, Lori. Mountain weather is pretty changeable. It's best to be prepared for everything."

I silently added frostbite to my lengthening list of holiday hazards.

Toby hoisted the day pack to his shoulders and reached for my carry-on bag.

"I can manage, thanks," I said, backing away a step. Aunt Dimity's journal and Reginald were in my bag. I wouldn't let Annelise carry it, much less a total stranger.

"I guess we're all set, then." Toby looked down at the twins. "Are you buckaroos ready to head for the hills?"

Will and Rob nodded eagerly and took hold of Toby's outstretched hands, hoping, no doubt, that he'd take them straight to the nearest rattlesnakes. They seemed mildly disappointed when he informed them that we were going instead to the parking garage. I signaled for the skycap to follow, and we set off, with the three boys in the lead.

It felt good to stretch my legs after the ten-hour flight, but the parking garage was a long way away from the Arrivals barrier, and I was soon struggling to keep up with the trio ahead of me. The twins seemed fine, if a bit pinker than usual, but Annelise and I were red-faced and gasping before Toby noticed that we were lagging behind.

"Sorry," he said, slowing his pace. "It's the thin air. You'll get used to it."

I took a swig from my water bottle and plodded on, thinking darkly of Mr. Barlow's cousin and wondering how long it would take to be airlifted from Bluebird to Kansas.

We arrived, eventually, at a sleek, stream-lined black van liberally spattered with red-dish mud. It held three rows of comfortable seats, and it was equipped with four-wheel drive, heavy-duty suspension, a high clearance chassis, and many other features I associated with bad roads.

"Great," I muttered hoarsely to Annelise. "There may be no air to breathe, but at least there are plenty of potholes to look forward to."

Annelise simply nodded. She was probably conserving oxygen.

While Toby and the skycap piled our luggage into the van's rear compartment, Annelise and I strapped the twins firmly into the middle row's booster seats. Once we were satisfied that the boys wouldn't hit the roof if we encountered uneven pavement, Annelise climbed in to sit behind them, and I hoisted myself into the front passenger seat.

Toby finished loading the luggage and tipped the skycap, but instead of climbing into the driver's seat, he opened the van's side door and passed a wicker hamper to Annelise.

"Sandwiches," he explained. "In case you're hungry. We've got a two-hour drive ahead of us."

"Did you make the sandwiches?" Annelise asked, peering into the hamper.

"Nope," said Toby. "I picked them up in Bluebird this afternoon, from Caroline's Cafe. Carrie Vyne makes the best sandwiches in the world. She packed some of her chocolate chip cookies, too. She makes great cookies."

Toby closed the side door, circled the van, and slid behind the steering wheel. After a brief glance at the boys, he turned the key in the ignition and called out, "Wagons, ho!"

"Yee-ha!" they yodeled.

Their father would have been proud of them.

The interstate highway out of Denver was in reassuringly good condition, but the scenery left much to be desired. Although the mountains beckoned, our immediate surroundings consisted of great swathes of boring tract houses separated by forlorn-looking patches of prairie. Since there was nothing much to look at, we concentrated on the sandwiches and the cookies. They were delicious.

"Do you *know* any cowboys?" Will asked hopefully, when we'd emptied the hamper.

"I sure do," said Toby. "They live one valley over from Bluebird, at the Brockman Ranch. Mr. Auerbach's arranged for you two to ride there while you're here."

"Will there be cows?" asked Rob.

"Not as many as there were in the old days," Toby said, with a reminiscent sigh. "I remember when the boys drove fifty thousand head of cattle from South Dakota all the way to Texas. It was rough going in those days. Cowpokes had to face all sorts of obstacles: floods, grass fires, storms so vicious they'd snatch the teeth right out of your mouth —"

"Were there Indians?" Rob interrupted, enthralled.

"Whole tribes of them," Toby confirmed. "Most of them were friendly, but even the bad ones weren't as bad as the rustlers."

"There were rustlers?" Will asked, wide-eyed.

Toby snorted. "More than you could count, all armed to the teeth and meaner than a bear with a blistered paw. I remember one time . . ."

I gave Toby an amused, sidelong glance as he went on to describe a hair-raising battle with a gang of desperadoes. I was no expert on American history, but I was pretty sure that the great cattle drives had ended in the late nineteenth century, when ranchers began transporting livestock by rail. If Toby could remember those days, he was remarkably well preserved, but I suspected that he was simply introducing the boys to the fine western tradition of telling tall tales.

"How high is Bluebird?" I asked, when the twins had fallen into a bedazzled silence.

"About eight thousand feet," Toby replied.

"Eight thousand feet," I said weakly. The caffeine had definitely worn off. "How long will it take us to get used to living at eight thousand feet?"

"No more than a few days," he assured

me. "It's normal to feel a little lightheaded at first, but if you feel a headache coming on — a serious headache, that is, as if someone were driving a chisel into your skull — let me know right away. It could be a sign of altitude sickness, and that's no laughing matter."

I closed my eyes and decided that it would be much better for my peace of mind if I refrained from asking any more questions. When I opened them again, I was swaying slightly from side to side and squinting in the glare of oncoming headlights.

The broad interstate and the wide open spaces had vanished, replaced by a two-lane highway that wound halfway up the wall of a twisting, serpentine canyon. In the dim light of the dying day, I could see a white-water stream foaming below us, while above us pine trees appeared to cling by their root tips to whatever soil they could find in the rocky terrain.

The road seemed to be made up entirely of blind curves bordered intermittently by bent and dented guardrails. As cars, campers, and trucks hurtled toward us out of nowhere, it became bloodcurdlingly clear to me that my husband had been both wise and farsighted to hire a local driver for us. Had I been foolish enough to take the wheel, I would have sent the van crashing into the canyon wall or plummeting into the rushing stream before we'd rounded the first bend.

I must have flinched, because Toby noticed that I was awake.

"Enjoy your nap?" he asked softly. He jutted his chin toward the backseats. "The others have dozed off, too."

"I wish I were still asleep," I confessed, tightening my seat belt. "I enjoyed the drive more when I was unconscious."

"It takes getting used to," Toby conceded, "but we're almost there, and you wouldn't want to miss this next part."

He'd barely finished speaking when the canyon opened out onto a scene of such startling beauty that I caught my breath. We'd entered a long valley surrounded by high mountain ranges. A black lake filled the valley floor, reflecting the handful of stars that had appeared in the darkening sky. The lights of a town twinkled at the lake's western tip, like birthday candles set in black velvet, surmounted by the serried silhouettes of peaks backlit by the setting sun.

"Welcome to the Vulgamore Valley," said Toby. "Bluebird's just ahead. Nice, isn't it?"

"It's gorgeous," I said softly. "Absolutely

gorgeous. I didn't expect a lake."

"Technically, it's a reservoir," said Toby. "But we call it Lake Matula, in honor of Annabelle Matula, the first woman to settle in the Vulgamore Valley."

"Are there fish?" asked a sleepy voice behind us.

"Lots of them," Toby replied. "And you'll find fishing poles at the cabin."

"Good," murmured Will. "I like fishing."

"Me, too," Rob chimed in, though he sounded even more drowsy than his brother.

When I next looked over my shoulder, they were both nodding in their booster seats, fast asleep. It had been a long day for my little guys.

The two-lane highway followed Lake Matula's northern shore, but trees grew right down to the edge of its southern shore. Search as I might, I could discover no glimmer of light in the forest, no sign of habitation anywhere but in the cluster of buildings to the west. It looked as though every human being in the Vulgamore Valley lived in Bluebird. Where, I wondered, was the cabin?

The posted speed limit fell from fifty to twenty when we reached Bluebird, at the far end of Lake Matula. The town had looked tiny from a distance, but it was at least three times larger than Finch. I could tell at a glance that it differed from Finch in many other ways as well. The golden limestone used to build Finch's houses had come from one quarry, so the village possessed a pleasing homogeneity that attracted world-class artists to its cobbled streets.

The same could not be said of Bluebird, which seemed to pride itself on the helter-skelter individuality of its dwellings. We drove past tiny Victorian cottages, stark cinderblock huts, ramshackle wooden houses, and at least one geodesic dome. It was too dark to pass judgment on the church, and I had only the briefest glimpse of the business district, but the gas station was a brightly lit eyesore flanked by heaps of dirty snow.

Toby turned left at the gas station onto a side street that became a dirt road at the edge of town. The stars vanished from view as we entered the dense, pitch-black forest bordering Lake Matula's southern shore. Toby followed the dirt road for about fifty yards, then slowed the van to a crawl and turned onto an even narrower dirt road that zigged and zagged upward.

"Lots of deer in these woods," he explained. "I wouldn't want to hit one on your first night here."

"Or any other night," I said, and peered anxiously ahead, hoping that our bouncing, juddering headlights would discourage all woodland creatures from crossing the road.

After what seemed an eternity, we reached a level clearing in the forest. Toby promptly shut off the engine and doused the headlights.

"Wait here," he said. "I'll be back in a minute."

I waited nervously while he disappeared into the gloom, wondering if bears knew how to open car doors; then I shrank back, blinking, as a blinding blaze of light drove away the darkness.

There, in the clearing, illuminated by a constellation of floodlights, stood Danny Auerbach's log cabin.

It wasn't a shack.

FIVE

Danny's cabin was unlike any building I'd ever seen. It sprawled across the clearing and climbed up the hillside like the roots of a gigantic tree, bending itself around boulders, bridging small gulleys, and encircling saplings.

In some places the cabin was one story tall; in others it rose to three, but each level bristled with balconies, decks, and porches. There seemed to be hundreds of sparkling windows, and they came in all shapes and sizes: portholes, stars, octagons, massive sheets of plate glass, tiny panes of leaded glass. At least six stone chimneys, three weathervanes, and a flagless flagpole rose from the irregular roofline. The largest chimney belonged to the cabin's central feature: a soaring A-frame structure, with a front wall made almost entirely of glass, that extended into the clearing like the prow of a ship.

"Wow," I said faintly.

"Pretty cool, huh?" said Toby.

"It's . . . it's *wonderful,*" I managed, wishing I could think of a bigger word. "It's magical, incredible, better than I —" I broke off, pricked by a sudden suspicion, and turned toward Toby so quickly that the seat belt snapped taut across my chest. "Does a crazy neighbor live nearby? With a shotgun?"

Toby eyed me in puzzlement. "The Auerbachs have owned the south side of the valley for five generations, Lori. They've never allowed anyone else to build here. Our nearest neighbor is Dick Major, and he lives at the edge of town, where the dirt road begins." Toby pointed to the east end of the cabin. "My apartment's behind the garage, and I don't own a shotgun."

"Just checking," I said, and settled back, relieved to know that two of my biggest worries had failed to materialize. The cabin wasn't a dilapidated shanty, and I wouldn't have to deal with a crazy neighbor. So far, so good, I thought. Now we'll see about the drains.

Toby restarted the engine, drove past the central A-frame, and parked the van in front of a short, broad staircase that led to an imposing wooden door incised with images of soaring eagles.

"Welcome to the Aerie," he said. "I'll get the luggage while you and Annelise bring the boys in. We can take them straight to bed, if you like."

I turned to look at the twins, who were still fast asleep. "Bed is where they need to be, but I can't lift either one of them. I hurt my shoulder a few weeks ago and it's still a little weak, so would you mind . . . ?"

"No problem," Toby said and stepped out into the crisp night air.

An hour later, the boys were in bed, Annelise was enjoying a well-earned bubble bath in a bathroom fit for a queen, and Toby and I were sitting on a huge, soft leather sofa in the great room, sipping hot chocolate in front of a roaring fire.

"Are you *sure* we're supposed to use the family's bedrooms?" I asked for the third or fourth time.

Toby nodded. "James left a note instructing me to put you in the family rooms. He thought you'd like being on the same corridor, but if you want to move —"

"No, no," I said hastily. "I don't want to change a thing."

Will and Rob would have disowned me if I'd moved them from the room James

Blackwell had assigned to them. The boys' bedroom was a *boy's* bedroom. The furniture was child-sized and made from rough-hewn logs. The chest of drawers had horseshoe handles, the twin beds had cartwheel headboards, and the metal bases of the bedside lamps were shaped like bucking broncos. The wide-planked floor was covered with Navajo-style rugs, the beds with Navajo-style blankets, and colorful paintings of hardworking cowboys hung on the walls.

The pièce de résistance was the open archway in the rear wall that led to an enormous playroom. The playroom's cupboards were filled with toys and board games, and a freestanding tent stood in the back corner, but the main attraction was the log fort with its rope ladder, slide, and tower. Annelise and I agreed that the fort would be a godsend if summer blizzards kept the twins cooped up indoors. The playroom also had a large picture window, but, thankfully, no porch, deck, or balcony from which my adventurous offspring could tumble.

Annelise, too, would have objected to any suggestion that she move from the room James Blackwell had selected for her, for practical as well as aesthetic reasons. Her bedroom was conveniently located directly across the hall from the twins' and next door to a splendid family bathroom, but it was also charmingly furnished and had its own little balcony.

The master suite, at the end of the same corridor, was sparely but beautifully furnished with simple pine furniture. White curtains hung at the windows, fluffy white rugs covered the polished plank floor, and the king-sized bed was draped with a crocheted white coverlet over a white duvet. A pair of white-upholstered armchairs sat before a corner fireplace made of smooth river stones, and the bathroom was a spacious oasis of comfort, with a cedar-clad Jacuzzi tub, a glass-walled shower stall, and double sinks set into an antique sideboard. A set of French doors in the bedroom led to a deck that overlooked the clearing in front of the Aerie. I had no desire whatsoever to exchange the master suite for another room.

"It's just a bit strange," I said, turning to Toby. "I mean, there are clothes hanging in the closets. I feel as if we're intruding."

"You're not," he assured me. "James Blackwell was supposed to ship the Auerbachs' stuff to them, but I guess he never got around to it. I'll take care of it tomorrow. But if you want to move to one of the guest suites —"

"No, thanks," I said firmly. "James Blackwell made the right call. I like being near my sons and Annelise. How many children does Danny Auerbach have?"

"Three," he replied. "Two young sons and a teenaged daughter."

I looked around the great room and sighed. "They must be the happiest kids on earth."

The great room was the A-frame structure at the center of the Aerie, a vast open space divided by furniture into three distinct zones. The ultramodern kitchen and the dining area took up the back half of the room, separated by a granite-topped breakfast bar, and the living room filled the front half — and I do mean *filled.*

The living room was jammed with leather sofas and chairs, wooden benches, pine tables, Indian rugs, carved chests, and a gaily painted upright piano that looked as though it had once seen action in a bordello. Rustic, glass-fronted cabinets held family photographs, rocks, feathers, bones, old spoons, antlers, and interesting bits of wood. Indian baskets, kerosene lamps, old cowboy hats, and tin plates filled shelves that had been mounted at various heights on the log walls, and quilts lay across the backs of chairs and on ottomans, as if to provide an extra source of warmth on chilly evenings. Some of the furniture was clustered before the enormous plate-glass windows, and some sat before the magnificent stone hearth, but none of it was formally arranged, and all of it looked well used.

The great room was cluttered beyond belief, and I fell in love with it at first sight. The Aerie wasn't a model home decorated by a fashionable designer. It was a real home where real people really lived, exuberant people who found the world fascinating and surrounded themselves with its colors and textures and their happy memories.

"It's wonderful," I murmured. "Just wonderful."

"I think so, too," Toby said agreeably. "Were you able to reach your husband?"

"Yes," I said. "He wanted me to use a laptop to do videoconferencing while we're here, but I'm not very good with computers. Fortunately, my mobile, er, my cell phone is working just fine. I know how to use a telephone."

"What time was it in England when you spoke with him?" asked Toby.

"Half past five in the morning," I said with a guilty wince. "Bill was pretty groggy, so we didn't have a long conversation."

"I'm surprised *you* aren't groggy," Toby commented.

"I will be, but I need to wind down a bit first." I raised my mug to salute him. "Hot chocolate always does the trick. Thanks for making it." I took a sip, then asked, "Do your grandparents still live in Bluebird?"

"No, but they're buried in the cemetery," said Toby, and when I looked distressed, he continued, "It's what they always wanted. They loved Bluebird. Granddad was the town doctor. He hoped Dad would take up the practice after him, but Dad went to school back east and decided to stay there. I grew up in Connecticut, but I came back here every summer. I love it here. I don't ever want to leave."

The double doors to the foyer opened, and we both looked over the back of the sofa as Annelise appeared, dressed in her robe and nightgown, with her luxuriant auburn hair streaming down her back.

"Lori?" she said. "May I have a word?"

"I'll refill your mug," Toby offered, and busied himself in the kitchen while I crossed to speak with Annelise.

"How's your shoulder?" she asked quietly.

I glanced toward the kitchen, to make sure Toby wasn't listening. My gunshot wound was a private matter. I didn't want him or anyone else I met on holiday to know about it.

"My shoulder's stiff," I said, lowering my voice, "but so's the rest of me. I feel as though we crossed the plains in a covered wagon instead of a wide-bodied jet."

"I recommend a hot bath." She stepped closer to me and went on very softly, "If you have any . . . bad dreams . . . you know where to find me."

I bristled slightly, but kept my voice low. "Did Bill ask you to look after me as well as the boys while we're here? He shouldn't have. I'll be fine."

"You weren't fine on the plane," she reminded me.

"But I *was* fine in the van," I countered. "I napped and I woke up, just like a normal person. I intend to do the same from now on."

"Of course you do," said Annelise, "but if you have any trouble —"

"Thanks, but I won't," I snapped, straightening. "Good night, Annelise."

"Good night, Lori." She called good night to Toby, closed the double doors, and went to her room.

As I returned to the sofa I made a mental note to tell Bill that I was in no more need of a nanny than I was of a babysitter.

"Do your parents fuss over you?" I asked Toby as he returned from the kitchen.

"Sure." He handed the refilled mug to me and resumed his place on the sofa. "It's what parents do. That's why I loved staying with Granddad. He always treated me as if I were a grown-up. I used to chop firewood when I was eight or nine, with a real axe." Toby's blue eyes twinkled delightfully as the old memories came back to him. "Granddad would have been charged with child neglect back east, but no one in Bluebird even noticed. It was the best place imaginable to be a kid."

"I wish I could have met your grandfather." I turned to stare sullenly into the fire. "It would be nice to be treated like a grown-up."

"It was great," said Toby. "I had the run of the valley. The only place I couldn't go was up here."

"Why?" I asked.

"The Aerie was built on the site of the old Lord Stuart Mine," he explained. "Until two years ago, the clearing was filled with half-ruined buildings and rusty machinery. Mr. Auerbach used some of the timber from the old mine buildings when he built the Aerie, but when I was a kid, the place was a death trap. Granddad made it clear that if he ever caught me up here, I wouldn't be allowed to visit him again. He was afraid I'd fall down a mine shaft."

"Mine shaft?" I echoed hollowly. "Are there mine shafts up here?"

"Hundreds of them," said Toby, "but most of them are fenced off, and when Mr. Auerbach built the Aerie, he had a whole team of engineers seal the entrance to the Lord Stuart Mine. It's tight as a drum, Lori, so you don't have to worry about Will or Rob getting into it. Mr. Auerbach has children, too," he reminded me gently.

Chastened, I took a calming swig of hot chocolate. "How often do the Auerbachs use the Aerie?"

"They haven't been here since Christmas," Toby replied. "Mr. Auerbach is a busy man."

"If he's too busy to use the cabin," I said, "why did he build it in the first place?"

Toby grinned. "He told Granddad that his parents wouldn't allow him to have a tree house when he was a child. The cabin's his tree house."

"Some tree house," I said admiringly. I pointed to a door beside the hearth. "What's through there?"

"The library," said Toby.

"There's a *library?*" I heard the squeak of

disbelief in my voice and smiled wryly at my own foolishness. "To be perfectly honest, Toby, I thought the cabin would be sort of . . . primitive. I wasn't sure it would have indoor plumbing, let alone a library."

Toby rolled his eyes. "You wouldn't catch Mrs. Auerbach using an outhouse. She likes her comfort. She added the outdoor spa and the home theater to Mr. Auerbach's building plans, and the library was her idea, too. She collects books. Would you like to take a tour?"

"Let's save it for tomorrow," I suggested, and we lapsed into a comfortable silence.

Several moments passed before I realized that I was staring fixedly at a lock of Toby's pale blond hair gleaming in the firelight and decided that it was time to go to bed. I quickly drained my mug, but before I could carry it into the kitchen, Toby took it from my hand.

"I'll do the dishes," he said. "You've had a tough day. Don't worry about the lights, either. I'll turn them off after you've gone."

"Do we have plans for tomorrow?" I asked, getting to my feet.

"If I were you, I'd take it easy for a few days," he advised, rising. "Let yourself adjust to the altitude before you attempt anything strenuous. Slow and steady wins the race."

"Slow and steady it is, then," I said. "Why don't you join us for breakfast? We should be up by eight," I added, though I knew I'd be up much earlier, "and we'll have breakfast on the table by nine. You can give us a tour of the Aerie afterward."

"Sounds good to me." Toby took a ring of keys from his pocket and handed them to me, saying, "They open every door in the Aerie. I have a duplicate set, so don't worry about losing them. My apartment's through there." He pointed to a passageway at the end of the kitchen. "If you need anything, come and get me." His eyes crinkled adorably as he smiled down at me. "I'm glad you're here, Lori. The Aerie's too big for just one person. I'll see you in the morning."

"Good night," I said. "And thanks, Toby. I've never met James Blackwell, but he couldn't be better than you."

"Aw, shucks, ma'am." Toby let his silky blond hair fall forward to hide his face. "You're making me blush."

I peered at him suspiciously. "Have you ever said 'Aw, shucks' before in your life?"

"Never," he said, raising his head and grinning playfully, "but it seemed appropriate."

I smiled, punched him lightly in the shoulder, and headed for the master suite. It was very late, so I settled for a hot shower instead of a bath, pulled on a flannel nightie, lit a fire in the corner fireplace, and sat in the armchair before the hearth, with Reginald in the crook of my arm and the blue journal in my lap. Aunt Dimity's old-fashioned copperplate began to spin across the page as soon as I opened the journal.

Is there a dirt floor? Does the roof leak? Is the loo out of doors?

"No, no, and definitely not," I replied. "It's wonderful, Dimity. The valley is wonderful, the cabin is wonderful, our rooms are wonderful, and Toby is wonderful. Everything is absolutely wonderful."

You seem giddy, my dear. Have you been drinking?

"Yes, but only hot chocolate," I told her. "I'm not drunk, Dimity. I'm ecstatic, euphoric, incredibly relieved that the cabin is so wonderful. . . ." I paused to get a grip on myself, then added, "Or maybe it's the altitude."

Rapture of the heights? Perhaps. Who, may I ask, is Toby?

"Toby Cooper," I replied. "He's the last-minute replacement for the original caretaker."

And he's wonderful, is he? Am I to assume that he's also good looking?

I shifted uncomfortably in the armchair. Aunt Dimity knew all too well that my track record with attractive men who were not my husband wasn't as spotless as it should have been. I'd never actually forgotten my wedding vows, but my memory had grown hazy from time to time. If I told Dimity that Toby Cooper was as cute as a cocker spaniel — a tall, broad-shouldered, manly cocker spaniel — she would get the wrong impression, so I elected to downplay his good looks.

"He's a child, Dimity," I said airily. "A nice kid. He's twenty-one years old and still in college."

Good. You've never shown much interest in younger men. What happened to the original caretaker?

"James Blackwell?" I said. "He quit two days ago. I don't know why. According to Danny Auerbach, he left unexpectedly."

Perhaps he grew tired of dealing with the crackpot neighbor.

"There isn't one," I said happily. "We have the whole mountainside to ourselves."

Perhaps Mr. Blackwell was overworked.

"Are you kidding?" I said. "No one's been here since Christmas."

He might have been lonely.

"The cabin's awfully big for just one person," I agreed, recalling Toby's words. "But it's splendid, Dimity. It has every luxury, but it still feels like a family home. I don't know why the Auerbachs don't use it more often. They left so much stuff behind that they wouldn't have to pack much more than an overnight bag."

What did the Auerbachs leave behind?

"This and that," I said. "A blouse and two pairs of trousers in my closet, a few T-shirts and a pair of sneakers in the boys' room."

It sounds like an abandoned ship. Why didn't the family take their clothes with them after their Christmas visit?

"They're rich," I said. "They probably have multiple wardrobes for multiple residences."

Did they leave entire wardrobes behind?

"No," I said. "Just odds and ends."

They left odds and ends, here and there. It suggests to me that they packed hastily. How very interesting.

"Is it?" I said vaguely. It was past midnight and the long day was catching up with me. I was suddenly too tired to follow Aunt Dimity's train of thought.

It's extremely interesting. If the Auerbachs packed in a rush, then we're dealing with two abrupt departures — the family's and James Blackwell's. If the cabin is as wonderful as you claim, why did they leave it in such a hurry?

"Don't know," I said.

You might ask Bill to look into it. He might know of some family emergency the Auerbachs experienced at Christmastime. And Mr. Auerbach may have told him why James Blackwell quit.

"I will," I said, suppressing a yawn. "I'll ask Bill tomorrow. Or today. I can't keep track anymore."

Of course you can't. Forgive me for prattling on, my dear. You must be exhausted. We'll continue our discussion after you've had a good rest. But don't forget to speak to Bill about it. I don't like abrupt departures, especially when they're unexplained.

"I'll remember, Dimity," I promised.

Sleep well, my dear.

"I think I might manage it tonight," I said to Reginald as the lines of royal-blue ink slowly faded from the page.

I placed the journal on the bedside table and brought Reginald to bed with me, to ward off my recurring nightmare. I lay awake for a short time, watching the firelight dance on the beamed ceiling and wondering why anyone would abandon such a lovely ship, but Toby's image kept swimming through my mind, distracting me.

"Like a cocker spaniel," I murmured, and smiling drowsily, I drifted into sleep.

Six

I awoke from a confused dream involving heroic dogs and sinking ships to find bright sunlight streaming through the French doors and the windows. A glance at the bedside clock told me that it was half past eight. I pushed the duvet aside, rolled out of bed with Reginald in my arms, and walked slowly toward the French doors, unable to believe my eyes. I hadn't slept past sunrise since I'd been shot.

Cold air rushed in as I threw open the doors, but the view made me forget that I was barefoot and wearing only a nightgown. My deck was no more than two feet off the ground, but I could see the entire valley from it: the glittering lake, the deep green forest, the snow-streaked peaks against a sky so dazzlingly blue that I couldn't look at it without squinting. The landscape was grandiose, extreme, almost frightening in its immensity. Nothing was tame or understated.

"Reginald," I said, under my breath, "I don't think we're in Finch anymore."

I shivered and wrapped my arms more tightly around myself and my pink rabbit, then realized with a start what the bedside clock had been trying to tell me.

"Eight-thirty!" I yelped. "Toby'll be here at nine!"

I hightailed it back into the suite, sped through my morning routine, and pulled on jeans, a T-shirt, a warm woolen sweater, and sneakers. I tried to run to the great room, but gave up halfway down the corridor. Once I'd stopped seeing pinpoints of light dance before my eyes, I continued at a more sedate pace and opened the double doors to the mouthwatering scent of frying bacon. The twins were perched on stools at the breakfast bar, Annelise hovered over several frying pans on the stove, and Toby stood across the granite-topped bar from the twins, filling their glasses with orange juice. I'd arrived just in time to hear him laying down the law to Will and Rob.

"First rule of the Aerie," Toby was saying. "Don't leave food lying around outside — not a peanut, not a hot dog, not a potato chip, *nothing.*"

I paused with my hands on the doorknobs

and held my breath. If Toby explained that human food attracted wild animals, the boys would probably create a trail of leftovers to guide bears to the playroom window. But Toby didn't fail me.

"It's unhealthy for the squirrels," he went on. "If we feed the squirrels, they'll get fat and fall out of their trees, *splat*." He smacked his hand on the breakfast bar, making the boys jump.

"We won't leave food out," Will promised, round eyed.

"We *like* squirrels," Rob said earnestly.

"Second rule of the Aerie," Toby went on. "No playing with matches. Forest fires are a very real danger in the high country. One careless match and" — Toby snapped his fingers — "no home for the squirrels."

"We *never* play with matches," Rob declared.

"Never," Will asserted.

"Then we'll get along fine," said Toby.

"Morning, all," I called, crossing to give my sons their morning hugs.

"Good morning, Lori." Annelise favored me with a penetrating glance. "How did you sleep?"

"I don't remember," I said triumphantly. "I was asleep."

"I'm making tomato and spinach omelets

to go along with the bacon," said Annelise, turning back to the frying pans. "You'll never guess what Toby brought for breakfast."

"Rattlesnake steaks?" I ventured, climbing onto a stool.

"Not for *breakfast,*" Toby scoffed, and pushed a large plate across the breakfast bar toward me.

"Scones?" I said, staring incredulously at the pile heaped on the plate. "You brought *scones?*"

"He brought homemade strawberry jam as well," said Annelise, sliding omelets onto our plates.

I looked from her to Toby. "Where on earth . . . ?"

"Caroline's Cafe," Toby answered. "Carrie Vyne makes her own jams and jellies, and she makes scones from scratch every morning. I ran down there in the van and bought a batch fresh from the oven. I thought you'd enjoy a taste of home."

I beamed at him. "If anyone had told me that I'd spend my first morning in the Rocky Mountains feasting on homemade strawberry jam and made-from-scratch scones, I would have told them they were dreaming."

"That's my job." He spooned jam onto a

scone and offered it to me. "Making dreams come true."

Our fingers brushed as I took the scone from him, and I felt a distinctive jolt that had nothing to do with the altitude, so I passed the scone quickly to Rob, cut Will's omelet into bite-sized pieces, and ordered myself sternly to act my age.

"When do we get to see the cowboys?" Rob asked, through a mouthful of scone.

"Not for a couple of days," I said. "We have to get used to the altitude before we go riding. But there are plenty of other things to do while we're here. Toby's going to give us a tour of the Aerie after breakfast."

Rob and Will were seriously under-whelmed by the prospect of traipsing through the Aerie, looking at rooms — the playroom was the only room that interested them, and they'd already seen *that* — so I suggested that Toby take them on a short hike after breakfast while Annelise and I poked around the Aerie on our own.

"Great idea," said Toby. "We'll go up to see the eagle's nest."

The boys brightened visibly, gobbled their breakfast, and ran off to fetch their hiking boots. I would have bundled them up in their warmest winter jackets as well if Toby hadn't stopped me.

"Light windbreakers over their sweatshirts will do," he said. "Hiking's hot work."

"But there's snow on the ground," I protested.

"It'll be gone by noon," he said, laughing. "We have four seasons every day in Colorado. Granddad used to say it should be the state motto. You'll see."

Annelise and I spent an hour exploring the Aerie before we were spent. After meandering through three guest suites, the laundry room, the arcade game room, the billiards room, the home theater, the library, the outdoor spa — which included a sauna and a massage cubicle as well as a beautifully landscaped hot tub — and myriad decks, balconies, and porches, we staggered back to the great room for a gulp of water and a well-deserved rest.

"Too many stairs," said Annelise, her chest heaving. "It's like climbing Mount Everest."

"Without oxygen tanks." I peeled off my sweater and sprawled on the sofa. I'd just put my feet up when my cell phone rang.

"Lori?" Bill sounded far more alert than he had when I'd called him in the middle of his night. "Why are you out of breath? You're not overdoing things, are you? You've only just arrived."

"You'll be happy to know that I'm reclining on a couch as we speak," I said. "Will and Rob are out hiking with Toby, but Annelise and I are taking it easy."

"Then why are you out of breath?" Bill pressed.

"Annelise and I have been hiking through the cabin," I said. "It's like Versailles. Glorious, but *big.*"

"I knew you'd like it," said Bill. "Danny never does anything halfway. About Toby Cooper — I didn't know the other caretaker had quit until I read Danny's e-mail last night. Is Toby okay?"

"He's great. The boys are crazy about him." So are you, muttered my conscience. I told it to shut up and hurriedly changed the subject. "It's strange about James Blackwell, though. Did Danny tell you why he quit?"

"Danny doesn't have a clue," said Bill. "Blackwell had worked as his caretaker since just before Christmas. The pay was good and the job was relatively undemanding, so Danny can't understand why he took off the way he did, without giving notice. Danny's pretty upset about it, but he assured me that Toby Cooper would take good care of you."

"He brought us fresh-baked scones this

morning," I said.

"Say no more," said Bill, sounding relieved. "I'll tell Danny you're happy with him."

I sat up on the couch and looked toward Annelise, who was standing at the window wall, dutifully drinking water while surveying the stunning scenery. Since she wasn't privy to the secret of the blue journal, I couldn't mention Aunt Dimity while she was within earshot, so I acted as if the next question were my own.

"Bill," I said, "did Danny have a family emergency last Christmas?"

"I don't know," Bill replied. "I wasn't in regular contact with him back then. Why do you ask?"

"He and his family spent Christmas at the cabin," I explained, "and they left some of their clothes behind. It looks as though they packed without double-checking the drawers and closets. I was wondering if something happened to make them leave in a panic."

"They're probably just absentminded." Bill's voice was edged with concern. "What's all this about a panic? You're not getting spooked are you, Lori? How did you sleep last night?"

"Like a log," I said flatly. "Until half past

eight."

"No nightmare?" Bill asked incredulously.

"Abaddon took the night off," I told him. "I'm not spooked, Bill. I'm curious. Would you ask Danny if anything happened at Christmas?"

"I will." Bill paused. "You really slept through the night?"

"I really slept through the night, undisturbed by my creepy nighttime companion," I told him. "You're a genius. The mountain air is like a tonic."

"Yay," he cheered softly, and went on to bring me up to date on affairs in Finch.

Nell Harris had returned from France but wedding bells hadn't yet chimed for her and Kit Smith, Peggy Taxman had made a ludicrously low offer for the greengrocer's shop, and the weather had been drizzly. I tried to describe the Aerie and the view from my deck, but failed so miserably that I gave up in the end, and told Bill he'd simply have to fly over and see it for himself.

"I wish I could," said Bill. "I know you had doubts about the trip, Lori —"

"And I was a fool to have them," I interrupted. "Your brilliant idea was truly brilliant, Bill. The only thing missing is you."

After promising to pay closer attention to

the time difference when calling him, I rang off.

"The snow's all but gone," Annelise observed, turning away from the window wall. "And there's hardly a puddle to be seen. There's something to be said for dry air." She strolled toward the sofa. "All's well at home?"

"I'll fill you in while we fix lunch," I said, getting to my feet. "The boys will be famished when they get back."

"I'm a bit peckish myself," said Annelise. "And I intend to take a nap after lunch."

"We'll *all* take naps after lunch," I said determinedly. "Slow and steady wins the race."

We stayed in or near the Aerie for three full days, but no one was bored. We took long hikes after breakfast, naps after lunch, and slightly shorter hikes before dinner. While we napped, Toby packed the Auerbachs' possessions and took the boxes to the Bluebird post office for shipping. He came back from town each day with something new to round out our wardrobes: wide-brimmed hats with ventilated crowns, shock-absorbing hiking poles, and lightweight headlamps for night hiking. Since my injured shoulder made wearing a day pack uncomfortable, I asked Toby to buy a waist pack for me; it came with pouches for two water bottles and a zippered compartment for small essentials.

Toby joined us for every meal and spent the evenings with us around the fire pit near the outdoor spa, singing songs, telling stories, and making beautifully gooey s'mores. It seemed a shame not to take advantage of the arcade games and the home theater, but no one wanted to stay indoors when the outdoors was so enticing.

When I finally took the time to explore Mrs. Auerbach's library, I found that it contained books on Colorado flora, fauna, geology, art, architecture, folklore, photography, and history, as well as biographies of prominent Coloradans. I selected a volume on Colorado pottery to read in bed, but I never made it beyond the first paragraph of the introduction because I couldn't keep my eyes open long enough to read further. The thin air was like a narcotic.

The trails around the Aerie were narrow, rock-strewn, and crisscrossed with tree roots, which made them far more challenging than the smooth, well-trodden paths surrounding Finch. Since I'd been all but bedridden for six weeks, I had trouble keeping up with the others, but Toby was never in a hurry and he always found clever ways to keep the twins occupied while I plodded slowly uphill, wishing I had an ice pack for my throbbing shoulder.

Toby was the ideal guide, extending our hikes gradually each day as our stamina increased. He pointed out famous landmarks and repeated their names until we knew them by heart: Ruley's Peak, Mount Schroeder, Chaney Canyon, the Bartos Range. We waded in Willie Brown Creek, picnicked in Getty's Gulch, and snapped photographs of mule deer grazing near the defunct Luddington Mine.

Toby had us stand stock-still and listen as the leaves chattered in stands of white-barked aspens. He drew us close to ponderosa pines, to smell the vanilla fragrance in the deeply creviced bark. He spotted a pair of luminous Mountain Bluebirds perched atop an old fence post at the edge of a meadow, and told us that an early prospector had named the town after a pair that had guided him to his first gold strike.

Toby also taught us to wear gallons of sunblock, to *stay with the group,* and to bring extra water on every hike. Thanks to his sage advice, and good fortune with the weather, we managed to avoid dust storms, sunstroke, rattlesnake bites, hypothermia,

89

altitude sickness, and a host of other woes that awaited unwary travelers in the mountains.

Rob and Will were so carried away by their high altitude adventure that they insisted on "camping out" in the playroom every night. They got a huge kick out of crawling into the sleeping bags in the freestanding tent and furtively switching on their headlamps after I'd called for lights out. I didn't mind. I liked knowing that the only bears in their wilderness were plush and toothless.

Bill called after breakfast every morning, but he was unable to answer Dimity's most pressing question. Danny Auerbach had switched his e-mail to auto-reply while he negotiated a new deal somewhere in Alaska, and Bill had been unable to reach him by telephone, so we still didn't know whether or not a family emergency had cropped up for the Auerbachs around Christmastime. Dimity found Danny's sudden inaccessibility deeply suspicious. I thought the altitude was making her daffy.

At our campfire on Friday, Toby made the momentous announcement that the boys were fit enough to ride the next day.

"I called ahead to the Brockman Ranch, so they'll be expecting us," he informed us. "They're providing two English-trained ponies, according to the instructions your husband gave them."

"Do they have English-trained ponies?" Annelise asked, surprised.

"Sure," Toby replied. "The Brockman used to be a working ranch, but beef isn't as profitable as it once was, so Deke and Sarah Brockman run it as a dude ranch now. They cater to riders from all over the world."

Will and Rob didn't like being thought of as dudes — once we'd explained to them what a dude was — but they were so anxious to climb into the saddle again that they *asked* to go to bed early. I left them zipped into their sleeping bags in their tent, to dream about horses, and shortly thereafter went to my bed, to dream about sweet-natured, blue-eyed cocker spaniels. Abaddon couldn't compete.

SEVEN

Toby did a double take on Saturday morning when Will and Rob paraded before him, nattily attired in tailored black riding coats, white turtlenecks, fawn-colored breeches, and tall black boots, with sturdy black riding helmets in their hands.

"You were expecting blue jeans and cowboy hats?" I said, raising an eyebrow at him.

"It's what most people wear at the Brockman Ranch," said Toby, "wherever they come from."

"Well, my boys learned to ride in England, and they're accustomed to English riding clothes." I folded the twins' distinguishing bandanas and tucked them into their breast pockets, so that only the tips protruded. "I may pick up some western gear for them to wear after they get used to their new ponies, but for now I'd like everything to be as familiar as possible. But I'm bringing clothes for them to change into when they've finished riding."

"Can they ride?" Toby asked, eyeing the boys' formal outfits doubtfully.

"Like the wind," I said proudly. "Don't worry. No one who sees my sons on horseback will make fun of the way they're dressed."

Since it was our first nonhiking day, Annelise had donned a pretty sun dress, a pale blue cardigan, and a pair of canvas slip-ons that were entirely unsuited for the trail. I'd dressed in shorts, a T-shirt, and sneakers, with a zippered sweatshirt on top to ward off the morning chill, and Toby was clad in his usual ensemble: T-shirt, flannel shirt, multipocketed trousers, and hiking boots. We all wore our wide-brimmed hats and copious sunblock, and carried our trusty water bottles in our packs.

The morning was a carbon copy of the three that had preceded it. The sun shone like a blowtorch, the sky was preposterously blue, and the air was so crisp it almost twinkled. Bill called after breakfast with nothing to report but the vicar's decision to leave rock and roll alone and ask the old reliable brass band to play their usual selection of familiar tunes at the village fête, a decision which had met with the villagers' heartfelt — and loudly expressed — approval. After the boys had taken turns telling their father about their plans for the day — "We're going to ride with cowboys!" — we all piled into the van.

Toby took the two-lane highway west out of Bluebird, over a mountain pass and down into a rolling valley dotted with stands of aspen and bisected by a willow-lined creek. As we came down from the pass, we could see the Brockman Ranch laid out before us.

A dirt road led from the highway to a sprawling log house with a deep porch, three stone chimneys, and a huge rack of elk antlers nailed over the front door. Spread out behind the house were a large barn, a spacious riding ring, and assorted holding pens, paddocks, outbuildings, and sheds. A row of rustic-looking cabins sat among the willows along the creek, with cars and campers parked beside those that were, presumably, occupied by dudes. Rob and Will nearly popped out of their booster seats when they saw a herd of buffalo grazing in the distance and a string of horses munching hay in one of the paddocks.

"The Brockmans had to go to Denver today," Toby informed me, as he parked the van in front of the ranch house, "but I spoke with the head wrangler, Brett Whitcombe, and he said he'd look after Will and Rob personally. Ah, here he is now."

A tall, slender man with short-cropped gray hair had emerged from the house. He was dressed predictably, in faded jeans, a red-checked shirt, a tooled leather belt with a big silver-and-turquoise buckle, and pointy-toed boots. He carried a battered straw cowboy hat in one hand, but he put it on as he strode across the porch and came down the steps to greet us.

"Welcome to the Brockman," he said as he opened the passenger door for me. He looked as though he might be in his midthirties — too young to have gray hair, in my opinion — and his voice was gravelly but gentle. "I expect you'll be Ms. Shepherd."

"Lori," I said, staring up at him as I stepped out of the van. "Please, call me Lori." I pointed haphazardly over my shoulder. "Annelise, the boys' nanny, and Will and Rob, my sons."

"How do you do?" he said, tipping his hat in their general direction. "I'm Brett Whitcombe, head wrangler at the Brockman. Everyone calls me Brett. Good to see you, Tobe," he called as Toby came around the back of the van.

Toby nodded amiably, acknowledging the nickname. "Likewise, Brett."

While Annelise and Toby helped the twins

95

out of the van, I stood frozen in place, unable to tear my gaze from Brett Whitcombe. The straw hat threw a shadow across his face, so I leaned in for a closer look.

"What color are your eyes?" I asked.

"My eyes?" Brett seemed surprised by the question, but he replied, "My wife tells me they're violet, but I've always thought of them as blue."

"No," I said, shaking my head decisively. "They're violet. It's an unusual shade. I've seen it only once before, back in England. My sons' riding instructor." I stepped back to survey the head wrangler's long lean body, short gray hair, and extraordinary eyes. "You're not related to an Englishman named Kit Smith, are you? His full name is Christopher Anscombe-Smith."

Brett threw a mystified glance in Toby's direction, then said politely, "I guess it's possible, but I couldn't say for sure. I've never taken much of an interest in genealogy."

"You could be Kit's brother," I marveled. "His *twin* brother. The resemblance is uncanny. Do you see it, Annelise?"

"Do I see what?" she asked, herding Will and Rob along until we formed a half circle in front of Brett.

"Doesn't Brett look like Kit?" I asked.

Annelise shrugged. "I suppose he does, a bit."

"A *bit?*" I pointed at Brett's face. "He's got *violet eyes!*"

"They're blue," said Annelise, elbowing me in the ribs. "You'll have to forgive Lori, Brett. She's still recovering from jet lag."

"It's a long flight from England," Brett said sympathetically. "Will you need a horse today, Annelise?"

"Not today, thank you," said Annelise. "Lori won't be riding, either."

"Mummy's afraid of horses," Will piped up.

"I'm *not* afraid of horses," I protested.

"Yes, you are," said Rob. "You're afraid to give Toby carrots, and he doesn't hardly have any teeth."

"He doesn't?" said Brett, with a bewildered glance at Toby.

"Toby's a pony," Annelise explained quickly. "An elderly pony. Back in England."

"We learned to ride on Toby," Rob informed the head wrangler.

"But we have our own ponies now," Will added. "They're faster than Toby."

"And they have more teeth," Rob continued. "They're called Thunder and Storm."

"We have a cat, too," said Will. "His name is Stanley. Do you have a cat?"

"Do you know Cowboy Sam?" Rob inquired.

Brett looked from one identical chattering boy to the other, grimaced slightly, and rubbed the back of his neck. "My wife has quite a few cats. I've known two or three cowboys named Sam, but they don't work at the Brockman. The ponies I rounded up for you are out back, in the riding ring. Want to meet them?"

"Yes, please," the boys chorused.

"Let's go," said Brett.

He and Toby strode off with the twins, but Annelise gripped my arm firmly and held me back until they'd disappeared around the side of the house.

"Honestly, Lori," she scolded. "You embarrassed that poor man to death, pointing at him like that."

"But —" I began.

"No *buts*," Annelise interrupted sternly. "And no more staring. And no more talk about Kit Smith. The poor man doesn't know Kit from a hole in the ground, so there's no use going on about it. He'll think you've lost your mind."

She released my arm and marched off to join the boys.

I replayed the scene in my head, realized that Annelise had been quite right to take me to task for my rude behavior, and trailed slowly after her, feeling as though I'd embarrassed myself far more than I'd embarrassed Brett Whitcombe. Kit Smith, whose manners were impeccable, would have been ashamed of me. I resolved to say nothing more about him to Brett.

A five-bar wooden fence encircled the riding ring. Brett and the twins stood inside the ring, near the swinging metal gate, where a pair of ponies were tethered. Annelise and Toby had taken seats on a set of wooden bleachers on the far side of the ring, in the shade of some cottonwood trees. A half dozen teen-aged boys in scruffy cowboys hats had gathered on the near side of the fence to watch the proceedings, attracted no doubt by the novelty of my sons' riding apparel. I edged my way past them until I was within a few yards of Brett, the twins, and the ponies.

Brett had rounded up a pair of palomino ponies for Will and Rob. They were called Nip and Tuck, and they didn't seem too ferocious. While Brett explained the rules of the riding ring, the twins ran knowing eyes over their prospective mounts.

"We'll take it one at a time, to begin with," Brett concluded. "And I don't want you to move till I say so."

He tightened Nip's girth, gave Rob a leg up into the saddle, and adjusted the stirrups, but when he took hold of the lead rope, to guide Nip into the ring, Rob objected.

"I know what to do," he said impatiently.

Brett gave me an inquiring glance, I answered it with a nod, and he released the lead rope. Rob walked Nip sedately once around the ring, then put him through his paces, going from a walk to a trot to a canter, bringing him smoothly back to a walk, and halting him smartly beside Tuck. Will gave Brett an arms-folded, I-told-you-so look, and the head wrangler gave him a leg up onto Tuck without further delay.

"Your boys have been well taught," Brett commented, as he climbed out of the ring to stand beside me. "My long-lost twin must be a fine instructor."

I felt myself blush a stunning shade of raspberry.

"You got a twin, Brett?" said one of the spectators.

"So I'm told." Brett grinned at me, then gestured to the knot of young men. "Let me introduce the crew. Lori Shepherd, this is Dusty, Lefty, Happy, Sneezy, Dopey, and Doc."

I was on the verge of saying good morning when it dawned on me that Brett was joking. I ducked my head sheepishly and joined in the general laughter that ensued. When the ranch hands had finished guffawing, they introduced themselves to me properly, welcomed me to the Brockman, and drifted off toward Annelise. I wondered if they were going to try the same gag on her.

Annelise had the video camera, and I was in charge of the digital camera. While she filmed the action, I snapped still shots of the twins, then settled down next to Brett to watch them enjoy their favorite pastime.

"How're you liking it up at the Aerie?" Brett rested his folded arms on the top bar of the fence. "Toby working out all right?"

"Toby's great," I said. "Very eager to please. If I didn't stop him, he'd cook our meals and do our laundry along with everything else he does. And I absolutely love the Aerie. If it were mine, and if I didn't have to fly so far to get here, I'd use it every weekend. I can't believe the Auerbachs haven't used it since Christmas."

"Me, neither." Brett shook his head. "Mrs. Auerbach and the kids used to spend every school holiday up there, and most weekends, too, but we haven't seen hide nor hair of them for six months now. In fact, no one's been there since the Auerbachs left, no one but the caretaker."

"Really?" I said. "I was under the impression that the Auerbachs let friends use the Aerie."

"They haven't had any takers lately," said Brett. "I reckon Bluebird isn't fashionable enough for the kind of people the Auerbachs know. They get bored looking at the lake, want fancy shops and restaurants. Caroline's Cafe serves up some mighty tasty grub, but I wouldn't call it fancy."

I watched Will and Rob steer their steeds through a series of figure eights, then asked, "If the Aerie's been empty since Christmas, why did the Auerbachs hire a live-in caretaker?"

"The caretaker's main job is just to be there," Brett explained. "You can't leave a place like that sitting empty. You never know what'll happen to it — frozen pipes, wind damage. Someone has to be on the spot to fix things when they break, and James could turn his hand to anything."

My ears pricked up. "Did you know James Blackwell?"

"I wouldn't say I knew him," Brett temporized. "James used to drop in on us now and again. He took an interest in local history. Asked all sorts of questions. Wanted to know what Bluebird was like in the olden days."

I recalled the books on Colorado history in the Aerie's library and asked, "Was James an amateur historian?"

"I suppose he may have been," said Brett, "but I'm not. I told him if he wanted to know about Bluebird, he should go to Bluebird. That's when he told me about Dick Major." Brett tilted his head toward me. "You met Dick yet?"

"No," I said. "I haven't been to town."

Brett's eyes narrowed. "Dick Major is a loudmouthed pain in the neck. Wish he'd go back where he came from, but it looks like he's dug in, in Bluebird. From what James said, he couldn't have a beer in the bar or a cup of coffee in the cafe without Dick's turning up. Parked himself at James's table without an invitation; told James he was a lazy good-for-nothing, a slacker who was taking money from the Auerbachs for doing nothing. Kept telling James to get a real job and stop sponging off his rich employers. Called him a worthless bum, right there, where everyone could hear him."

"Why did Dick Major pick on James?" I asked.

"Because he could," Brett said simply.

"James wasn't from here, so he didn't have family to back him up. Didn't have any friends, either —"

"Why not?" I asked. "Why didn't he have any friends?"

"He was kind of shy," said Brett. "A nice enough guy, but quiet, studious — a prime target for a meathead like Dick."

"I *hate* bullies," I said vehemently.

"So do I." Brett shook his head. "If I'd seen Dick picking on James, I'd've put a stop to it, but Dick's sneaky. He never put a foot wrong in front of me. So after a while, James avoided Bluebird. He just stayed at the Aerie or came out here. I reckon he spent too much time on his own. Got to believing the stories he heard."

"What stories?" I asked.

"Tomfool stories," said Brett, snorting derisively. "He was always trying to find out if they were true. Then he up and left without saying a word to anyone. It's lucky Toby was free to take his place. Toby's a good kid. Known him since he was younger than your sons." Brett rested his chin on his folded arms, then gave me a sidelong glance. "Is it true that you're afraid of horses?"

"Uh, yes," I said, caught off guard by the abrupt change of subject. "My sons never lie, even when I wish they would."

"And this is your first time in the Rock-ies?" Brett went on.

"Yes," I said.

"Well, then," he said, turning to face me, "I have a suggestion to make. Why don't you leave Will and Rob here for the day? Annelise is welcome to stay with them. They can eat lunch with the rest of the guests and come along on the group trail ride this afternoon. In the meantime, you can take off with Toby, let him show you around. He knows every sight worth seeing in these parts. I'll have the twins back to the Aerie in plenty of time for dinner."

"Is your vehicle equipped with booster seats?" I asked.

"It can be," said Brett. "We have them on hand for people like you: overseas guests with young children. It won't take me but a minute to rustle up a pair for your boys. They work just fine in the family cab of my pickup."

"Sounds good to me," I said, "but I'll have to discuss it with Annelise. She's still get-ting used to the altitude. She may need a nap later on."

"She can use one of the guest cabins," said Brett. "My wife will make sure she's com-fortable, and I'll look out for Will and Rob."

"You're very kind," I said, "but Annelise

may not want to stay."

"On the other hand," said Brett, turning to look across the riding ring, "she may not want to leave."

I followed his gaze and saw that at least a dozen men had gathered around Annelise. Some were ranch hands, while others appeared to be dudes, but they'd all doffed their cowboy hats and they seemed to be vying with each other for her attention.

"Your sons' nanny has a fan club," Brett observed mildly. "Must be that pretty dress she's wearing. Most of the gals here wear jeans."

"She's engaged," I told him. "And she's extremely levelheaded."

"It does a young woman good to know she's admired," said Brett. "Even a level-headed young woman who's engaged."

Brett evidently knew a lot about women, because Annelise was perfectly willing to remain at the ranch until the twins were ready to leave. Toby was equally willing to escort me wherever I wished to go. And I was more than willing to let the twins ride to their hearts' content while I went back to the Aerie. I had a lot to tell Aunt Dimity.

Will and Rob were eventually persuaded to dismount long enough for me to kiss them good-bye. Annelise fetched their extra clothes from the van, and Toby and I drove off, leaving Brett to field a multitude of questions from the twins about the upcoming trail ride.

Toby and I were halfway down the dirt road when a girl came toward us, riding an Appaloosa mare. The girl was in her late teens, long legged and slender, with a flawless oval face framed by a mane of golden curls that gleamed like corn silk in the sun. She reined in as we approached and regarded us with eyes that shone like dark sapphires.

"Howdy, Belle!" Toby shouted as we drove past.

"Belle?" I said faintly. "Who is Belle?"

"She's Deke and Sarah Brockman's daughter," said Toby. "She and Brett Whitcombe got married last fall. It took Belle two years to get him to the altar. Brett just couldn't believe that a lovely young thing like her could care for an old crock like him. Not that Brett's old, but he thought he was too old for Belle. Belle got through to him in the end, though. As they say, true love conquers all." Toby glanced at me. "What's wrong, Lori? You look as though you've seen a ghost. You don't disapprove of Belle and Brett, do you?"

"Me? Disapprove of true love? Not in a

million years," I said, and let the subject drop. If I told Toby that Belle Whitcombe was the spitting image of Nell Harris, a teenager bent on marrying a man with violet eyes who was twice her age, he'd airlift me to the nearest lunatic asylum. But I was certainly going to tell Aunt Dimity. "I know we're supposed to be sightseeing, Toby, but do you mind if we go back to the Aerie instead? I'm a little tired."

"Has your shoulder stiffened up?" he asked.

My head snapped in his direction. "What do you know about my shoulder?"

"You told me you injured it a few weeks ago," he said. "And you rub it whenever you get tired. If it's bothering you, I'd recommend a long soak in the hot tub."

The thought of inviting Toby Cooper to join me in the hot tub was appallingly appealing, but I couldn't risk it. If Toby saw my scar, he'd inevitably ask questions I had no intention of answering. My brain had been blissfully Abaddon-free for four nights in a row and I wanted it to stay that way. To rehash the shooting would be to risk luring my black-eyed demon back again.

Apart from that, I felt an urgent need to tell Aunt Dimity everything I'd seen and heard at the Brockman Ranch, and I couldn't take the blue journal with me to the hot tub. I wasn't sure if Dimity's particular brand of ink would run when wet, but I didn't want to chance it.

"My shoulder's fine," I said brusquely. "I just need a nap. Let's go back to the Aerie."

"Your wish is my command," said Toby, and turned the van toward Bluebird.

EIGHT

When we reached the Aerie, Toby stayed outside to prune underbrush and chop down a small stand of saplings that had sprung up too near the fire pit, as if to illustrate Brett Whitcombe's observation that a place like the Aerie couldn't be left unattended for too long. The Aerie, Toby informed me, as he doffed his T-shirt and hefted his axe, needed constant attention to keep it from being overrun by the surrounding forest.

A weaker woman might have stuck around to watch him work up a sweat, but contrary to Aunt Dimity's belief, I was capable of exercising self-discipline. I excused myself and went to the master suite. The morning was so beautiful that I would have opened the French doors if I hadn't been worried about Toby passing beneath my deck and accidentally overhearing a lively conversation between me and thin air.

"I couldn't explain Aunt Dimity to him even if I wanted to," I said to Reginald as I retrieved the blue journal from the bedside table. "So we'll leave the French doors closed for now." I tweaked my pink bunny's ears, sat in the white armchair near the fireplace, opened the blue journal, and said excitedly, "Dimity? Are you there? I have so much to tell you!"

The curving lines of royal-blue ink zoomed across the page.

Have we heard from Danny Auerbach at last? Do we know why he and his family left the Aerie?

"I'll get to Danny in a minute. First, I have to tell you about" — I paused for dramatic effect — *"doppelgangers."*

I know what a doppelganger is, my dear. Why do you feel the need to tell me about them?

"Because I saw *two* doppelgangers this morning, at the Brockman Ranch." I launched into a detailed description of my encounters with Belle and Brett Whitcombe, then awaited Dimity's reaction. It wasn't everything I'd hoped it would be.

They sound very much like Nell Harris and Kit Smith.

"They're *exactly* like Nell Harris and Kit Smith," I said. "Isn't it incredible?"

It's said that everyone has a double, Lori.

"But they don't just *look* alike," I persisted. "Belle's father owns the Brockman Ranch, where Brett's the head wrangler. Nell's father owns Anscombe Manor, where Kit's the stable master. Even their names are similar: Belle and Nell, Brett and Kit. And Brett didn't want to marry Belle because he thought he was too old for her — just like Kit! It's amazing, isn't it?"

Coincidences do happen, Lori. I wouldn't read too much into them.

"I'd read a lot into *these* coincidences," I retorted. "Don't you see, Dimity? It's an omen, a *good* omen. Everything worked out for Belle and Brett, so everything will work out for Nell and Kit." I cocked my head to one side and went on thoughtfully, "Maybe I should ask Belle how she persuaded Brett to marry her. Nell might appreciate a few tips."

You must promise me that you will do no such thing. Honestly, Lori, you can't pry into a stranger's intimate affairs simply because she reminds you of someone you know.

"I suppose not," I conceded reluctantly. "But if I get to know her better . . ."

You would have to know her well for several years before you could ask such a question. Are you planning to extend your stay at the

Aerie until Will and Rob have outgrown their ponies?

"No," I said, laughing. "Okay, Dimity, I'll let it rest. And if I see anyone else who reminds me of home, I'll keep my mouth shut. I don't want Annelise to yell at me again. She made me feel as if I'd been caught red-handed scrawling graffiti on the vicarage."

Thank heavens for Annelise's good sense, as well as her good manners. Take it from me, Lori, no one wishes to be told that he or she is exactly like someone else. We all like to believe that we are unique. In nine cases out of ten it isn't true, but it's what we like to believe. Do your encounters with doppelgangers form the sum total of your news?

"I'm just getting started," I told her, and settled back in the chair. "Do you remember asking me to find out why James Blackwell and the Auerbachs left the Aerie so abruptly?"

I do.

"Well," I said, "I think I have the answer. Or part of the answer. Or something that might be the answer after I've investigated it more thoroughly."

You shouldn't be investigating anything, Lori! You're on holiday. You're supposed to be relaxing. I wish I'd never mentioned my

113

misgivings.

"But you did mention them," I pointed out, "and there's no use telling me to forget about them, because I won't."

Of course you won't. You're like a dog with a bone when it comes to rooting out mysteries, but you're also like a kangaroo when it comes to jumping to conclusions. We've been here before, Lori.

"I know," I said, "but this time I'm sure I'm onto something. Well, I'm almost sure."

All right, then, let me hear your theory, or what might pass for a theory after you've investigated it more thoroughly.

I grinned at the page and continued confidently. "I found out some very interesting things while I was at the ranch. Brett Whitcombe told me that a bigmouthed blowhard named Dick Major used to make life miserable for James Blackwell whenever James went into town. Dick Major used to taunt James in public. He called James lazy and worthless and told him he should get a real job instead of taking money from his employers for doing nothing. I think Dick Major drove James away from the Aerie."

Are you suggesting that James Blackwell quit a comfortable and no doubt lucrative position because a local bully taunted him?

"Yes," I said. "Brett Whitcombe told me

that James was quiet and shy, just the sort of meek little mouse who'd be cowed by a loudmouthed bully."

But James Blackwell held the position of caretaker for six months before he quit. If he was so meek and mild, why did it take so long for Dick Major to shame him into leaving?

I regarded the question uncertainly, then shrugged. "Everyone has a breaking point, Dimity. Maybe it took James Blackwell six months to reach his. Or maybe . . ." I nodded as a new and better explanation occurred to me. "Maybe James heard stories about Dick Major that frightened him. Brett Whitcombe told me that James wanted to know if some stories he'd heard were true."

Did the stories concern Dick Major?

"I don't know," I replied. "Brett didn't repeat them to me. Maybe he didn't want to make me nervous about staying at the Aerie. But what if James Blackwell left the Aerie because he'd heard rumors about Dick becoming violent? What if James was afraid Dick's taunts would turn into punches?"

I applaud your creativity, Lori, but I can't help wondering if your own recent experiences might be coloring your interpretation of events. It wasn't so long ago that you were forced to run for your life after being threatened by a

115

homicidal maniac.

"Coincidences happen," I reminded her airily. "If Kit and Nell aren't the only Kit and Nell in the world, then Abaddon can't be the only murderous madman."

You're in kangaroo mode, my dear. With one fearless leap of the imagination you've transformed Dick Major from a loudmouthed bully into a murderous madman.

"But what if he *is* a murderous madman?" I asked. "It might explain why the Auerbachs left in such a hurry. They might have been afraid of him, too."

But why would Danny Auerbach leave his caretaker in the clutches of a murderous madman? Why would he allow you, Annelise, two small children, and young Toby Cooper to come to the Aerie if he was convinced that a murderous madman lived nearby? And why on earth would Danny run away from a murderous madman in the first place? Danny's a wealthy, high-powered businessman. If he thought his family was in danger, he wouldn't pack his bags in a hurry and flee. He'd contact his lawyers and go straight to the police. He's undoubtedly on good terms with the more influential members of the law enforcement community. I wouldn't be at all surprised to learn that they play golf together.

"I take your point," I said philosophically.

"I'm rather fond of my theory, but I suppose it does have a few holes in it."

Your theory has more holes than a colander. I suggest you plug them before you leap to any more conclusions.

"No problem," I said. "I'll ask Toby if he's heard any scary stories about Dick Major. If he hasn't, I'll head into Bluebird and hook up to the local grapevine. One of the townspeople will be able to fill me in. Nothing goes unnoticed in a small community."

An excellent idea. I'd wish you luck, but I doubt you'll need it. You've become quite adept at monitoring grapevines since you moved to Finch. You'll bring Toby with you when you go to Bluebird, won't you?

"Of course," I said. "I'll need him to introduce me to the locals. Why?"

I'd rather you didn't run into Dick Major on your own. I don't want an obnoxious bully to spoil your holiday.

I smiled as Aunt Dimity's elegant script faded from the page, then I returned the journal to the bedside table and rubbed my palms together energetically. I hadn't swapped gossip since I'd been shot. I was looking forward to getting back in practice.

It was nearly two o'clock by the time I returned to the great room. Toby was in the kitchen, preparing a late lunch. He'd already set two places at the teak table on the breakfast deck, so we went out there to enjoy the sunshine and the scenery as well as our meal. I waited until we'd finished the fruit salad and started in on the rosemary chicken–stuffed croissants to ask if he'd heard any stories about the infamous Dick Major.

"Stories about Dick?" Toby gave a low whistle and rolled his eyes. "I've heard too many to count. I've never actually met the man, but he's made a real name for himself since he moved to Bluebird — several names, in fact, none of which should be repeated in polite company."

"Not Mr. Popular, huh?" I said.

"He's about as popular as a swarm of mosquitoes." Toby speared a piece of chilled asparagus. "Where did you hear about Dick Major?"

"Brett Whitcombe," I replied. "When we were at the ranch this morning, Brett told me that Dick used to bully James Black-well."

"I'm not surprised," said Toby. "From what I hear, Dick's the kind of guy who gets his kicks out of intimidating people."

"Is he dangerous?" I asked.

"Dick's a pest, not a mobster," Toby said dismissively. "He started so many arguments with his next-door neighbor that the guy finally moved to a house on the other side of town, just to have a little peace and quiet. But word gets around; the house next to Dick's is *still* empty."

"When did he move to Bluebird?" I asked, wondering if Dick's arrival had coincided with the Auerbach's sudden departure.

"A year ago, I think," said Toby.

"A year ago?" I echoed disappointedly. "Not just before Christmas?"

"I'm pretty sure he was here way before Christmas," said Toby. "Why are you so interested in him?"

"I've been wondering why James Blackwell quit his job," I said. "I think maybe he got sick of being bullied by Dick."

"You could be right, though I'd hate to think I owe my job to someone like Dick Major." Toby grimaced adorably and went on eating.

"How have you avoided meeting Dick?" I asked.

"Just lucky, I guess." Toby pointed his fork at my plate. "How's the chicken?"

"It's delicious," I said. "Everything's delicious, but you shouldn't have gone to so much trouble."

"I didn't," said Toby, grinning. "I picked it up at the cafe."

As I took another bite of croissant, it occurred to me that if Caroline's Cafe was anything like Sally Pyne's tearoom in Finch, it would be the epicenter of gossip in Bluebird — a perfect starting point for my tour of the local rumor mill. Before I could suggest a quick run into town, however, my cell phone rang. I apologized to Toby and went into the great room to answer it.

"Lori?" Bill's voice came through as clearly as if he were standing beside me. "I finally managed to get ahold of Danny."

"Did you find out what happened at Christmas?" I asked eagerly.

"Not exactly," Bill answered. "Apparently *Florence* insisted on leaving."

"Who's Florence?" I asked.

"Danny's wife," said Bill. "She refused to explain why she wanted to leave, and she isn't the sort of woman you cross-examine, so Danny doesn't know what happened. Whatever it was, Florence has taken such a dislike to the Aerie that she refuses to go back there. In fact, Danny's put the place on the market."

"The Aerie's for *sale?*" I felt as if the wind had been knocked out of me. "I don't believe it."

"It's what property developers do, Lori," said Bill. "Build and sell."

I looked around the great room and shook my head. Feathers, bones, and interesting bits of wood, the harvest of many family hikes, had been lovingly arranged in the rustic cabinets. Rambunctious children had left their marks on the comfy furniture. Family meals had been prepared in the kitchen and eaten around the large dining table. It took no imagination whatsoever to picture Danny, his wife, sons, and daughter gathered around the fireplace, singing Christmas carols, roasting marshmallows, and sipping hot apple cider.

"Not the Aerie," I said firmly. "He didn't build the Aerie to sell. It's Danny's tree house, Bill."

"His what?" said Bill.

"His pride and joy," I clarified. "If you ask me, the Aerie's as important to him as the cottage is to us. I can't believe he's selling it. When did it go on the market?"

"Just after Christmas," said Bill.

"What are we supposed to do if prospective buyers show up?" I asked. "Hide in the woods until they leave?"

"Danny's put everything on hold while you're there," said Bill. "To tell you the truth, he's having a hard time attracting buyers. He's lowered the price twice in the past six months, but no one's made him an offer. I think he's beginning to regret his decision to build in such an out-of-the-way place."

"It's a *beautiful* place," I insisted.

"But it's not Aspen," said Bill.

"It's *better* than Aspen. It would break Danny's heart to sell the Aerie," I said sadly, and at that moment my own heart hardened. I didn't know what had happened to spoil the Aerie for Florence Auerbach, but I was determined to find out. If Dick Major was to blame, I'd find a way to make him mind his manners. I knew what it was like to be forced to leave a place I loved. I didn't want the same thing to happen to Danny and his family.

"Danny told me about the sale in confidence," Bill was saying, "so don't mention it to anyone, all right?"

"Does Toby know?" I asked.

"Toby Cooper?" said Bill. "I doubt it."

"But Toby was planning to spend the whole summer here," I said. "If Danny sells the Aerie after we leave, Toby will be out of a job."

"Danny hasn't had a nibble in six months," Bill said patiently. "Unless a miracle happens, Toby will be able to keep his job until it's time for him to go back to school."

"I hope so," I said worriedly.

"We'll just have to wait and see," said Bill. "It's an unfortunate situation, but try not to dwell on it, Lori. You're there to enjoy yourself. I don't want you to get your knickers in a twist about something that's beyond your control."

My knickers were already in a twist, and I was far from convinced that the situation was beyond my control, but I knew better than to say as much to Bill. He'd only feel guilty for upsetting me.

"Are you at the ranch?" he asked.

"No," I replied, "but you won't believe who I saw there. . . ."

Bill's reaction to my descriptions of Belle and Brett Whitcombe was even more infuriatingly blasé than Aunt Dimity's had been. He seemed to think I'd perceived a strong resemblance between them and Kit and Nell simply because I was homesick. I was so incensed by his patronizing tone that I vowed to take photographs of Belle and Brett the next time I went to the ranch in order to document my claims.

"Don't let Annelise catch you at it," Bill advised. "She'll confiscate your camera and make you sit in the corner until you promise to behave yourself. I'll speak with you again tomorrow, love."

I could have sworn I heard him chuckle as he ended the call.

I was in a somewhat grumpy mood when I returned to the breakfast deck, but Toby restored my cheerfulness by asking if I planned to attend church in Bluebird the following day. I told him that I could think of no better way to spend my first Sunday morning in Colorado.

A church lawn after Sunday services was, in my experience, a splendid spot to fish for local gossip. Although Toby had dealt my pet theory a blow by placing Dick Major in Bluebird well before Christmas, I remained certain that the town bully had had something to do with James Blackwell's departure as well as the Auerbachs'. I was determined to get the dirt on him before the week was out.

My fishing expedition was, alas, delayed by one day because Will and Rob insisted on attending the cowboy church at the Brockman Ranch, which turned out to be an all-day affair. After the guitar-twanging, yodel-filled service came the huge picnic lunch, then a rodeo in which my sons demonstrated trick riding skills I didn't know they possessed and wished I'd never seen. I managed to keep smiling during their bravura

124

performance, but I gripped the bleacher seat so hard I lost all feeling in my fingers.

The rodeo went on until the evening barbecue, which was followed by a bonfire, the singing of many cowboy songs, and the dramatic recitation of cowboy poetry. As we were getting ready to leave, Brett Whitcombe offered to pick up the boys and Annelise the next morning and bring them to the ranch for another day of riding.

After conferring with Annelise, I accepted the offer gratefully. I knew that the twins would be perfectly content to spend the rest of their vacation in the saddle. I'd also noted that Annelise, levelheaded though she was, was thoroughly enjoying her first taste of cowboy charm.

It was approaching midnight when we returned to the Aerie with a pair of sleepy-headed but happy little cowpokes as well as a dozen covertly taken photographs of Brett and Belle. If I'd known how to use a laptop computer to transmit images, I would have e-mailed them directly to Bill.

NINE

Our late-night festivities had not the slightest impact on Will or Rob. They crawled out of their tent bright and early on Monday morning, pulled on their freshly laundered riding clothes, and chattered like magpies with their father when he called at nine o'clock. After a quick breakfast, they stood by the window wall to keep watch for Brett Whitcombe's truck. He showed up at nine forty-five and took off with Annelise and the twins, leaving me and Toby to our own devices.

"Would it be okay if we went into Bluebird today?" I asked Toby as we loaded the dishwasher. "I'd like to explore the town."

"Sounds good to me." He closed the dishwasher and leaned back against it, with his arms folded across his chest and a challenging gleam in his eyes. "Walk or drive?"

"Walk," I said bravely. "Unless you think it's too far."

"It's not too far," he said. "If we go by the easiest trail, it'll take us twenty minutes to get there, tops. You won't even break a sweat."

"Only because we'll be going downhill," I pointed out.

"You can handle it, Lori," Toby said bracingly. "Grab your hat and pull on your hiking boots. It's another beautiful day in Colorado."

As far as I could tell, every day was beautiful in Colorado. I hadn't seen a cloud in the sky since we'd arrived, and the snow that had filled me with dread at the airport had disappeared from all but the shadiest nooks in the forest. Even though it was barely ten o'clock in the morning, it was already warm enough for me to dress in shorts and a T-shirt, but I took the precaution of adding a rain jacket to Toby's day pack before we took off, bearing in mind his oft-repeated, though still unproven, warning that mountain weather was nothing if not changeable.

The trail to town started at the western edge of the Aerie's clearing. It was wide and smooth and carpeted with pine needles that smelled like incense in the splashes of hot sunlight falling through the sheltering trees.

"We're on the Lord Stuart Trail," Toby informed me. "There used to be a narrow gauge rail line running along here, linking the mine head to the processing mill in Bluebird."

"Was the Lord Stuart Mine a big operation?" I asked.

"Biggest in the valley," said Toby. "Granddad told me that it employed a couple hundred men, all told. They used to walk along the sides of the track on their way to the mine from their lodgings in Bluebird. The Lord Stuart Trail was a major thoroughfare in its day."

"No wonder it's so easy," I said. "I *like* major thoroughfares."

"I knew you would," said Toby, with a satisfied nod.

A profusion of wildflowers bloomed in unkempt tangles along the well-trodden path. I tried to memorize the flowers' colorful names as Toby pointed them out — Orange Sneezeweed, Witches Thimble, Shooting Star, Fairy Trumpet — but when he reached Rosy Pussytoes, I burst out laughing.

"Rosy Pussytoes?" I exclaimed. "You've got to be kidding."

"That's what it's called," Toby insisted. "There are Alpine Pussytoes as well. In fact, if you stick *alpine* in front of any plant's name, you won't go far wrong. Alpine sunflower, alpine lily, alpine clover —"

"Alpine magnolia," I put in, "alpine euca-lyptus —"

"— alpine palm tree, alpine rutabaga," he continued.

By the time we reached alpine bougainvil-lea, we were giggling so hard that we had to stop walking. While I leaned against a fir tree to catch my breath, it occurred to me that I hadn't had a good giggle since I'd been shot. Bill had been as caring as any human being could be, and my best friend Emma had been wonderfully sympathetic, but Toby, who knew nothing of my harrow-ing brush with death, was giving me some-thing I hadn't realized I needed: a healthy dose of silliness. I felt a rush of gratitude toward him as we continued downhill.

The Lord Stuart Trail was so pretty and we were having such a good time that it came as something as a letdown when we finally reached the edge of town and the paved surface of Lake Street. The first house we saw would have had a lovely view of Lake Matula if it hadn't been surrounded by piles of highly unattractive junk. I stared in dismay at rusty bedsprings, an assort-ment of old washing machines, several rot-ting mattresses, a couch covered in split vinyl, a car radiator, and a myriad of other items that would no doubt fascinate some future archaeologist but which filled me with revulsion.

"Don't judge Bluebird by Dick Major's house," Toby advised.

"Dick Major lives here?" I stopped dead in my tracks and swung around for a closer look at the house. The roof seemed to be intact, but the paint on the walls was peeling badly and most of the windows were boarded up. "What a slob."

Toby hushed me and tugged gently on my elbow. "Keep your voice down and keep moving, please, Lori. I haven't had a run-in with Dick yet, and I don't want to push my luck."

"Sorry," I said, but as we walked away, I kept looking over my shoulder. It was hard to believe that anyone would willingly live in the midst of such a mess. "What does he do for a living? Collect garbage?"

"No idea," Toby replied.

"If you ask me, his next-door neighbor moved just to get away from the smell of moldy mattress," I commented.

"Could be," said Toby and increased our pace.

The houses became progressively tidier as we walked on. None reached the level of tidiness routinely maintained in Finch, but there was a certain careworn charm to most of them. I was particularly fond of a tiny Victorian cottage that had been painted lavender with bright purple trim. Its picket-fenced front garden was overflowing with a shaggy collection of lupines, columbines, and fluttering poppies as well as an assortment of vivid "alpine" flowers.

Most of Bluebird's businesses were located on Stafford Avenue, one block over from the highway that split the town in two. The buildings were made of wood or brick, in a Victorian style that suggested they'd been built before the turn of the last century. Whatever their original purposes, the buildings now housed a mixture of useful shops and places favored by travelers.

The hardware store stood beside Eric's Mountain Bikes, the grocery beside the Mother Lode Antique Mall, the post office beside an art gallery featuring watercolors by local artist Claudia Lechat. Sweet Jenny's Ice Cream Emporium specialized in Olde Tyme Fudge and Crazy Chris's Camping Supplies offered special deals on bait to those who fished Lake Matula or the trout streams that ran through the Vulgamore Valley.

Toby and I stopped at Dandy Don's Discount Pharmacy & Gifts, where I bought a handful of postcards depicting mountain scenes similar to those we'd seen during our hikes. Since I was a great believer in supporting local businesses, I didn't even try to resist padding my order with a packet of columbine seeds for Emma, a pair of gilded aspen-leaf earrings for Annelise, a pair of suede moccasins for me, and two adorable stuffed animals — buffalo — to remind Rob and Will of their first visit to the Wild West.

Tourists weren't exactly thronging the sidewalks on Stafford Avenue, but a fair number of them were moseying in and out of the shops, slurping ice-cream cones, studying maps, or snapping photographs of one another behind the hitching post in front of Altman's Saloon, HOME OF THE WORLD-FAMOUS ALTMAN'S BURGER. As I watched a family group posing for the camera, I thought of what a shame it would be if a bigmouthed bonehead like Dick Major spoiled their fun with rude remarks or crude gestures.

I was pleased to see that a real effort had been made to dress up the main drag. Baskets filled with multicolored pansies hung from the old-fashioned, cast-iron street lamps, and wooden benches with fancy scrollwork arms and legs sat next to many of the store entrances. A large banner strung across the street proclaimed BLUE-BIRD GOLD RUSH DAYS JULY 8-9-10 in bold print, but I had eyes only for a modest wooden sign hanging above a storefront on our right.

"Caroline's Cafe," I said, pointing to the sign. "Let's go in. I could do with a cold drink, and you can introduce me to Carrie Vyne. I'd like to tell her how much we've enjoyed everything we've tried from her cafe."

"After you," said Toby.

Tinkling bells jingled as he pulled the lace-curtained door open for me. I stepped inside, stopped short, and peered around the room in wonder. Caroline's Cafe re-minded me so poignantly of the tearoom back in Finch, with its charmingly mis-matched china, chairs, and tables, that a wave of homesickness threatened to over-whelm me.

"Where's Carrie Vyne?" I whispered to Toby.

"Behind the bakery counter," he whis-pered back. "What's wrong?"

"Nothing," I said, and breathed a sigh of relief as we made our way to an unoccupied table.

If Carrie Vyne had looked like Sally Pyne, the proprietress of Finch's one and only tearoom, I would have fainted dead away right then and there. Fortunately, she didn't. Both women were middle aged, but while Sally was short and round, Carrie was tall and stately. Sally's garish tracksuits were a favorite topic of caustic conversation in Finch, but Carrie would have aroused no comment at all, being tastefully dressed in blue jeans, sneakers, and a pale-pink, short-sleeved cotton blouse. And Sally wore her iron-gray hair clipped quite short while Carrie wore her white hair in soft waves that framed a lined but very kindly face.

"Back again, Toby?" she said, coming to our table to fill our water glasses. Her voice was light and musical, quite unlike Sally Pyne's staccato bark.

"Where else would I go for my midmorning munchies?" Toby responded, with a grin. He drew a hand through the air between Carrie Vyne and me. "Carrie, this is Lori Shepherd. Lori, this is Carrie. Lori's the woman I told you about, Carrie. The one who's staying at the Aerie."

"Pleased to meet you, Lori," she said.

"Likewise," I said. "*Very* pleased. We've loved everything Toby's brought up from the cafe — the scones, the jams, the croissant sandwiches. You're a brilliant baker and a wonderful cook."

"Why, thank you," said Carrie, blushing rosily. "Are you enjoying your stay at the Aerie?"

"I am," I said. "I wish my sons were here so that I could introduce them to you, but they're spending the day at the Brockman Ranch."

"I've heard they're good little riders," said Carrie.

I almost said, "Of course you have," but caught myself just in time. I was delighted to know that Carrie Vyne had her ear to the rail, but I didn't want to risk insulting her by implying that she was a gossip.

"They do okay," I acknowledged.

"Better than okay, I'd say," said Carrie. "From what I've heard, they'll be roping calves before the week's out."

"Oh, Lord, I hope not," I said weakly.

"Brett'll watch over them," Carrie said reassuringly. She finished filling our glasses and left the water pitcher on the table for us to use. "What can I get for you, Lori? I already know what I'm going to bring Toby, but what kind of snack would you like?"

"I'll have whatever Toby's having," I said.

"Won't take but a minute."

Carrie returned to the bakery counter and came back five minutes later with two tall glasses of ice-cold lemonade, two small, mismatched plates, and a larger plate filled with cookies that looked disturbingly familiar.

"Calico Cookies!" Toby exclaimed. "My favorites! Thank you, Carrie. What's in them today?"

"You tell me," she said with a wink and went to serve another customer.

Toby seized a cookie, took a large bite, and chewed slowly, with a look of deep concentration on his face.

"Chocolate chips," he murmured, "dried cranberries, and . . . sliced almonds?" He came out of his trance and gestured for me to sample a cookie, explaining, "Carrie adds different goodies to the basic recipe every time, so you never know what you'll find. But she always leaves out the coconut when I'm in town. She knows I can't stand coconut."

I stared at the cookies as though they were hand grenades. If Toby was telling the truth — and I had no reason to think he wasn't — then Carrie Vyne's Calico Cookies could quite easily be mistaken for Sally Pyne's Crazy Quilt Cookies, right down to the absence of coconut. I raised a cookie slowly to my lips, bit into it, tasted the familiar blend of sweet, tangy, and faintly spicy flavors, and lowered it gingerly to my plate.

"Do you know where she got the recipe?" I asked, my voice trembling slightly.

"I think she made it up," said Toby. "Aren't they great?"

"They're great," I said, and turned to look over my shoulder as the front door's bells jingled and a large woman with a weathered face and rhinestone-studded glasses barreled into the cafe.

Toby followed my gaze, heaved a small sigh, and muttered, "Buckle your seat belt. Maggie Flaxton has arrived."

"Carrie!" bellowed Maggie Flaxton. "Why don't you have a sign in your window for Gold Rush Days? How are we going to draw a crowd if we don't advertise?"

"The banner is working fine," Carrie answered mildly. "All of my customers ask about the festival."

The large woman sniffed doubtfully and rounded on me. "What about you? Did *you* ask about the festival?"

"I only just got here," I said, fighting the urge to snap to attention. "I was *going* to ask —"

"You're up at the Auerbach place, aren't you?" Maggie Flaxton interrupted.

"Y-yes," I managed, cowed by her commanding voice.

"I don't suppose you'll stay long," she

137

roared. "None of them do, and who can blame them? I wouldn't spend five minutes there if I could help it. But if you're still around in July, we could use your help. It's all hands on deck during Gold Rush Days. Toby's running the wood-splitting contest." She turned back to Carrie Vyne. "I want to see a sign in your window before the day is out, Carrie."

"It'll be there," Carrie promised resignedly.

"It had better be," shouted Maggie. "I can't do everything myself, you know." Frowning fiercely, she spun on her heel and stomped out of the cafe.

"Whew," said Toby, leaning his head on his hand. "She could rule the world if she put her mind to it, Maggie could."

"Does she run the grocery?" I asked.

"Yes," said Toby, "and everything else in town. How did you know?"

"Lucky guess," I replied.

I popped the rest of the cookie into my mouth and told myself sternly *not* to tell Toby that Bluebird's Maggie Flaxton was very like Finch's Peggy Taxman. I'd promised Aunt Dimity that I wouldn't mention doppelgangers to anyone, and I intended to keep my promise, but apart from that, I didn't want Toby to think that the sun had fried my brains.

"I wonder why she wouldn't spend five minutes at the Aerie?" I said.

"I don't," said Toby, with a wry smile. "The Aerie's too far away from town for her liking. Maggie prefers to crack her whip at close range."

A moment later the bells jingled again and a small balding man put his head cautiously into the cafe.

"It's all right, Greg," Carrie called to him. "Maggie's gone."

"Greg Wilstead," Toby murmured, for my benefit. "The shyest man in Bluebird."

"Lori," Carrie said brightly, looking in my direction, "if your boys are interested in trains, you should bring them to visit Greg. You've got an amazing set of tracks laid out in your garage, haven't you Greg?"

The little man ducked his head, mumbled something incoherent, and refused to meet my eyes.

"Thanks, Carrie, I'll keep it in mind," I said dazedly, envisioning the shy and balding George Wetherhead, Finch's local expert on railroads.

"Lori's staying up at the Auerbach place," Carrie added.

Greg Wilstead's head came up and he peered at me, his eyes wide with something that closely resembled horror.

"Oh, my God," he whispered, and left the cafe without buying so much as a bread roll.

"What was *that* about?" I said, looking after him.

"Don't know," said Toby. "Drink your lemonade, Lori. It's squeezed fresh every morning."

I'd taken only a sip of the lemonade, which was splendidly refreshing, when the jingling bells announced the arrival of a middle-aged, deeply tanned, and extremely overweight couple dressed in brightly colored T-shirts and baggy shorts. They went straight to the bakery counter and ordered a dozen doughnuts, a dozen elephant ears, and a dozen blackberry tarts to go. While they waited for Carrie to put their order together, they turned to survey the cafe. Their faces lit up when they saw Toby.

"Howdy, Tobe," called the woman.

"How the heck are you, Tobe?" said the man.

"Just fine. Pull up some chairs while you're waiting." Toby turned to me as the couple joined us at our table. "Nick and Arlene Altman run Bluebird's most popular watering hole, Lori."

"Altman's Saloon?" I guessed. "Home of the world-famous Altman's burger?"

"That's right," said Nick proudly. "Arlene makes the biggest, juiciest burgers in the Rockies."

"We run a family-friendly bar, Lori," Arlene informed me. "Feel free to bring your little ones with you any time."

"And their good-looking nanny," Nick put in. "Heard all about her from the boys at the Brockman."

"Men," said Arlene, clucking her tongue.

"I'm sure Tobe's told you that I make my own beer," Nick said, ignoring his wife and turning toward me. "Are you a beer drinker, Lori?"

Behind him, Toby and Arlene were shaking their heads frantically.

"Uh, no," I said, reading the signal. "In fact, I don't drink much at all."

"You may start if you stay at the Aerie too long," said Nick, chuckling.

"Our order's ready, Nick," said Arlene, and they heaved themselves to their feet.

"Nice to meet you, Lori," said Nick. "You be careful up there, you hear?"

"Hush, Nick," said Arlene. "Pay no attention to my husband, Lori. He's full of hot air."

"No, I'm not." Nick patted his ample stomach. "I'm full of your big, juicy burgers."

He chuckled merrily as he and Arlene paid for their order and left.

Once they'd gone, Toby leaned in close to me.

"Do not *ever* try Nick Altman's beer," he said. "I had to drink a whole bottle of it on my eighteenth birthday, just to be polite. My head nearly fell off the next day. The stuff is *deadly*."

I steadfastly refused to dwell on the startling similarities between the rotund Nick Altman and the equally plump Dick Peacock, who ran Peacock's Pub in Finch and made wine that could be used to strip paint, and focused instead on Nick's somewhat alarming comment concerning the Aerie.

"Why did Nick tell me to be careful up at the Aerie?" I asked.

"He's probably afraid you'll overexert yourself," said Toby. "He and Arlene don't believe in exercise."

"Really?" I said, in mock astonishment.

Toby began to laugh, but when the bells jingled again, he stopped abruptly.

"Oh no," he said under his breath. "My luck's run out."

"You're in early today, Dick," Carrie called. "What can I get for you?"

I took a surreptitious look over my shoulder and caught my first glimpse of the infamous Dick Major.

TEN

Dick Major didn't look like a murderous lunatic *or* a garbage collector. He looked like a jolly grandfather, and to my intense relief, he didn't remind me of anyone in Finch.

His face was round and pink, silver-rimmed glasses framed his pale blue eyes, and he wore his grizzled gray hair in a precisely clipped crew cut. He was neatly dressed in a short-sleeved yellow shirt, lightweight tan trousers, and a well-worn pair of brown suede shoes. He wasn't a tall man, but he was imposing, thanks to broad shoulders and a barrel chest that strained the buttons of his shirt. His voice, when he replied to Carrie Vyne's question, was higher pitched than I would have expected from a man with his burly build, and it held an unexpected undertone of general bonhomie.

"The usual?" said Carrie.

"You bet," he said. "Black coffee and a couple of jelly doughnuts to go. You got elephant ears today?"

"I sure do," Carrie said.

"Throw in a couple of elephant ears, too," said Dick. "And make it a *large* black coffee."

"Coffee'll take a few minutes," Carrie warned. "I'm making a fresh pot."

"That's okay. I'll wait." Dick Major turned away from the bakery counter to cast a seemingly benevolent gaze on the cafe's customers. His pale blue eyes lit up when he spotted Toby and me, and a wide grin spread across his face. As he approached our table, I felt a flutter of unease. There was something strange about his eyes. He opened them too widely, and he seemed to wait too long between blinks. I wondered if he was on some sort of medication.

"Dick Major," he said, extending a large, thick-fingered hand to me. "You the little lady staying up at the Auerbach place?"

"Yes." I took his meaty hand with some trepidation, but his grip turned out to be pleasantly firm rather than crushing. "Danny Auerbach is an old friend of my husband's."

"But your husband ain't there," Dick observed, still grinning. "Just you and those little tykes of yours and that . . . What do you call her? A nanny? Must be nice to be able to afford a nanny."

I didn't know how to respond, but Toby saved me the trouble.

"They're not alone at the Aerie," he said staunchly. "I'm staying there, too."

"So I hear." Dick's upper lip curled disdainfully as he looked Toby up and down, but his manic grin flicked back into place when he returned his attention to me. "Having a fine time, are you? Enjoying yourself? Seeing the sights? Planning to stay long?"

"We're having a wonderful time, thanks to Toby," I replied, carefully emphasizing Toby's name. "I don't know how long we'll stay. Maybe a couple of weeks, maybe a month, maybe the rest of the summer. We'll just have to see how it goes."

Dick leaned forward and planted his ham-sized fists on the table. "I wouldn't let my wife and kid stay up there with nothing but a little pip-squeak of a college boy to protect them. But maybe you're braver than I am."

Toby stirred, but I signaled for him to keep his seat. I didn't want him to tangle with Dick Major. It would be like a choirboy going head to head with a professional wrestler.

"I'm quite sure that Toby could protect us if the need arose," I said haughtily, "but why should it?"

"Ain't you heard?" Dick leaned closer, until his large, pink, grinning face was mere inches from mine. "The Auerbach place is *cursed.*"

I stared at him openmouthed for a moment, then broke into a peal of laughter. Dick Major couldn't possibly know that I had a foolproof curse-alert system sitting on my bedside table at the Aerie. If Aunt Dimity had detected the slightest trace of evil in our holiday home, she would have sounded the alarm. Her silence turned Dick's dire pronouncement into a harmless joke.

My reaction seemed to unnerve him. He pulled back, his grin faltering, and looked down at me uncertainly.

"I guess I *am* braver than you," I said, when I could speak. "I don't believe the Aerie's cursed."

"Your order's ready, Dick," called Carrie Vyne.

"Be there in a minute," Dick called back to her. His grin returned full force as he chucked me gently under the chin, saying softly, "Beliefs change, little lady. You'll see."

He left the table, paid for his coffee and pastries at the counter, and gave me a jovial, finger-waggling wave as he left the cafe.

"Wow," said Toby, gazing at me in respectful disbelief. "You could give Maggie Flaxton a run for her money, Lori. I've never heard of *anyone* laughing in Dick Major's face."

"I *wanted* to break his wrist," I said heatedly, rubbing my chin.

"So did I," Toby assured me.

"What did he think I'd do?" I said indignantly. "Tremble in my boots? Did he expect me to pack up and head for the airport because *he* believes in some stupid superstition?"

"I think that's *exactly* what he expected you to do," said Toby. "He was trying to frighten you."

"Well, he failed." I gazed reflectively at the sunburned tourists strolling past the plate-glass window at the front of the cafe. "So the Aerie's cursed, is it? How ridiculous. I've never stayed in a place that's *less* cursed, except for my cottage back in England. The atmosphere up there is good and wholesome. I feel *safe* up there. I've been sleeping through the night for the first time since I was —" I broke off, caught Toby's curious glance, and went on. "I've been sleeping through the night for the first time since I hurt my shoulder."

"How *did* you hurt your shoulder?" he asked.

"I fell off a horse," I lied, avoiding his eyes.

"Oh," Toby said, as if he'd had a sudden revelation. "So *that's* why you're afraid of horses. It must have been a bad fall."

"It was pretty bad, yes, but my *point* is that the Aerie has good vibes," I said.

"I agree," said Toby.

"Mind you," I continued, after a brief, thoughtful silence, "Dick Major's not the only one in town who thinks the Aerie's cursed. It seems to be a popular belief. It would explain why Maggie Flaxton wouldn't spend five minutes up there, and why Greg Wilstead gave me such a frightened-rabbit look when Carrie told him I was staying there."

"Greg *always* looks like a frightened rabbit," Toby put in.

"I'll bet Nick Altman believes in it, too," I went on, ignoring Toby's remark. "He thinks the curse will drive me to drink." I finished my first cookie and reached for a second one. "Why didn't you tell me about the curse, Toby? The kids in town must have clued you in during your summer vacations. Did you ask your grandfather about it?"

"Of course I did." Toby laid aside his

fourth Calico Cookie and regarded me intently. "Granddad told me that no rational person would waste so much as a single brain cell thinking about it. He was a doctor, a man of science. He had no use for superstitions."

"What about you?" I pressed.

"I'd like to think I'm a rational person," Toby replied, "not someone who perpetuates idiotic beliefs by passing them on."

"So that's why you didn't mention it to me," I said, nodding.

"That's right," said Toby. "Ghost stories around the campfire are one thing, but curses can get inside people's heads. Granddad would be ashamed of me if I even *pretended* to believe in such tripe, and I'd be ashamed of myself for . . . for worrying you."

"I promise you, I'm not worried," I said. "I'd just like to know more about it. Even rational people take an interest in local legends." I smiled coaxingly. "Come on, Toby, tell me about the curse. I'm not going to swoon. I'm the woman who laughed in Dick Major's face, remember?"

Toby heaved an exasperated sigh, but gave in, grudgingly. "According to Granddad, a fair number of accidents happened at the old Lord Stuart Mine over the years, a few of them fatal. So many kids and idiot adults got hurt messing around up there that some people — a handful of gullible, superstitious people — started to believe that the place was jinxed."

"How did the accidents happen?" I asked.

"How do you think?" Toby retorted. "When people climb on old mining equipment and goof around inside unstable old buildings, someone's bound to get hurt. It *was* dangerous. That's why Granddad wouldn't let me go up there when I was little. He didn't want me to spend the rest of the summer with a cast on my leg — or worse."

As Toby spoke, I recalled something Aunt Dimity had told me only a few weeks earlier, though it seemed a lifetime ago: *If you want to keep people from visiting a place, you scare them off. You tell them the place is haunted or cursed or unlucky.* It seemed to me that the curse had served a good purpose in the past — to scare children away from an extremely perilous playground — but it was also clear to me that although the curse had outlived its purpose, belief in it lingered on.

"It's not dangerous up there anymore," Toby went on, "not since Mr. Auerbach cleared the site and sealed the mine. And whatever anyone tells you — Maggie, Nick, Greg, Amanda, Dick —"

"Who's Amanda?" I interrupted.

"The local loony-tune," Toby answered shortly. "She has a lot of crack-brained beliefs. But I don't care what *anyone* says, the Aerie *isn't* cursed."

"I never thought it was." I stretched out a placatory hand to him. "Thanks for filling me in."

Carrie Vyne appeared suddenly at our table and seated herself in the chair Arlene Altman had vacated. Although business was picking up, she seemed content to let her two matronly assistants handle the influx of new customers.

"I hope Dick Major didn't say anything to upset you," she said, her kindly face filled with concern. "He doesn't usually show up until dinnertime. I would have chased him off, but —"

"But you've got a business to run," I interrupted, with an understanding nod. "You can't afford to chase off regular customers, even when they're as . . . unusual . . . as Dick."

"He's not from here," said Carrie, as though Dick's nonnative roots explained his uncouth behavior. "He moved to Bluebird two years ago with his wife and teenaged daughter. The daughter got away from him just as soon as she got her driver's license, and his wife took off a couple of weeks later. I reckon she just couldn't take it anymore."

"Take what?" I prompted.

"Living in that dump." Carrie jutted her chin in the general direction of Dick's house. "The whole town's embarrassed by it, but Dick won't lift a finger to clean it up. And he was always quarreling with his neighbors. I reckon his poor wife just got fed up with the whole thing and took off."

"Any self-respecting woman would," I said. "Do you know where he came from?"

"Some place back east," said Carrie. "Claims he moved to the mountains for his health. I wish he'd picked some other mountains." She smiled mischievously. "There's been talk on the town council about officially designating his part of town the Grumpy Old Man Zone."

I chuckled appreciatively, then asked, "What's wrong with his health?"

"He claims that he had some sort of work-related accident back east," Carrie told me. "He must have gotten a good settlement out of his employer because he's been living off of it ever since."

"Is he on medication?" I asked, recalling Dick's strange, unblinking gaze.

"If he is, he doesn't get it from Dandy Don's," said Carrie. "And I haven't heard of him getting any packets in the mail."

I was beginning to love this woman. She was better informed than an FBI agent.

"I wonder what happened to him?" I said. "He looked pretty fit to me, apart from the beer belly."

"Could be his back," Carrie reasoned, cocking her head to one side. "Back troubles are hard to see, but they can lay you out in no time flat. They can make you pretty grouchy, too. I had sciatica once, and I was a perfect misery to everyone in sight until it cleared up."

We discussed the agony of sciatica for a while, moved from there to arthritis and rheumatism, and wound our way through the perils of asthma, allergies, and migraines before I managed to steer the conversation back in the direction I wanted it to go.

"I've heard that Dick was pretty hard on James Blackwell, the guy who used to have Toby's job at the Aerie," I said.

"Oh, he was just terrible to James," Carrie acknowledged, nodding sadly.

"Did he get physical?" I asked.

"Do you mean, did he beat James up?" Carrie shook her head rapidly. "Oh no, Dick's not like that, not like that at all. He's never raised a hand to anyone. He just enjoys getting under people's skin." Carrie crossed her forearms on the table and leaned forward, the classic pose of the experienced rumormonger. "He used to pass remarks to James when James was in here. Arlene Altman said he used to do the same thing to him at the saloon. After a while, James just stopped coming to town. The next thing I knew, he was gone. It's a pity. He was a nice man."

I folded my own forearms on the table to signal that I, too, was ready to get down to some serious gossip-swapping. "Dick told *me* that the Aerie was cursed."

"Not *that* old thing again!" Carrie snorted impatiently. "No one hardly talked about it until the Auerbachs built their place, and then it all started up again, same as before. I tell you, some people will believe anything. I hope Dick didn't rattle you."

"He didn't," I said, "but maybe he rattled James. I heard that James was trying to find out if some stories he'd heard were true. Maybe the stories were the ones Dick told him about the curse. Maybe Dick got under his skin deeply enough to make him *believe* in the curse."

"I doubt it," said Carrie. "Only dimwits and children take things like that seriously, and James Blackwell wasn't a dimwit or a child. He had a good head on his shoulders. He was a well-educated, well-read man. Always had a book with him when he came to my cafe, and he was polite, well spoken. I miss him."

Her words tweaked a memory that had been lurking in the back of my mind, a memory I'd failed to mention to Aunt Dimity. It was something Brett Whitcombe had said while we watched the twins ride at the Brockman Ranch. *James used to drop in on us now and again. He took an interest in local history. Asked all sorts of questions. Wanted to know what Bluebird was like in the olden days.*

"An amateur historian," I murmured, half to myself.

"Pardon?" said Carrie.

I put even more weight on my forearms and peered intently at her. "I heard that James Blackwell was interested in local history. Maybe he learned something about Bluebird's past that made him believe in Dick's story about the curse."

"I can't imagine what it could be," said Carrie, "but if you want to know about local history, you should talk to Rose Blanding. She's Pastor Blanding's wife. She runs the Bluebird Historical Society in the old school building, where the tourist information office is, but only from nine to one, when Claudia Lechat takes over."

"The artist," I said, recalling the sign in the art gallery's window.

"Claudia does a little bit of everything." Carrie chuckled softly. "She even designed a road sign for the Grumpy Old Man Zone. But if you want to know about local history, talk to Rose Blanding. She's the expert. She and Pastor Blanding live right next door to Good Shepherd Lutheran, out along the lake. Toby can show you the way. She'll be home by one-fifteen."

"I wouldn't want to bother her at home," I protested.

"It's no bother," Carrie assured me, waving off my objection. "Rose is a pastor's wife. Her door's always open to everyone. You don't even have to be a Lutheran." She looked around at the rapidly filling tables and smiled apologetically. "Well, I could sit here and talk with you all day, Lori, but I guess I'd better get back to work. The lunch crowd's arriving."

"You can take our order before you go," Toby suggested. He looked at me and shrugged. "We may as well stay for lunch. We have an hour to kill before we visit Mrs. Blanding."

"I'll have whatever Toby's having," I said without hesitation. "I'd also like to bring a box of Calico Cookies back to the Aerie. My sons have noticed that the cookie jar up there is depressingly empty."

Carrie lowered her eyes modestly. "Do you think your little boys will like my cookies?"

"I know they will," I said with absolute conviction.

Mindful of my promise to Aunt Dimity, I didn't explain that Will and Rob had already fallen in love with Carrie Vyne's cookies, half a world away.

ELEVEN

Carrie Vyne presented Toby and me with the perfect meal to carry us through until dinnertime: a bowl of tasty cream of broccoli soup, a hunk of sourdough bread, a generous wedge of quiche lorraine, and a small bunch of sweet red grapes, all of it homemade, except for the grapes, but even they came from a Colorado vineyard. At one o'clock we gathered up our belongings, paid our bill, thanked Carrie for her hospitality, and departed.

Toby pointed out various landmarks and reminisced about his childhood as we strolled down Stafford Avenue toward the lake, but I was too preoccupied to give him my full attention. He carried the box of Calico Cookies, I had my bag of goodies from Dandy Don's, and we both wore wide-brimmed hats and dusty hiking boots. We would have looked like a pair of carefree tourists if I hadn't been so pensive and so silent.

The more I thought about it, the more certain I became that I'd been wrong to blame James Blackwell's abrupt abandonment of the Aerie on Dick Major's bullying. I was now convinced that James had fled the Aerie because of the celebrated curse. Danny Auerbach's former employee might have been the most sensible person in the world, but I knew better than most that the right set of circumstances could spook anyone.

If a man had ever been in the right place at the right time to be well and truly spooked, I told myself, it had been James. He'd lived alone at the Aerie for nearly six months. He'd been just far enough away from Bluebird to feel isolated, and since neither the Auerbachs nor any of their friends had come to stay at the Aerie during that time, he'd had nothing to keep him occupied but a few routine chores. He would have had plenty of free time to wonder if the rumors he'd heard were true. And he'd heard those rumors, as I had, not just from Dick Major, but from responsible adults all over town.

It seemed to me that if James Blackwell was as well educated as Carrie Vyne thought he was, his natural inclination would be to find out more about the rumors. He'd ask Brett Whitcombe questions, look through the books in the Aerie's library, perhaps bring one with him to read while he sipped coffee at the cafe. He might also pay a visit to the local historical society.

He'd be told by some that the curse was blatant nonsense, by others that it was God's own truth, but with a hungry mind and plenty of time on his hands, he'd go on searching until, somewhere, he'd find a clue that tipped the balance away from reason and toward superstition. It wasn't hard to imagine what could have happened next.

James would lie awake in the dead of night, turning the clue over in his mind, and odd noises that had never bothered him before would make him flinch. A simple stumble would remind him of the host of injuries — some of them fatal — that had inspired the local legend. He'd begin to sleep less, to stumble more, until fear finally overcame common sense.

As an educated, intelligent man, he'd be too embarrassed to explain his misgivings to his employer. In the end, he'd pack his bags and leave, without giving notice, without leaving a forwarding address — he'd leave as suddenly and inexplicably as the Auerbachs had left.

"I wonder if Florence Auerbach knows about the curse?" I mused aloud.

"I have no idea," said Toby testily. "And I don't know how you can fill your head with such drivel when you have" — he swept his arm through the air — "*this* to look at."

"Huh? What?" I snapped out of my reverie and realized with a start that Toby had led me away from Stafford Avenue to the gravelly west shore of Lake Matula and one of the prettiest sights I'd yet seen.

The long, narrow lake lay at our feet, a light breeze wrinkling its surface into a million fluid facets that sparkled like fool's gold in the sun. To our left and slightly above us stood a white-painted church, its spire gleaming against a backdrop of dark pines. Next to it stood a large Victorian house with a wraparound porch, a turret that rivaled the church's spire in height, and a veritable sampler of lacy gingerbread trim. The house was painted a demure shade of dove gray, but nothing could disguise its flamboyant architecture.

"It's fantastic," I said, laughing with delight. "Like something out of a fairy tale."

"I'm glad you noticed," Toby said sarcastically. "It's the parsonage, where Mr. and Mrs. Blanding live." He scuffed the toe of his hiking boot in the gravel. "I wish you'd never heard about the curse, Lori. If you're not careful, you'll become obsessed by it."

"If I show the slightest sign of obsession," I said lightly, "you have my permission to throw me in the lake."

"I'll do it," Toby warned, shaking an index finger at me.

"I know you will." I hooked my arm through his. "Come on. Let's see if Mrs. Blanding is at home."

It took us five minutes to walk the rest of the way to the parsonage. The front door was open, as Carrie Vyne had told us it would be, but the screen door was shut. As I raised my hand to ring the doorbell, we heard voices approaching from within. Toby recognized them at once.

"It's Rufe and Lou Zimmer," he said, his face brightening. "You'll like the Zimmer brothers, Lori. There's no one else like them on earth."

After my experiences at the Brockman Ranch and Caroline's Cafe, I was more than ready to challenge the veracity of his last statement, but I held my tongue, a feat that became increasingly difficult to do when the men in question finally tottered into view.

The Zimmer brothers were tiny, ancient, and utterly identical, from the tips of their brown wingtip shoes to the tops of their bald heads. They carried matching straw boaters in their identical right hands and wore matching gold cuff links in the cuffs of their starched white shirts. Their shirts were tucked into pleated cream-colored trousers held up by matching pairs of red suspenders. When they spoke, they sounded so much alike that I wouldn't have been able to tell them apart in the dark. The only reason I could tell them apart in daylight was that one of them held a brown briefcase in his left hand.

". . . mighty kind of you, Rose," said the one holding the briefcase. "We'll be sure . . ."

". . . to bring the maps back when we're done with them," continued the other. "Shouldn't take us too long . . ."

". . . to work out where the Escalante forge used to be," the first went on. "Old Lou thinks it was on First Street . . ."

". . . and old Rufe swears it was on Third," said Lou. "But we'll work it out. We surely do . . ."

". . . appreciate the loan," finished Rufe.

"Oh . . . my . . . Lord," I breathed.

Despite my previous encounters with Bluebird's army of doppelgangers, I was dizzied by déjà vu. Rufe and Lou Zimmer appeared to be the exact male equivalents of the ancient, identical Pym sisters, who lived up the road from me in Finch. They even talked in the same ping-ponging fashion. If I hadn't been clinging to Toby's arm, I would have keeled over from the shock.

Rufe and Lou were accompanied by a slender, middle-aged woman with salt-and-pepper hair and a sun-burnished face. She was dressed for the warm weather in a rose-colored linen skirt, a sleeveless white silk blouse, and extremely sensible shoes. Although she had the refined, slightly pedantic manner of an old-fashioned schoolmistress, I assumed that she was Rose Blanding, the minister's wife.

"Please, take your time," she urged the brothers. "There's no need to bring the maps back quickly. I know you'll take good care of them." She glanced up, saw me and Toby through the screen door, and smiled broadly. "Why, look, boys, I have more visitors."

"It's young Tobe!" Rufe exclaimed.

Identical smiles lit the Zimmer brothers' faces as Mrs. Blanding ushered them out onto the porch. They greeted Toby fondly, asked after his family, and told him he'd grown at least two inches since they'd last seen him. Toby then conducted a round of introductions that turned out to be for my benefit rather than theirs. The Zimmers and Mrs. Blanding already knew who I was, where I was staying, and with whom.

"Rufus and Louis are Bluebird's oldest citizens," Mrs. Blanding informed me, beaming at the two elderly men. "Though, technically, Rufe is older than Lou by two minutes. Their birth certificates are on display at the historical society."

Rufe nodded. "Some people think we founded the town . . ."

". . . but we're not *that* old," said Lou.

The brothers chuckled wheezily, then turned to Toby.

"So, tell us, Tobe," said Rufe, "have you had any trouble . . ."

". . . up at the Auerbach place?" Lou asked.

"None," Toby declared, with a touch of impatience. "Everyone's healthy, happy, and having a great time."

"Hope your luck holds." Rufe glanced down at the briefcase. "Well, we'll get out of your way. We got us some map-reading to do. Mighty pleased to meet you, Lori. Hope to meet your boys . . ."

". . . one of these days," said Lou. "*And* their pretty nanny."

The Zimmer brothers winked simultaneously, placed their boaters on their heads at identical angles, and tottered down the stairs. I shook my head to clear it, but it didn't help because Rose Blanding reminded me so forcibly of Lilian Bunting, who was married to the vicar of St. George's Church in Finch. In this instance, however, the resemblance made a certain sort of sense to me. The wives of vicars and ministers probably had a lot in common, I reasoned, no matter where they lived.

"Will they get home all right, Mrs. Blanding?" I asked, observing the brothers' unsteady progress along the lakeside path.

"They'll be fine," she assured me. "Rufe and Lou may look frail, but they're as tough as old axe handles."

"Of course they are," I murmured. "Just like the Pyms."

"If I'm to call you Lori," she went on, "you must call me Rose. Please, leave your things in the hall and come into the front parlor. Can I get you a bite to eat or a cold drink? It looks as though you hiked down from the Aerie."

We left our packs and packages on a table in the entrance hall and followed Rose into a high-ceilinged, spacious room overlooking Lake Matula. While Toby refused her offer of refreshments, explaining that we'd had lunch at the cafe, I took in the front parlor.

There was a lot to take in. The house's demurely painted exterior concealed an interior that paid unrestrained tribute to grand Victorian style. The tables were made of heavily carved walnut, the chairs and sofas were upholstered in lush fabrics, and the walls were covered in a flocked wallpaper that imitated silk brocade. Layers of drapes drawn back by tasseled cords hung at the tall windows, and a large rug with a swirling floral pattern covered the polished hardwood floor.

Dainty whatnot shelves displayed a splendid collection of Victoriana: beaded reticules, kid leather baby shoes, embroidered gloves, tiny spectacles, cobalt-blue medicine bottles, impossibly elaborate Valentine's Day cards, and feathered fans. A stereopticon sat on a small, marble-topped table near the love seat in the bay window and a voluminous silk paisley shawl had been draped over the baby grand piano. Toby and I sat on the fringed, bottle-green velvet sofa, and Rose sat opposite us on a button-backed easy chair with low arms and braided trimming.

"You have a lovely home," I said, as soon as we were seated.

"Do you like it?" Rose asked, as her gaze

made a leisurely circuit around the room. "It was once a bordello."

"A . . . a *bordello?*" I gaped at her in astonishment. "Next door to a *church?*"

"Not originally, but the situation did occur." Rose leaned back in the easy chair and shrugged nonchalantly. "It could hardly be avoided. At one time houses of prostitution outnumbered schools and churches in Bluebird by a factor of twenty to one."

My eyebrows shot up. "That's a lot of . . . entertainment . . . for such a small community."

"Bluebird wasn't small back then," said Rose. "Nearly eleven thousand people lived in the valley in 1865, and the vast majority of them —" She stopped short and tilted her head toward Toby. "Forgive me, Toby, I cast no aspersions on your noble sex, but the truth remains that the vast majority of the early residents were men. I'm sure there were some who didn't require such *entertainment,* as you so delicately put it, Lori, but evidently many of them did."

"Evidently," I said, smiling wryly.

"So many of them were single, you see," Rose continued, "or acted as if they were. Gold fever struck office workers, salesmen, farmers, and factory workers not only because it offered them a chance to get rich

169

quickly, but also because it offered them a chance to escape the restrictive lives they'd led back East — to throw off their traces and kick up their heels."

"Hence, the multitude of bordellos," I put in.

"And drinking establishments and gambling hells. But respectable women came to Bluebird, eventually, and tamed some of its wilder aspects." Rose paused, lowered her eyes, and smiled self-consciously. "Forgive me. I'm lecturing. It's an occupational hazard when one is both preacher's wife *and* president of a historical society."

"Don't stop," I said. "It's fascinating. I had no idea that Bluebird used to be a metropolis."

Rose seemed only too pleased to carry on. "From 1865 to 1870, Bluebird's population doubled. Butchers, barbers, bakers, blacksmiths — every type of tradesman was needed to serve the mines and the miners, and many of the tradesmen brought their families with them."

"Families that needed schools and churches," I said, nodding.

"And much more," said Rose. "In its heyday, Bluebird had an opera house, a theater, a newspaper, two hotels, five boarding houses, seven law offices, four debating societies, countless gambling hells, saloons, and brothels, and no fewer than seven churches. I'd have to consult a reference book to give you the exact number of shops that once lined Bluebird's streets, but you could find almost anything here that you could find in Denver. Passenger trains stopped here seven times a day."

I gazed at her incredulously. "What happened? Not that Bluebird isn't lovely as it is," I added hastily, "but it's not exactly *metropolitan*."

"Boom and bust," Rose replied succinctly. "The price of silver plummeted in 1893, when the country went on the gold standard. The silver claims dried up, the miners moved on to other jobs, and businesses failed. Bluebird shrank. By 1930, there were fewer than a thousand people living in the Vulgamore Valley. The state authorities selected the valley as a good place to build a reservoir partly because there were so few people left to displace."

"Hold on a minute," I said, glancing toward the bay window. "Are you telling me that the town of Bluebird used to be where Lake Matula is now?"

"Yes," Rose said brightly, "and I can prove it. Would you like to see a photograph of Bluebird at the height of its prosperity?"

"Very much," I said.

Rose left the front parlor and returned a moment later carrying a framed, oblong, sepia-toned photograph that was at least three feet in length. Toby and I made room for her to sit between us and she propped the photograph on her lap for us to see.

"It's a composite photograph," she explained, "a collage made in 1888 by a photographer named Mervyn Blount. Mr. Blount came to the valley in the early days to document the prospectors' lives, and stayed on to photograph the burgeoning town. He was quite the outdoorsman. He took these photos from a vantage point halfway up Ruley's Peak, and that's a difficult mountain to climb."

I peered curiously at the panoramic view Mervyn Blount had pieced together from separate photographs. The Vulgamore Valley was scarcely recognizable. Buildings of all shapes and sizes jostled for space along streets that ran parallel to a narrow stream — "Bluebird Creek," Rose informed me — at the very bottom of the valley. Railroad tracks emerged from the serpentine canyon we'd passed through on the way from Denver to Bluebird, and great swathes of forest were missing from the surrounding slopes.

"Where are the trees?" I asked in dismay.

"Propping up mine shafts, heating stoves, housing machinery and people," Rose replied matter-of-factly. "Mining was not kind to the environment in those days. It still isn't." She pointed to a blurred complex of wooden buildings halfway up the northern wall of the valley. "The Lord Stuart Mine stayed open a bit longer than the silver mines because it produced gold, but the gold vein played out, as gold veins always do, and it closed in 1896."

"And forty years later, they built the reservoir and drowned the town," I said sadly.

"There wasn't much of a town left by the time they flooded the valley." Rose's fingers drifted from left to right over the photograph. "Long before the reservoir was built, a series of flash floods had driven the remaining townspeople to higher ground at the valley's western end. They'd already salvaged what they could from the ruins of the old town."

"Danny Auerbach followed their example," I commented. "He reused timber from the old mine buildings when he built the Aerie."

"Waste not, want not." Rose pointed to the photograph. "The parsonage was built where it now stands, but Good Shepherd's loyal congregation dismantled the church in 1934, a year before construction began on the reservoir, and moved it to its present location."

"Next door to a bordello?" I said questioningly.

Rose laughed. "My house was used as a bordello for only a few years, after which it was occupied by a series of fine, upstanding families. Still, my husband and I had to do a great deal of restoration work on it when we came to Bluebird, thirty-five years ago. Fortunately, the town was in the midst of a resurgence then, thanks to the outdoor adventure trade. We mine tourists now, instead of gold and silver." She swiveled her head from side to side. "Iced tea, anyone? Please say yes. I've talked myself dry!"

"Iced tea sounds great," said Toby, "but let me carry the photograph for you."

After he and Rose had left the room, I walked over to the bay window to gaze at the reservoir. I tried to superimpose Mervyn Blount's sepia-toned image of the bustling town onto Lake Matula, but I couldn't manage it. It was almost impossible for me to imagine clouds of smoke fouling the crystalline sky, train whistles blotting out birdsong, a vigorous community filling the

Vulgamore Valley from end to end.

Rose and Toby returned, with Toby balancing a cut-glass pitcher and three tall glasses on a rosewood tray. He placed the tray on a round table next to Rose's easy chair, and resumed his seat while she filled glasses and passed them to us. I hadn't realized how thirsty I was until I took my first sip of iced tea, and Rose appeared to enjoy hers thoroughly.

"Ah, that's better," she said, after she'd drained half her glass.

"You know," I mused aloud, "Danny Auerbach would never have been allowed to tear down and recycle the old mine buildings in England, where I live. There, they'd be praised for their historic value and preserved by the National Trust."

"The site of the Lord Stuart Mine was a hazardous eyesore," Rose stated firmly. "It's also private property, so Mr. Auerbach was well within his rights to do with it as he pleased. The Auerbachs have owned land up there since 1860, when they bought out the claims of a few hardscrabble prospectors. Fortunately, they invested the profits from the mine wisely, so even when it closed, they prospered. Unlike their workers," she added, a note of disapproval entering her voice, "most of whom lived a hand-to-mouth existence. But don't get me started on working conditions in the mines. I'd bore you to death."

"You haven't so far," I told her earnestly. "You've opened my eyes to a whole new world. I've enjoyed every minute."

"Thank you," said Rose. "I'm always glad to share my knowledge of Bluebird's past."

"What about its folk legends?" I asked.

Toby heaved a despondent sigh, as if he knew where my question would lead and wished I wouldn't go there. Ice clinked as Rose took another sip of iced tea before answering.

"It's said that on a still night church bells can be heard beneath the waters of Lake Matula," she said, her eyes dancing. "There's even talk of a ghost train running along the tracks at the bottom of the lake." She chuckled indulgently and shook her head. "Long winters make for tall tales."

"Have you heard the church bells?" I asked.

"Certainly not," Rose said good-humoredly, "and those who think they have, have spent far too much time in Altman's Saloon."

"So I suppose a sighting of the ghost train is out of the question," I said.

"You suppose correctly. Even if I believed

in the legend, the water isn't clear enough for anyone to see all the way to the bottom of the lake." Rose's gray eyes narrowed shrewdly. "I think I can guess why you're interested in ghost trains and phantom church bells, Lori. You've heard about the curse, haven't you?"

I nodded. "I'd like to hear more."

"Why?" Rose asked sharply. "Do you believe in such things?"

"No," I said, "but I find them interesting. Why do so many people in town still believe in the curse when it no longer serves a useful purpose?"

Rose placed her glass on the tray, rested her elbows on the easy chair's arms, and tented her fingers. "What useful purpose did it serve?"

"If it scared children away from the site," I said, "it probably saved a few lives."

"I see." Rose frowned slightly. "Who told you about the curse?"

"The usual suspects," Toby interpolated, rolling his eyes, "but I plead guilty to giving Lori the gory details, after she badgered me for them."

"What details did you give her?" Rose inquired.

Toby shrugged. "I told her what my grandfather told me. Kids used to get hurt playing on the old mining equipment. So many children were injured that people began to believe the site was jinxed."

"If only it were so simple. . . ." Rose tapped the tips of her thumbs together, then stood. She crossed to a small secretaire in the corner and took a modern brass key from one of its drawers. She slipped the key into her skirt pocket before asking, "Are you up for a walk?"

"You bet," I said, getting to my feet. "Toby's whipped me into shape."

"I'm always up for a walk," Toby chimed in.

"Good." Rose turned toward the entrance hall and motioned for us to follow her. "If you want to hear the true story behind the Lord Stuart curse, come with me."

TWELVE

Toby and I retrieved our hats and sunglasses as we passed through the entrance hall, and Rose donned a straw hat that could have served as a small parasol, tying its rose-colored ribbons firmly beneath her chin before we went outside. There was no need for her to change into hiking boots. Her chunky, thick-soled shoes looked sturdy enough to handle all but the roughest terrain.

Although she pulled the front door shut as we left the parsonage, she didn't lock it.

"Have you ever been burgled?" I asked, as Toby and I followed her down the stairs.

"Not once in thirty-five years." She pointed to the rows of houses that rose in terraced ranks along Bluebird's steeply inclined streets. "Burglars don't prosper in Bluebird. There are too many eyes watching from behind too many curtains. It's one of the great advantages of having nosey neighbors."

"True," I said, thinking nostalgically of Finch's ceaselessly twitching curtains. "Nothing goes unnoticed in a small town."

"Not for long, at any rate," Rose added wisely.

She led us through Bluebird's back lanes, pausing to greet everyone we met along the way, to St. Barbara's Catholic Church, which stood at the top of Garnet Street, on the north side of the valley. Behind the church a dirt road climbed up the mountainside and disappeared into the forest. When Rose turned toward the dirt road, Toby stopped abruptly.

"I know where we're going," he said, eyeing the road unhappily.

"I knew you would," said Rose, "but let's keep it as a surprise for Lori."

"Some surprise," Toby muttered, but he walked on.

The road was wide enough for the three of us to walk comfortably side by side and shady enough for me to wish I'd brought my sweatshirt. It was properly maintained, as well, and cut at a gentle grade that made walking uphill a breeze. We'd climbed for no more than fifteen minutes when a ten-foot-wide iron gate came into view. Patches of rust showed through the gate's flaking layers of white paint, and above it an arch-way of lacy ironwork contained the words: BLUEBIRD CEMETERY.

"We're going to a cemetery?" I exclaimed, clasping my hands to my breast. "I *love* cemeteries."

"You do?" Toby looked at me as though I'd slipped a cog.

"I *always* visit cemeteries when I travel," I told him. "They're quiet and serene and —"

"Filled with dead bodies," Toby inserted, wrinkling his nose in distaste.

"They're filled with the past as well," I said, bubbling over with enthusiasm. "You can learn a lot about a place by visiting its graveyards. Isn't that right, Rose?"

"I couldn't have put it better myself," she said. "Shall we proceed?"

The gate was chained and padlocked, but Rose opened the lock with the key she'd taken from the secretaire, slid the chain around the gate post, and left it dangling. When she'd finished, Toby pushed the gate aside, and I stepped into a glade so lovely it took my breath away.

It was like a small cathedral, with pillars of white-barked aspens and a roof of sun-drenched leaves that glowed as richly as stained glass. The dirt road served as the center aisle, with a web of sunken paths winding from it through a maze of head-stones, crosses, markers, and monuments. Above us, choirs of birds twittered among the shivering aspen leaves, as if to emphasize the sylvan silence that descended when they stopped.

"It's beautiful," I said softly.

Rose nodded her agreement, but Toby was clearly unmoved by our surroundings.

"For heaven's sake, Lori," he said impatiently. "You don't have to whisper. You won't disturb anyone."

"It's a sacred place," I retorted.

"For worms, maybe," he countered.

"What kind of comment is *that?*" I said, frowning at him.

"An honest one." He frowned back at me, then hung his head and muttered angrily, "We buried my grandparents here last year. It's not my favorite place to be, okay?"

"Oh," I said, brought up short. "I didn't realize . . . I'm so sorry, Toby. Do you want to leave?"

"No, he doesn't." Rose placed a comforting hand on Toby's shoulder. "Try to think of this place as your grandfather thought of it, Toby — as a repository of history. He used to spend a lot of time up here."

Toby's head came up. "He did?"

"He found it fascinating. You will, too, if

you give it a chance." Rose gave his shoulder an encouraging squeeze. "Are you staying?"

"Yeah." Toby took a deep breath and glanced at us apologetically. "I'm staying."

"Then come along," Rose said briskly.

Toby and I followed Rose along the dirt road and onto a sunken path that branched off from it, to our right. I suspected that she would have moved at a faster clip if I hadn't expressed a keen interest in graveyards. As it was, she walked slowly enough for me to read the headstones whose inscriptions hadn't been obliterated by the passage of time.

It was like reading a roll call of nineteenth-century immigrants: Evgeny Krasikov, Padraig Doherty, Helmut Grauberger, Esteban Fernandez, Miroslav Simzisko, Leslinka Turek, and Alexis Laytonikis were just a few of the resoundingly ethnic names that caught my eye.

"It's like the United Nations up here," I marveled.

"It is," Rose agreed. "People from all over the world came to the Rocky Mountains to seek their fortunes. Bluebird even had a small Chinese community as well as a handful of Sikhs from northern India. Imagine the journeys they made to get here."

"In England," I said, as we continued

down the path, "the old graveyards are near churches. Why is Bluebird's so far away from town?"

"Economics, for one thing," Rose replied. "At the time the cemetery was created, town property was too expensive to waste on the dead, and much of the rest of the Vulgamore Valley was being mined. The ground here is relatively easy to dig, fairly level, and as far as we know, devoid of valuable gems or minerals." She paused before a row of twelve simple stone markers, each bearing the name Shuttleworth. "People were also afraid of contagion. Epidemics were not unknown in mining communities."

"What kind of epidemics?" I asked.

"Dysentery, cholera, measles, malaria, diphtheria, smallpox . . ." Rose kept her eyes trained on the headstones as she reeled off the long list of diseases. "The scourges that spring up wherever malnourished people live in overcrowded conditions with poor sanitation. Influenza killed the entire Shuttleworth family, from the infant son to the grandmother. Their church had to bury them."

"The good old days," murmured Toby, gazing somberly at the Shuttleworths' graves.

"It wasn't Disney World," Rose acknowledged. She bent to lay a hand on the smallest headstone, then walked on. "Miners' lives were difficult and dangerous. Those who weren't killed by disease died in mining accidents or froze to death or drowned. Some drank themselves to death, some committed suicide. Others were shot or stabbed in drunken brawls. A few were hanged."

"Frontier justice at work?" I said.

"So-called frontier justice was swift and sure," Rose said sardonically, "but I'm not sure how often it was just. And, of course, silicosis took many miners' lives." She noted my puzzled expression and explained, "Silicosis is a form of pneumonia caused by breathing air filled with silica dust. Respirators didn't exist back then."

"Good grief," I said, pressing my hands to my chest. Rose's litany of woes seemed at odds with the earlier picture she'd painted of Bluebird. "How could they build an opera house in the midst of so much misery?"

"They needed the opera house — and the debating societies and the baseball teams — to take them away from the misery," said Rose. "Besides, their expectations were different from ours. They had no antibiotics, no advanced surgical techniques. To them, disease and death were an accepted part of life — dreadful, yes, but accepted."

"Not everyone died young, though." Toby had crouched down to examine the inscription on an unusually elaborate marker: a white marble plinth surmounted by a kneeling, weeping angel with folded wings. "Hannah Lavery lived to be eighty-five."

"Dear Hannah." Rose spoke with real animation for the first time since we'd passed through the entrance gate, as though she were speaking of a friend she'd known and loved. "Hannah Lavery was the daughter of a wealthy mine owner, an exceptional girl who became a truly remarkable woman. When Hannah saw suffering, she refused to look the other way. She spent her entire life working for the welfare of miners and their families. She died in Washington, D.C., still lobbying for humane labor laws, but she wished to be buried here, among the people whose struggles had first awakened her conscience."

"She never married," I observed.

"Victorian men of her class preferred passive women to rabble-rousers," said Rose. "But I find that crusaders in every age have difficulty finding suitable mates. It isn't easy to give one's heart to a man as well as a cause."

I ran my fingers along the angel's folded wings, then walked ahead of my companions, drawn by a monumental monument that stood silhouetted against a ponderosa pine at the end of the path. The gleaming white marble obelisk towered over the phalanx of rough-cut red-granite headstones that surrounded it, and its inscription had been beautifully chiseled.

Cyril Pennyfeather
1859–1896
A LIVING SACRIFICE, HOLY,
ACCEPTABLE UNTO GOD
Romans 12:1

Erected to honor the memory
of a devoted teacher by the
grateful families
of those whose lives he saved

"Who was Cyril Pennyfeather?" I asked when Toby and Rose had caught up with me.

"He was a schoolmaster," Rose replied. "He came to the United States from England in 1880 and made his way to Bluebird in 1884. He and the men who lie buried near him died in the Lord Stuart mining disaster of 1896."

I blinked at her, looked back at the obelisk, and began silently to count the red-granite markers surrounding it.

"Twenty," I said finally. "Twenty men died in one accident — twenty-one, counting Cyril." I turned to Rose. "What happened?"

"A catastrophic cave-in," she answered. "No one knows what caused it. Some claimed that the mine manager had bought poor-quality wood to prop the shaft in which the cave-in occurred, but nothing was ever proved. The shaft was never excavated, and the mine closed shortly thereafter."

"What was a schoolteacher doing in a mine?" asked Toby.

"Many of his pupils or former pupils worked there," Rose told him. "When he heard about the cave-in, he went up to see if there was anything he could do to help. He led at least a dozen men to safety before he, too, was killed by falling rock." She nodded toward the inscription. "As you can see, the families of those he rescued raised money to pay for his memorial. He was much loved even before his death. After it . . ." Rose looked from me to Toby and back to me again. "After it, rumors of a curse began to circulate."

"Ah," I said as understanding dawned. "The Lord Stuart curse."

"Correct," said Rose. "I'm convinced that the Lord Stuart Mine closed because there was no more gold to be had from it, but others believe differently. When my husband and I first came to Bluebird, Rufe and Lou Zimmer took us up to the old mine site and told us about the disaster. Afterward, they brought us here, to show us the graves of those who'd died. They explained to us that the cave-in was the culmination of a series of fatal accidents that had plagued the Lord Stuart Mine almost from its inception. They held that the mine would have closed in 1896, even if the mother lode hadn't played out."

"Because of the curse?" I said.

Rose nodded. "Miners are superstitious, as men in hazardous occupations frequently are. If they came to believe in the curse, they might have been reluctant to work in the Lord Stuart."

"You can't run a mine without miners," I commented.

"I don't think the curse had anything to do with the mine closing," said Toby, shaking his head. "Don't you see? It was a cover-up. The mine owner closed the Lord Stuart to keep people from finding out about the substandard wood. A scandal like that wouldn't sit well with his investors."

"Maybe he invented the curse to keep inquisitive people away from the mine," I suggested, "and the accidents your grandfather told you about — the ones that happened in later years — reinforced the original lie."

"But why do they *still* believe in the curse?" Toby demanded. "The mine closed over a century ago. There's not a trace of it left aboveground. No one's ever been injured at the Aerie, much less died, but people *still* think it's risky to stay there."

"We still celebrate Gold Rush Days in Bluebird," Rose reminded him. "For some people, the past is always present. Your predecessor, for example, was deeply interested in the history of the Lord Stuart Mine."

"James Blackwell?" I said, suddenly alert.

"James came to the historical society toward the end of February," Rose said. "He wanted information about the mine. He already had reference books — Mrs. Auerbach collects them, apparently — so he didn't need to borrow ours, but I lent him newspaper clippings, photographs, town records, pamphlets, and other ephemera. He returned a few weeks later to ask for details about the 1896 disaster."

"Did you tell him about the curse?" I

asked.

"I didn't have to," said Rose. "He'd already heard about it in town — yes, Toby, from the usual suspects. James wanted to know if the legend was based in fact. I told him exactly what I've told you and left him to draw his own conclusions."

"Did he seem disturbed by the information you gave him?" I asked.

"Not particularly." Rose shrugged. "But I have to confess that I didn't monitor his reactions very closely. I was busy at the time, developing the society's summer event and exhibition schedule." She glanced at her wristwatch. "I'm sorry to say it, but I have to get back to the parsonage. Maggie Flaxton is dropping by at four o'clock to discuss my role in Gold Rush Days. I don't want to keep her waiting."

"No, you don't," said Toby, shuddering. "Rub Maggie the wrong way and you'll find yourself cleaning up after the burros in the petting zoo. Let's go."

"Wait," said Rose. "I think we have enough time to make one more stop before we leave. Toby, you can lead the way."

Toby's grandparents had been buried beneath a large red-granite boulder, the kind the twins had clambered over on every one of our hikes. A square patch on one side of the boulder had been smoothed, polished, and etched with his grandparents' names and dates, as well as a simple outline of the mountain range that contained Mount Shroeder's distinctive profile.

"We climbed Mount Shroeder when I was ten years old," Toby recalled. "It was Grand-dad's favorite one-day climb. He loved the view of the valley from the summit."

"He passed his love on to you," I said. "It's a wonderful inheritance."

Toby squatted down to brush dead leaves from the grave. "I wonder why he didn't tell me about the disaster when I asked about the curse?"

"Being a man of science, I expect he refused to connect the two," I said.

"Yeah." Toby stretched out his hand to touch the boulder. "Because there is no connection, right, Granddad?"

We made sure the gate was firmly chained and padlocked before we left, then started back down the dirt road toward town. After spending so much time in the cemetery's cool shade, it was good to feel the sun's warmth on my skin again.

"Rose," I said, "did Mrs. Auerbach ever ask you about the curse?"

"I've never met Mrs. Auerbach," said

Rose. "She wasn't a churchgoer and she didn't spend much time in town. She kept herself very much to herself when she and the children were at the Aerie. I imagine Bluebird's attractions pale in comparison to the Aerie's. I've been given to understand that it's a marvelous place."

"Given to understand?" I repeated, surprised. "Do you mean you've never been to the Aerie?"

"Never." She gave me a sidelong glance and a half-guilty smile. "To be honest, I'm hoping to wangle an invitation from you. I've always wanted to see what it's like inside. Apart from that, I'd like to pick up the material James Blackwell borrowed from the society."

"He never returned the papers he borrowed?" I said.

"He left so suddenly that it probably slipped his mind," said Rose.

"I'll bet it's in the library," I told her. "I'll look for it this evening. If I can't find it, you can help me look for it tomorrow, when you come to lunch. Will one-thirty work for you?"

"I can come earlier, if it's more convenient," Rose offered. "Due to lack of funding, the society is closed Tuesdays, Thursdays, and Sundays."

"How about high noon, then?" I suggested.

"High noon will work perfectly," said Rose, and she walked with a bounce in her step all the way back to the parsonage.

THIRTEEN

Toby and I collected our bags and packages from the hall table and thanked Rose Blanding sincerely for sharing her time as well as her incredible wealth of knowledge with us. I had no trouble believing her when she said that it had been her pleasure. She was a born lecturer, and Toby and I had given her a splendid opportunity to hold forth on a subject that was close to her heart.

We left by the front stairs, but we didn't take the lake path back to town. Instead, we followed a rough track through the stand of pines that shielded the parsonage and the church from the two-lane highway leading into town. Toby explained that, although the alternate route was slightly longer and marginally less scenic than the lake path, taking it would greatly increase our chances of avoiding a run-in with Maggie Flaxton. I backed his decision wholeheartedly, having employed the same tactics frequently in

Finch, to avoid a rampaging Peggy Taxman.

Before we left the shelter of the trees, I asked Toby to stop.

"Look," I said, "I didn't know that your grandparents had died so recently. If I'd known, I wouldn't have been so idiotically chirpy when we reached the cemetery. I'm really sorry if spending time there upset you."

"It's okay," said Toby. "It turned out to be pretty interesting. I guess Grandma and Granddad are part of the . . . the repository of history, now."

"They are," I said. "A hundred years from now people will find their headstone as fascinating as we found Cyril Pennyfeather's."

"Only if they have a tour guide like Mrs. Blanding," said Toby.

I was ready to move on, but Toby stayed put, gazing down at me with a faintly troubled expression on his face.

"What's up?" I asked.

"When we were in the cafe," he said slowly, "you told Carrie Vyne that James Blackwell was interested in local history. You knew it *before* Mrs. Blanding told us about his visits to the historical society. How did you find out?"

"Brett Whitcombe," I replied. "He told

me that James used to pester him with questions about what Bluebird was like in the olden days. He also told me that James was investigating some 'tomfool stories' — Brett's words, not mine. I think James went to Brett Whitcombe as well as Rose Blanding, looking for information about the Lord Stuart curse."

"Right." Toby pushed his hat back on his head. "The thing is, James left some stuff behind in his apartment — the apartment I'm using now. I would have shipped it to him, but I don't know where to send it."

"No forwarding address," I said, nodding. "Is it the material he borrowed from the historical society?"

"No," said Toby. "It's not books or papers, and I'm sure it belongs to him, not to the historical society — he left the receipts behind, too. I thought he was using it for . . ." His voice trailed off and his gaze wandered to a point somewhere over my right shoulder. "But after hearing Mrs. Blanding, I'm not so sure."

"Not so sure about what?" I asked.

Toby's eyes came back into focus. "I could be wrong. I'll show you when we get back. I'd like to know what you think."

My cell phone rang, frightening a camp-robber bird that had flown over to see if we had any crumbs to share. It flew off, twittering irritably, and I took the call. It was from Annelise, who wanted to know if she and the twins could have dinner at the ranch.

"They're having a cookout," she explained. "Will and Rob are dying to try buffalo burgers."

"What about you?" I asked.

"Belle Whitcombe took me out to see the buffalo calves today," said Annelise. "I'm planning to have a salad for dinner."

"A farmer's daughter turned vegetarian?" I said, feigning surprise. "Those calves must be cute."

"They're *adorable,*" she said. "We'll be back by seven, half past at the latest."

"Have fun," I told her. I put the cell phone back into my pocket and turned to Toby, announcing, "We're on our own for dinner. Annelise and the boys are eating theirs at the ranch."

"We can pick something up at the cafe," he suggested.

"Good idea," I said. "I wanted to go back into town anyway. I need to hit the grocery to pick up a few things for lunch tomorrow, and I'd also like to find a gift for Bill." I held up the bag from Dandy Don's. "Strange as it may seem, my husband isn't into stuffed animals, flower seeds, or earrings."

Toby laughed and we turned our steps once more toward Stafford Avenue. Fortunately, Maggie Flaxton was too busy browbeating a hapless neighbor into participating in Gold Rush Days to notice our presence in her store, so our shopping there went off without a hitch. I then spent twenty minutes meandering in and out of shops, rejecting one tacky souvenir after another, before Toby came up with his brilliant idea.

"How about a geode?" he proposed.

"Fantastic," I gushed. "What's a geode?"

"It's a round, hollow rock," Toby explained. "It doesn't look like much on the outside, but the inside's lined with crystals. When you break a geode in half, it looks like a twinkly cave inside. They're really pretty, but not in a girlish way. Granddad used one in his office as a paperweight."

"A man can never have too many paperweights," I said. "Where do we find geodes?"

"Mystic Crystals," Toby said promptly. "Also known as the rock shop." He began to walk rapidly toward the top of Stafford Avenue. "I hope it's still open. Amanda keeps her own hours."

"Amanda?" I said interestedly, scrambling to keep up with him. "The local loony-tune?"

Toby snorted disparagingly. "Amanda Barrow is Bluebird's resident hippie. She runs a commune in the geodesic dome with her cat, Angelique, and an ever-changing cast of crazies who think the dome sits on a vortex."

"Wouldn't it twirl around?" I said. "Like Dorothy's house in *The Wizard of Oz?*"

"It's not that kind of vortex," said Toby. "According to Amanda, it's a focal point for the mystical energies of the universe. According to me, it's a focal point for people who smoke too much wacky-weed — organically grown wacky-weed, of course."

"Do I detect a faint note of skepticism in your voice?" I asked, suppressing a smile.

"You detect a deafening roar of skepticism in my voice," Toby returned. "Don't get me wrong, I like Amanda well enough, but you never know what belief system she'll subscribe to next. Granddad used to say that she belonged to the goddess-of-the-month club. Grandma called her the queen of hocus-pocus."

"I'll bet she has some interesting theories about the Lord Stuart curse," I said, grinning.

"I'm sure we'll hear all about them," said Toby, "so brace yourself."

"I'm braced," I told him.

I probably could have found Mystic Crystals without Toby's assistance, but I wouldn't have known it was a rock shop. Amanda Barrow ran her business from a small Victorian house that stood between Eric's Mountain Bikes and the Mile High Pies pizza parlor. The house had been painted an eye-catching shade of hot pink that clashed resoundingly with the fluorescent orange and lime-green sandwich board sitting next to the front door.

The sandwich board advertised a well-rounded menu of metaphysical services — palm reading, tarot-card reading, aura reading, rune casting, crystal-ball gazing, psychic healing, dream analysis, and past-life retrieval — along with aromatherapy, medicinal herbs, meditation aids, and yoga classes. A long-haired white cat lounged in the shop's prominent bay window beneath a dangling display of spinning prisms, wind chimes, dream catchers, and multifaceted crystals.

"Angelique," said Toby, nodding at the white cat.

"I didn't think it was Amanda," I said dryly.

"Couldn't be," Toby joked. "Amanda's a redhead."

I felt as though I'd stepped into the vortex.

"Whoa, hold on, stop . . ." I seized Toby's arm to keep him from entering the shop. "Are you telling me that Amanda Barrow has *red hair?*"

"Yeah," said Toby. "She's got freckles, too. So?"

I put a hand to my head in an attempt to stop the whirling, but the pressure only seemed to magnify the image spinning in my mind of Miranda Morrow, Finch's red-haired, freckle-faced witch, who lived with a black cat named Seraphina.

"Are you okay, Lori?" Toby asked.

"Yes," I managed. "Just a little dizzy."

"I shouldn't have walked so fast," he said contritely. "I always forget that Stafford Avenue goes uphill."

"I'll be fine in a minute," I said.

"Take your time," he urged me. "There's no hurry. The shop's still open."

I closed my eyes, breathed slowly and steadily, and forced myself to concentrate on the myriad of differences between Finch's Miranda Morrow and Bluebird's Amanda Barrow. Miranda conducted her business over the telephone and via the Internet, not in person. She lived in a modest stone cottage, not a geodesic dome, and she didn't have a garish sign on her front gate advertising her profession. The only time I'd seen her read palms was at the Harvest Festival, when she'd played the role of a gypsy fortune-teller in order to raise money for the St. George's Church roof repair fund. No one in Finch — not even Peggy Taxman — had *ever* referred to Miranda Morrow as a loony-tune.

"Okay," I said, when I'd regained a modicum of mental stability. "All better. Take me to the geodes."

"This way," said Toby.

He opened the front door and we stepped into a high-ceilinged, rectangular room filled with the cloying, sickly sweet fragrance of sandalwood. A handful of joss sticks burned in a brass holder next to the cash register on the rear counter. The smoke trailing up from the joss sticks was the only sign of life in the shop, apart from Angelique, who took one look at us, gave an unearthly yowl, and streaked through a bead curtain behind the counter.

"I'll be right with you!" a woman's voice called from beyond the bead curtain.

"Amanda," Toby murmured. "She really shouldn't leave incense burning unattended. If Angelique knocked it over, the place would go up like a tinderbox."

"She shouldn't be burning incense at all,"

I murmured back. "It's an insult to the pure mountain air."

The room was divided into two distinct spaces. To our right, bathed in the sunlight pouring though the bay window, freestanding glass shelves held candles, stone pyramids, bottles of aromatic oils, packets of incense, brass incense holders, onyx Buddhas, chunks of quartz crystal, strings of stone beads, and baskets of polished rocks. Necklaces, earrings, and bracelets hung from a Peg-Board behind the counter, and a wooden bookcase against the far wall was filled with books on a wide range of metaphysical topics. CDs featuring New Age music complemented the book display.

To our left, shielded from direct daylight by a gauze curtain, sat four wooden chairs, a round wooden table covered with a circle of star-spangled black velvet, and a tall dark-purple cupboard in which, I imagined, Amanda Barrow stored the tools of her trade: crystal ball, tarot cards, rune stones, possibly a Ouija board and some dousing wands as well. The walls on either side of the purple cupboard were decorated with posters illustrating acupuncture points, meridian lines, and the constellations.

Toby ignored the left side of the shop and went directly to a glass shelf displaying a selection of geodes that had already been split in half. They were exactly as he'd described them: dull and boring on the outside, but alive with twinkly amethyst crystalline formations on the inside. I picked one up and carried it to the bay window to look at it in the sunlight.

"It's like the Big Rock Candy Mountain," I said, smiling delightedly. "Bill will love it. He's one of those guys who has everything, but he doesn't have anything like *this*. Thanks, Toby. It was a great idea. I think I'll get one for my father-in-law as well. It'll add a certain something to his law office in Boston."

The bead curtain rattled and I looked over my shoulder as a short, stout, middle-aged woman emerged from the back room. She had to be in her late fifties, but she dressed as if she were still in her teens, wearing a low-cut, embroidered peasant blouse; a flouncy, ankle-length muslin skirt; clunky leather work boots; an apple-seed necklace; and a pair of huge hoop earrings accented with feathers. Her face, chest, and arms were plastered with freckles, and her henna-enhanced red hair fell almost to her waist.

"Hi, Amanda," said Toby.

"Hello, Toby," said Amanda, coming out from behind the counter. "You'll have to forgive Angelique. I don't know what's gotten into her. She's in the back room, hiding under the sink. I tried to get her to come out, but —" Amanda broke off abruptly as she caught sight of me. She gasped, her green eyes opened wide, the color drained from her face, and she raised a trembling finger to point at me.

"Death!" she cried. "You bring *death* with you!"

FOURTEEN

Amanda's arm fell and she tottered as though her knees were about to buckle. Toby sighed impatiently, but he thrust the box of Calico Cookies into my hands and hurried over to guide the wobbling woman to a chair at the velvet-covered table. I stood in shocked silence for a moment, then returned the geode to its place on the glass shelves and crept quietly past the gauze curtain to stand a few feet away from Amanda and Toby.

The red-haired mistress of Mystic Crystals sat hunched over the table with her eyes squeezed tightly shut, massaging her temples and talking to herself.

"Yes, yes, I understand now," she muttered. "Angelique saw him, tried to warn me, to prepare me. . . . I should have listened, but how was I to know? Death comes to us unbidden, when we least expect it. Even those of us who see beyond can be taken unawares. . . ."

Toby rolled his eyes expressively, as though to reassure me that Amanda's histrionics were par for the course, then bent over her and asked, "Amanda? Can I get you a drink of water or anything?"

"Water, yes, water," Amanda whispered. "Water to cleanse, to clarify, to purify, to —"

"I'll get it," I said quickly.

I placed the cookies and my bag of souvenirs on an empty chair and headed for the back room. I didn't relish the prospect of facing a yowling Angelique again, but I didn't want to be left alone with Amanda Barrow, either. If she passed out, I doubted that I'd be strong enough to keep her from hitting the floor.

The back room turned out to be a small and remarkably tidy kitchen. After a hasty search, I found a clean glass in a cupboard and approached the sink. I did so with some trepidation, expecting at any moment to feel a set of sharp claws sink into my calf, but Angelique had evidently gotten over whatever had startled her. She leapt onto the draining board and sat there, watching interestedly, while I filled the glass with water. I stroked her fluffy back, then brought the glass to Toby to pass to Amanda. I wasn't sure she'd take it from my hand.

Instead of drinking the water, Amanda dipped her fingertips into it, pressed them to her eyelids, her forehead, and her breast, dipped them again, and flicked little splashes into the air, to the north, south, east, and west. Finally, she opened her eyes, threw her hennaed hair back over her shoulders, and turned slowly toward me. Her green eyes searched the empty space around me avidly before coming to rest on my face.

"He has gone," she announced. "His energy has traveled to another sphere. He didn't like being seen by me or by Angelique. He prefers to move undetected through the physical world."

"Who?" I asked.

"The male spirit who accompanies you," she replied. "Couldn't you sense his presence?"

I felt a prickling sensation on the back of my neck, as if a chill breeze had blown through the room. I knew of only one male spirit who would frighten cats and freak out psychics, and I didn't want him hovering within a hundred miles of me.

"Describe him," I said warily.

Amanda closed her eyes, spread her palms on the table, and breathed deeply through her nostrils. "Light hair. A slight build. The glint of spectacles. No." She frowned in concentration, then corrected herself. "Pince-nez. On a chain."

Tension drained from me. Whoever Amanda was describing, it wasn't Abaddon.

"I'm afraid I don't know what you're talking about," I said.

"He has not yet made himself known to you, though I sense . . ." Amanda peered at me intently, almost hungrily, as if she suspected that I, unlike most people who walked into her shop, had some experience in her chosen field of expertise. "Have you ever been in touch with the other side?"

"The other side of what?" I asked.

"Eternity," she whispered dramatically.

"I don't *think* so." I pursed my lips and frowned slightly. "No, probably not. I'm sure I would have noticed."

Toby sniggered and Amanda waited for me to go on, but I had nothing more to add. I wasn't about to tell the queen of hocus-pocus that I'd been in touch with "the other side" nearly every day for the past seven years. Aunt Dimity was a dear friend, not a psychic phenomenon. I didn't want her name bandied about by a bunch of aging hippies holding seances in the geodesic dome.

Amanda waved a freckled hand toward an empty chair. "Come. Sit with me. Tell me about your dreams."

"Sorry," I said, refusing the invitation. "I never remember my dreams."

It was a bald-faced lie, but my nightmare was strictly off limits, and no power on earth would compel me to speak of long, languorous dreams starring heroic, blue-eyed cocker spaniels while Toby Cooper was within earshot. He was a bright boy. He wouldn't need Amanda's help to interpret the symbolism.

"Perhaps the sphere will guide our sight," she suggested.

"Actually, we just came in to buy a geode," I told her.

"You may *think* you came into my shop for a mundane purpose," Amanda said, smiling complacently. "But I believe a greater power guided your steps. Shall we consult the orb?"

"Oh, why not?" I said carelessly.

I unbuckled my pack, added it to the pile on the chair, and took a seat at the table. After a brief hesitation, during which he no doubt struggled manfully to keep from voicing his opinion on orb consultations, Toby followed suit.

Amanda rose and removed from the cupboard a round object covered with a fringed, jacquard-silk cloth. She placed the object in the center of the table, resumed her seat, and swept the cloth aside to reveal a large and quite beautiful crystal ball on a little wooden stand. As she bent over the crystal ball, she bracketed her face with her hands, as if to block everything else from view.

Toby sat back in his chair with his arms folded, looking askance at the proceedings, but I leaned forward, propping my elbows on the table and resting my chin in my cupped hands. If Amanda had seen Abaddon's unholy ghost dogging my footsteps, I would have been nervous. As it was, I felt calm, relaxed, and ready for a bit of fun.

"I see a long journey," Amanda intoned. "You have come from afar."

I almost laughed out loud at her pathetic attempt to impress me. Anyone linked to Bluebird's highly efficient grapevine could have learned that I lived in England.

"You will meet a short, dark stranger," she went on.

"Isn't it supposed to be a *tall,* dark stranger?" Toby muttered.

Amanda continued to peer intently into the crystal ball, as though Toby's words were beneath her notice.

"Those you love most will surprise you,"

she said.

Again, I had to restrain the urge to laugh. There was nothing remotely mystical in Amanda's mumbo jumbo. I had every reason to believe that she, like everyone else in Bluebird, knew all about my five-year-old sons. It didn't take psychic powers to predict that little boys would at some point surprise their mother. Will and Rob surprised me every day. It's what five-year-olds *do*.

"Death came to claim you," Amanda murmured, "but you escaped his grasp."

I sat upright and the laughter died within me. Amanda might be throwing darts blindly, but even blind throws struck the target from time to time. This one had hit a bit too close to home.

"He will come for you again," she continued. "You risk all by sleeping beneath the eagle's wings. The killing curse will not leave you unscathed."

"That's enough." Toby pushed his chair back and got to his feet. "I knew you'd get around to the curse sooner or later, Amanda, but I didn't think you'd give it such a sick twist. You're supposed to use your alleged gifts to do good, but I don't see anything good in scaring people. Did James Blackwell come here, too? Did you try to scare him?"

Amanda looked up from the crystal ball. "All of my consultations are private and confidential."

"How convenient," Toby scoffed. "It means you don't have to defend yourself when you're wrong."

"I describe only what the orb reveals to me," Amanda said serenely.

"*And* what you hear in the cafe, *and* what you make up," Toby snapped.

"The inner eye does not lie," said Amanda.

"I hate to interrupt such a rousing debate," I said, with forced nonchalance, "but the closest I've been to death lately is a stroll around the cemetery with Rose Blanding — although I may die of starvation if I don't have dinner soon. Lunch was a long time ago and we've done quite a bit of walking since then." I stood. "Thanks for your time, Amanda. If you don't mind, I'd like to buy two geodes and get back to the Aerie. I really like sleeping beneath the eagle's wings. Should I, er, cross your palm with silver here or at the cash register?"

"Neither," she said, as unfazed by my reaction as she'd been by Toby's. "Take the geodes as my gift. To commune with your spirit has been payment enough."

"You're very kind," I said, avoiding

her gaze.

Toby and I were back on Stafford Avenue in less than ten minutes. I'd seldom been happier to breathe smoke-free air, but Toby looked angry enough to spit fire.

"I'm sorry about that," he said. "Amanda's always seemed harmless to me, but I guess she couldn't resist making the most of the curse."

"The *killing* curse," I corrected him. "It has a certain ring to it, don't you think?"

"I think," Toby said grimly, "that Amanda had better clean up her act or she's going to go out of business. Tourists don't enjoy being frightened. *You* weren't frightened, were you?"

"No," I said. "Personally, I think there are enough real horrors in the world. I don't have to go looking for them in crystal balls."

Toby gave me a searching, sidelong glance, as if to convince himself that Amanda's unsettling pronouncements hadn't upset me. My neutral expression must have reassured him because he relaxed and changed the subject.

"I'm glad you remembered dinner," he said. "I'm starving."

"Me, too," I said.

If I'd been completely honest with Toby, I would have admitted that I'd used dinner as an excuse to get away from Amanda Barrow and her orb. Amanda might rely on educated guesswork for most of her predictions, but she saw some things much too clearly for my liking.

Death *had* come for me, and I *had* escaped his grasp. Was he lying in wait for me at the Aerie, to complete the job he'd left undone in Scotland? Would I be the killing curse's next victim?

As we entered Caroline's Cafe, I felt a sudden rush of empathy for James Blackwell, lying alone in his bed, wondering what would happen next.

FIFTEEN

Toby and I decided to have dinner at the cafe, to save ourselves the trouble of cleaning up afterward. We returned to the Lord Stuart Trail at half past five, stuffed to the gills with Carrie Vyne's excellent fried chicken, mashed potatoes, and three-bean salad. As we started up the trail I saw something I hadn't seen before in Colorado.

"Do my eyes deceive me?" I said, squinting at the sky. "Are those . . . clouds?"

Toby followed my gaze and nodded. "Looks like a cold front's moving in. We may have a rainy night."

I nodded, secretly reassured. I hadn't dealt very well with thunderstorms since I'd been shot — every lightning bolt ignited flashbacks of Abaddon's creepy, pale face hovering over me on the storm-wracked cliffs in Scotland — but I could handle a rainy night.

"What thoughtful weather you have here," I commented. "No rain until we're done hiking — or trail riding or cooking out."

"It's not always so considerate," said Toby. "Which is why —"

"We always bring our rain gear," I finished for him.

A brisk wind was swooping through the treetops by the time we reached the Aerie, and the temperature had dropped by at least fifteen degrees. I was very glad we'd departed from the cafe when we did. If we'd stayed a half hour longer, I would have seriously regretted wearing shorts.

I left Toby to fill the cookie jar with Calico Cookies while I put Annelise's aspen-leaf earrings on her dresser and propped the pair of fuzzy buffalo against the twins' pillows in the playroom tent. When I reached the master suite, I glanced thoughtfully at the blue journal, but decided to postpone my chat with Aunt Dimity until after Annelise and the boys had returned from the ranch. I knew that our conversation would be a long one — it had been a remarkably eventful day — and I didn't want to be interrupted in the middle of it.

After changing into a pair of soft jeans and a long-sleeved cashmere sweater, and swapping my hiking boots for the blissfully supple moccasins I'd bought at Dandy Don's, I brought the geodes back to the dining room and placed them on the table, where everyone would be able to see them.

While I'd been distributing largesse, Toby had changed into clean jeans, sneakers, and an old gray-plaid flannel shirt. I returned to the great room to find him kneeling before the hearth, laying a fire.

"No fire pit tonight," he said. "It's too windy."

"I wasn't planning on it anyway," I said, crossing to lend him a hand. "It'll be baths and bed for Will and Rob when they get back, and I doubt that Annelise will want to stay up late." I passed logs to him from the bin until the pile was ready for lighting, then stood back. "The geodes will look fantastic by firelight, won't they?"

"Yes," Toby said, but he spoke as if he had other things on his mind. He closed the fire screen, straightened, and turned to me. He studied my face for a moment, then said, "Lori, tell me the truth. After everything we've heard today, does the Aerie seem different to you?"

"No." I smiled up at him and raised my hand as if I were taking an oath. "Scout's honor, Toby, the Aerie feels just as welcoming now as it did when I first set foot in it. Even if I did believe in curses, I couldn't believe that this place has ever been anything but loved."

"I really could strangle Amanda," he said darkly.

"Let's forget about Amanda," I told him. "Weren't you going to show me the stuff James Blackwell left behind? You may as well do it now, while we have the place to ourselves."

"Okay," said Toby. "Come with me."

I followed him through the passageway at the end of the kitchen and up two flights of stairs to the caretaker's apartment. Since I was scrupulously respectful of Toby's privacy, I would never have invaded his space without his permission, but once I was there, I couldn't help taking a look around.

The caretaker's apartment turned out to be a small, self-contained unit with a kitchenette, a living/dining room, a bathroom, a bedroom, and a private deck. The rooms were comfortably if not extravagantly furnished and clearly intended to be used by one person. Toby had personalized his somewhat spartan living quarters by lining the windowsills with chunks of quartz crystal he'd collected during our hikes, but apart from that, the rooms were as immaculate and impersonal as a hotel suite.

I was a bit taken aback by the apartment's cleanliness — Toby was, after all, a college student — until I remembered that Toby had spent nearly all of his waking hours at the Aerie with us. If the rooms looked unlived-in, I reasoned, it was because he hadn't really lived in them yet.

Toby must have noticed my inquisitive glances because he grinned and said, "It's humble, but it's home. Come through to the bedroom."

The bedroom seemed to be the only room Toby used on a regular basis. The bed-clothes on the single bed were rumpled, his hat hung from a bedpost, and his hiking boots sat next to the dresser in a circle of dirt and dust from the trail. Pine cones, rocks, and feathers littered the top of the dresser, and the nightstand was piled with books. When Toby opened the closet door, I caught a glimpse of flannel shirts on hangers and blue jeans on built-in shelves. His red jacket hung from a hook inside the door.

"Have a seat," he said.

Since there was nowhere else to sit, I sat on the bed. I was beginning to wonder why he'd brought me to the bedroom when, grunting with the effort, he dragged a large, open wooden crate out of the closet and pushed it to the side of the bed. Small though the apartment was, it would have taken a lot more effort to drag the crate all the way to the living room.

"Well?" he said, standing over the crate. "What do you think?"

The crate was filled with dirty, scratched, and dented tools: several pointy-ended hammers, a crowbar, a shovel, a sledgehammer, and a pickax along with a coil of nylon climbing rope, a battery-operated lantern, and a hard hat with a built-in headlamp.

"It looks like the kind of stuff a miner would use," I said.

Toby nodded. "When I found it, my first thought was that James had taken up prospecting as a hobby. A lot of people spend their free time smashing rocks for fun."

"And your second thought?" I inquired.

Instead of answering right away, Toby took several slips of paper from the drawer in the nightstand. He handed them to me, and I saw that they were credit card receipts from a hardware store in Denver, where James M. Blackwell had purchased everything he'd left in the wooden crate.

"See the dates?" Toby said. "He bought the crowbar and the lantern in mid-April and the rest of the stuff a couple of weeks later."

I shuffled through the receipts, then handed them back to Toby, saying, "Okay, I'm with you so far."

Toby put the receipts on the pile of books on the nightstand and sat beside me on the bed.

"I may be way off base," he began, "but the way I see it is, James went to the historical society in late February to ask for information about the Lord Stuart Mine. He went back in March to find out more about the mining disaster. In mid-April he bought a crowbar and a lantern. A couple of weeks later he bought a sledgehammer, a pickax, a shovel — tools he could use to . . ." Toby's voice trailed off, as if he couldn't bring himself to speak his thoughts aloud.

I pulled the crowbar onto my lap for a closer inspection. It was nicked and abraded, as if it had been used for some heavy-duty prying. As I ran my hand over the deep, gritty scratches, I recalled what Toby had told me while we sat before the fire on my first night at the Aerie: *Mr. Auerbach had a team of engineers seal the entrance to the Lord Stuart Mine. It's tight as a drum. . . .*

I put the crowbar back into the crate and turned to Toby. "Do you think James was trying to break into the Lord Stuart Mine?"

"He'd be crazy to try," said Toby. "It's dangerous down there."

"*Could* he break into the mine?" I asked.

"Not by the main entrance," Toby answered. "But he could have tried to reach it by a secondary tunnel. I told you before, the mountains around here are riddled with mine shafts."

"You're right," I said, brushing the grit from my hand. "He'd have to be crazy to try a stunt like that."

"Crazy or . . . greedy." Toby chewed his lower lip worriedly, then went on. "You heard Mrs. Blanding. Men came from as far away as northern India to look for gold in the Vulgamore Valley. James had a gold mine on his doorstep. All he had to do to find his fortune was to break into it."

"But the Lord Stuart Mine was played out," I reminded him.

"What if it wasn't?" Toby swung around to face me. "What if the Lord Stuart Mine closed *before* it was played out, to cover up the truth about the cave-in? James had done a lot of research. He could have decided that it was worth risking his neck to find out if there was still some gold left down there."

"And if there was?" My eyes widened as I realized where Toby's argument was headed. "Are you saying that James quit his job because he'd filled his pockets with gold?"

"If he had, he wouldn't mention it to Mr.

Auerbach," said Toby, "because the gold would rightfully belong to the Auerbach family." He leaned forward, his elbows on his knees, his hands tightly clasped together. "I hate to accuse a man I've never met of theft, but it would explain an awful lot: why he was so interested in the mine, why he bought the tools, why he left so suddenly without giving notice and without leaving a forwarding address . . ."

"But he was a nice guy," I protested. "Carrie Vyne, Brett Whitcombe, Rose Blanding — they all thought James was a good guy, and good guys don't steal from their employers."

"Gold fever does strange things to people," Toby observed sagely.

"He was an amateur historian, not a miner," I insisted.

Toby thrust a hand toward the crate. "What was an amateur historian doing with these tools?"

I pondered the question for a moment, then replied, "He was investigating history. Do you remember what Rose Blanding told us? James wanted to know if the Lord Stuart curse had some basis in fact."

"Not the curse again," said Toby, groaning.

"The curse is a part of the Aerie's history,

whether you want it to be or not," I said sternly. "If James went into the mine, I think it was because he wanted to know what really happened down there. He wanted to establish the facts about the disaster in order to . . ." I glanced hesitantly at Toby, then took a deep breath and plunged ahead. "In order to *exorcise* the Aerie. He wanted to free it from the curse. He wanted to prove that the mine had collapsed for perfectly reasonable reasons, not because someone had cast an evil spell on it."

"You're not telling me that *James* believed in the curse, are you?" Toby said scornfully.

"It doesn't matter whether he believed in it or not," I said. "Enough people *did* believe in it to make him want to prove them wrong."

"Then why did he leave so suddenly?" Toby asked.

"Because *we* were coming," I said, struck by a blazing flash of insight. "He hadn't found the proof he needed, but he was afraid that Annelise or I or maybe even the twins would find out what he was doing. He knew that Danny Auerbach would be furious with him for reopening the mine — Danny doesn't want his kids falling down an abandoned shaft, right? — so he took off before Danny could fire him."

"I don't buy it," Toby said flatly. "Your scenario doesn't ring true to me. James would have to be a structural engineer *and* an archaeologist to figure out what caused the cave-in. He couldn't just stroll in there and say, 'Aha! Weak braces!' "

"He's an intelligent man," I argued. "Maybe he found some books in the library that —"

"Books?" Toby interrupted. "If books taught James anything, it would be that he'd need years and years of special training to excavate the site and determine what went wrong. Sorry, Lori, but your explanation doesn't make sense."

"I like it better than yours," I said, eyeing him grumpily.

"I like it better than mine, too," said Toby. "But I think my explanation is closer to the truth. James found gold in the Lord Stuart Mine, stole it, and took off before anyone could catch him."

We lapsed into a somewhat prickly silence that lasted until my cell phone rang. I answered it, but the signal was so broken up that Annelise had to repeat her message several times before I could make out what she was saying.

". . . bad storm. . . . hail . . . high winds in

the pass . . . stay the night?"

"Yes!" I shouted back. "Stay there! Don't even *try* to come back! I'll see you tomorrow!"

". . . tomorrow!" Annelise hollered and hung up.

"Wow," I said, looking down at the cell phone. "It sounds as if they're getting hit hard at the Brockman. Brett Whitcombe wants Annelise and the boys to spend the night there because of high winds in the pass. It's hard to believe they're only one valley away from us."

"The front's moving in from the west," Toby explained. "If the storm's hit the Brockman, it'll be here within the hour."

"You told me it would be a rainy night," I said, eyeing him reproachfully. "You didn't say anything about a thunderstorm."

"A rainy night in the Rockies usually involves a thunderstorm," he said. "You'll love it, Lori. The lightning's fantastic and the thunder makes the floors shake."

Toby's peppy words made me feel sick to my stomach because I knew how I'd react to a thunderstorm that shook the floors. I could already feel my hands growing clammy. Experience had taught me that the only way to keep myself from curling into a pathetic, shivering ball during a really bad storm was to distract myself, to bury myself in a project so absorbing that the lightning would fade into the background.

"Thanks for showing James's stuff to me," I said. "Try to remember that we don't really know why he bought it. For all we know, he may have been hunting for geodes."

"Sure," said Toby, sounding thoroughly unconvinced.

I got up from the bed. "Get some rest, Toby. It's been a long day."

"Where are you going?" he asked.

"To the library," I replied, "to look for the stuff James borrowed from Rose Blanding."

"I'll come, too," he said, jumping to his feet.

"You will not," I said, pushing him down again. I hated to pull rank on him, but I didn't want him to see me lose it if the lightning *didn't* fade into the background. "You've got the night off. Listen to music, watch a movie, read a book, enjoy yourself. I *order* you to relax."

Toby looked down at his hands and asked in a subdued voice, "You're not angry with me, are you?"

"Why would I be angry with you?" I asked, nonplussed.

"Because I disagree with you about James," he said.

"Oh, for pity's sake, Toby," I said, laughing. "If I got angry with everyone who disagreed with me, I'd never *stop* being angry. I just want you to have some time to yourself for a change. You must be sick to death of looking after us."

"That's my job," he said.

"Not tonight it isn't," I declared.

"All right, I'll read a book or something," he said dully. He leaned forward to lift the lantern from the wooden crate. "You'd better take this with you. I've checked the batteries. It works. The emergency generator will kick in if the storm knocks the power out, but it takes a few minutes to get going. If you need me —"

"I now know *exactly* where to find you," I said, taking the lantern from him. "Good night."

I let myself out of Toby's apartment and made my way back to the great room. Roiling black clouds had filled the sky beyond the window wall, and cracks of thunder reverberated from the mountainsides, as if warning me to get away from the enormous plate-glass window before the lightning arrived. I darted into the library, turned on the lights, closed the draperies, and put the lantern on the banker's desk. I hit the lantern's on switch just to be on the safe side. I didn't want to be plunged into darkness if the power went out, even for a few minutes.

I'd visited the library several times since we'd arrived at the Aerie, so the room was familiar to me. Custom-made bookshelves lined three of its walls. The banker's desk rested before the fourth, beneath the window I'd so hastily covered. A mahogany map case stood beside the desk, and four oversized armchairs, each with its own reading lamp and cozy afghan, provided comfortable places to curl up with a book.

I sank into the nearest armchair and allowed my gaze to travel back and forth across Florence Auerbach's collection of books. When a sudden onslaught of rain peppered the window, I ordered myself to ignore the sound and concentrate instead on Danny Auerbach's perplexing wife.

I hadn't been able to tell Toby about Florence Auerbach's curious behavior because I'd promised Bill I'd keep it to myself. I hadn't told Toby that Florence had for some unknown reason interrupted her family's Christmas holiday at the Aerie, that she refused to set foot in it again, or that she'd ordered her husband to sell the Aerie without explaining *why* she wanted it sold, but I knew that even if I'd told Toby all of those things, I wouldn't have been able to convince him that she'd turned against the Aerie because of the curse. Toby didn't want to hear about the curse.

James Blackwell, I argued silently, might have been more open-minded than Toby. James had been living and working at the Aerie at Christmastime. He'd witnessed the family's precipitate departure. As the days ticked by with no sign of their return, he must have asked himself why they'd abandoned a place they'd once used so often. He could have concluded that their flight had something to do with the curse he'd heard about in town. It was clear to me, if not to Toby, that James had decided to mount an investigation of his own.

Since James liked to read, it was logical to assume that he'd combed through the books in Mrs. Auerbach's library for information on the curse, but he hadn't confined himself to books. He'd gone to the ranch, to speak with Brett Whitcombe, and to the historical society, to look for newspaper clippings, photographs, anything that might tell him more about the curse. He'd also purchased the tools he'd needed to take a firsthand look inside the mine — the place where it had all begun.

The more I thought about it, the more

convinced I became that James had gone into the mine for a very specific reason: to prove to the Auerbachs that their fears were groundless. Granted, he wasn't a structural engineer or an archaeologist, but he could have come across something in the library that told him what kind of proof to look for and where to look for it.

I had no intention of following James's footsteps into the mine, but I could try to reconstruct the thought process that had led him there. I wanted to prove to Toby that he was wrong about James Blackwell. I wanted to convince Toby that James had gone into the mine to investigate the true cause of the mining disaster, not to steal from his employers.

Hail was hammering the window when my eyes finally came to rest on the lowest shelf of the bookshelves to my left, where a gray archival box marked BLUEBIRD HIS-TORICAL SOCIETY had until now sat unnoticed in the shadows.

"Right," I said, getting to my feet. "We start there."

I pulled the box from the shelf and placed it on the desk, beside the lantern. As I removed the box's lid, several things happened at once. An earsplitting crack of thunder rattled the window, the power went out, and I saw by the lantern's stark white glare Abaddon's evil eyes staring up at me.

Sixteen

"Lori? Lori, wake up! Talk to me, Lori."

I opened my eyes. I was lying flat on my back on the rug in the library. Swirling sheets of rain were still battering the window, but the lights had come back on. Toby was kneeling beside me, clasping my right hand in both of his, looking very young and very terrified.

"Hi, there," he said, with a heroic attempt at a smile.

I peered up at him woozily. "W-what happened?"

"I don't know," he said. "I heard you scream and came running."

"I screamed?" I said, frowning.

"Oh, yeah." Toby nodded earnestly. "I heard it all the way upstairs, with my door closed."

"But why would I —" A muted flash of lightning lit the draperies, and the memory slammed into me like a tidal wave. I clutched Toby's hand convulsively and whispered, "It's him, *him!*"

Toby's eyes widened in alarm and he glanced over his shoulder. "Is someone here? Did someone *attack* you?"

"Yes . . . no . . . not here . . . in Scotland . . . his face, I saw his *face.*" I closed my eyes again and shuddered.

"Scotland?" Toby put the back of his hand to my forehead, as if he thought I might have a fever. "Are you feeling dizzy, Lori? You may be dehydrated. I've told you a thousand times to drink plenty of —"

"I'm not *dehydrated,*" I said crossly. I brushed his hand aside and pushed myself into a sitting position. *"I saw his face."*

"*Whose* face?" Toby asked.

I groaned, slumped forward, and covered my own face with my hands.

"You're shivering, Lori. Let's get you up off the floor." Toby lifted me bodily and set me down in an armchair. He pulled the afghan from the back of the chair and draped it around my shoulders, then stood peering down at me anxiously. "Should I call your husband?"

"No!" I barked. "Absolutely not. I don't want you to call anyone. Not Bill, not Annelise, not *anyone.*"

"Okay, okay, I won't." Toby scratched his head and looked around the room helplessly. "How about a cup of tea?"

I pulled the afghan closer and smiled wanly. "You sound just like my husband."

"Do you faint a lot at home?" he inquired.

"No, but I wake up screaming every morning." Tears began to blur my vision. "And Bill always makes me a cup of tea. He's so *kind.* Like you." I bowed my head. "I'm sorry, Toby. I ruined your night off."

"I didn't *want* a night off. What do you want me to *do?*" Toby's voice held a hint of desperation.

I dashed the tears from my eyes and pointed a trembling finger at the banker's desk, saying, "Bring the box to me."

Toby hesitated, then lifted the gray archival box from the desk and placed it carefully on my lap. I gripped the arms of the chair, took a shuddering breath, and lowered my gaze slowly to the old, sepia-toned photograph I'd last seen by the light of James Blackwell's lantern.

The man in the photograph stood ramrod straight against a backdrop of busy Victorian wallpaper, with one hand clutching the lapel of his ill-fitting suit coat, the other resting on the back of a dainty, velvet-covered chair. He had a thin, pale face; a halo of curly, black hair; and dark, piercing eyes — *crazy* eyes, eyes as black and fathomless as the pits of hell.

"Abaddon," I breathed.

"Aba who?" said Toby.

I couldn't tear my eyes away from the man's pale face. "Do you know who he is?"

Toby leaned over my shoulder to peer at the photograph, then picked it up and turned it over. "I have no idea, and there's nothing written on the back. Since the picture came from the historical society, my guess is that he came to Bluebird to strike it rich. A lot of men had portrait photographs taken in those days, to show the folks back home how successful they were, even if they weren't." He dragged an armchair close to mine, slid the box from my lap onto his, and began pulling out photo after photo. "See? There are lots more just like it."

He seemed relieved to have something to do, even if he didn't understand why he was doing it. He showed me one sepia-toned photograph after another, formal portraits of nameless men wearing suits that were too tight or too baggy or too short or too long for them. As their frowning, intent faces passed before me in rapid succession, I wondered if any of them had struck it rich, or if they'd all died the mean deaths Rose

Blanding had described in the cemetery.

A guttural rumble of thunder rolled from one end of the valley to the other and I shrank back in the chair. Toby must have noticed my reaction because he waved a photograph under my nose like smelling salts.

"Look," he said, with determined cheerfulness. "I've found a picture with a label. It's Emerson Auerbach. He must be Mr. Auerbach's great-great-great-grandfather or something. Pretty interesting, huh?"

Emerson Auerbach had clearly struck it rich. He was vastly proportioned and meticulously attired. He wore a top hat, a pinkie ring, and a monocle, and a multitude of fobs hung from the watch chain that spanned his elegant, outsized waistcoat. He held his many chins high and regarded the camera with a look that seemed to say, "I am a man to be reckoned with."

"And here's a group shot taken at the Lord Stuart Mine," said Toby, pushing a larger photograph into my hands.

I peered down at the picture and for a moment forgot the storm. Twenty-one men in shirtsleeves sat on a parched and rock-strewn hillside, facing the camera. They were thinner, scruffier, and much dirtier than Emerson Auerbach. The hats they wore were shapeless, their shirts had no collars, and their fingernails were caked with grime, but they exuded an almost palpable air of cockiness. They, too, I thought, were men to be reckoned with. I bent low over the photograph to examine each individual face, then caught my breath and sat back with a start.

"It's him," I said, trying not to panic. "The man in the first picture."

"Where?" said Toby.

I pointed to the back row. "He has a beard and he's wearing a hat, but the eyes . . . the eyes are the same."

Toby took the photograph from me, studied the figure at the back of the group, and nodded. "It's the same guy, all right. He must have showered, shaved, and dressed in his Sunday best when he had the portrait taken. I wouldn't have recognized him if you hadn't." He shifted the archival box from his lap to the floor and held the photo out to me. "Does he remind you of someone, Lori? Someone in England? Like Brett Whitcombe did when you first saw him at the ranch?"

"The man Brett reminds me of is as close to a saint as I'll ever meet," I told him. "The man in the photograph reminds me of . . . death."

"I *knew* it," Toby said, under his breath. He stood abruptly and began pacing the room, muttering angrily, "I *knew* Amanda had messed with your head. I could see it in your face when she talked about death coming to claim you. I swear, I'm going to strangle that woman the next time I —"

"But Amanda was right," I interrupted. "Death came to get me, and I got away from him."

"What?" Toby stopped pacing and swung around to face me. "When? Where? *Tonight?*"

"Not tonight. It happened seven weeks ago." I sighed heavily. I didn't want to tell Toby about the shooting, but I didn't want Amanda Barrow to shoulder the blame — or to take credit — for my strange behavior, either. Apart from that, I was heartily ashamed of myself for lying to someone as open and honest as Toby. If anyone had earned the right to hear the truth, he had. I motioned him to his chair and said, "Please. Sit down."

Toby resumed his seat, and I looked fixedly at the floor. I didn't want to see the mingled horror and pity that would soon fill his eyes. I'd seen it too many times before.

"I didn't hurt my shoulder falling off a horse," I began. "I was shot. By a lunatic.

In Scotland. During a thunderstorm."

"Ah," Toby said softly.

"The bullet nicked an artery. I almost bled to death." I heard a sharp intake of breath and pressed on. "The man who shot me called himself Abaddon. He wanted to kill Will and Rob, too, but I stopped him. His face . . ." I glanced down at the gray archival box, then quickly averted my gaze. "His face was as pale as milk. He had wild black hair, and his eyes didn't seem to have any whites. They were as black as pitch, without any spark of emotion, like tunnels to hell."

"*Jesus,*" Toby said in a hushed voice. "What happened to him?"

"He was struck by lightning," I said, "and he fell hundreds of feet into the sea. He couldn't have survived, but his body was never recovered. I know it's absurd, but there's a part of me that thinks he's still out there somewhere." I swallowed hard and forced myself to go on. "I have trouble with storms. I have trouble with nightmares — or I did until I came here. I haven't dreamed about Abaddon once since I got here. I thought I'd made some progress on the road to recovery, but then I saw the man in the photograph and . . . back to square one."

"Why didn't you tell me?" Toby asked.

"I'm sorry I lied to you, but I don't like to

talk about it," I said gruffly. "I don't want people who don't know me to think I'm weak."

"Weak?" Toby gave a short, incredulous laugh. "You took a bullet to save your children. You nearly bled to death for them. You're one of the bravest people I've ever met."

"Brave people aren't afraid of thunderstorms," I said.

"Wounded people are afraid of all kinds of things," he countered swiftly. "But wounds heal. You won't always be afraid of thunderstorms. But you'll always be brave."

I wiped away a tear that had trickled down my cheek and glanced at him. "I don't feel very brave at the moment. I feel like a quivering puddle of pudding."

"This, from the woman who laughed in Dick Major's face?" Toby tossed his head disdainfully and shoved the group photograph under my nose. "Look at the man who scared you, Lori. *Look at him.*"

I stared down at the man in the back row.

"He's not the man who shot you," said Toby.

"No, he isn't," I said, and with a faint sense of shock I realized that the man didn't even look as much like Abaddon as I'd first thought. "His eyes still give me the creeps, but his face is rounder than Abaddon's, he's shorter, and he's not as thin."

"He's also been dead for over a hundred years," Toby pointed out, with his usual, unassailable, common sense. "The man who shot you is dead, too. He was struck by lightning. He fell off a cliff. He's not out there anywhere."

I tapped my temple. "Too bad he's still in here."

"He won't always be," said Toby.

I raised my eyes to meet his gaze. "Because wounds heal?"

"They do," he said. "Trust me, Lori. I know about healing. I'm the son and the grandson of doctors."

Another burst of lightning brightened the draperies, but instead of flinching, I gave a snort of mirthless laughter. "Do you know how many doctors I've seen since I was shot?"

"But *I'm* Dr. Toby," he said, pressing his palm to his chest. "And *I* know what's good for you." He got up, threw the photograph into the box, seized my hands, and pulled me to my feet. "You know what they say, Lori. When you fall off a horse —"

"But I *didn't* fall off a horse," I protested.

"Don't be pedantic." He picked up the afghan that had tumbled from my shoulders and wrapped it around me again, then put his arm firmly around my waist and steered me out of the library. "Come on. We're going to enjoy the greatest light show on earth."

We stood at the window wall for twenty minutes watching a display of lightning that would have had me crawling under the bed a week ago. Every time I twitched, Toby tightened his hold on me and let out a whoop and a holler.

"That was a great one! Did you see *that?* Way to go, Zeus!"

"Way to go, *Zeus?*" I echoed, amazed to hear myself giggling.

"Make up your own cheers," he chided, and raising a fist, bellowed, "Rock on, Jupiter!"

The tumultuous thunderstorm finally worked its way out of the Vulgamore Valley, leaving a calmer and much less showy rainstorm pattering in its wake.

"We need the rain," Toby said quietly. "If you listen hard, you'll hear the trees sucking it up." He tilted his head toward me. "How're you doing?"

"I'm still trying to invent a good cheer," I said. "But I don't think I can beat 'Rock on, Jupiter!' "

Toby smiled tolerantly, but continued to

look down at me.

"How am I doing?" I gazed at the rain-streaked window and inspected my mind for any new dents or scratches. "To tell you the truth, I'm surprisingly okay. I don't think I'll sleep with that photograph under my pillow, but I think I'll be able to sleep." I looked up at him. "You're awfully wise for a twenty-one-year old."

"Grandma used to say that I had an old head on my shoulders," said Toby.

"Your grandmother knew what she was talking about," I said. "Your treatment seems to be working."

"It never fails," he said.

"Do you have many patients?" I asked teasingly.

"Just the kids in my dorm. Compared to them, you're a model of mental stability." He paused, then added without a trace of facetiousness, "I'm so sorry you were hurt, Lori, and I'm so glad you're still around to talk about it." He gave me no chance to respond, but glanced at his watch and went on in more businesslike tones, "It's only ten o'clock, but I think I'll turn in."

"I'm sorry I spoiled your night off," I said remorsefully.

"I told you before, I didn't *want* a night off," he responded. "But I *do* want a good night's sleep. We have a big day ahead of us tomorrow."

"Do we?" I said blankly.

"Mrs. Blanding," he reminded me. "Lunch."

I clapped a hand to my forehead. "I'd completely forgotten about her."

"You've had one or two other things on your mind," said Toby.

"I suppose I have," I agreed, dropping the afghan on the sofa. "Do you think Mrs. Blanding will be able to identify the man in the photograph?"

"I think she'll be able to identify *all* of the men in *all* of the photographs," said Toby with a sigh. "And she won't leave until she's told us their life stories in excruciating detail, so if I were you, I'd grab at least eight hours of good, sound sleep."

"I'll do just that," I said, "thanks to you."

I caught his hand in mine, squeezed it gratefully, and made my way to the master suite, where I took a hot shower, slipped into a flannel nightgown, and lit a fire in the corner fireplace. I turned back the bedclothes as well, but although I was tired, I had no intention of climbing into bed.

I wasn't afraid of nightmares, curses, or lurking lightning bolts, but I was rather anxious to avoid the volley of sarcasm that would come my way if I postponed my chat with Aunt Dimity a moment longer.

SEVENTEEN

After an evening rife with alarms and diversions, it was heavenly to curl up with Reginald before a crackling fire, with the blue journal in my lap. The familiarity of it all was infinitely comforting. If I closed my eyes, it was easy to pretend that we were at home in the cottage, sitting before a crackling fire in the study.

"Here we are," I murmured to Reginald, "my two old friends and me. No surprises, no shocks to the system, just a pleasant, peaceful conversation to round out the day." I chuckled wickedly as a fresh thought struck me. "I'll bet Amanda Barrow would go green with envy if she could see how easily I get in touch with 'the other side.' "

Reginald's black button eyes twinkled merrily in the firelight, as if he found the notion as amusing as I did. I touched the faded grape juice stain on his snout, tucked him into the crook of my arm, and opened the journal.

"Dimity?" I said. "Are you there?"

The curving lines of royal-blue ink spun across the page with a certain sense of urgency.

I'm most certainly here, and I wish to be brought up to date on everything you've learned since our conversation last night. Is Bluebird's grapevine less or more efficient than Finch's? Is Dick Major a murderous madman or simply a cranky old fusspot? Have you gleaned any new information about James Blackwell or the Auerbach family? As you can tell, my dear, I'm agog to hear about your day.

"It's been *such* a strange one, Dimity," I said, with feeling. "I mean, I should have known *he'd* show up because everyone else has — not just Kit Smith and Nell Harris, but Peggy Taxman, Christine and Dick Peacock, Mr. Wetherhead, and Lilian Bunting —"

Lori?

"— not to mention Ruth and Louise Pym, but they were identical, tottering old men instead of identical, tottering old women —"

Lori!

"— and the Calico Cookies. You won't believe me when I tell you about Carrie Vyne's Calico Cookies because it's just too

250

coincidental to be believed. They're *exactly* like Sally Pyne's Crazy Quilt Cookies, right down to the different nuts and things she puts in them every time, but thank heavens Carrie Vyne isn't one bit like Sally Pyne, except that they both run similar businesses and make wonderful pastries and simply *ooze* gossip, so I suppose they're sort of alike, but the main thing is, they don't *look* alike."

LORI!

I paused to take a breath, glanced down at the journal, and realized that Aunt Dimity had been trying for some time to gain my attention.

"Yes?" I said.

Good evening. When I expressed an interest in your day, I rather hoped I'd hear about it in a coherent fashion, but your account has so far been baffling rather than enlightening. You make it sound as though your neighbors in Finch have come to join you in Colorado, bringing with them a supply of your favorite biscuits. Although I don't for one moment doubt the sincerity of their affection for you, it seems to me highly unlikely that they would leave the village to languish in their collective absence for no reason other than to satisfy your sweet tooth. I must conclude, therefore, that I've misunderstood you. Would you

251

please gather your thoughts and begin again?

"Sorry, Dimity," I said, abashed, "but as I said, it's been a strange day. I guess I got a little carried away."

There's no need to apologize. Just start from the beginning and move on from there. Slowly.

I silently reviewed the parade of familiar strangers that had passed before me in Caroline's Cafe, then carefully described them to Aunt Dimity, adding telling details I'd left out earlier.

"You already know about Dick Peacock's homemade wine," I said. "Well, Nick Altman is just as fat as Dick, and *he* makes undrinkable *beer.* And Greg Wilstead has a model train layout in his garage that sounds a lot like the one George Wetherhead has in his living room. And Maggie Flaxton is big, loud, and pushy, just like Peggy Taxman. The only person in Bluebird who doesn't remind me of someone in Finch is Dick Major, for which I am profoundly grateful, because although Dick *isn't* a murderous madman, he *is* a jerk who likes to intimidate people, and we don't need someone like that in Finch."

Did he succeed in intimidating you?

"Certainly not," I said. "To tell you the truth, he came as something of a relief — a fresh face in a cornucopia of clones. Honestly, Dimity, I'm expecting to run into *me* pretty soon."

Would it be so strange if you did? Bluebird and Finch are small towns, and small towns tend to be populated with stock characters: the bossy organizer, the plump publican, the vicar's wife, the train enthusiast, and so forth. You, my dear, are the amiable foreigner. I wouldn't be at all surprised if you discovered someone in Bluebird who closely resembles yourself.

"I'd need a medic to revive me if I came face-to-face with myself," I said flatly. "It was bad enough when I came face-to-face with Abaddon."

I beg your pardon?

"Okay, it wasn't Abaddon," I admitted sheepishly. "But before I get ahead of myself again, let me tell you about the Lord Stuart mining disaster, the Lord Stuart curse, the set of tools James Blackwell left behind, and the box of photographs he borrowed from the Bluebird Historical Society."

I recounted everything I'd learned at the cafe, at the parsonage, in the cemetery, in the caretaker's apartment, in the Aerie's library, and afterward at the window wall in the great room, watching lightning with Toby by my side; then I waited in silence while Dimity digested the information. After some time, the old-fashioned copperplate began to curl across the page again, but the topic Dimity chose to address first surprised me a little.

What a remarkable young man Toby Cooper is turning out to be. He picked you up from the floor in more ways than one tonight.

I nodded. "When he told us at the airport that he could fix things, I didn't think he meant broken minds. But he has a gift for healing. I don't think I'll ever be afraid of thunderstorms again."

Toby seems to be a true caretaker — in every sense of the word. How fortunate that he was nearby when you saw the dark-haired man in the sepia-toned photograph.

"The one who scared the bejabbers out of me," I said.

Indeed. It's possible, I suppose, that the man in the photograph reminded you of Abaddon because he's one of Abaddon's ancestors. After all, Abaddon was an Englishman and Englishmen helped to settle the American West. I think it more likely, however, that you exaggerated the resemblance because Abaddon has been so much on your mind of late.

"The lantern light and the storm may have influenced my eyesight," I conceded with a wry smile. "I was already on edge when I saw the photograph. After I'd calmed down a little, Toby had me take a closer look, and I realized that the man wasn't Abaddon's twin. He still gives me the willies, but he's not the creep who shot me on the cliffs."

From your account, I gather that the dark-haired man is featured in two photographs in the archival box — the individual portrait as well as the group portrait. Does the same hold true for the other men in the group photograph? Is each man in the group represented by an individual portrait?

"I don't know," I said. "I didn't compare the group shot to the other photographs in the box. Does it matter?"

It might. If the dark-haired man is the only individual singled out from the group, it may mean that James Blackwell took a particular interest in him. I wonder who he was? I hope you'll make a point of asking Mrs. Blanding about him when she joins you for lunch tomorrow.

"I intend to," I assured her. "I'll check out the other photographs, too, to see if they're of men in the group shot."

Excellent. As for the curse . . . I've detected no trace of it, yet I feel certain that something frightened Mrs. Auerbach.

"What else could it be but the curse?" I said. "Why else would she suddenly decide to sell a place she'd grown to love? And why would she refuse to explain her decision to her husband? She was probably afraid that he'd laugh at her for being scared of a silly superstition."

James Blackwell knew all about the silly superstition. He made it his business to learn as much about it as he could.

"And he didn't start looking into it until *after* Florence Auerbach had left the Aerie," I said. "Which suggests to me that her fear triggered his interest."

I agree. Still, we must ask ourselves: Did James enter the Lord Stuart Mine in order to investigate the curse or simply to line his pockets with ill-gotten gold? If he's a common thief, we can wash our hands of him. If, on the other hand, he was an honest man searching for the truth behind the curse, then why did he leave the Aerie so hastily?

"I've told you what I think," I said. "James went into the mine to investigate the curse, and he left the Aerie because he knew Danny Auerbach would fire him for reopening the mine. It might even be illegal to go into old mines. He might have been afraid that Danny would have him arrested."

James had no reason to believe that Danny Auerbach would discover his scheme. Danny hadn't visited the Aerie in six months, and he gave no indication of returning.

"But James knew that other witnesses were on the way," I reminded her. "I refer, of course, to me, Annelise, Will, and Rob."

Why would you worry James? He was forewarned of your arrival. He had enough time to conceal his excavation project and enough sense, one imagines, to steer you away from it while you were here.

"What if Annelise or I had stumbled across it accidentally?" I asked. "We might have given him away."

I doubt it. Neither one of you knows the first thing about mine entrances. If you'd seen one that had been reopened, James Blackwell could have told you that it was a colorful relic of the Old West, and you would have believed him. You would have avoided the hazard, certainly, but you wouldn't have reported it to Danny Auerbach. You would have assumed — or James could have told you — that Danny knew about it already. James Blackwell would have had nothing to fear from you or Annelise — or the twins, for that matter.

"All right," I said reasonably. "If James wasn't a thief, and if he wasn't afraid of being fired or arrested, then why *did* he take off in such a hurry?"

I believe he discovered something in the mine that seemed to confirm Mrs. Auerbach's worst fears.

"He found proof that the curse is *real?*" I frowned in confusion. "But you just said —"

I've detected no trace of a curse, but facts have never stopped people from believing in fantasies. James Blackwell had witnessed Mrs. Auerbach's sudden flight. He'd spent months on his own, immersing himself in local lore. When he finally descended into the darkness of the mine, his mind might have betrayed him. A strange shadow, a queer sound, an oddly shaped rock could have taken on a terrifying significance.

I glanced at the shivering shadows on the ceiling and understood at once what James might have gone through, alone in the mine's pitch-black depths. If I'd been in his shoes, it wouldn't have taken much to make me believe in every superstition known to man.

"He convinced himself that the Aerie was cursed," I said, "without finding any real proof."

I believe he did, but I wonder . . . Was he frightened by a mere trick of the light or by something more substantial?

"If you think I'm going down there to find out," I declared, "you've got another think coming."

I would never ask you to engage in such a

dangerous undertaking. But you must admit that it's an intriguing question.

"It'll be a cold day in Panama before I risk my neck to answer an intriguing question," I said firmly.

Naturally.

"Bill would kill me if I even *thought* about poking around in a collapsed mine shaft," I insisted.

I don't want you to set so much as a toe in the old mine, Lori. As I said, there may be nothing down there but shadows and dust.

"And bats. I'm sure there are bats." I shuddered theatrically, then frowned. "If James Blackwell believed in the curse, he should have warned us. It wasn't very nice of him to leave us in the dark, so to speak. It's as bad as leaving us at the mercy of a murderous madman."

Before you condemn him, Lori, please try to remember that we're indulging in pure speculation.

"Our speculation is based on fact," I retorted. "We're not pulling ideas out of thin air. We're not making things up as we go along, like Amanda Barrow."

Amanda Barrow? I don't believe you mentioned her.

"Didn't I?" I clucked my tongue at my oversight. "Amanda would be crushed if she knew I'd forgotten her, but it's hard to remember everyone in a sea of doppelgangers."

Not another one, surely.

"Yes, another one," I said, smiling. "Amanda Barrow is Bluebird's version of Miranda Morrow, but Amanda's more flamboyantly psychic than Miranda, and she uses more props."

What do you expect? She's an American.

"Are you implying that Americans lack subtlety?" I asked, feigning indignation.

As a rule, yes, but there are, of course, exceptions to every rule.

"You're supposed to add, 'and I count you among the exceptions, Lori dear,' " I hinted.

But I don't count you among the exceptions, Lori dear. As you've just demonstrated, subtlety is not your strong suit.

"Ah, well," I said, shrugging, "I can't be good at everything."

Tell me more about Amanda Barrow. I adore flamboyant psychics. They have such vivid imaginations.

"Like me," I said without rancor.

I've never known anyone quite like you, Lori. What props does Amanda Barrow use?

"You name it," I said. "She specializes in palmistry, tarot-card reading, rune casting, crystal-ball gazing, past-life retrieval, and dream interpretation, but I don't think she'd turn down a chance to read tea leaves if one came her way. Oh, and let's not forget about her inner eye. You should have seen the act she put on when I walked into her shop. She went all wobbly and mystical because, according to her, I was" — I raised my arm in a melodramatic gesture — "accompanied by a spirit from the great beyond."

That would be me, I'm afraid.

I glanced down at the journal, did a double take that nearly sent Reginald flying, and lowered my arm very slowly.

The last sentence hadn't been written by Aunt Dimity. The handwriting was more flowery than hers, and the ink was bottle green instead of royal blue. I closed my eyes, hoping that fatigue had produced a fleeting hallucination, but when I opened them again, the sentence was still there.

"Who . . . who are you?" I managed.

An excellent question. Who are you and what are you doing in my journal?

Cyril Pennyfeather, at your service. I'm frightfully sorry to intrude on your private conversation, but there's something I simply must tell you!

EIGHTEEN

As I gaped, dumbfounded, at the page, Amanda's words came back to me with stunning clarity.

"Light hair?" I said unsteadily. "A slight build? Pince-nez on a chain?"

Again, that would be me. I fit your excellent description in life, and under the right set of circumstances it applies to me still.

"Are you the . . . the male spirit who accompanies me?" I asked, my voice cracking like a teenaged boy's.

Only when decency allows, I assure you. I may have many faults, but I am not a voyeur, Mrs. Shepherd.

I giggled weakly and fastened on the one thing my shocked brain could handle.

"Please, call me Lori," I said. "May I, er, introduce Miss Dimity Westwood?"

I'm delighted to make your acquaintance, Miss Westwood. And may I tender my compliments on the wonderful means of communication you have devised? It's so much more civilized than disembodied voices.

"Disembodied voices?" I said faintly and looked around the room, half expecting an invisible army to start whispering on cue. My befuddlement was such that the reappearance of Aunt Dimity's old-fashioned copperplate seemed like a welcome return to normalcy.

Cyril Pennyfeather? The name seems familiar. Are you the schoolmaster who led the miners to safety after the Lord Stuart mining disaster?

Indeed, madam, I am he.

Forgive me if my next question is an indelicate one, Mr. Pennyfeather, but would I be correct in saying that you died in 1896?

You would be entirely correct, my dear lady. I have been dead for well over a century.

"Reginald," I muttered, "forget what I said about no shocks to the system."

Aunt Dimity carried on as if I hadn't spoken. *Are you by any chance English, Mr. Pennyfeather?*

I am. I was born and raised in Bibury, in the county of Gloucestershire, the third son of a vicar who could scarcely afford to send his first two to university. Without a university degree, I had little hope of advancement in England, so I made my way to America and eventually to the American frontier, where the educational standards were less rigid. I was twenty-five years old when I opened my school in the boomtown of Bluebird, Colorado, and I taught there until my untimely death ten years later. They were the happiest ten years of my life.

It must have been a fascinating experience to live in an American boomtown, Mr. Pennyfeather.

It was, Miss Westwood. To witness firsthand a young, dynamic country growing by leaps and bounds, unfettered by outmoded social constraints

The handwriting stopped when I cleared my throat, and I had the eerie sensation that Cyril Pennyfeather was standing mutely beside the hearth, regarding me attentively through his gleaming pince-nez.

"I'm sorry to interrupt, Mr. Pennyfeather," I said, "but how long have you been, er, accompanying me?"

I've looked in on you from time to time since the first night you arrived at the Aerie, though I assure you that your privacy

"Yes, yes, I understand about my privacy," I cut in. "What I want to know is, was Amanda Barrow telling the truth this afternoon? Did she see you with me when I walked into her shop?"

I'm afraid so. Her cat saw me as well. I don't know why the cat made such a fuss. I was quite fond of cats when I was alive, and they were fond of me. Be that as it may, when I became aware of the commotion I'd created, I immediately made myself as inconspicuous as possible. I'm a shy soul, really. I dislike being the center of attention.

"If Amanda Barrow and her cat can see you, why can't I?" I demanded, feeling distinctly shortchanged.

It does seem unfair, doesn't it? I can, alas, offer you no conclusive answer, although I suspect it may have something to do with genetics. I'm sure you have gifts Miss Barrow lacks.

"I certainly have better dress sense, but that's beside the point," I said. "You've been hanging out with me for nearly a week, Mr. Pennyfeather. Why haven't I been able to sense your presence?"

More to the point, Mr. Pennyfeather, why haven't I sensed your presence?

You have both sensed my presence, dear ladies. You simply didn't recognize what you were sensing.

"Sorry?" I said uncomprehendingly.

I'm afraid you're going to have offer a more detailed explanation, Mr. Pennyfeather.

I will do so gladly. When you arrived at the

Aerie, Lori, your nerves were standing on end, and you, Miss Westwood, were too anxious about Lori to be conscious of anything else. Your mutual distress touched my heart, so to speak. I decided, therefore, to exert a . . . calming influence . . . on Lori. I'm rather good at that sort of thing, you know. Virtually unflappable, in fact. I was always able to calm a frantic pupil.

"Good grief," I said softly. "You made my nightmare go away."

It would be more accurate to say that I created an atmosphere of tranquility and security in which you found it easier to sleep, and sleep, saith the Bard, is the balm of hurt minds, great nature's second course, chief nourisher in life's feast. Macbeth, Act two, Scene two. But I digress.

I'm afraid you do, Mr. Pennyfeather.

I beg your pardon. To sum up: Once Lori found respite in rest, you, too, relaxed, Miss Westwood, but by then you'd grown so accustomed to my presence that it failed to catch your attention.

In other words, Mr. Pennyfeather, you flew in under my radar.

Radar, Miss Westwood? What is radar?

Forgive me, Mr. Pennyfeather. The word wasn't coined until 1941, but never mind. Suffice it to say that you've taken me quite by surprise.

"Me, too," I put in. "Although I did see your obelisk in the cemetery."

My obelisk is rather handsome, isn't it?

"It's lovely," I said and since I'd only mentioned it in passing to Aunt Dimity, I went on to describe it in more detail. "It's at least ten feet tall, made of polished white marble, with a beautiful inscription carved into it, a quotation from the Bible, something about a living sacrifice —"

Holy, acceptable unto God. They chose Romans Chapter twelve, Verse one., Miss Westwood.

How very humbling, Mr. Pennyfeather.

Indeed. More humbling still was the second inscription.

"It's below the Bible verse," I explained to Dimity. "It says that the obelisk was erected by the families of the men Mr. Pennyfeather saved, to honor his memory. Mrs. Blanding told Toby and me that the families took up a collection to pay for it."

They must have gone without bread to raise such a sum. I'm more deeply touched than I can say. I had no idea that they'd gone to so much trouble on my behalf.

"You didn't?" I said, frowning in confusion. "Haven't you seen the obelisk before?"

I'd never seen it until today. No one from

the Aerie has ever gone to the cemetery. Therefore, I could not go.

"Why would you need someone to take you there?" I asked. "I hate to state the obvious, Mr. Pennyfeather, but it's *your* grave."

You are under a slight misapprehension, Lori. The obelisk does not mark my grave.

"It doesn't?" I said, feeling more perplexed than ever.

I'm afraid not. I wasn't interred in the cemetery after my death because there was nothing to inter. My body, you see, was never recovered from the mine.

I instinctively lifted my feet and glanced uneasily at the floor. "We're living on top of your *grave?*"

Not directly, no, but we're not far from it. After the dust had settled, they managed to retrieve every corpse but mine. Mine was in a rather tricky location, you see. To remove it would have caused another cave-in, so they left it where it was.

"I'm so sorry," I said.

As am I, Mr. Pennyfeather. Truly sorry. I'm perfectly content to remain as I am, but I sense that you are not.

It's true. I wish to move on. If I'd received a proper burial, I might have proceeded to the next stop in my journey. Instead, I'm stranded in a way station between this world and the next. I cannot leave the mine site on my own, and I can accompany only those people who, like you, Lori, have a sympathetic and tolerant nature.

"I know a few people who would be surprised to hear me described as sympathetic and tolerant," I commented dryly.

You didn't shriek when you saw my handwriting. You didn't slam the book down and run from the room. Your acquaintance with Miss Westwood has broadened your mind in a very special way.

"I guess I do have gifts Amanda Barrow lacks," I said, lifting my chin proudly.

If you didn't, I would not have been able to visit the cemetery with you. I'm grateful to you for allowing me to go there, Lori. I've long wished to pay my respects to Hannah.

"Hannah Lavery?" The name hadn't come up in my conversation with Aunt Dimity, so I continued, "Hannah Lavery was the daughter of a rich mine owner. She became a social activist, a reformer who worked to improve the lives of miners and their families. Toby and I saw her grave at the cemetery. Rose Blanding called her a rabble-rouser."

Were you referring to Hannah Lavery, Mr. Pennyfeather, or to another Hannah?

In my eyes, there was no other Hannah.

Hannah Lavery made my work possible, Miss Westwood. I taught grown men and women as well as children, you see. The mine owners frowned on educated workers — it's harder to cheat a man who can read — but Hannah defied them. She supported my school with her own funds. My doors would not have stayed open if not for Hannah.

"You were both rabble-rousers," I observed, smiling.

We were also engaged to be married. But the call went out that the mine had collapsed, and I went up to lend a hand. I had to, you understand. My pupils needed me. I helped extricate a handful of men, but too many died. I wish I could have done more, before the second cave-in caught me.

I'm sure you did everything you could, Mr. Pennyfeather.

I pictured the angel weeping over Hannah Lavery's grave and remembered Rose Blanding's comments about Victorian men preferring passive women, and how difficult it was for a crusader to give her heart to a man as well as a cause. I knew now that in one particular case, Rose had gotten it wrong. Cyril had loved his crusader, and she'd given her heart to him. Only a tragic twist of fate had kept them apart.

"I don't know if you noticed," I said

quietly, "but Hannah Lavery never married."

I noticed. Foolish girl.

The flames in the fireplace quivered, as though Cyril had released a melancholy sigh. I sighed, too, at the thought of what might have been, but Aunt Dimity was more interested in history than in heartache.

Why did the Lord Stuart Mine close so soon after the disaster, Mr. Pennyfeather? Was it because the miners believed the mine to be unlucky? Or was it because the owners were afraid of the scandal that would ensue if their use of inferior wood was discovered?

I sincerely doubt that fear of any kind influenced the decision to close the Lord Stuart, Miss Westwood. In those days, scandals didn't matter to investors as long as there was money to be made. And although the miners were a superstitious lot, they also had families to feed. They couldn't afford to leave their jobs simply because the mine they worked in happened to be accident-prone. The only reason a mine ever closed was that there was no more gold to be had from it.

"So the mine *was* played out," I said happily. "James Blackwell couldn't have been a thief because there's no gold left to steal. He *must* have been investigating the curse."

At last, we come to the curse.

What can you tell us about the curse, Mr. Pennyfeather?

Quite a lot, actually, but I'm not sure where to begin.

"From the beginning," I said, to save Dimity the bother of writing it.

Very well. I will begin, then, by telling you that prospectors came from all walks of life, but very few came from well-to-do families. It was not uncommon, therefore, for a rich vein of gold to be discovered by a man who could not afford to exploit it properly. If he could, he found investors to provide him with capital. If he couldn't find investors, he had little choice but to sell his claim to the highest bidder. Just such a situation arose in the Vulgamore Valley in the year 1864. The prospector was a poor Polish immigrant named Ludovic Magerowski, and the highest bidder was a prosperous businessman called Emerson Auerbach.

"I saw Emerson Auerbach's photograph in the library," I said. "He looked like a high bidder."

Emerson Auerbach was extremely wealthy. He bought Ludovic's claim to the Lord Stuart Mine for five thousand dollars. It must have seemed like a vast sum to Ludovic, but it was a pittance compared to the mine's actual worth. By 1890, the Lord Stuart had yielded two hundred million dollars in gold.

"Wow," I said, impressed. "That's a spanking return on an investment."

Did Mr. Magerowski realize what he'd done, Mr. Pennyfeather?

Eventually. He returned to Bluebird some twenty years later, with a wife and young child, having tried unsuccessfully to strike it rich elsewhere.

I gave a low whistle. "It must have killed him to see someone else reaping such outrageous profits from a mine he'd sold for chump change."

It angered him, certainly. He initiated a lawsuit, claiming that Emerson Auerbach had swindled him, but the lawsuit was dismissed for lack of evidence. He took his complaint to the newspapers, but they ignored him, as did everyone else in Bluebird. They'd grown accustomed to hearing a prospector cry foul after a claim he'd sold fairly and squarely had yielded a fortune. No one but Ludovic believed that Emerson Auerbach had done anything wrong. Apart from that, no one liked Ludovic.

"Why not?" I asked.

He was a blustery, self-aggrandizing fellow. He claimed to have an English benefactor — the famous Lord Stuart, in whose honor he'd named the mine — but when I asked him why an English nobleman would deign to sponsor an impoverished Polish immigrant in a venture as risky as prospecting, he had no answer. Since he had no money, either, I concluded that the famous Lord Stuart was a figment of his imagination.

What happened to Mr. Magerowski after the lawsuit failed?

Strangely enough, he went to work in the Lord Stuart Mine. I can only assume that the mine manager felt sorry for his wife and child, because Ludovic had gone quite mad by then. I remember seeing him just before I died.

I gasped. "He was *there?*"

Yes, Lori, Ludovic was there on the day of the disaster. When I saw him, he had a look of insane triumph in his eyes.

"His eyes," I whispered, as the hairs on the back of my neck rose. More loudly, I asked, "Did he have dark curly hair? And a beard? And intense dark eyes?"

Yes. He grew the beard after he came to work in the mine.

"I think I've seen his photograph, too," I said. "He reminded me of someone, a homicidal maniac I, um, ran into once."

I don't know if Ludovic was a homicidal maniac, Lori, but I do know that he put a curse on the mine. He raised his lamp, looked directly at me, pointed to the bloodstained rocks, and growled, "No accident. I did it. I damned it all to hell. If I can't have it, let the devil take it." He gave an unearthly howl of laughter, then sprinted to freedom. A moment later, the shaft's roof collapsed, and I was buried inextricably beneath a ton of debris.

"What an evil-minded little man he must have been," I said heatedly. "Your final moments of life were stressful enough, Mr. Pennyfeather. Ludovic had no right to make them worse with his ranting."

You said earlier that you had something to tell us, Mr. Pennyfeather. Did you wish to warn us about the curse?

Why should I wish to warn you about something so trivial?

Do you believe it to be trivial?

Naturally. I know that Ludovic cursed the mine — I heard him do it — but I do not believe that a lunatic's ravings can affect affairs in the tangible world. No mere mortal has such power.

"Then why was the Lord Stuart so prone to accidents?" I asked. "And why were so many people hurt at the site after the mine was shut down?"

One needn't turn to the metaphysical realm to explain mining accidents, Lori. Mining is a hazardous occupation in and of itself, an occupation rendered even more hazardous by managers who cut corners when purchasing building materials, which the Lord Stuart's manager most certainly did.

If you knew the mine was unsafe, Mr. Pennyfeather, why didn't you bring it to someone's attention?

I did. Hannah and I wrote to congressmen, senators, and newspapers, decrying the perilous state of the Lord Stuart Mine, but no one listened. Profits, as I mentioned earlier, were worth more than men's lives.

"Hannah Lavery kept fighting the good fight right up to the day she died," I said.

Of course she did. She was indefatigable. There was a pause, as though Cyril was taking a moment to collect himself, then the flowery handwriting continued. As for the accidents that occurred after the mine closed, they, too, happened for entirely mundane reasons. Indeed, when I remember the foolhardy risks taken by those who explored the site, it seems incredible to me that so few were killed or injured. I would also point out that no accidents have occurred since the site was cleared.

"I agree with everything you've said," I said stoutly. "I've never believed that anything was wrong with the Aerie."

If you don't wish to warn us about the curse, Mr. Pennyfeather, why have you made yourself known to us?

I'm afraid I have news that you may find a

bit disturbing.

"Well?" I said eagerly. "What is it?"

Very well, then. Prepare yourselves for a shock. The Lord Stuart Mine has been reopened!

"Oh," I said, unable to disguise my disappointment. "I know that it's been reopened, Mr. Pennyfeather. Toby figured it out."

You don't seem disturbed by the knowledge.

"That's probably because I'm not," I admitted. "I'll keep the twins away from the danger zone and let Danny Auerbach — the present owner — know about it. The Lord Stuart is really his problem, not mine."

I suppose it is. Forgive me for alarming you unnecessarily. My big news seems to be old news.

A sense of anticlimax lingered in the air, but only for a moment. It had suddenly dawned on me that Cyril Pennyfeather might be able to answer a question I'd been asking almost from the moment I'd arrived in Colorado.

Why had Florence Auerbach and James Blackwell abandoned the Aerie? I no longer believed that they'd been chased off by a bully, but while I still held out hopes for the curse as the root cause, Cyril's unanticipated appearance suggested another explanation for their flight. Had they run as if they'd seen a ghost because . . . they'd seen a ghost?

"Mr. Pennyfeather," I said, "have you tried to contact other people who've stayed at the Aerie?"

I have not. It would be a most imprudent thing to do. Not everyone would welcome me as warmly as you have, Lori. Most people would react like Miss Barrow's cat if I revealed myself to them in any way.

I accepted his answer philosophically. After all, I still had the curse to fall back on.

"Well, it's their loss," I declared. "I think you're a perfect gentleman."

Thank you, Lori. I've always felt that there's no need to forget one's manners simply because one has lost one's life.

In the interest of good manners, Mr. Penny-feather, I must point out that we are keeping Lori up rather later than we should. Have you noticed the time, my dear?

I swung around to face the clock on the bedside table and realized to my dismay that it was nearly half past eleven.

"Whoops," I said. "I've enjoyed meeting you, Mr. Pennyfeather, but you'll have to excuse me. If I know Annelise — and I do — she and the twins will be back from the ranch bright and early tomorrow morning, and I don't want to be groggy when they get here."

I understand completely, Lori. Would you care to stay a while longer, Miss Westwood? I was rather hoping you'd explain radar to me.

It would be my pleasure, Mr. Pennyfeather, though I'll have to explain a great many other things first.

I smiled as I watched both sets of handwriting fade from the page. Neither Cyril Pennyfeather nor Aunt Dimity needed the journal to continue their conversation. I had a feeling that they'd communicate more easily without it, which was just as well — Cyril had a lot of catching up to do.

I left the blue journal on the chair, damped the fire, and took Reginald to bed with me. My mind should have been spinning like a top, but as my head hit the pillow I felt nothing but a great sense of relief. My private demon seemed to be in full retreat, I had Cyril's reassurance that the Aerie was untainted by evil, and I would never, for as long as I lived, have to break the news to Toby that the queen of hocus-pocus — and her cat — had been telling the truth.

NINETEEN

I awoke refreshed and well rested at eight o'clock the following morning, threw on shorts, a T-shirt, sneakers, and a lightweight cardigan, and met Toby in the kitchen for breakfast. It was yet another picture-perfect Colorado day. The air was crisp, the sky bluer than blue, and leftover raindrops hung like diamonds from the branches of every tree.

I stayed in the kitchen after breakfast to assemble the lasagna I intended to serve for lunch. I planned to throw together an artichoke salad later, while the lasagna was baking, but I asked Toby to run into town to pick up a fresh loaf of crusty bread to serve with the meal — I was unwilling to foist my first attempt at high-altitude bread-baking on an unsuspecting guest.

I'd just put a pitcher of sun tea out to brew on the breakfast deck when Bill called. I flopped onto a cushioned lounge chair and propped my feet on the railing while I told him everything that had happened since we'd last spoken. It was a joy to be able to speak freely about Cyril Pennyfeather to a tangible human being, but Bill, bless his heart, was far more impressed by my ability to weather the thunderstorm than he was by my encounter with the great beyond.

"Why should I be astonished by Cyril?" he asked, when I teased him about his nonchalant reaction. "I was sure that some-one like him would show up sooner or later. Dimity can't be the only one of her kind in the world, or in between worlds, or wherever she is."

"Amanda Barrow would know the proper term," I said, laughing. "Think I should ask her?"

"Only if you want her to camp out on your doorstep with her crystal ball for the re-mainder of your vacation," Bill said sardoni-cally.

I wrinkled my nose. "Nah. Doesn't sound appealing. I guess I'll keep the news about Cyril between you and me."

"It's too bad you can't share it with Flor-ence Auerbach," said Bill. "If she had Cyril's guarantee that the Aerie isn't cursed, she might change her mind about selling it."

"I can't see myself trying to explain Cyril

to a complete stranger," I said, shaking my head. "I'll just have to find another way of convincing Florence."

"Are you sure this curse business isn't bothering you?" Bill asked suspiciously.

"Do I sound bothered?" I asked back.

"You sound great," Bill admitted.

"I sound even better in person," I said, sighing. "I wish we were talking face-to-face."

"You may get your wish sooner than you expect," said Bill.

I carefully removed my feet from the deck railing and sat forward in the lounge chair. "What do you mean?"

"I mean that I have to fly to Boston next week to confer with Father about a few clients," he replied. "If all goes well, I should be in Colorado in ten days."

"Oh, *Bill* . . ." I grinned so hard I nearly strained my face. "That's *brilliant.* Will and Rob will do backflips when they see you, but be warned — they'll run you ragged, showing you the sights."

"Don't tell them I'm coming," Bill cautioned. "I don't want them to be disappointed if I'm delayed."

"I won't say a word. It'll be a big surprise." I perked up even more as another happy thought occurred to me. "Just think, Bill,

I'll actually have a chance to prove to you that the Bluebird doppelgangers aren't a product of my homesick imagination."

"I look forward to meeting every one of them," said Bill. "With the possible exception of Maggie Flaxton."

With an especially cheery good-bye, he rang off. I sat for a moment, savoring my good fortune, then went to the laundry room, where I sang cowboy songs at the top of my lungs while I folded the clean laundry. Toby returned a short time later with a loaf of Carrie Vyne's Italian bread and a box full of her exquisite lemon tarts.

"The twins and I can dig into the Calico Cookies after lunch," he informed me. "But I thought the ladies might prefer a more sophisticated dessert."

"You are a pearl beyond price," I told him, beaming.

"I'm not bad," he agreed complacently.

Brett Whitcombe brought Annelise and the twins back to the Aerie at half past nine. The three prodigals had already eaten breakfast at the ranch, so they went straight to their rooms to change into fresh clothes. Annelise emerged first, wearing beige shorts, a short-sleeved cotton blouse, the aspen-leaf earrings, and a big smile.

Will and Rob were distracted by the

stuffed-toy buffalo I'd left in their tent, but I eventually managed to get them into clean shorts and T-shirts. They thought the geodes were the coolest things they'd ever seen, apart from the *real* baby buffalo they'd seen at the ranch, but after examining the sparkling crystals and telling me all about their day in the saddle and their stormy night in the bunkhouse, they were ready to tackle the next adventure.

"We're going fishing," Will announced.

"Excellent," said Toby. "We'll go up to Willie Brown Creek, see if we can hook a few rainbows."

"We don't want *rainbows*," Rob objected. "We want *fish*."

"Rainbows *are* fish," said Toby. "Come on, I'll tell you all about rainbow trout while we pick out some poles."

When Toby and the twins had left the great room, Annelise beckoned to me to join her at the breakfast bar. I could tell by her expression that something was troubling her, so I quickly took a seat beside her.

"I wanted to have a word with you before I went off again with the boys," she began.

I nodded, wondering what was wrong.

"I put the idea of fishing into the boys' heads," she went on.

"It's a great idea," I said. "They love to fish."

"Yes," said Annelise, "but I put the idea of fishing into their heads because I think they should have a few days off from the ranch."

"Problems?" I said quietly.

"As a matter of fact —" She broke off as the menfolk returned to the great room, bristling with fishing poles. "Never mind. I'll tell you later."

"I'll come with you. You can tell me on the way." I got up, intending to change into my hiking boots, but I'd moved no more than a few steps away from Annelise when the doorbell rang. I stopped short and looked toward the foyer in surprise. "Who on earth can *that* be?"

"Don't ask me," said Annelise, shrugging. "I didn't even know we had a doorbell."

"It can't be Mrs. Blanding," I said, glancing at my watch. "It's only ten o'clock. She's not supposed to be here until noon."

"Maybe she decided to come early," Annelise suggested.

"Two hours early?" I said doubtfully.

Toby strode across the great room to peer through the window wall. "There's a pickup parked out front, but I don't recognize it."

The doorbell rang again.

Toby turned toward me and squared his

shoulders protectively. "Do you want me to answer it?"

I looked from the twins, who were dancing impatiently from foot to foot, to Annelise, who was clearly anxious to get going before Will or Rob started casting for trout in the kitchen sink, and reluctantly shook my head.

"No, you guys run along," I said. "I know how to get to the creek. I'll catch up with you later."

Toby glanced once more at the mystery truck, then led the others to the mudroom behind the kitchen. The mudroom door opened onto the trail that would take them to Willie Brown Creek, so when I heard the door open and close, I knew they were on their way.

The doorbell rang again, and I felt a surge of annoyance with the ringer for interrupting my conversation with Annelise. If there'd been problems at the ranch, I wanted to hear about them, not waste time with a casual caller. As I hastened into the foyer and flung the front door open, I was already devising ways to get rid of the man I found standing on the doorstep.

He was short and stocky, with short, dark hair, green eyes, and a face so deeply tanned it looked like leather. His faded black T-shirt fit snugly across his muscular shoulders, but hung loosely over the waistband of his faded jeans, and his work boots were dusty and well broken in. He looked as though he might be in his early thirties.

"May I help you?" I said crisply.

" 'Morning," he said. His voice was deep and resonant, and he spoke with a western twang. "My name is James Blackwell."

The man's lips kept moving, but a faint buzzing in my ears obscured his words.

"*James Blackwell?*" I squeaked, grasping the door jamb for support.

"Yes, ma'am," he said. "As I was just saying, I used to work for Mr. Auerbach. I have a paycheck and a letter from him, and my driver's license, too, if you want proof of who I am."

"James Blackwell?" I repeated, dazed with disbelief. "The caretaker?"

"Yes, ma'am," said James. "I've come to pick up a few things I left here. I'll be out of your hair in a minute."

"Oh no, you won't," I said, snapping out of my daze. I seized his wrist determinedly and pulled him into the foyer. "I have about a thousand questions to ask you, James Blackwell, and you're not going anywhere until you've answered them."

"But ma'am —" he began.

"Resistance is futile," I declared, tugging him toward the great room. "I'm the mother of twin boys."

"Yes, ma'am," he said, and came along docilely.

As soon as the great room door was closed behind us, I introduced myself and offered James a cup of tea, which he declined.

"I wouldn't say no to a cup of coffee, though," he added.

"You'd say no to my coffee," I said flatly. "I don't make it very often and when I do, it looks like mud. God alone knows what it tastes like."

"No problem," he said. "I'll make it."

I could tell by the way James moved around the kitchen that he'd been there many times before. He knew where to find the coffee and the coffeemaker, and he selected a large blue mug from the cabinet as if it was the one he always used. He certainly didn't seem nervous or fearful. From what I could see, he was completely at ease in the Aerie.

I sat at the breakfast bar and watched him mutely, glad to have a chance to recover from the shock of meeting a man I'd never expected to meet. By the time we'd settled on the sofa before the hearth, I'd calmed down enough to feel a twinge of guilt for lunging at him and dragging him into the Aerie against his will.

"I suppose you're wondering why I greeted you so . . . unceremoniously," I ventured.

"Not really." James took a sip of coffee and cradled the blue mug in his large hands. "A man can't just vanish like I did without leaving a trail of questions behind him. I expect you want to know why I quit my job."

"I have no right to interrogate you," I admitted, "but yes, I would *really* like to know why you quit your job, and so would everyone else within a fifty-mile radius of the Aerie."

"I expect word'll get out quick enough once I tell you, so I may as well get it over with." James smiled briefly, then pursed his lips and sighed. "The first thing you have to understand, Lori, is that I'm a married man. The second thing is that I was laid off from my job last September. I was still out of work at the end of November, when my wife told me she was pregnant with our first child."

"I'm so sorry," I said, adding swiftly, "Not about the baby, of course, but about your losing your job."

"Thanks." James took another sip of coffee. "The caretaker's job sounded like it was

289

custom made for me. I work construction, so I can fix almost anything, and I'm right at home in the high country. The only catch was, Mr. Auerbach didn't want to hire a married man."

I recalled the single bed in the caretaker's apartment and nodded.

"I'd heard from a friend that Mr. Auerbach paid top dollar, and with a baby on the way, I needed the money," said James. "So I lied. I told him I was single. And I got the job."

"Didn't your wife mind being separated from you?" I asked.

"Sure, but when I told Janice — that's my wife — how much I'd be making, she went along with it," said James. "Besides, we live in Denver, so I wasn't too far away. I went to see her whenever I could think of an excuse to drive into the city. It wasn't an ideal situation, but we both thought it would pay off in the long run."

"Did Mr. Auerbach find out about Janice?" I asked. "Is that why you left?"

"No, that's not why I left." James put the blue mug on the coffee table and swung around on the sofa to face me. "I got a call from Janice last week — three days before you were due to arrive at the Aerie. She'd gone into labor. The baby's not due until

August, Lori. Since you're a mother, you can imagine the state my wife was in."

"She must have been scared," I said.

"She was," James acknowledged. "As for me, I panicked. I threw my stuff in a bag, left a short message on Mr. Auerbach's answering machine, and hightailed it out of here. I met up with Janice at the hospital in Denver."

"Is she all right?" I asked solicitously.

"They managed to stop the contractions," he said, "but she'll have to stay in bed until the baby comes. So I can't work here anymore. I can't work at all. I have to stay at home with my wife."

"How are you paying your bills?" I asked worriedly, then held a hand up to forestall his answer. "Forgive me, James. It's none of my business."

"No offense taken," he said easily. "Janice and me'll be fine. As I said, Mr. Auerbach pays top dollar. I earned enough here in seven months to get us through till I can go back to work. And next time I'll find a job closer to home."

"I'm glad to hear it," I said, smiling. "I'm glad about Janice and the baby, too."

"Thanks," said James, reaching for his coffee.

"You'll probably laugh at me," I said, "but

I was convinced that you'd left the Aerie because you thought it was cursed."

Instead of laughing, James compressed his lips into a thin line and looked faintly disgusted.

"I wouldn't let a curse run *me* out of the Aerie," he said. "Mrs. Auerbach did, though. Stupid woman. She shouldn't have listened to Tammy."

"Tammy?" I said inquiringly.

"Tammy Auerbach," James explained.

"The teenaged daughter?" I guessed, glancing in the direction of Annelise's room.

"That's right," said James. "Tammy didn't like being cooped up with her little brothers — what fifteen-year-old girl does? — so she started hanging out with a crowd of crazies in Bluebird."

"Amanda Barrow's crowd of crazies?" I said, intrigued.

James nodded. "Tammy Auerbach thought every word that came out of that fool woman's mouth was the gospel truth, so when Amanda told her about the curse, she took it to heart."

"So *Tammy* Auerbach believed in the curse," I said, half to myself.

"Tammy Auerbach would've believed that cows laid eggs if Amanda Barrow said it was so." James's face darkened. "When I got wind of what was going on, I went into town to tell Amanda to lay off the kid, but the damage had already been done. Tammy was having trouble sleeping, and Mrs. Auerbach started acting all weird. She had me check the plumbing and the floorboards in the family suite."

"Why?" I asked.

"No idea," answered James. "Everything was fine in the family suite, and I told her so, but next thing I knew, she upped stakes and took off out of here."

"She left some clothes and other things behind," I said. "Why didn't you ship it to her?"

"She didn't tell me to," said James, "so I thought she'd be coming back. She didn't, though. I haven't seen or heard from the Auerbachs since Christmas. Rumor has it that they're thinking of selling the Aerie."

I suppressed the urge to confirm or deny the rumor and said instead, "You must have wondered about the curse."

"I did," said James. "I don't believe in it any more than I believe pigs can fly, but once I'd seen with my own eyes how it could affect people, I got interested in finding out more about it. With the Auerbachs gone and nobody else coming, there wasn't much else to do. I spent a fair amount of time in Bluebird, asking folk about the curse. One guy in town took a sort of ghoulish interest in the subject, so I spent a lot of time listening to him."

"Was it Dick Major?" I ventured. "I heard that he was harassing you."

"Dick *thought* he was harassing me," said James, "but I was pumping him for information. When I finished with the folk in Bluebird, I drove out to the ranch to find out if Brett Whitcombe knew anything. Brett's a good guy, but he didn't want to talk about the curse, so I went to the historical society to find out more. I struck pay dirt there. Have you met Mrs. Blanding, the pastor's wife?"

"I have," I said.

"She can talk the hind leg off a bull elk once she gets going," said James, shaking his head, "but she knows her stuff. She loaned me all kinds of old photographs and newspaper clippings. They're in a box in the library. I'm planning to return it to the parsonage on my way back to Denver."

"There's no need," I said. "Mrs. Blanding is coming here for lunch today. She'll take the box with her when she leaves. I'll explain why you didn't return it. I'm sure she'll understand."

"Thanks. Give her my thanks, too, will

you?" James finished his coffee and took the mug to the dishwasher.

I followed him into the kitchen. His mention of the gray archival box had reminded me of another box — the wooden crate Toby had discovered in the caretaker's apartment — and another question. I wanted to know what James had done with the tools he'd left in the crate. Had he used them to steal gold from his employer? Or had he used them to find out what had caused the Lord Stuart Mine to collapse? After a brief inner debate, I decided to tackle the issue head-on.

"James," I said, leaning on the breakfast bar, "while you were investigating the curse, did you try to break into the Lord Stuart Mine?"

James turned toward me, grinning sheepishly. "I guess you found my tools, huh? Well, yes, I did open the big steel door Mr. Auerbach put on the mine entrance. As I said, with no family and no guests to cater to, there wasn't much else to do. I'd learned an awful lot about the Lord Stuart and here I was, living right on top of it, so I figured, why not take a look-see?"

"Did you find gold?" I asked, leaning forward.

James gave me a quizzical look, then

cocked his head toward the forest beyond the breakfast deck. "Come with me and I'll show you what I found."

One part of me watched in startled dismay while the rest of me responded like a cat to curiosity's call.

"Lead on," I said.

TWENTY

We didn't have far to go, which was fortunate since I was wearing sneakers instead of my trusty hiking boots. The entrance to the Lord Stuart Mine was no more than fifty feet from the back wall of the third guest suite, but it was so well hidden by trees, shrubs, and boulders that I would never have spotted it if James hadn't pushed branches aside and led me to it.

A square arch some ten feet tall and eight feet wide had been carved into the side of the mountain. Within the arch, Danny Auerbach's team of engineers had installed a steel door painted in a swirly camouflage pattern. The door's left edge had been bent outward in uneven scallops, and it had no handle, only a heavy-duty hasp from which hung the broken remains of a once imposing padlock.

"I smashed the lock with the sledgehammer," said James. "I would have replaced it with a new one if I hadn't left in such a hurry."

I nearly swooned at the thought of what might have happened if the twins had discovered the metal door with the broken lock.

"Don't worry," I said unevenly. "I'll replace it."

"You don't have to," James told me. "I managed to pry the door open with the crow bar, but after that . . ."

He stepped forward, slipped his hands into two of the larger scallops, and heaved with all his might, but he could only pull the steel door open a foot or two before it came up against a boulder. He then stood back and gestured for me to take a look inside.

I stepped over a low shrub, ducked under a branch, and crept up to peer timorously into the Lord Stuart Mine. I expected to see a yawning, bat-and-rat-infested hellhole. I saw instead a slightly chipped concrete wall that completely blocked the entrance.

"But . . . but . . ." I sputtered. "Where's the *mine?*"

"Somewhere behind the concrete plug." James tapped the wall with his knuckles. "I thought I might break through it with the pickax, but I gave up pretty quick. The angle makes it hard to take a good swing, and only Mr. Auerbach knows how thick the plug is. He made damned sure his sons couldn't get into the mine, so I don't think you'll have to worry about your twins."

I pressed my palms against the cool concrete and nodded. "Since Rob and Will are only five years old and not *quite* as strong as you are, James, I'd have to agree." I withdrew my hands and heaved a little sigh. "I have to confess that I'm a tiny bit disappointed. I was kind of hoping to see a glint of gold in the darkness."

"If any gold's left inside the Lord Stuart, it's out of our reach," said James. "But you should watch yourself, Lori. Gold fever's a nasty bug. You don't want to get bit by it."

I moved out of his way, he pushed the door shut, and we walked back to the great room in the Aerie. Since it was already eleven o'clock, I made a detour to the kitchen to put the lasagna in the oven, then helped James carry the wooden crate to his truck. After we'd loaded the crate, James closed the tailgate and turned to survey the Aerie.

"I liked it here," he said. "One day Janice and me and the kid are going to have a cabin in the mountains. It won't be as fancy as this one, but it'll be ours."

"With scenery like this, you don't need fancy," I said, sweeping a hand through the air to indicate the lake, the forest, the snow-capped peaks, and the dazzling blue sky. "Are you sure you can't stay for lunch? There's plenty of food and you're more than welcome. I know for a fact that your replacement, Toby Cooper, would love to meet you."

"Thanks, but I'd better be going," said James. "I left Janice with one of her girl-friends, but she gets fretful if I'm gone too long."

"You're a lucky man," I said, clapping him on the shoulder. "You have so much to look forward to. Give Janice my best."

"I'll do that, Lori." James climbed into the cab of his truck, started the engine, and drove down the steep lane toward the dirt road that would take him back to the high-way.

It wasn't until the truck was out of sight that I remembered the lantern I'd left in the library. I felt a stab of guilt for forget-ting to give it to James, but there was noth-ing I could do about it, so I went inside to make the artichoke salad and set the dining room table for lunch.

While I puttered from one task to another, I reran the past hour in my mind, rehearsing the revelations I planned to share with Bill, Aunt Dimity, Toby, and Rose Blanding. I was fairly certain that I could rely on Rose to share my news with every living soul in and around Bluebird.

The fishermen returned from Willie Brown Creek at half past eleven, crowing over the trout they'd caught and thrown back. Rob and Will were wet, muddy, and in dire need of baths, so I had no chance to speak privately with Annelise or to inform Toby of James Blackwell's unexpected visit. While Toby put the salad and the bread on the table, filled water glasses, and added ice to the sun tea, Annelise and I whisked the boys first into the bathtub, then into their room to dress them in clean, dry clothes.

I ran back to the kitchen to check on the lasagna, and Annelise brought the boys and their buffalo into the great room to play quietly — and cleanly — while we waited for the doorbell to ring. At precisely twelve o'clock, it did.

Rose Blanding stared avidly around her as I ushered her into the great room and introduced her to Annelise, Will, and Rob.

"How lucky you are to have such a lovely place to stay," she said to the boys.

"We slept in a *bunk bed* at the ranch," Rob informed her airily.

"And we saw *two* snakes," said Will.

"But they weren't rattlers," said Rob, with a wistful sigh.

The twins continued to extoll the ranch's virtues while we ate, but Rose seemed to be preoccupied with the Aerie's. She appeared to listen attentively to the boys' chatter, but her eyes roved around the room as if she were memorizing every detail of her surroundings. I was confident that a minute description of the Aerie's interior would find its way onto the local grapevine before sunset.

After we'd finished the meal, I left Rose to wander at will while Toby and I cleared the table and Annelise took the boys outside to hunt for fossils. Rose seemed captivated by the objects displayed in the rustic cabinet. She was still peering at them when I joined her.

"The twins took naps when we first got here," I told her. "But they don't seem to need them anymore."

"They're acclimatized," Rose observed knowledgeably. "It's amazing how quickly children adjust to the altitude." She favored me with an inquisitive, sidelong look. "Did I see James Blackwell's truck pass by the parsonage this morning?"

"James Blackwell!" Toby exclaimed from

the kitchen. He threw down a dish towel and hurried over to where Rose and I were standing. "Did *he* ring the bell this morning? Did you get a chance to speak with him, Lori? Did you find out if he" — he glanced at Rose and finished cautiously — "did what I thought he did?"

"Let's all have a seat," I said. "James's visit was extremely informative. I have a lot to tell both of you."

Toby perched on the hearth ledge while Rose and I made ourselves comfortable on the sofa. They listened raptly while I told them a slightly abbreviated version of James Blackwell's story. I enjoyed shooting a significant look at Toby when I described James's unsuccessful assault on the Lord Stuart Mine. I had no intention of discussing Toby's unworthy suspicions in front of Rose, but I relished the prospect of forcing him to admit — after Rose had gone — that he'd been wrong to accuse his predecessor of theft.

Rose was shocked to learn that Amanda Barrow had played such a pivotal role in the Auerbachs' departure, but Toby wasn't even mildly surprised.

"Amanda tried to pull the same stunt yesterday," he informed Rose indignantly. "She tried to use the curse to scare Lori."

"But it's nonsense," Rose protested. "The curse is utter nonsense."

"So is everything else Amanda does," said Toby, "but it doesn't stop people from believing in her."

Rose's gray eyes narrowed. "I'll have to have a little talk with Amanda. I don't mind it when she practices her profession on adults, but when it comes to frightening an impressionable teenaged girl . . ." She gazed fiercely into the middle distance, then cleared her throat and turned a much gentler visage toward me. "I'm sorry for the Auerbachs, of course, but they'll be all right. People with money always are. James, on the other hand, may find himself struggling to make ends meet once the baby arrives. I'm worried about him."

"I am, too," I admitted. "What if he can't find a job after the baby's born? Danny Auerbach won't hire him back."

"Leave it to me," said Rose. "I'll think of something. James was well liked in Bluebird. I may be able to find a way to bring him back — with his family, of course."

"That'd be great," I said. "He loves it up here."

Rose folded her hands in her lap. "You certainly had an interesting morning, Lori. Thank you so much for telling me about

James. The lasagna was delicious, by the way. And your sons are adorable, so big for their age and so articulate."

Rose added a few more compliments before it dawned on me that she was waiting to be taken on the promised tour.

"Would you like to see the rest of the Aerie?" I asked.

"I would," she replied instantly.

I took Rose Blanding from one end of the Aerie to the other, leaving out only the caretaker's apartment and cleverly making the library our last stop. I wanted her full attention when I asked her about the photographs in the gray archival box.

Rose's face lit up when we entered the library. She walked straight to the shelves to look over the books and uttered soft cries of delight when she found ones she knew to be rare or out of print.

"I realize that envy is a sin," she said, sighing deeply, "but I can't help being envious of Mrs. Auerbach. Her collection is truly priceless."

"Here's your box, Mrs. Blanding," said Toby, drawing her over to the banker's desk. "Lori and I were looking through it last night. We wondered if you could identify any of the men in the pictures."

"I can identify *all* of them," Rose assured

us, opening the box.

My eyes met Toby's over Rose's bowed head, but we looked away quickly, suppressing smiles.

"James Blackwell was interested in the Lord Stuart mining disaster," said Rose, "so I gave him contemporary accounts of it: articles from the local newspaper, photocopies of relevant correspondence, and so on."

"Toby and I are interested in the photographs," I reiterated, to keep Rose from going off on a tangent.

"The group portrait is the key," she explained. She lifted the large photograph out of the box and showed it to Toby and me. "Every man in the photograph, but one, died in the disaster."

"Oh, my gosh," I said, peering down at the proud faces of the doomed men. "I should have guessed. Twenty red granite headstones in the cemetery, twenty-one miners in the photograph."

"I included an individual portrait of each man in the group portrait." Rose passed the group portrait to Toby and raised a handful of photographs from the box, fanning them out like playing cards. "I also included a portrait of Cyril Pennyfeather, whose obelisk we saw in the cemetery." She plucked one photograph from the rest and handed it to me, then put the others back into the box.

A wave of affection tinged with sorrow swept over me me as I took in Cyril's narrow chest and shoulders, his wavy blond hair, and the pince-nez perched on the bridge of his rather prominent nose. He was dressed in a serviceable tweed suit and held an open book in one long-fingered hand, as if he'd looked up from his reading to have his picture taken. He stood at a slight angle to the camera, before a backdrop that included a classical bust on a truncated Doric column. If I hadn't already known he was a schoolmaster, I would have guessed it.

"He has such intelligent eyes," I murmured.

"He was, by all accounts, a highly intelligent man," Rose said. "He could speak French, German, Latin, and Greek, and he knew most of Shakespeare's works by heart."

"Macbeth," I murmured, returning the photograph to the box. "Act two, Scene two."

Toby was still examining the group portrait. He handed it back to Rose and asked, "Which one of the men survived?"

A shiver traveled up my spine as Rose

pointed unerringly to the wild-eyed, bearded man in the back row.

"He brought water to the other miners," she said. "He was refilling his can when the mine collapsed and so escaped unharmed. His name was Ludovic Magerowski."

"I *knew* it!" I cried, as Cyril Pennyfeather's words came rushing back to me. "I *knew* he was crazy."

"How did you know?" Rose asked in mild surprise.

I blinked at her, then said quickly, "His eyes. He has crazy eyes."

"You do judge men by their eyes, Lori," Rose commented, looking amused. She turned back to the photograph. "But you were right about Cyril Pennyfeather, and you're right again about Ludovic. He was deranged. That's why they wouldn't allow him to handle tools or to have anything to do with explosives. No one trusted Ludo to do anything but deliver water."

Rose went on to describe Ludovic Magerowski's life. Her account tallied with the one Cyril Pennyfeather had written in Aunt Dimity's blue journal, but Rose had one enormous advantage over Cyril — she knew what had happened after the disaster.

"Rumors flew," she said. "The most popular one was that Ludo had sabotaged the mine to exact revenge from Emerson Auerbach for cheating him out of a fortune." She rifled through the box and came up with a frail newspaper clipping encased in a protective clear plastic envelope. "As you can see, Ludo didn't help matters. He gave an interview to the Bluebird *Herald* in which he claimed to have special powers."

"Like Amanda's?" Toby hazarded.

"Just like Amanda's," Rose confirmed. "Ludo announced that he had, indeed, sabotaged the mine, but that he'd done so with mind power alone. In other words, he'd *willed* the mine to collapse."

"That must have gone over big in Bluebird," I said sarcastically.

"They couldn't arrest him for the illegal use of willpower," Toby pointed out. "What happened to him, Mrs. Blanding? Did the townspeople take the law into their own hands?"

"I'm sure they would have, if they could have gotten to him in time," said Rose. "Fortunately — or unfortunately, depending on your point of view — the *Herald*'s editor arranged for Ludo to be spirited away to an asylum near Denver before the interview appeared in the newspaper. I suppose he didn't want Ludo's blood on his hands."

"What happened to Ludo's wife?" I asked.

"She had relatives in Ohio, but she chose to stay on in Bluebird. I imagine it was easier for her to stay here, where the story was already known, than to confess the awful truth about her husband to her family. There was a great stigma attached to mental illness in those days." Rose sighed as she returned the group portrait and the newspaper clipping to the archival box. "A year to the day after the mining disaster, her body was found floating facedown in Bluebird Creek. The coroner ruled her death accidental, but I suspect that he was being kind. Suicide would have barred her from being buried in the cemetery."

"And the child?" I asked.

"He was sent to an orphanage. As for Ludo, he was never seen in Bluebird again. He died two months after he entered the asylum." Rose replaced the lid on the box. "It's been said before, but it bears repeating: Gold fever is sometimes a fatal illness."

Toby and I stared down at the archival box in somber silence, but our thoughts were interrupted by the doorbell.

"Three times in one day?" I said, astonished. "I'm going to have to hire a social secretary."

Toby must have been hoping for a return appearance by James Blackwell because he ran to answer the door before I could make a start toward it. A moment later we heard him bellow angrily, "What are *you* doing here?"

Rose and I exchanged alarmed glances and hastened into the great room, arriving just in time to see Amanda Barrow, in full gypsy regalia, sweep in from the foyer with Toby hot on her heels.

"I did not come here of my own volition," she declared. "I was *summoned!*"

TWENTY-ONE

"I didn't summon you," said Toby, eyeing Amanda contemptuously.

"Nor did I," I said.

"You misunderstand." The bangles on Amanda's wrists rattled as she spread her arms wide and gazed toward the ceiling. "I was summoned by no earthly power. I responded to a call beyond the reach of human hearing."

"Like a dog?" Toby said scathingly.

I didn't even try to disguise my hoot of laughter with a cough. I had no idea what had brought Amanda to the Aerie, but her timing couldn't have been worse. The baleful influence she'd exerted on young Tammy Auerbach was still fresh in my mind and although I couldn't bring myself to send her packing, I wasn't inclined to give her a warm welcome.

Toby, on the other hand, looked as though he might take a swing at her, so I hurried over to place myself between them.

"Amanda," I said, "what can I do for you?"

"You can do nothing for me," she said, lowering her arms. "But *I* can do something for *you*."

"Thanks, but we've already washed the dishes," said Toby, in tones of withering scorn.

Amanda spared him one disdainful look, then focused her attention on me. "I do not, of course, refer to a mundane chore."

"Pity," said Toby. "The mudroom could use a good scrub."

"Good afternoon, Amanda," Rose said, crossing to join our merry group.

"It is afternoon, Rose, but whether it be good or bad I cannot yet tell." Amanda sidled past me and began to prowl around the great room with her eyes half closed and her arms stretched at full length in front of her.

"If you want to see the Aerie, we can schedule a tour," I said.

"I do not wish to see the Aerie," said Amanda.

"Then what in heaven's name *are* you doing?" Rose demanded. "Playing blindman's buff?"

"I am allowing myself to be guided," Amanda replied, continuing her circuit of the room. "I sense your hostility, Rose, but you and I are not so very different."

"Aren't we?" Rose said skeptically.

"We both believe that the supernatural plays a role in everyday life." Amanda paused to wave her palms over the rustic cabinet, then moved on. "We believe in a power greater than ourselves. We believe in revelations, prophecies, and the continuation of the spirit after death."

"I *don't* believe in using fear to intimidate innocent children," Rose said tartly.

"Yes, you do," Amanda countered evenly. "You believe in hellfire and eternal damnation, and you use those beliefs to intimidate children in every Sunday school class you teach."

"I beg your pardon," Rose began heatedly, but I decided to redirect the conversation before things got out of hand. I didn't want the pastor's wife to take a swing at Amanda, either.

"Sorry," I said firmly, "but my guests aren't allowed to discuss religion or politics under my roof, even when I'm only borrowing the roof. Since you're an uninvited guest, Amanda, the rule applies doubly to you."

"But I *was* invited," Amanda insisted, moving her hands in a circular motion over the dining room table. "I was summoned soon after you left me yesterday. Your unwillingness to accept the orb's insights made me hesitant to respond to the call, but ultimately it became irresistible. Ahhhh . . ." She let out a hair-raising moan and glided toward the foyer as if an invisible force had seized her by the wrists and pulled her there.

"Good," said Toby, standing aside. "The exit's to your right."

But Amanda didn't turn toward the front door. Before anyone could stop her, she plunged through the foyer, up the stairs, and into the family suite corridor. Rose and Toby stood rooted to the spot, as if they couldn't believe what they'd just seen, but I tore after Amanda, half afraid that the invisible force would take her straight to Aunt Dimity's blue journal. I didn't want the inner eye that had "seen" Cyril Pennyfeather to get anywhere near the journal's pages.

"Get back here, Amanda!" Toby roared, finding his voice.

I heard scurrying footsteps behind me and knew that he was on his way, with Rose Blanding bringing up the rear. I would have knocked Amanda down with a flying tackle if she'd attempted to enter the master suite, but she didn't. She allowed herself to be dragged along until she reached the boys' room, where she stopped so suddenly that I had to hop sideways to avoid running into her.

"Here," she whispered loudly. "The vibrations emanate from *here.*"

Rose collided with Toby, who collided with me, and before we could sort ourselves out, Amanda was off and running again, with her bangles rattling, through the boys' bedroom and on into the playroom. By the time we caught up with her, she was standing stock-still in front of the freestanding tent. Her stillness was so absolute, her concentration so razor-sharp, that instead of ordering her to leave the room, as I'd intended, I found myself hushing Rose and Toby and motioning for them to keep back.

"The curse lingers in the very fabric of the building," Amanda intoned.

She raised her arms slowly, lowered them inch by inch until her palms faced the floor of the tent, then snatched them back, as if they'd been scalded. I jumped, Rose clucked her tongue irritably, and Toby scowled.

Amanda inhaled deeply, then closed her eyes and addressed the ceiling. "Dark things abide here."

"I'll have you know that my *sons* sleep here," I said, bristling.

"I see darkness, I see flames, I see a hate-filled heart seeking to destroy." Amanda pivoted on her heels, raised a hand to point at me, and cried, "A full moon rises tonight. Heed my warning! Escape while there's still time!"

My companions' furious gasps made me hope that Amanda would heed her own warning, but she didn't move.

"Amanda Barrow," Rose said awfully, sparks of hellfire dancing in her eyes. "I've never in all my life seen such a revolting display of cheap theatrics. Your circus act may impress fifteen-year-old girls and inebriated acolytes, but I can assure you that it does not impress us."

"Actually, I thought she did it pretty well," I murmured, but Toby talked right over me.

"Listen up, Amanda," he said coldly. "If you ever mention the curse to either one of Lori's sons, I'll throw your crystal ball *and* your rune stones *and* your entire stock of tarot cards into Lake Matula." He raised his arms and wheeled around slowly until his palms were facing the corridor. "Hey, look, Amanda, you've been summoned again! A voice beyond the reach of human hearing is telling me it's time for you to leave."

"I will go," said Amanda, drawing herself up with great dignity. "I have done my best.

317

I can do no more."

"I'll walk you to the front door," said Toby and followed Amanda out of the playroom like a prison guard escorting a fractious inmate.

"Well, *really . . .*" Rose released an indignant breath, then turned to me. "I feel as though I should apologize, Lori, though I don't know why I should. We've always exercised tolerance toward Amanda and her band of followers, but it looks as though she needs to be reined in. It's completely unacceptable for her to march into a private home and carry on in such an appalling manner. She'll be disrupting church services next."

"No, she won't," I said soothingly, hoping to head off a witch hunt. "She won't invade the church or the parsonage or any other house in Bluebird. Don't you see, Rose? The Aerie holds a special attraction for Amanda because of the so-called curse. She simply can't resist performing on such a ready-made stage."

"What if she drops by while your sons are here?" asked Rose.

"Maybe I'll let her conduct an exorcism," I said with an easygoing shrug. "It'd be worth it to get her out of my hair."

"You're more generous than I am," said

Rose. "The *nerve* of the woman . . ."

"Let's not let her spoil the day." I nodded toward the corridor. "Why don't we cool our tempers with a couple of tall glasses of iced tea?"

"I'd love to, but I can't," said Rose, looking at her watch. "I have to attend a Gold Rush Days committee meeting in less than an hour. Besides, I don't want to overstay my welcome. I'll just collect my box and be on my way."

We met Toby in the foyer, where he was keeping an eagle eye on Amanda's car as it disappeared down the twisting drive. After she'd gone, he fetched the archival box from the library and stowed it in the trunk of Rose's car. Annelise and the twins joined us as we waved good-bye to Rose.

Neither Will nor Rob had discovered any fossils, but they'd found enough rusty nails, railroad spikes, and leftover bits of mining machinery to make me thankful that their tetanus shots were up to date. They lovingly arranged their finds on the hearth ledge in the great room, then asked if they could go to town with Toby, who'd volunteered to pick up dinner at the cafe. Toby didn't believe that anyone on vacation should have to cook two big meals in one day, and I agreed with him, but before giving the twins the go-ahead, I took Toby aside.

"I need to speak with Annelise," I said quietly. "Can you handle both of the boys on your own?"

"Sure," said Toby. "They're great kids. I won't have any trouble with them at all."

"I hope not," I said and gave my sons the thumbs-up.

Toby and the twins headed for the van while Annelise and I settled down on the breakfast deck with glasses of iced tea, to discuss her reasons for keeping the boys away from the Brockman Ranch. I was a bit apprehensive about what I would hear. Annelise didn't usually consult with me or Bill about the twins unless she needed serious backup, which she very seldom did. Will and Rob really were great kids.

"Okay," I said, gripping my glass with both hands. "What happened at the ranch?"

"Two things," said Annelise. "First, we had a little language problem while we were on the trail ride."

I smiled with relief, though I was frankly surprised that she'd felt the need to bring such a trivial complaint to my attention.

"The boys can't help using English words and phrases," I said reasonably. "They've grown up with them. Besides, you were there to translate."

"I didn't have to translate," said Annelise. "The Americans on the trail ride understood Will perfectly when he called the little boy ahead of him a 'son of a bitch.' "

My jaw dropped and iced tea sloshed onto the table. *"What?"*

Annelise nodded. "They understood Rob, too, when he used the word that rhymes with 'duck.' "

"He . . . *what?*" I sputtered, spilling more tea.

"I don't have to spell it out for you, do I?" Annelise shook her head bemusedly. "They weren't even angry. The words just popped out of their mouths as if they used them every day. Heaven knows what the other adults on the ride thought about their upbringing."

"My sons have had an *excellent* upbringing," I said, shaking drops of iced tea from my hands. "You know very well that we don't use that kind of language at home. They must have picked it up from someone at the ranch."

"I'm sure they did," said Annelise. "Two of the guest children are foul-mouthed little beasts, and their parents are just as bad, if not worse."

"Did you have a talk with Rob and Will about good manners and polite language?"

I asked.

"Naturally," said Annelise. "That's when we ran into the second problem. When I asked Will and Rob where they'd heard those words, they told me they'd heard them *here,* at the *Aerie.* Now, you and I don't use that kind of language, and I don't think Toby Cooper does, either."

"Toby would never swear in front of children," I agreed.

"Will and Rob assured me that they didn't learn the words from Toby," said Annelise, "but they can't say who they *did* learn them from. They insist that they heard them in their *tent,* in the *playroom,* during the *night.* They must be lying, Lori, and to tell you the truth, the lying troubles me more than the smutty language." She paused. "Lori? Are you listening?"

I nodded vaguely as I stared into the middle distance at an image only I could see — the image of Amanda Barrow's hands recoiling from the playroom tent as if they'd been scalded.

"Those you love most will surprise you," I said under my breath.

"Sorry?" said Annelise.

"Nothing." I cleared my throat and stood. "I'm sure you handled the situation perfectly, Annelise. I don't think we should make a big deal out of it, but I'll . . . I'll call Bill to see what he thinks." I drummed my damp fingers on the teak table. "Yes. I'll call him right now. I'll be in the master suite, and I don't want to be disturbed."

"All right," said Annelise. "Give him my best."

"Who?" I said blankly.

"Bill," said Annelise, eyeing me curiously. "Give Bill my best."

"Oh yes," I said. "I'll do that."

I left the breakfast deck and crossed the great room at a rapid pace, breaking into a run as soon as I reached the foyer. I dashed up the stairs, through the corridor, and into the master suite, where I snatched the blue journal from the white armchair and opened it without bothering to sit.

"Dimity," I said urgently. "I need to talk to you. You, too, Mr. Pennyfeather, if you're around. Something really weird is going on."

Twenty-Two

Aunt Dimity's familiar handwriting was the first to appear on the page, followed closely by Cyril Pennyfeather's flowery script.

What seems to be the problem, my dear?

May I help in any way?

"Are both of you one hundred per cent *sure* that the Aerie isn't cursed?" I asked.

I think I can speak for both Mr. Pennyfeather and myself when I state categorically that the Aerie is curse-free. What's troubling you, Lori?

"Amanda Barrow." I lowered myself into the white armchair and stared pensively at the ashes in the grate.

The psychic? Aunt Dimity clarified.

The hysterical psychic? Cyril added.

"She may have been hysterical, but she gave me a pretty accurate description of you, Mr. Pennyfeather," I reminded him. "After you took off, she looked into her crystal ball and started telling me things. I thought it was a big joke at the time, but

324

I'm not so sure anymore."

What sort of things did she tell you?

"She said I'd come from afar," I began, "and she was right — I came to Colorado all the way from England."

She could have heard of your journey from any number of sources.

"That's what I thought," I said. "But she also predicted that I'd meet a short, dark stranger."

Shouldn't it be a tall, dark stranger?

I glanced down at Cyril's polite inquiry and remembered that Toby had muttered the same thing as Amanda had peered into her orb, but I was too distressed to crack a smile.

"Amanda predicted that I'd meet a *short,* dark stranger," I said, "and she was right again. James Blackwell showed up at the Aerie this morning. He's short, dark-haired, and deeply tanned, and until today he was definitely a stranger."

James Blackwell, the missing caretaker, returned to the Aerie this morning?

"Yes, but let's stick with Amanda for the moment," I said, refusing to be distracted. "She also said that Death had come to claim me, but I'd escaped his grasp."

How clever of her. After Abaddon attacked you, you came as close to dying as anyone can come, but you rallied and recovered. Have you mentioned the incident to anyone who could have passed the news along to Amanda?

"Annelise knows about the shooting, of course," I said, "but she'd never breathe a word about it to anyone here. Toby knows about it, too, but I didn't tell him about it until last night, *after* Amanda had said her piece."

I see. What other interesting tidbits did Amanda Barrow share with you?

"She told me that those I loved would surprise me," I said, "and guess what? She was right *again.* Bill surprised the heck out of me this morning when he told me that he'd be arriving at the Aerie next week."

Why were you surprised? It's exactly the sort of thing Bill would do.

"True," I allowed, "but he wasn't the only loved one who surprised me today. Annelise just finished telling me that Will and Rob not only used smutty language at the ranch yesterday, but lied to her when she asked them where they'd learned it."

Will and Rob don't use smutty language or tell lies.

"I know," I said emphatically. "That's why I was surprised."

To summarize: Amanda Barrow was correct

about Mr. Pennyfeather, your long journey, your meeting with James Blackwell, your close encounter with death, and the twins' surprising naughtiness. Perhaps she does have a gift after all, over and above her ability to accurately describe ethereal escorts.

"If she does," I said, "then something's seriously out of whack because, unlike you and Mr. Pennyfeather, Amanda thinks the Aerie's cursed. She convinced Tammy, the Auerbachs' teenaged daughter, that the Aerie is cursed, and she came here today to inform me of the same thing."

Amanda Barrow is mistaken.

No one can be right all the time.

"Amanda's batting average is pretty spectacular so far," I said anxiously.

True. What, exactly, did she tell you about the curse?

"She seemed to sense something underneath the tent in the playroom," I said. "There's nothing under the tent but floorboards, but Florence Auerbach was so concerned about the floorboards in the family suite that she asked James Blackwell to take a look at them. Why is everyone taking such a keen interest in floorboards?"

Floorboards make noises, Lori, especially when a new building is settling onto its foundations.

"The Aerie was built only two years ago," I said. "It must still be settling."

A new building's normal noises can seem quite eerie, especially if they're heard in the dead of night by a listener who is predisposed to hear eerie sounds.

"So if Tammy Auerbach heard a floorboard creak or a door squeak, she'd think it was a manifestation of the curse," I said.

The poor child must have been a nervous wreck. Florence Auerbach probably asked James Blackwell to check the family suite's floorboards in order to convince Tammy that nothing was wrong with them.

"But Tammy was too far gone by then," I said, nodding. "James Blackwell told me that Tammy was so jittery she was losing sleep —"

The balm of hurt minds.

"That's right, Mr. Pennyfeather," I said. "And without her nightly dose of balm, Tammy got more and more jumpy, just like I did."

I suspect that Florence Auerbach took her daughter away from the Aerie for much the same reason Bill sent you away from the cottage.

"She didn't want Tammy to have a nervous breakdown," I said. "But Tammy was so afraid of the curse that she refused to return to the Aerie, so Mrs. Auerbach decided to sell it."

If Tammy told Amanda about the strange sounds she'd heard at the Aerie, Amanda would naturally make a fuss over the floorboards. Their curious creaks and moans would lend credence to her claim that the Aerie is cursed.

"But Amanda went to the playroom when she came here today," I said. "Why didn't she go to Tammy's room?"

I imagine she chose a room at random. As long as it was in the family suite, it would serve her purpose, which was to give a convincing performance.

"I suppose so," I said reluctantly.

You still sound troubled, my dear.

"I am," I admitted. "According to Amanda, the curse is in the fabric of the building. I can't help remembering that Danny Auerbach recycled lumber from the old mine buildings when he constructed the Aerie. What if the curse is still . . . clinging to the old wood in the floorboards under the tent?"

There is no curse, Lori. There is only a woman who needs to convince others of its existence. Amanda Barrow is a local. She's known about the recycled lumber ever since the Aerie was built. If I were her, I'd use that knowledge to give my false claims the ring of truth.

Aunt Dimity's argument made good sense, but I was still worried.

"Will and Rob told Annelise that they learned their smutty vocabulary in the playroom tent," I said. "When Amanda came here, she made a beeline for the tent. She may be blowing smoke about the curse, but what if she actually sensed something sinister in the playroom? You mentioned disembodied voices when we spoke the other night, Mr. Pennyfeather. What if a foul-mouthed spirit is hanging around the tent at night, teaching my sons to swear?"

Miss Westwood and I are the only spirits currently in residence at the Aerie, Lori, and we are not in the habit of using rude language.

"Can you be sure there's no one else?" I persisted. "Maybe a demon flew in under your radar."

Ah yes, I know about radar now, thanks to Miss Westwood's excellent explanation, and I can assure you that no demon has flown under ours. A demon's signal, so to speak, is quite distinctive. I would be instantly aware of it, as would Miss Westwood.

"My sons don't lie, Mr. Pennyfeather," I said stubbornly. "And you admitted only a moment ago that Amanda might have real gifts, Dimity."

So I did, but she also appears to crave attention almost as much as she enjoys upsetting people. I repeat: There is no curse. Since Mr. Pennyfeather and I seem unable to reassure you on that score, however hard we try, might I suggest an experiment?

"Go ahead," I said.

Sleep in the playroom tonight, Lori. I strongly doubt that you'll hear a demonic chorus serenading you with obscenities, but I'm certain that a night spent with your ear pressed to the floorboards will convince you that Mr. Pennyfeather and I are more reliable than Amanda Barrow when it comes to the detection of curses and evil spirits.

"I'll do it," I said. "I'll spend the night in the playroom. It's not that I doubt you, Dimity —"

I understand, Lori. You're protecting your sons. It's what mothers do. I wouldn't have it any other way.

Nor would I.

"Thanks," I said. "I'll let you know if anything happens."

If a demon happens, you won't have to let us know.

I smiled wryly as the two sets of handwriting faded from the page, then closed the journal and put it on the bedside table, next to Reginald.

"Do you think I'm being silly, Reg?" I asked my pink rabbit.

Reginald was understandably noncommittal. The notion of spending a night on a cold, hard floor when I had a warm, soft bed at my disposal was already beginning to strike *me* as silly.

"Nevertheless, I can't afford to take chances where Will and Rob are concerned," I said staunchly, then bent low to whisper in his ear, "But don't tell Toby or Annelise what I'm planning to do, okay? They'll think I've gone off the deep end."

Reginald's black eyes gleamed supportively. I touched the faded grape juice stain on his snout and cocked an ear toward the corridor, listening for the thunder of little feet that would signal the twins' return from Bluebird. When I heard nothing, I left the master suite and returned to the playroom.

I gazed speculatively at the freestanding tent for a moment, then grabbed hold of it with both hands and slid it to one side. I was so afraid that my sons had spent the past week sleeping on a bloodstained, curse-ridden, demon-haunted remnant of the Lord Stuart mining disaster that it took every bit of courage I had to look at the spot where the tent had been.

It was indistinguishable from every other patch of floorboard in the playroom. I got down on my knees and rapped the floor with my knuckles. It sounded reassuringly solid. I pushed on the floorboards, stomped on them, and hopped up and down on them, but they didn't emit so much as a squeak. I was beginning to wish that James Blackwell had left his pickax behind instead of his lantern when I heard telltale noises coming not from the floor, but from the foyer.

Toby and the twins had returned. I stomped on the floor one more time, then gave up and went to join the others in the great room.

Toby had decided that Caroline's Cafe wasn't the only local eatery that deserved our patronage, so we dined on pizzas from Mile High Pies and peach ice cream from Sweet Jenny's Emporium. The ice cream eliminated any possibility of s'mores at the fire pit, but I eased the twins' disappointment by announcing that they would spend the night in the great room.

Will and Rob were enthralled by the idea of mounting an expedition to another part of the Aerie and ran off after dinner to help Toby move the tent from the playroom to their new camping spot.

Annelise, by contrast, was . . . Annelise. After considering the vast number of things the boys could break, dismantle, and/or wedge their heads into in the great room, she elected to sleep on the sofa, where she could keep a close eye on their nocturnal activities. Since it would be easier to sneak into the playroom after lights-out if I had the family suite all to myself, I put up token resistance, then happily allowed her to have her way.

I pushed furniture aside to make room for the tent, Toby set it up in the space I'd created, and the twins furnished it with foam pads, sleeping bags, headlamps, and fuzzy buffalo. After Annelise had made up the sofa and I'd popped the boys into their jammies, Toby said good night and retired to his apartment.

Will and Rob were so tired that it didn't take long to get them settled in their tent. I kissed them good night, thanked Annelise for taking the night shift, turned out the lights, and went into the foyer, where I stood listening at the double doors. When the boys' drowsy whispers died down, I tiptoed to the master suite, changed into blue jeans and a thick woolen sweater, gathered up a pillow, a blanket, and my headlamp, and carried them to the playroom.

The full moon shining through the tree branches outside the picture window cast an intricate pattern of shadows across the room. I felt a twinge of guilt as I thought of Annelise trying to sleep in the bright moonlight streaming through the great room's window wall, but after a few moments on the floor, I would have gladly traded places with her. It didn't take long for me to realize that it was impossible to sleep comfortably on a floor while fully dressed, though I doubted that a pair of silk pajamas would have made any difference.

I was on the verge of retreating to my cozy bed when a queer sound brought my heart into my throat. I couldn't tell whether it was the creak of a door or the tenor in a demonic chorus, but it seemed to come from the corridor. I sat up, turned my headlamp on, and nearly jumped out of my skin when a shadowy figure loomed over me in the darkness.

"I knew I'd find you here," said Toby. "Is it time for me to throw you in the lake?"

TWENTY-THREE

"What are you talking about?" I demanded, pressing a hand over my galloping heart.

"Keep your voice down or you'll wake Annelise," said Toby.

"What are you talking about?" I whispered.

Toby switched on James Blackwell's lantern, set it on the floor, and sat next to it. "You gave me your permission to throw you in the lake if you showed the slightest sign of being obsessed by the curse."

I scowled at him. "I'm not obsessed by the curse."

"Uh-huh," Toby said disbelievingly. "Amanda's act this afternoon had no effect on you whatsoever. You changed everyone's sleeping arrangements simply because you thought it would be fun to sleep in here instead of in the master suite. I admire your spirit of adventure."

"I didn't change the sleeping arrangements because of Amanda's act." I lied without hesitation. I did not intend to tell Toby, of all people, that I was on the lookout for a lurking demon. "If you must know, Will and Rob used some pretty ripe language at the ranch yesterday."

"I know," said Toby. "While we were waiting for the pizza they reviewed all the words they mustn't say."

"Audibly?" I said, wincing.

Toby grinned. "Don't worry, I shushed them before they got too far down the list."

"How long was the list?" I asked, horrified.

"Not very long," said Toby. "But what does their cursing have to do with the curse?"

"Nothing," I said. "I'm not here because of the curse. I'm here because Will and Rob heard those smutty words while they were sleeping in the tent. I'm convinced that they're telling the truth, so I want to find out what's going on and put a stop to it."

"Okay," Toby said, drawing the word out to twice its normal length. "You want to find out how the twins learned to swear in the middle of the night while they were all by themselves. Shouldn't you be searching for a hidden tape recorder left behind by the Auerbach boys?"

"Gosh," I said, brightening. "I hadn't thought of that."

"You don't have a very high opinion of the Auerbach boys," Toby said dryly.

"I've never met the Auerbach boys," I said. "For all I know they could be potty-mouthed pranksters. They could have rigged a tape recorder to come on when the clock strikes midnight. The twins wouldn't know it was weird. They'd think it was just another fantastic feature of the Aerie."

Toby stared at me wordlessly for a few moments, then got to his feet and picked up the lantern.

"Where are you going?" I asked.

"To get a couple of lawn chairs," he replied. "It's only ten o'clock. If we're going to be here past midnight, we might as well be comfortable."

"You don't have to stay," I said, though I hoped he would, not only because I enjoyed his company, but because I'd be less tempted to abandon my vigil if he shared it with me.

Fortunately, Toby had already made up his mind to keep me company.

"If you think I'm going to miss the Auerbach boys' nightly tutorial on swearing," he said, "then you're not the model of mental stability I thought you were." He chuckled softly to himself as he left the room.

He returned a short time later with two folding chaise longues, which he set up side by side on the spot where the tent had stood. I offered him half of my blanket as we stretched out on the chaise longues, but he refused, so I covered myself with it and leaned back with a contented sigh. The chair was a great improvement over the floor.

We doused the lights to save the batteries and endured five grueling minutes of utter silence before one of us couldn't stand it anymore. Much to my surprise, it wasn't me.

"You know," Toby said softly. "It's possible that Will and Rob could have heard a *live* voice in their tent."

"Whose?" I asked. "The smut fairy's?"

"No," said Toby. "A real, live human being's."

I snorted derisively. "Are you suggesting that some pervert crept into the Aerie in the dead of night in order to teach my sons how to swear?"

"He wouldn't have to enter the Aerie," said Toby. "Did I ever tell you about the mine shaft underneath the Aerie?"

"There's a *mine shaft* underneath the Aerie?" I said, sitting bolt upright.

"I've been trying to picture it in my

mind," Toby murmured. "It's a horizontal shaft, and I'm pretty sure it runs beneath the family suite."

"We've been *sleeping* over a *mine shaft?*" I said, thunderstruck.

"Relax, Lori," said Toby. "It's a small shaft and it's been underpinned, so it's perfectly stable."

"How do you know so much about it?" I asked.

"I've been in it," he replied.

I switched on my headlamp, swung my legs to the floor, and sat sideways on the chaise longue. "I thought your grandfather ordered you not to go into the mines."

"He did," said Toby, "but I went into them anyway."

"Toby," I said, scandalized.

"What else was I supposed to do?" said Toby. "I was already the city kid, the kid from back east. You think I wanted to be the goody-goody as well? Forget it. By the time I was thirteen, I'd explored every abandoned mine on this side of the valley." He glanced heavenward. "Sorry, Granddad, but a kid's gotta do what a kid's gotta do."

"It's a miracle you lived long enough to go to college," I said, shaking my head.

"Anyway," he went on, "if someone was in the shaft, the boys could have heard a voice coming up through the floor."

"But how would anyone get into the shaft?" I asked. "I've seen the Lord Stuart's main entrance, and it's blocked good and proper."

Toby tilted his head to one side. "I can think of at least three other ways, if they haven't caved in."

"But —" I broke off suddenly and stared at the floorboards between our chairs. "Did you hear that?"

Toby nodded, swung his legs over the side of his chair, and seemed to hold his breath as he, too, stared at the floor.

A faint thumping noise sounded beneath our feet, followed by a few indistinct words uttered by a muffled voice.

"Somebody's down there," I whispered.

"I don't think it's the smut fairy," Toby whispered back. "I'll bet you anything it's one of the crazies from Amanda's commune."

"Why would . . . ?" My voice trailed off as the answer to my question exploded in my head. It didn't take a huge amount of brain power to figure out exactly why someone from the commune would prowl beneath the Aerie, frightening Tammy Auerbach and unwittingly entertaining my fearless sons.

"That conniving *cow*," I whispered furiously. "She's been sending her acolytes into the mine shaft to make spooky noises so we'd buy into her story about the curse. She's been *manufacturing* the curse."

Toby's jaw set in a grim line. "They're trespassing on private property. I'd love to catch them at it."

"Me, too," I said fervently.

He raised an eyebrow. "Well, then?"

"Well, then, what?" I said.

"Let's go." He pointed at the floor. "Let's go down there and get them."

"Are you out of your *mind?*" I squeaked. "No, no, no, and absolutely not-in-a-million-years *no.*"

"Fine," Toby shrugged. "I just thought you might want to get back at Amanda for teaching your sons to swear. I thought you'd want to punish her for scaring Tammy Auerbach. I thought you'd want to get even with her for trying to dupe you. But if you want to let her off the hook . . ."

I didn't consider myself an abnormally vengeful person, but Toby's words were having their desired effect. I could feel myself weakening.

"I know which tunnel we could use to ambush them," he murmured tantalizingly. "If we do it right, we'll give them as big a scare as they gave Tammy."

"If we do it wrong, we'll kill ourselves," I countered.

"We won't do it wrong," Toby insisted. "Trust me, Lori. I know my way around the shafts."

"Okay." I took a deep breath and let it out in a rush. "Let's go."

Toby stood and pulled me to my feet. "We'll leave through the master suite, to avoid disturbing Annelise."

"Good," I said as we headed for the corridor, "because I have to change my shoes. I'm not going into any mine shaft wearing sneakers."

Toby fidgeted impatiently while I pulled on my hiking boots, then led the way onto my deck. We climbed over the railing, jumped, and hit the ground running, though we slowed to a fast walk when Toby ducked into the trees and onto a trail downhill from the Aerie.

The moon was so bright that we didn't need the lantern or my headlamp to find our way, and in less than ten minutes we were standing before a sagging wire fence strung across a rough-edged hole in the mountainside. Toby pulled the fence aside easily and waited for me to join him in the mouth of the mine shaft. I stepped past the fence, then hesitated.

"Toby?" I said. "How cold do you think it is in Panama?"

"Huh?" he said.

"Never mind," I said and plunged in after him.

TWENTY-FOUR

The tunnel wasn't nearly as horrible as I'd expected it to be. The floor was surprisingly uncluttered by debris, there was ample headroom, and the rough-hewn walls were far enough apart for Toby and me to walk side by side. Better still, the wooden supports didn't look as though they were on the brink of giving way, I didn't hear or see a single rat, and the bats had apparently gone out for supper.

Granted, the thought of getting lost and wandering blindly from pillar to post until our lights failed made me want to howl with fear, but Toby seemed to know what he was doing. We passed several openings leading to other shafts, including a rubble-filled one that made me think of Cyril Pennyfeather. I was still contemplating Cyril's sad fate — and praying silently that we wouldn't meet with the same one — when Toby skidded to a halt before an opening that looked different from the others.

"Well, well," he said quietly. "Amanda *has* been industrious."

"What do you mean?" I asked.

"She's carved a new tunnel," he answered, shining his light into a shaft that was much smaller and more roughly hewn than ours. "I've never seen this one before."

"How could she dig a tunnel without anyone knowing about it?" I said doubtfully. "Where would she put the dirt and rocks?"

"They have a big garden up at the dome," said Toby. "They could have dumped the diggings there. And if the tunnel mouth is near the dome, they'd have no trouble keeping it secret. The townspeople leave the commune pretty much alone." He peered into the tunnel again and frowned. "Still, it seems like an awful lot of trouble to go to just to scare the Auerbachs."

"Oh my," I said softly, struck by a revelation that should have come to me much sooner. "It might be worth the trouble if it helps Amanda buy the Aerie at a bargain price."

"What are you talking about?" said Toby. "Mr. Auerbach would never sell the Aerie."

"It's been on the market for the past six months," I informed him. "No one's put in an offer, so Danny's lowered the price twice already. Bill told me about it in confidence, so I couldn't tell you."

Toby's stunned expression quickly gave way to one of outrage. "If Amanda Barrow conned Mr. Auerbach into selling —"

"Of course she did," I broke in excitedly. "Amanda wants to expand her empire by buying the Aerie. She targeted Tammy and dug the tunnel in order to scare the Auerbachs into selling it. She must think *I'm* interested in buying it now that the price has come down. That's why she tried to scare *me*."

"What did you call her?" Toby said darkly. "A conniving cow? Not strong enough, Lori. I'm thinking of a few choice phrases from the twins' list."

I waved a hand toward the new tunnel. "Let's not ambush her gang under the Aerie. Let's confront their ringleader, face-to-face, at the dome."

"I'm in," Toby growled.

He stiffened suddenly, then pressed a finger to his lips, reached over to turn off my headlamp, and switched off the lantern. The darkness was absolute, but the silence was broken by a faint clanking noise and the distant shuffle of footsteps farther down the shaft in which we were standing. Toby's voice came out of the darkness so softly that

I could scarcely hear him.

"Give me the headlamp," he said.

I slipped it off and passed it to him. A moment later a dim red glow shone in the darkness. Toby had wrapped the headlamp in a red bandana. It would provide enough light to guide us without giving us away.

"Useful," I breathed, pointing to the red bandana.

Toby grinned, handed the unlit lantern to me, and nodded for me to follow him into the freshly carved tunnel. It descended at a fairly steep angle, but my hiking boots kept me from slipping. Toby had to bend low to keep from hitting his head on the jagged roof, but the awkward position didn't hinder his speed. He'd clearly lost none of the skills he'd honed in childhood, while disobeying his grandfather.

After a few hundred yards, my thighs began to ache with each jolting, downward step and by the time the tunnel leveled out, my knees were pleading with me to stop torturing them, but I was too distracted by then to listen to them. A faint splash of light had appeared far down the tunnel.

Toby glanced over his shoulder to make sure I was still with him, then increased his speed, racing toward the splash of light as if he wanted to reach it before it went out. I jogged gamely in his wake, wondering what Bill would say when I told him where I'd spent the night. The words *stupid, hare-brained,* and *suicidally irresponsible* came immediately to mind.

We'd almost reached the source of the mysterious glow when Toby slowed to a walk, slipped the bandana from the headlamp, and let its beam play over a solid wall of rock directly ahead of us. The dead end was illuminated from above by light leaking past the edges of what appeared to be a fairly large trapdoor. The top rung of a wooden ladder had been nailed to the wooden rim surrounding the trapdoor, and its legs were planted firmly in two slots cut into the tunnel's floor.

Toby didn't hesitate. He shoved the bandana and the headlamp into his pocket, climbed the ladder, and pushed the trapdoor open. I had to close my eyes against the harsh glare that flooded the tunnel, and when I opened them again, Toby had vanished. I scrambled up the ladder after him, hauled myself through the opening where the trapdoor had been, and found Toby standing a few steps away, looking utterly perplexed.

I was just as confused as he was. I'd expected to find myself in Amanda's garden, surrounded by row upon row of organic wacky-weed, but there was nothing remotely organic about the tunnel's terminus, nor was there any sign of the geodesic dome.

We were standing in what appeared to be the living room of an oddly furnished house. Its oddness stemmed from the fact that, apart from a single bare lightbulb dangling from a ceiling fixture directly above the trapdoor, there were no furnishings. Instead, the room was filled from floor to ceiling with densely compacted piles of dirt and rubble. Swathes of cyclone fence nailed to sturdy posts held the piles in place and created a passageway that led from the trapdoor to a hallway off the living room.

"What in heaven's name . . . ?" I said, in a hushed voice.

"I don't know," said Toby. "Let's look around."

Toby closed the trapdoor, took the lantern from me, and held it high as we entered the hallway. The front door was to our left, but we turned right, to explore the rest of the house. The bathroom and the kitchen were spotless, but rubble filled the dining room and the largest of the two bedrooms at the back. A small, windowless storeroom behind the rubble-filled bedroom held tools similar to those James Blackwell had stored in the wooden crate at the Aerie, but these tools looked as if they'd been put to much harder use than James's.

We paused briefly in the storeroom, then retraced our steps to the second bedroom. It was, in its own way, the strangest room of all. The single bed in the corner had been so fastidiously made up that it would have passed muster in a Marine boot camp. The chest of drawers was aligned precisely with the desk opposite the bed, and both were neat as a pin. I found the room's excessive tidiness unsettling, but two other features made it seem downright weird: The window above the bed had been heavily coated with black paint, and the walls were papered over with maps.

Some of the maps were hand drawn, some were standard, government-issue topographic maps, and some were so old that they'd been sandwiched in clear sheets of plastic to keep them from falling apart. Toby crossed to the desk to examine the hand-drawn map that hung on the wall above it.

"Look," he said, tracing lines with his fingertip. "It shows the underground route between the new tunnel and the shaft underneath the Aerie."

"Does it tell you where we are at the moment?" I asked.

Before he could answer, a loud thud sounded in the living room.

I leaned close to Toby and whispered, "Someone's opened the trapdoor."

The first thud was followed by a second, as the trapdoor fell back into place. Toby quickly extinguished the lantern and stationed himself in front of me. I stared past his shoulder, spellbound, as the clump of heavy footsteps approached the bedroom. My nerves were strung so tight I could feel them twanging, and I nearly shrieked when a hand reached around the doorjamb to hit the light switch, but my reaction was tepid compared to Dick Major's.

He was dressed in coveralls, work boots, and a miner's helmet, and he carried a lantern similar to ours. His pink face contorted with rage when he saw us, and his pale blue eyes nearly popped out of their sockets. He let loose a string of expletives, as if to illustrate from whom my sons had learned them, and finished with the relatively mild, "What the *hell* are you doing in my house?"

"Hello, Dick," Toby said calmly. "We were just about to ask you the same thing."

"*You.*" I inched around Toby as comprehension dawned. "It wasn't Amanda. It was *you.*" I looked at the maps surrounding us and gave a satisfied nod, convinced that I'd finally seen the light. "Your house is on the edge of town, closest to the Aerie. You drove off your neighbors so they wouldn't spy on you, and you made yourself the most unpopular man in town so no one would ever visit you." I glanced at the blacked-out window. "Did you pile the diggings around the house when you ran out of room inside? Is that why you collected so much junk? Are the mattresses and old couches there to disguise the piles of rubble?"

Dick took a step toward me and balled his free hand into a fist. "You think you're pretty smart, don't you, little lady?"

"I do, as a matter of fact," I said defiantly and pointed a trembling finger at his face. "You're *pink!* Everyone else in Bluebird has a tan, but *you* don't, because *you* hardly ever see the sun. You dig at night and sleep during the day. That's why you never show up at Carrie Vyne's cafe until late afternoon. That's why your usual drink is strong black coffee."

Dick snarled, but I was on a roll and barely noticed.

"You're even built the right way," I said. "Look at your shoulders, look at your big hands. You don't get muscles like that *fishing.* You've been *digging.* You hacked a tunnel from your house to connect with the one leading to the Aerie because . . . because . . ." I fell silent, having run out of revelations.

"I know why you did it, Dick." Toby jerked his head toward the hand-drawn map above the desk. "You've been searching for gold, haven't you? You've been scavenging whatever's left down there. You've been stealing gold that doesn't belong to you."

Dick thumped his chest furiously, bellowing, "It *does* belong to me. It *all* belongs to me. My great-great-grandfather discovered the Lord Stuart Mine, and the Auerbachs *stole* it from him."

I staggered back a step and my mouth fell open. "You're Ludovic Magerowski's great-great-grandson?"

"The Auerbachs drove Ludovic *crazy*," Dick shouted, flecks of spittle flying from his lips. "They drove his wife to *suicide*. They put his son in an *orphanage*. My great-grandfather changed his last name to Major, but it didn't change our luck. Nothing's gone right for us since the Auerbachs stole the Lord Stuart."

"So you decided to balance the books?" said Toby. "You came here to take what's rightfully yours?"

"*Yes*. But I came too late." Dick's voice

sank to a hoarse whisper, and his eyes became bleak. "There's no gold left. The Auerbachs took it all."

"If there's no gold left in the Lord Stuart," I said, "why did you go back down there tonight?"

"If I can't have gold, I'll have justice," Dick shouted, shaking his fist at me. "I know how to get it, too. I worked bomb disposal in the army." He bared his teeth in a savage grin. "I left a surprise package under the Aerie tonight, a little thank-you gift for the Auerbachs. It's set to go off at midnight. By then I'll be on my way to Denver."

For a heartbeat, Toby and I stood as if carved out of stone. Then Toby launched himself at Dick, punching him so hard that the big man collapsed in a heap.

I leapt over Dick's prone body, dashed up the hallway, and flew through the front door. I didn't stop to check my watch or to see if Toby was following. I charged up the dirt road and onto the Lord Stuart Trail with only one thought thundering in my head: I had to get my sons and Annelise out of the Aerie before Dick's "surprise package" exploded.

Moonlight silvered the trail and scattered it with shadows. Aspen leaves chattered overhead, but I could scarcely hear them above my gasping breaths. My lungs ached, my legs burned, and flashbulbs seemed to pop before my eyes, but I ran on, hurtling myself upward, past the wildflowers, past the ponderosa pines, past the fir tree I'd leaned against, giggling with Toby, one day ago.

When the Aerie came into view, I realized with a sickening jolt that the front door would be locked. I instantly changed course, flung myself over the railing and onto my deck, sprinted through the master suite, and raced down the corridor, shouting for everyone to get out. By the time I reached the great room, Annelise had roused the twins and pulled them from their sleeping bags, though they were still clutching their fuzzy buffalo.

"Out!" I shouted breathlessly. *"Get out!"*

Annelise scooped Rob into her arms, I darted forward to lift Will, and we fled the Aerie as if the hounds of hell were after us. We nearly crashed into Toby as he bounded across the clearing, but he swerved in the nick of time, took Will from me, and led us back down the Lord Stuart Trail. We'd just spilled out onto the dirt road when a deafening explosion rocked the ground beneath our feet. I stumbled, turned, and saw a fireball billow gracefully into the night sky.

"*Reginald,*" I whispered, stricken. "*Aunt Dimity.*"

TWENTY-FIVE

I could feel my heart breaking as the devouring flames leapt skyward, taking with them my precious Reginald and the blue leatherbound journal that had connected me for so long to my dearest friend and wisest counselor, the remarkable, unforgettable Aunt Dimity. Tears filled my eyes and spilled down my cheeks. My breath came in rasping sobs, and when Toby spoke, his voice seemed to come from a distant planet.

"Well," he panted, "thank God for that."

"Thank God for *what?*" I snapped, rounding on him.

"Dick's aim was bad," he said. "He missed the Aerie."

"He . . . he *missed?*" I stammered as a knee-weakening wave of relief flooded through me.

Toby shrugged. "It's easy to get turned around in the tunnels if you haven't grown up exploring them. I'd say he planted his bomb about a half mile to the west of where he intended to plant it. If we can get the fire under control, the Aerie should be okay."

"Bomb?" said Annelise, raising an eyebrow.

"I'll explain later," I told her.

A siren howled in Bluebird and a cacophony of voices echoed over Lake Matula. The townspeople were awake. A truck from the volunteer fire department roared past us as we limped along Lake Street and Toby flagged down the local sheriff as he drove by.

"Hey there, Tobe," said the sheriff, running an eye over our little band of refugees. "Any idea what caused the explosion?"

"Yeah." Toby jutted his chin toward Dick Major's house. "You'll find him in the back bedroom. Lock him up, Jeff. I'll drop by the jailhouse and explain everything once we find beds for these kids."

"Carrie Vyne's got an empty guest cabin," the sheriff suggested.

"Thanks, Jeff," said Toby. "Fire service on its way?"

"You bet," said the sheriff. "Got 'em coming in from as far away as Boulder."

"Can we ride in your police car?" Will asked, rubbing his cheek against his buffalo.

"With the siren?" Rob added hopefully.

"Maybe another time, boys," the sheriff said kindly. "Right now I've got some business to take care of."

He put two fingers to his brow in a casual salute, then pulled over to park in front of Dick Major's house. As we continued to trudge up Lake Street, I wondered what he'd make of the place once he stepped through the front door.

I also wondered what Amanda Barrow would do when she realized how accurately she'd predicted the night's tumultuous events. She'd told me in her shop that Death would come for me again, and he had. She'd told me I risked all by sleeping beneath the eagle's wings, and she'd been right. She'd stood before the playroom tent, warning of darkness, flames, and a hate-filled heart seeking to destroy, and in no time at all, I'd encountered the darkness of the mine shaft, the flames on the mountainside, and a man so filled with hatred that he was willing to kill innocent women and children in his insane bid for revenge.

What would Amanda do when she discovered she'd been right from start to finish? I wondered. As we walked up Stafford Avenue toward Caroline's Cafe, I shuddered to think of Amanda Barrow camping out on the Aerie's doorstep, babbling nonstop about the great beyond, and hoped with all my heart that I'd be back in England long before she realized how truly gifted she was.

Carrie Vyne was in the cafe, preparing food and drink for the swarm of firefighters who would soon descend on Bluebird. She welcomed us with open arms, took us to the vacant guest cabin, put sheets and blankets on the beds, lit a fire in the living-room fireplace, and brought sandwiches and a thermos of hot chocolate out to us from the cafe.

Carrie also brought bandages, antibiotic ointment, and arnica cream for Annelise's feet. My intrepid nanny hadn't bothered to don bedroom slippers when my frantic call to action had startled her from sleep. She'd been so intent on saving my sons' lives that she'd run all the way from the Aerie to Bluebird *barefoot.* I wanted to pin a great big shiny medal on her nightgown, but since medals were in short supply, I simply tended to her cuts and bruises and helped her hobble to her bed.

"You're a bona fide heroine," I said as I smoothed her blankets.

"It's all in a day's work," she replied, smiling.

I hugged her, turned out the light, and

joined the boys and Toby, who'd gathered around the fireplace to drink hot chocolate. Despite the fact that they had bunk beds in their bedroom, Rob and Will fell asleep curled up in blankets on the floor while Toby and I watched a seemingly endless stream of emergency vehicles speed through the streets of Bluebird.

"I have to go back to the Aerie," I said quietly, after the boys had fallen asleep. "Tonight."

"The road will be blocked off," Toby warned.

"I don't need to take the road," I said. "Will you stay here with the twins?"

"I'll keep an eye on them," he promised. "I hadn't planned on getting any sleep tonight anyway."

It took me less than an hour to hike to the Aerie, tuck a few necessary and two irreplaceable items into my carry-on bag, and return to the guest cabin. Toby was still awake when I got back, so I put the carry-on bag in my bedroom and sat up with him through the night. We didn't say much, though he did compliment me on my record-breaking uphill dash.

"You carried Will in your arms all the way to the edge of the clearing, too," he reminded me. "You were too weak to lift him out of the van a week ago."

"It's amazing what you can do when your children are in danger," I told him. "You'll find out one day, when you're a father. You'll give your life for your kids, one way or another."

I touched a hand to the scar on my shoulder, then turned to watch the burning mountain.

EPILOGUE

It took three days to put the fire out. By then it had burned a hundred acres, turning majestic trees into charred matchsticks, but thanks to the firefighters' skill and the recent heavy rain, it spread no farther and the Aerie was untouched. We moved back the day before Bill arrived, and although he could stay for only a week, the rest of us stayed there until the end of August, when Toby returned to college.

When news of the fire reached Danny Auerbach, he came to Bluebird to check on his property. While he was in town, I took him to Caroline's Cafe for lunch and a long talk, at the end of which he decided to have a still longer talk with his wife and daughter, take his beloved tree house off the market, and build a small cabin for James and Janice Blackwell and their child. He also decided to plug the mine entrance Toby and I had used, before his sons discovered it.

The Blackwells — with their healthy baby girl — moved into their cabin two months after Toby left. James resumed his caretaker's duties as if there'd been no interruption, and the Auerbachs are once again staying at the Aerie every chance they get.

Will and Rob spent much of the summer at the Brockman Ranch, though Toby coaxed them away every now and then to hike, fish, and hunt for fossils. When he offered to teach them how to pan for gold, however, I put my foot down. Gold fever was a nasty bug. I didn't want my sons to be bitten by it.

Maggie Flaxton bullied me into selling raffle tickets during Gold Rush Days, but Bill adamantly refused to participate in Nick Altman's beer-tasting contest. He wasn't as impressed as I was by Bluebird's doppelgangers, but he'd learned through hard experience to avoid anything that was both homemade and alcoholic.

I put an end to Amanda Barrow's visits to the Aerie by telling her straight out that I held long conversations every night with a magic book that talked back to me. She accused me of mocking her and never darkened my doorway again.

Dick Major followed in his infamous ancestor's footsteps when he entered a high-security prison for the criminally insane. Once there, he began to call himself Ludo Magerowski and to curse everyone who tried to help him. His house on Lake Street was demolished before the year was out and the rubble it contained was put to good use by the highway department.

Toby and I made one more foray into the Lord Stuart mine shafts that summer. On a hot and sunny day in early August, Toby used his local knowledge and a photocopy of Dick Major's hand-drawn map to help me find the cave-in that had killed Cyril Pennyfeather. I knelt at the spot to fill a plastic bag with handfuls of dust.

I took the dust to the cemetery the next day and sprinkled it on Hannah Lavery's grave. There must have been something of Cyril mixed in with it, because I never heard from him again.

"Do you miss Cyril?" I asked Dimity on our last night at the Aerie.

I do, but I'm not sorry he's gone. He fulfilled his purpose. It was time for him to move on.

"What purpose?" I asked.

I believe that Mr. Pennyfeather remained in the Aerie in order to save more lives, and he tried his best to do so. Do you remember? He warned us that someone had reopened the Lord Stuart Mine. We thought he was refer-

ring to James Blackwell at the time, but he was, in fact, speaking of Dick Major. If we hadn't jumped to the wrong conclusion, we would have heeded Mr. Pennyfeather's warning and thwarted Dick Major's plot.

"I never thought I'd live to see the day when you'd admit that you'd jumped to a conclusion," I said, grinning.

There's a first time for everything. And I am sincerely happy for Mr. Pennyfeather. Having fulfilled his purpose, he has continued his journey and rejoined the woman he loves. He's earned the right to rest in peace.

"Have you ever thought of continuing your own journey, Dimity?" I asked.

You're part of my journey, Lori. I don't mind putting the rest of it on hold. I have all of eternity at my disposal.

"Do you think I'll spend the rest of my life rescuing my children from homicidal maniacs?" I asked wistfully.

I imagine you'll have a few hours to spare for knitting socks and baking cookies. But if a situation arises that requires you to save your children's lives, you will. It's what mothers do. Besides, you've made progress — you came away from your latest feat of derring-do unscathed.

"Annelise didn't," I said. "Her feet are still sore. And Toby nearly broke his hand

367

punching Dick Major, but he enjoyed it so much that I don't think he feels scathed."

Toby Cooper is a remarkable young man.

"I tried to thank him today, Dimity, but I just got all teary-eyed," I said. "He looked as embarrassed as if I'd spit up on his shoes."

I'm sure he was embarrassed because he, too, was choked up. You, Annelise, Will, and Rob have been his family for several months. He'll miss you.

"I've invited him to visit us in England," I said. "We may not have rattlesnakes, dust storms, or snow in July, but we have pretty good thunderstorms. I hope he comes."

As do I. You haven't mentioned your shoulder lately, my dear. Is it still troubling you?

"My shoulder is completely healed," I said. "If the scar wasn't there, you'd never known I'd been shot. I'm happy to report that I have my brain to myself again, too. Abaddon has finally moved out."

On the whole, your visit to America has been most satisfactory.

"No one in Finch will believe it," I said. "When they think of America, they think of vulgarity and violence. To be honest, I did, too, but I don't anymore. With the truly gigantic exception of Dick Major, everyone I've met has been cheerful, helpful, and kind."

Including Maggie Flaxton?

"I may not be Maggie's biggest fan," I said, laughing, "but women like her make the world go round."

They do indeed. Will you miss Bluebird?

"I'll miss the Rocky Mountains," I acknowledged. "I'll miss the blue sky and the crisp air and the snowcapped peaks. I'll miss the wildflowers and the aspens, the mule deer and the buffalo."

But will you miss Bluebird?

I leaned back in the white armchair and gazed into the fire. I thought of gossip and Calico Cookies and scones. I thought of a place rich in history and blessed with great natural beauty. I thought of good people doing their best to keep their small town alive, and as always, my thoughts came around again to Finch. Bill might not see the similarities, Annelise might ignore them, and Aunt Dimity might discount them, but I knew what home felt like when I found it.

"No, I won't miss Bluebird," I said, smiling. "After all, I'm not really leaving it behind."

CARRIE VYNE'S
CALICO COOKIES

Preheat oven to 350 degrees F. Makes about 5 dozen cookies.

Ingredients
- 1 cup (2 sticks) butter
- 1/3 cup white sugar
- 1/3 cup brown sugar
- 2 eggs
- 2 teaspoons vanilla extract
- 1 teaspoon almond extract
- 1 1/2 cups all-purpose flour
- 1 teaspoon baking soda
- 1 teaspoon cinnamon
- 1/2 teaspoon ginger
- pinch of salt
- 2 1/2 cups oatmeal
- 1/2 cup each: chocolate chips, dried cranberries, sliced almonds, toffee bits.

May also use raisins, butterscotch morsels, peanut butter pieces, or white chocolate chips.

Mix and match to your heart's content!

Cream butter with sugars. Add eggs, vanilla, and almond extracts. Beat well. Add flour mixed with baking soda, cinnamon, ginger, and salt. Fold in oatmeal and beat well. Fold in the nuts, chips, and bits; mix well. Place teaspoon-sized rounds of dough on foil-lined cookie sheets. Bake 7–8 minutes. Freezes well.

ABOUT THE AUTHOR

Nancy Atherton is the author of eleven previous Aunt Dimity mysteries. The first, *Aunt Dimity's Death,* was voted "one of the century's 100 favorite mysteries" by the Independent Mystery Booksellers Association. She lives in Colorado Springs, Colorado.

We hope you have enjoyed this Large Print book. Other Thorndike, Wheeler, and Chivers Press Large Print books are available at your library or directly from the publishers.

For information about current and upcoming titles, please call or write, without obligation, to:

Publisher
Thorndike Press
295 Kennedy Memorial Drive
Waterville, ME 04901
Tel. (800) 223-1244

or visit our Web site at:

www.gale.com/thorndike
www.gale.com/wheeler

OR

Chivers Large Print
published by BBC Audiobooks Ltd
St James House, The Square
Lower Bristol Road
Bath BA2 3SB
England
Tel. +44(0) 800 136919
email: bbcaudiobooks@bbc.co.uk
www.bbcaudiobooks.co.uk

All our Large Print titles are designed for easy reading, and all our books are made to last.

SLEEP
BABY
SLEEP

Also by David Hewson

The Killing trilogy
The Killing
The Killing II
The Killing III

Nic Costa series
A Season for the Dead
The Villa of Mysteries
The Sacred Cut
The Lizard's Bite
The Seventh Sacrament
The Garden of Evil
Dante's Numbers
The Blue Demon
The Fallen Angel
Carnival for the Dead

Amsterdam Detective series
The House of Dolls
The Wrong Girl
Little Sister

Other titles
The Promised Land
The Cemetery of Secrets
(previously published as *Lucifer's Shadow*)
Death in Seville
(previously published as *Semana Santa*)

DAVID HEWSON

SLEEP BABY SLEEP

MACMILLAN

First published 2017 by Macmillan
an imprint of Pan Macmillan
20 New Wharf Road, London N1 9RR
Associated companies throughout the world
www.panmacmillan.com

ISBN 978-1-4472-9343-9

3 5 7 9 8 6 4 2

A CIP catalogue record for this book is available from the British Library.

Printed and bound by CPI Group (UK) Ltd, Croydon, CR0 4YY

Visit **www.panmacmillan.com** to read more about all our books
and to buy them. You will also find features, author interviews and
news of any author events, and you can sign up for e-newsletters
so that you're always first to hear about our new releases.

To Rienk Tychon, my Dutch editor,
without whose guidance, support and local knowledge
Pieter Vos could never have been brought to life.
Hartelijk dank.

SLEEP
BABY
SLEEP

ONE

The note was waiting for him, pinned to the door of the houseboat, when he came home that Wednesday night.

> You're a clumsy man, Vos.
> You miss things.

Two lines out of a printer, the page folded over then stuck to the rotting wooden frame with a drawing pin. Sometimes it seemed most of Amsterdam knew a solitary police brigadier lived in the run-down black-painted barge by the Berenstraat bridge. Sometimes that meant the odd act of vandalism. More often people knocking on his door asking for help. Or, worse, following him into the Drie Vaten bar across the road and trying to bend his ear when all he wanted was some peace and quiet away from the occasional tumult of the job.

'These things happen, Sam,' he told the white and tan fox terrier seated patiently on the grubby planks, watching him with keen, bright eyes. The dog didn't disagree.

Just after eight. Night was falling over the quiet stretch of the Prinsengracht where Vos lived. He'd slunk out of the medal ceremony at the police headquarters in Marnixstraat at the top of the street, tired, hungry, eager for a beer. Jillian Chandra, the new station commissaris, a stern woman recently arrived from national headquarters in Zoetermeer, hadn't much appreciated having a dog in the station garden for the presentation.

Vos wasn't sure Chandra appreciated much about him either, his attitude, his scruffy clothes, the long dark hair in need of a barber, something Vos was aware of and would get round to soon. But the event was to hand out long-service medals to a number of officers, among them Dirk Van der Berg, one of Vos's oldest colleagues, a firm friend of Sam's. The terrier had to be there.

Commissaris Chandra, faced with a curious message like this, would doubtless have reached for some disposable gloves and popped it into a plastic evidence bag just in case. She was a manager, not a front-line officer. Straight from the bureaucrat hive in the south where people looked at computer screens more than they did people, she didn't appreciate Amsterdam was different, a mutable, living metropolis where there was always something to catch the eye of the curious. What mattered was choosing your moments then picking at the threads that merited attention.

Two cryptic lines of text didn't. Vos tore the paper from the door, left the pin stuck there to make sure it came nowhere near Sam, then balled up the page and tossed it into the waste bin by the gangplank.

The lights of the Drie Vaten beckoned. It was getting dark. Just one person sitting at the little tables outside, a man in a long coat, fast asleep beneath a wide-brimmed hat.

Beer.

Jillian Chandra didn't approve of alcohol on police premises. They'd been offered coffee and soft drinks instead, and if she'd noticed the look of horror on Van der Berg's face she didn't show it.

'Let's have supper with your friend Sofia tonight, shall we?' Vos said, and the dog was tugging at the end of the lead before he'd finished the sentence.

At the door his heart sank. A sudden sharp bark from inside the brown bar stopped them in their tracks. In an instant Sam was yelping wildly, pulling hard on his lead. Like most of his breed, he was firmly convinced he was more human than animal. Other dogs he usually didn't like. The one that was yapping a desperate falsetto just then, a muscular black and white mongrel belonging to a large and equally vocal widow from a terraced house round the corner, he loathed in particular, as the mutt hated him.

With Vos struggling to hold Sam back, the pair set up a to-and-fro cacophony of angry, explosive barks. Four customers at the counter covered their ears, the widow among them, fixing Vos with a furious stare that said: *We were here first.*

True, he thought. He was still hungry and in need of female company. The rippled reflection of a three-quarter moon was already visible in the still black waters of the Prinsengracht by the gentle humpback bridge. But it wasn't cold and Sofia had Leon, her second-in-command, helping out behind the counter. He could get some beer, some bread, liver sausage and cheese, then the two of them would sit outside with Sam for a while, enjoying the evening.

'Can I help?' asked a voice by the door as Vos hesitated there. 'I'm good with animals.'

It was the man in the long coat. The broad hat was still over his face but he was awake enough and didn't sound drunk or stoned. His hand was raised, ready to take the lead.

Sam looked at him and to Vos's amazement stopped barking.

'Thanks. Won't be a moment.'

The stranger put out a long arm and led Sam beneath the table. Vos walked in, ordered a beer, some food, then tried to catch Sofia's attention. It wasn't easy. There was a big party at the back. He hadn't seen them from the door, or realized how busy the Drie Vaten was at that moment.

She came with the drinks and the liver sausage he'd ordered.

'We could sit outside if you like . . .' he began.

Sofia Albers was thirty-five. She'd rented the bar a few years earlier, just before he moved into the ramshackle boat outside the door. A brief marriage lay somewhere in the past, and a few boyfriends along the way. The Jordaan was her home and always had been. It was second nature to be generous to the motley band of customers who wandered through the Drie Vaten's worn wooden interior, young and old, rich and poor, decent and occasionally crooked. With a cheerful, inquisitive face, sun-tanned all year round and framed by a head of straight dark hair, she attracted plenty of admirers too, none of whom seemed to stay long.

The widow's dog started up again. Sofia shot it a savage glance. Sam was as much hers now, given how often she looked after him when Vos was working.

'Can't, Pieter,' she said briskly. 'Too busy.'

The mongrel stopped barking as suddenly as it had started.

'Can't Leon . . . ?'

'Another night.' She winced and he knew he wouldn't press her. 'Oh . . . one of your colleagues came down from Marnixstraat half an hour ago. He was trying to find you. His name was . . .'

She riffled through a set of scribbled notes next to the beer pumps.

'Ruud Jonker . . .'

'A police officer? I don't recall anyone called that. What did he look like?'

Still, he knew the name from somewhere.

'I didn't really notice. He had police ID. Hasn't he phoned?'

'No.'

A pair of British tourists interrupted, pushing their way to the bar, demanding a couple of beers then asking if she minded them smoking dope. They always put an imaginary joint to their lips with that question. Vos had seen it so often and still didn't understand why.

Sofia poured two Heinekens and told them to take it outside. There was a guilty look on her face at that moment, as if she'd realized she'd made a mistake.

'I'm sorry. He showed me a card and said he needed to talk to you. He'd lost your phone number.' She tugged at a lock of brown hair. 'I think it was a police ID. It had a photograph on it. I was trying to serve someone.'

'Don't worry . . .'

'But I gave him your number. I shouldn't have done that.' She smiled, nervous. 'Rushed off my feet for once. He sounded like one of yours. Still . . . At least the dogs have quietened down a bit.'

Vos glanced at the mongrel. It was curled up beneath the widow's sturdy legs, seemingly fast asleep. This seemed odd. The arguments never ended so easily.

A sudden flash of guilty panic struck him. He strode out through the Drie Vaten's battered wood and glass doors. The tables were empty apart from the two tourists giggling over weed.

Heart thumping, he walked onto the cobbled street by the boat, stood at the corner of Elandsgracht and Prinsengracht, close to the bridge, calling the terrier's name.

No answer.

No sign of a man in an overcoat and hat.

No Sam.

Something trembled against his chest. Then the trill of the phone reached him.

A new text there, from a number he didn't recognize.

Like I said, Vos. You miss things.

He dialled back straight away and got voicemail.

The phone trembled and sounded again. The second message was nothing more than a cryptic set of numbers.

52.366258, 4.896299.

The man put the phone on the passenger seat and pulled out into the night traffic on Marnixstraat, trams and buses, the bustle of the city.

The dog was a gift he hadn't expected. It had scraped its claws against the black Prinsengracht cobbles as he dragged it to the van, not barking, too proud and grumpily puzzled for that.

He'd meant what he said. He was good with animals. It was just people that got to him.

A red light came up on the way to Leidseplein so he checked his watch. Eight twenty-seven. It was important to manage every second. This was a kind of game after all. Hide and seek. Catch me if you can. Ninety minutes or less from hooking his quarry outside his houseboat on the Prinsengracht to the end of the first act.

He drove with the window down. The late September evening was unusually hot, close to cloying. The long coat lay on the passenger seat, a hat beside it.

An odour rose from the back, one he didn't much like.

Not a dog smell either.

Laura Bakker was still at the reception when Vos called, listening to the last of the speeches, the sound of the event coming down the crackly line like the buzz of surly bees. Late twenties, a tall and striking young woman with long red hair, an unusual taste in clothes and a loud, sometimes confrontational voice, she worked as a detective in Vos's team.

'You might have waited till the end . . .' she scolded him. Bakker had dressed for the occasion: a black flared trouser suit and white shirt. Conservative for her. 'Commissaris Chandra expected that.'

'I didn't know half those people. Why should I?' He looked up and down the Prinsengracht again. 'I think someone's stolen Sam.'

'Oh my God. Why?'

A ridiculous question in the circumstances. Not that he was going to say it. Vos forwarded her the mysterious text.

'Someone came into the Drie Vaten to get my phone number. Sofia barely saw who he was. He walked off with Sam and sent this message. It means nothing to me.'

He could hear Jillian Chandra's booming voice diminish as Bakker walked away from the ceremony. Then a beep as his text turned up.

'Numbers,' she said.

'I know that. But—'

'I'm thinking.'

There was a short pause then she said, 'Looks like decimal degrees.'

'What?'

'They use them for computer maps. Instead of latitude and longitude. You know what a map app is?'

'I suppose . . .'

He barely used the phone for anything but messages and calls. Why would he need a map? Amsterdam was where he'd lived and worked all his life. He knew just about every street and alley and canal.

'It's for a place. You put those numbers into the app and it takes you there.'

'I don't know how.'

He could hear her breathing, picture her nimble fingers tapping at the phone.

'Doesn't matter. I've got it. Rembrandtplein. The tram stop going west. If you . . .'

A dog barked. The mongrel was at the door of the Drie Vaten, staring out into the dark, looking for something to yap at.

'I'm on my way,' Bakker said as Vos looked to hail a cab.

The Albert Cuyp market had been Bert Schrijver's life for as long as he could remember. At the age of eight he'd started working for his father, shifting boxes of flowers and bulbs around the warehouse on Govert Flinckstraat, selling what they could through the stall one block away. The building ran all the way from Flinckstraat to the market, a sprawling terraced mansion in its day with a courtyard, storerooms, apartments, a shopfront and a flourishing wholesale trade. The 'castle', the family called it, home to the Schrijvers for more than sixty years since his grandfather started the business just after the war. Not that the old man would recognize the area now.

While Flinckstraat stayed quiet and allowed his solitary van to make the delivery rounds, the Albert Cuyp filled each morning, with tourists mostly, meandering around the stalls looking for cheap clothes, home-made cookies and pastries, all kinds of cheese, all manner of fish, fresh and cooked to order. Fancy restaurants offering expensive burgers and exotic food were springing up everywhere, along with cafes that sold kinds of coffee Bert Schrijver didn't even recognize. The quarter was coming to be occupied by a new, international crowd who'd decided De Pijp was the next corner of Amsterdam to patronize, to fill with trendy cocktail bars and organic bistros and pizzerias, to pillage for housing until the prices for working-class locals went through the roof.

Flowers they bought too, but not as many as before, nor were the commercial customers as easy to find as they used to be. Since the divorce Schrijver's meagre income had been stretched close to breaking point. As usual of an evening he was totting up a long day's paltry takings surrounded by the heady scent of tulips, lilies and roses, many of them wilting, unsold and unsaleable around him.

On his deathbed his father had delivered a damning verdict on his son: he was good at giving people what they wanted. The trouble was, as any born retailer understood, most of the time Joe Public simply stood there scratching its head, never knowing what it was looking for.

His son could haul around crates of blooms and bulbs all day long with his strong and tireless arms. But he could never spot that moment of hesitation in a customer's eyes then dash to fill it: buy this, try that. So they walked on, to settle for a crummy T-shirt from the foreigner down the way or throw silly money across the counter for a bag of cookies twice the price of the baker's round the corner.

As their income fell, Schrijver had been forced to butcher the castle piece by piece, sold off like a precious carcass over the years. When Schrijver was young they'd owned everything, all five floors on both sides, Flinckstraat and Albert Cuyp, top to bottom. The attics had gone a decade before. Now the upper floors were private apartments, most not even occupied by their owners at all but rented out, often by the day to tourists.

After the divorce he'd been forced to sell the family flat where three generations had grown up, then move a single bed into the ground-floor office. His daughter, Annie, the flower girl as all the locals called her, had the larger, smarter studio at the front across the small, dark courtyard. And still he teetered on the verge of bankruptcy each month, fending off creditors, begging early payment from the many who owed him.

That constant air of uncertainty affected his daughter. She craved escape from the grim, cramped warehouse where they lived cheek-by-jowl. Even if it was just for a night or two with a friend somewhere or on the couch at her mother's housing association apartment facing the open green space of Sarphatipark.

Bert Schrijver was forty-six, Annie twenty four years younger. He didn't mix much with the other market men any more. Couldn't afford the bar bills. And he missed her whenever she vanished. There was nothing left then except the accusatory bookkeeping, the dying flowers, the cloying scent of failure. He was typing the last line of the day's takings into their ancient laptop when the doorbell went. Schrijver was up in an instant. Sometimes she forgot her spare set of keys and had to be let in.

But it was Nina, her mother, who stood there clutching a cheap black jacket around her, looking the way she always did when she was forced to see him: miserable and disappointed. She was still the woman he'd fallen for as a teenager when she was selling *kibbeling*, raw herring and fried mussels on one of the market stalls. He'd long ago given up any hope she'd take him back.

9

'I can't find Annie,' she said, not looking at him. 'Haven't seen her since Monday.'

He tried to clear his head of numbers and the constant battle to juggle dates for paying bills.

'Come in.'

She peered round him into the dark interior, past the buckets of drooping flowers.

'I don't need to come in.'

'She said . . .' He was a slow man and knew it. 'She told me she was staying round your place last night. Today's her day off anyway. I thought maybe the two of you had gone shopping. Had to do the deliveries myself before I opened the stall. Jordi called in sick.'

Nina scowled at the mention of Schrijver's old bar mate, the only part-time help he could afford.

'Jordi Hoogland. I can't believe you're still throwing money at that bum.'

'Not much. Less than anyone else would take. Annie said she was at your—'

'She wasn't staying with me last night. How many times do I have to say it?'

The look he knew. It said: *You're being stupid again.*

'That's what she told me.'

'I've been calling her all afternoon.'

The phone came out of her pocket. She dialled. A cheery young voice came out of the tinny speaker and said, 'Hi, it's me. Just leave a message for the flower girl. She'll get back to you real quick.'

Schrijver got a familiar cold feeling in his stomach.

'She's not been hanging round with that bastard Sanders again, has she?'

Nina glared at him.

'Right. Blame Rob. She's twenty-two. Not your little girl any more. You've got to stop hating any man she—'

'He was bad for her.'

'And what do you know about that?'

Her voice had grown loud and high and shrill.

'I know Rob Sanders made her miserable.'

He brought this anger out in her. It was a talent he'd never wanted.

'I can't find her, Bert. I haven't seen her for two days. *Two days.*'

He had to think.

'She was here when I went out yesterday. When she said she was going to your place. Gone when I got back. Just Jordi round then.'

Nina stood by the green warehouse door. Schrijver went inside and found his jacket, wallet, phone and keys. When he returned she had her phone out again.

'I'm calling the police.'

'Do that.'

'Where are you going? Don't you want to be here?'

There were so many bars the young frequented in De Pijp. Annie knew every one of them, and plenty beyond too, in the Jordaan, the centre.

He'd start in the nearby places, the tavern in the square down the road, the beer cafe along the way, then, if he got nowhere, the streets around the park. Someone had to know. She was the flower girl of the Albert Cuyp.

'I'll find her.'

'Don't you go near Rob. I talked to him already. He's not seen her in days. They finished. Remember?'

Schrijver scowled at her and dragged on his jacket.

'And he always tells the truth, doesn't he?'

Then he slid the green door shut, put on the padlock, and looked up and down the half-deserted market street. Trash and scavenging birds. A bunch of young out for the night, happy, as if the Albert Cuyp belonged to them. This had been his world once.

Local families, growing up together. A sense this was a place people shared and cared for, a village that just happened to be set on the edge of the city. It was a community still, he thought. Just not his.

Rembrandtplein looked much as it did most summer evenings. Full of tourists brimming with drink or woozy from weed. The air was heavy with the smell of dope, the square littered with spent frites cones and beer cans. Vos's cab couldn't get close because of the crowds so he got out at the perimeter and headed for the westbound stop. Where the road gave way to pedestrians Laura Bakker was walking down the metal tram rails in the street, a tall figure, red hair loose down her back.

They reached the glass and metal shelter almost together, Bakker scanning the interior, looking for a piece of paper the moment she turned up.

Ruud Jonker.

The name kept nagging him.

'Pieter? How did it happen?'

'Outside the Drie Vaten. I asked someone to hold his lead. Went in to get a beer. Wasn't thinking. Next thing . . .'

There was a loud blast of rock from a band in one of the bars. A bunch of young men were stripping off their shirts and beating their bare chests.

'Maybe it's a horrible joke. They're just trying to scare you.'

'Some joke.'

There was no obvious piece of paper stuck inside or outside the tram stop.

'Does the name Ruud Jonker mean anything?' he asked. 'Is there someone called that in Marnixstraat?'

'Not that I know.'

An ambulance cruised along the pedestrianized square, headed for a bunch of men in the corner. A drunk was rolling round, throwing up violently amidst the trash on the ground. His mates seemed to think it was funny. Then a marked police car followed. She watched it and said, 'Stealing a dog's a crime. We could call in . . .'

He just looked at her.

'I'll do it,' she promised. 'If you won't.'

Vos didn't answer. He was staring at the advert next to the route map and timetable inside the stop. It was for a brand of jeans he'd never heard of before. One called 'Ruud'.

A handsome kid in too-tight denims stood in front of a boat in a harbour on a perfect sunny day in Spain or somewhere. He grinned with perfect white teeth and thrust out his muscled, tanned chest.

The only word printed there was the brand name. But beneath it someone had scrawled in thick black felt tip, 'Jonker'.

Then, in a balloon coming out of his mouth, 'Remember me, Pieter? If you don't, you will.'

In smaller letters below . . . 52.366466, 4.917661.

'There,' Vos said, pointing at the numbers.

Bakker yanked out her phone and started stabbing at the keys.

'Who the hell is he?' Bakker asked as she began to tap in the numbers.

Someone little, he thought. Someone he'd forgotten about altogether. Investigations were like that. The only live ones were the cases in front of you. The past was past. Dead and meant to stay that way.

'I think he was supposed to be a monster,' Vos murmured. 'Not that I ever really knew.'

He was grateful she wasn't listening.

'There,' Bakker said and presented him with the phone.

The place was close to the Artis zoo in Plantage. Vos liked trams. He used them all the time and knew every line in the city. Two services running through Rembrandtplein went close to there, the nine and the fourteen.

'Thanks.'

Bakker's fists went straight to her hips. He got what he now thought of as the trademark glare.

'What the hell is this about?'

There was the clang of a bell. A number nine rounded the corner.

'Me, I think,' Vos said, watching the blue and white carriage approach. 'Go back to Marnixstraat. Tell the night team I may call.'

She held out her phone.

'From the zoo?'

The tram came to a noisy halt in front of them. The doors opened with a familiar hiss and a gaggle of girls in short skirts and skimpy tees stumbled onto the Rembrandtplein cobbles.

'I very much doubt that,' he said and stepped inside.

The reception in the Marnixstraat garden was drawing to a close. Vos had slid out without anyone spotting. Bakker seemed to have copied the same trick, there one moment, gone the next. Dirk Van der Berg envied them both. But Commissaris Chandra had told him to hang around until the end so he did, clutching a plastic cup of cold coffee, nibbling at soft, stale biscuits and bad sandwiches.

Twenty-five years he'd spent in the police. A tall, heavy, worn man with a melancholic grey and pockmarked face, he had the paunch, the scars, the inner and outer wounds to prove it. All of them told him: getting ordered to wait behind like this wasn't good.

The new commissaris didn't look much like anyone else in Amsterdam police headquarters. Just turned forty, always smartly dressed, she had the sturdy build of an athlete and wore a permanently unconvincing smile. Her father came from Jakarta and had worked as a cook in an Indonesian restaurant. Her mother was

Rotterdam born and bred, a civilian executive in Zoetermeer police headquarters for a while, though Chandra was quick to emphasize this was not how she came to enter the service.

She was, as far as anyone knew, not so much unattached as aloof from everyone around her. When she wasn't working she seemed to spend most of her free hours in the gym, a habit she recommended at every possible occasion. Van der Berg had joked once that his fitness regime largely consisted of cycling to any of a number of the preferred bars he knew in the city. Her smile had remained frozen throughout but he'd got the message.

A single woman with few friends in Amsterdam would usually have attracted some sympathy. People might have tried to show her around, invite the new boss for dinner, offer to introduce her to a few places outsiders rarely saw. But no one had yet plucked up the courage or the enthusiasm. Jillian Chandra came across as polite, intelligent, and deeply committed to the job. She wrote morale-building memos that included every buzzword of modern policing. Eight weeks into her posting, she still seemed a stranger to most around her.

'So . . .' she said in her low southern voice after she guided him to the edge of the dwindling crowd.

Van der Berg tried to stop himself staring at her immaculate uniform with its too-shiny buttons.

'So?'

'Twenty-five years. If you had it all again what would you do differently?'

'Nothing.'

She laughed and wasn't amused.

'Surely . . .'

'Not a thing. I've made some mistakes. Who hasn't? But I've got a good wife. A nice home. Colleagues who happen to be friends. No complaints.'

Her green eyes flickered at that last.

'Vos,' she said, and nothing more.

'Among them.'

'I suppose I should be grateful to him. Vos is why I'm here, isn't he?'

Not exactly, Van der Berg thought.

'If there's anything I can do to help, Commissaris. This isn't Zoetermeer.'

'Same country.'

'Different place. Amsterdam's not black and white. It can turn prickly if you think that.'

She had a pleasant face, broad, with high, full cheeks, flawless olive skin, shrewd and interested eyes. He found it hard to work out how much sincerity was there but then you didn't step onto the management up escalator by being too open with your feelings.

'Vos was out of the service altogether for a while,' Chandra said. 'For more than two years. He'd still be in that grubby houseboat of his, smoking himself stupid, if it weren't for Frank de Groot. And how did he repay that?'

He'd half-expected this. Chandra's predecessor was still at home waiting to hear whether he'd face a criminal trial for covering up evidence in a sex scandal in Volendam. The grapevine said he'd get away with a caution and the loss of a big chunk of his pension. People were pulling strings, but a long and largely praiseworthy police career was over in disgrace.

'You can't blame anyone but Frank for that. Besides . . .' He so wished he was in the Drie Vaten clutching a decent glass of *tripel*, not a half-full plastic cup of weak coffee. 'What were we supposed to do? Turn a blind eye?'

'No blind eyes on my watch. If this place was being run properly De Groot would never have tried a stunt like that. It's a sign of laxity. Carelessness. Insufficient discipline. No rigour. From now on we do things by the book.'

'Which book is that, Commissaris?'

She smiled more broadly, pleased by the question.

'Mine, of course. All this time and you're still at the foot of the ladder.'

He nodded.

'Suits me. I like going out onto the street. Meeting people. Looking them in the eye. All this . . .' He glanced at the building behind them, the windows dotted with computer screens everywhere. 'It's important. But if people don't see us out there . . . you run a risk.'

The smile diminished.

'What risk?'

'The risk they forget we exist.'

Jillian Chandra thought for a second and said, 'Good point. But the book . . .'

'Your book, you mean?'

'It's what matters. I don't think Vos appreciates that. He seems to feel he can carry on the way he did with De Groot. Doing whatever he wants and informing me of it afterwards. Turning up dressed like a bum. That damned dog with him.'

Sam she'd tolerated in the office for a while until an unfortunate incident with a waiting-room sofa. Now he was banned and Vos forever on the end of sly comments about his scruffy jackets, the jeans, the unruly hair.

'Pieter's focused on what counts. Not the small things.'

'I'd never have handed him his job back the way De Groot did. You walk out of these doors and that's it. No second chances.'

This he believed to be true.

'In that case we would have been deprived of one of the smartest men I've ever worked with.' He glanced at her uniform and didn't care whether she noticed or not. 'Perhaps not Zoetermeer smart. But Amsterdam smart. Which we still need, whatever the people down south may feel.'

'Loyalty.' Her hand came out to his arm. 'A fine quality. Admirable. But only a fool wants to go down with the ship.'

She came close and whispered in his ear.

'We both know you're no fool.'

'At the risk of repeating myself, he's the best officer—'

'All the more reason for him to follow the book. All the more reason for you to tell me when he doesn't. One way or another he will toe the line. Or I'll have him back in that barge of his, staring at the walls, smoking weed. Have no doubts.'

He didn't. That had been coming all along.

'Good.' One last squeeze of his arm. 'I'm glad we understand one another. Now you can go.'

The van crossed the river by the ugly brown block of the Heineken brewery, kept to the busy road then, after a little way, bore right into De Pijp. He cruised slowly past the long straight street that, during the day, was given over to the Albert Cuyp market. The rubbish trucks had done their best. Most of the day's trash was gone. A couple of workmen were hosing down the asphalt, watched by a pack of hungry herons, stiff and straight as soldiers, wondering if there were any scraps left in the waste from the fish stalls.

Briefly the scent of flowers came to him: lilies and roses. Perhaps it was that odd perfume that summoned a sad, pathetic whine from behind. The van had no back windows and a cage-like mesh separating the front seats from the rear. It was important no one outside saw, and no one inside could move.

'This isn't about you,' the man muttered. 'You are . . .'

The word briefly eluded him.

'An innocent.'

Though innocents died too.

He'd never been quite clear how he could get Vos on the hook that night. Perhaps through the cruel bastard called fate. Or luck. Or coincidence. The note on the houseboat door was meant to be a start. After that a call. Another tantalizing breadcrumb, a message left at the bar, a place everyone knew the man frequented most nights.

Then opportunity had presented itself. Vos had handed him the dog's lead. Decision made.

In the back the little animal whimpered again.

He bore left and found the river. It was a circuitous route but a pleasant one.

The dog let out a low crooning yowl.

In a while the road called Amsteldijk would turn into a modest cobbled lane, not much more than a track beside the still, deep waters of the river that gave the city its name. There were places he could stop and leave the terrier. He could knock on the door of any number of houseboats, tether the lead to the railing and then flee.

But that meant risk, all for the well-being of a creature too simple to understand anything of what was at stake.

As the dog's claws scuttled round the bare metal floor the man thought of what lay by the animal's side. Bare flesh, warm and cold, and blood. He hadn't expected he'd be putting something else in there.

'Keep those sharp fangs to yourself,' he ordered and wondered why. It was a dumb creature and surely couldn't understand his words.

Something did though.

There was another sound from the back, a shuffling, mumbling moan.

'What's there's mine. No one else's,' he said, to whom he didn't know.

Trying not to worry about the conversation with Chandra, Van der Berg wandered down Elandsgracht to the Drie Vaten. The bar was heaving with some kind of party, people he'd never seen in his life. Sofia Albers was too busy to talk. Vos's houseboat was empty, all the lights off, which was odd.

For a moment Van der Berg thought of calling him and got far enough to take out his phone. He didn't like Jillian Chandra one bit, but then bosses of her ilk weren't there to be liked. Their purpose in life was to manage, to control, to be seen to be in charge. Not investigate or put themselves in the way of harm. Commissaris Chandra simply wanted to shepherd the men and women beneath her into the paddocks and enclosures the distant bureaucrats of Zoetermeer demanded then turn around to her own bosses with a triumphant flourish and say: *Look, job done.*

Vos was intelligent enough to know all this for himself. So Van der Berg stashed his phone, fought his way to the bar, got a beer out of a harassed Leon and found a rickety spare seat out by the pavement.

Drinking by yourself wasn't such fun. He avoided it normally, but not now because tonight, as summer gave way to autumn with one last burst of sweaty metropolitan heat, the city felt odd. It must have been Chandra's thinly disguised threats that affected his mood. There could be no other reason.

Van der Berg shifted his big legs beneath the table and his right foot found something soft. He reached down and picked it up.

A man's suede bush hat – Australian, he saw from the label inside the brim. The kind of thing a tourist wore he guessed, glancing back at the busy bar.

There were two British men smoking themselves stupid a couple of tables away, taking no notice at all. This was a fine hat in search of an owner.

Van der Berg tried it on and found the thing a decent fit.

Finders keepers, he thought, placing it back on the table. If someone came to claim it, fine. If not . . .

———

It took the tram four minutes to cross the Amstel, wind its way into the quiet residential quarter of Plantage, then work down the broad road by the side of Artis, the sprawling zoo that occupied much of the central area.

The coordinates were for what looked like a building site next to the public car park. Vos vaguely remembered there'd been construction going on hereabouts for some time. By the gates stood a couple of diggers and a small crane parked next to a set of corrugated iron hoardings and a large sign that spoke of a new apartment complex coming the following year.

The fencing was down at the front, revealing what must have been a yard for the builders, an expanse of concrete surrounded by low workers' cabins. A party was going on outside them, one of the improvised and illegal events the city had to deal with from time to time. Rarely with great success. They came and went like mayflies and it was never easy to pin down an organizer to take to court.

The long-established institution officially known as Natura Artis Magistra was as much a scientific body as a zoo for the curiosity and amusement of the public. It was obvious from the moment Vos pushed his way into the heaving midst ahead of him the event was designed to mirror the location.

He couldn't begin to guess how many people were there, chatting, drinking, eating, dancing to the deafening music coming out of a makeshift DJ desk set up on trestle tables in front of a cabin marked 'Manager's Office'. Every last one of them was in costume, with masks or faces painted for the occasion. Lions and zebras, giraffes, monkeys and apes, bizarre parrots, some beasts he couldn't begin to name.

The disguises made them anonymous in the hot and noisy night. Somewhere close by he heard a real animal noise. The squawk of a primate maybe, or a bird alarmed by the racket.

There was no stray piece of paper here, no message on a wall.

Vos knew he wasn't searching for anyone now. Someone surely had to be looking for him.

Laura Bakker sat in the office, face up to a computer screen. Rijnders was running the night team, bemused as to what he was supposed to do. Van der Berg she'd recalled to Marnixstraat just as he was ordering a second beer in the Drie Vaten.

Both men had listened to her odd tale about Vos and the missing dog.

'He loves that little animal more than anything,' Rijnders observed. Bakker waited for more: it didn't come.

Jillian Chandra stuck her head through the door and called out a cheery goodnight. She'd changed out of her uniform and was wearing a shiny chocolate shirt and jeans. A pair of long and lurid green earrings glittered in the office lights. She beamed at Bakker and Van der Berg and asked, 'Overtime?'

'No,' Van der Berg replied instantly, shuffling his new-found hat beneath the desk so she couldn't see. 'Just checking the holiday schedules. We're trying to juggle them between us.'

'You came to work to think about avoiding it,' she said with that constant smile. And then she left.

'I think the commissaris has a date,' Rijnders suggested. 'She looked quite . . . human.'

'Lucky date,' Bakker grumbled. 'Does she have to let us know she's got her beady eyes on us every minute of the day?'

'Boss class,' the night man pointed out. 'It's what they do.'

'It's all they do,' Van der Berg added. 'Do you like my new hat?'

He popped it on. Bakker told him he looked ridiculous.

'Back to Sam . . .' she said.

Rijnders didn't like any of this.

'If Pieter hasn't asked for help why are we trying to force it on him? We do have things to do, you know.'

'Much?' Van der Berg asked.

The night man frowned.

'Couple of muggings. Young woman missing in De Pijp. Probably late back from a party. Locals are taking a look. Not much if I'm honest. What's the problem?'

Her fingers rattled the computer keyboard.

'Ruud Jonker. The name seemed to ring a bell . . .'

Rijnders was known for his prodigious memory. Men and women, victims, witnesses and perpetrators, passed through Marnixstraat in their hundreds each year. Without good reason most officers would be hard-pressed to recall the name of some-one they'd dealt with a month before. A face perhaps. Not him.

'Ruud Jonker? Dead and gone.'

They waited for more.

'Got to be three, four years ago. Really nasty one. Started with some date rape cases. Some women died.' He nudged Van der Berg's elbow. The hat was off now, tucked in a drawer. 'Come on, Dirk. You remember. Those clubs. And the creepiest part—'

Van der Berg shook his head.

'That idiot in the press called them the Sleeping Beauty mur-ders,' Rijnders added. 'Remember now?'

There was a look of horror on Van der Berg's face.

'No, no. That was that sick bastard Vincent de Graaf. It was all done and dusted. Vos put him away. Three dead girls I think, that we knew about anyway. He never said sorry or anything. It was—'

'And the other bit?' Rijnders asked.

Van der Berg shuddered but before he could say anything Bakker started tapping the screen. The case files were there. Summer, four years ago. There was a spate of date rape com-plaints. Women claiming they'd been drugged in clubs and at impromptu illegal parties then woke up the next morning with-out a clue what had happened to them. Then three women fished out of the river, naked, stabbed to death, traces of a sedative in their bloodstreams.

The men read the screen over her shoulder.

'It was Vincent de Graaf . . .' Van der Berg repeated. 'He went down for murder. I don't recall anyone else—'

'Vos ran the case,' Bakker interrupted. 'These are his notes. He wasn't convinced De Graaf acted on his own. He wanted . . .'

'I was there,' Rijnders cried. 'The day it happened. We'd nailed De Graaf but he was a slippery bastard. One of those guys convinced of his own genius and not so good at convincing anyone else. No one believed a word he said. We got him through a mate he had living in De Pijp. Ruud Jonker. Ran a tattoo parlour in the Albert Cuyp. He was on CCTV in a club in Warmoesstraat the night one of the girls got taken. She was talking to De Graaf. Jonker was with him. Vincent we grabbed straight off. By the time we found out where Jonker was . . .'

Bakker had got there already. All the photos from the scene. A body hanging from a beam in a curious room. There was an old-fashioned barber's chair in the centre and walls covered with patterns for tattoos: death's heads, screaming skulls, fierce animals, butterflies.

'That's Ruud Jonker,' Rijnders said. 'Dead as dead gets. No tears shed for that one.'

'Someone used that name to get Vos's phone number out of the Drie Vaten. Then stole his dog.' She stabbed the screen. 'This isn't about Sam at all.'

When she called the dance music in the background was so loud she could barely hear him.

'Where the hell are you?'

'By the zoo,' Vos said over the noise.

'Ruud Jonker. We've worked out . . .'

'I know. I remembered.'

'But—'

'But nothing. I don't want you under my feet until I know what I'm dealing with.'

'Pieter . . .'

Then another blare of music and he was gone.

He pulled the van onto the grass verge by the river. Along the road the red and white coat of arms and the four crosses of Amstelveen stood illuminated above the black iron cemetery gate. Lights were on in the reception building behind. The only man alive in Zorgvlied, a security guard, was there somewhere, probably watching TV.

He liked this area. The quiet spider's web of the burial ground. Then, past the triple bridges that carried the busy southern ring road and the railway tracks across the river, the vast empty space of the Amstelpark, with its lakes and hidden bowers. A place a man could hide, get lost, then walk out free in any number of directions.

Curious tourists rarely found their way here. The locals had to go back into the city for entertainment. Not far beyond the park lay the Zuidas, with its tower blocks rising out of rubble and armies of multinational young. There, in skyscraper offices growing up from the ground like weeds, they manned banks and tech start-ups, and the trust companies used by everyone from foreign rock stars to web entrepreneurs to cut the tax they were supposed to be paying back home.

A stranger never got a second glance hereabouts. Perfect for what he needed.

One last check of his watch. This was like a ballet, a deadly dance to be choreographed. He knew pretty much how long it would take Vos to get here. There was time for one last cigarette and then he checked his things, the gun, the rope, the knife, the torch, the keys.

He threw the half-smoked cigarette out of the open window, pulled on his gloves more tightly, found the mask he'd put in the glove compartment and put it on. Fake fur and rubber with two ears sticking out of the top. A costume wolf. He got out, walked round to the back, threw open the doors and looked at what was there. The cowering terrier and two still shapes in the shadows.

The dog started whining. He yelled at the creature to shut up and to his surprise it did.

Then he reached inside and pulled back the sheets. Pale, grubby skin, slack face, a white cotton gag round her mouth. But she was breathing. Behind them in the shadows, up against the seat, a quivering bundle of fur.

'Wake up, sleepy head,' he said, and slapped her round the face.

Ten minutes Vos wasted wandering round the outdoor party by Artis. The noise was deafening, the air rich with the stink of weed. That didn't trouble him any more, didn't fill him with any pangs of longing as it once had when he first came back into the police.

All the lurid faces around seemed to stare at him. They were peacock figures, anonymous probably to each other so ornate were the disguises they wore. And he was just a man pushing forty in scruffy jeans, a jacket that had seen better days, dark hair longer than Jillian Chandra would have liked. A city sparrow in a flock of gaudy birds of paradise.

Vos worked his way back towards the street, ready to give in and call Laura Bakker. Then say . . . what?

I lost my dog. I gave his lead to a stranger who vanished with him, leaving curious messages in his wake. And the name of a murderer who killed himself years before.

Any ordinary member of the public who turned up at the doors of Marnixstraat with a story like that would get a raised eyebrow from the uniform officer on duty at the desk and told to come back in the morning when the drink had worn off.

'You,' said a young female voice, trying to make itself heard over the din. 'Vos.'

He turned and saw a slim figure in a black and white panda costume, rings around her eyes, white powder over her face.

'Me,' he said, seeing she had a scrap of paper in her hands. She turned it: a picture of him from the paper a few weeks back, running an update on De Groot's dismissal from the service. 'You know my name. How about yours?'

She grinned then, a line of fine white teeth, straight like those of a child.

'You can call me Li Li.'

He turned his head to one side and tried to imagine her without the face paint. She didn't look Chinese.

'A panda name,' the girl said, turning round in front of him, twirling a stumpy white fake fur tail in her fingers.

Vos pulled out his police ID and flashed it in her face.

'I'm a brigadier with the Amsterdam police. I want a real name. Not a pretend one. If I don't get it you're coming with me . . .'

Three tall figures came and cast a shadow over her from the strobe lights behind. A couple of gorillas, a tall, muscular lion. Maybe two hundred people here. He was on his own.

'Pandas like to have fun,' the girl said. 'You don't seem fun at all.'

'Beat it,' the lion ordered in a low American grunt. 'You're damaging the mood.'

Twenty minutes and he could have teams out to close the whole thing down. In other circumstances he might have considered it.

'I think you've got a message for me. Hand it over and then I'm gone.'

The panda face frowned.

'No message.'

The three men shuffled closer.

'What then?'

She leaned forward, stretched up and whispered in his ear.

'A present. He left you a *present*.'

'Who?'

A shrug.

'Some guy.'

She reached into a pouch on her belly and pulled out a fifty euro note. 'A present for me too. Just to deliver it.'

Vos held out his hand. She went back into the pouch, pretended she couldn't find it while the three men around her started to laugh. The music got louder. He would put in a call about this place. Once he was on his way.

Then she retrieved an envelope, plain brown, something thick in it, held the thing in front of her, teased him with it, giggling all the while.

'Thanks,' he said when she finally handed it over.

He walked through the broken fencing, away from the noise and the cloud of weed smoke. Inside was a pamphlet about somewhere familiar.

Vos stared at it and all thoughts of calling a team to break up the party behind him vanished. It was a brochure headed by a black and white shield with four crosses, the coat of arms of Amstelveen, the suburb to the south of the city. Beneath that two words, 'Begraafplaats Zorgvlied', a photo of a high iron gate, another picture of trees, scores and scores of grey slabs beneath them stretching into the distance.

He'd been there often enough in the past. It was one of the oldest cemeteries in Amsterdam, a sprawling burial ground set in parkland by the banks of the Amstel. Maybe four kilometres south.

A cab was crawling towards him hunting business. He flagged it down.

Back in the midst of the music and dope the panda called Li Li sipped her cocktail and watched him go. One last thing to be done.

She texted the number she'd been given. The single word he'd asked for.

Delivered.

Schrijver tried the bars the young liked in the busy square of Gerard Douplein. No one remembered seeing a young woman like Annie: tall, slim, striking with a blue streak in her blonde hair and a little ring in her nose. Unusual features, he thought, but looking around him: not so much any more. His daughter was pretty, vivacious, talkative. Would chat to anyone. That came from selling flowers in the street. She was so much better at it than he. But she was trusting too, and Bert Schrijver had lost that facility a long time ago, before the divorce even, when he was starting to realize the family castle was built on sand, with only his own feeble talents to shore it up against the coming storm.

He went to another place near the Heineken brewery, pulled out his phone for the friendly barman to show him a picture of his daughter, beaming in the busy market, holding out a bunch of roses like a bouquet for a lover.

'You're sure you've not seen her?'

The man was busy.

'That's the flower girl, isn't it?'

'Annie.'

'Annie,' he agreed. 'She was in here a few nights ago.'

'When?'

He rinsed a beer glass with water, half-filled it from one of the pumps and placed it in front of Schrijver.

'I don't recall. Here. Have one on me. It's ours. We're trying—'

'I'm not here for beer. I'm trying to find my girl.'

'Sorry,' the barman said.

Schrijver tried to frame a question but there wasn't a good one in his head.

The phone trembled in his pocket. Annie's number was flashing on the screen. He marched out into the street, short of breath, heart pumping and he didn't know why.

'Love,' he said. 'We've been looking—'

There was a dog barking high and scared in the background. 'Where am I?'

Her voice sounded wrong. Confused, dazed, half-asleep.

The dog yelped again then fell silent. Something was happening, something was moving.

A muffled voice came on the line and Bert Schrijver fought to answer the question: *Do I know this man?*

'You're her father, aren't you? Do you understand what she does at night? Where she goes?'

'No,' he found himself replying. 'How would I? She's a grown—'

'Time you did.'

Annie moaned again, sounded barely conscious.

'Don't touch her,' Schrijver said. 'Don't you dare. I'll—'

'What?' the voice interjected. 'You'll send me some flowers?'

'Please.' The words just seemed to form themselves. 'She's all I've got.'

'All the more reason you should take care. The cemetery. Zorgvlied. Among the graves. Come and get her.'

A drunk stumbled along the pavement and bumped into him, almost knocking the phone from his fingers.

'For God's sake don't hurt my girl—'

The line went dead.

The cab got caught in traffic. At the river it shook off the night-time crowds and ten minutes later turned onto the single track lane that ran by the Amstel, past empty parks and solitary houses set behind trees on one side, the wide and placid river, dimly lit by occasional houseboats, on the other.

The driver kept moaning, first about the sluggish road, then, when they turned onto the narrow dark lane, the fact he had to pull in every time he met an oncoming car. After a while that stopped, most of the lights too and the houses with them. Through the open window Vos could hear the odd bird call and the distant bark of a dog. A deep tone, not that of a frightened terrier. The crowded, sweaty city seemed distant here. The night was cooler, filled with the sounds of nature, not man.

The phone sat in his hand. A photo of the panda girl was there, snapped without her knowing before he fled the strange party in a corner of Artis.

As the taxi slowed, a tall structure appeared ahead on the right, the reception building for Zorgvlied, a familiar coat of arms in front illuminated by a few street lights. They had to stop. A car was coming towards them, another cab. As the vehicles met the oncoming one stopped. The driver wound down the window, popped his head out and asked, 'What's with this place? Pitch dark and two rides to a cemetery. Are the dead having a party or something?'

Vos didn't wait to hear an answer. He threw some money onto the front seat and got out.

A torch was shining near the tall black iron gates at the front of the cemetery. There were two men there, one in uniform behind the railings, quiet, listening. On the river side another, thickset and yelling in a coarse accent, slamming his fist on the bars.

The guard aimed his torch beam at Vos as he reached the gate, sighed and said through the railings, 'This is a graveyard. It's the middle of the night. I don't know who you are, friend, but the message is the same as I gave this lunatic here. Piss off. Come back in the morning. If you don't I'm calling the police.'

Vos pulled out his ID and clamped it to the bars.

'The police are here.' He glanced at the man next to him. Burly, muscular, wayward hair and beard, he looked frantic. 'Who are you?'

It took too long to get the story out of the man called Bert Schrijver. Everything came out in a jumble with names – Annie, Nina, the Albert Cuyp – that Vos had to check and recheck along the way. The security guard listened all the while, in silence. The man's pain was clear to see.

'My girl,' Schrijver said in the end. 'She's in trouble. He said she's here somewhere. If he's hurt her . . .'

Vos ordered the guard to open the gates then phoned Bakker and told her to come straight to Zorgvlied with six officers, all the blues flashing.

She was still at her desk, going through the reports on the case from four years before. There was a note for Vos in the log. Vincent de Graaf, the man jailed for the Sleeping Beauty Murders, was now in the prison hospital, undergoing tests for cancer. Seriously ill, perhaps dying. Marly Kloosterman, the prison medical officer, had called to tell Vos that De Graaf kept hinting he had something to say. As far as Bakker could see, Vos had never received the message.

'There's a girl here somewhere,' Vos said. 'Her name's Annie Schrijver. I think . . .'

The father was staring at him, face wracked with fury and grief.

From somewhere in the vast dark of the graveyard came a sharp, high sound. A familiar one. The bark of a little dog.

'Bring along a medical team too.'

Zorgvlied was a maze of winding paths and gardens, leafy bowers, ponds and fountains, seventeen hectares bordered by the Amstel to the south and the narrow canal called the Kleine

Wetering around its land side. Sam – Vos was sure it was him – kept barking sporadically but from a distance; it was impossible to pinpoint where.

The messages, the chase across the city. This was all a kind of game. A challenge, a puzzle set for him alone. And puzzles came with clues.

'A grave,' Vos said. 'How do I find out where someone's buried?'

'Easy,' the man said and walked to the half-open door of the reception.

'Where's my girl?' Schrijver cried and looked ready to dash off into the endless dark.

'She's wherever that dog's barking,' Vos answered. 'Stay there.'

He followed the uniformed man inside. There was a computer just by the door. Already the guard was rolling the mouse to bring it to life.

'You've got a name?'

'Jonker. Ruud Jonker.'

'They're all here. Hundreds, old and new. It takes a few seconds. If . . .'

A map flashed up, footpaths straight and meandering, trees, monuments, statues, water features, numbers and names that meant nothing. It seemed more like a guide to a vast and busy theme park than the topography of a graveyard.

'Paradiso,' the guard said, placing a finger on the screen. 'Where they put the funny ones.' He sighed. 'About as far away as you can get from here. The eastern corner, by the water.'

A page started to pop out of the printer. Then he moved into a different app. Colour CCTV screens came up. Ten of them covering all the roadside entrances, nothing in the cemetery itself. The only activity was their own.

'This is crazy. I don't see how anyone could get in. If—'

'He's here,' Vos insisted.

The guard grabbed the printout, opened the drawer, pulled out two more torches, handed them over and said, 'Stay close. It's dark out there and you really don't want to get lost.'

Along the gravel path they went, beneath trees, branches gently moving above them, owls hooting, creatures stirring unseen. Sam barked again. No human cry at all. Bert Schrijver kept marching like a man possessed. In a few minutes Bakker ought to be outside, with backup.

'Annie,' Schrijver called into the night. '*Annie . . .*'

The cry sounded like a plaintive howl.

Torch beams flashing in a radius ahead, trying to spot something that wasn't grey stone or black marble, they walked on.

It was five minutes to the sector called Paradiso. Vos remembered now: this was where they buried the eccentrics and a few of the famous. Graves with photographs, tiny Buddhist temples, poems, mementoes, toys and plants, scattered flowers, fresh and old, casting the faintest perfume against the dank smell of nearby water.

The guard checked the sheet in his hand, shook his head, swore, stopped.

'I nearly took you down the wrong path. This place . . . in the dark . . .' He turned to his left. 'Over there.' The beams of their three torches swung round over headstones. Then stopped when together they caught sight of a pale shape, naked in the half light, lying across a grave at the very edge of the plot.

'*Annie . . .*'

Schrijver was shrieking, running, arms outstretched.

Vos told the guard to go back to the gate and wait for the police teams to arrive. Then lead them here immediately.

'Are you sure?' the man asked, a frightened note in his voice. 'This place is like a maze. In the dark—'

'I'm sure.'

Vos strode to the Jonker grave, looked at the headstone and thought . . . *tattoos.*

That was another memory coming back from the grim events the papers called the Sleeping Beauty case.

Schrijver was on his knees on the gravel. The headstone had a photograph of a man, his face covered in scrolls and patterns like a Maori warrior. A name: Ruud Jonker. Born in De Pijp, died there thirty-seven years later. Across the middle of the low grave border there was a body, naked, muddy, face down, blood leaking onto gravel.

'Schrijver,' Vos said, kneeling next to the shaking, weeping man. He pulled a pair of latex gloves from his pocket and tried to edge the man back with one hand while checking for life with the other. Through the thin latex he could feel how cold the flesh was. The skin was wet and there was weed plastered everywhere. 'You need to step away. We've help on the way. Your daughter—'

'It's not my daughter,' Schrijver spat at him. 'Are you blind?'

All the rules he'd learned over the years told him: you don't move a corpse. You wait. He wondered why Sam wasn't barking any more, felt guilty that he should even be thinking of the little dog at that moment.

Vos reached out and gently gripped the grimy, mud-stained hair, lifting the head so he could see. It was a man, thin-faced, neat hipster beard, perhaps thirty, long dark hair, glazed eyes that seemed frightened even in death. There was something on his naked shoulder: a tattoo, the ink so raw and new there was blood around the wound.

Three words.

Sleep Baby Sleep.

In the darkness beyond the fringe of bushes at the edge of the graveyard an engine stuttered into life, weak and uncertain, like an outboard on a dinghy. Vos was barely on his feet when the throttle opened up. Then came the sound of Sam, yapping furiously.

This time he could fix the direction. It was along the canal, back towards the heart of the cemetery, just outside the curious area called Paradiso. Vos edged the torch beam along the path. Between a row of low cypresses was one of the grander monuments, large enough to boast a rectangular lily pool surrounded on two sides by Doric columns, a broken pediment at the top. The silhouette of an angel with broad wings and a bowed head was just visible at the nearest point, something like a vine trailing from one of the wings.

Vos could smell fuel, close by. He pulled out his phone and got Bakker.

'Where are you?'

'On the little lane. Not far away. A minute maybe.'

'Tell control we've one dead. Maybe two. Then . . .'

Ahead of them a ball of red and yellow flame appeared by the bank then a blazing brand dipping down to the grass. There was a soft roar of ignition and a line of fire began to run towards the rectangle of the pool tomb, outside the line of columns. The flickering yellow light revealed the little terrier tethered to one of the columns, struggling frantically to get free. Sam started to shriek and scream. Schrijver saw something too, dashed forward crying his daughter's name over and over.

It took a moment for Vos to understand. There were two naked muddy arms just visible past the winged statue. Sam yelped again, straining, biting against the rope. Then the line broke and he was racing free into the dark night.

Vos ran too. The flames were confined to the low line of conifers some distance from the grave. They were for show, for terror, nothing else.

Schrijver was by the body on the ground by the time Vos got there. It was a young woman, naked, muddy, unconscious in a huddle in the sight of the angel's bowed gaze.

Annie . . .

Bert Schrijver carried her, weeping, muttering, away from the grave, back to the grassy path. There Vos placed his jacket on the cold gravel while Schrijver lowered her gently onto it, wrapping the fabric round her muddy form. Vos was on his knees by her face in a second, head down to her mouth, fingers feeling for a pulse. The girl coughed, rolled her eyes, turned to one side and puked on the dry late summer grass.

In the dark the boat engine revved more loudly.

He left Schrijver with his daughter, raced through the dying flames out towards the canal. Muddy tracks ran up from the bank to the raised edge of the cemetery. This was how the man had entered, avoiding the CCTV around the entrance gates. Delivering his cargo: a body, a semi-conscious woman, a dog.

Vos pushed through the undergrowth. His torch beam fell on a small dinghy manoeuvring in the water, heading along the channel. Straight away he tried to work out all the exit routes. It was impossible. This area was polder, reclaimed land criss-crossed by a skein of narrow waterways. The canal could lead anywhere, back to the Amstel, out into the complex network of ditches and canals that ran through the neighbouring Amstelpark all the way to the Zuidas. He could be back in the city or south in the suburbs under the cover of darkness and no one was going to follow him.

A figure in the back stood up. Sirens were rising close by, a harsh rattle in the quiet night. They'd chase this man but that, Vos knew, was a contest lost already. It had been from the start.

'Another day, Vos,' cried a cheery male voice, middle-aged, confident, amused. 'You will hear from me again. That I promise.'

The engine surged into a soprano whine, the nose of the dinghy bucked up, the boat vanished into the darkness.

Figures ran through the shadows: Laura Bakker's familiar tall form to the front as usual. Behind her, medics in white with a stretcher. Van der Berg struggling to keep up behind.

Vos jumped as something brushed against his leg. Sam was there, leaning against his shin, feet on Vos's shoes, muddy, wide-eyed, trembling, a length of crude rope still attached to his neck, the end bitten through with those sharp terrier teeth.

'It's all right now, boy,' he said then loosened the cord and placed it carefully on a nearby grave. After that he scooped up the shivering little dog, held him tight and close and walked back into the field of graves where a man was bent low over his daughter, uttering a frantic prayer. Torchlights were gathering round, police and medics swooping on the pair by the lily pond and the frozen angel that stood above them, arms open, dead eyes fixed upon the scene.

His phone beeped. A text there, from a new number, an international one.

A wise man learns more from pain than pleasure. And so our education begins.

TWO

The hospital was a sprawling network of buildings next to the busy A10 ring road, a medical city in miniature set on both sides of the tram tracks running from the centre to the Zuidas.

Bert Schrijver had sat in the ambulance that took his daughter there from Zorgvlied, trying to cling to her hand all the way. Nina had joined him in admissions, tearful and full of questions he couldn't answer. The two of them had spent the next seven hours in the emergency wing, stuck in a corridor watching medical teams come and go. Around four they were allowed to move into the intensive care unit and watch their daughter through the window of the single room she'd been allocated. Now it was seven thirty on a bright September morning. They sat on the same hard chairs, stiff, tired heads aching, hungry, thirsty, watching the still figure in the gown behind the glass, unwilling to step away out of an irrational fear of what might happen.

A uniform police officer was with them, a kindly woman who kept offering to fetch coffee and something to eat. Vos, the brigadier who'd come to Zorgvlied for his own reasons, had appeared around two in the morning, checking on Annie's condition, asking questions about the dead man found with her in the odd graveyard section called Paradiso. The Schrijvers had no idea who he was and neither, it seemed, did the police.

Three years before, Schrijver's parents from the castle in the Albert Cuyp had died here, six months apart. He hated every corner, every ward, every room, the cloying antiseptic smell of the place, the sound of it, the steady whir of fans, the chirp of electronics, even the presence of the doctors and nurses whose practised smiles of sympathy were rarely followed by news that was welcome.

Somewhere in this endless maze of corridors, wards and theatres Rob Sanders worked, a nurse who might have made a son-in-law once. At thirty-three he was more than a decade older than Annie, an off-and-on lover. Until the day he hit her and it was only Nina who'd stopped Schrijver beating the living shit out of Sanders for that.

'You should step away for a while,' the policewoman said again. 'Let me get you something. We could go to the cafe.'

'She's right,' Nina said with a sharp glance in his direction. 'We're doing nothing here.'

Doing nothing.

The feeling of helplessness was the worst part. During the night, while Nina briefly slept, greying head on the hard hospital bench seat, he'd got down on his knees and prayed to a god he hadn't spoken to for years, one that never listened before and doubtless wouldn't now.

Take me, Bert Schrijver had whispered, tears filling his eyes behind lids squeezed tight. *Not Annie. Not my little girl. Take me. A worthless, useless piece of shit who's screwed up every opportunity he's ever been given. And will screw up the next if it ever comes along. Because that is who I am. For pity's sake, for the love of my daughter, take me.*

'Bert . . .'

He pulled himself out of this memory and said, 'I don't leave my girl when she needs me. You go.'

Nina sighed and shrugged her jacket more tightly around herself.

'Annie doesn't need you. She's no idea we're here.'

'And if she wakes?'

She wore a gentle though condescending expression. One he hadn't seen in a long time. He had got it a lot when they were married and he was struggling to maintain the business the way his father had. The look said: *I know you're doing your best. But you're an ineffectual man at heart. You don't see it. But we do. All of us. We forgive you. What else is there to do?*

Nina reached out and touched the back of his hand. He looked at her fingers: wrinkled, thin, ever-wrestling. His own were fat and ugly, dirty with the previous night's mud.

'You're filthy, Bert. You stink. You need a shower and a change of clothes. The doctors said . . .'

He'd heard all that. Had listened to every word. Annie had been given some kind of date rape drug. An overdose. Maybe she'd been drinking too. Maybe doing hard drugs, not that he was inclined to believe that. By the time they got her to the hospital her breathing had turned shallow. If she didn't recover soon . . .

They never said it but he guessed what they were getting at. He and Nina might face a terrible decision. Life or death delivered through a simple switch on the wall. Their daughter gone for no good reason, just twenty-two years old.

A familiar harsh, cracked voice rang down the corridor, an old, tobacco-stained tone he'd been hearing around the market since the two of them were kids together. Jordi Hoogland, the one outside employee the business could still just about afford.

He was walking towards them, arms outstretched, the biker's black leather jacket on him, jeans, greasy grey ponytail down his back.

'Oh Christ,' Nina muttered then picked up her bag and told the policewoman she was going to the hospital cafe.

Still, she watched as Hoogland stumbled up to Bert Schrijver and hugged him, choking on his words. The man smelled of stale beer, sweat and cigarettes.

'What happened? I heard. In the market. Everyone's talking.'

'Don't they have anything better to do?' Schrijver grumbled.

Hoogland was staring at Annie through the glass. She lay on the bed, a still, slim shape in a hospital gown. No ring in her nose now. They must have taken that out when they put in the lines.

41

There were wires everywhere, monitors rising and falling by her side. The blue streak in her hair looked dead already.

'What kind of bastard would do something like this?'

'I don't know. If I did . . .'

'Tell me what you want,' Hoogland said, taking his arm. 'A friend in need . . .'

'A friend?' Nina Schrijver echoed. 'Out of money again, Jordi?'

Hoogland's eyes narrowed.

'Came to help. That's all. Whatever you want. Just ask.'

'Ask you?' One last look at the still, sad shape beyond the window. 'I need a break from this,' she said then left.

Back in Paradiso, Vos was fighting to keep his eyes open among the outlandish graves and other-worldly tombstones. Three hours' sleep was all he'd managed.

Laura Bakker was on the phone to Marnixstraat constantly, asking questions, getting few answers. Schuurman, the best pathologist Marnixstraat possessed, had led a team through the hours of darkness. Aisha Refai, the young and talented forensic officer, was by his side as they began the painstaking task of searching and scraping for material among the mud, the gravel and the eccentric graves. Two scientific officers in white bunny suits were going over the pool tomb with the stone angel. Zorg-vlied's director and security officer had turned up, baffled, full of impossible questions, offended by the intrusion into this peaceful corner of the city.

The steady glare of morning made the headstone of Ruud Jonker appear brighter, almost cheery. The colour portrait attached to it, a late picture of the man buried beneath the stone chips, seemed defiant, as if the tattoos and grin were trying to prevail against death itself.

Vos recognized the photo. It had been pinned to the wall of

Jonker's tattoo parlour when they arrived to find him hanging from a beam next to the old barber's chair he used for his customers. Like the note left on the door of his houseboat the evening before, this dead man's features seemed designed to taunt him.

You're a clumsy man, Vos.

You miss things.

'Usually because people lie,' he murmured.

Schuurman said his people would be here all day. Possibly tomorrow too. The Zorgvlied people weren't happy. The whole of Paradiso would have to be off-limits to the public. There'd be complaints. This corner of the cemetery, outlandish in parts, funny even, was quite an attraction for those who knew about it.

'They do,' Laura Bakker agreed.

The words took him by surprise. He hadn't noticed she was off the phone.

'You look worn out, Pieter,' Aisha Refai observed. 'How much sleep did you get?'

'Enough. What do you know?'

In the concise, professional fashion he'd come to expect, she told him. There was little in the way of physical evidence at the moment, and what they'd found probably came from the victims. But they'd worked out how the two had been brought here. A small boat had steered through the narrow canal that ran from the river round all three sides of Zorgvlied, then back to the Amstel, branching off beneath the busy road into the neighbouring park. The channel was little used but just about navigable. Breaks in the weed and mud tracks up from the bank suggested one man was responsible. There were slide marks that indicated he'd dragged both victims up into Paradiso, placed them there for someone to find, laid a line of diesel around the stone angel then waited in the boat for the show to begin.

'Quite a show too,' she concluded.

'No arguing there. What killed him? I thought I saw a wound.'

Like all forensic people she hated guesswork.

'A little early to say. He'd been hit on the head. Schuurman doesn't think that would have been fatal. There were facial bruises, scrapes on his knuckles. He'd been in a fight. And lost. You asked us to look for date rape drugs.'

Vos waited as she checked something on her phone.

'We haven't had time to work on him yet. But I passed that suggestion on to the hospital. They found GHB in the woman's urine.' She looked at him intently to make sure he understood. 'If she lives you may well have saved her.'

GHB. The same drug used in the Sleeping Beauty cases.

There were so many things awry here. The timeline for one. A neighbouring stallholder saw Annie Schrijver leave her home in the Albert Cuyp around five two nights before. The next day she wasn't due to work so it took a while for her mother to get worried. If someone had slipped her a date rape drug the night she disappeared it would have worn off, or had more serious consequences, by the following morning. Yet she wasn't found until the evening, still drugged.

His phone went. Jillian Chandra.

'I want you to keep me up to speed with what's happening,' she said before he could utter a word. 'We could have two murders soon, a lunatic loose in the city—'

'Of course. But—'

'Do you have a lead yet?'

If only. Murder was often predictable, the product of anger or envy, drugs or drink, lust or hate. It was usually close and spur of the moment. Careful planning and deliberation were rare. Even the most common kind of homicide outside domestics – gangland killings – came with a history, a lineage, like footprints in the blood. Though men and women who took the lives of others never appreciated it, they tended to work to an unspoken template. And for that the police were deeply grateful.

This had the same feel as the Sleeping Beauty case that preceded it. Like jazz, it appeared at first to be improvised. Yet

behind the casual ad-libbing lay structure and some kind of careful plan. At that moment he couldn't begin to discern either.

'Ask me in an hour or two,' he replied and knew it sounded
desperately weak.

'I'm asking you now. The media are going to give us hell. I
looked at the files from four years ago. If we're going through that
nightmare all over again . . .'

If, he thought.

'Perhaps it's someone with an axe to grind. Maybe a friend
of Jonker's. Maybe . . .' Aisha Refai wandered back to the stone
angel and the pool. There were carp in it, Vos saw. Fat orange fish
swimming lazily in the greenish pond set among the many
corpses in the Paradiso earth. 'Whoever it is they're organized.
They know their way around.'

'What about the girl?'

'She's in intensive care. We're going there next.'

'Don't know much, do we?'

There was a long, dissatisfied sigh and then she hung up.

Vos looked around him. In the daylight Zorgvlied seemed
more like a well-manicured park than a cemetery. Finding
Jonker's grave hadn't been easy. The narrow canal around the
burial ground wasn't an obvious way in.

He called the office and got Van der Berg.

'This is a rare one, Pieter,' he said. 'How's Sam?'

Vos had a feeling he was going to get asked that question a lot.

'He's with Sofia. He wasn't hurt. I don't want to keep saying
that to people all day long. So tell everyone, will you?'

'Sure.' Van der Berg sounded vaguely offended. 'What else
can I do for you?'

'See if there are any listed sex offenders living within spitting
distance of Zorgvlied. If there are check whether there's even the
slightest connection with Ruud Jonker or the Sleeping Beauty
case.'

'Anything else?'

'This,' Vos added, sending him the photo he'd snatched on his phone. The girl from the rave at Artis.

'Pretty panda,' Van der Berg said.

'There was an illegal party near Artis last night. See if we pulled in any of the organizers. Anyone who might know this kid. She passed on the message.'

The clatter of keys came over the phone.

'Seems we had a couple of calls from the neighbours moaning about the noise.'

'Did we do anything?'

A pause and then, 'We sympathized. No arrests. No names taken.'

Wonderful, Vos thought, recalling the way the creatures crowded round and stood ready to leap on him if he'd persisted in trying to talk to the girl.

'If you don't get anywhere in an hour give that photo to the media. Tell them we don't think she did anything wrong. All the same we—'

'We'd like to eliminate her from our inquiries.'

'Quite.'

Van der Berg paused for a moment then asked, 'Is it all happening again? Like before?'

'I don't know.'

'The commissaris is getting very jumpy. The media are sniffing round like crazy. It's just the kind of story they like.'

'We don't even know what the story is yet.'

'No.'

Something in Van der Berg's voice indicated he had something to say.

'What is it?'

'I've been going through the notes. About the Sleeping Beauty case. It seems someone from the prison left a message for you two weeks ago. They thought maybe you'd want to interview Vincent de Graaf again. He was hinting he wanted to talk.'

'And?'

'It was that doctor. Marly Kloosterman. The one you . . . and her . . . well, I don't want to pry.'

'I never got any message.'

'No. Sorry. Well, you know now.'

There was one last word with Schuurman and Aisha then he walked back to the car by the entrance to Zorgvlied and tried to picture the previous night's movements in his head.

'Jesus. I'm being slow,' he moaned as Bakker came and unlocked the car.

'Why?'

He didn't answer, just looked up and down the lane, trying to think this through.

'Pieter. We're due at the hospital. Will you kindly tell me what's going on?'

If he hadn't been so exhausted and confused by the long night he'd have seen it earlier. Annie Schrijver and the unidentified victim had been taken to Zorgvlied in some kind of small boat or dinghy. But Sam had been snatched in the centre of the city. Whoever took him couldn't have got there on the water. There wasn't time. So a vehicle must have been involved.

'Maybe he came back and got it after he left in the boat?' Bakker suggested.

'Maybe.'

'Perhaps there were two of them.'

Except it didn't feel like two. Not that he was going to say that. It sounded ridiculous. For all he knew there might have been an entire team teasing him, sending him racing through the city the night before.

She was right, though. They needed to be at the hospital. Vos called Van der Berg again and told him to get some uniform officers down to Zorgvlied to check the river banks.

'Looking for what?' asked the voice on the other end of the line.

'Tyre tracks,' Vos said.

The moment they got to the hospital they went to find the duty consultant. There was an awkward question to be asked. A thin middle-aged man of Chinese appearance, heavy-eyed as if he'd been up all night, the medic was scrolling through data on a computer screen in his office. It seemed there wasn't a lot new to say about Annie Schrijver's condition. It was serious. All they could do was wait.

'If you could persuade the parents to go home for a while that might help,' the doctor said. 'Her father needs a shower. And a change of clothes. Some manners might not go amiss but I guess that's asking a lot.'

'Do you have any idea what they're going through?' Bakker asked.

'Yes,' the man replied with a curt smile. 'I do. Part of my job. Part of yours too, I imagine. Or do you lie to people?'

'We try to help.'

Vos glanced at her and Bakker fell quiet.

The doctor picked up his clipboard.

'They can't just sit in a corridor here day and night. We don't have room to put them up. The best thing is for them to go home. Sleep. Get clean. Wait until we have a clearer picture—'

'How much GHB was she given?' Vos asked.

'Too much. Beyond that I can't say.'

The timeline still bothered Vos.

'She was last seen late on Tuesday afternoon. When we found her last night she was unconscious. Would one dose . . . ?'

'No,' the consultant answered, getting the point straight away. He gave them a brief lecture about gamma-Hydroxybutyric acid, one Vos didn't need. He remembered most of the details from four years before. GHB acted directly and swiftly on the central nervous system. In small doses it could be a stimulant or aphrodisiac. In larger quantities, especially when mixed with alcohol, the chemical could lead to a sleep so deep it was hard to rouse the victim. Overdoses, intolerances or simple allergies could lead to breathing difficulties, unconsciousness and death.

'The young still seem to think it's a sweetie of choice whatever we say. GHB's odourless, though I gather it's got a mildly salty flavour.' The doctor stared at Bakker. 'Remember that if your drink tastes funny in a nightclub.'

'I don't do nightclubs,' she replied. 'Where do you get it?'

'Anyone who knows a bit about chemistry can knock it up,' Vos told her. 'They make it at home. Give it names like Lollipops. Juice. Desert Rose.'

'True,' the man agreed. 'We have it here as well. Not knocked up in someone's bedroom. Mainly it's used to treat narcolepsy. Severe disruption of sleep patterns. A drug's a drug. It's the way you administer it that makes the difference.'

Vos's phone buzzed. It was a text from Jillian Chandra asking for an update.

'So if she got doped on Tuesday night,' he went on, 'that still wouldn't explain why she was in a semi-conscious state last night?'

'No.'

'But if he administered a second dose yesterday?'

The doctor thought about it.

'Depends how much. If it was small she'd sleep like a log for a while. If it was bigger . . .' He checked his phone for messages. 'Then I'd call it murder. Two heavy doses would kill anyone. But these kids . . . they think this stuff is just harmless fun. You go clubbing. It makes you feel good. If you find a girl you like you slip it in her drink. Get her home. Do what you like. She sleeps it off and in the morning she doesn't really have a clue what went on. How often do they complain to you?'

'Hardly ever,' Vos replied. It wasn't just the shaky memory. There was the shame, and the nagging feeling that dogged so many victims of sexual assault, male and female. The idea that somehow, in their carelessness and stupidity, they were to blame.

'Is Annie Schrijver going to live?' Laura Bakker asked.

'Hopefully,' the doctor answered, heading for the corridor. 'I do have other patients to deal with. You'll excuse me.'

One last point had to be settled. Vos stopped the man and said, 'Do you know if she'd been assaulted?'

It was clear from the response in his eyes it wasn't a welcome question.

'By assaulted you mean . . . what?'

'Had she been beaten up?'

'Not that I could see. Few bruises on her shins. From what I heard she got dragged through a graveyard naked. Probably from that. I don't think she was in a fight if that's what you're getting at.'

'Had she had sex recently?' Bakker added.

The man took a deep breath and stared at her.

'We're trying to save her life. To do that I need to focus on medical priorities. Nothing else.'

'This is a criminal investigation,' Vos said. 'One murder. Maybe soon it will be two. We need to answer those questions.'

'You mean you want to examine her? You'll need consent. That girl can't give it. Nor me. If—'

'What about the parents?' Bakker wondered. 'If they say yes?'

He didn't answer.

'We'll deal with it,' Vos told him.

'Ask nicely,' the consultant said as he headed off. 'Those two are in a state. And afterwards . . . get them out of here. They need that. So do we.'

Back in Marnixstraat Van der Berg was wondering if there was a way he could side-track Jillian Chandra's efforts to follow Vos and Laura Bakker's every move. The serious crimes unit had a way of working, one that had been established over decades under a succession of station heads, all of them male, all of them from Amsterdam. Everything was primarily hands-off, delegated to a front-line team. Murders and other high-level crimes couldn't be tackled by committee. The commissaris of the day gave the job to a suitable brigadier then stepped back and, for better or worse, left the troops to the task.

Chandra wasn't cut out for that arrangement. She was the kind of boss who stood behind you as you worked, watching every keystroke, waiting for the moment she could stick her nose in and say, 'No. Not like that.'

It hadn't happened yet. But the moment couldn't be far off.

He'd pulled out every file he could find on the Sleeping Beauty case from four years before. There were surprises there, lacunae and oddities that were easily visible to someone fresh to the facts and blessed with the benefit of hindsight. It was clear, as Rijnders had said, that Vos hadn't been entirely convinced by the result. One suspect, Vincent de Graaf, a high-level mover and shaker in financial circles, convicted of murder, sexual assault and the illicit administration of drugs. The second, Ruud Jonker, owner of a lowly tattoo parlour in De Pijp, dead, suicide it seemed.

The three murdered women were in their twenties, dumped in the Amstel river not far from the Zuidas, dead from frenzied knife attacks. Each of them – and this was the creepy part Rijnders had recalled – had a message tattooed on their shoulder. The same three words, 'Sleep Baby Sleep'.

Once the story started to hit the papers several other women came forward to complain they'd been drugged in nightclubs in De Pijp and the Zuidas and thought they'd been sexually assaulted afterwards. But none had tattoos, any clear recollection of where they'd been taken, what might have happened there. A couple pointed out De Graaf in an ID line-up. Most didn't. Jonker was dead. Trapped, De Graaf was happy – almost proud – to confess to three murders as part of what he claimed was violent love-making that went too far.

For four years nothing like the Sleeping Beauty deaths happened again. There had to be a reason for that gap. Van der Berg was checking with a couple of the intelligence people going through the sex offender records when Aisha Refai came up from forensic, grinning ear to ear.

'Please tell me you've got a name,' he said.

'For our customer on the slab? No. Names are your field, Dirk. Not ours. Getting anywhere?'

When he didn't answer she waved her tablet at him and Van der Berg let her get on with the show.

Photos.

A corpse. Neat hair, fashionable trimmed beard. White, fit, muscular, athletic perhaps. Maybe thirty. Probably good-looking when he was still breathing. Cleaned up ready for the pathologist's scalpel, eyes closed, a line of dried blood running from his left nostril, he just looked dead. Then some close-ups. A wound at the side of the head, probably a blow from a hard object like a hammer.

The tattoo on his shoulder was very like the ones from four years before. The familiar single line of text, 'Sleep Baby Sleep'.

Van der Berg felt out of his depth.

'Don't you need, like, a shop or a parlour or something to give people tattoos?'

She closed her eyes and ran a palm across her forehead.

'My God. Where do you start?'

'Don't tell me you've got one.'

Aisha laughed.

'In that case I won't. This is a very simple thing to do. A single colour, just three words. I talked to someone who runs a parlour this morning. He says it's a piece of cake. Probably used what's called a portable line gun. You can pick them up online for forty euros. If you can write your name you can tattoo someone. Especially if they're dead.'

'Damn.'

So they didn't need special premises. It could happen any-where.

'We are going to get DNA from the Schrijver girl, aren't we?' she asked.

'Vos and Laura are at the hospital right now. We need permission.'

'Good. Do you really have no idea who he is? A boyfriend . . .'

'Why would a boyfriend want to drug her?'

He got that hint of condescension again.

'You'd be amazed, Dirk. If she was hitting some of the clubs. All sorts of stuff goes on. Want to know how he died?'

'Let me guess. That date rape drug he used on the girl. GBH—'

'GHB,' she corrected him. 'No. At least if he did get that on Tuesday night it's probably gone from his system by now. We don't have all the results back.'

He tried to tell himself murder inquiries always started this way. Too many questions, too few answers. But Aisha had one. It was written on her face.

'One result I do have though. Whoever our friend downstairs is . . . he was poisoned.'

She pulled up a photo on her tablet. A close-up of his mouth. Blue skin, black lips. Something on his gums that looked like dried, caked powder with brown flakes in it.

'You're sure?'

'Not a shadow of doubt. Potassium cyanide killed him. The stuff the Nazis used to use in suicide pills. Secret agents too if they thought they might get caught. So long as your stomach acid's not too high it's a really quick death.'

She hesitated then said, 'I'm guessing here, and this is beyond my remit. But I'd suggest this wasn't suicide. From the way the stuff was caked in his mouth he was probably unconscious anyway. No sign he tried to spit it out. It just went in and . . .' She made a cutting gesture with her hands. 'Gone.'

'Wonderful. Date rapes. Poison. Tattoos. Cases that were supposed to be dead. What the hell . . . ?'

'Something else.' She zoomed in on the powder. 'What does that look like?'

'Sawdust. And . . . some grey . . . stuff.'

'Well done! I may be hiring an intern soon if you want the job. It's plaster. The kind you can buy from a builder anywhere.'

He stared at the fatal mixture on the dead man's black lips.

'What the hell does it mean?'

'That,' she said, 'I cannot tell you. All I know is this. There's only one place I've found where people habitually mix potassium cyanide, sawdust and plaster.'

A flick of her fingers and another photo came up. A large glass vessel with a sealed top, a beautiful butterfly flapping its wings inside, at the bottom a layer of brown and grey.

'It's a killing jar. For moths. And butterflies.'

'Oh,' he whispered. 'That really helps.'

One of the intelligence people, a bright woman who'd just joined from Lelystad, overheard. She'd been checking out the sex offender records.

'Butterflies?' she asked then hammered the keyboard in front of her.

People argued around the sick and dying. Out of earshot of everyone else, or so they hoped. Sullen, aggrieved huddles in hospital corners, in funeral homes, at crematoriums. Vos had seen this many times before and knew there was no easy way to alleviate their pain. They didn't want to share it. They craved to pass it on, find someone near to blame. All too often he couldn't help. Maybe it was an accident, bad luck, simple fate. Or perhaps the world at large had failed them and those responsible had fled. The best thing to do was let the grief and fury expend itself then hope to pick some sense out of the emotional debris left behind.

Even so, there was something strange about the way Bert Schrijver, the woman Vos took to be Annie's mother, and a third younger man in a blue medical uniform stood stiff and angry in the long corridor by reception. The policewoman was doing her best to keep the older man calm. It didn't matter. Bert Schrijver needed to let off steam and whoever the medic in the blue suit was he seemed to make a fine and easy target.

An older individual in a studded black leather jacket detached himself from the shouting the moment he saw Vos approach, walked down the corridor the way people did when they didn't want to be seen, never realizing how visible this made them. Curious, Vos told Bakker to follow and find out who he was. Then he strode up, waited for a gap in the yelling, showed his ID card and waited.

The man from the previous night looked exhausted, a mess. Unshaven. In need of a shower as the consultant had said. The woman introduced herself as Annie's mother Nina. She was striking, with high cheekbones, shoulder-length dark hair turning grey and darting, anxious eyes. Vos couldn't help glancing at the unconscious figure on the bed. A nurse was checking the monitors and making notes. Schrijver watched, tired eyes damp with tears, grubby fingers to the glass.

'I've been trying to calm things down,' the uniform policewoman objected. 'I keep telling them . . .'

Vos held up a hand and looked at the man who was the object of Schrijver's anger. He was early thirties, spiky short fair hair, a face that looked as if it might be genial most of the time. Fit and tough if he wanted to be. A name badge read: Rob Sanders.

'You're a doctor?'

'A nurse. Annie and me. We were . . .' He sighed. Schrijver swore. Sanders closed his eyes. Staff in hospital met the sick and dying every day. They didn't normally look quite so pained by the sight. 'What the hell happened?'

'We're trying to find out,' Vos told him. 'Someone abducted Annie. On Tuesday night probably. The man with her was killed.'

'The man?' Sanders wondered.

'I thought you were done with my daughter,' Schrijver spat at him. 'Don't think you had any rights there.'

'I never did. Never would.' He turned to Vos. 'How is she?'

'You work here,' Schrijver cried. 'You tell me.'

'Let it go, Bert!' Nina Schrijver yelled. 'It's not Rob's fault she's like this.'

Sanders nodded thanks then headed for the door to her room. Schrijver stopped him.

'You don't go in there. I don't want you near her.'

The woman was close to tears.

'He's a nurse, for God's sake. He's every right—'

'No,' Sanders said. 'I don't. I just . . . wondered.'

Vos leaned against the glass and watched him.

'When did you and Annie stop . . . stop being friends?'

That didn't go down well. Rob Sanders wasn't the calm, kind hospital face just then.

'Is that important right now?'

'I don't know. We're trying to work out her movements. When you all saw her last.'

Tuesday afternoon, Bert Schrijver said, when she was leaving the shop. She'd stopped working Wednesdays a few months before; a six-day week was too much for her. Annie had told him she was staying with her mother that night. He'd assumed the two of them were together. But Nina Schrijver hadn't seen her daughter since Monday when they had lunch in a cafe by the park.

Sanders came last.

'We bumped into each other in the market a couple of weeks ago.' He checked his watch. 'I'm off shift and clearly doing no good here.' Nina Schrijver waited, expectant. Then he came and embraced her, kissed her on both cheeks. 'Tell me if I can help. I know this place like the back of my hand. If there's anything—'

'You can stay away from her,' Schrijver interrupted. 'That's what you can do.'

Sanders wandered off down the corridor with a wry, regretful smile.

'You're a stupid, ungrateful man, Bert,' Nina snapped. 'Did I ever tell you that?'

'Morning, noon and night. If—'

Vos said, 'You should go home, both of you. Get some sleep. The hospital will call if her condition changes.'

He got mobile numbers out of them then asked the question that brought him here.

'We really need to get your daughter examined by one of our forensic team. It's important. If that's OK—'

'Why?' her father asked.

'Jesus Christ,' Nina Schrijver swore. 'They found her naked in a graveyard. Why the hell do you think?' She nodded, staring sad-eyed through the glass. 'It's OK.'

Vos's phone rang. He walked away from the Schrijvers for some privacy. Laura Bakker marched up the stairs, holding up her notebook, a name scribbled on it: Jordi Hoogland.

'He doesn't like us,' she said. 'Also he's got a ponytail. At his age. I ask you.'

It was Van der Berg calling.

'Are you still at the hospital?'

'On my way back. Tell forensic they can come and take a look at the Schrijver girl. The parents have given permission.'

'How is she?'

'Much the same. Anywhere with an ID for the man?'

'Nowhere. We're releasing a photofit they've run up in the morgue. The commissaris wants us to put out a warning about spiked drinks in clubs.'

'Why?'

'We've got the TV and newspaper people banging on the door asking if the Sleeping Beauty killer's back in town.'

'The Sleeping Beauty killer's stuck in prison, dying by the day.'

'Then a copycat maybe. She still wants that warning out there.'

His phone beeped. It was a photo sent by Van der Berg. A man about forty, wispy beard, thinning hair. A butterfly tattoo running up one side of his neck.

'You asked for a sex offender living near the river, didn't you? Well, here you are. Jef Braat.'

Bakker was craning to get a look at the picture.

'Sentenced to two years for sexual assault a while back. Served half, released two months ago. Records think he did a lot more than that. Whoever our dead man is he was killed with some poison you find around butterfly people. At least the kind that use killing jars. Braat was working at Artis until two weeks ago. In the butterfly house. Left suddenly.'

'Got an address?'

'Houseboat on the river out in the wilds on Amsteldijk Noord about a kilometre beyond Zorgvlied. Right now he should be at work in some new little butterfly house they're building at the kid's zoo in the Amstelpark.'

Just across the highway from Zorgvlied, attached to the network of narrow canals running out from the cemetery.

'I'll tell the commissaris you're on it. She's very interested in your movements right now. Want a few officers to keep you company?'

'For a kid's zoo? Send Laura all the background you've got. See if we have anything on a man called Rob Sanders. He's a nurse at the VU hospital. Used to be Annie Schrijver's boyfriend. And someone who works down the Albert Cuyp. Jordi Hoogland.'

As soon as he was off the phone the Schrijvers came up to talk.

'We're going to take your advice and go home for a while,' the mother said. 'You will find who did this, won't you?'

'Of course,' Bakker answered straight off.

'In time,' Vos added.

'Time,' Bert Schrijver grunted and made the word sound like a curse.

The Zuidas was the new home for money in Amsterdam, a budding Dutch Wall Street or Canary Wharf. Among the towers for banks, financial specialists, trust houses and global insurance firms, tall cranes stood like giant storks feeding on stumps of half-built office blocks. Corrugated iron fences hid patches of bare grass waiting for the next construction crews. Fancy corporate offices loomed over minimalist apartment complexes purpose-built for the area's new residents: the single, the unattached, the wealthy, the foreign.

Vos drove through the construction traffic out towards the Amstelpark, a pleasant sprawl of greenery, lakes and play areas next to the growing financial suburb. Laura Bakker went through the information coming over from Marnixstraat, reading out the details as they crawled through the lines of cars and trucks. Jef Braat was thirty-eight, jailed for assaulting a tourist outside a bar in the red light district. The attack fell somewhere short of rape but that may have been because he was beaten up by a couple of men who'd intervened when they saw what was happening.

'Should have gone down for more,' Bakker grumbled.

There was no point in moaning about the length of sentences. A working officer could waste all day on pointless gripes. What was interesting was the date of Braat's release. There had to be a reason why a long-dead case like this had suddenly reignited now. Perhaps it was simple: the man who lit the fire had just come out of jail.

Her phone beeped.

'Dirk's been through records,' she said. 'Rob Sanders is clean. Jordi Hoogland's got a couple of convictions for drunkenness and assault. Nothing recent.'

'What did Braat do for a living before he went to jail?'

She went through the file.

'Driver for a financial company in the Zuidas. The De Witt Trust. The boss was a character witness in court. Said he was a good employee, trustworthy, loyal. Helped cut the sentence.'

Vos pulled into the entrance to the park. They couldn't take the car any further.

'He did some volunteer work for Artis while he was inside,' she went on. 'They gave him a job in the butterfly house when he was released. He got fired for some reason.'

'The De Witt Trust? You're sure?'

She tapped her phone.

'That's what it says here. Why?'

'Vincent de Graaf founded the De Witt Trust. They must have known each other.'

She checked the report on her phone.

'De Graaf was in prison himself by then. The man who spoke up for Braat in court was the general manager. Willem Strick.'

As far as they knew the Sleeping Beauty case had never come near Vincent de Graaf's work. There'd seemed no reason to chase that line at the time. De Graaf's deadly hobbies appeared to be part of a private fantasy acted out with Ruud Jonker. And perhaps others they never found.

They left the car with security then stepped inside the park gates. Bakker looked at a map of the area set up by the entrance.

'This place is huge. How do we—?'

Vos had taken his daughter Anneliese here from time to time when she was little. In fifteen years the place had hardly changed.

'We catch the train.'

When they walked ahead they met a miniature track running from a tiny platform. There was a sleek white engine that must have looked like a futuristic rocket when it was made decades before. A handful of excited young children sat with their parents in the open carriages behind, begging to leave. In the cab of the engine stood a cheery driver in a striped cap who saluted as Vos flashed his ID and got on board.

'The police always ride for free,' the man said with a grin. He looked happy to play train driver for the kids. Then he squinted at Vos. 'Don't I remember you from years back? With a little girl?'

The visits here were part of a different life when Vos had a family, a settled home. Something that seemed like stability. He didn't recognize the man at all.

'Your memory's better than mine,' he said as Bakker climbed into the open carriage beside him.

The driver tooted his whistle. The kids cheered. For a moment Vos was back with Anneliese, excited by his side. A proud father who wanted nothing more for his daughter than for her to be well and happy and settled. Just like Bert Schrijver who was now, he hoped, at home, getting some sleep, more likely half-awake, praying for the phone to ring.

'This Braat character's got to be involved,' Bakker insisted as they set off.

'You think?'

'Too many connections for it to be a coincidence. Vincent de Graaf. Artis.'

'Connections . . .' Vos murmured.

She looked exasperated. He could do this to her sometimes.

'You think I'm wrong, don't you?'

'No. I just don't know if you're right. Anyway . . . I hate jumping to conclusions. Cases are like . . . like . . .'

He was supposed to mentor a junior officer like Bakker. To teach her the ropes. There was little need. She was quick, incisive. But she was young, which meant she saw things in black and white. And Amsterdam was rarely so accommodating.

'Like what?' she asked.

'They're narratives. Like a story. Lots of little pieces of string tied together loosely, hopefully, as you go. Then . . . at the end.'

Vos leaned back and closed his eyes. It was warm, the end of summer. The park was empty save for a few families. Away from Marnixstraat and the angry, frightened family in the hospital, there ought to be time to think. Except the more he tried, the more things didn't add up. He kept seeing Jillian Chandra's persistent, demanding face asking . . . why? Was the Sleeping Beauty killer really back in business? He kept remembering Marly Kloosterman too, the one woman he'd nearly fallen for when he came back into the police and was struggling to find his feet. That had blossomed briefly until nothing but his own timid reluctance had brought the brief affair to a close.

'At the end you pick it up and pull. Either the knots hold. Or they fall apart in your fingers.' He opened his eyes, smiled at her and shrugged. 'In which case you return to the beginning and try to tie them back together. Just differently.' The stop was coming up, and beyond it a playground where three kids were lounging on a roundabout looking bored. 'Until you find some context they're nothing more than little pieces of string. Maybe useful. Maybe not.'

They got off next to the kid's zoo, asked an attendant selling tickets for the rides how to find the butterfly pavilion. He pointed to a modest wooden building on the far side of the complex then wished them luck.

There was a sign on the door promising a grand opening in a week's time. A man in grey overalls was sweeping up sawdust and plaster from the building work. He was sixty at least with a thin silver beard and a narrow, almost skeletal face. Bakker asked where they could find Jef Braat.

'Who wants to know?' He looked at their ID cards and introduced himself as Erik de Jong. The money and the organization behind the little butterfly house in the making. Given it looked little more than a large shed with a glass roof and a few plants inside, that seemed a stretch. 'He's supposed to be here. With his damned pets.'

Vos walked over to a glass case by the door. There were racks running from one side to the other, and photos of exotic butterflies. Four bright green shapes like bulbs from a Christmas tree were hanging on wires.

'Pupae,' Bakker said.

'Chrysalises,' De Jong corrected her. 'They were supposed to have hatched by now. Or so Jef told me when I paid for them. I came in yesterday and found out the heat had failed. He was supposed to be looking after that, checking it every night.'

He'd last seen Braat two days earlier. Since then . . . nothing. Not that he'd called.

'Why not?' Vos asked.

De Jong shuffled on his feet.

'Jef's a big guy. I took him on because the probation people said he'd be fine. He knew about butterflies too. Supposedly. I've seen him get mad. You don't want to get close to that.' He glanced at the river. 'I thought about going down to his boat. It's just ten minutes. Take the path down to the Amstel. But I don't . . . I don't like arguments. Not with his kind.' He tapped a finger on the glass case. The green shapes looked waxy and dead. 'I've got fifty thousand tied up trying to get this place off the ground. That bastard's screwed me. Artis and their lawyers yelling at me too.'

'Artis?' Bakker asked.

'They say he stole these things from there. That's why they fired him. I never knew. How would I? Who steals butterflies?'

The narrow waterway from Zorgvlied was no more than fifty metres away. The Amstel lay at its foot. A little boat like the one Vos saw the night before could easily move around here unseen in the dark.

'Where exactly does he live?'

'Why are you so interested in Jef Braat?'

'We're nosy like that.'

De Jong huffed and puffed, took out a pen and a little pad then scrawled a drawing of the river bank, a location some way along from the bridge. A name: *Sirene*.

'Only been there once. It's a wreck. Amazed the thing's still afloat. He's got those rich young finance folk from the Zuidas living all round in neat and fancy houseboats. Gin palace cruisers. They must love him.'

'Thanks,' Vos said and set off towards the river.

There was a long, winding path down towards the Amstel. It was more than ten minutes to Braat's houseboat, he thought. Erik de Jong was wrong there. Perhaps about much else too.

Commissaris Chandra didn't look up from the computer.

'Where's Vos?'

'Following up on a suspect,' Van der Berg said. 'Could be a good one.'

'Could be? He's had most of the day working on this and we're nowhere.'

She sat back and stared out of the window. Elandsgracht was across the canal, the long street leading down to the Drie Vaten and Vos's houseboat. She'd got rid of Frank de Groot's comfy leather chair and replaced it with something trendy made out of tubular steel and canvas. It didn't look comfortable at all but maybe she liked that.

'How many people do we have working in serious crime?'

He stuttered over the answer. It wasn't his job to do a head count.

'I'm not exactly certain how many are on duty at the moment. Enough.'

A smile surfaced, one of victory.

'Quite. Enough for someone else to check out that lead. And Vos to be here, in the office, in charge.'

'The thing is . . . he was at the hospital. Talking to the parents of the Schrijver girl. The lead's in the Amstelpark. Just round the corner. A few minutes away. It seemed to make sense—'

'This was his decision?'

It seemed a strange question.

'It's his case.'

'Under my command. Bring him back. Someone else can go knocking on doors. I want him in the office. Senior officers should be here keeping me in the picture. How's the girl?'

'She's twenty-two. I don't think you'd call her a girl.'

Chandra looked at him and said, 'I stand corrected.'

Van der Berg had remarried in his mid-thirties. His first wife, a woman out of the clerical pool, was sweet and charming when they first met. A few years of being shackled to a cop who worked all hours and sometimes came home stinking of sweat and beer with nothing to talk about but work had changed her. In the end it had been much like this. There were times when everything he said was going to be wrong. It didn't matter what the words were. Just the fact he was the one uttering them.

He told her about Jef Braat and how they were looking at some other men close to the Schrijver family. Chandra didn't seem much interested in hearing more. She was management. Details were beneath her. All that counted was that some day soon she could phone her distant bosses in Zoetermeer and say that, thanks to her fine, wise leadership, the job had been done. Case closed. Move on to the next.

'You know . . . there's nothing much Vos can say that you can't get from me. I've been on top of the files all day. He's been out of the office and—'

'He's the officer in charge.'

'They're nearly there,' he cried and realized this was why Chandra was asking. If Vos was on to something it would now be found by another officer, one acting on her orders.

'Get someone else. Just do it, will you?'

He shuffled out of her office, took the back stairs, went into the garden where she'd handed him the long-service medal the day before. There he lit a cigarette and wondered how Jillian Chandra was going to work out in Marnixstraat. Hers was a world where mistakes were never made, only detected. It took old school Amsterdam officers, set in their ways, ignorant of the methods of modern policing, to foul up. She knew by heart the most important lesson of the modern brigade of management: the simplest way to avoid doing wrong was to do nothing at all and wait for those beneath her, men and women who did not have such liberty, to fail.

By the fountain in the middle of the garden he made the call.

Vos was breathing hard. Van der Berg was sure he heard the sound of a duck quacking madly.

'Our new mistress, the dragon from the south, requires your presence in the office immediately. She says someone else can take over the Braat lead.'

There was a long pause.

'That's very generous.'

'I wouldn't cross her, Pieter. She's adamant you get back here now.'

There were ducks. Or geese. Some kind of wildfowl anyway, along with the gentle whir of a puny outboard carried on the breeze.

'Tell the commissaris I'll be back just as soon as I possibly can.'

'Pieter . . . *Pieter.*'

The quacks came one last time and then the line fell silent.

It was the end of the afternoon and they were breaking the market. Gone were the busy crowds of shoppers who packed the Albert Cuyp six days a week. Men in overalls scrambled over stalls dismantling iron frames, packing gaudy shades. Cleaners patrolled the street washing it down with powerful hoses. Greedy herons pecked for scraps of discarded herring and *kibbeling*. Paper and discarded fruit and vegetables ebbed on a damp tide towards the gutter and the sweepers with their carts.

Nina Schrijver had grown up with this sight. One so normal she took it for granted. Took everything for granted when she thought about it. The marriage. Bert. The idea that Annie would somehow amble along as the market's pretty flower girl, selling cheap and sometimes faded blooms with a smile and an occasional wink, until a lucky man claimed her for his own.

There was no reason that shouldn't happen. Annie had the same flirty skills Nina had used to shift fried fish back when her father had his stall there. But now he was dead, like her mother, the space he'd once occupied taken by an Indonesian family selling sambals and pickles they made at home. And she no longer lived in what was left of the Schrijver castle, instead got by in a studio apartment overlooking the green space of Sarphatipark down the road.

Bert gave her money every week, not that he could afford it. Some part-time work packing shelves in a supermarket made up for the rest. There'd been a man for a little while. Bert never knew – at least she hoped he didn't – but he'd been there not long before the marriage failed. He worked shifts for the council which meant sweaty afternoons of mindless passion in his flat in the Jordaan, the flower van parked outside, her phone turned off in case Bert rang to ask why she was late. Guilt killed off that miserable affair, along with the absence of any real love or joy.

She leaned against the wall of a bar recently sprung up in a shop that had been closed and derelict for a few years. There was little in the way of a social life at all except when Annie came round and they went out for a cheap meal in one of the working-class Indonesian cafes near the tram stop in Ferdinand Bol. But Rob Sanders had phoned from the hospital and said he wanted to meet without Bert around. She watched him ride his sports bike down the street then clamp it to one of the lamp posts while a hungry heron watched as if offended by the intrusion. He felt at home even if she didn't any more.

The baggy blue nurse's uniform had been replaced by smart jeans and a tan leather jacket. He came over, kissed her on both cheeks. He was young, fit, handsome in a laddish way. But that was just his manner. Sanders understood how to treat women, to make them feel special. It was a rare talent among the men she knew.

'I need a drink,' he said and they went inside the bar. It was early and the music was quite soft and gentle. The Eagles. The place seemed to want to pretend it was California.

'Speaking as a medical man, this,' he said, pointing at the cocktail list, 'is what I prescribe for such occasions.'

The barman made two tumblers of Bloody Mary, flavoured with something fiery and sour called kimchi. She'd never have guessed the Albert Cuyp could provide a drink quite so exotic. Even the Indonesian cafes with their cheap, basic meals of chicken and rice and potatoes seemed Dutch to her these days.

But Sanders was single, free. He had the time and the money. She was glad he hadn't grown the neatly manicured beard that some of the local blades thought essential. Still, he fitted in with this new De Pijp.

'How is she?' she asked. 'No one's called.'

Annie's ward wasn't in his part of the hospital. He still knew people who worked there, had talked to them.

'She's stable. That place . . . it's the best care Annie can get. It doesn't help having relatives around all the time. You and Bert need to stick to the visiting hours.'

'Will she be all right?'

'Yes. She will.'

'I'm sorry, Rob.'

'About what?'

'About Bert. All the fuss he made.'

Sanders sipped at his spicy drink, went to the counter and came back with some tortillas.

'What does he know? About us?'

'What she told him. You hit her.'

'Doesn't he want to know why?'

Men were so logical somctimes.

'Of course not. Annie's his little girl. She went crying to him. Hysterical.' It was a black day. Schrijver was working. Nina had to deal with the immediate aftermath, not that she could stop her daughter running to the Albert Cuyp in tears. 'Let's face it. I don't know either.'

'We had a row. I didn't hit her. Just shook her.'

Annie had backtracked on the whole thing later. She didn't want to lose him but in the end they broke up all the same.

'That's all it was, honestly. A lover's tiff. Water under the bridge now. Next you'll be telling me Bert's never touched you.'

That took her aback.

'Of course he hasn't. Never came close. Even when I went for him.'

He raised his glass and chinked it against hers.

'Now we know where Annie gets it from.' He stroked his cheek. 'You should have seen the scratches.'

'That was it? You shook her? Nothing else?'

The question seemed to offend him.

'That was it. You don't think we'd have tried again if it was anything more, do you? Annie wouldn't. She's strong. Like you.'

'Even if that's true, Bert isn't. This could break him. God knows he's got trouble enough with the business as it is. I look at him and it's like . . . like he's aged ten years lately. I think things are worse than he lets on.'

Sanders sipped at his drink and kept quiet.

'When will they let us see her again?'

'You're going to have to wait for them to call. They got very pissed off about Bert losing his temper. We've got strict rules about threats to staff. If I hadn't gone and argued maybe they'd have banned him altogether.'

'Thanks,' she murmured.

'Least I can do. Jesus. I still can't believe it. What was Annie doing hanging round sleazy bars with creeps who do that sort of crap?'

That was a surprise.

'The police said that?'

'No.' There was an awkward, almost childish clip to his answer. 'That's where these things happen, isn't it? Pickup joints where some bastard drops dope or whatever in your drink. Where the hell—?'

'I don't know. Do you?'

'Wouldn't be asking if I did.'

There was a short fuse to him sometimes. Just like Bert.

'No. Sorry. Stupid of me. It's just . . .' Just what? No one had offered them any answers. So the questions kept dancing round her head, teasing, nagging, taunting. 'I always thought she stayed local. Around De Pijp.'

He scowled.

'Don't ask me.'

'No.' She poured the rest of the drink into his. It was too spicy and too strong. 'I say all the wrong things. You're being very supportive. I appreciate that. Bert would too if he could see straight.'

'Jordi Hoogland,' he said out of nowhere.

'What about him?' she wondered.

'Why was he hanging round the hospital? What's Annie to him?'

It seemed an odd question.

'Not a lot. I don't think she likes him much to be honest. Him and Bert have known each other since they were kids. Bert's soft when it comes to things like that. Jordi works for next to nothing.' She watched him and asked, 'Why do you ask?'

'Just wondered.'

He downed the cocktail in one and choked a little on the heat.

'You've got my number,' Sanders said. 'If there's anything you need I want you to call. Don't think twice. When they let you and Bert into the hospital it's best I stay clear. If he loses it again they really will kick him out for good. Nothing I can do.'

'I just want Annie back. Will that happen?'

Out in the street one of the cleaners accidentally upended a fish bin. Herons pounced on it, spearing at the pieces with their broad sharp beaks.

Sanders didn't say anything and she thought of Bert's furious words in the hospital earlier that day. How all they did was make you wait, say useless things that told you nothing. Never let you near the truth.

'Did you hear? I want her home. With me. Where I can keep an eye on her.'

'I want that too.'

He kissed her cheek. He liked kissing, she thought.

'Take care.' Sanders got to his feet, pointing a finger at her the way some men did. 'Call. I'm here for you. And Annie. Always.'

'Thanks,' she said, watching him go.

Some people walked through the door. Four young men, beards, the old-fashioned clothes that seemed in vogue. The same number of women, a couple of them drunk or stoned already. The volume of the music went up a notch. Perhaps you didn't need to wander so far from the Albert Cuyp to find trouble if you wanted it.

She went to the counter and bought herself a glass of wine. Twice the price of a local cafe. The barman looked at her as if to say: *Are you sure?*

'I came from here,' she told him. 'A while ago. When things were different.'

'Nice,' he replied and stifled a yawn.

———

71

Jef Braat's home was just as the butterfly pavilion man had predicted: a wreck. An old barge listing in the green water of the Amstel a kilometre along from Zorgvlied, on a bend of the river surrounded by open fields and the flat landscape of polder.

'Makes your pad look positively swish,' Bakker observed as they waited in a clump of trees to see if anyone was coming or going. 'The commissaris isn't going to be best pleased we're out here watching ducks when she wants you in her office.'

'Depends.'

'On what?'

'On what's inside.'

The *Sirene* was grey and black, a long rectangular cabin set on what looked like an industrial hull. Vos got hassle enough for his own shabby houseboat on the Prinsengracht. The city authorities would have towed this wreck to the scrapyard without a second thought.

Grey curtains covered all the porthole windows. The gang-plank was rotting timbers running through a patch of overgrown irises. A post-box hung off a pole on the bank. It didn't look as if Braat got much mail. Maybe the place had stayed empty while he was in jail. Neglected for a couple of years. Forgotten.

Bakker had her handgun out and was checking it, getting ready for a forced entrance. Vos didn't like weapons. The thought of what they might do distracted him. Besides, the place looked empty. Unless Braat was the kind of man who slept through the afternoon.

With Bakker squawking behind he crossed the rickety timbers from the rough grass bank and stood beneath the rusty shelter above the door. There was, to his surprise, a bell. He put his finger on it and kept it there. No sound came from inside. Vos put his ear to the timber hull, heard nothing at all, then stepped back and looked.

'Please tell me you're not going to do something stupid,' she begged.

'Such as what?'

'Going all macho on me and trying to kick the bloody door down.'

'Promise,' he said and took a pair of latex gloves from his pocket then nodded at her to do the same.

'I don't trust your promises.'

She came and stood by him, the weapon raised. Vos pushed the barrel to one side. Then stepped back as if he was going to kick the door anyway.

'That's why—' she began.

He reached forward, lifted the latch, put his shoulder to the door and pushed. The timber moved with a crack then came to a halt against something solid. There was just darkness beyond the door. A smell came to them, organic and vaguely foetid.

'I really wish we could wait for a team,' she said in a low and determined whisper.

Vos put his shoulder harder to the wood. It gave easily, sending something metal crashing to the floor, and after that came the sound of breaking glass. Everything happened so quickly he stumbled forward into the warm, rank darkness ahead.

Something soft and hot and alive met him as he fell forward. Hit Laura Bakker too as she rushed in behind. There was a sound like a million tiny creatures stirring into motion. Soft wings rose to meet their faces. She screamed. A tiny furry body fell into her mouth and then she screamed some more.

'Light,' Vos said as they struggled against his lips too.

'Can't take this,' Bakker cried. 'Sorry.' And rushed outside, kicking the old door wide open.

Now he could see. A little anyway. The thing he'd bumped into was a metal rack for hatching insects, the kind they'd noticed in the pavilion in the Amstelpark. He'd knocked it over, shattering the panes that kept the creatures trapped. Freed from their prison, a cloud of whirring anxious insects rose to swamp the interior of the old barge in a cloud of soft and feathery wings.

73

The butterflies that should have been in the pavilion. Here they'd been for a day or two at least, hatching, filled with hunger and a need for sun. All the colours of the rainbow as they reached daylight, some large with ornate markings, some small, almost plain, they fought among each other to race into the brightness ahead of them.

They'll die, Vos thought, watching them. They were exotic, tropical creatures meant for another climate on the other side of the world.

A bright beam broke the darkness ahead. Bakker was back, still coughing, right hand over her mouth, a tissue to it. In her left she held an LED torch, the pure white light stabbing into the cabin interior.

'Just butterflies,' she said through her fingers.

'Or moths,' he added.

'Oh, thanks for that. I really . . .' Bakker fell silent. The beam had fallen on something by the far windows. Vos took the torch and asked her to go outside, take a few deep breaths, then call in a team.

'We should get out of here,' she said without moving. 'They're going to want to look at every inch of the place.'

Then she was coughing again. He led her out of the door, got her seated on the grass, tried not to look while she gagged on all the things that had found them: the flimsy, fibrous insect wings, the stench from the dark maw of the rotting hulk called the *Sirene*.

Bakker was in no fit state to talk to anyone at that moment. So he phoned Marnixstraat himself as he walked back, shone a light inside again, took in what was visible there. Straight through to control he asked for Jef Braat's photo and description to be circulated immediately to all stations and patrol beats throughout north Holland, with an order to detain immediately with caution.

'Should I inform the commissaris?' the operator asked. 'She seemed very anxious to hear if you called.'

Jillian Chandra's presence appeared to have worked its way through the entire building.

'I'll tell her myself soon enough. Put me through to forensic.'

Aisha Refai answered. He gave her the rough address. There was no road here, just a lane. The scene of crime team would arrive in a small fleet of vans. Very soon the place would be over-run with people in white bunny suits, elbowing everyone to one side while they pounced with their cameras and evidence bags, their chemicals and probes.

'What is it?' asked the voice on the other end of the line. 'Another body for me?'

'Hundreds,' he said. 'Thousands.' The butterflies were swarming over the river bank. Bakker was feebly trying to swat them away with her arms. 'But not the kind you think.'

He went back inside and swept the cabin. The torch beam fell upon a big office chair, beside it on a table what looked like a drill, a couple of needles shining in the dark.

'This is where he inked them. Did lots else besides, I guess.'

Beyond the chair were more metal frames full of chrysalises, some still emerging, some hatched, giant wings beating against the glass. Next to that was a double bed covered in crumpled sheets. Dark stains on the grubby cotton. Blood on the fabric, blood spattered up the cream timbered walls.

'You're going to be here a while.'

Bert Schrijver was fast asleep in his office when she woke him. Nina looked different. Clean hair, neat and tidy, smart skirt, white blouse.

'I seem to recall I asked you to get a shower. Smarten yourself up,' she said.

He'd been so exhausted when he got back he'd just gone straight to the computer, checked for messages, put his head on the desk and that was it. Schrijver glanced at the clock on the screen. It was almost six.

'Any news?' he asked.

'She's stable. They're pissed off with you for picking a fight with Rob Sanders. We can still go back there when they let us but you've got to behave.'

'I will,' he mumbled.

Jordi Hoogland opened the office door and stuck his head through. He'd done the rounds, he said. Caught up with some of the late orders. But because it was just him making the calls more than half the day's stock still hadn't been delivered.

'I'll freshen it up with the hose. They won't know the difference.'

'Chuck out anything that's bad,' Schrijver said automatically. 'I don't want people paying because I fouled up.'

Hoogland frowned at that and said he'd spray the flowers anyway. They could talk in the morning. Then he went back into the warehouse and soon after they heard the sound of water, could smell it in the air along with the sweet scent of roses and jasmine.

Schrijver got out of the chair, stretched, felt old and weary.

'I don't know why you keep him around,' Nina said.

'Because he works for peanuts. And that's all I've got to pay people with these days.'

'Do you trust him?'

'With what?'

'He's got the run of this place, Bert. Money. Stock. Your computer.' She hesitated. 'Annie's never liked him.'

He threw up his arms in despair.

'What is this? I can't do everything.'

She seemed to back down at that.

'Go and get showered,' she repeated. 'Find some fresh clothes.'

Thirty minutes later he came back to the office. Hoogland was still out in the warehouse, sweeping up, washing down the one van Schrijver had left.

Nina was at the PC. He hadn't bothered to lock it down. All the records were there. Sales and expenses. Nagging emails from the bank.

'I hope you're not paying him overtime,' she said without looking up.

'Couldn't run this place without Jordi. Especially not now.'

'Oh Christ, Bert.' She pushed the mouse to one side and blanked out the screen. 'I'll come in and help out if you'll let me.'

Three generations of Schrijvers had sold flowers from this place. Now the castle was in its death throes. He'd realized that already, not that he'd told them. A woman from an estate agency was due round the following morning.

'I can cope. I've got customers to think of.'

'They'll drop you like a stone if you keep screwing them around. And anyway,' she gestured at the PC, 'you're not making anything out of them. I just went through the numbers. They're worse than ever. This whole place is leaking money. Pretty soon . . .'

'Hard times all round. For everyone.'

She laughed and there was a cold and unsympathetic timbre to her voice that disappointed him.

'Hard times? Do you actually walk around here with your eyes open? There are fancy hipster restaurants out there charging ten euros for a cocktail you and I have never even heard of. Foreigners with cafes selling fast food shit for more than I used to get for fresh *kibbeling* I'd cooked myself. It's just hard times for people who are too dumb to move with them. Annie knew that.'

'She never told me.'

Beyond the door Hoogland started the industrial vacuum to sweep up the dust. Schrijver wanted to tell him to pack up, go back to the little studio he rented on the other side of the Albert

Cuyp, do whatever he did of an evening. Sell dope. Steal. Rip off a few tourists. Everything away from the shop was his business.

'What the hell happened to her?' he wondered. 'If that bastard Rob Sanders did this I swear to God I'll kill him. Coming up to us in the hospital like that. Like he cares . . .'

'How do you know he doesn't?'

'He . . . hit . . . her!'

His voice had turned too loud. Jordi Hoogland opened the door, broom in hand and asked if everything was OK.

'Everything's fine,' she said. 'You should go home.'

Hoogland was muscular, gruff, ugly. He didn't like being told what to do, especially by a woman.

'If Bert doesn't need me—'

'Go home,' Schrijver said. 'And thanks.'

'I'll be back in the morning.' Hoogland glowered at her. 'You just say what you need, Bert.'

There was a tense silence for a while. Then they heard the sliding door to the warehouse open and close and she said, 'No one knows what happens between two people. Not even themselves sometimes. We didn't.'

'I know I'm stupid. You don't need to tell me. That bastard hit her. Him a nurse too . . .'

She reached forward, took his hand and that silenced him.

'No one knows, Bert. No one's got the right to judge. Rob wouldn't really harm her. He wouldn't dream of it. I'm sure.'

He wanted to ask the obvious question: how?

But then his mobile rang. Only a handful of people ever called: customers, suppliers, the bank, Annie and Nina mainly. He had their numbers in the address book so he knew who it was before he answered.

The phone didn't recognize this one.

'Is Mr Schrijver there?' asked a woman who sounded busy, as if she'd rather be doing something else.

'Speaking.'

'It's the hospital. We need you to come. And your wife too.'

'What's happened?'

'There's a change in your daughter's condition.'

'What kind of—?'

'The doctors say you should come here straight away if you can. Both of you.'

'If—'

'It's quicker if you go straight to intensive care reception. I'll tell them you're on your way.'

Then she hung up. He looked at Nina. Her face was lined now and sometimes he thought she hated him. But she was still the woman he fell in love with when she served fried fish in the market, trying to ignore his pathetic attempts at courtship.

Pity was the reason she went out with him in the first place. Then Annie came along by accident and with her a marriage that happened almost without thinking. The Schrijvers were big in the Albert Cuyp then. His father wasn't having any bastards fouling up the line. If it hadn't been for the pregnancy Nina would never have become his wife in the first place. She'd have dumped him and gone back to serving *kibbeling*, pretty face, white nylon coat, plenty of men, better, smarter, more handsome, begging for her hand. That knowledge, the certainty of his own inferior status, ate at him daily when they were together.

'They want us,' he said. 'The hospital. They wouldn't say why.'

Night was falling over the river. Clear sky, faint moon, a stiff chill breeze running through the ragged trees. The sounds here were quite unlike those of the city. Somewhere in the hedges busy owls hunted, hooting. Along the banks wildfowl squawked. Cattle lowed in the adjoining fields. By the boat, beneath harsh flood-lights, the team of forensic officers talked in low tones, lost in the tasks before them.

This was their stage now. Vos and Bakker were spectators waiting on results. His mind had drifted to the houseboat and the Drie Vaten, to taking Sam for one last walk along the canal. He'd no idea when that would happen again. The terrier would stay with Sofia Albers for the duration. This case was going to be protracted, he felt, even if they managed to pull in the fugitive Jef Braat from wherever he'd fled.

To his surprise he'd heard nothing from Jillian Chandra's office at all. Or Dirk Van der Berg. This didn't worry him. He had Bakker, quickly recovered from the shock of the swarm of insects that flocked to them as they broke into Braat's barge. And as good a forensic team as he could have wanted: Schuurman and Aisha Refai at its head. There was blood on the sheets and walls. A tattoo machine and needles. The scene of crime people had almost whooped with joy when they saw how many promising prospects there were for DNA inside the wreck called the *Sirene*.

Perhaps there would be answers. There ought to be, Vos knew. But something about this case bothered him, much as the Sleeping Beauty murders had four years before. Sometimes homicide refused to fit the templates. It could be like life itself, asymmetrical, unpredictable, reluctant to dance to the tunes the legal and investigative systems preferred. There were rough edges, dangling threads. Occasionally they were visible. More often they lurked unseen, nagging doubts in the back of an officer's mind, chafing there for years however hard you tried to dismiss them.

The media were carrying warnings about spiked drinks and advice for women to take care in nightclubs. It was a logical and understandable reaction to the possibility that one of the killers from the Sleeping Beauty case had now re-emerged, undetected over the years. Yet crimes carried their own watermarks, like fingerprints and DNA. And this was different. A man was dead, a young woman lucky to survive. Not dumped in the Amstel river in the hope they'd disappear but laid out almost for exhibition in Paradiso, the curious corner of Zorgvlied where one of the original murderers, Ruud Jonker, was buried in a colourful tomb.

Odder still was his own involvement. The night before he'd been tempted into the discovery in Zorgvlied in an intricate and deliberate manner. Jillian Chandra, who'd never worked homicide in her career, could not comprehend this. But there was another story building here, one he had yet to begin to recognize.

Bakker filled the empty hours by nagging forensic for information and, when that proved fruitless, calling back to Marnixstraat to chase for updates. Mostly Vos sat on a decrepit wooden bench seat by the path, watched and waited, taking in the shape of the boat's interior, trying to imagine what might have happened.

All the clues were there. A crumpled bed, not that there seemed any evidence of sex from the forensic sprays and lights and probes. There was violence though. The needles and the ink were used, just as they were four years before, a teasing line of text but only on an unidentified man.

The logical narrative was that someone – Jef Braat, perhaps in concert with the unidentified man – had taken Annie Schrijver to the houseboat after spiking her drink. She was attacked, doped again and the second man murdered. The following evening a message had been left on Vos's houseboat and Sam snatched from outside the Drie Vaten.

After that . . . Rembrandtplein. Artis and the panda girl. Then Zorgvlied.

But why? He hadn't a clue and that offended him because the why mattered more than anything. It was the knowledge, the line that led from deed to doer. Understanding the train of that narrative eluded Vos entirely at that moment. A man had hoodwinked two young people, abused them, damaged them, killed one and left the other struggling for life. The obvious recourse was to dump their bodies somewhere distant. Instead he'd lured a police officer into the web, perhaps stolen his dog on a whim to reel him in. Run such unnecessary risks. Then fled.

You're a clumsy man, Vos.

You miss things.

The man's spoken words were educational too. Loud and firm and confident they had rung out over the graves of Zorgvlied through the dark the night before, taunting him.

Another day, Vos. You will hear from me again. That I promise.

An educated voice.

Someone nudged his shoulder. It was Bakker, phone in hand. 'Anything?' he asked.

'They can't find Braat anywhere. Artis don't have any other address for him. Can't find any relatives yet.'

There was still no word on the identity of the dead man found with Annie Schrijver.

'You may as well go home, Laura. We'll pick this up in the morning. Bang your head against the wall for too long and it just ceases to work.'

He tugged at his long hair, realized he did need a trip to the barber, and perhaps he'd been putting it off because Jillian Chandra had been scolding him on the subject. That thought prompted another puzzle: why had she not been nagging him now? Why so silent all of a sudden?

'Have we heard anything from the commissaris?'

'Not a squeak. Nice, isn't it?'

Vos phoned Van der Berg. He was in a bar somewhere. It sounded as if beer had been taken.

'You got me sent off with a flea in my ear, Pieter. She really didn't like you running round all over the place and never a word back on what you're up to.'

'We had good reason, for God's sake. We found Braat's place. Annie Schrijver and that man were here. I've got forensic. Chandra knows that.'

'Yes but she wants to be told. By you. Directly. Don't you get that?' Van der Berg stopped for a swig. Vos could picture him. He'd seen this often enough. 'Also you're not the only one who can swan off on their own.'

'What do you mean?'

Van der Berg's voice, normally so calm, rose in volume.

'Jillian Chandra is the boss, remember? She calls the shots. When that call came in telling us to look for a van in the water she said she'd deal with it.'

'And you didn't think to tell me?'

That was as close to a yell as Vos got. Aimed at someone who was much more than a colleague too.

There was a long silence then Van der Berg said, 'No. Sorry about that. She said you were obviously too busy to be disturbed. For once I did as I was told.'

'Dirk—'

'Don't take this out on me. At least with De Groot we knew where we stood. To hell with it . . .'

The line went dead. Vos swore and got through to Marnixstraat. A somewhat embarrassed night team officer came on the line. A uniform patrol had come across tyre tracks going into the Amstel two kilometres along the bank from where he now stood. Commissaris Chandra had taken control of the recovery herself.

'No one told me,' Vos pointed out.

'I guess . . . well . . . that was up to her, wasn't it? They're waiting on a crane or something.'

Another curse. Vos marched over, took Bakker's arm and told her to requisition one of the forensic team's vehicles.

'Where are we going?' she asked.

There were more lights now in Braat's houseboat, figures in white suits moving through the low interior like busy ghosts.

'You're going home. Leave this to me.'

———

83

There were so many parked vehicles along the bank he had to leave the car by the road and walk the last few hundred metres to the river. Jillian Chandra was there in a dark coat, directing a team of people he barely knew. A small crane was dangling a lifting hook over the black water beneath tall floodlights, a set-up that must have taken a couple of hours to put into place.

He told himself to stay calm, then walked into fray.

'Fancy seeing you here,' she said, glancing at him then turning back to watch the crane hook swing towards the river.

'If I'd known—'

'When I ask to be kept in the picture I expect it to happen.'

In eighteen years he'd worked under four different heads of Marnixstraat. All Amsterdammers, officers who'd risen through the ranks and knew the ropes and the city around them. Each had his foibles and could, on occasion, turn awkward. None of them would have behaved like this. Jillian Chandra was making it up as she went along and didn't mind who knew.

'We've got the place where they were attacked. Braat's boat.'

'So I gather.'

He looked round. There was no sign of any divers.

'Have you sent anyone down to look inside the van?'

She shrugged.

'One of the uniform people came down here and saw the tracks.' Two men in waders, the kind fishermen used, were guiding the hook towards its target. 'We get it out and then we take a look.'

'May we speak, Commissaris? Privately?'

Beneath the fluorescent glare of the floods she looked at him, thought for a moment then said, 'Of course.'

They walked away from the bank and the mill of people there.

'You should have sent divers down first.'

'Why?'

'Because there may be something there we don't want to disturb.'

'I don't think that's likely, is it? You've found the man's boat. I've got his van. We've checked the plate. It is registered to him. I've got Braat's details circulated everywhere. Once we pick him up—'

'You can't run a case this way,' Vos said and knew immediately he was in the wrong.

'I can do what I like.'

'If you want me to lead this investigation you mustn't intervene like this. Without my agreement—'

She stared at him.

'I need your agreement?'

'Without my knowledge, then. This is a complex matter. More so than we understand. If an investigation gets pulled in different directions . . .'

'Complex?' She looked amazed. 'A stinking pervert you should have jailed four years ago gets out of jail and does exactly the same thing again? You call that complex?'

'We don't know for sure—'

'I had Schuurman phone me from the boat. It's clear what happened there. We've got this Braat creature nailed. You just have to find him. Any ideas on that front?'

The officers in waders were struggling to attach the hook to something beneath the black water.

'Not right now.'

'Best come up with something in the morning. Eight o'clock. My office. You will be there.'

'Divers,' he said. 'You always use divers. One step at a time. We need to be patient.'

She laughed at him.

'Patience? Is that what let this bastard skip free four years ago? When you—'

'Commissaris,' he said with some force. 'I don't know what happened four years ago. Not fully. And if I haven't got a clue then neither have you.'

In the harsh artificial light Chandra glared at him and asked, 'How did you find out I was here?'

'I asked control.'

She was the kind of woman who was probably very good at spotting a lie.

'It wasn't Van der Berg who put you onto this, was it? I specifically ordered him not to.'

'I said. It was control.'

Another dry, humourless laugh at that.

'God. You really are living in the past, aren't you? The way things were once upon a time. Keep the people above you in the dark. Get on with it in your own sweet way. Just watch each other's backs and everything will be fine. Because the fools upstairs will never know any better.'

She leaned forward and prodded his shoulder with a stubby finger.

'What century is this? Remind me.'

'One where people get drugged and murdered and God knows what else. All in some foul little dump of a houseboat when no one's looking.' He was aware immediately he'd risen to her bait and didn't mind. 'Same as any other.'

Chandra smiled, victorious.

'Not for you, Vos. Not any longer. I hope you can find it in you to work with me. If not, I'll sort out a little place for you in the provinces. You can take your ego there. Maybe look for lost dogs or something.' A thought. It amused her. 'You like dogs, don't you? Got experience losing them too.'

'Anything else, Commissaris?'

She was on a roll and enjoying it.

'People like you are what's wrong with the service. You lack discipline. A sense of order. You're blindly loyal to those who are close to you. And the rest of us . . . well, we don't really count, do we?' The finger came out and jabbed him once more. 'I'm here to fix you or fire you. Never forget it. Now . . .'

The crane engine kicked into life, sending up a scattering of noisy ducks from the rushes. Their wings flapped across the starry sky.

Chandra left him and walked to the bank. The van was coming out of the river, water dripping out of its doors, pouring out of a shattered front window like blood from a freshly opened wound.

Halfway through their argument he'd felt a buzz in his jacket pocket. The phone. A message.

Another foreign number, impossible to trace he felt sure.

Are you suffering yet, Vos? Has it begun?

He typed an answer.

I believe so. What do you want?

There was a pause and he wondered for a second whether it might have been worth trying for a trace. But it was hard to imagine whoever was taunting him had left any pointers there.

Then came the reply.

What we all want. Fulfilment. Recognition. Joy.

By the river someone started to yell for the crane to move.

Hospitals.

Bert Schrijver would never lose that picture of his parents dying slowly, hour by hour, in this self-same antiseptic complex, the air filled with that sickening clinical smell, the corridors echoing to the slow steps of nurses and doctors striding from ward to ward, never stopping to talk to patients or relatives any longer than was necessary.

He couldn't believe they'd actually managed to make the experience worse. Annie was locked away in the intensive care unit behind a set of double doors only the medical staff could open with their ID cards. The nurse who'd summoned them had gone home. The woman on reception wasn't sure why they'd been called at all. When she tried to find out, quite half-heartedly, all she got was a blank.

Intensive care was in the throes of an emergency. The medical staff were too busy to find out why he and Nina had been told to come to the hospital straight away. In the endless corridors and wards beyond the double doors it seemed someone was fighting for life. Perhaps, Bert Schrijver thought, losing the battle. And just maybe it was their daughter, that one bright light he had, smiling, happy Annie, the flower girl of the Albert Cuyp. The only precious gift left to him, so irreplaceable that a small, much-hated voice had whispered in his ear for ages: *One day something dark and evil will snatch her from you and there's nothing an idiot like you can do to stop it.*

In the corner an old woman, straggly grey hair, dishevelled clothing best suited for winter not September, sobbed loudly, rhythmically into a grubby handkerchief. Snatches of her words came to him from time to time. A man's name. *Thomas.* Fragments of a whispered prayer to a god whose attention was surely oversubscribed hereabouts.

After a while he couldn't listen any more. So he left Nina, got a cup of water from the dispenser and sat alone by the toilet door, sipping at the drink, then stuffing his fists in his ears to keep out the racket.

The cries of the living. The whirr of machines. The asthmatic breathing of the air conditioning. Hard footsteps on harder floors.

Three times he'd tried to argue with the woman on reception, demanding to know what was happening. Three times he got knocked back, the last with a firm warning backed up by a wagging finger: *Get any more aggressive and security will be round to kick you out for good this time.*

Angry, lost, ashamed at his impotence, Schrijver let his head fall between his hands, dripped some of the cold water against his cheeks hoping it would make him feel just the least bit alive.

Cold liquid met skin. Then warm. He realized he was weeping and that made his head fall even further down and the half-full cup fall to the floor.

A soft hand stroked his forehead. Nina was there retrieving the cup, wiping away the little puddle it had left. She sat next to him, moved her fingers from his thinning hair down to his hand and took it.

'Bert. If we can't learn how to wait we can't be here. That's what you do in hospitals.'

All he needed was for Rob Sanders to walk in and his misery would be complete.

'Why won't they tell us?'

'Maybe because Annie's not the only one here. There might be . . .' She glanced at the double doors. 'Tens of them. Hundreds for all we know. Lot worse than how we saw her too. They're busy. An emergency.'

'And Annie's not? What do they care?'

'Of course they care,' she said and the don't-be-stupid tone in her voice was back. 'It's just all that sympathy gets shared around among lots of people. Patients and relatives like us. You can't expect every last bit of it. That would be greedy and you've never been a greedy man.'

The doors opened. Two nurses walked out, half-running, pushing some kind of a machine in front of them. Then came a man in a wheelchair, blue hospital gown around his skinny frame, a bottle of something on a pole by his shoulder, lines in his arm.

Schrijver couldn't stop himself staring at his face. Grey and bony, white whiskers against pockmarked skin. Marked by something else too. Fear and resignation.

You're dying, he thought. *I know they say we all are. Right from the moment we're born. But you're dying here and now, second by second, breath by breath. Won't ever set foot out of this place again. See the sunlight. Laugh and cry in the open air, somewhere green and cheerful.*

'Worst thing is,' Nina added, watching the nurses, the ward orderly, and the sick man pass, 'it all kicks off again tomorrow. Day in, day out. God knows how they deal with it. You get hard, I guess. Otherwise you'd never manage.'

She sighed to herself then, to his astonishment, kissed him quickly on the cheek.

'One other thing they'll never say about Bert Schrijver. That you turned hard. Not in you, is it?'

'Sure about that?' he asked and regretted it in an instant. She pulled back from him and there was that look of regret, of self-loathing, on her face. Something they both could manage when they wanted.

The door opened. The consultant they'd seen earlier bustled through dictating to a nurse scribbling on a pad by his side. The man barely saw them. Schrijver was up before Nina, standing in front of him, blocking his way.

The doctor scowled at him then apologized.

'Oh, right. The Schrijvers. I didn't recognize you.'

'Someone called. They said Annie's condition changed. We've been sitting here hours.'

'I'll be in theatre if you need me,' the nurse said and walked off.

The consultant had dead eyes. He looked as if he hadn't slept in days.

'It all got hectic,' he said, clearly trying to marshal his thoughts. 'Coach crash out near Schiphol. Didn't you hear the news?'

'Had enough news of our own,' Schrijver said.

'They called about Annie,' Nina repeated.

He thought about this then nodded.

'Right. Follow me.'

Heart pumping, breath coming in short gasps, they went through the double doors.

They never tell you out straight, Bert Schrijver thought. *There's always a roundabout route. Maybe they just don't want to say it. Because that might steal away a little of their own lives too.*

They rounded a corner. Annie's room was two doors along. A couple of nurses were bustling through, sheets in their arms, and straight away he told himself.

Too late again, you useless bastard. Did nothing for her when she was alive. Couldn't even make it into the room when she gasped out that last pained terrified breath.

He was crying again and couldn't help it, the warm thick salty tears running down his bristly cheeks.

Schrijver stumbled into her room, heard the hated machines laughing at him in their tinny electronic tones.

'Annie . . .' Nina said by his side. 'Oh, Annie. Darling . . .'

She lay on the bed. Fewer wires and lines now, not so many bleeping machines.

Eyes wide open, blue he remembered, not that he'd been able to recover that particular memory before. Her face was so pale it was hard to believe warm blood flushed her cheeks. Fair hair tousled and greasy, that silly sapphire streak in it.

'Mum,' Annie Schrijver said and started to weep. Careful to avoid the lines and cables, Nina approached and threw her arms around her daughter, held her as close and tight as she could.

Bert Schrijver could only watch, lost for words at that moment as the consultant spoke calmly and clearly about how the worst was over. That perhaps as quickly as a day from now Annie would be free to go home.

Home.

Wherever that was. A dump by the Albert Cuyp full of flowers he'd been mentally ticking off for a funeral. The Schrijver castle, now teetering on the edge of bankruptcy. Or her mother's little flat more likely.

He'd failed her. Schrijver knew that, accepted it now, and that knowledge seemed to piss upon all the relief and joy he felt that she still lived.

'What happened?' he asked.

The words just came out. As soon as they did he knew Nina would turn on him with that familiar, accusatory look.

'I'm sorry, Dad,' she whispered. 'I'm so . . .'

The two of them were blubbing, more than he'd ever seen since Annie's grandparents passed away.

He sat on the edge of the bed and took her hand. The consultant said something none of them heard and left.

Schrijver squeezed his daughter's fingers. There were marks still there, the little cuts she got from handling thorny rose stems. Stigmata were all he'd given her over the years.

'What . . . ?' he began and could think of nothing else.

'Not now,' Nina told him as the three of them came close on the hard white cotton sheets, amidst the electronic drone of the machines above the bed.

Maybe never, he thought. Perhaps it was the best, the kindest way.

Vos watched the van swing above the river leaking filthy water as it travelled to the bank. Jillian Chandra was in charge. He'd no desire to start a public fight with her. No wish to do anything except get to the bottom of the strange sequence of events that had begun with Sam's disappearance the night before. Which meant going back to the Sleeping Beauty case. He hadn't managed to get to the bottom of that four years before. If he was honest with himself, he'd known it all along.

That also meant undertaking the delicate task of renewing his acquaintance with Marly Kloosterman, the doctor in the prison hospital. An interview with Vincent de Graaf, now her patient, was called for. De Graaf had asked for it. Time to give him what he wanted.

The men working the crane were starting to yell for the van to come down. Vos had seen countless vehicles recovered from the drink. Canals usually. It was a tricky task, dangerous sometimes. Best left to the experts. Not that Commissaris Chandra would have agreed. She was running Marnixstraat. She knew best.

The crane chugged and heaved. He'd watch this all the way through then return to the Drie Vaten, sink a couple of beers, talk to Sofia Albers and try to remember what the real world was like.

'Bring it down to the ground now,' one of the recovery team yelled.

A sturdy man, someone Vos recognized from occasions like this in the past. The waders that reached up to his beefy chest were drenched and covered in weed. Putting a tentative hand to the van's rear nearside wheel he turned and asked Chandra to move back from the area they were going to use to land it.

She did, reluctantly accepting there were a few things here beyond her. At that moment Vos felt a twinge of sympathy. There'd been a common refrain in Marnixstraat since she'd arrived, one he quashed whenever he heard it. A whisper that said it was only gender and foreign blood that made a woman like her rise so rapidly through the ranks, buoyed by a fashionable tide of political correctness.

All of which might be true. Still, it didn't lessen the difficulty of being both female and from an immigrant background. Life must have been tough for Jillian Chandra when she was starting out. She'd never acknowledge the fact, or that it had shaped her. Or, and this had only just occurred to him, that it left scars, something brittle, almost fragile, behind the steely facade of which she made such a visible show.

The van landed on the muddy grass with a crash. Chandra didn't wait before moving towards it, pulling on a pair of latex gloves.

'Oh, for God's sake,' Vos murmured. 'Please . . .'

He dashed over, determined to stop one more breach of protocol. Forensic were always first to deal with evidence like this. They knew what they were doing. The rest stood back.

'Commissaris,' he said, trying to reach out and stop her as she approached the door. 'You have to leave the entry to—'

'Don't tell me what to do!' she said out loud, determined everyone around would hear.

Fine, he thought and stood back to watch her anyway.

It was an old Renault. White once, now covered in river mud and weed, the nose dented, front windscreen shattered. Water still stood halfway up the side window, kept in by the closed door.

He saw something there and checked himself.

'I'd really advise . . .'

Chandra wasn't listening. Watched by the shocked forensic officers she grabbed hold of the driver's door handle, jerked on it, got nowhere, jerked hard again and then it began to move.

She briefly turned to grin at him, triumphant.

Grubby water tumbled out around her knees. Before she could step back something flopped sideways out of the van, fell against her legs, hanging there, half held by a failed seat belt. A long shape, that of a man, naked from the waist up.

Dead eyes staring, dead mouth grinning, teeth yellow and broken, biting on slimy green weed.

Jillian Chandra started screaming, a long, high frightened yowl quite unlike her usual breathy tenor. She stumbled away, shrieking at the corpse as a pair of dead arms slipped out from beneath the belt and flapped at her face and neck. One of the uniforms raced up and fought with the body, releasing it from the van. It dropped to the damp ground with a sudden thud. Chandra was fleeing through the band of forensic officers who'd automatically come to crowd forward, peering at what she'd found.

'Their job,' Vos told himself. 'Not ours.'

Scene of crime people were always curious, never daunted. Experience did that to you and experience – of the city, the dark world around her – was something the new commissaris so visibly lacked.

Since the rules of conduct had vanished Vos joined them, down on his knees by the side of the body.

A well-built man of middle age. It looked as if something, a pike, a wandering zander, had nibbled at his lips and eyes, taken a bite out of his shoulder. The last wound wasn't far from the butterfly tattoo that ran across most of the right side of his neck. Above was a face that, even in death, seemed easily recognizable from the photo Bakker had shown him.

There were scratches on his right shoulder and they had to be important. On Annie Schrijver, nothing. This man . . .

Vos pushed forward and saw.

Sleep Baby Sleep.

He stood up, took out his phone and got through to control.

'You can call off the search for Jef Braat.'

'You've found him?' asked the woman at the other end.

Jillian Chandra sat on the muddy grass, hands to her mouth, shaking.

'I believe we have,' he said.

THREE

He got in the office early, determined to be on time. It was no surprise Laura Bakker was there already but he hadn't expected to see Van der Berg an hour before the shift was due to begin.

'Everything OK, Dirk?'

Van der Berg was in a creased dark pinstripe suit that had seen better days. His eyes were a touch bloodshot. Perhaps it had been a long night.

'Wonderful.'

There was something odd by his computer. A bush hat. One that looked familiar.

'Where did you get that?'

The thing was dark brown, broad-brimmed and made of suede.

'It looks stupid,' Bakker chipped in from the adjoining desk. 'By the way . . . the summons is off. That posh bloke she brought with her from Zoetermeer. The PR man. Den Hartog. He came in to say she's called a press conference at nine thirty. First off he's got her doing some preparation. Then a couple of TV interviews.' She screwed up her nose, thinking. 'Never been stood up by a commissaris going into make-up before. Den Hartog says we're going to have camera crews wandering round the office for a while so we're supposed to be on our best behaviour. I don't know what he thought we'd be doing. Pole dancing?'

A shifty look on Van der Berg's face suggested he knew this already.

'A press conference?' Vos asked. 'About what?'

Van der Berg smiled a quick, sardonic smile and said, 'Sleeping Beauty case put to bed. First trophy on the wall. Best not argue. Pointless.'

'Sounds like it's good news all round,' Bakker added. 'Annie Schrijver's come round in hospital. She's lucky. No long-term damage. They'll probably allow her home soon.'

There was a bustle at the door. Outside the office a cameraman was filming Jillian Chandra walking down the corridor beaming broadly in a uniform so pressed, the buttons shining like little silver beacons, it had to be brand new.

'Whole thing didn't turn out so bad in the end,' Bakker went on. 'She's OK. Sam's fine. That sick bastard who got away four years ago is out of our hair for good and . . .'

'There's a corpse in the basement,' Vos pointed out. 'A murder victim. We don't have a clue who he is. Unless something's happened I haven't been told about.'

Silence then.

'Has it?'

Van der Berg went back to squinting at his screen. Bakker shrugged.

'The hat, Dirk?'

Vos waited until the truth came out. Found underneath a table outside the Drie Vaten two nights before, just after Sam had been snatched.

'I asked in the bar,' he explained. 'I told Sofia. If anyone came back to claim the thing I'd happily hand it over. But—' He glared briefly at Bakker. 'I like it.'

Vos reached into the drawer and pulled out a large evidence bag. Then, very gingerly, he picked up the crown between pinched fingers and dropped the hat inside.

'Is there a DNA record anywhere with your name on it?'

'What?'

'This looks like the hat he was wearing. The man who took Sam. Who lured me all the way to Zorgvlied. Two bodies there and a can of petrol.'

Bakker laughed. 'Jef Braat left it there? Oh, come on. That can't be right. It's just a coincidence, Pieter.'

'Take this down to forensic,' Vos told Van der Berg. 'Get yourself swabbed. Ask them if they can find someone else's DNA on the thing. Start with the sweatband. Maybe we'll get lucky.'

'If you'd mentioned we were looking for a hat . . .'

The two men had worked together for almost two decades with barely an argument along the way. Now there was a distinct chill between them.

'I sent a team down to the Drie Vaten to see if anyone remembered the man. They might have found it.'

'I didn't know! Like Laura says. It's probably not his anyway.'

Vos picked up the bag with the hat in it.

'Take this downstairs. You know what to ask for.'

Van der Berg grunted something then grabbed it and headed for the stairs.

'You didn't need to talk to him like that,' Bakker said.

'Like what?'

'Like . . . he's in the wrong. If no one told him you were looking for stuff down there . . .'

'Why's everyone so touchy today?'

'We weren't until you turned up.'

He ignored that crack and started to read some of the overnight reports. News of Annie Schrijver's recovery. The night team had taken a brief and remarkably uninformative statement from her in hospital. She said a man who'd bought flowers in the market had invited her out for a drink somewhere in the centre. She'd no idea who he was. Couldn't even remember a first name. Or much about the bar either. Some time later she'd been woken in the back of a van and told to talk to her father. By a man wearing an animal mask. A dog or a wolf. After that she'd passed out again and knew nothing until she came to in the hospital. The interview had ended early at the insistence of the medical team.

There were no missing person reports that matched the cadaver still lying without a name tag in the morgue. But Braat's houseboat was gradually coughing up evidence. The place contained weed and cocaine alongside scores of butterfly chrysalises seemingly stolen from Artis. And a recently used portable tattoo kit. Clean of prints but there were traces of blood and ink.

The forensic nurse who'd visited Annie in hospital had found none of the usual evidence of violent assault. There was no sign yet of sexual activity anywhere in the boat. The victim's clothes were missing which meant they had none of the usual sources of DNA.

Braat's movements before his death remained a mystery. No one had seen him since he'd briefly turned up at the Amstelpark making excuses to the owner of the butterfly pavilion being built there.

Cases often ended messily, with partial solutions and awkward questions left unanswered. This one didn't feel it had attained even that status yet. Yet Jillian Chandra had decided it was over bar the details. That much was obvious from a quick look at the web. The news services were running stories already, ones that could only have come from her pet PR man Den Hartog. They'd dug up the cuttings on the Sleeping Beauty case and declared that the team involved four years before had failed to close it properly.

The media were predicting the police would soon name a third murderer, an Amsterdammer who'd escaped the earlier investigation and gone on to kill again. One victim, an unidentified male, had died already. A young woman from De Pijp had narrowly escaped with her life.

Bakker came and sat by his side as he read.

'Where do they get this stuff?' she asked. 'Do they just make it up?'

The report said that, under pressure from the new commissaris, the Sleeping Beauty case had been reopened and seemingly resolved. The perpetrator was a recently released sexual offender who had been missed by the earlier investigation. His body had been recovered from the Amstel by a team led by the commissaris herself the night before. Suicide, the reports were hinting.

'Sometimes,' he said.

There was a sound beyond the door. Chandra was walking into the far side of the office, being filmed all the way by the crew.

'Please get me out of here,' Bakker begged. 'I don't want my picture on the TV. My nan will be on the phone straight off wondering why I'm not wearing a nice dress.'

Van der Berg nodded at the two of them as he came back in then sat down in front of his PC without a word.

'The morgue,' Vos said. 'After that . . .'

He walked up to Van der Berg and put a friendly hand on his shoulder.

'Laura and I are going to Bijlmerbajes.'

A pause, a nod, a sly glance then, 'Oh yes. The prison hospital. I remember now. Is that doctor there still sweet on you?'

Bakker said gleefully, 'Ooh. Gossip. Do tell.'

'Nothing to tell,' Vos said, aware he might be blushing. 'I want to talk to De Graaf. He asked for us. Besides . . . I don't think Laura's ever been inside the jail. Have you?'

'Always a first time. This doctor—'

'No one's sweet on me,' Vos snapped.

They went quiet at that until Bakker said, 'Perhaps we ought to have another go at talking to Annie Schrijver. That statement says so little. She has to remember more.'

'Maybe,' Vos agreed.

Bijlmerbajes wasn't far from the hospital in the Zuidas. Any more than Zorgvlied, the Amstelpark, the river. It was as if everything was happening in a specific defined area. Like a village. That in itself was interesting.

Marly Kloosterman, who ran the medical unit, was interesting too. A bright, practical, attractive woman who'd briefly skirted his life. They'd met at one of the social evenings the prison organized with the police from time to time. It wasn't long after he returned to the job. Life seemed complicated enough. He wasn't ready for a relationship and in his own inept way he'd tried to tell her that before anything got too serious.

Van der Berg still didn't look happy.

'This is all very well. But you ought to clear it with the commissaris first. She specifically asked me to tell you. No more surprises. No more . . .' He looked up, trying to recall something. 'What were her exact words? Oh yes. We don't fly solo any more.'

Across the room Jillian Chandra swept through the office with an imperious smile on her face, followed by the TV people.

'She's busy,' Vos said. 'You tell her.'

Schrijver slept in the office next to the desk. There was no other room left in what remained of the castle. A single bed, a hard mattress. Usually the early morning market traffic woke him but not today. He was starting to rouse, still half-dressed from the night before, when Jordi Hoogland rapped his knuckles on the desk.

'You've got a visitor.'

He tried to shake himself awake, head full of confused, dazed memories. Relief that was somehow tainted with pain. For a moment he doubted himself. Was it really true Annic would be fine? The doctors had allowed them so little time with her. She was too tired, they said. But they still ushered the two of them out and let in the police.

They'd hung around until three, waiting in a private room for someone to allow them back to their daughter's bedside. It never happened. A sympathetic officer gave them a lift back to De Pijp. An odd journey, next to his ex-wife, both of them too drained to speak.

Then he'd fallen on the single bed and tumbled into a black enveloping sleep.

He signalled to Hoogland to wait for a moment, got up, stiff and aching, found his phone on the desk.

There was a message from Nina. Annie was still resting. The doctors thought it best she had no visitors for a while. They were carrying out more tests. The prospects looked good but they wanted to be sure.

Hoogland remained at the door, leaning on the frame, burly arms crossed. Black leather jacket, black jeans, black T-shirt. Grey hair drooping down his back in the usual greasy ponytail.

'I grabbed one of the immigrants from the market to help out. Afghan kid been hanging round asking for work. Says he knows flowers. He's hasn't got a licence to drive but he can man the stall. I'll do the rounds. You OK with that?'

'Can you trust him?'

Hoogland snorted.

'He's dead if he screws with me. Knows it too.'

Fine then, Schrijver said, and asked who the visitor was.

Hoogland's wrinkled, unshaven face creased in a frown.

'Says she's from the estate agents round the corner. You made an appointment.'

'Right.'

'Anything I should know about?'

No, Schrijver told him. Then asked for a few minutes to get ready.

When he came out, shaved, washed, new clothes that were old, she was looking at the pile of previous day's flowers the way people did sometimes.

That's not fresh. Who do you think you're fooling?

He could almost hear her say it.

A smart woman in a pristine navy blue suit, she came over and gave him a business card: Lies Poelman from the agency he'd walked into the week before. Big office. Lots of fancy places in the window. They'd said the going rate for apartments in the area was around five thousand a square metre. Schrijver had come back and tried to estimate the size of the remaining ground floor space left over from the castle. It must have been more than seven hundred with the yard, the bare warehousing, the office, the boxed-in storeroom that was now Annie's. Then the shop-front on the market.

Even though it was a dump it surely ought to be worth two million or more. The bank had a charge against the property for the debts the business had run up. It was the only way he could keep afloat. Schrijver hadn't looked too hard at those numbers of late but the debt probably amounted to somewhere north of two hundred thousand. Even so there ought to be enough money to get out of the market, split the proceeds with Nina, then give his half to Annie. She could buy a nice little flat somewhere close by, find a proper job. De Pijp was her home. His too, but he could throw himself on the mercy of the city and go wherever they wanted to put him.

'You told us you had a property to sell,' the Poelman woman said, sounding a little puzzled.

He gestured at the scruffy warehouse full of fading flowers. The smell wasn't too good. Strong perfume, rotting foliage.

'This is it. The yard. The shop the other side of that.'

She gazed at him, mouth half-open. Lots of lipstick and very white teeth.

'These are commercial premises. Do you have permission for residential use?'

'What?' He didn't understand. 'It's mine. We live here. Been in my family for years. The people upstairs bought those places off us.'

'Who handled the sale?'

'Some agent.' Who swindled me, Schrijver nearly said. That man had rattled on about permissions and change of use too, then battered him down on the price. 'They said in the office you get five thousand a square metre round here. God knows what idiot would pay that . . .'

'For apartments. Legal. Converted. Modern heating. Fitted kitchens. Bathrooms. Rain showers.' She gestured at the sliding wooden door. 'Views.'

'The shop at the front's got a view. I'll show you.'

They crossed the grubby courtyard. There was a dead pigeon by the drain. She stepped away from it then walked into the part that looked out onto the Albert Cuyp. Jordi Hoogland was behind the stall they set up each day, talking to a foreign kid amidst the buckets of tulips and lilies.

'This could be a nice place for someone,' he suggested.

'A view of the market.' She laughed. 'I have to say . . . it's not something we get asked for much.'

She pointed to a bar that had opened down the street. A new place for the new crowd. Cocktails and burgers. He'd never been in. Never thought about it. He slept on the other side of the building and didn't go near the shop till the morning.

'You know the Mariposa?'

'What?'

'The cocktail joint. Really popular.'

He cursed himself for not looking there the night Annie went missing.

'Not with me.'

'Right. Not with you. They're open till three in the morning some nights. You'd need to be deaf to live here. This place is a shop. Nothing else.'

'If it fetches more that way . . .'

She shook her head, walked back into the courtyard and looked around. There was nothing there but grey grubby walls, mostly belonging to people he didn't even know.

'Would you want to carry out the conversion yourself?' she asked and looked as if she knew the answer.

'How much?'

He loathed these people. They could size up something, anything, and turn it into money in their heads.

'The place at the front needs refitting even for commercial use. Proper heating for one thing. They'll make you put in a toilet and basin. The back?' She scowled. 'The thing is . . . people want windows. Maybe you could get two places out of it. At a push three.'

'What about here? The yard?'

'The yard's a place for dead pigeons. Share it between the apartments. Or hand it over to the biggest. Won't make any difference to the price.'

'How much?' he repeated.

That wince again and she said, 'Permission, plans, architect, builders, materials. Big job. Got to be two fifty up. Four if you want it premium. Not that I'd go for premium. Lipstick on a pig as they say.'

'I'm handy. I can manage.'

She looked straight at him.

'We don't handle do-it-yourself, Mr Schrijver. Besides, the city will want major work like this signed off. Electricians. Plumbing. Plans. Proper architect ones. You can't bring in your drinking mates and let them scrawl something on a beer mat.'

He was struggling to imagine how he might make this happen.

'I'd need to raise that money before I started?'

'Would you work for someone who wasn't going to pay you till he'd sold the place? You could always take out a loan set against the property.'

Debt. That was the answer they offered for everything. He was drowning in it already, every penny willingly given with a smile. Schrijver took a deep breath and asked, 'How much would I get for them? Finished? All of them?'

There was a deliberate and professional pause. Then she said, 'The front wouldn't go for much. Market retail. It's not big enough for a restaurant or a bar. If you're lucky two fifty. If we got two units out of the storeroom about the same, maybe a bit more.

Squeeze in a third and perhaps I could get the whole deal up to about seven or eight hundred. I can't guarantee that of course.'

Numbers usually foxed him but not these. He'd lazily counted in the yard and thought the whole block was worth two million. On what she was saying he'd be lucky to clear a fraction of that. After selling costs and bank debts there'd be barely three hundred thousand to split between them.

'I need to share this with my ex-wife. My daughter. She lives here right now. I'd hoped she'd buy herself a place close by. If she had maybe two hundred . . .'

'You might find a little studio. There are better deals if she's willing to move further out. Some real bargains in the north.'

'This is her home. Where she grew up. She shouldn't have to live in a shoebox.'

The estate agent shrugged and looked around her as if to say: *She's putting up with this dump, isn't she?*

It was a pipe dream anyway. He'd no idea how he could raise the money to convert the place. Or supervise the work without getting ripped off.

Hoogland had come back in from the street and was lighting a cigarette on the other side of the yard, juggling the keys to the van. The young, dark-skinned man he'd found, the Afghan, Schrijver presumed, was working the stall now.

'Sorry I wasted your time. I need to get to work. Got to see someone in hospital soon.'

The woman didn't move. He knew what that meant. There was an offer coming.

'Your other option is to sell up lock, stock and barrel to a developer. Let them take the risk on planning. Pick up all the hassle and the bills.'

'How much?'

She suddenly looked interested.

'Actually now I think about it there is someone on the books who's been looking for an opportunity round here. A Chinese investor. It's a lot rougher than they wanted but they've got ready cash. You'd need to move quickly. They don't like hanging about.'

'*How much?*'

She smiled at that in a way that told him she'd been angling towards this moment all along.

'They're new to the market. Still a touch . . . naive. What if I could get them up to half a million? Quick and easy money. Probably as much as you'd make doing it yourself anyway. Without the pain.'

'Without the pain,' he murmured.

'Your choice.' She looked round the scruffy yard. 'Buildings are funny. They always carry memories with them. But you can't live off memories, can you? Best pass these old bricks on to someone else to find their own.'

'Five fifty,' he said and knew straight off it should have been more.

'Let me see what I can do. If I get an offer in a matter of days will you settle it swiftly? There are no . . . impediments? Nothing I need know about?'

'He can have it tomorrow if he comes up with the money.'

'It's a woman actually.'

'I don't care who the hell it is.'

Already he could picture the end of the business. More than half a century of the Schrijvers selling flowers gone for good, all because he wasn't up to the job his father and grandfather had managed without a second thought. There'd be people picking over the pallets and the crappy office furniture seeing if there was anything they wanted. New locks, the smell of fresh paint, not tulips, lilies and roses. He'd be loath to walk through the market after that. It hurt just to think about it.

The woman rattled off some commercial details, commission and other charges, not that he listened. Then she left by the shopfront, stopping to buy something from the kid on the stall.

Schrijver watched, interested. She was smiling for the first time, had her purse out, looked more engaged than she had for a single moment with him.

Schuurman was back in the morgue after a night spent out by the Amstel. He was a dapper middle-aged man of studied manners, little humour and precise language. Long hours never seemed to dim his determination. Vos liked him. Laura Bakker feared him a little. But so did most of Marnixstraat.

The resting place for the dead lay in the station basement and possessed an atmosphere of its own: cold, chemical, noisy with the racket of old air conditioning and the beep of many machines. Vos found there were usually answers here, if only one could frame the right question.

Aisha Refai was tapping at a keyboard as the two of them approached.

'I can't tell you yet,' Schuurman said without looking up. 'There's no guarantee I'll be able to next week. Or ever.'

This was the game and it had to be played.

'I don't recall asking a question,' Vos pointed out.

The pathologist looked up and raised a bushy eyebrow.

'But you will. And knowing you it will always be an impossible one.'

'Sorry.' Vos bent over the PC to see what Aisha was entering there. 'I don't suppose you have a time of death for our friend Braat? Or is that too difficult?'

The young forensic officer showed him a photo. A watch, stopped at five to midnight on Tuesday.

'Very cheap timepiece, the kind you'd buy for five euros down the market. The case leaked. Seems pretty obvious it stopped when he went into the Amstel.'

'Obvious,' Vos agreed.

'And then he drowned?' Bakker asked.

'And then he drowned,' Schuurman agreed.

'Any sign of sexual activity?' Vos wondered.

Schuurman wouldn't commit to an answer on that. Still, they knew Annie Schrijver and the unidentified victim had been in his boat. The man's blood was on the sheets and walls in quantity, hers in smaller amounts. Braat's too, as if there'd been a fight. There was physical evidence both victims had been in the back of his van. Vos was beginning to understand why Jillian Chandra, anxious as she was for answers, felt she'd found her man.

'Why would you kidnap two people, kill one, then commit suicide?' Bakker asked.

'I deal in facts. Not interpretation,' Schuurman replied without looking up from the desk.

'What else?' Vos wondered.

'What else do you want to know?'

'Did he have GHB in his blood?'

'Traces,' Aisha said. 'Very small traces.'

Laura Bakker was going through some of the photos on her desk. A crumpled corpse on muddy grass, illuminated by floodlights. An old van dripping water.

'What does that mean?' she asked.

'It means he had traces of GHB in his bloodstream at the point we checked,' Schuurman replied with mock patience.

A short lecture followed. The drug never stayed long in the body. Especially one that had been sitting in the murky waters of the Amstel river for more than a day.

'So there's no way of estimating what kind of state he was in when he went into the water?' Vos asked.

Schuurman nodded.

'None. He might have taken a small dose to . . . enhance his fun. If indeed there was fun. A bit more to help him sleep.' He had a craggy, academic face. It was turned on both of them. 'The question you really want to ask is one I wish I could answer. Was he conscious when he went into the water or doped like the

Schrijver woman and the others from four years ago? I can't tell you. Sorry.'

'The commissaris felt sure he killed himself,' Bakker pointed out.

Schuurman gazed at her and said simply, 'Such are the prerogatives of power. May we return to our work now? If we know more you'll hear it.'

Then he went back to his notes.

Bakker kept shuffling through the photos from the previous night. Vos picked up a couple too, looked at them then announced it was time to leave.

Out in the car park they picked up a pool Volvo. She could drive, he said. It was a bright morning, sunny and still unusually warm. TV vans were lined up all around the station. Bakker had to bark at one to let them out.

'You saw something,' she said as they turned into the heavy traffic along Marnixstraat.

'Did I?'

'Yes. You did. And I didn't. Care to tell me?'

It was easy for him. He'd been there the previous night when the van had come out of the water. The vehicle was old. But it still had airbags. He'd checked the make and year when he got home. Neither of them had blown. So the van had gone slowly into the water, with no real impact.

Maybe people killed themselves that way. Especially if they were drowsy with GHB.

'When Chandra opened the door I was there. Braat was wearing a seat belt. One of the uniforms popped it open after she started screaming blue murder. It was dark. People were panicky. Maybe it was just an automatic reaction. Get the man off her. Next thing you know he's on the grass. Very dead.'

A tram loomed up ahead of them. Vos leaned over and gently turned the wheel to ease them away from it. Laura Bakker still struggled with city traffic from time to time.

He waited. She was thinking and that was what he wanted.

'Who puts on a seat belt to kill themselves?' she wondered.

'Someone's who's doped up? Running on automatic? Not thinking straight?' He recalled Van der Berg and the discovery that morning. 'Someone who forgets his hat?'

A young man on a bike wobbled in front of them. A tourist. Bakker wound down the window and yelled at him.

'So Jef Braat got strapped into the driver's seat doped up then someone pushed his van into the water?' she asked when the chastised cyclist rode past.

'That would appear to be one possibility.' He pointed out another oncoming tram. Her fingers stiffened on the wheel. 'Though it seems Commissaris Chandra has other notions. As she's about to tell the world.'

'Oh dear,' Bakker said. 'That *is* a shame.'

The foreigner Hoogland had picked up from the market had scribbled out a sign and stuck it to the front of the stall: bouquets made up on the spot for five, ten, fifteen or twenty euros. In all the years Schrijver had worked the flower trade they'd never done that. Bouquets had to be ordered or bought ready-made. If you just turned up, you got flowers out of the buckets or what was there already.

The young man had a pleasant, soft and gentle foreign voice. Schrijver listened as he upped the estate agent from the five-euro bunch to ten then whipped together a pretty little bouquet so quickly he could only have done this before.

The flowers on their own were worth maybe half that. But put together neatly . . . she seemed happy enough.

When she wandered off Schrijver walked outside and introduced himself. The kid wasn't a kid really. He looked early twenties, maybe more close up. Skinny, smiling, but with the dark, weary eyes a lot of the recent immigrants had.

'I'm Bert,' he said, holding out his hand. 'Thanks for helping out.'

He had hard hands, leathery from labour, and said his name was Adnan.

'You're from Afghanistan?'

He laughed at that.

'No, sir. Syria.'

'Sorry.'

'No need to be sorry. You give me work. I'm glad of that.'

His father had run a florist's shop in Aleppo, lived above the place, he said. A bomb took it out during the war, his parents with it. Schrijver glanced back at the building behind him. In some ways he'd been lucky, he guessed.

The Syrian pointed to the sign he'd made about the bouquets, asking if it was OK.

'You do what you want, Adnan. If it shifts flowers it's fine with me.'

Then he ambled back inside and moved a few empty boxes into the yard. Hoogland stopped loading the van and came out. He didn't look happy.

'That kid's from Syria,' Schrijver told him. 'Not where you said.'

'So what?'

'So he knows flowers. If he can pay his way, I'll keep him while Annie's away.'

'Fucking hell,' Hoogland snapped. 'I'm having to work alongside a rag head now, am I?'

He was casual, not even on the books. Paid in cash the way he wanted.

'You can do what you want, Jordi. You found him. If he makes my life easier—'

'That why you're selling the place?' Hoogland nodded at the building. 'Giving up? Too hard for you?'

'I didn't realize it was any of your business.'

'Been working here off and on forever.'

'Plenty of other people who'll have you.' He looked Hoogland in the eye. This was something he should have said years ago. 'Just keep your hands out of the till. They might not be as forgiving as me.'

That brought a bitter scowl.

'True. But if you weren't so desperate you wouldn't have let me, would you? And if you paid proper wages I wouldn't need to.'

This moment of frankness between them felt strange, unwanted. They were friends of a kind. Or rather men who'd grown up together and never quite escaped each other's company. Different in many ways, Schrijver with his scruffy work clothes, Hoogland with the thuggish black leather and ponytail, the look he'd affected as a teenager, one that was ridiculous now. It had worked with the women once. But that was long ago.

'I don't have time for this shit,' Schrijver said. 'The hospital's going to want us back.'

This time he'd try to keep a handle on his temper. Whether Rob Sanders showed up or not.

Hoogland came and stood in his way. He was just a touch shorter than Schrijver but beefy, strong like all the market porters.

'You're doing all this for that girl of yours, aren't you?'

'Maybe. Some of it.'

Hoogland looked around, nervous suddenly.

'Do you think she's worth it, Bert?'

'What . . . ?'

The remark, said in half a whisper, was so strange, so unexpected, he couldn't even get angry.

'Do you think she'd do the same for you?'

Schrijver pushed him away and walked outside. The market was getting busy. A tall man with a ridiculously coiffured beard was at the front of the bar called Mariposa chalking up specials for the day. Cocktails or food maybe. The names were so foreign Schrijver had no idea.

To his astonishment there was a small crowd around the flower stall. The Syrian was running up a bouquet for a bunch of women tourists wearing matching T-shirts for a hen party. He was a good-looking kid. Nice smile even though there must have been more pain packed into his years than Schrijver could begin to imagine. If it had damaged him he hid it well.

'Abracadabra!' Adnan cried and finished the spray with a flourish. It was a good mix, well done, attractive, put together so quickly Schrijver could scarcely believe it. Then, as he passed it over, he reached up with his left hand and placed a single dwarf lily behind the ear of the woman at the front.

'You should let us do your wedding, lady,' he said in good English. 'Excellent price, beautiful flowers.'

'You'd need to ship them to Scotland, love,' she answered with a laugh.

'All things are possible, with a little effort,' he replied in a deep and sincere voice.

They laughed. They ordered another ten-euro bouquet to take with them. Out of pity more than need, he thought.

On the way out Schrijver stopped and patted him lightly on the back.

Adnan looked a little scared at that.

'I just try to sell flowers, boss. You OK with that?'

'Very. Carry on like this, young man, and you'll earn yourself a job.'

The Syrian grinned then returned to working the passing crowd.

Schrijver went to the pavement and watched him. He'd never been easy with customers. His father had once told him he couldn't sell a fifty guilder note for five cents. You either had that talent or you didn't. Annie possessed it, and her mother's winning smile. This stranger had it too.

His phone rang.

'Where are you?' Nina asked.

'Work. How is she?'

'Sleeping. They say we have to wait.'

Waiting.

'Bert. The news is saying they got someone last night.'

'Who?'

'I don't know. They didn't say. He's dead.'

'Good.'

'Have you heard from them? That detective and the woman we saw at the hospital?'

'No. You?'

'Not a thing,' she said with a rare note of bitterness in her voice.

'Well, isn't that a surprise? You don't think they're bothered about us, do you?'

Little people. Dregs of the market. What did they matter?

'You can be very unkind sometimes,' she said. 'When they let us back into the hospital, you behave.'

At the end of the street he saw the van heading off into the city, Hoogland on his rounds. Maybe he could get rid of him altogether. Use the Syrian instead.

And that would save the Schrijver castle. Just the idea of it made him want to laugh.

'When are we going?' he asked.

'When they let us. I want a promise. No more fights. No more arguments.'

'Sure,' he said. 'I'm going for a coffee in the Schaapskooi. Two euros a cup. Don't have to pay stupid tourist prices. I'm buying.'

'Can't,' she said, so quietly he could barely hear. 'Call you later. Bye.'

A smiling Jillian Chandra took the press conference in Marnix-straat's media centre, standing room only for the hacks among the camera crews. She'd learned how to work the press when she ran the public relations team in Zoetermeer. One thing mattered above all else: control.

This came courtesy of the publicist she'd brought with her from headquarters. A tall, officious man, grey-haired though in his early thirties, steely-eyed behind rimless glasses, always in a smart dark suit, Den Hartog was the slickest manipulator of news she'd ever encountered. No one knew better when to leak and when to stay silent, the moment to cajole, the instant to pick up the phone and threaten a hapless reporter.

He'd arrived two weeks after she took control in Amsterdam and already disposed of two long-serving locals from media relations. Now he was in the front line. And loving it.

Den Hartog had rapidly taken charge of his own little publicity empire while she still struggled over the grander stage at large. There was, for her, a more delicate balance to be struck between old and new. To kick out too many established Amsterdam officers might signal a reckless impetuosity. Caution was required. Over the months to come she'd slowly bring in more civilian support from Zoetermeer. Before long they'd be followed by serving police officers too.

The locals had to know their place. One, at least, was hers. Vos's friend, Dirk Van der Berg, a genial man, known to the press, probably a drinking companion for a few. Now he was tamely seated by her side, a familiar face required, Den Hartog said, to show she was at one with the existing team.

In his scruffy, ill-fitting suit Van der Berg looked out of sorts. Not that she cared. He'd bend or break. As would Vos eventually. By Christmas Marnixstraat would be transformed.

She smoothed down her jacket and looked straight into the gleaming eyes of the cameras as Den Hartog introduced her. Then his minions handed out the prepared statement. Chandra did as he'd suggested and waited for the assembled hacks to get their copies before slowly, deliberately, reading it out word-for-word.

The document was concise and as factual as they could make it. A man had been killed two nights before, and a young woman attacked. She had been knocked out with the same date rape drug used in the Sleeping Beauty murders. Chandra didn't mention the tattoo on the man, or the odd fact Annie Schrijver had somehow escaped that indignity. All she said was that other factors in the case led them to believe that Vincent de Graaf, jailed for the earlier killings, had a previously undiscovered accomplice: Jef Braat, a driver who'd worked for him and escaped prosecution only to be jailed for a less serious offence for which he was released eight weeks before.

The woman he'd assaulted was due to be released from hospital in a day or two, lucky to escape with her life. During an operation Chandra had directed personally the night before Braat's body had been recovered from the Amstel river. His houseboat was being investigated but it was already clear that he was responsible for the latest attacks, and appeared to have committed suicide as the police closed in on him.

With that a hand went up in the front row.

'Why would he kill himself?' one of the reporters asked.

That wasn't on Den Hartog's list.

'We're still working on the case,' she said. 'Braat had recently lost his first job on release from jail. He was about to be fired from the second one and faced questions over some thefts from Artis. He was a man at the end of his tether. Or so it seems.'

'But . . .' the man came back.

'What I have to tell you is that, on the information we have at present, we are no longer looking for any other parties in connection with the attacks of two nights ago.'

An odd silence greeted her final words. These men and women must have reported on Marnixstraat for years. They knew officers here. Had certain expectations. Den Hartog was right: they needed winning over.

A bespectacled middle-aged hack in the front row waved his

phone around and said, 'I heard it was Pieter Vos who found the people in Zorgvlied. And the boat too.'

'It was a combined operation,' Chandra said, still smiling. 'Under my command. We work as a team. Credit is shared. As is blame if it's called for.'

A woman from one of the TV crews chipped in, 'So four years ago Vos closed down the Sleeping Beauty case with one of these animals still at large? Is that why he's not here?'

'Brigadier Vos is busy.'

'Will there be an inquiry?'

'We're a learning organization. We'll always endeavour to understand why things work. And why they don't. Then take any necessary corrective action.'

The room had a buzz about it. They had something to feed on. The possibility of a fall from grace.

'I wasn't here four years ago so I can offer no direct insight. Though . . .'

She looked at the uncomfortable figure by her side and said, 'Detective Van der Berg was.'

He wriggled in his bad clothes, stubbly cheeks turning crimson.

'Perhaps,' she added, 'now's not the moment . . .'

'Vincent de Graaf confessed for God's sake,' Van der Berg said, grabbing the microphone, bringing it so close to his mouth the words boomed out over the room. 'The only other party we could connect with those cases killed himself. There was never anything to suggest—'

'We will look to deal with any procedural mistakes, never fear,' Chandra interrupted. 'Of more immediate importance . . .'

Den Hartog nodded at the two admin assistants he'd brought with him and they moved through the rows of seats handing out photos.

'We still haven't identified Braat's victim. His *final* victim,' Chandra went on. 'These are mock-up images we have from our forensic people. We'd like to hear from anyone who thinks they may know this man. I have time for two questions only.'

They were fixed. A pair of friendly faces he'd arranged.

A young woman from a radio network asked, 'Do you think there may be other attacks you don't know about?'

Chandra nodded.

'It's very possible. Women who suffer this way are often reluctant to come forward. They fear the publicity. The experience. Wrongly they blame themselves. All I can say is . . .' Her eyes roamed the room. 'The victim is never at fault. Whatever may have happened here in the past, under my watch we have all the procedures in place to deal with sexual assault cases in a sympathetic and caring fashion. This man has raped and murdered women. He may have come close to killing others. If anyone believes they've been drugged in a bar or nightclub, then assaulted in this way, they should contact us immediately. We'll give you details of a hotline number shortly. It will be staffed by women officers trained to deal with these issues in the strictest confidence.'

The second plant, a newspaper hack, raised his pen and asked, 'Is Vos still leading the investigation?'

'For the moment. Thank you.'

With that she turned abruptly and left by the side door back to the executive offices. Van der Berg rushed to catch up.

'You're not very good at these things, are you?' she said as they walked together.

He had his phone out and was working through the messages.

'I wasn't aware I was supposed to be. If I'd known you were going to hang me out to dry . . .'

Chandra stopped in her tracks and stared at him.

'I thought we had an understanding.'

'And what was that?'

'Do I really need to spell it out?'

He brushed away some texts on his phone.

'I'm just an idiot at the bottom of the food chain, Commissaris. So yes. I think you do.'

She looked up and down the corridor. There was no one around.

'I want Vos brought into line. I want you to help me put him there. If you don't . . .'

'Then what?'

She laughed.

'Oh, come on. You're not stupid. Get him in my office. We can start now.'

'Can't,' Van der Berg told her.

'Why not?'

'Because he's gone out. With Bakker. He wanted to see Vincent de Graaf in Bijlmerbajes. Then the Schrijver woman.'

A flash of sudden fury rose in her cheeks.

'I specifically said—'

'I know what you said. But you were too busy having your photo taken. Vos is the brigadier in charge of this case. This isn't Zoetermeer. If he thinks he needs to see someone . . .' Van der Berg looked at his phone again and shook his head. Whatever he was waiting for wasn't there. 'You have to let him do it. If this comes to something disciplinary they'll run a ruler over you, boss. Just as much as him.'

Boss.

That felt good. She touched his arm.

'Sound advice. Thanks. We move slowly.' Her finger ran down the old, rough wool of his sleeve. 'You might want to find yourself a new suit. This one's seen better days.'

From a distance the jail called Bijlmerbajes looked more like a seventies public housing estate than a prison. It stood behind high razor fencing close to the Amstel river, not far from Zorgvlied on the opposite bank. Six fourteen-storey off-white tower blocks

joined by an underground tunnel the staff and inmates had nick-
named 'Kalverstraat' after the city shopping street. The inmates
ranged from small-time crooks to violent criminals who might
never be released.

Vos knew the place intimately, the name of each tower, the
lift systems, the visitor rules. The authorities divided the blocks
according to prisoner type, trying to keep the minor convicts
engaged in work and rehabilitation programmes away from their
more dangerous counterparts. Vincent de Graaf was in the medical wing of Het Veer, the highest security tower of all, one mostly
restricted to prisoners with severe psychological problems, often
sent to Bijlmerbajes from other institutions unable to cope with
them.

Bakker had watched, fascinated, as they negotiated security
at the main entrance. Then two guards took them through the
tunnel to a second checkpoint at the entrance to Het Veer. Marly
Kloosterman, the duty doctor assigned to meet them, was waiting on the other side of a high iron gate. She was a cheery-looking
woman in contrast to the surroundings. In a white medical jacket,
with short fair hair and a lively, smiling face, she looked more like
a genial local doctor greeting a familiar patient. Beaming from
behind the bars she waved and cried his name as they turned up.

'We're old friends,' Vos said before he was asked.

'So I see.'

They cleared the scanners, Bakker handing over her weapon.
Then Kloosterman came and hugged him, a brief embrace that
seemed to leave Vos embarrassed. Which made her hug him once
more, giggling at the effect.

'I only ever see you for work these days, Pieter. It's been
months. So how are things?'

Bakker was watching them, arms folded, amused.

'Um, fine, thanks. This is Laura. Laura Bakker. My um . . .'

'Detective Bakker,' she said as he stumbled over the words.

Marly Kloosterman winked at her.

'I hope you're keeping him in check.'

'Doing my best. It's not easy.'

The two of them looked him up and down.

'I can imagine. You should come and see my new home, Pieter. I joined the houseboat club too. Plantage. Not far from Artis. I can hear the monkeys at night. At least I *think* they're monkeys. When you live on your own you sometimes get funny ideas.'

'I hope your place is in a better state than his,' Bakker told her. 'The city council are going to throw the book at him if he doesn't do something about it soon.'

'Another time, Laura,' he said with a quick smile. 'De Graaf...'

The smile vanished.

'Oh yes, him. We need a chat.'

They took the lift to the third floor and walked down a long corridor, on either side cells that could have doubled as private hospital rooms were it not for the heavy locks on the doors and the tiny barred windows.

'This is what jail's like?' Bakker whispered.

'No,' Vos said. 'It's not.'

And Vincent de Graaf would hate it, he thought. Until he became sick he'd been in the wing reserved for sex offenders. It was secure, quiet, a place they could be safe from attacks from other prisoners. This was a kind of solitary. One he presumed was forced upon a dying man by circumstance. Nowhere else in Bijlmerbajes could offer the twenty-four-hour medical care he needed.

Kloosterman opened the door of her office and ushered them in.

They took the two seats in front of her desk, feeling more like patients than visiting cops. She got them coffee from her espresso machine and then the story began.

De Graaf was terminally ill, with three or four months to live at the most. Pancreatic cancer diagnosed too late for anything but palliative care.

'Had he been a free man . . . a rich man getting all that expensive medical cover . . . perhaps things would have been different. That's the way he sees it. But who knows? It's a sly disease. We don't run medical insurance check-ups in here. Not part of the service.'

Vos said, 'I gather he wants to talk to us.'

'I passed on the message. As he wanted.'

'You don't believe him?'

She thought for a moment then went to her filing cabinet, opened a drawer and pulled out a plastic bag with a phone in it.

'I really don't know. Vincent de Graaf is as cunning as a fox. A few weeks ago we discovered he'd got hold of this. He's been communicating with someone on the outside. Here . . .'

She passed the handset over.

'Any idea how he got it?' Vos asked.

'Oh, come on, Pieter. This is a jail. You know as well as I we can't keep out everything. And maybe . . .' She shrugged. 'We did run him over to the hospital in the Zuidas for some scans. We don't have the equipment here. I wondered if someone slipped it to him on the way.' She stopped, as if surprised by her own thoughts. 'Like I said . . . he's a cunning bastard. I've worked here for five years. In all that time I never felt I'd met anyone who was . . . beyond explanation. We've got murderers and rapists, you name it. Most of them, you can see the way they got here. Drugs, drink, a psychosis that perhaps we should have picked up earlier. Then along comes Vincent de Graaf . . .'

She put down her coffee and folded her arms.

'I have to believe no one's born evil. I *have* to. Because if that's possible then what we're doing here's different. We're not trying to help damaged human beings become whole enough to let them back into the world. We're just prison guards in white coats administering sedatives.'

Bakker growled something.

'I'm sorry?' Kloosterman said.

'I think most people will just be happy they're off the street.'

'Most people don't see them the way I do. Even you. All you see is a criminal and send them to court. I have to deal with them afterwards. Witness their misery. Their guilt. Their shame. They're human beings. Most anyway. The man you've come to see is sick and weak and desperate. But even so . . . he's not like all the rest.'

'I put him inside,' Vos told her. 'He's nothing special.'

She nodded and smiled at him again.

'We ought to discuss that some other time. Till then we'll have to disagree. The real reason he wants to talk to you now is this.'

She reached into a drawer and retrieved a glossy brochure. It was for a private medical facility in the Zuidas, attached to the university hospital.

'Copernicus Cancer Centre,' Bakker said, reading the cover. 'He thinks it can help him?'

Kloosterman thought carefully about her answer.

'That's what he says.'

'And he can pay for it?'

'I don't doubt that.' She nodded at the brochure. 'And he's furious I won't give him access.'

'Why not?' Vos wondered.

'Two reasons. First . . . it's pointless. He's terminally ill. There's nothing anyone can do for him that we're not doing here. They'd probably use the same machines we did when we sent him there, give him the same drugs. Second, if I allow him to order up private medical treatment how can I deny that to someone else? I might be setting a precedent. Next thing they'll be sending out for pizza.'

A dying man might not be much interested in precedents, Bakker pointed out.

'What Vincent de Graaf's interested in is immaterial. I'd rather not have my hands tied. So if someone's going to make the decision it's you. Not us.'

She retrieved the pamphlet and put it away.

'The deal he will offer you is this. Allow him treatment at that place and he'll talk. Tell you something he should have told you before. It may well turn out to be his personal recipe for pancakes. That's all I'm saying.'

'Is he an escape risk?' Vos asked.

Marly Kloosterman thought about that.

'Let's take a look at him,' she said, getting to her feet. 'You tell me.'

Chandra was back at her desk, nagging Van der Berg about the unidentified victim. Den Hartog had come in to listen.

'I can't believe we haven't a clue who he is,' she said. 'After two days.'

'We do,' Van der Berg replied.

'Really?'

'He's probably not from Amsterdam. Foreign perhaps. Doesn't know many people here. Otherwise someone would have been on the phone.'

'Not a lot, is it?' Den Hartog complained.

'It's something. We're passing on his description further afield. Fingerprints. DNA. We'll get there.'

Chandra didn't respond to that. Instead she said, 'This girl in hospital . . .'

'Twenty-two,' Van der Berg cut in. 'Not a girl.'

'This *woman* then. The one who hangs around places where they slip dope in your drink. It would really help if she went public. Made a statement on TV.'

'I like that idea,' the PR man said, suddenly enthusiastic. 'A lot.'

'May I ask why?' Van der Berg wondered.

'She'd make it personal. It could show how much we care

about sexual assault cases. And demonstrate that she puts her trust in us too.'

Van der Berg shook his head.

'You can't do that. You can't even ask it. We don't release the names of victims in sex assault cases.'

'If she agrees . . .' Den Hartog pointed out. 'It's her choice.'

'Are you serious? What kind of state is she in to make a balanced judgement? She's in hospital. Lucky she's alive. It's going to be hard enough for her to put this behind her as it is. Stick her on TV and she's public property. The kid will have to live with it for the rest of her life.'

Chandra looked as if the decision was already made.

'I thought she was a woman. Not a kid. This is up to her. Not you.' She turned to Den Hartog. 'Get out there. Talk her round. Put her on the phone to me if you need to. Could you get one of your tame TV people down there quickly?'

Den Hartog's face broke into a rare smile.

'For that? Like a shot . . .'

There was a knock on the door and Schuurman walked in. Before he could speak Chandra said, 'Do you have an ID for that man yet? It's all we need to close this thing down.'

The pathologist took a seat without being asked.

'No. I'm afraid not.'

'Oh.'

One short exclamation, and it was as damning as she could make it.

'Commissaris. Your press conference this morning.'

'What about it?'

'I wasn't aware you were going to broadcast our preliminary findings quite so quickly. I'd really rather you hadn't.'

Den Hartog then produced a short lecture about media responsibilities and where they lay. Schuurman listened, visibly beguiled.

When the PR man was finished he said, 'Oh, I don't object to your . . . decision tree or whatever you want to call it. Just the release of initial findings as if they were facts.'

Chandra glared at him.

'What do you mean?'

'What I mean is . . . you effectively told the media Braat was the perpetrator here. He killed our unidentified friend and damn near murdered the Schrijver woman too.'

'That's what you said.'

He shook his head firmly.

'No. Not at all. What I said was that it was clear the two victims were physically assaulted in his houseboat. That Braat was definitely present and had been involved in some kind of fight.'

'That's as good as saying—' Chandra began.

'No. It isn't. It's a simple statement of the facts. The implications you drew from those were yours and yours alone. Had I known about them in advance . . .'

Silence. Then Schuurman took out his tablet and started to consult his notes and photos.

'I would have told you to wait.'

She went quiet. So did Den Hartog. Van der Berg had his hand over his eyes.

'First off,' Schuurman continued, 'I now discover Braat was inside the van wearing a seat belt. I was unaware of this fact because we were at the houseboat. Though I gather one of your uniform officers removed the belt after his corpse fell against you. A great shame. We would have much preferred him kept in place. You really must leave these things to us in the future.'

She was glancing at Den Hartog.

'I was . . . I didn't ask for the belt to be . . .'

'No matter now,' the pathologist went on. 'Damage done. In itself the seat belt is simply rather puzzling. Of more importance, it's clear the engine wasn't running when the vehicle went into the river.' He held up a photo of a key in an old-fashioned ignition lock. 'Turned to off.'

One more photo. A bottle of wine on the table in Braat's houseboat.

'Two thirds gone. The rest very heavily dosed with GHB. So much I suspect it would have affected the taste. But it was a nasty cheap Spanish Tempranillo and I suspect they'd been drinking already. So perhaps . . .'

More pictures. Muddy marks, on the bank by the crane that lifted out Braat's van, by the man's houseboat too.

'Our corpse has large feet. Size forty-seven. These were forty-three, from thick-soled industrial boots.'

He indicated the footprints on the river bank near the van.

'These are heavier than the others. That would indicate pressure. Consistent with someone pushing the van into the water while Braat was conveniently drugged senseless inside, strapped into the driving seat to keep him upright.'

'The houseboat?' she asked. 'What happened there?'

Schuurman sighed.

'As I seem to have to say rather too often, I can only address the facts. There was violence. We've yet to find any evidence of sexual activity. The bottle of wine was doped. If we assume . . .' He slapped his forehead theatrically. 'No. I really mustn't make assumptions. So many people here to do that for you . . .'

'Cut it out, Schuurman,' Chandra barked at him. 'I've got Vos's name on the list already. Don't make me add yours.'

Den Hartog took a deep breath and said nothing.

'Ah,' Schuurman replied. 'A list. Very well. Put my name on it if you like. My wife's always complaining I spend too much time at work anyway . . .'

'I need to know. What might explain it?'

He hesitated for a moment then went on.

'Were you to ask Vos I suspect he'd say this. The woman was

drugged elsewhere and brought back to the houseboat for the enjoyment of those who abducted her. There, perhaps before setting about their unconscious victim-to-be, our gentlemen celebrated with a bottle of cheap wine. Which was drugged too. Braat and our nameless friend were rendered semi-conscious by one of their party. Fisticuffs ensued when they realized what was happening. They lost. This same third party later rubbed potassium cyanide in the mouth of our unidentified guest then lugged an unconscious Braat to his van and pushed it in the river, presumably hoping we'd believe this was all down to him.' A smile. 'You obliged.'

He flicked through the notes quickly.

'We've found no trace of potassium cyanide in the houseboat or any pinned butterflies, by the way. Braat seemed to prefer his alive. So it would appear our third party came prepared.'

'You're guessing.'

'I'm ashamed to say I am.'

Van der Berg asked, 'The man had a tattoo. The woman didn't. Seems odd.'

'Your patch, not mine,' Schuurman told him. 'There are needles in the houseboat. A kit you can buy online very easily. Everything's been very carefully wiped clean. Isopropyl alcohol all over the place. He knew what he was doing.'

'Where do you get something like that?' Chandra wondered.

Schuurman glanced at Van der Berg. A look that said: *Is she serious?*

'A pharmacy. A hospital. A morgue. Common wash-down stuff. There are traces of recent blood and skin on the needles. Our unidentified gentleman only, I'm afraid. Braat had a butterfly on his neck as well. That was old. Several years. I checked back and it looks like a pattern we found in Jonker's studio, by the way. Perhaps he was part of that particular game. Before you ask you wouldn't need to be a genius to track down potassium cyanide either. It doesn't just kill butterflies. There are quite a few industrial processes that use it too. Anyone who really wanted it . . .' He shrugged then shut the lid on the tablet. 'All this is conjecture, of course. Which, as I emphasized, is not my field at all. But you requested it and you're the commissaris. It may be true. Or half-true. Or pure fiction. However, one thing I can state with absolutely certainty.'

He waited.

'What?' she asked.

'The story you gave so readily to the media this morning without my knowledge bears absolutely no resemblance to reality. Jef Braat may be a murderer. I don't know. But he's certainly a victim. That's beyond doubt.'

Den Hartog took to scribbling furiously on his notepad.

'Any more questions?' the pathologist wondered.

She looked shell-shocked.

'Vos knew there was something up with this all along,' Van der Berg said. 'If we'd—'

'Then why the hell didn't he say so?' Chandra cried.

'Did you ask him?' Schuurman wondered.

Silence. He paused at the door.

'Oh, and that list of yours. A word of advice, Commissaris.'

'What?' she grumbled.

'The longer it gets the more people around here will want to be on it.' He glanced at Van der Berg. 'Most of us anyway.'

When he was gone Chandra turned to Den Hartog and asked what they were going to do. He'd make calls, he said. Soften the story. Make it clear the case was still open and being actively pursued.

'I'll go round the hospital and get this Schrijver girl on TV whether she wants it or not,' he added. 'If we can put her face up there and a name to it we'll get them off our backs.'

'Do that,' Chandra told him. 'And next time you want to put me in front of the media make damn sure I'm in possession of the facts.'

Van der Berg stood up and raised his phone.

'I'll get hold of Vos, shall I?' he said.

The last time he'd seen Vincent de Graaf was in court. Even there it seemed the man was acting out a part, that of a dissolute, rich and middle-aged Amsterdammer caught playing games that went too far. Standing, almost smirking before the judge, he'd appeared lean, fit and healthy, fifty-two when he was arraigned, used to affluence, single, occasionally featured in the gossip pages with a glamorous woman on his arm. A partner in a trust firm in the Zuidas, with business interests in property and other financial concerns throughout the city. He owned a terraced mansion on the Herengracht. Still did. Vos had checked. But now the place was rented out to Russians and Vincent de Graaf was sick.

When they entered the hospital cell he barely looked up from the bed. Stick-thin with a skeletal wasted face and staring eyes, sallow bony limbs poking out from blue and white striped pyjamas, hair gone except for a few greying hanks.

'You look terrible, Vos,' he said as Kloosterman left, ordering the guard to lock the door. He puffed out cheeks that looked like waxy parchment. 'How is the world out there? Must be dull without me in it.'

Vos pulled up two chairs by the bed and said, 'I gather you want to talk.'

De Graaf's eyes were as keen as ever. They were on Laura Bakker, running up and down her long frame as she took a seat, pulling her skirt over her knees.

'Don't see many worthwhile women in here.' She glared at him. 'I do apologize.' He shuffled upright on the sheets, pulled a pillow behind his back and waved a hand at her, beckoning. 'You come with a name?'

'Bakker.'

'Bakker.' He said it very slowly, eyes on her all the time. 'Do tell. Have you any . . . tattoos?'

'In all honesty . . . do I look the tattoo sort to you?'

His eyes narrowed.

'Oh, my God . . . that accent. You really must do something about it, Bakker. An innocent from the wild green spaces of Friesland. A stranger in these parts. Lacking in sophistication. Thinking we're all debauched, corrupt animals. Perhaps you're right. Why exactly do you want her around, Vos? Personal amusement? Of one kind or another?'

Bakker bristled. As she was meant to.

'You asked to see us,' Vos said.

'First things first. I'd like my question answered.' He leaned forward and stretched a bony finger towards Bakker's legs. 'Do you have a tattoo? Come on. Somewhere private. A crevice. A little patch of intimate skin. A woman from Friesland would never advertise it, I imagine. But . . .'

Her cheeks were going red.

'It's there,' he added. 'Where exactly?'

'I don't have a tattoo.'

He raised his eyebrows, smiled. His teeth were yellow. It was as if the man was rotting from the inside out.

'I didn't ask to see it, dear. Let alone touch it.' His fingers waved and then retreated. 'Not much point any more. Though there was a time . . .' He closed his eyes for a moment, pleased with himself. 'They let me get the news in here. I gather your problem's returned. Dead bodies in the night. Wicked acts. Pharmaceuticals misused.' He laughed to himself. 'Sleep Baby Sleep. Can't blame me this time, can you? Though perhaps I should be consulting a copyright lawyer. What do you think?'

'You're starting to bore me, Vincent,' Vos said.

He leaned back against the pillow and glared at them.

'That bitch Kloosterman told you I'm dying, I presume.'

'She did,' Vos agreed.

'Did she tell you there's a private clinic at the hospital that might give me a few months more?'

'She thought that unlikely. The treatment you've been getting—'

'What treatment?' he asked with a sudden savagery. 'Painkillers and prison food?'

'I'm sure they're doing all they can.'

'Are you? And I'm supposed to trust the word of these people? A low-grade prison quack? Against the opinion of a consultant who earns ten times the pittance she gets?'

The cell had a small barred window. He struggled to his feet and put his fingers against the glass.

'All I'm asking for is one appointment. Drive me there yourself if you like. Bring me back.' He looked at himself then shook a skinny ankle in their direction. 'I won't be running off. Don't worry.' His eyes went to the grey world beyond the window. 'I imagine it's starting to smell of autumn out there. A chill on the breeze. The leaves turning. I won't see it again, you'll be pleased to hear. Not that I'm asking out of sentiment, you understand. Three more months those people can give me. Maybe. Even in this dump it's better than being dead. If it's wasted . . . what's lost?'

'And in return?' Vos asked.

'What do you want?'

'The truth would be a start.'

He nodded.

'The truth. People always think they want that. I wonder sometimes . . .'

De Graaf sat down on the edge of the bed. Just that small amount of effort had cost him much. His breath was short and rapid. There was sweat on his yellow, stubbly cheeks.

'You know it wasn't just the two of us. That clown Jonker. He was just a lackey. We used him for the premises. The tattoos. That dump of his was my private little Cabinet of Curiosities. Would have been out of place on the Herengracht. If the fool had been more circumspect you'd never have known.'

'This other man,' Bakker cut in. 'He's still alive then?'

A brief, grim laugh.

'Oh, very much so. Living life to the full and keen for things to stay that way. You'll be grateful, trust me. Perhaps it'll bring a little much-needed credit to the brigadier's somewhat chequered career.'

He looked at Bakker very closely then asked, 'I must ask, sweetheart. Has he had you yet? Was it any good?'

Vos's phone trilled. He gave it to her and nodded at the corridor.

She left in silence with a face like thunder. De Graaf watched her every inch of the way. When the guard slammed the heavy door shut he said, 'It seemed a reasonable enough question.'

'It wasn't.'

Another shrug.

'Maybe not. Still, I got my answer, didn't I? How extraordinary that you should find a junior as priggish as yourself. In the police of all places. You should get out more. Take that from someone who knows.'

Vos retrieved his notebook and pen then placed them on the table.

'Write me the name. I'll have you in that clinic by this afternoon.'

'Kloosterman won't let you.'

'This will be my call. Not hers.'

De Graaf picked up the pen. An office ballpoint. He stared at it as if the thing were too cheap for him to use.

'I've got a cancer eating at my guts. It hasn't reached my brain.' He put down the pen and folded his bony arms. 'The clinic first. Then you get it.'

Vos retrieved the ballpoint and the notebook, stood up and pressed the bell for the guard.

'You want to know!' De Graaf cried, and his voice was almost breaking. Then, more quietly, 'He's back in business. I read about it. Don't screw with me, Vos. A couple of hours in the clinic then he's yours.' He shuffled along the sheets, jabbed a finger at the window. 'There's a woman out there thinking about tonight. Going out on the town. A few drinks somewhere. He's waiting for her. I know. I invented this game. I was good at it and I taught my pupils well.'

Vos hesitated.

'Why those women in particular?' he wondered. 'You must have doped and raped . . . I don't know how many. Three you killed. And marked.'

'Three you know of . . .'

'Why?'

De Graaf looked interested, leaned forward on the bed.

'You're the clever one. All the papers used to say it. Until you . . . um . . . had your little breakdown. You tell me.'

Vos said, 'Because they woke. Because they saw you. And when you'd stabbed them to death you couldn't resist doing something you wouldn't have dared if they were going to live. Because then they'd be sure to come running to us, pointing to that tattoo on their shoulders. Instead of living a life of shame and doubt not knowing quite what happened. Or who to blame.'

Bakker was at the door with Kloosterman.

'Very good,' De Graaf said, glancing at the two women. 'Impeccable logic. So if you'd like to stop it happening again let me out of here. Just for a few hours. Let me see real daylight, go to that clinic in the Zuidas, then I'll tell you . . .'

'Jef Braat's dead,' Bakker broke in. 'We fished him out of the Amstel last night. His name's worth nothing to us at all.'

That news took the man in the blue and white pyjamas by surprise.

'Braat?' he whispered. 'What the hell are you talking about?'

'Your old company driver. We don't need a name.'

De Graaf scowled.

'Oh please, Vos. Is your little girl serious?'

He was a cunning man but a lousy liar. When the evidence stacked up against him four years before he'd confessed readily. Perhaps too quickly. He didn't look as if he was faking it now.

'It's serious, Vincent. We found the dope and the tattoo gear in his houseboat. Lots else besides.'

De Graaf began to laugh. The effort seemed to pain him. When he'd recovered sufficient breath he looked at Bakker and said, 'Jef Braat's not the name I have in mind and Vos here knows it. That idiot was scum. Lowlife. Easily led. A spear carrier in a greater drama beyond his comprehension. I'm offended ... deeply ... that you should believe I'd dream of bartering a name like his for a life like mine.'

Vos put his notebook in his pocket, checked his watch, sighed, and said, 'Tell me now. Or you can rot here till they cart you out to Zorgvlied.'

'No, no.' He grinned. 'Cremation for me, dears. Sorry. So many people would love the opportunity to dance upon my grave. Regrettably I must disappoint them.'

They walked out. The door slammed shut. De Graaf's furious yells barely made it through the metal and glass.

Marly Kloosterman looked at him, astonished.

'You mean you're not going to give that evil bastard what he wants?'

Before he could answer Bakker held up the phone.

'The commissaris is very anxious to speak to you.'

'I'll call her from the hospital. After we've seen Annie Schrijver—'

'No, Pieter. She says you've got to talk to her right now.'

The summons came in a text from Nina: the doctors were willing to let them in. That was all. She was there already when Schrijver turned up at the hospital front desk. A different set of dark old clothes this morning: brown sweater, black trousers. In his head she looked just the way she did when he first began to admire her secretly, shyly, as she worked on the fish stalls a little way along. He'd put on weight, lost hair, got jowly, didn't bother to shave as much or as carefully now she was gone. The years had crept up on him and with them their damage. But not on Nina. Just a few grey hairs and the shadow of crow's feet around her eyes, a sadness there, a sense of loss, for which he felt responsible in ways he couldn't quite name.

Of all the things he'd screwed up over the years – and there were many – the divorce hurt the most. And still he didn't fully understand why she'd left him. Because he was stupid. A failure. Maybe that explained all.

'Hanging around again,' he grumbled, clutching the plastic cup of coffee she'd brought him. 'That's all these places make you do. Sit there, twiddling your thumbs. Until one of them comes out and breaks the news. Like God. Or a priest or something.'

'That's a lot of words for you, Bert.'

'Got lots of words in my head. Just don't say them out loud too often. They're not worth much.'

'Says who?'

'Says me. Says everybody. Why did they ask us here if we can't go in?'

She didn't know the answer to that, though the waiting didn't seem to bother her as much as it did him. Annie would recover. That was all that mattered. Nina was patient, calm, resigned. He'd never be any of those things. Schrijver sniffed at the coffee and wrinkled his nose. It was weak, lukewarm out of a machine. She got the message without a word, took the cup and disposed of it in the toilet. Nina was always tidy, always clearing up. The remnants of the castle he'd held on to were never as neat after she left.

Her eyes crept to the double doors that led to Annie's room.

There'd been activity there. A tall, distinguished-looking man in a grey suit going to and fro, not that he spoke a word to them. Then a brisk, smartly dressed woman Schrijver thought he vaguely recognized though he didn't know from where.

Nina watched her go and said, 'Isn't she on the TV news?'

'Don't watch the news,' Schrijver answered. 'It's just depressing.'

'Maybe you should have said more,' Nina murmured, barely listening to him. 'Maybe I should have asked.'

'Too late now.'

'It's never too late to be friends. Annie's going to want that. She'll need both of us when she comes out of here.'

'Yes,' was all he could think of.

'She won't be able to help out in the shop for a while either. Perhaps . . .' She steeled herself and said it. 'If you're OK with it I could come round again. Work the stall. I know we rowed before but we can put all that behind us. Been a while since I sold anything in the market. I used to be good at it. Or so they said.'

'You were the best. I mean it. I never ate so much fried fish in my life trying to pluck up the courage to ask you out.'

She laughed at his words and he wondered when he'd last managed that.

'I remember one day you had *kibbeling*. Then you came back for mussels. Then calamari. Something else . . .'

'Prawns. I never really liked them.'

'You probably said they were for your dad.'

He was twenty-three when they started courting. There hadn't been anyone before. He was too shy, too tongue-tied, too wrapped up in the flower business for a girlfriend.

'I lied. Couldn't think of anything else. Sorry—'

'No, no. Don't apologize. I knew. It didn't matter. It was . . . nice really.'

He thought of the woman from the estate agents. How hard,

how calculating she was. How he'd bite off her hand if she could get the money he'd asked for.

'Don't take this wrong, Bert. I know you need some help with the business. I'm happy to do it. You don't need to pay me any more than the maintenance. Maybe I've got some ideas about other things we could sell. Times change. You change with them. It's not so hard.'

'For me it is.'

The thought returned: perhaps the Syrian lad called Adnan could help them put things right. New ideas, fresh enthusiasm. And with that idea Jordi Hoogland's face came to mind, staring at him sourly, uttering the bitter words, 'You need a rag head to save you now, do you? A foreigner I picked up on the street? Some man Bert Schrijver turned out to be.'

She patted his hand just briefly.

'Well, you think about it. It would be nice to get that place back on its feet again. Everyone else in the Albert Cuyp's busy. No reason not to join them.'

But I'm the reason, he thought. And one way or another I'm selling the place from under you because that's all there is left.

'Thanks,' Schrijver told her. 'How much longer are these bastards going to keep us hanging around before we get to see Annie?'

Her face fell. Her hand moved away. The wrong words again.

'I'm sure they're doing their best. They saved her life for God's sake . . .'

There was a commotion then. An angry male voice he recognized too well. Rob Sanders, still in his blue nurse's uniform, was bustled through the ward doors by a couple of uniformed cops. Schrijver hadn't even realized they were there. He could see now there were more people down the corridor. Men with cameras, cables, mikes, gathering round Annie's room.

Sanders stormed over, glared at both of them.

'Are you a party to this? Nina? I know that idiot would fall for anything. But you?'

Bert Schrijver blinked. He was always slow to anger. But it happened and when it did he was just as slow to back down. He didn't say a word, just got to his feet, grabbed Sanders by the collar of his thin blue jacket and slammed him against the wall.

The woman on the reception desk was on the phone already. Schrijver really didn't mind.

'I should have punched your lights out when you hit her,' he said, face so close up to Sanders' he could smell the hospital on him, that chemical cloud supposed to keep you healthy. And still people died.

'Maybe you should, Bert,' Sanders cried, struggling in his arms. 'Time you did something.'

He pushed Schrijver away. The two men stood there, face to face, squaring up, fists half-raised.

Uniforms were coming through the door. Cops and hospital security people. Nina was up by then, pushing her way between them. The smart man in the grey suit hovered round the back, whispering into his phone.

Then the woman they'd seen earlier emerged through the door, red-faced and angry too, yelling for quiet.

'Den Hartog!' She went to the suit and prodded him in the lapel. 'This is difficult enough as it is. Do something.'

Schrijver realized Nina was right. He had seen her on the news. She was one of the presenters, a woman known for tough interviews and controversy.

'Who are all these people?'

'They're putting Annie on TV,' Sanders yelled. 'Face, name, everything.' He glowered at the scrum of bodies around them. No one looked back. 'Do you lot know what you're doing?'

'The TV?' Nina whispered.

The uniform cops rounded on the Schrijvers and Sanders. Reluctantly maybe. But what they wanted was clear.

'You've got to go,' one said. 'This is a hospital. You can't disturb the place . . .'

'Annie doesn't deserve this!' Rob Sanders barked at him.

'She's agreed,' the grey man said. 'That's all we need.'

Sanders flew at him.

'You can't put her up there for everyone to gloat over. Not after what she's been through.'

The TV woman turned on him.

'And you are?'

'A friend,' he answered. A nod to the Schrijvers. 'And these are her parents. Do you want this, Nina?'

'No,' she said straight off. 'Annie won't want it either . . .'

'She's already signed the waiver,' the grey man chipped in. 'She's a brave young woman. She wants to do what she can to help. She'll be a heroine after this.'

Sanders pushed through the uniforms and got to him, jabbing a finger towards the TV crews.

'She's not free entertainment for these bastards. Nina. Bert. You can't allow this . . .'

'She's twenty-two years old,' the man said. 'She can make her own decisions. She has.'

'You think?' Sanders replied. 'You know that?'

But the uniforms were moving, pushing them down the corridor, out into the grey day beyond.

Schrijver couldn't think straight, couldn't work out who to yell at.

Then they were on the pavement, listening to the racket of the traffic on the busy road, the construction crews working on the next line of buildings for the financial companies trying to turn the Zuidas into a new Dutch Wall Street.

Hands shaking, Nina pulled out a pack of cigarettes from her bag. Bert Schrijver looked back at the vast plain building behind, hating it more than ever. There were two TV vans parked in the space for ambulances, people milling around them. Men with well-trimmed beards and trendy clothes, the kind who hung around the bars of an Albert Cuyp he no longer recognized.

'Are you going to do something or not?' Sanders asked him.

'Like what? Go in there and slap her around the way you did? That worked, didn't it?'

The nurse glared at him.

'You're so dumb, Bert. Really. You don't have a clue what's going on.'

Schrijver thought of punching him out then. It would have been so easy, and satisfying too in a way. But you couldn't pass hurt on like that. All you did was double the pain, not halve it. A part of him said that was just what Rob Sanders wanted.

'Why do you keep hanging round her?' he asked. 'You dumped her months ago.'

'I still want her to be happy,' Sanders answered in that sly, evasive way he had. 'I want her to be safe. How's that going to work if her face is on the TV, on every front page, people knowing what happened to her? How's she going to stand out in front of everyone in the Albert Cuyp after that?'

Schrijver had got on him with him once. Liked him enough to wonder if they'd ever marry. But Sanders was more than ten years older than Annie and he'd never understood why a man like him, seemingly solid, decent, good job, good prospects, had never settled down. Why he couldn't stick with his daughter either. As if she wasn't good enough.

'I don't know what to do,' Schrijver muttered. 'I'm an idiot. How would I? Nina?'

She was weeping and that always made him feel bad.

'There's nothing we *can* do . . .'

One of the TV crew came over and introduced himself. Schrijver didn't even get the name. Just the message: they wondered if he and Nina wanted to give an interview as Annie's parents once the cameras were through with her.

The fury came out of nowhere. He was on the man, fists flying without a second thought. It took Nina and Sanders to pull him off. The TV hack retreated, hands up, bleating about only doing his job.

'What kind of job is that?' Schrijver yelled at him.

The uniforms marched out again, barking orders. Come back when you can keep your temper, they said. Not before. And even then the staff might not lct you in.

A phone rang. It belonged to Sanders. He answered it, walked away so they couldn't hear him, then wandered off into the adjoining hospital block with just a nod to Nina. Then the police pounced once more, telling them to get off the premises straight away or face arrest.

As they walked down to the busy road Schrijver stared up at the first floor where they were keeping her. Blinds closed. A bright light behind them. Something for the cameras, he guessed.

My girl, he thought. *I should be there. Her mother too. No one else.*

'Bert,' Nina whispered, tugging at his arm. 'We'll try again in a little while. When those TV people are gone. It'll be easier. Leave it to me.'

'The damage will be done by then.'

'I guess.' The tears stood glistening in her eyes and he could feel how much they were stinging. 'You're not as dumb as you think, you know.'

Together they walked through the diesel smog of the construction trucks, the racket of hammers and cranes, into the tower blocks and building sites of the Zuidas. She'd find them a coffee, she said. Somewhere in this strange and foreign place not far from home.

Vos went out to the car to take the call. Something was wrong with Bakker but he couldn't guess what. So he phoned Marnix-straat, got straight through to Jillian Chandra, listened to what she had to say about Schuurman's findings and said nothing at all.

'You don't seem surprised,' she noted.

'Sorry about that.'

'What did De Graaf say?'

He told her about the deal on offer: one trip to the private clinic and then a name.

'When can you get him over there?'

'The moment he gives me a name.'

A long pause and then she said, 'Do you understand the situation? I told everyone today we were closing this case. That Jef Braat was the final link in the Sleeping Beauty murders. Now we know he isn't. We have a murderer out there, preying on young women in nightclubs.'

'One woman. She's alive. Two men dead. It's not the—'

'I don't have time to play intellectual games. Neither do you.'

'Neither does Vincent de Graaf. He's got less time than any of us. So why won't he just give me the name?'

Bakker was staring at him.

'Are you always this stubborn?' Chandra asked.

'It's nothing to do with being stubborn. There's something he's not telling me . . .'

'Yes! The name!'

'Will you please listen?'

'Is he a flight risk?'

Vos thought of the man he'd first arrested and the shell of a human being they'd just seen, eking out his final days.

'Not in the least. I doubt he can walk far, let alone run.'

'Then give him what he wants. Drive him over there and get that name out of him afterwards.'

Not possible, he said. They'd found an illicit phone in his room. He'd been in contact with unknown parties on the outside, perhaps in the very hospital complex he now wanted to visit.

'Wait,' Chandra cut in. 'You said he wants to go to a private clinic.'

'Yes. A clinic next to the university hospital, where he's been treated already. Dammit . . . his old office can't be far away. The prison doctor says there's no medical reason for him to go there.'

'I don't give a damn whether there's a reason for it or not. We need that name.'

'If he's serious he'll be back with it before the day's out. If he isn't . . . this is about something else. I don't—'

'Jesus Christ!' she shrieked. 'Are you under the illusion this is a discussion or something? I told you. I *ordered* you. Tell Bijlmer-bajes to take him to this damned appointment. When that's done put him in the smallest, nastiest cell you can find and keep him there until he talks.'

Behind the wheel Bakker had heard the shrill voice rising from Vos's handset.

'I caution against that, Commissaris,' Vos said.

'Your caution's noted. Just do it.'

'We need to interview Annie Schrijver again. Properly this time.'

'Is this a bad line or something? Did you hear me?'

He turned to Bakker and asked her to call Marly Kloosterman and tell her Commissaris Chandra had decided to comply with De Graaf's request. Transport and an appointment needed to be arranged as soon as possible. Vos put his hand over the phone so Chandra couldn't hear her caustic response.

'Best do it outside,' he said and waited until she'd climbed out of the car. 'Yes, Commissaris. I heard. Annie Schrijver . . .'

'You can't interview her right now,' she said and told him why.

He was speechless.

'If she's on TV making a personal appeal perhaps that will loosen a few tongues,' she went on. 'More than I ever will.'

'We don't identify rape victims.'

'No we don't. But they can identify themselves. She's going public out of a sense of duty. Brave girl.'

'I cau—'

'Yes, yes, you caution against it. Let me remind you. We've got a killer out there. For all we know we'll be facing up to another dead girl, another tattoo tomorrow.'

But only if she wakes, he thought.

Bakker was having a difficult conversation. He waved at her to wait until he could take over the call.

'The media will crucify me over this if I'm not careful,' Chandra added.

The words just came out.

'But not if they're drooling over an interview with a rape victim.'

There was a long deep breath on the line.

'You know, Vos, I've been very patient with you. Right down to the damned dog. But I have my limits. Get that name out of De Graaf. Then find the bastard. You've got time before that happens. What do you intend to do?'

He'd worked that out already.

'Braat was fired from the butterfly house at Artis. Someone led me to that party next door to the zoo on Tuesday night. We'll stop there on the way back. Maybe there's a link.'

'You're chasing butterflies?'

'Unless you'd like us somewhere else.'

'Happy hunting,' Chandra told him and was gone.

He got out of the car and took the phone from Bakker as she mouthed at him, 'Your friend wants a word.'

Marly Kloosterman sounded disappointed.

'I don't get it,' she said when Vos took the phone. 'I thought you were waiting to get a name . . .'

'I thought so too. I've been . . . overruled. Commissaris Chandra has decided. Her mind's made up and it's not the sort you change. How quickly can you arrange it?'

'The clinic will see him at the drop of a hat if he's got the money. And he has.'

'Try and arrange it for this afternoon. When he gets back we'll talk to him.'

'One condition,' she added.

Nothing was ever easy.

'Which is?'

'I want you to come round to see my new houseboat. We can have a glass of wine on the deck. You can give me a few tips. It's your fault I bought the damned thing.'

Bakker had her arms folded and was watching him.

'My fault?'

'Yes. You and your little dog. You always looked so snug in that place of yours. I guess that's why I never got invited back. I was intruding.'

It all began the Christmas before. A party, police and prison staff, and suddenly, he realized, she was interested in him. A beautiful winter evening, frost on the pavement outside the Drie Vaten. He'd started a little coal fire in the barge burner. Then, the next morning, found the idea of closeness, of ties and the demands of another, too daunting to face.

A few difficult conversations had followed. After that nothing but a handful of meetings in the course of work, uncomfortable for him though Marly Kloosterman dealt with them gently, as if she understood.

'I'd like that,' he said. 'I'll try and do better this time round.'

'Me too. Sorry if I was a bit needy.'

He didn't remember her being needy at all.

The woman from the TV was called Lucie Helmink. She was one of the anchors for the nightly news, a station veteran of everything from chat shows to war zones, forty-seven though she dressed younger and, on the screen, looked it too. Den Hartog had worked with her before. It was often rewarding but never easy.

Now she stood with her crew in the hospital corridor, arguing about the way the transmission was going to be handled. Helmink had talked to the station about running it live in the next newscast. Den Hartog was adamant that wasn't going to happen.

'Why not?' she asked, arms folded, eyes fixed on his.

Inside the room a make-up artist was working on Annie Schrijver, brushing her hair, trying to hide the blue streak, using powder to put some colour in her cheeks. A production assistant was bringing in bouquets of flowers to set around the room. The lights were ready, the cameras. Helmink said she was confident she could play this whole interview by ear, improvising questions as Annie Schrijver began to talk.

'Because there's a criminal investigation in train,' Den Hartog said wearily. 'If you go live there may be something she says we don't want out there.'

'And yet your new commissaris told us this morning this was all done and dusted? You'd got the guy?' She leaned forward and tapped a bright red fingernail against the lapel of his grey suit. 'Dead. If there's no trial coming there's nothing we can prejudice.'

'Situations change,' was all he said.

'Not for me. Live broadcast's got impact. We can key it into the news.'

Den Hartog looked at his watch.

'Lucie, please. I can still throw you out of here and get in someone else.'

'You wouldn't dare.'

'Don't test me. I'm not asking you to hold off for long. Just give us the chance to take out anything we don't want out there.'

He was always surprised by how the TV people looked close up. All the hard glamour and star quality the screen gave them was gone. What was left was a tough, determined mask, seeking one thing only: ratings, a story that beat all the others. A win.

'The longer I hold this back the more we'll have to run with the package we did this morning with Chandra.'

Smart woman. She'd guessed the situation.

'How long to edit the interview before you let it go?' he asked.

'Fifteen minutes. We can do it in the van here.'

'Thirty,' he insisted. 'I may have to check some things with Commissaris Chandra first.'

'Agreed,' Lucie Helmink muttered then walked into the room.

The crew had put baffles over some of the medical equipment to deaden the noise, though it looked as if most of it was no longer connected anyway. Annie Schrijver was still under the hands of the make-up woman. Helmink stood back, stared at her and tut-tutted.

'What's wrong?' Den Hartog asked.

'She's supposed to look sick. Like someone who's just been through hell.' A scowl then, a glance around the room. 'Not some nightclub chick with nothing more than a hangover.'

Helmink told the make-up woman to stop.

'Not finished,' she objected. 'The lights . . .'

'You're done. Leave it.'

Annie Schrijver sat upright in the bed. She wore a hospital gown covered with a blue diamond pattern. There was a single line in her arm. An attractive young woman but exhausted, scared, confused. Den Hartog had prepared the way for the interview, through a long, persuasive discussion with her alone. Now she was Helmink's.

'You're very brave, sweetheart,' the TV woman said, pulling up a chair by the bed. 'People will be saying that tonight. Not everyone has this kind of courage.'

'Maybe I don't.'

She had a flat, weak voice.

'But you do. I can tell. Believe me. I've worked everywhere. Libya. Syria. Places you wouldn't believe. I know what courage looks like. You've got it.'

'I don't know if I want to—'

Helmink began barking instructions at the crew. The cameraman was checking the lights. Ready to go. Everything was in motion.

'No need to go into details,' Den Hartog cut in. 'We wouldn't want them anyway. All you have to do is run through what we said. You went out for the night. Someone spiked your drink. That one little slip and . . .' He shrugged. 'Say what we agreed. You want women like you to be careful. To know the cost if they're not. That's all.'

She sat up in bed and ran a hand through her hair. It was so clean, so carefully brushed it looked wrong.

'My mum's OK with this?' she asked. 'Dad too?'

Helmink glanced at Den Hartog, a look that said: *Your question, not mine.*

'They're behind you every step of the way,' he told her.

'So why aren't they here?'

'Soon,' he said. 'Can't have too many people in the room. Just say it in your own words. How women like you need to avoid getting into the same . . .'

He was hunting for the right word when she cut in bitterly, 'Mess. Same stupid fuck-up as I did, you mean?'

'No language, darling,' Helmink warned her. 'Looks awful if we have to bleep things out. Please. We want sympathy here. You are a victim after all.'

She didn't get a response to that. So Lucie Helmink looked at the crew, the camera, smiled, checked her face in a mirror by the bed, grinning to make sure her teeth were OK.

'Let's get this started,' she said. 'We don't have all day.'

There were rules about prison transport but they didn't apply to a dying man. Two nurses and a private ambulance were all that would be needed to ferry Vincent de Graaf to and from the private clinic in the Zuidas. The place was ready to make an appointment that afternoon once they knew they could name their price. Within an hour he'd be out of Bijlmerbajes. A visit to a consultant, perhaps another two hours for scans. Then back to meet his end of the bargain.

Marly Kloosterman stayed in the room as he struggled into outside clothes: baggy khaki chinos, loose white shirt, bright blue nautical sweater, all from the time he was brought into the medical wing from the sex offenders' block.

'You might at least give a man some privacy,' he grumbled, fighting with the zips, the buttons, the effort.

'I'm your physician while you're here. It would be remiss of me to leave you to your own devices.' She watched him sweating as he tried to pull the sweater over the scraps of grey hair on his shiny bald head. 'I can help if you want.'

'No,' he said with a quick savagery. 'I don't need help from the likes of you. Every minute I've been here you've enjoyed watching me. Every second.'

She sighed and took a seat.

'That's very unfair, Vincent. It's part of my job. As far as I'm concerned you've received the best treatment money could buy. If you feel otherwise I can find the complaints forms. Let you file—'

'As if they'd listen to me.'

'Oh, we all listen to you. Don't have much choice, do we? Given you whine every minute of the day.'

'When do I go?'

A glance at her watch and she said, 'Presently.'

He got the sweater over his chest and struggled to pull it down, panting with the effort. Exhausted, he sat down on the bed, trying to get back his breath.

When he finally managed it he glared at her and said, 'I hate to spoil your fun, Dr Kloosterman, but you can leave me now. I'll wait on my own.'

'You mean you don't want company?'

'Not yours, thanks.'

'Shame.' She didn't move. 'When you get back . . . when Vos comes to meet you . . . what are you going to tell him exactly?'

He placed a skinny finger against his nose.

'That's between him and me.'

'Not really, Vincent.'

'What do you mean?'

'I mean if this is just a game . . . if you screw him around the way you've been screwing us ever since you set foot in this place . . . there will be consequences.'

He laughed and looked at himself. The machines, the lines, the medication by the bed.

'What do you think I care for consequences?'

'So you are going to give him a name?'

'Definitely,' he said, nodding his head. 'On my life. Any more questions?'

'Only one.' She walked up, looked into his dim, glassy eyes. 'Do you ever think about them? All those women. The ones you killed. It wasn't just three, was it? We both know that. Then all the lives you ruined along the way. Women who never quite knew what happened to them. Only that it was disgusting and some-how you managed to make them feel it was down to them. Their fault. That they're the ones to feel guilty and bear the blame.'

He scratched his neck, screwed up his face and said, 'I hate to disappoint you but . . . no. Can't say I do.'

'Then why do we hear you screaming through the walls at night?'

He laughed.

'Oh, that? Bad dreams. I keep having this nightmare that I'm trapped in some hellhole with a bitch of an ice maiden who takes enormous pleasure sticking needles in me day in and day out. Understandable in the circumstances.'

'Very funny.'

He tried to sit more upright.

'You know, Marly, ordinarily I wouldn't consider a woman of your age. There's nothing left to . . . spoil. But for you I'd happily make an exception.' He glanced at his skinny frame. 'Not person- ally you understand. But it could be arranged. Just ask—'

'You're not going to tell him a damned thing, are you?'

He hesitated for a second then said with a grin, 'The appoint- ment's booked. Nothing you can do to stop it now. Vos is an unusual man, don't you agree? He likes to see the best in people. Extraordinary if you think about it.'

She retreated to the door without a word then leaned on the bell. One of the male nurses came in pushing a hospital wheel- chair. There were grey blankets folded neatly over the back and an oxygen kit on the seat.

'We'll let you know when it's time to leave,' she said on the way out. 'If you disobey one word the nurses tell you they're under orders to bring you back here instantly. No clinic. No appointment. No possibility of a rerun. Do I make myself clear?'

His right hand rose in a salute.

'I promise not to run away, dear doctor,' Vincent de Graaf said, then hobbled over, found the wheelchair, sat in it and closed his eyes.

Bakker had returned to the car, still upset at something. Vos asked what was wrong.

'Is that what monsters look like?'

He'd called ahead to Artis and got through to the keeper of the butterfly collection. His name was Lucas Kramer. The man had grunted something inaudible when Vos mentioned Jef Braat then said he was happy to speak if they met him in the butterfly

153

house. They were still dealing with problems in the stock records. Braat's legacy from the sound of it.

'Not really,' he said. 'Monsters look like you and me. Like the person sitting next to you on a tram.'

'The way he asked if I had a tattoo . . .'

'Let it go. You'll meet much worse.'

'He knew,' she murmured.

'Knew what?'

'I do have one.'

Vos couldn't think what to say. Laura Bakker was a conservative, level-headed woman, without the least concern for fashion. The last person he'd expect to get a tattoo.

'None of my business,' he said.

'A boyfriend wanted me to do it. Something . . . personal between us. I just went along with it. Don't know why.' She shook her head and looked out of the window. 'It's like we're conditioned. Programmed not to think. A man asks. A woman complies.'

'We've all done something stupid when we're young, Laura. You put it down to experience. Consign it to the distant past. Friesland. When you were a kid.'

She started up the Volvo and they set off back into the city. The events of Wednesday night remained sharp in his memory. There was surely something there he'd missed.

'This isn't the distant past. It happened six months ago,' Bakker said. 'Not in Friesland. Here.'

Vos sighed, looked at her, said, 'Sorry.'

There was something in the way he did it that made her laugh.

'No. I'm sorry. I'm being stupid. It's just a little tattoo. A humming bird. No need to know where. What does it matter?' They were on the long straight road to Artis. Not far from the impromptu party where the panda girl had dispatched him to Zorgvlied two nights before. 'Marly Kloosterman really likes you. Were you two once . . . ?'

'No. At least . . . not any more. Not ever really. I'm not good at all that. Never was.'

'Relationships,' she grumbled. 'More trouble than they're worth. You get pressured into feeling . . . if you don't have one there's something wrong with you. And there isn't.' She caught his eye. 'Is there?'

Vos pointed out the lane by the canal that led to the staff gates into Artis. Marly Kloosterman's new houseboat had to be nearby. He wondered what it was like. Whether she enjoyed living there on her own, a bright, lively woman, sociable in a way he'd never be. Divorced too and he couldn't for the life of him imagine how any sane man could fail a woman like that so much he'd come to lose her.

He and Bakker never talked about their private lives. It was easy for him since he didn't have one. The subject wasn't off-limits. Just irrelevant. This sudden frankness was awkward, unwanted yet somehow needed too.

'What do I know? If it happens it happens,' he said. 'If it doesn't then . . . perhaps you save yourself a lot of pain.'

'And a tattoo,' she added, turning into the gate.

They walked past a rock pool full of noisy sea lions, barking and honking, then entered the Artis butterfly house, a modern two-storey glass building at the very edge of the zoo. The atmosphere hit them the moment they stepped through the plastic sheet doors, a wall of hot air so humid the moisture seemed to stick to them. A world of lush green vegetation lay ahead, gigantic palms and succulents stretching two floors to the roof. Through the leaves and branches gaudy shapes flitted, some the size of a hand, some like tiny flying flowers darting to and fro. The noises of the zoo outside, animals, exotic birds and excited visitors, were gone entirely. It was as if they'd entered a verdant tropical jungle recreated in the chilly northern clime of Amsterdam.

Kramer was there to meet them. He was a stick-thin, silver-haired man of fifty or so, smart in a white lab coat and steel-rimmed glasses. With him was his assistant, Rik Loderus. He looked the perpetual student with a head of bubbly dark hair atop a round, beaming, bespectacled face. A pair of baggy hiking shorts and a T-shirt covered in bright butterfly designs completed the outfit. The two men could scarcely have seemed more different.

Straight from a school party, Loderus explained when Bakker stared at the bizarre clothing.

'I dress for the occasion,' he added then took off his glasses and wiped away the moisture.

A gaggle of kids in uniform was filing along the winding path to the floor above. Loderus called out to them and got happy waves back.

'I trust this won't take long,' Kramer said then ushered them through to the office, pointing out the frames of chrysalises set out for public display along the way.

'Half of them empty,' he said with a dismissive wave. 'Thanks to that thieving bastard. I should never have let him set foot in this place. It was only on the recommendation of others . . .'

He glared at Loderus.

'Not me, boss. I thought you took him on,' his assistant commented as they went through the double doors into a small and tidy room where the busy air conditioning brought some welcome cold. 'Besides, he's dead. Saw it on the news. Seems he did a lot worse than pinch our butterflies.'

'Well,' Kramer said. 'That's the last time we take a convict here.'

Loderus sat on the edge of his desk and raised an eyebrow.

'Lucas. We've had ten, eleven men from prison helping out before. None of them caused any problems. A couple are still here. Very good workers.'

'Never again in my department,' Kramer repeated. He stared at Vos and Bakker. 'What do you want?'

'We'd like to know about Jef Braat,' Vos said. 'What he did, where he came from, who he hung around with.'

Kramer looked at his sidekick and said, 'I've got a budget meeting. You can deal with this.'

With that he walked out of the door.

'Lucas is very busy,' Loderus explained. 'Don't take it personally.'

'We're police,' Bakker told him. 'We don't.'

He smiled at her.

'Good. There's not a lot I can tell you really. We give ex-cons a chance from time to time. Braat was one of them. Spent some time in the reptile house then talked his way in here. He seemed . . . OK. I wouldn't have gone out for a beer with him to be honest with you.'

'Why not?' she asked.

'Not my type. A touch aggressive if you rubbed him up the wrong way. That big butterfly tattoo on his neck didn't look right either. I doubt he'd have lasted. Even if he wasn't taking our babies.'

'Babies? They're insects.'

'Beautiful insects,' he said, pointing at the window. Something had landed there. It had huge wings, strange patterns on them in lurid red and blue and yellow.

Vos asked if Braat had any friends.

'Doubt it. He was only with us a few weeks. Then someone noticed things were missing. Security confronted him. Lucas and I decided it would be best if we left it to them. After which he was gone. Cleared his locker that same day. I kind of thought he might punch someone on the way out but . . .' Loderus frowned. 'Most of the guys we get from prison are fine. They deserve a break. If we lose a few butterflies along the way . . . we can always get more.'

A second shape fluttered in front of the glass, then clung to a vine running down the pane, long spindly legs, fat furry body.

Vos looked at it and asked, 'How do you kill them?'

That seemed to surprise him.

'Why do you ask?'

'It may be important.'

Loderus went to a door at the back of the room, pulled a set of keys out of his pocket and opened it. They followed him into a storage area full of filing cabinets running almost to the low roof. Bakker opened the nearest drawer. There were lines and lines of dead butterflies inside, pinned to paper boards, Latin names beneath, desiccated bodies, some ancient, a few more recent. By a blacked-out window stood a row of killing jars. On the wall was a poster: an old pastel drawing of butterflies. She glanced at Vos. He'd seen it too. The images resembled the tattoo on Braat's neck.

'We only do it when we really need to,' Loderus explained. 'God knows we've got enough specimens from way back when people used to pin them up for fun. I hate it . . .'

'How does it work?' she asked.

'We put poison in a killing jar and drop the poor thing in.'

'Potassium cyanide,' Vos said.

'Exactly. How did you know?'

'Where do you keep it?'

Loderus pulled out his set of keys again and went to a cupboard secured with a single padlock. Inside were bottles and packs of chemicals. He rooted through a few and muttered, 'It's here somewhere.'

The two of them came and stood behind him.

'It should be.' Nervous, he pulled on his long dark hair. 'I don't understand . . . Ah.'

He retrieved a brown jar and pointed to the skull and crossbones on the label.

'Almost gone,' Loderus said, unscrewing the lid. 'Need to order some more.'

Vos looked inside. A thin layer of white powder lay on the bottom.

'Let me guess. Jef Braat had access to this locker.'

'I imagine so.'

Vos asked about records. Loderus checked a book. The last time the killing jars had been used was two months before. There was no way of telling if more poison had been taken from the bottle since then.

'Lot of use that is,' Bakker said. 'And he really had no acquaintances here? No one he talked to?'

Loderus shook his head.

'Don't think so. I know this looks like a zoo. Show business or something. But we're a serious scientific operation. The visitors help pay for real research. And maybe we educate them a little too. Lucas is one of the top men in his field. I'm not exactly without qualifications myself. Jef Braat was . . . a man who swept up and took out the rubbish.'

Bakker kept on at him. Vos poked around the boxes. Dead butterflies, pictures on the wall. Poison. Braat could have taken some, could have used it too. And then someone murdered him in turn. It was all conjecture. They needed something positive. A name from Vincent de Graaf might be a start. Perhaps Jillian Chandra was right.

His phone trilled. A message from one of the night team just coming on duty.

I don't know if you've been told or not. But the Schrijver girl's going on the news. Right now. You may want to watch.

'Damn,' he murmured and walked back into the office, found the PC, sat down at the desk and pulled up the live news feed.

A familiar face came on the screen. Lucie Helmink standing outside the hospital, mike in hand, telling people that what they were about to see might shock them.

Then the scene switched to Annie Schrijver upright in bed, eyes darting everywhere. The make-up artist and the hair stylist had made her look as if she was in a TV studio. Still, she seemed drained and frightened.

'Can't believe we put her up to this,' Bakker whispered. 'I'm not even sure I can watch it.'

She went back into the storeroom. They could hear drawers getting opened, her low complaining voice.

Loderus sat down to watch. In spite of the distressed face on the screen he seemed amused.

'Something's funny?' Vos asked.

'Not that,' Loderus said with a nod at the computer. 'Your friend. She's different. Is she . . . um . . . ?'

He stopped as if he'd gone too far.

'Is she what?' Vos asked and felt he was speaking like a cross father interrogating a potential boyfriend.

Annie Schrijver had started talking. She had a quiet, monotonous voice, something unexpectedly hard to it too.

'Nothing,' the butterfly man said. 'Sorry I asked.'

The sky was getting darker, rain was starting to fall as they took Vincent de Graaf down in the lift to the Bijlmerbajes car park. The pair of prison nurses handled the wheelchair. Marly Kloosterman accompanied them in silence. The man himself wore a bored smile throughout, clutching his sweater around him against the cold.

A silver Mercedes ambulance had been booked for the short trip to the Zuidas. The driver remained behind the wheel while two medics came and signed the paperwork. Kloosterman talked to them, ran through the arrangements. The ambulance would drive into the clinic car park at the side of the public hospital and there be met by local staff. They were to remain on site until De Graaf's examination and any scans were complete. After that he'd be returned by a clinic nurse and taken back to Bijlmerbajes.

One of the men gazed at De Graaf in his wheelchair and chuckled.

'I don't think he'll be doing a runner, will he?'

'If he does I'll have your heads on a block.'

'Thank you, ma'am.'

'No. I mean it. You take him there. You bring him back. No screw-ups.'

He handed over the signed documents and said nothing. She returned to De Graaf and the local nurses then went through the journey ahead. He couldn't take his eyes off the sky, the blocks of the prison, the walls, the van. It was if he'd forgotten what the outside world was like.

'Enjoy your treat, Vincent,' she added. 'It's more than you deserve.'

'You don't know what I deserve. You've no idea.'

'As soon as I get news you've left the clinic I'll bring Vos back here. You're going to talk to him the moment you turn up.'

'I do so hope I'll feel up to it. These things can be terribly tiring.' He looked up at her and winked. 'I don't suppose you could put back that appointment till tomorrow, could you? Give me time to recover. To . . . um, think.'

'You promised him a name.'

'Oh, I'll give him a name.' He eyed the nurse's badge. 'Robin.' He looked up at the man and smiled. 'That's a nice one.'

'I could stop this—'

'No you can't. Wheels in motion, Doctor. A prison quack must know her place.'

'Take him,' Kloosterman snapped and watched them load the wheelchair up the ramp.

There was a crack of thunder somewhere in the east. Autumn was coming and with it the cold and wet, the smell of damp leaves, the promise of dead winter.

Two minutes later the Mercedes was through the heavy gates of Bijlmerbajes, heading out into the early evening traffic. De Graaf sat in his wheelchair, smiling at the nurses, amused by the stern way they returned his gaze.

'Windows,' he said. 'It would have been so nice if I'd had a vehicle with windows. Perhaps on the way back . . .'

'This is what you get,' the senior medic told him.

The sound of traffic. Music from the ambulance dashboard up front. A waft of diesel on the damp evening air.

It was as close as freedom would ever get if the likes of Pieter Vos and Marly Kloosterman had their way.

'Very well,' De Graaf said then folded his skinny arms over the blue jumper and tried to peer through the windscreen up ahead.

Bert and Nina Schrijver found themselves in a trendy cafe set in the midst of the finance blocks springing up all over the Zuidas. It felt like another city, a different world. Thirty-somethings in expensive-looking casual clothes, bent over laptops and tablets, tapping constantly at their giant phones.

He'd given up trying to apologize. She wasn't much interested in listening anyway. Schrijver had stopped counting the hours too. If he moaned about waiting one more time she'd scream. The entire afternoon had vanished in silent recrimination, overpriced coffee they couldn't drink, fruitless calls to the hospital pleading for entry only to be told to phone back later.

After a while you ran out of things to say. All that was left was the guilt and the dark thoughts that came out of nowhere, laughing at the back of your head.

Annie was alive and yet somehow a shadow still hung over them. He couldn't name it, couldn't quite see it, but he knew for sure it was there.

Hoogland came on the phone. Schrijver went outside to take the call. The stall was busy. It seemed the Syrian kid was proving popular, bringing in more money than even Annie had managed with her sweetest of smiles.

'Keep him,' was all Schrijver said when he heard.

'What do you mean?' Hoogland asked. 'Keep him?'

'I mean bring him back tomorrow. He's got no other work, has he?'

'Have you lost your mind? He's living in a hostel somewhere. We don't even know who he is. He might be a terrorist.'

'Don't be stupid. Does a terrorist want to work a flower stall? He's making me money. More than you ever do. Maybe if I watch him I can learn how to stay afloat.'

'He's smiling at people and running up bouquets on the spot. Neat trick but I don't need him to do it.'

'You should check your smile in the mirror, Jordi.'

That didn't go down well.

'Annie can smile at them,' Hoogland replied. 'She's good at that.'

'Annie won't be back on the stall for a while.'

Maybe never, he thought.

'Then I'll do it. Or get some other market bum . . .'

'You make shit bouquets. Even I can manage better.'

'If we wind up needing a rag head to fix things . . .'

'We?' Schrijver yelled. 'Since when was it . . . we? This is my business. Not yours. You can piss off and take your thieving fingers elsewhere for all I care.'

It was a cruel, unnecessary thing to say. Hoogland was no angel but at least he'd been loyal. Or, more accurately, turned up to work for pennies, paid late on occasion, when no one else would bother.

'If he's illegal and you employ him they'll fine you. Put you out of business.'

'I'm almost out of business already. Let me worry about that.'

'You're a fool, Bert,' Hoogland barked. 'Bigger than you know.'

The line went dead.

'Handled that well,' Schrijver muttered to himself.

He looked back in the cafe. People were standing up, going to a huge flat-screen TV set against the back wall. Nina was among them, hand to her mouth, tears in her eyes.

On the TV he saw the reason. Annie was there staring into the camera, looking sick and scared. Something else too that was obvious now she was blown up four times life-size on the screen, something that seemed alien, wrong in the child he'd always raised to be polite and decent and truthful. But that was on the surface and the surface was all a stupid man saw. Not the private life, the seething hidden world that lay beneath.

Evasive was how his daughter seemed. There was no other word.

He marched back into the cafe and took Nina's arm.

'We're going to see her. I don't care what they say.'

'Laura,' Vos called. 'Get in here. I need you to watch this.'

She wandered into the office and joined the two men at the computer.

Annie Schrijver was nodding as the interviewer went through what she called 'the story so far'.

'Story?' Bakker murmured. 'It's a bloody outrage . . .'

Vos shushed her. Lucie Helmink was pushing the mike closer to the figure on the bed, urging her on.

'Now tell us, Annie. What do you think happened? In your own words.'

'As if they'd be somebody else's!'

'Laura . . .' Vos said.

'Laura,' Loderus echoed more softly.

She was silent then. So was Annie Schrijver.

'What exactly do you remember?' the TV woman asked.

A frown, a pained look at the camera then she said, 'Nothing much. Going out for a drink. With a guy. Waking up.' She rolled her eyes. 'In a van somewhere. Blacking out. Coming to . . . here.'

'You didn't know this man?'

'No.' It was said with the slow, extended petulance of a child. 'He bought some flowers. Seemed nice. A . . . guy . . . I didn't know. It happens.'

'You didn't think . . .'

'He wasn't wearing a shirt with the word rapist on it. I'd probably have noticed.'

'This sleeping beauty's got claws.' Bakker whispered.

'Where did you meet him?' echoed Lucie Helmink.

'Some place.' She screwed her eyes tight shut, looked as if she was struggling for a memory. 'Nearby I guess. I don't remember a car. Or a taxi. My bike . . .'

'Just any place?' Helmink asked. 'This man was a stranger. You went with him—'

'Not just any place!'

Her eyes flickered from side to side, as if looking to someone for comfort.

'Couldn't have been. I wouldn't . . .'

'Somewhere you thought you were safe?'

'Must have done.'

'And what happened?'

'Had a drink,' she said, close to a whisper. 'Talked. He was . . . OK, I guess. Otherwise I wouldn't have stayed. Not stupid . . .'

'No one thinks you're stupid.'

Annie Schrijver glared at her but didn't speak.

'The drink . . .'

'It was a drink. A beer. No. A cocktail. And then I don't remember. What—'

Bakker jabbed a finger at the screen and said, 'Wait . . .'

'Laura,' Vos warned. 'Will you keep quiet?'

'But—'

'They taste funny,' Annie Schrijver said. 'Don't they?'

'I don't know,' Lucie Helmink answered. 'What kind of funny?'

'Like someone put salt in them.'

'But you didn't notice?'

'It was a cocktail. They taste funny anyway. A—'

The audio bleeped out something.

'Missed that,' Loderus complained.

'A fuck-me cocktail, she said,' Bakker told him.

Annie Schrijver was laughing at her strange little joke, a short, mirthless sound. It was painful to see.

'What do you think he did?'

There was a long pause then nothing. Helmink asked again.

'Maybe you should ask the police. Or the doctors. They've been prodding and poking me.'

'You think he raped—'

'What do you reckon?' she cried. 'We played cards? He did what they always do. It's not like this was the . . .' She stopped herself and there was sudden colour in her cheeks. 'Not like I'm the first.'

There was a break then as if something had been cut. Helmink returned, face to camera. It wasn't even clear if she was talking as part of the interview at all.

Vos had his phone out and looked ready to go.

'It's very brave of you, Annie, to talk about this,' the TV woman was saying very slowly. 'What's your message to women like yourself . . .'

'Laura,' Vos cried. 'Come on. We're off. Let's find the car.'

'But, but . . .' She pointed at the screen. 'It's not finished.'

'Seen enough.'

He shook Rik Loderus by the hand. So did she. The butterfly man was blushing and seemed to be mumbling something about her number.

'Oh, for God's sake,' Bakker grumbled. 'Not now.'

Outside they headed through the back of the zoo into the staff car park. Vos was on the phone, through to Jillian Chandra.

'The interview—' he began.

'Wasn't so great, was it? You'd think that TV woman could have made more—'

'Annie Schrijver was lying.'

They got to the car. He nodded at Bakker to take the wheel.

'Any directions, sir?'

'The hospital.'

Chandra was listening.

'What is this, Vos?'

'I said. She's lying. She knows damn well where they went. Maybe she's got a good idea who did this. Who that corpse in the morgue is too.'

'Oh, please. Once again the great detective sees something the rest of us are blind to. Shame you didn't manage this four years ago.'

They began to edge out onto the road by the narrow canal, past the building site and the houseboats. From somewhere behind an animal bellowed.

'Can't believe we never got to see a giraffe or an elephant or something,' Bakker complained with a shake of her head.

'No,' Chandra barked down the phone. 'This is not a priority. We've interviewed Annie Schrijver. He gave her that date rape drug. She knows nothing.'

'I'm telling you—'

'Listen to me. I want you at Bijlmerbajes for when De Graaf returns from the clinic. I want a name from him. That's something solid. Not you playing detective with some amnesiac victim while we still have that bastard out there.'

Bakker bounced over the speed bumps too quickly. It took a moment for him to get his breath back.

'De Graaf won't be back for an hour at least. There's time. Maybe I can grab him when he comes out of the clinic. I'll let you know how it goes.'

'Did you hear me?'

He cut the call and put the phone in his pocket. Then to be sure took it out and turned the thing off.

'It could just be an awkward interview,' Bakker said. 'You might be reading too much into it, Pieter.'

He wasn't listening.

'She lied,' Vos said. 'Though why . . .'

For the life of him he couldn't imagine.

The Copernicus Cancer Centre was a two-storey block tacked to the side of the public hospital complex, close to the rising forest of towers of the financial district. The ambulance pulled into the small car park at the back. The doors opened and Vincent de Graaf caught his first sight of evening sky outside Bijlmerbajes since three months before, when Kloosterman last sent him to the public hospital next door for a scan.

The lights were on in the Zuidas buildings. As they man-oeuvred his wheelchair he found the familiar silhouette reaching up into the darkening sky like a giant concrete finger and said, 'You see that one? Third in. I built that. The De Witt Trust. Paid some stuck-up architect. Had to. But I built it. Ten floors, all rented now. Upwards of three hundred and fifty a square metre last time I checked.' He grunted. 'Not that it's much use to me.'

'You're talking to yourself, pal,' the nurse said.

The chair bounced on the hard car park ground. The Zuidas was different four years on. The financial centre must have doubled in size, eating up the green polder fields, replacing meadow with asphalt, glass and brick.

It didn't smell sweet any more. There was smoke and tar on the rainy breeze and the noticeable whiff of pollution. He liked that.

'I know I'm talking to myself. Do you think I'd waste my precious breath on you? Christ . . . !'

The idiot had gripped him hard around the shoulders and by accident dragged out the needle-like cannula in De Graaf's left arm. The pain was brief but sharp.

'You want me to put that back?' the medic asked, reaching for his gloves.

'I'll wait,' De Graaf snarled. 'For a doctor.'

They pushed him to the rear doors of the Copernicus clinic. A figure in blue scrubs was waiting there half hidden in the shadows. He came out with a clipboard, a pen, a steady, knowledgeable manner, walked behind the wheelchair, signed the forms the ambulance man gave him, then pushed De Graaf up the slope.

They went into a tunnel by what looked like a private staff car park in the bottom of the building.

'Stop,' De Graaf said, raising a weak hand.

He told the man to turn the wheelchair round. He wanted to see the Zuidas again. The tower he'd built. The way the place was rising out of nothing but green meadow.

Vincent de Graaf stared at the urban landscape before him, all lights and glass and concrete. He'd been praying to see it again for months. Now he was here it seemed disappointing. This was once his world, a place he ruled, where he did whatever he felt like. But carelessness had robbed him of that prize and now a wicked, cruel thing inside would take the weak and flimsy husk that was left.

'We have to go,' a confident male voice said from behind.

'How did he find you?'

'Does it matter?'

The messages he'd received in Bijlmerbajes were vague invitations. Difficult to interpret, hard to refuse. That need he had for freedom, albeit briefly, had consumed him. Just the thought of seeing the night sky without those damned prison blocks around . . .

'We need to go.' The wheelchair squeaked into motion. 'The time—'

'I know about time,' De Graaf cut in, shocked by the sound of his own voice, how close it was to breaking. 'I know more about that than you ever will.'

Around the corner stood what looked like a white golf buggy. When he worked down the road De Graaf had seen them use these to transport patients around the hospital complex, from X-Ray to MRI, theatre to intensive care.

Strong arms came down and lifted him gently from the chair. De Graaf's hands reached out like those of a sickly child, rising to the neck of a parent. Then stopped as he felt foolish, and clutched them instead to his bony chest.

'I don't know you,' he said, looking at the face above him. Then wondered, 'Do I?'

'Doubt it,' the man said as he carried him to the buggy.

The fake leather cushion of the back seat was at least soft. The stranger found a blanket, laid it over him, up to the chin, and gingerly raised it to his face.

'No,' De Graaf said, surprised to find that suddenly he was scared. Now. When he was free. 'Don't cover me.'

'I've got to.' He lifted the blanket over De Graaf's sweating, trembling face, went to the front, brought the electric motor to life, and trundled out into the night's steady rain.

Annie Schrijver's parents were with her when Vos marched through the door, Bakker at his heels. Her father looked up. Her mother didn't. The room was full of the flowers the TV people had placed there for effect. Roses, lilies and tulips, their heady scent filling the air.

'She wants some peace,' Bert Schrijver said, glaring at them. 'You people have done enough already. Leave her be.'

He came and stood in front of Vos.

'You hear me?'

'Bert,' Nina whispered. 'Remember what they said when they let us in. No more . . .'

'They think they bloody own us. Put Annie on the TV like that . . .'

'Not our decision, Mr Schrijver,' Bakker broke in. 'We did our best to fight it.' She looked at him hard. 'She could have said no.'

'But people don't, do they?' he yelled. 'Not when they've got all manner of clever folk like you standing round, telling them what to do.'

Vos eased past, caught Nina Schrijver's eye, took a seat, pulled it up by the bed. Her daughter wouldn't look him in the face.

'I'm Brigadier Vos, Annie. I was the one who found you that night . . .'

'The one who saved your life,' her mother added.

'I'm sorry you were pressured into this. I wish it hadn't happened. All the same . . .' His phone was still switched off. In his head he could see Jillian Chandra getting mad somewhere, perhaps even on her way here already. 'A very dangerous man's still out there. We need to find him. To stop him. For that . . .' She looked at him then. 'For that you have to tell us the truth.'

'What do you mean, the truth?' Bert Schrijver roared.

A nurse stopped by the door, looked in, asked if everything was OK. Bakker flashed her ID and got her out of there.

Schrijver seemed to get the point. More quietly he said, 'She told you everything she knew. That bastard doped her. She doesn't know what's happened. If she did . . . if . . .'

He went quiet. Something in his daughter's face had stopped him. Vos put a hand in his pocket and turned on his phone. Nothing Chandra could do to stop him now.

'Guilt's a funny thing,' he said, watching the way she hung on his every word. 'We all get it. We all think we understand it. We've got it under control. But then it comes out from nowhere and bites us. Tells us however innocent we think we are really it's us to blame. For being careless. Or stupid.'

Nina Schrijver's hand went out and took her daughter's fingers.

'It doesn't matter how often you say . . . you're not to blame, it's not your fault. Nothing that happened was down to you. You're forgiven. That sense of shame just stays there like a stain inside. One no one else can see. Just you.'

'Stop it, please,' the mother whispered.

'I can't,' he said. 'Annie knows something. I need her to tell me.'

'What in God's name is this about?' Bert Schrijver asked, voice low for once.

'Where did you go, Annie?' Bakker asked. 'Who with?'

Head down, chin on her pale neck, glassy eyes staring up at them, childlike and full of resentment, she mumbled something.

'Can't hear,' Vos said.

When she spoke her face was contorted, full of pain and anger like a child.

'The Mariposa! It's where they all go. All the rich ones from the Zuidas. Ten-euro cocktails and clothes I'll never afford. Lives I'll never have.' Just saying that seemed to lift some weight from her. 'He was a foreigner who chatted me up in the market when he bought some flowers. I just went for a drink . . .'

'We need a name.'

'If he told me I don't remember.'

'There's more,' Vos said.

'Is there?'

She wasn't going any further so Vos said straight out, 'You stumbled over your words, Annie. You were going to say this wasn't the first time it happened.'

'Wasn't,' she snapped.

'He's still out there,' Vos added. 'If you can help us find him . . .'

Bert Schrijver let out a low and mournful groan, long and pained, just one word after, 'What?'

'We've all got secrets,' Bakker added. 'It's just that yours are about more than you. We need—'

'Rob did it just the once!' she cried. 'Years ago. When me and him first met. He put something in my drink. It wasn't . . . wasn't like you think.'

Schrijver turned to his ex-wife, face full of thunder and shock.

'Sanders? That bastard was part of this? You knew and never told me.'

'Of course I didn't know! How could I? Christ, Annie. He did that and you still . . .'

'It was just one of those things! Happens all the time. For God's sake, Dad, don't look so fucking angry. You got mum pregnant while you were pissed, didn't you? The pair of you . . .'

'Not the same,' Nina whispered.

'You're sure about that? It would have happened anyway. I wanted him.' More quietly, 'Rob never tried anything like that again. Never needed to. He said sorry. He meant it. *Dad!*'

Schrijver was out of the room. Vos told Bakker to find any uniforms around and keep him away from Sanders.

'How many years ago?' he asked.

'Four.'

'Where?'

'In the city. De Wallen.' She peeked at her mother. 'The kind of place I wasn't supposed to go. It was different. I was on my own. Nothing to do with this. *Nothing* . . .'

'It was just him?' Vos asked. 'Just Rob? You're sure?'

Annie was hesitating over her answer when Vos's phone rang. Chandra, he guessed, picking it out of his pocket. He'd try to get the news in before the argument started.

'Pieter,' said a gentle, concerned voice in his ear.

He had to think for a moment. Then it continued, 'It's Marly. What's going on?'

'Sorry?'

'I just got a call from the Copernicus people. De Graaf didn't show up for his appointment. I checked with the paramedics. They're still in the car park. They say they dropped him off with a nurse almost an hour ago. In his wheelchair. They don't know where he is. He can't just vanish . . .'

Nina Schrijver was back at the bed, arms around her daughter.

'Can't he?' Vos whispered.

Outside in the corridor he heard the commotion. Two uniforms wrestling with a furious Bert Schrijver, Bakker with them. He called control and told them to bring a search team to the hospital, then assign some people from the night crew to pick up Rob Sanders.

'Where's the CCTV room?' he asked the woman on reception.

Same floor, four hundred metres along the corridor. Restricted access.

'Get us in there,' he ordered. 'Laura.'

Thirty seconds later they were in a small office watching a security guard flick through the screens. Cameras covered the sprawling complex, more than a hundred in all. Vos got him to look at the Copernicus car park and scroll back an hour. It took a little while but he found it. An ambulance turning up, two men unloading a wheelchair. They vanished into a blind spot, came back, just the medics, pulled out cigarettes, little red lights darting on the screen.

'Get me inside,' Vos said.

Up came a view of a corridor to the lift that was supposed to take De Graaf to Copernicus reception. Nothing.

'Where could someone push a wheelchair from there?' he wondered. 'Without being seen?'

'Not inside, that's for sure.' The security officer scratched his neat hair. 'It has to be the other side of the staff parking area.'

He played with the keyboard and brought up another gloomy exterior. Cars glistening under the rain, splashes of light on puddles. Then, in the dark, something like a golf buggy moving steadily down the pathway between the vehicles.

'That goes nowhere,' the guard said, baffled. 'In this weather? In one of those things?'

'Let me see it live,' Vos ordered. 'Pull back and give me the area.'

The screen changed. No buggy. No movement.

'Pieter,' Bakker said, pointing at the picture. 'There.'

A neon sign on the tower block at the very edge of the screen.

De Witt it said, in vertical red neon letters.

'That was his company, wasn't it?'

He went for the door. She followed, checking her weapon.

His phone was ringing. It had to be Jillian Chandra this time. She could wait.

Holding hands in the flower-filled room, listening to the whir of the air conditioning, the dwindling yells and cries down the corridor, the silence between them.

'They're going to throw Dad out for good, aren't they?' Annie said finally.

Nina Schrijver was there already, thinking of how she'd handle things.

'Probably. Doesn't matter. You'll be out of here before long.'

'He'll hate me for not telling him. You too . . .'

'All I knew was you and Rob had a bad start. Not the details. Never wanted them. Don't now.'

'Dad's going to hate me—'

'Don't be ridiculous,' Nina Schrijver snapped. 'Your father doesn't have it in him to hate anyone. Except maybe himself. We'll get you home soon.'

'Home.'

There was a message in that single word.

'Come to my place, then. Or maybe we could go away for a few days. I've got the money.'

Annie glared at her, something in that look: *I'm a Schrijver. I don't run.*

She said, 'I did this. I made him lose it like that. My fault. Whatever that policeman said . . .'

Nina's fingers tightened on hers.

'Don't think that way, love. It won't help.'

Annie nodded, closed her eyes, took a long, pained breath.

'What will?'

It had to be said.

'The truth. Like that police man told you.'

Annie laughed, a short, dry, mirthless sound.

'The truth? No one tells you everything. There's stuff you don't even say to yourself.'

'Someone did this to you. Someone put you in here.'

'It wasn't Rob. What's Dad going to do to him?'

'Nothing. I'll make sure of it. Make sure he understands.'

She was close to tears.

'You think you do? Or me? I've screwed up everything . . .'

'I understand,' Nina Schrijver answered, 'that you and Rob had a difficult relationship. It started bad. It ended bad. You're not the only one it's happened to.'

'Guess not,' she whispered.

'Do you really not know his name? The one who . . .'

She couldn't say it.

'The one who doped me? Raped me?'

'Him.'

Annie hesitated. She was better at lying than her father. But Nina Schrijver had raised her. She recognized that glance to one side, the sly and culpable cast in her eye.

'I asked a question. You're going to have to face it some time—'

'His name's Greg Launceston. American.' She nodded at the window. 'Works for a computer company around here some-where. Loaded. More money than you could imagine. Thought it could buy him everything.' She sighed. 'In the end I guess it did.' A brief and bitter laugh. 'And if he did rape me I don't remember a thing. Or feel it.'

'He's dead.'

'Am I supposed to be sorry?'

Nina couldn't think of an answer to that.

'Anything else you want to know?' Annie asked.

'Save it for the police—'

'He'd been coming to the market nagging me for ages. I went out for a drink with him last week. He tried it on. Had his little bag of coke with him. Full of himself. I played along for a while then told him where to get off. He got all shouty. Called me a . . . prick teaser. Lots of other names too. Not so nice ones.'

Nina squinted at her, trying to work this out.

'And you still went out with him again?'

A sarcastic nod then, 'And I still did. What a little slut your daughter is, eh? Why couldn't I have stayed home in that tiny little room of mine watching the TV?'

Old fingers tightened on clammy young skin.

'You weren't to know. Don't torture yourself—'

'I really have to tell them, do I? When they come back.'

The doubt in Annie's voice amazed her.

'Of course. Everything. Get it off your chest. Once you're out of here we'll start again. I'll help Dad get back on his feet. You don't have to work until you want to. We'll cope.' She bent forward and peered into her daughter's face. 'That's what we do. Market people. We manage. We get by.'

'Everything.' Annie Schrijver spoke so softly the word was barely audible.

'It's like poison. You want it out of yourself. You heard what they said. There's a monster out there somewhere.'

Annie was staring at her, not pleasantly.

'There's always been monsters. Nothing new there. No one's

got the right to know everything. Not even you. Stuff happens, Mum, and you wish it never did. Wish you could forget it . . .'

Words were funny. Sometimes they came so easily. Sometimes they wouldn't form at all. With strangers. With people you'd known all your life.

Then occasionally they lurked at the back of your head, daring you to utter them, wondering if you had the guts to hear the answer you dreaded in return.

The question she really wanted to ask was . . . *And what the hell does that mean?*

Nina Schrijver lacked the courage to say it. Instead she asked, 'Is there anything I can get you?'

Her daughter sniffed, wiped her face with the sleeve of the gown and looked around.

'A bedpan might come in useful.'

A blustery wind greeted them when they emerged from the Copernicus car park, biting rain in their face, nothing moving ahead. The De Witt building seemed a long shot. A coincidence too many.

'Could have got him in a car,' Bakker said.

'Could have,' Vos agreed. 'But where's the wheelchair? Where's the buggy?'

She looked around, scanning the hospital perimeter, the finance blocks further on.

'I don't get it. The man's sick. Dying. He must need medical treatment every single day. He can barely walk. What possible motive could he have for doing a runner now?'

'"Do not go gently . . ."' Vos murmured.

'Pardon?'

'It's a poem. Nothing.'

Vincent de Graaf was counting down the days. Immobile, dependent on others. Dying slowly, certainly, trapped inside a clinical prison cell. Vos felt he could usually think his way into the minds of the people he was chasing. But one in that position . . . he didn't know where to begin.

The phone trilled. Another text message, another obscure foreign number.

Are you suffering, Vos?

He looked around, wondering who might be watching them from the many shadows, then tapped the number to make a call.

Three rings, nothing he could hear nearby. An answer. Silence except for the wind somewhere.

'Are you suffering, Vos?'

The voice was digital, robotic. There had to be some kind of software between them, an app that changed the way he – or perhaps even she – spoke.

'No. I'm lost.'

The thing laughed. It sounded like a creature out of a child's cartoon.

'You're closer than you think for once,' it said and then was gone.

The entrance to De Graaf's office building was a black glass frontage with a desk and one lone man in uniform behind it. The floors above were mostly in semi-darkness. The Zuidas worked twenty-four hours a day, buying and selling financial services around the world. But not, it seemed, the De Witt Trust.

Vos pressed his police ID to the door until the guard came.

'We're looking for someone,' he said. 'A patient in a wheel-chair. Someone with him. Perhaps . . . more than one.'

The man stared at him and said, 'Is this a joke?'

'No joke,' Bakker told him. 'Vincent de Graaf, the man who started this company, has just gone missing from the hospital. We wondered if maybe he came . . . home.'

'De Graaf?' the guard asked, wide-eyed. 'He's supposed to be in jail. Murdered some girls. You let him out?'

'No,' Vos answered. 'We didn't let him out. When did you last admit someone to the building?'

He was heavily built with a sour, florid face, a thick dark moustache above a mouth that seemed set in a permanent sneer. The kind of man who wouldn't admit the Pope without seeing a photo ID.

'Just before six. Two cleaners. They're still in the downstairs office behind me. Next question?'

Bakker grunted something and wandered outside into the dark.

'So who else is still here?'

'Five or six people working on the top floor. Software outfit who rent space from the management company. They work any hours they feel.'

'I meant for De Witt . . .'

'De Witt barely exist any more. Not since you lot put the boss inside. It was a trust company and who's going to trust some-one like that? They just own the building and rent it out. Only Mr Strick's left from the old days.' He sniffed. 'Used to be De Graaf's partner. One of the rich blokes. More like office manager now. Hate it when that happens, don't you?'

Somewhere in the distance rose the angry wail of a siren. Marnixstraat was sending out the troops. They could flood this area. But it was a faceless, labyrinthine place, half office and hospital complexes, half building site. In the dark, without a clue where to look, it was going to be hard.

'Is Strick here?'

'No. Left at five as usual.'

The phone in Vos's jacket rang.

'I'm round the back,' Bakker said. 'Found a hospital buggy in the bushes. Near what looks like the tunnel for an underground car park.'

'Coming,' he said and looked at the security guard. 'There's a car park beneath the building?'

'Well spotted.'

'We need to check inside.'

The guard shrugged.

'Can't help. Don't cover that bit. Not on my round. Different company and—'

Vos reached out and tapped him on the chest.

'I want to go in there. I want to go in there now. If you can't open it up find someone who can.'

The man laughed at him.

'In that case I'll give you a number you can call.'

Before he could take it further Bakker was on the line again.

'Pieter? There's a set of steps hidden behind the bushes. They go down to a fire door or something. It's open. I can just about make some light. I think there's someone's inside . . .'

'Stay where you are,' Vos ordered.

'I'm not sure but—'

'*Stay where you are!*'

She was waiting for him by a thick stand of conifers set by the sloping drive to the underground garage, gun out low by her side. A white and blue hospital buggy sat halfway up the pavement, driven into the hedge, front wheels deep in mud.

The rain was turning denser, heavier.

A line of steps ran down from behind the trees. Perhaps fifteen or so, slippery with algae and rain. At the foot was a narrow metal door, half-open.

He took out a torch, set off first, ignoring her bleats about the fact she was the only one with a weapon.

At the foot of the greasy steps he pushed open the metal door, listened to it creak on dry hinges then turned the beam down a corridor so narrow they'd have to walk single file. Ten metres ahead lay another door, just cracked open. No sound of machinery ahead, no heat from any boiler. There seemed little purpose to the place at all.

Then, faint on the dank breeze, it came to him: a man's laboured, shallow wheezes.

He flashed the torch round the walls. Bare cement, thick cobwebs dangling from the low ceiling. Then the floor. Grubby concrete, deep with dust marked by recent footprints as if the place had been unused for years then recently rediscovered.

He thought of De Graaf struggling for breath on his prison hospital bed. A ghost of what he once was.

A man in that condition couldn't walk down these steps.

Vos got to the second door and poked it open with his foot. Bakker squeezed beside him, gun in one hand, torch in the other. Their two beams swept the space ahead.

'Jesus,' Bakker murmured.

Three uniformed officers had Bert Schrijver in the back of their van. Cuffed, manacled to the side rail, unable to move much, which meant he banged his big feet on the metal floor, shouting and screaming all the time.

When he stopped for a moment one of them said, 'You know. We'd really like to be sympathetic here. But you're making it very hard.'

'Screw your sympathy,' Schrijver bellowed. 'What use is that to me?'

The oldest of the officers sat down opposite, looked at him and sighed.

'We don't want to arrest you, mate. We certainly don't want to charge you. But if it goes on like this we will. If you could just cut the threats . . .'

'That bastard Sanders raped my daughter!'

The men exchanged glances.

'We are looking for him, you know,' the officer told him. 'May take a while but we'll find him. Vos is on his case. Bit of an oddball but he's the best man we have.'

That calmed him a little.

'If Rob Sanders isn't here why am I in this bloody van? In handcuffs like a criminal?'

'Because you've been yelling and screaming blue murder all day. The hospital told us. They don't want you on the premises.'

'My girl—'

'Your daughter's coming out tomorrow. You can wait for her at home. Or in the station. You choose.'

He didn't answer.

'Do you want me to phone your wife? She says she'll come and help.'

'Ex-wife,' Schrijver snapped. 'We're divorced. She never told me. *Never told me—*'

'For God's sake,' one of the younger men broke in, exasperated. 'Make it easy for us, will you? Else we can chuck you inside a cell for the night, shut the bloody door and see what you look like in the morning.'

The sirens were everywhere, their radios alive with chatter. From what he'd heard the commissaris was on the way. The big boss. These men thought they had better things to do than deal with the likes of him, Schrijver guessed. They were probably right.

'You say you haven't found him?'

'No,' the officer moaned. 'We only just put out the call. You got any idea where he might be?'

Schrijver thought about that.

'You might want to try some dive called Mariposa in the Albert Cuyp. Seems popular with that sort from what I can gather.'

One of them got on the radio with the tip straight away.

'Thank you,' he said when he'd finished. 'Cooperation. That's what we like to see.'

183

A rattle of the cuffs then, a silent plea.

'If I get your wife . . .'

'Ex-wife.'

'She still uses your name. If I get her here and she takes you home do you promise to stay there? To behave? Like a good boy? Who knows? When you wake up tomorrow it might be a bright new day.'

'Fat chance.'

The man growled, 'Well in that case it's a cell for you—'

'I meant . . . fat chance about . . . the day.' He rattled the cuffs again. 'You can let me go. He's not here. I won't go looking.'

'Fetch her,' the officer told the other two. 'I'm going to find out what's going on. Don't let him free until the wife's turned up. Sorry . . .' He corrected himself before Schrijver could. 'Ex-wife. If we've got a spare car someone can drive them home. If not . . . Get them in a taxi. I want them gone and I don't want to hear another squeak from *him* this side of Christmas.'

'Your fault . . .' Schrijver muttered.

The man came and crouched in front of him.

'What was that?'

'I said it's your fault. Police were supposed to have dealt with all this years ago. The papers said. If—'

A hefty fist came out, strong fingers grabbed Schrijver's jacket.

'Don't push it.'

Silence then, on both sides. Bert Schrijver hung his head, kept his mouth shut and waited.

The chamber hidden deep in the dark Zuidas polder was as cold as the tomb and stank of mould and damp, of earth and rank decay. At its centre, beneath a single fluorescent tube, a man lay on a red leather barber's chair much like the one Vos had seen in Ruud Jonker's tattoo parlour in De Pijp four years before, a corpse dangling from a rope by its side. A dusty mattress, stained with fungus and filthy drips of water, was set on a bed by the near wall. Next to it was a row of rusting green metal cabinets with narrow drawers, most of them open, contents strewn everywhere as if by a child playing a wicked game.

The man was Vincent de Graaf and he was naked, a yellow skeletal shape reclined on the dusty leather, ribs sticking through waxy skin, one hand at his groin though the fingers were covered by sheets of cards scattered like leaves across him. For a second Vos couldn't take his eyes off the filing cabinets. He'd seen something like them before, and recently. Then it came back: the dead butterfly collection in the zoo.

There were faces on the cards, photographs, all of them women, naked, some eyes closed, some half-open with black and staring pupils. Their mouths stood agape. In a few a hand intruded, the back of a man's head, a penis erect like a fleshy exclamation mark there to insult the sleeping and the dead.

These were his prizes, Vos thought, and this the place he liked to win them. Not Ruud Jonker's dismal den in De Pijp at all. Being an organized, meticulous man he kept his trophies for future enjoyment in his own private Cabinet of Curiosities, the proof of them pinned to card like trapped insects, a record of his conquests to be enjoyed at leisure. Though surely never, even in his febrile imagination, in circumstances like this.

De Graaf's face was half-turned in their direction, a gaping grin halfway between terror and ecstasy; it was impossible to tell. The man's right arm was caked and smeared with blood. Midway between wrist and elbow stood the red plastic mark of a cannula, its needle straight into the vein. Above was a medication stand, a bag of clear liquid, some kind of machine, a pump Vos guessed, hooked onto the metal rig, beeping, lights flashing, feeding the drug into him much as something similar would once have done in Marly Kloosterman's clinic.

There was more blood on his naked shoulder as well and Vos

understood what he'd see when he looked there. Beneath the gore and scratched skin a fresh tattoo, crude and hasty.

Sleep Baby Sleep.

'Does it suit me?' De Graaf whispered in a voice that was weak but full of venom. 'I ask because I can't quite turn to see.'

Vos ignored him, looked at the label on the clear plastic bag attached to the stand. It was a tag with a brand name and a declaration of the contents: morphine. The thing was half-empty. It seemed to be working overtime.

He bent down to the man on the chair, put his head to his chest, listened to his shallow breathing.

'You need to see this,' Bakker said.

She was going through the cabinet drawers, pulling out more pieces of card.

'Not now. Do you know anything about morphine?'

'Not really. I . . . This is where he took them, isn't it? And he came back here . . .' She glanced towards De Graaf's right hand, where it was, what it seemed to be trying to do in the midst of all the photographs, the naked faces, submissive skin. 'Christ. The sick bastard—'

'Not now,' he repeated and pulled out his phone. Half a bar of signal. It was enough to get through to control, say where he was, demand immediate emergency medical help.

'There are some steps near the private car park behind the De Witt building. If you get problems, ask the security guard.' A thought. 'Tell Chandra she doesn't need to worry about Vincent de Graaf. We have him. If . . .'

He stopped. De Graaf was laughing out loud. The effort faltered, fell into a cough, then subsided into short and shallow breaths.

'Get here quick,' Vos added. 'He's bad.'

With his free hand De Graaf was trying to lift a photo stuck to his chest. One among scores, picked at random. All white, all young. All unconscious or dead.

An echo rolled down the long damp corridor. Voices and sirens getting near.

Vos couldn't think straight. Couldn't take in all the possibilities here. So he did what came easily, bent down over the skinny, yellow creature on the chair, tore the photo of an unconscious teenager from his crooked fingers.

'I want that name,' he said, staring into Vincent de Graaf's bleary, liquid eyes.

The pupils were dilated, the whites tinged yellow. Still they seemed to be mocking him.

De Graaf laughed and mumbled, 'Do you?'

The intravenous pump clicked and shot out another dose. De Graaf let out the faintest whinny as the drug hit him.

Decisions, Vos thought. In a moment a medic might be here and take De Graaf from him.

'We had a bargain, Vincent. A good businessman always keeps his word.'

'You never did business with me. What do you know?'

'I know we had an arrangement. And if you don't deliver I'm going to rip that line of morphine out of your arm right now.' He leaned closer, aware of the stink on the dying man's breath. 'Will that hurt?'

A pause, a hateful look in two failing, jaundiced eyes and then, 'Too late, Vos. You are always too late.' A glance at the plastic bag, the clear line running into his arm. 'Hurt's beyond me now.'

'I want that name.'

De Graaf closed his eyes, smiled a pained smile.

'I want that name.'

Feet coming down the corridor, voices, the loud, stern tones of Jillian Chandra among them.

'Stop this,' Bakker said, putting a hand gently to his arm.

'Can't,' was all he could say before, with one violent movement, Vos ripped the line out of the dying man's arm. There was the briefest, saddest, softest scream. Blood pumped up, spattered them both.

'Tell me, for fuck's sake,' Vos hissed, a finger's width from the sallow, shiny cheeks.

But all that came from his mouth was a single gasp of breath, no words at all.

De Graaf couldn't move, couldn't look, couldn't speak. His eyes were turning still and glassy.

Vos threw away the torn cannula and gripped his bony bleeding wrist, yelling, shaking, screaming. Shapes flooded through the door, blue medical scrubs, doctors. Uniforms and voices he half-recognized.

Arms gripped him, forced him aside, pushed him towards the rusty green cabinets, through the photos strewn everywhere like leaves shed by a cruel autumn gale.

Jillian Chandra was there, Van der Berg with her. Both looking at him in shocked silence. Bakker too and that hurt most of all.

'We need the name,' Vos shouted, pointing at the naked clammy figure as the medics swarmed around. 'I told you not to let him go until we had it. We need it now . . .'

'Get Vos out of here,' Chandra ordered.

'Listen to me . . .'

Medics swarmed around the stick-thin shape in the chair, taking away the morphine stand, the pump. A doctor in a white jacket was barking orders.

'He's gone, Pieter,' Laura Bakker said. 'Let's get out of here.' He didn't move. 'I've something to show you. Outside.'

He followed her across the strewn cards and photographs, rustling testaments to human misery kept close beneath the cold Zuidas earth.

Up the greasy steps the rain had stopped, the clouds had cleared. Half a moon cast a silver light on the trees, the cars, the damp roads around them, the tower block above.

'I should have got it out of him,' he whispered.

'Well, you didn't. *We* didn't. But he left us something. Those pictures.'

A sea of lost faces, the sleeping, the vanished.

'What use are they? Even if we could find them . . . what good would it do? With any luck they've mended their lives. The last thing they need is the likes of us bringing all that poison back again.'

'True,' she said. 'In principle. But . . .'

She'd brought one picture from inside and held it out in front of him.

Vos fell silent, unable to imagine what this might mean.

They must all have come from the same camera. A cheap instant one, he imagined from the shiny square paper. Someone had written dates in a neat hand – blue ballpoint – in the corner of each.

The picture in Laura Bakker's fingers was from four years before. Not long before the Sleeping Beauty case broke.

The face there was younger but recognizable all the same.

Annie Schrijver, slimmer, paler, with longer hair, almost a schoolgirl.

Eyes half-open.

Awake.

Vos's phone throbbed and he knew what he'd see there: another text from another untraceable number.

Any the wiser?

Vos hit the redial button. Four ring tones and then an answer.

'Not much,' he said. 'Are you?'

A laugh. A man. Dry. Not young. Then something switched in, the robot voice.

'Nice try,' it said. 'Goodnight, Brigadier. Sweet dreams.'

FOUR

The dreams weren't sweet. They were dark and discomfiting. Naked bodies, dead, unconscious, some crooked in a leather barber's chair, others floating in a swirling river that rose to swallow them. And Annie Schrijver everywhere, the face of a victim but something knowing about her too.

That last had stuck with him all the long morning, through the awkward briefing with Chandra, Van der Berg by her side. No one mentioned his tantrum the previous night. It wasn't that they were being considerate. The case had simply moved on to fresh and more difficult pastures.

Working on a tip from Annie Schrijver's mother, the night team had finally got a name for the man found dead in Zorgvlied. An American, Greg Launceston, who'd been working for one of the tenants in the De Witt building. Rob Sanders hadn't been seen since clocking off at the hospital the previous afternoon. Every duty officer in Amsterdam now had his photograph and instructions to arrest him on the spot. A small team had broken into his flat in De Pijp and found nothing incriminating so far.

Vos had a hunch Sanders would turn up one way or another. More than anything though he wanted to pick up where he'd left off with Annie Schrijver and that was proving impossible. The hospital said she'd be allowed home shortly but every request for an interview was being rebuffed. To Chandra's disgust the parents were directing inquiries to a law firm notorious for handling anti-police cases. There were questions about the pressure Den Hartog had placed on Annie to go on TV. At least that meant Chandra was more occupied with thoughts of damage limitation than interfering in an investigation that seemed to grow murkier by the hour.

The photos from De Graaf's subterranean lair were posted around the walls of the serious crimes unit, a team of desk officers and civilians set on identifying the victims they so cruelly portrayed. Four women had been traced, all missing, now presumed dead.

'We're not going to find them all, are we?' Bakker asked, staring at the sea of faces. 'They weren't human to him. Just trophies to gloat over.'

They'd fixed an appointment with Willem Strick, De Graaf's former partner, in his office at the De Witt building.

'Um . . .' She nudged him and pointed discreetly across the corridor. Marly Kloosterman was there getting out of the lift, bright-eyed, scanning the office. 'Your friend's here. Do you want me to . . . ? Look busy?'

He didn't answer. Just got some coffee and found a desk where the three of them could talk.

'I'm genuinely sorry, Pieter. Sorry we fouled up. Sorry he's dead.'

Marly Kloosterman was flicking through the preliminary report from the morgue. It said Vincent de Graaf had died of pulmonary oedema. He'd effectively drowned as his lungs filled up with fluid caused by the massive morphine overdose administered through the pump.

'Not your fault,' Bakker told her.

She didn't look as if she agreed.

'Did you get anywhere with that phone I gave you?'

Forensic said it had been remotely wiped. Someone had a way into it from elsewhere. The moment they thought it was compromised they sent a command which restored the thing to factory defaults.

'That's a shame.' She placed the papers back on the desk. 'I really haven't been any help at all, have I?'

'He was still alive when we got there,' Vos said. 'If I could—'

She shook her head.

'He was a very sick man.' She tapped the printout. 'Nothing was going to keep him alive after that.'

'I could have got a name.'

'Vincent was never going to give you anything. He as good as told me when he left.' She grimaced, scraped nervous fingers through her short hair, looked worried for a moment. 'I think he maybe threatened me too.'

'Threatened you? How?'

'It was just a stupid thing. He said . . . He said he wouldn't usually be interested in someone my age.' She smiled. 'Nothing left to spoil apparently. But for me he'd make an exception. Not for himself, you understand. His friend.'

'His friend's still out there,' Bakker said.

'His friend killed him, didn't he?'

'Looks that way,' Vos agreed. 'We can still get someone to keep an eye on you.'

'No. I should never have mentioned it.' A thought; she glanced at him. 'But if you want to come along . . .'

'Marly . . . this is serious.'

'Oh, please. Whatever drove Vincent on . . . whatever's driving this accomplice of his now . . . it's not vengeance, is it? Nothing quite so noble.'

'I still think . . .'

'No. I don't want any of you wasting your time on my behalf. You've better things to do. I've got to get back. The shit's going to be flying over this. Not your way. I'm the one who fixed that transportation.'

But it was just what the prison did in the circumstances, Vos said.

'It was. And it went wrong. I put my hand up. I'm to blame.'

'Obvious you don't work round here,' Bakker growled. 'You'd be busy finding someone else to carry the can.'

There was a difficult atmosphere in the office. Jillian Chandra had been taking calls from her superiors in Zoetermeer. Word was they were less than impressed by results so far. Den Hartog was stomping round the corridors like a man with a hangover. Van der Berg seemed to be out of Vos's team for good, working by her side, barely talking.

Vos pulled up one of the autopsy pictures on the computer. It was something he'd seen briefly in the angry confusion of the previous night. He pointed to the photo: Vincent de Graaf's right arm, the one that had taken the morphine line that had killed him. The drug went in through a small needle fixed into the vein. But his arm was covered in bruises and puncture marks from near the shoulder to the wrist, dark red blood marks on them. More than a dozen. Not a man fond of injections, or even the thought of them, Vos found it hurt just to look.

'This thing you put in a someone's arm,' he said, pointing to the tiny plastic and silver device.

'A cannula,' Kloosterman told him.

'Are they hard to insert?'

'Can be if you want to get it right.'

'So many—'

'De Graaf's veins were like him. They never wanted to co-operate. I used to struggle sometimes and I must have inserted thousands of those things.'

Bakker, less squeamish, rolled up her sleeve and pinched the blue line beneath her pale skin there.

'Can anyone do it?'

Kloosterman thought about that.

'In theory I suppose. It's just a short, sharp needle with a tube on the end. You find the vein, you drive it in. If the arm doesn't work you try the back of the hand. I insist a doctor does it. We have the time and we have the staff. In an emergency you'd leave it to a nurse.'

She peered at the photo more closely.

'Some of those marks probably date back to someone in the clinic struggling to get one into him. I really don't know. It's not something we record.'

'Would it have hurt?' Bakker asked.

Vos had gone a little ashen-faced. Kloosterman noticed and it amused her.

'Needles,' she said. 'When you don't have many they terrify you. If someone sticks them in you day in and day out most people barely feel them. When I was a medical student my flatmate used to let me practice on him. Although . . .' She looked a little coy. 'It is possible he had other reasons for cooperating. We did end up married. For a while.'

'You're saying it wouldn't have hurt?' Bakker persisted.

'Vincent de Graaf was a very sick man. He was no stranger to needles. Can you blow that picture up?'

Bakker did and they looked at the map of bruises, yellow and purple, on De Graaf's bony dead arm.

'I'd say you're looking for a very clumsy nurse who's well out of practice. Or a rank amateur who discovered it wasn't as easy as he thought.'

Vos flicked over to the general photo of the scene. The naked skinny corpse on the barber's chair, the stand, the equipment behind.

'A rank amateur couldn't set that up.'

Marly Kloosterman patted his knee.

'It's a bag, a pipe and a pump, love. You could pick up how to use it on YouTube if you wanted. Oh dear. I'm not being helpful, am I?'

Bakker had the car keys out. She wanted to be gone from

Marnixstraat, hunting round the place where Vincent de Graaf died such a strange and mysterious death. So did Vos, if he was honest.

'You're a lot of help,' he said. 'We have to go. Is there anything else?'

'Not that I can think of.'

He had to say it.

'I need to know you're safe. De Graaf met this man. If he really did pass on your name then—'

'Oh, please. I'm a big girl now. Unless a certain brigadier I know is in the neighbourhood. It's quite a boat. Did you see *Het Parool* at the weekend?'

The question threw him. He hadn't.

'I was in the Beautiful Homes section.' She pulled out her phone and showed them a picture of the two-page spread. The place looked impressive even though the photos were tiny: a long, shiny green boat, elegant rooms, a bedroom with a double divan, ornate linen and a chandelier. 'I do tours, but only for special friends.'

Bakker had her long arms folded and was staring at the two of them.

'Would you like a quiet moment together?' she wondered.

Silence.

'Obviously not,' Kloosterman announced. 'Still. Can't blame a girl for trying.'

She wandered off with a little wave. Bakker up scooped her bag, checked her gun, got her jacket.

'I really like your friend. Not sure about that houseboat. Bit over the top.'

'Thank you.'

'No. I mean it. About liking her. She's different. Sense of humour. You could use that. Been a bit grumpy of late.'

'Thank you again.'

On the way downstairs his phone bleeped: an email. It was

from Marly Kloosterman. A copy of the article from the paper and a message.

Just a reminder, Pieter. One day. Please . . .

The lawyer called Petra Zomer had phoned Nina Schrijver the night before after seeing the interview on TV. She was partner in an activist firm based in the city centre, keen to take on social cases, everything from immigration appeals to child custody and police persecution issues. By the time Annie was ready to leave hospital Zomer was behaving as if she owned them already. Her firm organized the transport. One of its seniors warned off the media as much as was possible while Zomer fielded calls from Marnixstraat demanding a fresh interview, staying non-committal, promising she'd get back to them.

Bert Schrijver wondered where the money for a fancy lawyer was going to come from. The police, Zomer said. In the end. Until then the firm would work for free, no win, no fee. With long black curly hair and a lively, ever-smiling face she looked like a student of twenty-three, dressed even younger, had tattoos running up her thin, taut arms. Nina was sold on her already. Annie didn't have – or want – much of a say. The debate was over before he realized it had even begun.

Annie's return home was quiet in the circumstances. A blacked-out Mercedes took her round the side. Zomer got her to pull the hood of her jacket over her head then walked her in through the back door. Her mother and father followed. There were still plenty of photographers and reporters around, all looking for new pictures of the rape victim who'd been brave enough to go public, but they'd been sent a fake tip-off to look for Annie going in the front.

Inside, Zomer told them she'd had four offers from magazines and TV stations, promising big sums for 'the full story'. Not now, Nina insisted. Maybe not ever. What mattered was getting

Annie settled, getting her well. Bert Schrijver watched and stayed quiet. There was still a distance between the three of them, something unspoken, a place no one much wanted to go. At least he and Nina were equal there for once.

He'd closed the doors to the market side of the building. Adnan was selling hard on the stall. Hoogland was nowhere to be seen. Perhaps he'd given up on the flower trade finally and tagged onto one of the other businesses. Or joined the team that broke the market nightly, taking down the stalls, scouring the filthy street with sweepers. There was always casual work to be had and Jordi Hoogland knew everyone hereabouts. Even if they didn't like him they needed hands from time to time.

Then they sat round the desk in the office, the lawyer taking a chair as if she was family already. Vos had been on the phone nagging for an interview, she said. He wanted to clear up some points from the previous night. She'd stalled.

Annie listened and asked if they'd found Rob Sanders.

'Still missing,' Zomer told her. 'They've been round his apartment. I imagine they're trying to connect him to the Sleeping Beauty case.'

'Rob wasn't part of all that,' Annie cried.

'You seem very sure,' the lawyer said.

'I am. I know him. We've been close a long time.'

Schrijver scowled and muttered, 'After what he did.'

'You don't know what he did,' Annie snapped at him. 'I do and I'm not taking him to court. I don't care what they say. What happened . . .' She glanced at her father. He didn't look her in the face. 'What happened was a long time ago. I put it behind me. If I hadn't do you think we'd have stayed together all that time? This is my decision. My life—'

'It's not unknown for abuse to lead to relationships,' the lawyer told her. 'That doesn't make it right. Doesn't mean he's not liable. Perhaps in a civil court—'

'Rob Sanders hasn't got two cents to rub together,' Schrijver broke in. 'If you're thinking of suing him you'll be sticking your fingers into empty pockets.'

There was a smile between the lawyer and Nina. One that said, 'There. Now you see what he's like.'

Then Zomer said, 'This isn't about money, Mr Schrijver. It's about justice. If anyone deserves to be hauled into civil court it's surely the police. They need to understand they can't treat victims any way they want. Besides, they really want to find Vincent de Graaf's accomplice. If—'

'That wasn't Rob!' Annie said. 'How many times do I have to tell you?'

'Just drugged you up on your own. And then . . .'

Schrijver regretted his words immediately.

'Yes,' she said. 'Rob just spiked my drink and on it went from there. Shame really. Shouldn't have wasted his money on those drugs. I'd have slept with him anyway. Guess he was being a bit shy.' She looked exasperated. 'Dammit, Dad. Don't you get it? Sometimes people make mistakes. They regret them. They're sorry. I never saw anyone as sorry as Rob was and . . .'

She stopped there. Nina swore under her breath. All four of them went quiet for a while. Schrijver just knew it was going to be the lawyer woman who'd break the silence.

Zomer leaned forward, reached out to Annie with her long thin fingers. The tattoos on her arms were flowers and dragons, all colours. Schrijver couldn't for the life of him work out why she'd want them.

'When you agreed to that interview? Was it your idea?'

'Course not,' Annie snapped. 'Do I look stupid?'

'No. You don't. But—'

'They said it was the right thing. Other women might come forward. I'd be helping them.'

'Very decent of you,' Zomer said. 'But did they outline what effect it might have on you? The publicity. You were still in a vulnerable state. Did they offer any counselling?'

Annie calmed down a little.

'That man from the police. Den Hartog. He said Mum and Dad were fine with it. They thought it was a good idea. If they—'

'What?' Schrijver roared.

Nina had her hands to her mouth.

'We never told them that, love,' she said. 'They never asked. If they had we'd have wanted you to stay clear of it. So would Rob. He was dead mad too.'

'Hardly surprising in the circumstances,' Bert Schrijver muttered and was glad his phone rang since it saved him from the filthy looks coming his way.

He went out into the courtyard to take the call. It was Lies Poelman, the estate agent.

'Mr Schrijver. Good news.'

'You don't watch the TV. Or read the papers. Do you?'

'I'm sorry?'

'Doesn't matter.'

'I have an offer. From our Chinese client. She's willing to pay the asking price. Five hundred and fifty thousand. Cash. No need for a mortgage. We can start on the paperwork this afternoon if you like—'

'Not now.'

There was a long silence and he could just see her mouthing a curse on the other end of the line.

'What do you mean . . . not now?'

'I mean I've got a lot on my plate. Personal issues. Look at the news, woman. See if you can work it out.'

There was another breathy pause then she said, 'Clearly this is a bad time. When will be a good one?'

The lawyer had come out into the yard too and slunk off to the other side, phone in hand.

'You tell me.'

'Mr Schrijver. My client is enthusiastic but needs to close this down quickly. There are other options. I'd be loath to see you lose this sale to someone else. To be perfectly frank I don't think your property is going to be easy to shift. It's in a state. There may be regulation issues. You grasp at this now or it could be months . . .'

'I'll get back to you.'

The Zomer woman was on the phone too, talking to someone in tones so low he couldn't hear.

He went inside. Annie had gone into her room and was picking up some things, putting them in her rucksack. Nina still sat at the desk. She looked up when Schrijver walked in. A touch guilty, he thought.

'Going then, are you?' he asked.

'We think it might be best if Annie stays with me for a while.'

'Whatever you want. I've got to do the van run. Leave the stall to the lad outside. But no worry . . .'

'We're not abandoning you, Bert. Petra reckons the police have really screwed up. Putting Annie on the TV like that. Lying to her about us two saying it was OK.'

'I don't give a shit about the police. What about her? That bastard Sanders? How do we get her over that?'

Nina wasn't even listening.

'She reckons they put Annie up there to take the heat off that new woman running the place. We can sue for damages. All the pain that interview's caused. She just needs a witness.'

'A witness?' he murmured.

The young lawyer was still talking outside in the courtyard, looking their way. Petra Zomer caught their eye, raised a hand and then a victorious thumb.

They were ten minutes from going on air when Zomer got through to the TV newsroom to say she was representing Annie Schrijver.

'That was quick,' Helmink told her. 'Congratulations. At least

I assume congratulations are in order. I mean . . .' She laughed. 'You don't take on losers, do you?'

'I take on victims. People the others won't touch because it's too awkward.'

'Sure. Things are really busy here. We're running a story saying Amsterdam's got another Sleeping Beauty killer. What do you have for me?'

A choice, Zomer said. Watch the police take all the blame for the way Annie Schrijver's been treated. Or stand with them in the dock.

'You're threatening me?' Helmink asked. 'Get serious. We're big. You're a mouthy little bunch of unwashed students pretending you've got a social conscience. It wouldn't be an even contest.'

'Don't like those, Lucie. More a David and Goliath type.'

'Get to the point. Like I said. We have stories to run.'

'The point is this: were you under the impression Annie's parents had given their blessing to her talking to you? Did Den Hartog tell you that?'

The producer was making clucking noises and pointing at his watch. He could wait. Helmink had a cold feeling in her gut. She was there when the parents screamed blue murder at the idea the girl might go on TV. A witness to Den Hartog lying to Annie Schrijver, telling her the opposite. More than that, a beneficiary too. Journalists lost their jobs over stunts like that.

'She's an adult. I didn't need their permission.'

'I know that. But she was in a distressed state. Annie's put herself in the public domain without understanding the consequences. She's adamant she asked Den Hartog if Nina and Bert thought it a good idea to give that interview. He told her they were right behind her. They were sure it was the best thing to do. If he said that he was lying. They wanted her to have nothing to do with it and he knew it too.'

She remembered the conversation well. Without that lie

Annie Schrijver could well have pulled out of the whole thing. Rape victims were never identified. If some form of subterfuge had been used to get her to give up her anonymity the fallout could be massive.

'And?'

Zomer sighed in exasperation.

'Did you hear him say it?'

'What if I did?'

'Then you need to choose sides.'

'I already have. I'm on mine.'

'So were you there?'

'What's that worth?'

The briefest of pauses. Helmink guessed the calculation was made already.

'If you're willing to put it in a statement . . . Annie on a plate. When the air's cleared you can interview her again. There's a better story you don't even know about. I promise. Much better.'

That was good bait.

'There are legal issues, Petra. You of all people should understand that.'

'I do. We play a long game.'

'So when the police have finally nailed that bastard,' Helmink said, 'like they should have done years ago, then I get to talk to her? Exclusively?'

'Quite,' Zomer agreed. 'See. We're in this together. All the blame gets shifted back to the police. Where it belongs. And this is serious. Annie can sue big time. Play ball and I guarantee it won't be you.'

Dealing with stories you got wrong had become harder over the years. It was no longer acceptable simply to ignore the errors and hope they'd go away. Some form of public *mea culpa* was required. What better than a reflective face-to-face with Annie Schrijver? Maybe a tearful one on both parts? A confession from

Lucie Helmink that she was too trusting in what the man from Marnixstraat had told her. A reconciliation with the victim she'd unwittingly wronged.

'If you're right this could take down Jillian Chandra,' Helmink said. 'Not just her lapdog PR man. Daughter of an immigrant. A woman at the top of Amsterdam police for a change.'

Zomer snorted.

'She's still police. I want justice for Annie.'

Helmink swore beneath her breath. She could ladle on the bullshit herself when needed, but rarely with such skill and never at such a tender age.

'Besides,' the young lawyer added, 'wouldn't that make for an even better story?'

'I'll forget you said that. Let's just stick to the justice stuff, shall we?'

'Sorry. I didn't mean to—'

'I was there when Den Hartog told Annie her parents supported giving the interview. I heard him say it. If he hadn't I might have pulled back from talking to her. She was obviously in quite a state. It was hearing they wanted her to do it that made her go on. Truly, if I'd known . . .'

There was a silence between then. Perhaps some embarrassment on both parts.

'I'll need that in a formal statement at some stage,' Zomer said.

'You'll get it. We have a deal?'

The producer came and stood over her, pointing to the studio.

'You bet.'

'Got to rush,' Helmink told her. 'Call me when you can.'

Midday traffic, sluggish and angry, so bad it took almost forty minutes to get to the De Witt building. The car park was full of police vehicles. Forensic were swarming over the basement, officers in white suits everywhere. TV vans were parked up at the perimeter, a few reporters holding mikes, talking to camera.

Nothing new had come from inside. So the two of them wandered back into the main building, got no grief from the security guard they'd met the previous night, and went to the office of Willem Strick, once business partner to Vincent de Graaf in the trust company that had built the place. Now, as the guard had said the night before, little more than an office manager.

He looked the part: a tall, skeletal man in a drab black suit, white shirt, red tie, gloomy narrow face with a protruding chin that bore a small Van Dyke beard. His staring grey eyes scanned them up and down as they came in.

Strick started off slow and bureaucratic, going through the succession of events that had toppled him from the executive office on the top floor of the building down to this cubby hole behind reception, counting the rent receipts, fixing the plumbing. It all began with De Graaf's conviction and the flight of De Witt's customers to other trust firms. They ranged from tech giants to rock bands, all keen to avoid the curious eyes of international tax authorities. The last thing any of them needed was a welter of publicity thanks to a man who'd promised them privacy and charged a fortune for those desperate to hide behind the company's walls.

'And so.' He swept his long arm around his small, bare office. 'I'm left with this.'

'You could have sold the building,' Vos pointed out.

'And come away with pennies. It's mortgaged to the hilt. The rent just about covers that. Better to wait on capital appreciation. Vincent . . .' He pulled a face. 'He was brighter with money than I ever was. Somehow he managed to syphon a lot more out of De Witt than I knew about. When the boat went down I was left alone at the wheel. So now I draw a salary and collect the monthly dues.'

'What was the rent on that place downstairs?' Bakker wondered. 'The little hidey-hole where he used to take the women?'

Strick briefly closed his eyes as if the question pained him.

'I'm an accountant, not an architect. The first I knew of any basement was when you people called me last night—'

'There are steps down there. And a door! You're telling me you never even had a look?'

Strick turned to Vos and said, 'Is this serious? Because if it is I'll get a lawyer in here right now . . .'

'People have died. It's serious.'

'I meant . . . are you really asking me whether I knew Vincent had that place?'

'Yes. We are.'

He looked aghast.

'I'm a happily married man. Two kids. Both at college. Struggling to keep them there. I've no need of a . . . hidey-hole. No reason to look for one. Don't you get it? We had an office manager. When the sky fell in I fired him and took his job. I do what he did. Fix things. Collect bills. Kick people out if they can't pay. Vincent never mentioned any basement. Understandable in the circumstances, don't you think?'

'I suspect one of your tenants found that place,' Vos said. 'Greg Launceston. American. Worked for a software company . . .' He checked his notes. 'The Syclamen Group.'

Strick shrugged.

'Not aware I ever met the man. What does he look like?'

Bakker pulled up the passport photo they'd retrieved from the US authorities overnight. A thirty-year-old Stanford graduate, moved to Amsterdam six months before to work on a mobile app start-up located on the top floor of the building. Funded by US venture capital money and a group of Dutch angel investors.

Strick frowned at the photo, a clean-shaven unremarkable man with neat, businesslike dark hair and a glint of a smile.

'He grew a beard here,' Bakker added. 'The usual bushy sort.'

'May have seen him come and go. Don't really recall. They're just tenants. I don't wish to be part of their . . . social scene. If he wanted to poke around in the bushes looking for a basement I never knew about, that was down to him.'

'What social scene is that?' Bakker asked.

He laughed.

'Oh, come on. This is the Zuidas. Hipster central. They're burning through other people's money and spending it any way they like. Dope. Drink. Hookers. Unpaid bills. I've kicked out two of these software outfits in the past year. What they do in their spare time is up to them but I don't want it on the premises.'

'You had much worse than that,' Vos observed. 'You had murder. And rape. You had Vincent de Graaf's accomplice putting him to death down there last night. Just when we thought we were about to get a name out of him.'

'And,' Bakker said, 'you gave a character reference to Jef Braat when he was in court on a sexual assault charge?'

Strick glared at her.

'A character reference? I was asked if he'd done anything wrong when he worked here. I told his lawyers the truth. Not that I knew. He drove for us. That was all.'

'Where were you last night?' she added.

'At home. With my wife. Listening to the Berlin Philharmoniker. Live. We have a web subscription. You can check with her if you like.'

'We will,' Vos promised.

'Shostakovich. Violin Concerto No. 1 in A minor. Richard Strauss. An Alpine Symphony. That's my . . . *our* idea of a congenial evening. Vincent and I were business partners only. He made me money for a while but frankly I never liked him. Nor did I make a habit of meeting him outside these walls.'

'And now he's dead.' Vos watched him. 'Will you go to the funeral?'

'I'm busy that day. Whenever it is. He screwed up my life . . . and yes, before you say it, plenty of others' too. Much worse.'

He scribbled a name on a card and a phone number.

'Syclamen's run by a woman here. Louise Warren. From London. Formidable. If you want to know about this Launceston character, I suggest you talk to her.'

Vos took it, they went outside. Bakker was busy working her phone.

'Shostakovich and Richard Strauss in Berlin last night. Maybe he is telling the truth. I can't see a cold fish like that getting caught up in Vincent de Graaf's kind of games.'

'Maybe not,' Vos said and called the number on the card. Louise Warren, it seemed, was expecting them.

The Saturday market was busier than usual, crowds cramming the narrow street, squeezing between stalls to find space on the pavement then stumbling back when they couldn't find room there. Which was all Bert Schrijver needed. The flower business had a large frontage, too big for the business he now had. Most of it was wasted on storage for the stall outside. That meant his was one of the few spots along the Albert Cuyp where people could gather without being constantly bustled or hassled by shop-keepers.

Every day it happened. Smokers, drinkers, people who just wanted to chat. They got in the way between the street and the building and he didn't have the heart or the will to move them.

What added to the bustle was the young Syrian. He was loving the job Schrijver had given him, chatting up the women shoppers, flourishing bouquets at strangers, offering to make one for them. Schrijver heard him flit between English, French and Dutch. He was bright, enthusiastic, a born salesman. The business hadn't seen anything like it since Schrijver's father was around.

He had ideas too. A lot.

Not long after the lawyer headed off to her office, and Nina and Annie for a coffee somewhere, Adnan was inside going through the storage area. Schrijver was cautious about stock. There was little he could do with a bloom that was past its prime except send it off for recycling. But Adnan had been selling so hard they were running out of several key lines: roses, lilies, chrysanthemums. There was even a limited range of tulips left. By the time it came to break the stall at five he'd probably be out of most of his reserves, something that hadn't happened in years.

'Boss,' the Syrian cried, hunting through the flowers. 'We need more roses.'

'My name's Bert. Don't call me that.'

'Bert. I'm out of . . .'

'The stock you see is the stock we've got. Live with it.'

Adnan was always busy, always anxious, always thinking. Different ways to keep the boxes to make them more accessible. Another range of flowers to stock for more ambitious – and expensive – bouquets.

'Back in Aleppo we used to do things a bit different.'

'This is Amsterdam. It's how we do things here.'

Adnan looked a bit taken aback by the sudden caustic tone.

'Sorry,' Schrijver said. 'Bad time. Lot going on. Don't suppose you read the papers either?'

'Papers are full of stories about people like me. Not easy reading. And why? I know what happened. Even if they don't.'

Put in my place again, Schrijver thought. This time by an immigrant Jordi Hoogland had picked up off the street.

Adnan pulled a slim dog-eared photo album out of his pocket and found a picture of a young dark-haired woman and a toddler with a round and smiling face. His wife and little girl, he said. With him now in Amsterdam and grateful a kind local had offered him some work. Schrijver didn't have the time to deal with all that.

'You've got a customer,' he said and nudged the Syrian back out into the street.

Twenty minutes later the estate agent called again. The Chinese woman wanted an answer by Monday. If he was still dithering then she was out.

He didn't say a thing.

'You could decide now,' Lies Poelman told him. 'Just say it. I'll get on with the paperwork.'

It was tempting, but of all his many faults rashness wasn't one of them.

'I'll call on Monday.'

'It needs to be the morning. I'm out in the afternoon.'

'I'll bear that in mind.'

The bank emailed asking about the overdraft. Then the wholesalers wondering when they might get paid. Nina came on the line and said that Annie didn't want to work the shop again. Didn't much feel like being in the public eye after what had happened with the TV people. The Albert Cuyp had awkward memories. The little room on the ground floor behind the shop she used as a bedroom Schrijver could turn to storage or something else. Soon she'd be looking for a job. 'A real job', as Nina put it.

'Are you all right for money, Bert?' she asked.

'What's that supposed to mean?'

'I mean . . . that place looks like it's on its uppers.'

'I'm not bankrupt. May not be the brightest spark around but I can manage money well enough to know that.'

'Good,' she said. 'Will you be OK on your own? Till we get things sorted?'

Been on my own for years, Schrijver thought. What's the difference now?

'Forget about me. It's Annie we need to worry about.' He had to say it even if this was the coward's way, over the phone. 'You knew something was wrong with Rob Sanders, didn't you? You never told me. I had the right to know.'

There was a long gap. He wondered if she was getting mad. But she didn't sound it when she came back.

'I knew there was something funny there. That's all. If she'd told me what it was I'd have been as mad as you. Except I'd have tried to talk it through with her. What would you have done?'

'Don't know really.'

'I do. You'd have gone round and kicked his head in. Told yourself you'd done what any loving father would. In the circumstances.'

That was true.

'Maybe.'

Then Adnan was back at the street door, waving something in his hand. Schrijver walked outside. This conversation seemed better surrounded by the busy babble of Saturday.

'You need to get to grips with this, Bert,' Nina said, still nagging. 'Some things start off bad and turn good. Some go the other way.'

The Syrian was waving a US fifty-dollar bill.

'Annie loved that man,' she added, an audible note of regret in her voice. 'For better or worse. Doesn't matter what you think. Or me. Something in him, something maybe in what he'd done . . .'

'What he'd done! You know what he did! He drugged her. And then . . . then . . .'

He hadn't meant to shout. The shock and embarrassment were obvious on the Syrian's face. Adnan wasn't waving the note any more. He didn't know where to look.

'I don't really know what happened, Bert. I won't ask either. It was a long time ago. The young . . . they do things we don't understand. Always have done. Same with you and me . . .'

'I never slipped something in your drink. Never would have.'

'No. We just got stinking drunk a couple of nights and next

thing I know I'm pregnant. For quite a while Annie and Rob seemed happy enough. Did you really never notice?'

Too busy, he thought.

'I hope they find him before I do. Bye.'

Adnan just stood there, the fifty-dollar bill in his hand.

'What is it?' Schrijver snapped.

'An American, boss. I mean . . . Bert. She don't have euros. Just this. Can I take it?'

'What did you do in Aleppo?'

That came out all wrong, with an aggression he'd never intended.

'We took people's money. Didn't matter what kind. Money's money. Better in your pocket than theirs.'

'Do what the fuck you like,' Schrijver muttered, desperate to go back to the computer, to moving boxes of flowers, getting in the van for the afternoon run, a mindless, boring circuit of the city.

Head down, worried, maybe even scared, Adnan went back to the stall.

And there was Jordi Hoogland, tugging a cart through the sea of shoppers. He'd witnessed the angry exchange with the Syrian. Too far away to hear, thank God.

Hoogland smiled for a moment, an expression Schrijver couldn't interpret. Then tipped him a brief salute and moved on.

Louise Warren was European CEO of the software company Syclamen, fifteen people, all men except her, occupying the top floor of the De Witt building. A sharp-featured, brisk English-woman in her early thirties, elegantly dressed, cautious, she spoke to them in her office overlooking the car park that adjoined the hospital. Police vehicles filled it now. Half a kilometre away another team was going over Greg Launceston's plush penthouse in a new Zuidas block. Information was starting to come in from the US too, after his mother and the authorities had been told of his murder.

Launceston grew up in Palo Alto, son of a family wealthy from tech investments. After Stanford he went into marketing with a number of web start-ups, one of them successful. According to the police he'd fought off a date rape charge after a Halloween party in San Francisco the previous year. A young woman tourist out for the night claimed Launceston had drugged her then taken her to his apartment. When she woke up the next morning she couldn't remember a thing. Launceston was adamant, to her and to the police, that the sex was consensual.

The police team who worked the case had every reason to believe he was guilty. As they were preparing an indictment the victim withdrew her statement. They felt sure she'd been paid off by Launceston's family. Mud stuck though. No one would employ him locally afterwards. The move to Amsterdam and a company backed by his own family appeared to be the only way he could find work.

Warren didn't read the Dutch papers or watch TV. She knew nothing about the deaths that week, hadn't seen the photofits the media had carried in an effort to identify the body in the Marnix-straat morgue.

'Sorry,' she said with a shrug. 'I don't speak Dutch. How would I know?'

'Because he didn't turn up for work?' Vos suggested.

'He was Greg. He'd go missing for days on end. I'd never hear a thing.' She smiled. 'I preferred it that way.'

'Did you know you were employing someone who'd faced a rape charge?' Bakker asked.

She wriggled on her leather chair and glanced out of the window.

'He was accused. It never went to court. Twenty-five per cent of the equity for this company came from his parents. Need I say more?'

Beyond the glass partition of the office a young team was working. Men in their twenties, casual clothing, beards, more time spent looking at screens than faces.

'What did he do?' Vos asked.

'Greg was executive vice president, marketing.'

'What did he do?' Bakker repeated.

'Not a lot. To be honest he didn't come into the office much at all.' She hesitated then said, 'The security guard says there was some secret basement here. You think he found it?'

He must have, Vos told her. Somehow.

'You'd no idea?'

She shook her head.

'Greg was on the payroll because he had to be. I didn't mix with him. No one in the office did, as far as I know. We had work to do. Lots. He didn't. He'd come in with his laptop from time to time. Get his head down. Research, he called it. Mostly as far as I can gather he was chasing up the story of that creep who built this place. What was his name? They said he died here last night or something.'

'Vincent de Graaf,' Bakker said.

'Him. Greg kind of got obsessed. He used to show me the press cuttings he'd found. He'd even taken to mapping out the bars he'd used. The places the victims were found.' She shuddered. 'I never dreamed he'd actually do anything. I just thought he was a rich kid on the payroll to keep mummy happy.'

Friends, Vos asked. He didn't have any. As she said, he barely mingled with the office.

Bakker didn't quite believe this.

'You didn't socialize with him at all?'

Warren shook her head vigorously.

'No, I did not. Once he asked me to join him for a drink. I found an excuse. I think I was a touch outside his age range. Whenever I caught a glimpse of the photos he liked to ogle on his laptop they were . . . young. Almost childlike.' She thought for a moment then added, 'His family had better not think about pulling funding on us now I can't babysit their little boy. If they do, I'll run his name through the shit everywhere. I don't see why we should lose our jobs because of that creep.'

'Nice thought,' Bakker noted.

Warren wasn't impressed.

'You never met Greg. If you had—'

'I think he found out about that basement,' Vos said. 'It looks as if it hadn't been used for years. Since De Graaf went to jail. Any idea how?'

She shrugged.

'Like I told you. Greg was obsessed with all that Sleeping Beauty stuff. He seemed to think the fact we'd wound up occupying his old offices was fate or something. Smart guy. I'll give him that. When he wanted something he usually got it. Had the time too. Wasn't as if he had to work or anything.'

Something jogged her memory. She turned to her laptop, tapped the keys, then dragged the screen round so they could see. It was a digital map of the city covered with blue and black dots and three red crosses. A legend said the blue dots were for bars, the black ones for places victims who survived the attacks were left. The three red crosses were where the murdered women had been found. A skein of lines connected them all.

'Stats were Greg's thing,' Warren said. 'He sent me this when he still thought I might be interested in his little obsession. You get the picture? He's trying to form a mathematical analysis of the places involved to see if they tell him anything. See this?' Like the radials of a spider's web, the lines led to a shaded area over the Zuidas, around the De Witt building itself. 'He told me he thought the location of the attacks and the placing of the bodies suggested they originated from somewhere nearby.'

'So that's what led him to the basement here?' Bakker said.

'Maybe,' Warren agreed. 'Greg was always poking around the

place. He was quite keen I joined him for a while. Then . . .' She shrugged. 'He just stopped pestering me.'

'He'd found it,' Vos said. 'And lots more besides.'

Bakker passed over an email address and asked for the message to be forwarded, along with everything else they had from Launceston on their system. Warren shook her head.

'You can have this one. You'll need a warrant for the rest and I'll fight it. I'm not handing out our private correspondence just like that.'

'But . . .' Bakker began.

'But nothing. Listen to me. I put up with that foul bastard because I had to. I paid him. I listened to his creepy stories. I did my best to keep him away from decent people working here who didn't want to know him either. Now I'm going to have to deal with this car crash and try and keep this company afloat.' She tapped the laptop screen. 'That's what you get.'

Two minutes later they were outside. Bakker wanted to take another look at the basement. Vos waited for the beep on her phone. Louise Warren had been as good as her word. It was Launceston's map.

'So,' she said. 'He was probably a serial date rapist to begin with. Sent over here by his mummy to keep him out of trouble. As luck would have it he lands up in the office of someone even better than he is. Someone he can try and emulate.'

Vos was looking at the entrance into the underground room. With the tramp of forensic the way in was now obvious. It hadn't been before. But a man who went hunting could surely locate it. Find how to get inside too.

'He must have felt he was that archaeologist getting inside Tutankhamen's tomb,' Bakker said, echoing his thoughts. 'Finding all those treasures.'

True, Vos agreed, then zoomed in on the part of the map that interested him. One of the blue dots was in the middle of the Albert Cuyp. He showed it to Bakker.

'At a guess I'd say that's where the Mariposa bar is,' she said.

'Me too,' he agreed. 'One problem there.'

'It wasn't around four years ago, was it?'

Vos called the team going through Launceston's apartment. The place wasn't looking promising apart from one thing: they'd found a phone number scribbled on a beer mat there. It was Jef Braat's mobile.

When he came off the line he told Bakker.

'So Greg Launceston was trying to pick up where Vincent de Graaf left off,' she said. 'His habits. His right-hand man. His little lair here.'

But De Graaf wasn't alone. There was another partner. The name he'd promised them in return for the slim chance of a few more months of life.

'We need to take a look at that bar in the Albert Cuyp.'

His phone rang and he heard the angry tones of Jillian Chandra.

'I want you two back here straight away,' she said. 'No diversions. No excuses.'

Twenty minutes later they were in her office. Den Hartog was twitchy, Van der Berg making notes, still not looking anyone in the eye.

Eleven of the twenty-seven individual women in De Graaf's photographs were now known to be missing, murdered, they had to assume. Doubtless with the tattooed words on their shoulder, 'Sleep Baby Sleep'. The victims came from all over the Netherlands: Eindhoven, Rotterdam, Dordrecht, one from a small village near the Belgian border. Subtle differences in the pictures suggested they'd been attacked and murdered elsewhere, then snapped. Afterwards their pictures were taken back to the De Witt crypt to be part of De Graaf's collection.

Of the remaining sixteen women a dozen had been accounted

for. Five had been spoken to. None was willing to give a statement about what had happened to them.

'So,' Chandra said, 'four years ago we had the worst serial killer in living memory active here and no one noticed.'

It was bad, Vos thought. But in the circumstances understandable. The women were listed as missing persons in various parts of the country. There was nothing to connect them with Amsterdam or Vincent de Graaf.

'We put the man in jail,' he said. 'For life. Life meaning . . . life in this case.'

'He wasn't the only one, Vos! Was he? What about Braat?'

Braat was part of the game, he said. De Graaf confirmed that before he left for the Zuidas.

'They had Annie Schrijver's photo. Does that mean Sanders was part of all this too?'

'Commissaris . . . I have to get Annie in here. She's out of hospital. She knows something she's not saying. There's no reason for her to refuse an interview. If need be I'll arrest her for withholding evidence if it comes to—'

'No,' Chandra said emphatically. 'You won't go near her.'

Bakker was on that in an instant.

'What? You saw her on TV. There's a photo of her in that basement, wide awake, which means she ought to be dead. We've got to talk to her.'

It was Den Hartog who chipped in.

'You can't. There are legal issues.'

'Legal issues?' Bakker repeated. 'She's an important witness in a murder case.'

Van der Berg briefly raised an eyebrow at her before going back to his notebook.

'What's that supposed to mean?' she threw at him.

'It means there are legal issues.' He glanced at Den Hartog. 'Aren't there?'

'They're threatening us over the TV interview she gave,'

Chandra explained. 'Gave willingly, I might add. A lawyer from the awkward squad's sidled up to the parents and told them she can get some money out of this. She's claiming we coerced a vulnerable woman into going public with an admission that was not in her own interests.'

Silence then until Vos said, 'So I take it we did.'

'No one's making any admissions,' the PR man replied.

'But clearly she's got a point. Otherwise we wouldn't be sitting here discussing it. I'd have her in an interview room downstairs and we might be getting somewhere.'

Chandra turned to Van der Berg and told him to make sure he wrote down word for word what she was about to say.

'Vos. You go nowhere near Annie Schrijver until the lawyers say it's safe to do so. We'll try to negotiate something.'

Van der Berg scribbled at the page obediently.

'Then what do you want me to do?' Vos asked.

'You could start by telling me what you know. If you've any idea why this suddenly blew up out of nowhere. That might help.'

He understood quite a lot when he thought about it.

'What happened is Jef Braat came out of jail and met his biggest fan. An American. Greg Launceston. A rich kid from one of the software start-ups in De Graaf's old building in the Zuidas. Launceston had form for date rape back in California which is why his so-kind family dispatched him over here. Unfortunately – I'm assuming this is coincidence – he discovered our friend Vincent's hobbies and this rather fired a passion for them.'

He picked up his phone and showed them the map from the email Louise Warren had given them.

'Launceston didn't have a real job. He seems to have spent most of his waking hours chasing everything he could find out about De Graaf. The bars he used to haunt. The places the papers said he left his victims. He seems to have been very good at tracking things down. Eventually he came to believe De Graaf had some kind of base in the Zuidas. Unlike us he found it. I assume through Jef Braat.'

'How did he know Braat?' Van der Berg asked.

It was the first decent question Vos had had from him since Chandra snatched his old colleague away.

'Can't say. If he spent long enough digging, hanging round the bars De Graaf used, perhaps the two of them bumped into each other. Found common cause. Given they're both dead it may be hard to find out.'

Bakker was following all this too.

'So on Tuesday night Launceston met up with Annie Schrij-ver—'

'We have to ask her about that,' Vos broke in. 'And we can't.'

'Well, say he did,' she carried on. 'Launceston spiked her drink. Got her back to Braat's boat. The third man murders Launceston and leaves Annie with him in Zorgvlied. Then pushes Braat into the river hoping we'll think he did it all.'

'Very roundabout way of killing people,' Van der Berg chipped in.

Quite, Vos thought, wishing his old friend was back on the team, not wasting his time taking notes in Jillian Chandra's office.

No one spoke. Then Van der Berg asked, 'Why would he kill them?'

'Because our mystery man thought he'd put it all behind him,' Bakker suggested. 'De Graaf's in jail. The case seems closed. Having this pushy American come back wanting to kick things off again brings back the risk. It means we'll start looking again and this time round perhaps we'll find him.' She looked pleased with herself. 'So you kill anyone who knows. Braat and Launceston. Then he lures De Graaf out of jail to the Zuidas and kills him too. He's safe.'

'Could work,' Van der Berg commented, nothing more.

'Unless you have a better idea.'

'Not my case.'

'Annie Schrijver might know,' Vos pointed out.

'She's already said she only met the one man and then blacked out.'

'Maybe she's lying.'

Chandra grimaced and said, 'You're not going to get the chance to find out. Do you have any idea who this man might be?'

Some, Vos told her. He was clever, meticulous. All that choreography the night Sam was snatched showed that. The man was familiar with technology. The map coordinates. The phone he'd managed to smuggle to De Graaf somehow then wipe remotely. The text messages from an ever-changing array of untraceable foreign SIMs. An active man able to handle a boat, navigate the narrow waterways around the Amstelpark. That ringing cry through the dark next to the Zorgvlied cemetery.

Another day, Vos. You will hear from me again. That I promise.

'He's . . . educated.'

'What about Rob Sanders?' Chandra wondered.

'It can't be him. Forensic didn't find a single incriminating thing in his apartment. No foreign SIMs. No books. This man reads books.'

Chandra looked smug.

'Books? Really?'

'Really. Also . . .'

Two things he couldn't get out of his head. One was the picture of Vincent de Graaf's right arm covered in bruises and cut marks. The other the tattoos quickly scrawled on Launceston and De Graaf by their killer.

'Sanders is a nurse. He wouldn't need twenty or thirty goes to get a needle into someone's arm. And that tattoo . . . Sleep Baby Sleep. He puts it on the women because they're trophies. It's the final act of possession. Why go to the trouble of doing that to two men? Doesn't add up. It's not Rob Sanders.'

Van der Berg sighed and closed his notebook. Den Hartog

pulled out his phone and started to check his messages. Vos wondered what he'd said.

Then Chandra threw a blue forensic folder on the desk and told him to read it.

The report was an hour old. They'd taken DNA samples from the bathroom in Sanders' flat in De Pijp. They matched the traces in the felt band of the suede hat Van der Berg had picked up outside the Drie Vaten on Wednesday night.

By all rights she should have revealed that at the start of the discussion, not the end. He'd been set up.

'You need to cut out the clever stuff, Vos,' Chandra ordered. 'It'll be the death of you. Me too if I allow it. Just find Sanders and put this mess to bed. Do you have no idea where he is?'

'The best person to ask is—'

Her voice rose. Van der Berg's head went down. Den Hartog too.

'How many times do I have to say it? You can't go near Annie Schrijver. So what else?'

Before he could say anything Bakker leapt in.

'We need to check out a couple of bars. Starting with that one in the Albert Cuyp. What's it called?'

'The Mariposa?' Van der Berg said. 'You know what that means? In Spanish?'

'Butterfly,' Vos replied. 'Thanks, Dirk.'

Chandra scooped up the blue folder.

'Go near that family and you're digging your own graves. I'll be the one who pushes you in.'

Bert Schrijver had given the young Syrian a money belt for the market that morning. A leather pouch with a hundred-euro float in it. Ordinarily Adnan would have offloaded some of the cash back into the office during the day. But Schrijver's foul temper meant he was reluctant to come inside again. So, close to the end of the busy afternoon when the stallholders were looking round, getting ready to start the long and laborious task of breaking the market and looking forward to Sunday, the only day the Albert Cuyp closed, he went into the adjoining alley and quietly counted the takings.

Out of the way so no one could see. He'd lost track of how many times they'd been robbed on the long and arduous journey from Aleppo, across the sea to Greece then on through countries he could barely name until they wound up in Amsterdam. A kind of home. A place of safety for him, his wife Mariam and their four-year-old daughter Lia even if it meant sharing a single room with so many others in a squalid block near the IJtunnel.

Carefully he went through the notes. Almost fourteen hundred euros plus the fifty-dollar bill that was all an enthusiastic American woman could offer. Big money. Bert Schrijver looked as if he could use it. Adnan would be happy with his share: ten euros per hour. In his head he could already see himself proudly returning the takings to Schrijver in the office, placing the money on the table and hoping that might cheer him up.

As he was sorting the bills into some kind of order a shadow came and blocked out the light from the market.

'Thinking of running?' Jordi Hoogland asked.

He was a broad and powerful man. The kind Adnan and his family had met a lot on that difficult journey across Europe.

'No, sir. This is Mr Schrijver's money. I count it for him. I give it him. Then I get my wages.'

He smiled and brandished a fan of notes. Hoogland just stood over him, a bitter smile on his face.

'That was my job you took. Years I worked at it.'

Fear. It was always there. Always would be after the barrel bombs began raining down on Sulaymaniyah, the neighbourhood where they lived. His people had stayed out of the civil war. Perhaps the government planes made a mistake. Or they wanted to send a message. No one bothered much about motives when those metal canisters began raining from the sky on houses, schools and hospitals. They were just afraid, like now.

'I never meant to take anything from you, mister. You asked me to work here. I just did what I was told. If—'

He held out a fifty from the wad of notes. Most of what he expected to earn that day.

'Here. You take my wages. I never meant to offend you. Or anyone—'

One punch straight into the place they often aimed for. The soft belly beneath the rib cage. You winded a man that way. His head came down. Your knee came up, met with a chin or lips, it really didn't matter. Once you'd got those blows in you'd won.

Adnan went over with little more than a whimper. Somewhere along the way he'd learned that screaming just made things worse.

Hoogland's hard fists rained down on him until all he could do was wind himself into a tight, pained ball, crouch at the Dutchman's feet, hands over his dark hair, taking each punch and kick as it came.

After a while they stopped. His mouth was full of blood. His lips were swollen.

One more kick and Hoogland rolled him over, dragged his slender frame up against the black brick wall, patted him down.

The wad of notes went and the cheap phone Adnan kept for calling Mariam. She was struggling to find a kitchen job that included child care.

Hoogland's fist closed on his jacket, his other hand on Adnan's windpipe. Face hard against the wall he listened to the man's rants, wondering when they'd end.

One last knee to the groin. Hoogland's mouth came up. Spittle flying, he snarled, 'If I so much as see or smell you in the Albert Cuyp again I swear I'll rip your head off. Chuck you in the canal. Who's going to miss you? One more stinking rag head. I'd be doing the world a favour.'

Maybe that was true, Adnan thought, as Hoogland pulled him back to the point where the alley joined the emptying street.

'When I let you go you run. As fast as those skinny legs will take you. If you stop I'll be there. And then it all gets worse. With me?'

'Yes, sir,' Adnan whispered through swollen bloody lips.

Hoogland let go. The Syrian looked at the Albert Cuyp. He knew markets. Knew flowers. Thought perhaps just this once they might be in luck.

But run he did.

The market was pretty much over by the time Vos and Bakker got there. Cleaners were out hosing down the street, sweeping away the rubbish. Small electric trucks wove through the last of the customers, taking down stalls and shifting scaffolding and timber boards. A new crowd was turning up for the Albert Cuyp. The early shift of the Saturday night people starting to cram into the cafes and the cocktail bars that were springing up everywhere.

They stopped outside the Mariposa, a few hundred metres along from Schrijver's flower stall. That was closed already, just a few bare green stalks on the pavement betraying its presence. The sliding doors to the shop were shut. No sign of life at all.

'Not that we can go there anyway,' Bakker said, anticipating Vos's thoughts.

He was staring at the bar on the other side of the road.

'God, I'm an idiot,' he murmured.

The outside walls had been painted, desert scenes, cacti, mountains, bottles of tequila, glasses of margarita.

'That was Ruud Jonker's place. Where he had his tattoo parlour.'

'You're sure?'

'Not the kind of thing you forget,' Vos muttered and they went inside.

Stainless steel chairs, shiny mirrors, abstract art on the walls, stripped pine. A board full of exotic cocktails twice the price of a beer in a local dive. The early evening crew was starting to gather, three deep at the counter already. There were just a couple of men busy behind the bar and it was hard to tell them apart. Early thirties, combed brown beards, striped shirts with braces, heavy workmen's trousers. Vos went to the counter, flashed his ID and said he wanted to talk to whoever was in charge.

The two glanced at each other and the nearest said, 'We both are. Can it wait?'

'No,' Bakker told them. 'It can't.'

They'd remodelled the place so much it was unrecognizable, turning what was once a chaotic den into an open space with cramped tables and tall chairs. The clearest memory Vos had of that night four years before was of finding Ruud Jonker swinging from a beam by a rope next to a red leather chair. He couldn't place that anywhere here. The premises had changed so much.

Then one of the men led them into a small office at the back. A computer, a desk and a few chairs. A beam in the ceiling. No barber's chair, no drawings of butterflies on the wall. But this was where they'd found the individual they'd believed to be Vincent de Graaf's sole partner in a cycle of rape and murder, one much larger and wider than any of them had suspected. A man who'd killed himself when he knew they were closing in.

Vos left it to Bakker to get the story. The near-identical beards were the owners, Tom and Anton de Vogel, two brothers from what sounded like a fancy address in the Canal Ring. They'd opened the place eighteen months before.

'Where did the name come from?' Vos asked.

The one they were talking to was Tom.

'It's Spanish. We wanted a Mexican theme. We do some fancy tequila and mezcal.'

Vos glanced up at the beam, stared at the man in the blue

striped shirt and heavy trousers and asked the question again. Tom de Vogel tugged nervously at his long brown beard.

'We're not great believers in coincidence,' Bakker added when he kept quiet.

'There were all these butterfly posters on the walls when we took over the lease. Tattoo art.' He laughed. 'Still that leather chair too. I'm amazed you took away the rope. Seemed a good joke . . .'

'A *joke*?' she said.

'Sorry. Poor taste. I apologize. The truth is this place had been empty for a couple of years. No one wanted to take it on. It wasn't the history. Everything was a mess. Took us eighteen months to convert it the way we wanted. Get permission. Find the right architect. Came in at twice the budget we expected. Mariposa. It sounds nice.'

Vos wanted to know where the money came from.

'Family,' he said. 'Dad's in banking. He wanted to set us up in business. We didn't . . . We didn't want to trade on all that bad stuff. And we haven't. We're not ghouls. We sell drinks. That's all.'

Vos pulled up a photo on his phone.

'What about him?'

A file shot of Braat from criminal records.

De Vogel grimaced.

'So you do know him?' Vos said.

'Jef. Just a first name. Started coming in regularly a few weeks ago. Seemed to know a few people.'

Then a picture of Launceston from the morgue. De Vogel went white at that one and whispered, 'Jesus Christ. So it was him. In the paper. He's dead.'

'Let me get this clear. You knew we were asking for help identifying this man. You recognized him. You did nothing.'

'That wasn't the picture in the paper,' De Vogel objected.

'I mean . . . it could have been anyone. His name was Greg or something. Acted like he had money.'

'You knew him?'

He was getting twitchy.

'Not really. He just came in with Jef a couple of times. Creeped me out to be honest. We never went out of our way to talk up all that stuff about the tattoo guy. It was years ago. Most people round here have forgotten all about it.'

'Greg Launceston hadn't,' Bakker suggested.

He was back to tugging at the carefully coiffured beard.

'True. The idiot wouldn't shut up. He begged us to let him come in the office and take photos. I couldn't wait to get him out of the place.' He blinked, as if trying to remember something. 'He even talked about buying us out at one point. We thought about it too. Then everything went quiet. He said he'd found somewhere . . . more suitable. Whatever that means.'

Vos knew and so, from the look on her face, did Bakker. Launceston had discovered the hidden basement in the De Witt building.

'Listen,' De Vogel pleaded. 'It gets really busy in here of an evening. Anton and me try and run the place on our own as much as we can. It's just booze and finger food. We're trying to pay off Dad's loan—'

'Do you ever get women pass out?' Bakker asked.

The face behind the beard turned a shade rosier.

'We know the rules. We don't serve drunks—'

'Not talking about drunks, Tom. Are we?'

He was getting very nervous.

'I know what you're saying. If we caught anyone up to that kind of thing we'd throw them out. Hard enough making a living as it is what with the rent and stuff . . .'

'Throw them out?' she asked. 'You'd call us, wouldn't you?'

He laughed.

'And in the meantime . . . what? We're supposed to keep hold of them? Just the two of us? Be reasonable.'

Vos pulled up another photo on his phone: Rob Sanders.

'Seen the face.'

'When?'

'Er . . . recently. We don't keep a guestbook you know.'

'I want your CCTV. Last Tuesday.' Vos nodded at the computer. 'We'll wait.'

'What?'

'We know for a fact one young woman was doped here on Tuesday night,' Bakker said, pulling a memory stick from her pocket and waving it in his face. 'So put the CCTV on here. Unless you think we should go back through all the date rape complaints we've had from De Pijp over the last year. See how many of them happened to stop by too.'

'It's not that kind of place! We're just a bar, for God's sake.'

She pointed at the computer.

'Give us the video.'

'I can't. We don't have CCTV. People come here to enjoy themselves. We're not going to spy on them.' He curled a lip. 'We'll leave that to you people.'

Vos flipped him a card and said to contact him if he or his brother thought of anything else he might want to hear.

They walked back into the bar. Vos looked up at the board on the wall and asked her what she wanted. She got the idea. They weren't welcome. That meant they were going to stay.

Back behind the counter De Vogel groaned.

A virgin margarita for her, a cocktail with old tequila for him. They paid, almost twenty euros, no tip, then found two tiny stools by the window and placed their drinks on the ledge.

'Don't think Commissaris Chandra would approve,' Bakker said, then took a sip.

'Perhaps not,' he agreed, unable to take his eyes off the green doors of Schrijver's shop down the street. 'Don't you have something to do this evening? Washing? I don't know.'

She put down the glass and stared at him.

'I'm not leaving you here on your own. Don't think that for a moment.'

The cocktail was good. Another night he might have two.

The van route round the city, dropping flowers for hotels and corporates, picking up more stock from the wholesaler, seemed to take forever. Bert Schrijver's mind was working overtime and getting nowhere in the end.

It was always the same. He wanted to do something. To help. To make things better, for Annie and for Nina too. But knowing what the right thing was never came easy. All too often when he thought he was there the world turned and he realized all he had hold of was the familiar feel of failure.

Just do nothing, Bert. Make your life easy.

That's what his father used to say with a sarcastic sneer whenever he saw his son in agony over some decision. Schrijver would never have plucked up the courage to ask Nina out in the first place if the old man hadn't nagged him so much. That awkward, embarrassed courtship. The pregnancy. The marriage. Annie. Everything just happened, was never planned.

He turned into the parallel street at the back of the market and parked outside the rear doors. The photographers were gone. But Nina was there looking furious and with her a grim-faced Jordi Hoogland.

'Shit,' Schrijver muttered as he got out of the van.

Without waiting to hear what they had to say he walked through the storeroom, across the courtyard out towards the street. The doors were closed already. Just behind them, waiting to be stowed, was a line of buckets still full of flowers.

'Where's Adnan?' he asked as the other two turned up.

Hoogland sucked in a quick breath and caught his eye.

'We had to shut it up ourselves, Bert. I tried to tell you. He was a quick fix the day we needed someone. You can't trust those sly bastards. I never meant—'

'*Where is he?*'

'Apparently he's done a runner,' Nina said, nodding at Hoogland. 'With the day's takings. Over a thousand euros if the stock's anything to go by.'

And for Monday I've got a bigger order than ever, Schrijver thought. Bought only because the Syrian was shifting so much stuff.

'I don't get it. Adnan seemed a decent kid. I yelled at him a bit earlier. Caught me at the wrong time.'

'He saw his chance and took it,' Hoogland said. 'They're all like that. Steal the shirt from your back while you're trying to help them.'

Schrijver started to pick up the half-empty buckets of flowers and drag them back into the storeroom. Nina came to help. Then Hoogland too.

'He seemed a real nice lad,' Schrijver said again. 'If you don't trust anyone . . .'

'That's you,' Hoogland told him. 'Decent. Honest. Generous. Just the sort they go for. I'm gutted I ever found the little sod.'

'Not your fault,' Schrijver murmured. He looked at Nina. 'How's Annie?'

'She's having a drink with a couple of her market mates round the corner in the square. I thought it would be good for her. Didn't want her in that Mariposa place.'

He couldn't believe it.

'She'd go back there? After all that's happened?'

The look came then. The one that said: *You really don't understand a thing, do you?*

'This is where she's from. You can't expect her to run and hide. Not in her nature.'

Jesus, he thought. The young. They brought it on themselves.

'You need to tell the police about that Syrian,' she said.

'No.'

She lugged in the last of the roses, put her hands on her hips and stared at him, open-mouthed.

'What?'

'I said no. Those poor bastards have been through enough already. Put me in their shoes I'd nick the clothes off your back if I had to. He's got family. They looked lovely. I'm not having him going to jail and them homeless. Got enough on my conscience without that.'

Hoogland nodded.

'Police wouldn't do a damned thing anyway. Except give him more of our money to live off. Don't know where he's staying either.'

That didn't ring true.

'How can I have him on the books if he doesn't have an address, Jordi? I know you're always running jobs for cash. But you said he had the documents—'

'Yeah. Like he told me. But I didn't check. Did you? And let's face it . . . if we knew how to find him he wouldn't be running off with all your cash like that, would he?' He balled a big fist. It looked bruised and bloody already. 'Want me to look? I'll get it back. Let him know he can't pull those tricks round here.'

Nina shook her head and said she was going home. Before she set off she looked hard at Schrijver and said, 'We've got enough on our plate without your mate going round beating up thieving foreigners. Haven't we?'

'Always a wise woman,' Hoogland replied with a sarcastic salute.

When Nina left, the two men tidied away the spent flowers and put them in the recycling bins. Another week over. No money made. Schrijver felt bad about that. Adnan looked a bright lad and he wished he hadn't bawled him out. That temper was costly sometimes. Now it had left him back in the hands of Jordi Hoogland, with his stupid hair and ridiculous leather clothes.

He went and turned off the lights in the office then closed the door to Annie's room, wondering when it would get used again. Maybe he ought to give the whole thing to the Chinese woman and let her decide.

Hoogland was shuffling about in his big boots, awkward for once.

'I feel really bad about this, Bert. I was the one who brought that little shit in here.'

Schrijver thought he'd check the books later. Perhaps there was an address. He could go round, stay calm, try to reason with him. But Hoogland was right. If it was real, he wouldn't have walked off with the money.

'Shut up, will you? I was the one who asked you to find someone.'

Hoogland pulled a wad of notes out of his pocket. A big load.

'Water under the bridge. I did well out of here. Went down the docks and did a night shift. Bit of toing and froing round the market. Bloody hard work. Happier with you.'

Schrijver said nothing. He was looking at the notes.

A nervous tug at the ponytail then, 'Anyway, Bert. How about we pretend we're young again? You and me go out and blow this lot getting shit-faced. Do you a power of good to wake up tomorrow with a stinking hangover. Take your mind off things.'

Schrijver reached out and extracted the fifty dollar bill from the middle of Hoogland's wad. Then waved it in his face.

'Wonder where that came from?' Hoogland said, stashing the rest. 'Some sod must have . . .'

They'd never fought before though sometimes it had been close.

Schrijver swiped him with the back of his right hand. Then when Hoogland was still reeling from the shock he punched him hard, straight in the face, blood coming from the man's nose as he fell back towards the plastic buckets and trays they used for the flowers.

A minute it must have lasted. Less maybe. Had Schrijver thought about it he might have been worried but all the anger and the pain inside came out and Jordi Hoogland was unfortunate enough to bear the brunt of it.

He stopped the blows when they were amidst the upturned buckets, Hoogland's hands upturned. Surrender and it wasn't half the fight Schrijver had expected.

'What the fuck have you done, Jordi?'

Hoogland's right eye was swollen, closing.

'A favour for you. A big one. Here.' He took out the wad of notes and dropped them next to a bunch of expiring tulips. 'Have the bloody money. That's not why I did it. Don't even want any.'

Still no straight answer.

'Did what?'

'Did what was needed. Punched that little scumbag's lights out. Taught him a lesson. What his place is here. Not running round like he owns you. Like he's got a better idea how to run this shop than us.'

There it was again.

'Us? You're not part of this. You never were. I only gave you work because you were there. I felt sorry for you. Don't you even get that?'

Hoogland struggled out from underneath him, wiping his bloody face with the sleeve of his torn and tattered leather jacket.

'What I get is you're a loser, Bert. Always were. Always will be. Biggest I ever met. You lost Nina. You lost Annie. And now you're going to lose this place your old man left you . . .'

Schrijver's fist came back and it was all he could do not to hit him again.

'Get out. Don't come back. Don't ever come near me or mine, or anyone who works here, again.'

The man in leather made the yapping sign with his fingers and said, 'Yeah, yeah.'

Schrijver dragged him by the arm across the courtyard, pulled the shop doors to one side and held them open.

'They put you inside for beating up immigrants,' he said. 'Worse than picking on your own. Should be too. Coward's way. For pity's sake he was half your size and if—'

'Oh.' Hoogland was swiping his nose again and laughing. 'Like you care? Like it matters what Bert Schrijver, the biggest clown in the Albert Cuyp, thinks about a bloody thing? Don't kid yourself, mate. We all know what you are. The only one who doesn't is you.'

'Get out.'

Hoogland was staring at him, grinning through the blood.

'You really are the dumbest, Bert. Don't have two brain cells to rub together.'

'If you don't want me to kick your arse again just fuck off out of here and don't come back.'

Again the grin. Hoogland nodded towards the door to Annie's room, the partitioned storage area, flimsy wooden wall around it, windows at the top. He walked over and picked up one of the flower pallets, placed it by the door, turned it over and stood on it. Schrijver could see now. When Hoogland did that he could peer through the narrow window at the top.

'Not a clue what that girl of yours gets up to while you're out running orders round the place. Just me here having to watch her. And listen.'

He grabbed Hoogland by the grubby collar of his leather jacket and pulled him off the box. Still the market man couldn't stop laughing.

'Big dumb Bert Schrijver. Everybody's fool. Maybe you should ask her.'

A couple of punches, faint, weak sorry ones. He got Hoogland to the door and kicked him outside. The street was half-empty.

Lines of the young were walking along the pavement, headed for the Albert Cuyp nightlife, something that didn't even exist when he was their age.

Then, hurrying from the short road that led to the square on Gerard Doustraat, he saw her. She looked as if she'd been crying as she walked down the market with that fierce, determined gait she had.

'Annie!' he yelled.

Bakker saw him first. A shambling, slumped figure, head down, hood up, sidling nervously towards the Schrijver place. He had something in his hand.

She nudged Vos's elbow so hard the expensive cocktail spilled down the front of his jacket.

'Laura—'

A long finger, pointing.

'That's Rob Sanders over there.'

The figure across the road stopped by a Vietnamese noodle shop, phone to his ear, looking as if he was checking out the menu. Not convincing.

By the time Vos called control Bakker was outside by the door, leaning on the frame, telling a hipster with a glass of fruit drink that looked positively botanical exactly what she'd do if he didn't stop blocking the view.

The call must have gone out instantly to a car in the vicinity. From somewhere back in the main drag leading up to the Heineken Experience and the Singelgracht came the rise and fall of a familiar wail. Sanders twitched, dragged his hood around his head more tightly and looked around.

'Oh, for God's sake,' Vos moaned. 'A siren?'

Bakker was scanning the street.

'Our friend Rob's not alone,' she said and pointed.

A hundred metres along Annie Schrijver was marching towards him.

Bakker had started to move when Vos put out a hand stop her.

'We walk,' he mouthed, and walk they did. Steadily, keen not to alarm anyone. To begin with anyway.

Then a marked police car came screeching round the corner, sliding on the greasy asphalt, lights flashing, klaxon blaring.

Vos and Bakker ran out into the road, dodging the sweepers and the piles of trash.

There was a shout. A loud, aggressive male voice. Bert Schrijver yelling his daughter's name over and over.

'Too late,' Bakker muttered and in that moment the hooded man began to run. Straight away she was after him, red hair flying behind her, elbows working, legs pumping. She followed as Sanders raced south, pushing through the growing night crowds.

Vos tried to keep up. So did Annie Schrijver. But Sanders was too quick and so was Bakker. In a few moments the chase was joined by the two young uniforms from the car. Soon they were out of the market altogether, headed towards Sarphatipark, a patch of green in the midst of De Pijp's crowded streets and alleys.

At the end of the road, by the iron railings that marked the park edge, another police car pulled up, two more uniforms leaping out. Closing in they followed the fleeing figure, faster even than Bakker as the hunt led down the winding path into the heart of the tiny oasis, a place for lovers and dog walkers, the odd bum stopping for a smoke.

By the time Vos and Annie Schrijver got there, exhausted and out of breath, the four uniforms were circling their target in front of an elegant monument surrounded by fountains. The waters rose and fell. The tulips around them had seen better days. The uniforms were nervous, twitching, uncertain about what to do. Bert Schrijver turned up and put his strong arms around his struggling daughter.

Vos stopped, short of breath, then watched as the officers pounced, one taking Sanders down to the pavement, knee in the back, the other seizing his arms, getting out the cuffs.

Annie Schrijver flew from her father's grip, trying to get to the man on the ground. Vos just managed to get hold of her and keep her back.

'What is this?' she yelled, at Sanders, no one else, voice breaking, furious. 'What is it now, Rob?' Something flew from her hand. A phone, landing on the ground in front of the fountain wall. 'You say you want to talk—'

'And then you call the police,' Sanders yelled back, trussed now, incapacitated. 'Thanks for that.'

Vos stepped between them and said, 'We were here anyway. Looking for you. Annie never knew. It was just luck. Bad or otherwise—'

'Bullshit!'

She was crying. Sanders couldn't look at her.

'It's not bullshit,' Vos insisted. 'It's true. Not a word I can use about much at the moment. Unfortunately.'

Annie Schrijver stared at him, angry tears in an angry face, no words left.

Her father came up and tried to pull her away. Bakker was onto control telling them Sanders was coming into custody.

'Annie . . .' Schrijver begged, trying to pull her away.

'You don't get it,' she muttered. 'None of you.'

'No,' Vos agreed. 'We don't. We can't. Not until you tell us.'

She glared at him and there was that familiar, uncompromising look in her eyes he knew so well. The one that said: *You're police and we don't trust you. Because you refuse to understand. You won't believe a word we say.*

'Who are you to talk?' she snapped. 'That lawyer says you fooled me into making an idiot of myself in public. She'll take you to the cleaners for that. If you want to speak to anyone, speak to her.'

Then she shook herself free of her father, turned on her heels and walked away, past the dying tulips, past the locals watching puzzled and shocked at this sudden intrusion into their peaceful little world.

With a long and miserable face, Bert Schrijver followed, trying to catch up with her. There were more marked police cars turning up at the park entrance. Soon the place would be swarming with uniforms.

'There's gratitude for you,' Bakker said as Annie Schrijver headed back towards the Albert Cuyp. 'At least the commissaris will be happy.'

'You think?'

Annie Schrijver marched off to the Pilsvogel. Her father followed and didn't know why. It was a bar he'd used when he was a kid, back when the Albert Cuyp was nothing but a tight local community built around the market. All that had changed. Foreign voices, crowds of young hogging the tables on the street, cramming into the narrow interior. He guessed her friends had left. If they existed at all. He wasn't sure what to believe any more. Or who.

Nina was there though, seated at one of the barrel tables by the street, a glass of wine in front of her. She looked angry and upset as Annie stormed over.

Schrijver stayed back, wondering if a smarter man might know his place and retreat in silence to the lonely quiet of home. But that wasn't him. Something needed to be said.

'What the hell did you think you were doing, Annie?' he asked when he came up to them. 'You know the police were looking for him.'

A waitress in a short skirt came up and asked what they wanted. Stood there until Schrijver answered. It was a bar. You had to drink. Beer, he said, and Annie nodded at her mother's wine.

The girl vanished to the counter so he asked again, 'For God's sake. You were going to meet him. After what he's done—'

'What he's done?' she broke in.

Schrijver looked at Nina and asked her the question that had been nagging him ever since the scene in the hospital the night before.

'How much else is there an idiot like me doesn't know?'

'Search me, Bert,' she muttered and took a swig of wine.

The drinks came. The waitress stood there until she got some money. Annie knocked back half of hers in one go, closed her eyes briefly, then glanced at her mother and said, 'I need out of this place. De Pijp. This bloody city. I may need to ask for a loan.'

'Of course,' Nina said. Annie always got what she wanted.

Schrijver wagged a finger at her.

'You should talk to the police.'

'Why?' She looked angrier than he'd seen in ages. 'Really, Dad, after everything they've done . . . why?'

'That man Vos didn't put you on the TV. He told us. He's a decent sort. You deal with him. They've got Rob Sanders now. You can't keep avoiding them—'

'Can't I?' she cut in. 'I don't owe anybody anything. This is no business of the police. It's between me and Rob. No one else—'

'There were other girls,' her mother said quietly. 'It wasn't just you.'

'Not with him!'

'Really?' Nina asked. 'You believe that? And Tuesday night was nothing—'

'Nothing to do with Rob. Nothing at all. I just felt like some company. So I went for a drink with that American creep. Next thing I know . . .' Another big slug of wine went down. 'I'm in hospital. You two looking at me like I've done something wrong.

Everything else is a long bad dream. No Rob in it. Wish there was. Things might have worked out differently.'

She stood up and looked at her mother until Nina pushed away her half-finished drink.

Schrijver stopped them before they could flee.

'That lawyer won't hide you forever. You're going to have to talk to Vos. One day. None of this will go away until you do. Doesn't matter if you run off either.'

When she looked up at him like that, headstrong, wilful, awkward, he saw the child in her, the wayward, always active kid who dashed around what was left of the castle never doing as she was told. The only daughter he had and he'd loved her more than anything else in his life.

'You know that, do you, Dad?'

'I do.'

There was a brief and savage look of victory on her face.

'Well, if anyone would it's you. Let's face it. You're the king of hiding stuff. What's going on with the shop . . . with everything.'

'What does that mean?' he asked and prayed she wouldn't answer.

'It means we're all going down in the shit together, aren't we? Bust. Bankrupt. Finished. I'm not stupid and nor is Mum.'

There was such calculation behind the remark, such a deliberate attempt to hurt him. Schrijver didn't know what to say.

'Jordi Hoogland knows something about you,' Schrijver said and hated himself on the spot. It was meanness that put the words in his mouth, nothing else. Spite greeting spite.

'What?' Annie demanded.

'Don't know. Wouldn't say.' He stared at her. 'You care to tell me?'

'That's enough,' Nina said and took her arm. 'We're leaving.'

The waitress was back picking up their glasses. She looked at him and asked if he really wanted his untouched beer.

'Paid for it, didn't I?' Schrijver retorted.

When she was gone he left the drink, went back to the shop, dragged open the green doors, headed straight for the office.

So Annie knew they were headed for the rocks. He should have guessed. She was never slow.

Still there was something bothering him, something he needed to check.

Night was falling on Amsterdam and Rob Sanders was saying nothing at all. Chandra had ordered them to use the interview room with two-way glass. Now she stood on the observation side with Vos and Van der Berg watching Bakker and a statement officer trying hard to persuade the man at the table to speak. Even if it was just to confirm his name.

Swollen lips from the tumble he took in Sarphatipark. A plaster on his cheek to cover the graze there. He looked like a bum who hadn't slept in days. Vos suspected Sanders had taken flight the moment it became clear De Graaf's secret room had been found, stayed out for the night wondering what to do, where to go. Perhaps it was inevitable he would find his way back to De Pijp and the Schrijvers. Where else was there left to go?

All they knew for the moment was what they'd gleaned from the encounter in Sarphatipark: he'd phoned Annie Schrijver and tried to meet her. Why, they didn't know.

The commissaris was a dangerous mix of emotions. Relief that they finally had the man in custody. Intense frustration that she couldn't wrap up the case with a quick and informative confession.

'This has gone far enough. You need to put the evidence to him,' she demanded.

At Vos's orders they hadn't yet raised the question of the hat from the Drie Vaten.

'Not now.'

She sighed and came very close, a habit she had, a blunt attempt to intimidate people. Perhaps it worked in Zoetermeer.

'What do you mean, not now?'

'I'd rather save it until he's starting to talk.'

'Why?'

Van der Berg stepped in for once.

'Because if we introduce it when he's in this kind of mood he'll just shrink further into his shell. Then it'll take a lot longer to get anything out of him. When they clam up like this all that usually unclams them is time and patience.'

The way she reacted to the last word told Vos it was one she hated deeply. She glared at Van der Berg, then Vos.

'You think he date raped Annie Schrijver four years ago? With Vincent de Graaf?'

Probably, Vos said, remembering the photo of her they'd found in De Graaf's stash. That in itself was odd: eyes open, that frightened stare straight into the lens.

'And after something like that she went out with him? There has to be more to it . . .'

'There does,' he agreed.

But to charge Sanders with rape they'd need either a confession or an incriminating statement from her. Neither of which appeared forthcoming.

'Annie Schrijver formed a relationship with him afterwards. A long one. A close one, it seems. Even without recent events she's not minded to help us. Nor is he.'

Chandra was barely listening.

'I want this thing wrapped up. The hangover from four years ago. Zorgvlied. That American pervert. I want this bastard charged and in court as soon as we can manage it. There's too much bad publicity flying around already. The longer it goes on the worse it becomes.'

Vos stayed silent.

'Unless you're still persisting with the idea we have the wrong man.'

'There's nothing we can charge him with at the moment. We don't have the proof.'

Chandra gazed at him, astonished.

'Proof? We've got his DNA on the hat he dropped. It places him in the middle of everything.'

He shook his head.

'No. All it does is place a hat he once wore outside a bar. Nothing else. We don't have a print, a hair, not a single piece of direct physical evidence that says he was involved.'

'Which is curious,' Van der Berg agreed.

'Jesus Christ,' Chandra grumbled. 'I wish to God I had my people from Zoetermeer here. They'd have this in front of a judge in the morning.'

Vos waited to see if Van der Berg would chip in there. When he didn't he said, 'If we try to wrap this up on speculation rather than evidence some clever lawyer will take us to pieces in court.' He hesitated then said it anyway. 'We've enough trouble with lawyers as it is.'

He nearly added more but thought the better of it. Instead he went to the interview room door and called for Bakker. She was well over shift. Exhausted officers rarely got anywhere. It was time for someone else to take over.

'OK,' she said when he told her to go home. 'I don't think Mr Sanders is about to talk, I'm afraid. About anything. Doesn't even answer when I ask him if he wants a lawyer.'

Vos brought in Koeman from the night team and left instructions. Sanders would be told he was going to be detained for further questioning about two murders and a case of sexual assault. He would be allowed a few hours to sleep and to shower. In the meantime, they'd find him some fresh clothes. No belt, no objects he might harm himself with, and someone to keep a suicide watch throughout.

'If he looks as if he wants to talk, call me,' he told the night man. 'If he doesn't, don't push it. We'll come back in the morning when he's had time to think. Might be easier then.'

Chandra listened, arms folded, huffing and puffing. When Koeman left to tell his officers she said, 'This is deeply unsatisfactory.'

Bakker looked mutinous. She stared at Chandra and asked straight out, 'Have you worked investigations before, Commissaris? I mean . . . directly?'

That, Vos thought, really helped.

'As it happens . . . yes. I was acting commissaris in Leiden for a while—'

'Leiden?' Bakker almost laughed. 'Not exactly crime central, is it? If Rob Sanders doesn't want to talk there's precious little we can do. We either wait until he unbuttons his lip. Or we find something that'll do it for him.'

'Go home, Bakker,' Chandra told her. 'You're annoying me.'

Then she sniffed the air and turned on Vos.

'Have you been drinking?'

The tequila was good in the Mariposa. He'd say that for the two brothers running the place.

'Just the one. In the course of duty.' He checked his watch. 'Duty being well past I feel it's time for more.' He smiled, at her, at Van der Berg. 'Good night.'

Jillian Chandra moved to stop him leaving.

'Tomorrow you get somewhere with this farce. Or I'll find someone who can.'

The harder Bert Schrijver tried to unravel what had gone on that evening the more stupid he felt. So Rob Sanders had phoned his daughter. For reasons Schrijver couldn't begin to imagine she'd gone to meet him.

All the same he knew it was idiotic to worry about things you couldn't affect, couldn't control. Pointless to obsess over your own problems too when, however large they seemed, there were always others with worse.

Such as innocent refugees beaten up and robbed by a thug like Jordi Hoogland.

There was an address for Adnan. It was scribbled in what he presumed was the young Syrian's own careful handwriting in the books. Desperate to get away from the Albert Cuyp, Schrijver grabbed a tram to Centraal station and walked the rest of the way. Wouldn't have been a good idea to take the van. It was just possible he'd do what Hoogland suggested and drink himself into a stupor somewhere that night.

Adnan Mathan and his family lived near the docks. Third-floor room in a tenement that stank of bad drains and cooking. The scared-looking woman who answered the door wasn't keen to let him in. Nothing personal. This was a place for immigrants and people who helped them. Schrijver guessed he didn't look like either.

He stood there and called through, 'Adnan. It's Bert from the market. I know you're home.' He tried to find the right words. 'I know what happened. I came to apologize. Also I owe you some money.'

The woman opened the door a little wider at that and Schrijver saw: one big room that seemed to be packed with people. Adnan, his wife and their young daughter were huddled in the far corner on two single mattresses. Still Schrijver waited on the threshold. You had to be invited. That was only polite. Everywhere as far as he knew.

Eventually the young Syrian came over and took him out into the corridor. Beneath the weak yellow bulb of the landing his face looked swollen and bruised.

'Jordi Hoogland speaks for himself and no one else,' Schrijver told him. 'What he did was wrong and by God he knows it now. He won't be back our way for a long time. Here . . .' He held out

245

a hundred euros from the day's takings. 'These are your wages. A bonus as well.'

The Syrian stared suspiciously at the money.

'You don't owe me a bonus. You didn't do this.'

Schrijver took his hand and stuffed the notes into his palm.

'It's not sympathy. It's common sense. You got me more money today than we've had on a Saturday for as long as I can remember. Take it.'

The young man did and looked grateful.

'Can I come in?'

'Why?'

He wondered what their lives were like in Aleppo. Not fancy, he guessed. But not poor. Much like market people everywhere. Can't have been easy to move from that and find yourself confined to a hovel, crammed into a room with people you probably didn't know. Scratching a living in a foreign and occasionally hostile land, a family to feed.

'I want you back working for me. I'd like to know who you are. Your wife. Your daughter. I'd like to meet them.'

Adnan hesitated for a short while then stood back and beckoned with his arm. The room was badly lit, hot, airless. The curtains were little more than ragged sacks. Someone was cooking in the corner on a gas camping stove. Perhaps a dozen or more people, mostly young, mostly miserable Schrijver guessed, living in a single room. There were babies there. He could hear them, smell them.

His wife was Mariam. She looked older than her husband, or perhaps was just worn down, stick-thin with close-cropped, roughly cut black hair. Schrijver wondered if she was ill. The daughter Lia was four, tired but smiling. Not thin at all. That was where the food went.

'We're grateful you gave Adnan some work, sir,' Mariam told him in a voice that was serious and not in the least servile.

'I'm Bert. No one calls me sir. Any more than I call them that.'

His words brought the faintest of smiles to her dark face.

He wanted a drink. A beer. A couple of gins. Instead he said, 'There's a cafe round the corner. Keeps late hours. I use it sometimes if I'm working nights. We could go there to talk. Quietly. In private. If it's OK . . .'

'It's OK,' she replied with a grateful glance, then took her yawning daughter's hand and led the way.

It was a ten-minute walk, longer than Schrijver realized. But they didn't complain. The distance wasn't much for them, he imagined.

The place had been there years. Just three customers left and thirty minutes to closing time. Cheap white tables, uncomfortable chairs. Coffee all round. Without asking Schrijver bought some food at the counter: cheese toasties, biscuits, a fruit yogurt for the little girl.

'Who are you?' he asked when he came back and watched the way they fell on the plates.

Adnan opened his jacket and took out his little photo album. Best keep your belongings close to you on the road, he said.

Schrijver knew nothing of Syria except what he'd seen on TV. He'd have struggled to find it on a map. These were pictures from what they called the good times. Before the war. It seemed a warm and sunny place, full of happy people. Their stall looked bigger and smarter than his, with exotic flowers he'd never seen in the Albert Cuyp. There were pictures of them with relatives on a beach, cooking round a barbecue. He didn't ask who the others were and they didn't want to say. Then Lia as a baby, a toddler surrounded by so many furry animals she was almost drowned by them.

'The toys couldn't come,' the little girl announced, jabbing a finger at the picture. 'No room.'

'Sorry about that,' Schrijver said as if it was his fault.

Photos of Mariam, healthier, happier, wearing a white apron and a chef's mob cap. She was serving up exotic food from the

247

counter of an open-air restaurant. Old wooden tables in front, red and white chequered cloths on them, every seat taken by a beaming customer.

All of this was gone now, Schrijver understood. Not just gone but vanished. Never to be recovered. Lives and livelihoods all lost, disappeared in smoke and dust and blood.

Mariam was a cook in a restaurant run by her brother nearby, Adnan said.

What happened?

He didn't dare pose the question. The answer seemed to hang over them, live inside the little album of memories the Syrian kept in his jacket, one last link to a home they'd never find again.

'My mum's a good cook,' Lia told him with a wise and certain nod.

'I bet.' He looked at Mariam. 'You found some work?'

'Soon,' she said. 'Not easy finding a job with child care. We don't want to live on hand-outs. In . . .' Her face grew briefly hard. 'In a place like that.'

'Who would?' he murmured.

On Sundays the market was closed, he told them. The one day of the week when everyone stopped work. A time for family, for relaxation, for remembering why you spent the other six days shifting boxes here and there, trying to sell them. Struggling to put food on the table.

'But there *is* food on the table,' Lia said and pointed at the toasties.

Schrijver looked at the little girl and laughed out loud. So did she. Then her parents.

The idea came out of nothing. Maybe it was a good one. Maybe bad. But he had it and the notion wouldn't go away. There was something he needed, Nina and Annie too, and that was to look outside themselves and view the world from another perspective, with other lives in it.

'We've got a tradition,' he said. 'Every Sunday. We invite

round new friends. And . . .' He smiled at Mariam. 'If they can cook we ask them to. Their food. Not ours.' He reached into his pocket, pulled out the wad he'd taken from Hoogland, and placed five twenties on the table. 'We pay, naturally.'

They stared at the money, all three of them, and then at him.

'We've never eaten Syrian food. We'd like to. Me. My daughter Annie. Her mother Nina. We'd love that.'

Adnan didn't take the money.

'You're a kind man, Bert. But I heard you had trouble. People in the market. They were talking about it. We've got enough problems of our own—'

'They're my troubles. Nothing that need worry you. A couple of hours. We've got a little kitchen you can use to cook.' He tapped the money. 'You can find what you need, I'm sure.'

'A tradition?' Mariam asked.

A bad liar, always.

'One I just invented. Please. Say one o'clock.'

'Eleven if I'm to do the cooking,' she replied and scooped up the notes.

The little girl yawned and ran her fingers through her curly black hair then put her head on the table, ready to sleep.

'Can't wait,' Bert Schrijver said.

There was the faintest bite of autumn in the air as Vos walked down Elandsgracht to the Drie Vaten. It would have been easy to cross the road to the empty houseboat he called home. But he was a creature of habit. The place was quiet. Sofia Albers poured him a beer the moment he walked in. Sam looked up from his plastic bed by the counter, yawned long and noisily then closed his eyes.

His phone buzzed. A text from Dirk Van der Berg, the longest personal exchange they'd shared in days.

I imagine you've got the message already but for pity's sake tread warily. The Zoetermeer Dragon is searching for a scapegoat. She's a practical woman. The nearest sacrificial victim will do. Especially if he's dumb enough to offer his head on a plate.

'Language,' Sofia said when she heard his angry muttered response.

'Sorry.'

Sam looked at him, yawned again, stretched in his bed and went back to sleep.

Sofia came and placed some liver sausage and a bread roll in front of Vos. It went with the beer. Dinner.

'You're looking . . . stubborn tonight,' she said.

'Really?'

'Yes. Even more so than usual.'

'Thank you.'

From time to time he mused about abandoning Marnixstraat, not that he had the first inkling what he might do instead. But the idea the job might be snatched from him by a bureaucratic pen-pusher from Zoetermeer, one who thought front-line policing was a spell as acting commissaris in a quiet spot like Leiden . . . that was wrong. Offensive. Impertinent. Undeserved.

He was good at what he did. Most of the time anyway. He'd earned that brigadier's badge and wasn't inclined to give it up easily.

When he'd finished he bent down, stroked Sam, got a growl in return. No evening stroll along the Prinsengracht this night. The dog could stay in the Drie Vaten once again.

The houseboat seemed empty without him. Vos sat in the cabin looking at the photos pinned to the planks of the bows. Family pictures from before. There was one from the Amstelpark, Anneliese with her mother on the futuristic little train.

Another memory. Marly Kloosterman looking at these self-same pictures that night when, a little full of drink, she'd come back here, keen to do so, amused by his shy reluctance. It was all part of the delicate dance of courtship, the process through which strangers got to know one another, tested how much they needed closeness, how preciously they valued their independence. Not long after he'd shied away, daunted by the idea of a relationship so soon after the awkward return to Marnixstraat.

He still felt guilty about that.

It was late but there was an excuse.

A sleepy voice answered when he called.

'Pieter? Is that you?'

'I wanted to check you're OK. I'm still bothered about what De Graaf said. Maybe we should—'

'Oh, don't be silly. It was just him making idle threats. I'm here, aren't I?'

He asked about the prison management. What they were saying about De Graaf's escape.

'They're being very understanding. I mean . . . I did follow procedure. It wasn't as if anyone was expecting a man in his condition to try to escape.' He heard her move, tried to picture where she was, what a fancy houseboat was really like. 'It said on the news you have someone.'

'Someone. Yes.'

'You don't sound optimistic.'

That wasn't quite right. They were making progress. He just had the feeling there was a piece of the story they hadn't yet seen.

'It's OK,' she added when he stayed quiet. 'I won't pry. If anyone's going to get to the bottom of this, it's you. I'm sure of that. So are the people you're working with. I could see it in their eyes when I came round this morning. You're . . . admired. Needed.'

'The new commissaris doesn't quite see things that way.'

'I saw her on the news. She does like publicity.'

'It's the new way. You don't just do the job. You have to be seen doing it.'

'Putting that poor Schrijver girl on TV like that. Really. It's disgraceful. If I'm speaking out of turn I apologize—'

'No,' he interrupted. 'I'm the one who needs to say sorry.'

A long pause and then she asked, 'For what?'

'For what happened. The way I just retreated. Ran away. I could make the old excuse. Work. This job.'

She laughed.

'No problem. I know that one. I've got a bit of police blood in me too. But that's a story for another time.'

'The truth is, I wasn't ready. It was all too soon. I didn't know what I wanted.' The photos on the cabin walls stared back at him. 'From anything.'

'Do you now?'

She sounded interested.

'I'm getting there. First I need to find a man I should have put in jail four years ago. Work out what happened this week too. I really . . . really don't have a clue.'

'All in good time.'

'In good time I'd like to see that fancy boat of yours. I don't think *Het Parool* will be coming round taking pictures of mine. Maybe I can pick up some tips.'

She hesitated then said, 'Are you asking for a date? For real this time?'

'Seems so.'

'I've got tomorrow off.'

'I very definitely haven't.'

She laughed and he liked that sound.

'No. Of course not. Sorry. Anyway there's some neighbourhood party I have to go to. Later in the week . . .'

'I'll call. I promise. If—'

'No promises, Pieter. No guarantees. We're grown-ups, remember? We know how much they're worth.'

On that odd and cautious note, they said goodnight.

He sat for a moment, holding the phone, trying to work out how he felt. Excited. Relieved. Scared. Full of an odd anticipation.

The houseboat was too much of a mess for visitors. One day he'd tidy up. Perhaps get in a cleaner. It wasn't grubby, just disorganized.

A place he kept fond things. His own Cabinet of Curiosities, like the photos against the shiny black planks in the bows.

A couple of minutes rummaging through a cupboard full of old and dusty books, CDs and tapes and then he found it: a cassette of children's songs his daughter used to love when she was little.

Vos's hi-fi was so old it still had a tape deck. The song was the first on the list. Four young voices struggling to sing in harmony.

Slaap kindje slaap, daar buiten loopt een schaap.

Sleep baby sleep, outside there runs a sheep.

Three words from a nursery rhyme. Vincent de Graaf had used them to place his stamp, his mark of ownership, on the women he'd murdered for having the temerity to wake while he and his associates assaulted them.

There was a cruel and savage logic to that.

But why scrawl it on a man?

FIVE

The city was quiet on Sundays. Light traffic along Marnixstraat. Little in the way of business for the police headquarters at the top of Elandsgracht. One important customer only: Rob Sanders, still offering little but a sigh and a roll of the eyes.

At Vos's insistence they'd brought him some clothes from home, let him sleep, shower, try to bury the miserable lost figure they'd seen the night before. But still he wouldn't talk. Sanders just sat there through a string of interview attempts, a fit and intelligent man of thirty-three, white shirt now, black trousers, fair hair washed, clean-shaven. Silent except when he wanted something. It was almost as if he thought that at some point they'd give up, open the door, let him walk free then head off back to De Pijp and home.

Which might well happen. Nothing the night team had uncovered linked him further with either Zorgvlied or Braat's houseboat. There was the hat, which still hadn't been put to him on Vos's orders. And there'd been no taunting text for once. Did that mean the game was over? Work done?

Mid-morning Vos went in with Laura Bakker, a tray of coffees and some pastries from the canteen. It was her turn to try.

'Are you listening, Rob?' she asked. 'Anyone in?'

He had an alert, rugged face. Handsome in a way. Vos could imagine him plying the bars and clubs where the young went to flirt and more of a night.

Bakker placed the nurse's hospital ID card on the table.

'You get access to the medical stores. Easy to pick up GHB.'

Sanders shook his head.

'Isn't it?' she wondered.

Nothing.

'Where would you go to get some potassium cyanide?' she asked.

He sighed and just looked at them.

'You know,' she went on. 'The stuff you used to kill your new American pal, Greg Launceston. When you took your ex-girlfriend to Jef Braat's boat so you and your pals could gang rape her then blame the whole thing on Braat.'

There was a flash of anger in his eyes but not a word by way of reply.

'If that's what happened of course,' she went on. 'I mean, we have to assume it is because, let's face it, if it wasn't you'd surely say so. Something like . . .' She leaned back in her chair. 'Oh, I couldn't have been gang-raping my ex-girlfriend Tuesday night because I was down the Concertgebouw listening to Wagner. Or spiking the drink of some other brainless girl I felt like hitting on because it's so much easier with women if they're semi-conscious. Means you don't have to turn on the charm . . .'

'Won't work,' Sanders said in a low, gruff voice. 'Don't bother.'

'But it has,' Bakker replied with a grin.

Vos opened the box they'd brought and placed the hat on the table.

'Let's not talk about Annie for the moment. Let's talk about your hat.'

Sanders was staring at the thing, looking puzzled.

'It *is* your hat,' Bakker said. 'We know that. Found your DNA inside the band. You being a nurse and everything . . . you know what that means.'

'It was my hat. Was.'

Bakker turned to the video camera on the wall, held up two thumbs and let out a little cheer.

'Well,' she said with a sigh. 'That didn't hurt, did it?'

'When did it cease to be your hat?' Vos asked.

'Is this important?'

'Very.'

'Why?'

'We're not saying,' Bakker told him, folding her arms. 'Not until you tell us where you lost it. Three can play this game.'

He shrugged.

'In a bar somewhere maybe. I don't remember.' He frowned. 'I imagine drink had been taken. Weed had been smoked. One of those nights. It's not a great hat. Didn't notice for a while.'

'And you a medical man too,' Bakker tut-tutted.

'I'm just a nurse. That's all.'

Which bar, Vos wondered. The Mariposa?

'Maybe. Lots of bars in De Pijp. I do the rounds. Why do you want to know?'

Vos kept it short: the hat was left in the Jordaan on the night Annie Schrijver and Greg Launceston were found in Zorgvlied. There was a connection.

'I don't drink in the Jordaan. I don't know anyone called Launceston. What connection?'

'It was left by the man who drove them there on Wednesday night.'

That seemed to surprise him.

'Wednesday night I was at home watching television. On my own. I never went to the Jordaan. Or Zorgvlied.'

'What about Tuesday?'

'Same shift. Worked till midday. Did some shopping. Went home.'

'Watched TV?' Bakker suggested.

'Spot on.'

'Why did you break up with Annie?' Bakker wondered. 'Her father said you hit her. Was that it?'

A low mumbled, 'None of your business.'

'But it is, Rob. I'm always interested in why a man hits a

woman. There seem to be so many different reasons, all with the one outcome. Did she . . . *offend* you perhaps?'

'Annie asked for it.'

It was said so plainly she couldn't help but laugh.

'She *asked for it*? Didn't know her place or something?'

'I mean,' he snapped, 'she asked for it. She hit me. I hit her. It was a row. People have them.'

'Need a little more than that.'

He leaned forward and stared into her face.

'There is no more. We had a row. There was bad behaviour on both parts. That's why we broke up. My decision. Not hers.'

'What did you row about?' she persisted.

He waved away the question and gazed at the wall.

They waited a while then Vos pulled out a photo of the dump of a barge called the *Sirene* and said, 'Tell me about Jef Braat.'

Sanders blinked rapidly then closed his eyes.

'This is his houseboat.'

'I never went to Braat's boat. I loathed the man. He was just a barfly.'

Vos placed more pictures in front of him. Limbs and skin, intimate and medical.

'He was more than that. Braat was part of Vincent de Graaf's rape club. The Sleeping Beauty case. Remember?'

Not a word.

'The odd thing is . . . Annie wasn't seriously hurt beyond the drugs. Scrapes from the ground and getting moved. She was stripped naked and we haven't found her clothes. But she had none of the usual injuries, bruises, abrasions, cuts, we'd expect. So maybe it wasn't what it appears. Perhaps—'

'What do you think I am? An animal?'

'That,' Bakker said, 'is what we're trying to establish.'

He looked bored and stared at the table.

'Your hat was left by the driver who dumped her in Zorgvlied,' Vos said. 'After Annie was taken to a houseboat, drugged, not once but twice. And still survived while two men died.'

'Nothing to do with me.'

'A medical man would know how to do that. A medical man would have access to the drugs. To De Graaf too when he came in for a scan. Where were you Friday night?'

Silence. One last photo.

'Look at it.'

Sanders didn't.

'Look at it!' Vos yelled.

It was Annie Schrijver from the collection they'd found in De Graaf's basement. Wide-eyed, staring straight into the lens. A teenager, frightened for her life.

'Four years ago Annie Schrijver was raped by that bunch. I think it happened in that place right next to where you work. Where someone put him to death with a morphine drip in the arm just when you went missing. The kind of thing a medical man might know about.'

Sanders couldn't take his eyes off the picture.

'Most of the women De Graaf and his friends raped they didn't kill,' Vos went on. 'Do you know why?'

'You tell me.'

'Because they didn't wake up. They didn't *see*. But . . .' He put his finger on the photo. 'Annie did. And still she lived. Then she kept quiet. So maybe . . . maybe . . .'

'Maybe she wasn't a victim at all,' Bakker cut in. 'Maybe she was all part of the game. Along with you. I think we ought to arrest her. Bring her in here. See what she says and—'

He was on his feet, furious.

'After this week? The way you made her suffer . . .'

'We've got a job to do, Rob,' Bakker said, unmoved.

'And we'll do it,' Vos added. 'One way or another. With your help. Without it.'

Difficult interviews hung on moments, seconds like this where a suspect's resolve wavered, like an acrobat trembling on a high wire. They recognized it, waited, hoped.

'Whatever,' Sanders said then went back to staring at the wall.

They returned to the observation area behind the glass. Jillian Chandra and Van der Berg were there. Perhaps had been all along.

'We nearly had him,' Bakker grumbled.

'Give it time,' Vos said.

Chandra glared at them.

'Time? We don't have time.'

She'd been talking to the lawyers. The hat apart, they had nothing to link Sanders to the case. Without more evidence they'd have to release him.

'If you don't get somewhere with this today, I'll redraw the whole team and start afresh. There's a serial rapist, a killer out there—'

Something in his face stopped her.

'What was that look for?'

'Braat was murdered,' he said. 'Greg Launceston too. De Graaf's dead. That's all we know. Three men dead. Annie Schrijver lived. As I just said in there . . . we don't know she was raped at all.'

'You're not bringing her in. You're not even talking to her. Not until I get a grip on this damned lawyer.'

'It isn't the same as before, is it?' Bakker said. 'If you think about it.'

Chandra wasn't impressed.

'You two overcomplicate everything. We've had a homicidal sex criminal loose in the city. One you should have put behind bars four years ago. The press know it. Sooner or later they're going to throw all that shit my way.'

She tapped on the glass.

'It's him. Look at the DNA. The fact he can't account for where he was when any of this happened. Most of all . . .' One more rap on the window with her nails. 'If he didn't do it why the hell won't he say so?'

Good question, Vos thought. But any answer she might think overcomplicated so he didn't bother.

'I want progress,' she repeated. 'Today.'

With that she bustled out of the room, Van der Berg in her wake.

'I don't think we'll ever make that woman happy, will we?' Bakker said. 'Where do you get potassium cyanide by the way? Apart from a butterfly nut.'

He'd looked that up. It was a common enough chemical if people went looking. Used by the jewellery trade for gilding and polishing.

'Not a hospital,' he added. 'That's for sure.'

He told her to team up with Rijnders who was on a day shift. Give it an hour then the two of them could go back and try Sanders again.

'Don't push too hard. Don't get sarcastic either. It's counter-productive.'

'Sorry, sir,' she said with a quick salute. 'What about you?'

'I need to see someone. Call if he starts to talk.'

It was still quiet outside. The tram stop was right by the station front door. The number 10 ran all the way to Plantage and the zoo. Marly Kloosterman's boat couldn't be more than a few minutes away.

One was coming, a blue and white leviathan creaking down the deserted street.

Vos got in, found an empty seat at the back then took out his phone.

He worded the text carefully before he sent it off to the mobile number they had on file for Annie Schrijver. His name. His rank.

A reminder that he was the one who found her at Zorgvlied. Then a brief message.

Rob Sanders is facing charges of rape and multiple murder. Not that I think he's guilty but he won't talk to us so the lawyers will think we've no choice.

If you know otherwise, Annie, now's the time to speak.

Adnan Mathan, his wife and daughter turned up at the flower shop just before eleven. Gone were the busy stalls lining both sides of the street. Most of the shops and cafes were closed. Cars were taking advantage of the chance to park for free so close to the city centre for once. They ranged the length of the street and more were circling looking for spaces.

Bert Schrijver was waiting for the bell. He slid back the green wooden doors and greeted the family of three standing uncertainly in front of him. Schrijver wore a red waistcoat, braces holding up wide, baggy trousers with a sharp crease down the front.

'Sunday best,' he announced cheerily. 'Been a while since I had the excuse.'

Mariam had four bags of shopping with her. She handed over sixty euros in change. Syrians ate cheaply, Schrijver guessed.

The bruises on Adnan's face had gone down. Jordi Hoogland could have done much worse if he'd wanted.

'The kitchen?' his wife asked. She was wearing a threadbare purple cardigan and shapeless black trousers and looked thinner than ever in the bright sun. Adnan had a black fake leather jacket and jeans. Lia was in a red dress and pink jumper. Old clothes trying to look new, the best they had, Schrijver guessed.

'Later,' he said and showed them round. Annie's living space at the front, a studio effectively with a double bed, a sofa, table, two chairs and a gas hob, a little shower and toilet. Then the courtyard. He'd salvaged an old football from one of the bins in the street and kicked it for Lia, laughing as the little girl started to boot the thing round the worn cobbles. After that the office at the back, ashamed a little of his bed in the corner. There was another gas hob and kettle by the sink. Mariam could choose where she wanted to cook.

She thought about that.

'The front I think. You have table and chairs for outside?'

'The courtyard?' Schrijver frowned. 'We haven't eaten out there in years.'

'We can use the stall,' Adnan said. 'It's warm enough. I'll do it.'

Mariam went off to Annie's place and soon Schrijver heard the busy sound of chopping.

By the time Nina and Annie arrived a trestle table was set up in the yard. Fake green grass from the stall served as a tablecloth. Plastic knives and plastic forks. He didn't have enough proper cutlery to go round.

Adnan detected some awkwardness at their arrival and wandered off to help in the kitchen. Nina gazed at Bert and said, 'What is this? I thought that man had stolen from you. Are you going soft in the head now?'

'He didn't steal a thing. That bastard Hoogland took the money off him. Knocked him about a bit too. I got the money back. Would have phoned to tell you last night but it was late. You heard anything from the police?'

Annie walked off into the courtyard and started to kick the ball for the little girl, with no enthusiasm and not a shadow of a smile.

'Not a thing,' Nina told him.

'Maybe they won't call at all. Not with Petra Zomer on their case.'

'What the police did was wrong.'

'I still don't like having that woman running things. Anyway . . .' He gestured to the visitors. 'We've got guests. Don't know how long it's been since I could say that. Adnan's a good lad and I think his family's nice too. Been through hell from what I can gather. I'm using him in place of Annie. He can shift flowers like nobody's business. If he can keep it up we'll be making money here, real money, before long. And I was thinking . . .'

She had that look about her, suspicious, the one that said he might be about to do something stupid.

'Thinking what?'

'Thinking it'd be nice to hear some cheery young voices around for a change. Instead of me whingeing on to myself like an old misery.'

She didn't quite accept that.

'I don't want you asking Annie about Rob Sanders. If I can't talk to her about it, you certainly won't.'

He nodded.

'All right. What happened was between them. None of my business. Any more than what you do. I understand that now. Takes a while when you're an idiot but you get there in the end.'

He pointed to the trestle table with the green plastic grass and scratched his chin.

'You know what that needs? Flowers. A few nice bouquets. Got a bit of old stock out back. Bet there's something decent in there.' He winked. 'I knew a market girl who could run up a lovely bouquet out of a rubbish bin once upon a time. Wonder what happened to her?'

She looked at him askance.

'Are you all right, Bert? You haven't taken to the weed in your old age, have you?'

The smile vanished.

'Don't need that crap. Got a family here again, haven't I? Even if half of it's someone else's.'

She seemed amused at that and said she'd go and look. There were smells coming out of the shop at the front. Warm, rich spicy ones. Mariam walked out into the corridor to get something from a bag she'd left there. Schrijver felt embarrassed at seeing what came next. Adnan following, putting his arms round her, kissing her tenderly in the shadows behind the green doors.

That was what love looked like. All the trouble and terror they'd been through could only have made it stronger. Perhaps that's what marriage was really about. Building a barrier between you and the cold hard world, a wall the shadows and the blackness couldn't penetrate. Not easily.

Nina came back, her arms full of lilies, pink and spotted orange, carnations, tulips and a flourish of white roses. With all the care she'd once used in the market she primped and cut and then arranged them on the plastic grass using the big silver vases from the stall. Six chairs he found from the office and the storeroom, and three cushions to get Lia's little frame up to the table.

'Looks lovely,' he said when it was done, then realized his arm had gone round Nina's shoulders, his fingers briefly running through her fine fair hair the way they used to. She noticed and touched his hand.

'Going grey,' she said. 'Do you think I should do something about it?'

There were more flecks of silver he hadn't noticed before. That was another trick he'd forgotten. How to look, how to see the things that were precious before they vanished from your grip.

'Not for me. You look beautiful.'

A step too far. She backed off and said very carefully, 'I'll see if I can give her a hand in the kitchen. Keep an eye on Annie for me. She's . . .' Lia was back to kicking the ball around on her own. Annie was across the far side of the courtyard, staring at her phone, tears in her eyes, anger in her face. 'She's not good. I don't know what to say. What to do any more.'

'Me neither.' Nina was watching him, waiting for the rest. 'Hard to help people who won't help themselves.'

Just a few words, spoken in haste, and he knew from the look of disappointment on her face they were the wrong ones once again.

She walked off to the source of all those strange alluring aromas. Annie now had her back to him across the yard.

Schrijver walked out into the empty market, found the grocer's shop that opened Sundays, bought some beer and wine. He didn't know if Adnan and his wife drank booze or not. But he would. By four he'd probably be on his own with nothing but bottles for company.

The tram stopped at the back of zoo, close to the staff car park where he'd been with Bakker two days before. A genteel part of the city if it wasn't for the exotic bird shrieks and animal cries rising from the zoo. Water formed a natural border for Artis on half its perimeter here. On the other side of the canal called Entrepotdok stood a line of apartment buildings, a few houseboats in front of them. Marly Kloosterman's was a ten-minute walk away, further than he'd expected, almost opposite the patch of waste ground used for the rave where he'd met the young woman in the panda costume who'd sent him on to Zorgvlied.

A young woman they still hadn't traced, even with Annie Schrijver's tearful plea on the television.

Vos's home was a converted klipper barge that once worked the waterways of North Holland. Marly Kloosterman lived in a very different kind of vessel, a square green-timbered houseboat designed for nothing more than accommodation. It stood tall on the water, with French windows opening to the pavement and the canal beyond, a tidy garden at the back with deck chairs and a barbecue. Smoke was rising from the grill and he wondered for a moment if he was about to blunder in while she had a visitor. It seemed impossible such an attractive and intelligent woman was short of admirers.

Then a surprised voice behind cried, 'Pieter! What on earth . . . ?'

He turned. She was there in a pale cotton shirt and cut-off jeans, short hair damp and uncombed, looking younger than she ever did inside the prison hospital. A brown paper carrier bag hung off her right arm. A shiny scarlet scarf was wrapped loosely around her neck. He could barely take his eyes off her.

'You might have said you were coming. I'd have bought more food.'

'I don't need food, thanks.'

She picked something out of the bag. Sausages. The weather was changing. This might be the last chance anyone had to cook outside for a while.

'Well, let's see how it goes, shall we?' she said and guided him on board with a firm hand, pointing to the rear deck where the barbecue was starting to smoulder. 'Not inside please. I'm halfway through cleaning that mess and I don't want to be embarrassed.'

'It looks perfect,' he said, glancing through the French windows as she took him past. It did too. Modern, clean, organized. Just as it was in the photos in the paper. Everything his own boat wasn't.

'Far from it. Give me good warning, I'll happily let you inside.' A smile. 'If that's what you really want.'

God, Vos thought. It was so long since he'd been through this odd ritual, the little teases, the delicate tango.

He took a seat, said no to her offer of a beer.

'I wanted to make sure you were OK. What De Graaf said . . .'

She waved a dismissive hand in his direction.

'It was just him being . . . him. Why skip a threat if you could utter it? No one's come near me. No one's been hanging around. Don't worry. If they did I'd be straight on the phone. Besides . . .'

Silence then.

'Besides what?'

She looked very serious, the way she did in her white coat in the jail.

'I'm being presumptuous here. But from what I've read the man you're looking for went quiet for the best of four years.' A pause and then she added, 'It's OK, Pieter. I'm not prying. I'm not asking if I'm right.'

'I don't know if you're right or not.'

She frowned.

'Sorry. But it strikes me that if he could give it up just like that then maybe he can do it again. Just stop. Start again a few years down the line if he feels like it.'

'Then we might never find him.'

'Quite,' she agreed. 'I hope you do. If not . . . if he's just packed it in . . .'

'I haven't,' Vos said. 'I'm not retired. Not yet.'

The waste ground opposite was empty save for a few cars. He asked about Wednesday night, what she'd heard, what if anything she'd done.

'I put in a pair of ear plugs and tried to sleep. I gather some of the neighbours called you. Called the police, that is. Didn't do much good. I suspect I'll be hearing lots of complaints about that when I go to the neighbourhood party this afternoon. We like to keep things quiet here.'

She tipped out the contents of the bag onto the table. Salad, bread, mustard.

'We can share . . .'

'No. No. Really.'

'I said we can share.'

The charcoal was grey and ready. Vos had never got the hang of barbecues. Everything seemed to come out either undercooked or burnt. That never, he imagined, happened with Marly Kloosterman.

'Your colleague, Bakker.'

'What about her?'

267

'Is she . . . happy?'

It seemed a curious question.

'I think so. She's still new to the city in some ways. She's tough. Clever too.'

'Oh, I don't doubt that. You'd never have slow people round you. I doubt you'd have the patience.' She opened a pack of vegetable crisps, fancy ones. 'Is that why you kept avoiding me? I wasn't quite interesting enough?'

'I told you. I wasn't ready. The coward's way out. It's always easiest and being a lazy man I like the easy way. Consider yourself warned.'

She didn't seem happy with that answer.

'Also,' he added, 'you're so . . . sane. I couldn't work out why a woman like you would want to waste your time with a layabout living in a dump of a houseboat with nothing more to amuse him than a little dog.'

'A lovely little dog,' she corrected him. 'And I don't feel the term layabout quite works for you. Though what does . . .'

'Am I forgiven?'

She wrinkled her nose, thinking, then turned the sausages round on the grill.

'We'll have to see. Are you really not going to have a beer?'

'I'm working. And the new commissaris is rather strict on such things.'

'Best start then.'

'Start what?'

'Working. You clearly came here with something on your mind other than my safety. Time is therefore short. I'm going to eat, drink two beers, take a nap and finish my cleaning before going to this shindig across the road. It's for charity. I'll get a bad conscience if I bomb out. The . . . um . . . courtship or whatever this is will have to take place some other time, won't it?'

'Right,' he agreed and picked up a few of the crisps.

'Let's begin with you asking me a question,' she suggested. 'Anything you like.'

Schrijver didn't know what the food was, just that it tasted delicious. Kebabs and vegetables, flatbreads, grains and hummus. Mariam made them so quickly he knew cooking had to be in her blood. Adnan had said she ran a street food stall back in Aleppo. That, though he'd never mentioned it to Nina, was one more reason he'd asked them round.

They ate and ate. They talked, awkwardly to begin with, but after a little wine more freely. When the food was finished, they relaxed around the makeshift table, quietly amused at how the little girl had fallen on every dish that came in front of her. Even Annie looked a little better for some food. Pensive too. As if there was something going on inside her she didn't want to share.

When the meal was done Nina insisted on clearing the plates. Mariam, she said, had done enough. There was a brief tussle over that which ended in them both vanishing into Annie's old room and attacking the washing up together.

He chatted idly with Adnan. Annie read an old picture book with Lia.

Then, slow as ever, he remembered the surprise he had in store. Lia had left her toys behind in Syria. Annie's he couldn't bear to throw away so without telling her he'd kept them crammed inside a locker in the warehouse, long forgotten by everyone but him.

So many she'd had over the years. Every time they argued, every time he felt he'd failed her, another one turned up as if love could be bought and bargained for like fish and flowers in the Albert Cuyp.

'I've got something to show you two,' he said, guiding Lia and Annie into the back. 'We all need nice surprises from time to time.'

They followed him into the warehouse where the perfume of yesterday's flowers mingled with the diesel from the elderly delivery van. He'd thought he might give a little speech but now it was upon him the words just weren't there. Instead he found a set of keys and unlocked the dusty cabinet where he'd put Annie's belongings one by one as she'd abandoned them over the years.

It was worth it for the look on the little girl's face alone: joy, bemusement, shock. Annie too as Lia pounced upon the piles there, books and boxes of games, Lego and crayons, fur animals and a plastic pirate ship. Even a few dolls, not that Annie had ever liked them much.

Lia picked up a battered rag tiger and clutched it to her chest, beaming. Annie sat down next to her on the cold grey floor, cross-legged the way she did when she was a kid, and started sorting through the collection in the cupboard. Soon they were both at it.

Adnan and his wife came and watched, embarrassed. But grateful too. Then Nina joined them.

'We don't need this, Bert,' he said after a while. 'It's kind but—'

'We've no use for all this stuff,' Nina broke in. 'I'd forgotten it was even there. Annie too from the look of it.'

Bert Schrijver recalled a fragment of what he'd wanted to say.

'I always used to think happiness was about what you got for yourself. That's rubbish. For fools. Really it's about what you give away.'

Annie was brushing tears from her eyes again. She got up from the floor, patted Lia on the arm and told her very sweetly to take anything she wanted. Then went back into the courtyard, phone in hand.

'I have a suggestion for you and Mariam,' Schrijver added. 'Been thinking about it a lot ever since last night.'

The three of them waited. Their attention made him feel good. He wouldn't hit the booze even if this whole pipe dream fell to pieces.

'The truth is this place is on its last legs. If I don't do anything about it, I'll be bust by Christmas. This ship is heading for the rocks and for the life of me I don't know how to turn it round.' He smiled at Adnan. 'Maybe you do. Maybe between us we can work something out.' He nodded back towards the shop. 'Annie isn't using that room any more. I don't believe she'll ever come back. It's not big but it's better than what you've got. You move in there . . .'

'Bert,' Adnan said. 'We don't have money for rent. We don't have much at all—'

'I don't want money.' Schrijver tapped him gently on the side of the head. 'I want what's in there. You're bright. You're keen. Got ideas. And Mariam.'

That was the other part.

'You can cook. You ran a stall, didn't you?'

'In Aleppo,' she agreed.

'It's food. Good food. Different food, the kind no one else does round here. All that new crowd, they like stuff that's different. They pay loads for a lot worse than you just ran up for next to nothing. '

Nina was nodding. She was quick too. She could see it.

'Bert's right. The flower stall could be half the size it is. We can put flowers on one side. Food on the other.' A thought then. 'Don't know what the market bosses are going to say . . .'

Schrijver had run through that conversation in his head already.

'The market bosses are going to say we're helping people. A family of refugees who came here looking for something and are willing to work to get it. I'd like to see them argue with that.' He looked at Mariam. 'I can scrounge some second-hand kitchen gear from somewhere. For starters we can begin with what we've got. Tomorrow. The Albert Cuyp won't know what's hit it.'

He held out his hand, first to Adnan then to Mariam.

'If you're willing to take a chance on me I'll do whatever I can

271

to make it work. You can move in this afternoon. We'll take the van round that place of yours and get your stuff.'

'You don't know us,' Adnan said so softly it was hard to catch the words.

'And you know don't me. We're equal there. But we've got a lot in common. Both of us are screwed if we just sit on our arses waiting for tomorrow to come.'

They glanced warily at each other.

'Bloody hell,' Schrijver said, shaking his head. 'You dodge bombs and God knows what else to come all the way here. And now you can't make up your mind over a simple thing like this. Who'd believe it?'

He laughed then. And so did they.

'You're a kind man.' It was Mariam. 'Adnan told me that and he knows people.'

'I'll help you move then.'

There were tears forming in her dark, deep eyes. She walked back into the courtyard rubbing them. Her husband followed and put an arm round her.

Nina did the same to the big man next to her.

'You do come up with surprises sometimes, Mr Schrijver. I must say that.'

'Last chance for us. First for them. Here, anyway. Got to take it. Both of us.'

Annie marched back in. There was something in her face he hadn't seen since before she'd vanished. Strength. Determination.

'They told me what you said.' She nodded back towards the family gathered in the yard. 'I think you're right, Dad. I think it's a good thing to do.'

'If you want to be a part of it somehow—'

'I'm off now,' she cut in. 'Something to do. See you at home later, Mum.'

'Everything all right?' Schrijver asked.

She couldn't take her eyes off the little girl clutching the ancient fur tiger to her.

'It will be,' Annie said then left.

Vincent de Graaf. Start there, he thought. He'd been in the prison sick wing for months under Marly Kloosterman's care, aware from an early stage that he was dying.

'Did he change much in that time?'

'You mean the Kübler-Ross model?'

'The what?'

'The five emotional stages of dealing with death. Denial. Anger. Bargaining. Depression. Acceptance.'

That was new to him.

'Standard stuff,' she said. 'Works usually. For normal people. Vincent wasn't normal but then you know that. The denial part – you can't be serious, I feel fine – didn't last long. He was very sick. The anger was there to start with. I guess it began the moment you sent him to jail.' She wondered about the rest. 'I never felt he was depressed. That was something for other, lesser people, rather beneath him. Maybe that nonsense about offering you a name in return for visiting the clinic counts as bargaining. I don't know.'

'Acceptance?'

She rolled the sausages over on the grill. There were four of them, she pointed out. Nearly ready. He had to eat something to get an answer.

'One,' he said and she found a couple of bread rolls.

'He accepted the idea he was about to die more readily than any patient I've ever known. He was in jail. For life. He hated it. I think he'd have killed himself if he could. So maybe he didn't mind. Equally . . . if someone offered him the chance to get free one last time I think he'd have done anything for that. He did, didn't he?'

She picked up the sausages, placed two in a bun and wouldn't let him argue.

'He talked though. Quite a lot. About how much he enjoyed what he did. The old cliché, how rape's more about power than sex . . . he said that was all wrong. For him. It was the sex he liked. They were unconscious, weren't they? No great stretch to feel a sense of control over someone who doesn't even know what you're doing to them. *That* . . .' She waved a barbecue fork in his direction. 'That was what turned him on. There was a sexual charge in having a young woman stretched out before him. Someone he and his sidekicks owned. Could do with what they liked. He started to tell me a few things on that front from time to time. I told him to shut up or I'd walk out.'

'Did he ever hint he had another accomplice? One we never caught?'

She stared at him, the smile gone.

'Of course not. I'd have been on the phone to you straight away. Mostly he just talked about the . . . pleasure of it all. I've never met anyone so lacking in the slightest sense of guilt or conscience. I never want to again. If they send me another in Bijlmerbajes it's time for a career change. Maybe it is anyway.' She sighed and offered him some mustard. 'I've been thinking about that for a while. One of the overseas medical charities. Somewhere a long way away. Where I feel I'm actually achieving something. Keeping the likes of De Graaf alive may have fulfilled my Hippocratic Oath but I'm not sure it did a great deal for humanity.'

Whether you worked in the police or a prison you had to maintain some distance between the criminals you met along the way. Their victims too. It was never easy. He hadn't realized how much that struggle had affected her.

'I'm sorry,' he said. 'I never thought about that. It must have been depressing. You had every right to hate him.'

A flash of anger crossed her face then.

'Hate him? Don't be ridiculous. And even if I did I'd never have let him know. That would have made him so happy. I told you before. I work there in the belief we'll get a chance to change people. Bring them back to being something close to a safe and decent human being. Responsible, even. It's a slim chance sometimes but I never met anyone I thought beyond that hope. Until that man came along. He took immense and measured delight in the pain of others. A studied, intelligent form of pleasure. Nothing cheap or nasty or vicious. It was an intellectual pastime. A game. Like chess. Or backgammon. Except the pieces were naked women he'd rendered unconscious.'

She shrugged and took a bite of the roll.

'Besides . . . hating is for children and sickos. What I did hate was something intangible. The fact we couldn't change him. That he was just . . . elemental. One of those things. Like the weather. Hating Vincent de Graaf would have been as stupid as developing a loathing for cancer. Or death.'

Vos took a bite of the sausage. It was a bit fancy for him. Complex. Sophisticated. Unexpected. Like Marly Kloosterman.

'I could go and work in Africa maybe. Feel I'm changing something.' A glance at him. 'Doing my bit.'

'I'm sorry, Marly. I shouldn't have come. I thought maybe he'd let slip something. A word, a hint . . .'

'Vincent de Graaf was a very cautious creature. From what he said you'd never have caught him if it wasn't something stupid that sidekick of his did. The tattooist, I think.'

'Jonker. Ruud Jonker.'

'Killed himself, didn't he?'

A body hanging in a dilapidated shop in the market.

'Definitely. I've been over the files again. There's no chance it was anything else.'

'That's the only man he ever mentioned. Sorry.'

'I shouldn't have wasted your time.'

He needed to be back in Marnixstraat. There were no answers here.

'Pieter.' Her hand went out to his knee and stayed there. 'It's fine. Don't worry. We don't need to rush. We don't need to do anything at all. Not until you're ready.'

He couldn't frame the words.

'There is a chance you'll be ready at some stage, isn't there?'

His phone rang. It was Annie Schrijver.

'Vos here.'

A pause. She was in the street somewhere. He could hear the traffic.

'You're the one who found me?'

'I am.'

'Thanks. I never said that. Sorry. I've been a bit of a cow all round really.'

Marly Kloosterman got the message it was a private call and went inside the cabin.

'You've every reason, Annie.'

'What with lawyers and tantrums and everything . . . I'm amazed you want to waste time on me at all.'

He put down the food and went and stood on the gangplank. Across the canal people were erecting tents and laying down a dance floor by the side of the zoo.

'There are things I don't understand,' he said. 'I'm sure there are things you don't understand too. Perhaps if we shared them we'd begin to see—'

'You can't blame Rob for this. You're not the only one who's saved me, you know.'

A glimmer in the dark.

'I did wonder.'

There was the sound of a bell. A tram. She was surely not far away.

'Here's the deal,' she said. 'I'll come and talk to you. Two conditions. I get to see Rob. You can listen. I *want* you to listen.'

Vos closed his eyes. Allowing a witness to meet someone who might be charged with her rape would surely damage if not jeopardize any prosecution. Jillian Chandra would never allow it. If she knew.

'Agreed. But you need to talk to me and me alone when you turn up. Call me on this number when you get there.'

'Second . . . I want you to bring in Jordi Hoogland. Dad's old mate. If he was a mate. More a bloody parasite as far as I could see.'

'Why?'

'Because I asked for it. Because after we've talked to Rob I think you'll want to speak to him.'

'I need more than that, Annie. To bring a man in.'

'Well, that's all you get. Take it or leave it. If that bastard Hoogland's not there you can forget about the whole thing. Because he's behind this somehow. I swear it.'

Kloosterman had come out of the cabin and was putting more food on the barbecue. Perhaps expecting him to linger.

'Any idea where he might be?'

'It's Sunday, isn't it? Sleeping off last night if I know him.'

She read out an address. Vos scribbled it on his pad.

'An hour,' he said. 'Call when you're in Marnixstraat. I'll come out and meet you.'

'Got to go,' he said.

She looked up from the grill, disappointed.

'That's a shame.'

He glanced across the canal.

'Your party . . .'

'Starts at four. Goes on for hours, I suspect. Come along later if you get the chance. No need to dress up really. All in a good cause.'

Something in her face must have told her he thought that unlikely.

She came over and he never knew who moved first. Just that before he realized they were in each other's arms, so close, and then they kissed, tenderly, with all the odd reluctance of strangers.

Marly Kloosterman pulled back laughing, blushing.

'I'm terrible at this. Really. You're not the only one who's been out of the game for a while.'

He wanted to ask why. It seemed strange that she should ever be alone.

Her eyes strayed to the cabin.

'If you had the time. Jillian Chandra need never know . . .'

Vos sighed.

'Or you could head off to work. It's OK.' She was amused and he was glad about that. 'I know you have to. Another day.'

He took her hands, kissed her again, touched the soft fair hair at the nape of her neck, remembering this was what closeness felt like.

It was a long and pleasurable moment. And then she watched him walk to the dockside, back towards the trams. A wave, a look back, a smile and he was gone.

Ten minutes later her phone beeped with a message.

Do we still have a date?

She thought about the answer.

It's not a date. I thought I made that clear.

A second or two. Then . . .

But you are coming?

If only Vos had stayed. If only her frank invitation had won him over. She'd have been happy to have wasted an hour or two that way.

Or do you have something better to do?

Sunday afternoon. He must have guessed she didn't.

So long as you understand. It's not a date. It never will be.

A smiley emoticon came back then . . .

Just a pleasant drink, Doctor. I ask no more. I've got my costume. What are you?

She'd thought about picking up something from the fancy dress place the day before. Then decided against it.

Marly Kloosterman MD. That's all.

A picture of a grey vulpine head came up on the screen, long fangs extending from a grinning mouth.

Grrrooowwwlllll! Who's afraid of the big bad wolf, Marly?

She didn't have to think much about that one.

Not me.

Back in Marnixstraat Sanders had fallen silent again. Jillian Chandra was getting more and more nervous about when she'd need to release him.

'And who the hell is this Hoogland character you've picked up?' she asked.

He was downstairs in a room on his own, furious at being dragged out of bed for no apparent reason by the uniforms who'd come calling.

'He works for Bert Schrijver,' Vos explained. 'Or used to. He's known the family a long time. We've never ruled him out. He's hung around De Pijp for years. I'd put money on the fact he must have bumped into Ruud Jonker and Jef Braat at some stage. Same kind of bar crowd.'

That didn't impress her.

'God, you sound desperate. Don't do anything that's going to set another bunch of lawyers on us.'

'I'll do my best,' he replied and then his phone buzzed. Vos glanced at the number. 'I have to go.'

He was out of the office before she could object. Annie Schrijver was where he'd said, by the tram stop.

The depressed, damaged victim he'd seen in the hospital was pretty much gone. Out in the street, in black denims, trainers, a shiny red jacket, blonde hair brushed, tidy, the blue streak fading, she looked like one more young city woman out for the afternoon.

'I want to see Rob first,' she said.

Vos led her round to the back entrance into the station. Chandra's office overlooked the front. They might have been spotted already.

'This is . . . unorthodox, Annie. To say the least. So stick with me. OK?'

She stood back and looked at his scruffy clothes.

'You're trouble, aren't you? Are you sure you're police?'

'I am. For now.'

They took the stairs to the first floor. Two uniforms were in the interview room with Sanders, one of them reading the paper. Vos went into the empty observation area, called Bakker and told her to meet him there with coffee. Four cups.

'Four?' she repeated.

'That's what I said.'

Then they left Sanders on his own for a few minutes, watching him through the one-way pane. He looked bored, tired, depressed.

Bakker turned up with the coffee. Her jaw dropped when she saw Annie Schrijver staring through the glass at the man beyond.

'Is the commissaris aware of—?'

'Thanks,' Vos said, taking the tray, and they went in.

Annie was last. Sanders never looked up until she said very quietly, very calmly, 'Hello, Rob.'

Nothing more.

Fear and anger in his voice, he asked, 'What is this?'

———

One floor up Jillian Chandra was at the computer, going through the duty rosters. Van der Berg now had a desk next to her, a screen on it too. He was staring out of the window at Elandsgracht and the short walk down to the Drie Vaten.

'Your drinking days are over,' she told him, barely looking up from the machine. 'This is work. Not a social activity.'

'Sometimes the two mix.'

'Not any more.' She called him over and showed him the list of available officers. 'These are the people who can take over from Vos. Who do you recommend?'

He ran through the names and said nothing.

'A woman officer would be good,' she added. 'Only one there. Isn't that odd?'

'She's never worked a murder inquiry. Fraud, mostly.'

'And Vos has worked scores. Fat good that's done us.'

Van der Berg dragged over his chair, sat next to her, folded his arms.

'Sometimes these things take months. Years. Sometimes you never get there at all. It's not the fault of the officers. It's because we've got a world out there that doesn't want to talk to us even though they so much want us to deliver whatever they think of as justice. Just on our own.'

Chandra closed her eyes and laughed.

'We're here to *make* them talk. I've really got my work cut out in this place.'

'Commissaris . . .'

'Have I really not made myself clear? I am the new broom here. I sweep all before me. If I need a sacrificial offering to make that clear to all of you, high and low, then so be it.'

Van der Berg sighed and said nothing.

'Vos has repeatedly ignored my orders. He's a disruptive, anarchic presence in this organization.'

'He's also the best man most of us here have ever worked with. If you give him the chance, you'll see.'

She scowled at that.

'Man. It's always man, isn't it?'

'Sorry. It is. Term of speech. An antiquated one, I agree.'

'How many chances does he need? So he's popular. All the better. Don't worry. I won't sack him unless he really asks for it. A job somewhere else. In uniform. Out of my hair. Out of your way.'

'He deserves more than—'

'I don't give a damn what he deserves! This place will run the way I want it. Not him. Or you. Or anyone else.'

She stabbed a finger at the screen.

'Run me through these names. Tell me who they are. What they do. What they're like. Tomorrow's a new day. We start again.'

Vos found a seat for Annie Schrijver, then Bakker. After that he went to the video camera on the wall and turned it off. Bakker caught his eye. He shrugged and said, 'Let's talk frankly. For a while. Between us.'

Annie was staring at Sanders, unflustered, challenging. He wouldn't meet her gaze. Then, starting to sweat, he muttered, 'I can't believe they dragged you in here. After all they did . . .'

'Either you tell them, Rob. Or I will.'

His face flushed. His eyes closed. Nothing but a low curse followed.

'All those things we never said,' she added. 'All those years pretending the two of us could let it lie . . .'

'There was a picture of you, Annie,' Vos told her. 'In Vincent de Graaf's collection. The one he kept in the place he took women. We know you were among them.'

'We know you woke up too,' Bakker went on. 'It's all there. You, staring at the camera. As far as we know every other woman that happened to died. You didn't. Why is that?'

'Tell them, Rob,' she demanded.

Silence.

'Why won't you?' Annie yelled. 'What's stopping—?' She went quiet too then whispered, 'You were lying. All the time. About how I was the only one. Just a pack of fucking lies . . .'

Eyes on the table, Sanders said, 'Get her out of here. I've nothing to say.'

'He saved me.' Annie was looking at Vos and Bakker. 'Kind of. That I think is true. First time he'd played that game. Or so he reckoned. I believed him. I wanted to. They spiked my beer and took me somewhere. Did whatever. And when I woke up . . .'

She frowned, remembering.

'I saw this face. That one who went to jail.'

'De Graaf?' Vos asked.

'Him. I saw . . . he had a knife. My head was all over the place. I just thought . . . that's it.'

Her hands flew across the table and seized Sanders' arms.

'Tell them. Tell them I didn't imagine it, Rob. You saved me. If it wasn't for you he'd have killed me . . .'

'I didn't know!' Sanders yelled. 'He never told me he was going to . . .'

He looked at her across the table, pleading, unable to find the words.

'You're saying he never told you he'd kill any woman who woke up?' Vos asked. 'Who could identify any of you?'

No answer.

'What did you think would happen, Rob?' Bakker wondered. 'You'd all just shake hands and go home—'

'I thought we just put them to sleep.' Red-faced, he looked at Vos and Bakker. 'That's all. They stayed that way. Then we let them go. It was a bit of fun and nonsense.'

'Fun and nonsense?' Bakker echoed. '*Fun and nonsense?* You drugged those women until they passed out. Then you raped them. Raped Annie . . .'

'I didn't touch her! It was him. De Graaf. I watched and then she . . . opened her eyes. He got a knife out.' A line of sweat stood out on his forehead. 'I told him. I wasn't up for that. I'd punch his lights out if he tried.' He stabbed a finger at his chest. 'It was me that got her out of there! It's something, isn't it?'

Annie wouldn't let him avoid her eyes.

'First time, you said. First and last, and it was a shock. You were so . . . sorry. So furious with yourself. And I didn't know where to turn.'

Bakker bent down and glared at him, waited until he looked back.

'So you found your own way to keep her quiet. Told her you loved her. How it was all a big mistake. Never happened before. Never would again. But best not go the police, eh? That way your new boyfriend would only end up in jail and . . .'

'I did love her!' he yelled. Then more softly, 'I do . . .'

'Two months ago,' Annie said very plainly, turning to Vos, 'he finished with me. Said it wasn't working. That was it. We'd kept breaking up. There was always an argument about something or other. But this was for good, he said. I knew. He was hanging round the bars.' She leaned across the table. 'You and your friends were out again, weren't you? Back to your old tricks—'

'Annie, Annie, Annie!' There were tears in his eyes and that stopped her. 'No. Please. It wasn't that . . .'

'What was it then?'

He tried to take her hands across the table. She snatched them away.

'Jef Braat got out of jail. He kept following me. Taunting me whenever I saw him. Saying he had a new mate and they were going back to the old days. If I didn't join them they'd come for me. They knew . . .' He stared at Annie. 'They knew about us. I was trying to protect you.'

Bakker laughed a short dry laugh.

'But not enough to tell us, eh? You just dumped her. Ran away.'

'He did,' Annie said. 'But I wouldn't let him. I'd call. Nag. Sneak him into my room when Dad was out doing deliveries. I told Hoogland to run the stall. I was going to be busy. Never said no to that, did you? Not when no one knew.'

He kept quiet.

'This is important, Rob,' Vos said. 'It wasn't just De Graaf and Jonker and Braat, was it? There was someone else. Someone . . . on a par with De Graaf. Important—'

'Yeah,' Sanders agreed. 'But I never met him. Three times, that's all I did it, and the last one I said I'd punch that bastard's lights out if he didn't leave Annie alone. Braat and Ruud had gone by then. The other one never came. They said he picked his times. Busy man. Just when he felt like—'

'Who—?'

'Don't know.' He groaned and leaned on his elbows. 'Do you think they'd have told the likes of me? I was just a beginner, a hanger-on. I think maybe Vincent wanted to kill Annie exactly because of that. It was kind of a . . . a test for me. If I'd passed I'd have met the other one. But I didn't and I never saw any of them again until Braat poked his head into the Mariposa a few weeks back, grinning at me. He said the old days were back and I was in, whether I wanted it or not.' He tried to catch Annie's eye. 'I thought they'd come for me. Not you. If I'd known that bastard was going to do something to you, Annie, I swear . . .'

'You'd have done what?' she snapped. 'Told me? Everything? Don't lie.'

'Where does Jordi Hoogland come in?' Vos asked.

She was the one who answered.

'Tuesday Rob came round again. I begged him. We went to my room. Jordi was outside. That bastard had started spying on us. I should have guessed. When Rob was gone me and him had a big argument. About work. He reckoned he wanted more money if he was going to cover for me on the stall every time Rob turned up.'

She glanced at the door.

'I told him to get lost. Went out for a drink with that American afterwards because I was pissed off with everything. Rob sleeping with me behind everyone's back and pretending it never happened. Me for begging him to keep coming round. Next thing . . .' A shrug. A sigh. 'Jordi Hoogland didn't dare go running to my dad. He didn't know which way that would fall out. But he was muttering about doing something to fix Rob.'

Bakker asked him straight out, 'Where did you lose that hat?'

He hesitated for a moment then said, 'I couldn't find it when I left Annie's. I was dead worried. If Bert had seen it . . . Didn't dare go back to look.'

Vos told Bakker to get a statement officer into the room.

'What's going to happen?' Sanders asked.

'You're going to go through this all again for the record. What happened last week. What happened four years ago. Then you're going to sign it.'

Sanders laughed then nodded at the dead camera on the wall.

'What kind of idiot do you think I am?'

Marly Kloosterman chose a plain brown jacket, a fawn shirt and jeans, then wandered along the canal and crossed over into the wasteland where the party was starting up. It was for charity, they said. Something to do with animals. Fancy dress was suggested, not required. Most of those there had complied though, so she found herself surrounded by people with face paint, in costume, zebras and tigers, pandas and monkeys. And a few from fantasy movies just to add some spice to the mix.

She'd only moved to the area six months before after selling the apartment when the divorce settlement finally came through. A few people among the locals she knew but not well. Now they wore disguises it was hard even to guess who they were.

A man in a zebra costume came and tried to chat her up. She smiled, said nothing and after a while he got the message.

No wolves anywhere. Not that she could see.

She went to the little stage they'd set up by the water. It was almost opposite her houseboat. The band was playing jaunty pop. A few costume animals were starting to dance badly in front of them. For a moment she wanted to laugh. Then she checked her phone for messages, saw none, took out the plastic glass she'd brought with her and the small bottle of ready-mixed gin and tonic she'd brought. Poured some and took a sip.

'I can't believe you're drinking that dreadful muck,' said a low, amused voice behind her. 'Mine's so much better.'

She turned and saw him. A tall figure, grey leggings, grey overshoes, a white circle for the belly, long arms behind his back. And a comic wolf mask, fake fur round the head, large pointy ears, a black shiny nose, sharp white plastic incisors dropping from a grinning scarlet mouth.

He twirled round, a balletic movement.

'Got this specially for you. I hope you like it.'

'Oh my, Mr Wolf. What big eyes you have.'

'All the better to see you with, my dear.'

Except they weren't big. Just holes in the fabric, two dark, glinting shapes behind them.

She reached up and flipped one of the canines. It was nothing but flimsy plastic.

'And what big teeth.'

'All the better to eat you with.'

Though muffled by the mask he had the cultured, ironic voice she recognized. Hard to hear with the band so she took hold of the grey fabric on his chest and led him away to a quieter spot near the water, not far from the staff entrance into the zoo.

A monkey squawked somewhere and she wasn't sure if it was for real or one of the party guests having fun.

'I don't know why I'm doing this,' she said.

He tugged at the costume.

'Same here. Let's go.'

'You're a very tenacious man.'

She knocked back more of the gin and tonic. He watched then reached into the pockets of his costume and brought out a bottle full of scarlet liquid.

'This is better. Spritz. With Campari. Not that orange Aperol filth. I make it myself.'

'Are we in Venice then?'

The wolf's head nodded towards the water.

'Got the canals.'

She finished the gin and held out the plastic glass.

'This has been a shit day,' Marly Kloosterman said. 'Got nothing I really wanted. This is a bad thing for a doctor to say. But God I feel like getting drunk.'

He laughed at that and poured out a big slug of the scarlet concoction. Spritz was a curious drink, she thought, one that never tasted the same outside the Veneto.

It was booze all the same.

Hoogland looked up from the table, saw Annie Schrijver, loosed off a couple of curses and said, 'Did that little bitch put me in here? Whatever she said . . . it's a lie. It always is.'

He was wearing a green lumberjack shirt over a grubby white vest. Tatty old jeans. His right eye was black and yellow with bruises, swollen.

Annie looked ready to go for him. Vos put out a hand and kept her back.

'Simple question,' he said. 'You spied on Annie and Rob Sanders. Last Tuesday . . .'

'Spied? Hard to miss it. Those two going at each other like dogs on heat. Me outside trying to sell flowers when she was supposed to be there. Jesus . . .'

'Did you enjoy it, Jordi?' Annie yelled. 'Help you remember what it's like? With a woman who wasn't unconscious when you—'

He was on his feet then, waving a fist.

'I didn't do any of that stuff. Never. Talk to that boyfriend of yours. Not me.'

Bakker raced between them and pushed him back into his seat.

'But you knew about it, didn't you?' she said. 'Knew it was going on—'

'Half the men who hung around the bars knew what that lot were up to. Didn't know about the killing part, mind. Not my fault it took so long for you idiots to find out about that.'

'Tuesday. What did you do?' Vos asked.

A sly look at all three of them.

'Nothing you can drag me in court over.'

'What?' Bakker demanded.

He laughed and looked at Annie Schrijver.

'I met Jef Braat over the weekend. He kept asking about them. Said a mate of his, an American, fancied her. I told him what a slag she was. Two, three times a week . . .' He scowled at her. 'When Bert was out she'd get Rob Sanders round and shag the life out of him while I covered for them. Every time that dirty bastard came round he walked out of the place grinning at me like I was an idiot for covering for her. And them supposed to be finished.'

He licked his lips and asked for a coffee.

'You get coffee after we've had the story.'

'Huh.' Hoogland turned shifty. 'Jef hated Sanders' guts. Don't know why exactly. History there, I guess. He said him and the

American and some new mate of theirs were up to something. They could play a trick on Rob. Give him a little aggravation.'

Hoogland sat back and smirked.

'Next time he does it make sure you get something off him, Jef says. Tuesday that's what I do.'

Vos nodded.

'You took his hat and gave it to Braat?'

'It was a joke.' Hoogland opened his arms. 'Jef said he'd get it back. Wasn't like stealing.'

Annie shook her head and muttered, 'You sorry piece of shit . . .'

'After which,' Vos went on, 'this American friend picked her up, drugged her, took her to Braat's boat. Did what they felt like and planned to leave Sanders' hat wherever they were going to leave her. Scores settled with two people you hated, Jordi. Proud of yourself?'

Hoogland's coarse face flushed with fury.

'I didn't know any of that. Or they had their eyes on her. I just . . .' He shrugged. 'While she was pulling her knickers on I grabbed that hat and went off for a beer. What happened after that. Well . . .' Hands behind his head, he grinned at them. 'Nothing to do with me. Took a man's hat, for a laugh. That's all. As far as I knew they were going to give it him back. Can I go now?'

'No. You can wait here,' Vos told him and got them out of the room.

'What are you going to do?' Annie asked in the corridor.

'Not a lot I can do. It's a hat. I don't think Rob Sanders is going to complain or sign a confession, is he?' Watching her he added, 'We need you to make a statement.'

'No.' She shook her head. 'I'm not going through all that crap again, especially not in court. Besides . . .' She leaned against the wall. 'It doesn't change the fact Rob saved me. Maybe we both went a bit crazy afterwards but if it wasn't for him I'd be dead.'

'We can't ignore what went on,' Bakker told her.

'Maybe you'll have to. Rob wasn't playing their games any more, was he? That's why they hated him.'

'Four years ago he was,' Vos said.

'The only way you can prove that's through me. Not going to happen.' A smile, confident, the first time they'd seen that. 'Here's an idea. Let him go and I'll fire that pushy lawyer who came on to us. On the other hand you can drag me into court to testify and then I'll do the same to you. Won't be pretty for either of us, will it?'

'Think about it, Annie,' Bakker begged.

'I have. I want my life back. I won't let anyone take it from me again. Not Rob. Not you lot.'

They walked her downstairs then stood in reception and watched her leave. Vos phoned custody to tell them Hoogland was free to go. Sanders would have to wait, a few hours anyway.

'Can't believe she doesn't want that bastard in court,' Bakker muttered as she left the building.

Vos shrugged.

'I can. Imagine what she'd have to go through. Her private life out there for everyone to pore over. Besides . . . even with her testimony it could be a tough one to prove. If it was just his word against hers.'

'It's never the woman they listen to, is it?'

His phone rang and Jillian Chandra's hard and angry voice rang in his ear.

'I just heard you brought the Schrijver girl into the building. In spite of everything I said.'

'I was about to come and explain—'

'I'm sick of your explanations. Do I fire you now or wait until the morning?'

Bakker was tugging on his sleeve. There was someone waiting on the bench seats in front of the desk. A young woman he'd seen before.

Black and white costume, black and white face.

The panda girl.

'Morning would be best, I think.'

'What's your name?' he asked. 'And don't tell me Li Li.'

Nola van Veen, a university student at the VU. She looked as if she'd been crying and couldn't take her eyes off Annie Schrijver outside waiting for a tram.

'That's her, isn't it? The woman on the TV? The one it happened to?'

'That's her,' Vos agreed. 'You took your time.'

The white make-up was thick and streaked with grey tears.

'I take it you don't wear this stuff day in and day out?' Bakker added.

'No need to be horrible. I'm here, aren't I?'

She seemed much as Vos recalled from the noisy, crowded party on Wednesday night. Short with a round and featureless face. It was hard to imagine what she looked like out of the costume so he got an address out of her and Bakker wrote it down. His phone kept going: Jillian Chandra. In the end he turned it off.

'You do realize where you sent me?' he asked. 'What I found there?'

'Kind of.' She was squirming. 'I didn't know.'

'Dead people. Pain. Misery. Whoever got you to do that's a murderer and lots worse—'

'*I didn't know!*'

He sat down next to her on the bench. Bakker took the other side.

Her flat was near Artis so she'd got a tip-off about the party on Wednesday from a friend. It was organized by a bunch of people who thought it might be a good joke to try to steal a march on the charity event planned for the weekend. While she was there a man came up and offered her fifty euros if she passed on a message to someone who'd turn up later. He handed over the money there and then, the envelope and a cutting from the paper with Vos's photo.

'What was he like?' he asked.

The panda nose wrinkled.

'Tall. Grey. Furry.'

'Let's just chuck her in a cell for a while,' Bakker said. 'She can think it over—'

'It was a fancy dress party! He came as a wolf. Big fake head.' She made a face. 'Sharp teeth. Sounded quite . . . posh. Stuck up, I'd say. And old. Fancied himself. He gave me that thing to pass on. Fifty euros. Said you'd be along later. That was it.'

'No questions?' Bakker asked.

'He said it was a practical joke. If I'd known—'

'Why did he choose you?' Vos wondered.

'How would I know? He came up. He gave me those things. I did it. Sorry.'

'And that's it,' Bakker said. 'You wait four days to tell us that? Do you live in that stupid costume?'

The panda face glowered at her.

'Not exactly. I didn't know.'

Vos thought of Marly Kloosterman, the event she was going to by Artis.

'Didn't know what?'

She sniffed, scared.

'I'd see him again. This afternoon. He was staring at me. Same costume. Same shape. Same size. Then he came over and said . . .'

Her furry arm rose and wiped her nose. Black make-up smeared across the fabric.

'He asked me if I wanted a drink. Said if I liked he could get me into the zoo. All for free. A private tour or something. He worked there. I couldn't stop shaking.'

She pulled a bottle of water out of her little rucksack and gulped at it.

'Then he saw this woman just right by us and went off to talk to her instead. Didn't even say goodbye. Like I didn't exist. So I came straight here. It was him. I'm sure.'

Vos got out his phone and pulled up the cutting from *Het Parool*. Marly Kloosterman smiling in the elegant living room of her houseboat.

'That's her.' The girl's eyes were wide with surprise. 'How did you know?'

Bakker had her car keys out.

'Stay here, Nola,' he said. 'Someone will come down and take a statement.'

The tram rattled towards De Pijp. Annie Schrijver sat on her own, staring at the familiar city. The busy square of Leidseplein. The Paradiso where she went to see bands from time to time. Then the quieter, leafier quarter opposite the Rijksmuseum. Next stop and she could walk all the way home.

But not to the Albert Cuyp. That part of her life was over. Selling flowers in the market. Hanging round the little bars at night. Pleading with Rob Sanders never to leave her. Going through each unthinking day, running on empty, hoping the next might turn out better.

It was laziness that had kept her there. That and fear. Her parents had been just about together four years before when she'd so nearly died. They were bickering on holiday somewhere in Spain while she struggled to come to terms with what had happened, only Jordi Hoogland to watch her, puzzled, uncaring in the shop. And Rob Sanders. Coming round daily, guilt and kind words in equal measure. That took guts, she'd thought at the time. She could so easily have shopped him.

Except she was in a daze, unsure which way to turn. Her

mother was already in a state, her father too as their marriage crashed around them. To tell the police would be to invite strangers into an intimate part of her life, one that had shame enough without others to add to it. So slowly, idly, she let Sanders talk his way there instead. It wasn't love so much as need. Damaged, alone, she craved company and protection. A body to put between her and the cold hard world.

Did it occur to her that what he sought most was selfish? A silence on her part that might save him from discovery?

The stop loomed up. A decision to be made.

Perhaps. But need was need on both their parts and always won in the end. When Vincent de Graaf came to court, Ruud Jonker dead in his studio, they agreed: put the past behind them. Try to forge a future around what lay ahead. It was love of a kind, but with a fault line running through it. One that had to crack some day.

The tram bell rang. There was a bench by the stop. She sat down and called home.

'Love,' Bert Schrijver said and she could hear the concern in his voice. It had always been there. It was her spiteful choice to ignore it. 'Where are you? Is everything OK? I worry—'

'I know. I do that to you.'

'If a father can't worry about his daughter . . .'

'I'm on my way to Mum's. Nothing's wrong.'

He sounded in a good mood. Maybe the wine had helped. But it was more than that, she felt.

'Plenty's wrong, sweetheart. Always will be. That's why we've got each other.'

She thought of Lia, the little refugee kid with a history she couldn't begin to imagine. Playing delighted in the shop with toys two decades old.

'I'm sorry I screwed up, Dad. I'm sorry I've been an idiot. Some things are hard to say. To talk about—'

'No need. You're back. You're safe. That's all that matters.'

A woman walked past tugging at a poodle on a lead. Another day in the city.

'The funny thing is,' Annie said, 'you only see kindness in strangers. Not your own. You take them for granted. As if you're owed so it's nothing special.'

'You don't have to say this. Say anything—'

'I do. You're special, Dad. Kind and patient and generous. Mum too. I should have told you what went on ages ago. I just felt . . . ashamed. And puzzled too. It's like . . . like you walk into a tunnel and you never question why it's dark. You're just there and that's all there is.'

'There's no tunnel now. You're our daughter. We'll always love you. We'll always do what we can.'

She watched the woman with the dog potter off down the street.

'I'll stay with Mum for a few days. After that I'll find a job somewhere. Away from here maybe . . . I don't know.'

He didn't say anything.

'What you're doing with that foreign family . . . I think it's brave. Nice of you. I hope it works.'

Her father snorted.

'If it doesn't I'll just have to get a real job too, won't I? But I think we've got a chance. I've watched Adnan. His wife. They've got that lovely little girl. You always say to yourself . . . you want your kids to have something better than you had. They've got more reason than most. More than me.'

She had to say it.

'That man Vos wants to put Rob in jail. They need a statement from me. I won't give it to them. I don't want that. Don't want it for him. Or me.'

He didn't speak.

'I thought you'd be mad to hear that.'

'I thought so too. But I'm not. You're all that matters. If you're fine with it—'

'More than fine,' she interrupted. 'And that lawyer who came on to us. She can piss off too. I'm not having her badgering the police for what they did. I never made it easy for them. For any of you.'

A happy sigh and he said, 'Now *that* I'm glad to hear. We start again. All of us. We pick ourselves up from the floor, shake off the dust, get back in the fight. That's who we are. It's what we're meant to do.'

'Suppose,' she whispered. 'Got to go now. I'll pop in and see you tomorrow.'

Down the length of Ferdinand Bol she walked, past the old Heineken brewery and the ever-present queue of tourists outside.

Past the Albert Cuyp, empty for Sunday. Not that she looked.

In the car Vos tried to call.

Marly Kloosterman's unflustered, casual voicemail was all he got.

Bakker had been on to control asking for backup. Two marked cars in the area were directed to the zoo, told to wait for orders.

The traffic was light. The Artis staff car park almost full. From the waste ground came the sound of jaunty reggae. There had to be a couple of hundred people by the water, talking, dancing, drinking, eating. Half in costume, half in summer clothes. It was still warm for the time of year. The place had that Sunday after-noon feel to it: lazy, a little drunk, relaxed.

Vos recalled the dry cold laughter when he'd phoned after the text two nights before and then the sarcastic robotic voice. This was a man who thrived on laziness, who saw his opportunity when others let down their guard. A time like this, he thought as he slammed the Volvo onto a patch of waste ground by the canal.

Two security men were heading over already, yelling at them to move. Bakker came off the phone with her ID and a few choice words. The uniforms were the other side of the zoo, she said. Half a kilometre away.

'Tell them to get to the party,' Vos said. 'And what we're looking for.'

Then they walked towards the crowd by the canal and began to push through the sea of bodies there.

So many people, so many strange costumes. Deafening music and the occasional shriek from the zoo behind.

Not a wolf in sight.

He phoned Marly Kloosterman again and got the same calm recorded message.

Someone was forcing his way through the dancers towards them. A young man in a wide sombrero. He wore large red spectacles, a bright yellow tropical shirt and blue shorts. In his right hand was a plastic cocktail glass with fruit and a straw popping out of the top.

He came and stood next to Bakker, beaming.

'Fancy seeing *you* here!'

Bakker just stared.

'Rik. The butterfly house. Remember? Rik Loderus.'

'Vaguely,' she muttered.

Vos got straight on him, demanding to know who else was at the event from Artis.

Loderus waved his cocktail glass at the crowd.

'Everyone who can get away. We support local charities. Would be wrong if we didn't.' He grinned at Bakker. 'Can I get you a drink or something? If you've got the time maybe a dance . . .'

'For Christ's sake,' she snapped. 'We're looking for someone.'

'Oh.' He seemed disappointed. 'Can I help?'

'Only if you know a man who's wearing a wolf costume.'

He didn't say anything.

'Do you?' Vos demanded.

'Well . . .' He scratched his chin. 'I think maybe . . .'

There was a sudden deafening burst of feedback from the stage.

'Who?' Bakker asked.

'Lucas. Lucas Kramer. He sent out for one specially.' Loderus winked. 'Been behaving a bit funny all week to be honest. I think he's got a date.' He puffed out his cheeks. 'I got a right rollicking for sticking up for Jef Braat after you left. Don't know what that was about. Now . . .' He clapped. 'About that drink—'

Vos grabbed hold of his shirt front. Loderus went quiet, worried.

'Where is he?'

'I don't know.' He looked around. 'Could be anywhere. It's my day off. Can't say I was keen to spend it in the company of my boss.'

'The zoo's open?'

'Course it is. Sunday's busy.' He thought of something. 'But not the butterfly house. They've been doing some rewiring for the heating. We're keeping the public out until tomorrow and . . .'

Vos's phone rang. Kloosterman's number flashed up before he answered. Two steps away to try to get some quiet, he pressed the handset hard to his ear.

Someone in pain, a wordless moan, then a curse.

It was easy to picture things sometimes. Something had swept the phone away, sent it clattering across a hard stone surface. When it came to a stop all he could hear were her weak and distant cries.

Then the frantic barks of happy sea lions.

A 'no entry' poster was stuck to the wall outside the entrance to the butterfly house. Red and white tape attached to poles blocked the way. Vos ducked beneath, Bakker not far behind. The metal door beyond was ajar. He pushed through the thick plastic sheets and peered into the humid jungle ahead.

The air was so oppressive it felt as if they'd been hit by a warm and heavy cloud. Bakker bumped against him, pressed forward by Loderus, who was blinking at the interior, wiping his glasses clean with the edge of his tropical shirt.

Red and yellow wings fluttered around them as if the insects were curious at this intrusion.

'I've got to tell you,' Loderus said, throwing the sombrero to one side. 'This is a big place. A lot more to it than you can see.'

Vos looked around.

'He won't be here. Too obvious.'

The zoo man seemed to have sobered up on the spot. He pointed towards the area they'd visited before.

'That leads into offices and storerooms and all kinds of stuff. It's like a maze.' He put his glasses back on. 'I take it this isn't a social visit?'

'You take it right. Keep behind us,' Vos ordered. 'Stay out of our way. Do as you're told.'

Past the cocoon displays, past a plantation of lush and fleshy bananas, there was a notice that read, 'Private. Keep Out'. Vos elbowed the door open and stared into the gloom ahead.

This was the office they'd seen earlier. A computer was whirring somewhere to the right, the one on which they'd watched Annie Schrijver's awkward performance on TV. Its screen saver cast an eerie sheen across the desks and chairs.

Without being asked Loderus found the light switch. Fluorescent tubes flickered into life. The place was empty but there was something on the ground in front of them: a woman's scarlet scarf.

'Torch,' Vos said and waited until Bakker gave him one. 'Don't touch the light switches again unless I ask for it.'

Beam on the hard grey cement floor, he edged into the facing corridor. The next place was where they'd seen the butterfly collection stored so carefully in the metal cabinets around the walls.

No one.

Loderus led them to a second storeroom. A dead end. Nothing but filing cabinets lining the walls and storage shelves full of equipment and boxes.

They were running out of options.

'She tried to phone me . . .' Vos thought of the brief call. 'I heard an animal. A seal or something. Barking.'

'Not here,' Loderus said. 'There are sea lions in the pool out front. He wouldn't have come in that way. There's just an emergency exit and it's always locked.'

'Where, Rik?' Bakker asked.

He was thinking.

'The pump room next to the pool. There's an access passage the engineers use. Lucas used to go there sometimes. There's a viewing window. He liked to watch them.'

'There,' Vos said.

Back the way they'd come was an opening to a long dark corridor. The torch beam fell on algae, brick and metal conduits dripping condensation. Then, in the distance, a faint light emerged, leaking out from beneath a closed door.

The air was still damp and humid but colder now, with a different feel, a different smell: salt, the sea and something alive.

As he approached there were new sounds too, the gentle murmur of running water. Just audible behind it a pained, too-human whimper.

He ran on, the torch flashing, yelling words that came as second nature.

Police. Over and over her name.

One kick and they were through, into a small and tenebrous chamber, pipes and machinery burbling to the left, on the right a plate glass window shiny with blue-grey light. It was built into the side of the pool outside, two sleek black shapes swimming there, turning in the water, their raucous cries sounding through the pane.

The dark spatter running across the damp glass was as long as an arm, as random as a Rorschach stain.

Heart beating hard against his chest, Vos walked forward, felt his foot slip in something greasy on the floor.

Blood, a winding black trail of it, ran across the grubby slate tiles.

A long lounger was set in front of the glass, tipped back like a barber's chair. He caught sight of a head half-hidden, short hair matted, stained, face turned to one side, mouth agape.

Bakker was on the phone calling for medics.

'Marly,' he whispered.

She lay there, a curled and foetal shape on wrinkled black leather, eyes closed, no sign of life. Clothes torn and so soaked and strewn with blood he could barely believe there was no wound visible.

Vos bent down and took her wrist, feeling for a pulse on the cold damp skin. The rhythm eluded his shaking fingers. Then something pushed past, Loderus racing towards the far wall. Doors there. An emergency exit. The zoo man launched himself hard at the bars, stumbled through when they gave.

Daylight flooded in, leaving Vos blinking. Still she hadn't stirred.

Loderus stood there ashen, hands to his mouth, eyes wide with shock.

Vos bent down, as close to her face as he dared, tried to say something that mattered, to find the words.

Somewhere outside there were voices, taut and high, approaching.

'Pieter,' Bakker said, putting a hand to his shoulder.

'The bastard doped her. Just like the rest. I could have—'

Her hand gripped his arm.

'Will you listen to me? Will you look?'

He followed her pointing finger. A line of gore, thick and

viscous, running into the shadows by the corner. Where it trailed away a body was slumped against the wall, a man half out of a blood-soaked costume, mask off.

Bakker walked over, threw the doors wide open. Lucas Kramer lay there, eyes on nothing at all. Then a sea of bodies swarmed around them, pushing him back until Marly Klooster-man vanished in their midst.

SIX

Monday, midday in Jillian Chandra's office, running through an update on what looked to be the closure of the Sleeping Beauty case, for good this time.

Marly Kloosterman remained under observation in hospital, recovering from an overdose of the date rape drug GHB along with numerous cuts and bruises from a violent and prolonged assault. The worst wound, a shallow knife slash close to her collarbone, had been stitched but would still leave a scar.

While Vos was at the hospital the night team had broken down the front door of Lucas Kramer's terraced home by the Amstel, a few streets away from Artis. The butterfly man was separated. His wife now lived in a holiday property they owned outside Antibes.

They'd got through to her eventually, broken the news, received little in the way of a reaction in return. What she did offer was revealing: Kramer had been a close friend of Vincent de Graaf and a client of his trust company. The two had spent time together. It sounded as if De Graaf's prosecution had brought the marriage to a messy separation, full of unspoken suspicions and threats.

'Would have been nice if Mrs Kramer had told us something,' Bakker grumbled as Vos ran through the morning's findings in Jillian Chandra's office.

'Perhaps she was scared,' he suggested. 'Perhaps she had good reason.'

'If scared people don't talk to us how are we supposed to do our job? And they just keep on being scared.'

Chandra nodded. She seemed to like that idea.

'So Marly Kloosterman's going to be OK?' Van der Berg asked, one eye on Vos as he spoke. 'You spoke to her last night?'

Not then, Vos said. The doctors wouldn't allow it. But he got a call from the hospital at seven thirty that morning and went over there. Thirty minutes was all it took, Bakker making notes and recording the interview on her phone.

'She's doing fine. She was lucky. If she gets her way she'll be home soon.'

Bakker sighed.

'I guess you need to be tough working in Bijlmerbajes. Lucas Kramer picked the wrong woman this time.'

When they'd turned up at the hospital that morning she was already demanding to be discharged. A determined woman, with a professional opinion about her treatment, she seemed mostly recovered. Vos hadn't needed to press at all. She was desperate to say what she could, almost as if she thought it might be too diffi-cult if she waited any longer.

It was a mundane tale as rapes so often were, and she wouldn't look him in the eye as she recounted it. Kramer used to stroll past her boat from time to time. He seemed a friendly man, solitary, always keen to talk about his work in Artis. Earlier in the week they'd fallen into conversation when she was coming back with some shopping. He'd asked her if she was going to the Sunday afternoon party. Kramer seemed good with the hangdog look so, more out of pity than anything, she'd agreed she'd meet him there.

After Vos had left the previous afternoon she'd wandered over and he'd tracked her down. They'd laughed at his wolf's outfit. He'd offered her a drink, talked pleasantly and then offered her a private tour of the butterfly house. A peek behind the scenes.

She'd closed her eyes at that point, angered by the memory, cursing her own stupidity. And Vos had said what he had to: she wasn't the one to blame. Not that it seemed that way to her.

When Kramer invited her to the pump room to view the sea lion pool she was starting to realize she'd been drugged. She still had the will and the strength to resist as he came for her. When he attacked her with the knife she fought back, as hard as she could, kicking, punching. She didn't remember wresting the blade from him. Forensic said it was possible the knife was still in Kramer's hand when it sliced into his neck. He was, the morgue said, half-drunk at the time.

A more obvious case of self-defence it would be hard to find and Vos told her there and then. She'd looked up at him, confused, the bruises turning to yellow, the plasters stained with dried blood.

'I think I killed him, Pieter. I don't remember clearly. It was . . . it was a fight.'

'He had a knife,' Bakker said. 'You were lucky. God knows how many weren't.'

Still the words seemed to inflict a real and physical kind of pain.

Jillian Chandra was barely listening as Vos went through the statement Marly Kloosterman gave from her hospital bed. It was her day off as she'd said twice already. She looked very different. A smart navy jacket, red silk shirt beneath, gold necklace, brown hair down for once. Anxious to get this over with, she listened to him recount the conversation and said, 'Well, at least we don't have another dead woman on our hands.'

Van der Berg raised a finger.

'Actually we don't have any dead women. Not this past week. Just dead men. Damned risky thing to do as well. Attack a woman in a place like that and—'

'The butterfly house was closed,' Bakker interrupted. 'Nobody there to disturb him. Come nightfall he could have done whatever he wanted. Dumped her in the Amstel like they did with the rest, probably. If that panda kid hadn't spotted him and come in. If Marly hadn't managed to drop her phone . . .'

'Date rapists aren't scared to use their own premises,' Chandra added. 'They think it's easy. That the woman won't remember and if she does she'll blame herself.' A scowl and she looked at the office clock. 'Sometimes the way they behave . . . they just bring it on themselves. Then throw the mess in our lap and expect us to fix it. Not that . . .' They were all staring at her. 'Not that I'm suggesting that was the case here.'

'One way of looking at things, I suppose,' Van der Berg replied and went back to his notes.

There was a stash of porn in Kramer's house. A number of photos of young women that would, at some stage, have to be checked against the pictures of past victims in the Sleeping Beauty case. He'd died so quickly they couldn't have saved him even if they'd got there earlier. In the struggle the hunting knife had caught his neck and severed the external carotid artery. Unconscious in thirty seconds or so, dead in a minute or two, Schuurman guessed. Most of the blood they'd first seen on the semi-conscious Marly Kloosterman was Kramer's, not hers.

'I want this tidied up by the time I come back to work tomorrow,' Chandra declared. 'Can we really not get Sanders in court?'

He'd been released the previous night, striding out of the building with a sly smile. Someone must have leaked that to the media. By ten o'clock they were reporting that an earlier suspect in the case had been freed without charge.

'Not unless you want that lawyer throwing writs at us,' Vos said. 'Annie Schrijver's adamant she'll do it if we try to prosecute. Even if we put her on the stand . . .'

She shot him a hard look.

'That's what happens when you turn the damned camera off.'

'And if I hadn't . . . we might never have known.'

'Possibly,' she muttered.

It was, Vos knew, an act. Chandra had abandoned the idea of charging Sanders the moment she heard Annie Schrijver's offer.

Den Hartog was already drafting a statement saying the case was closed with Kramer's death.

'Things could have turned out worse,' she said grudgingly while checking the messages on her phone.

'A lot worse,' Bakker noted. 'Are we keeping you from something, Commissaris?'

'As I've already said, it's my day off. I shouldn't even be here.'

Vos got to his feet and said they needed to tidy up a few loose ends.

'Sit down,' Chandra ordered. 'I haven't finished with you yet.'

Annie Schrijver didn't wake till ten. After that she sat in her mother's flat trying not to look at the photos on the mantelpiece. Memories of a different time back when they were a family, struggling together to keep the market stall alive.

She put off listening to the news until midday. The TV said a man she didn't know was dead. And one she did had been released the previous evening, free as a bird.

No one called. Not the police. Not Rob. She was glad of both. A man had abducted her, saved her, seemed so contrite afterwards that, in her fear and confusion, she'd let him into her life. Later she'd come to believe the two of them had fallen in love. Then, when he'd abandoned her, she'd fought so hard to keep him.

How could you explain that to strangers when it was impossible to explain it to yourself?

Chastened by that thought she walked to the salon round the corner, asked them to change her hair colour to brunette, get rid of the blue streak, give her a new short cut. Maybe the girl who did it recognized her from the TV. Maybe not. It was hard to tell and she didn't want to know.

'Are you all right?' the kid with the scissors asked after a while.

'Yes.' Her voice didn't sound it. 'Why?'

'No reason.'

They always had to talk. This time it was about the coming winter, how cold it would be, how miserable. The girl, who didn't look a day over twenty, was going to escape. Flee south to the Canary Islands and warmer weather, spend the winter clipping the hair of expats there.

'Is it easy?' Annie asked.

'What?'

'Just going like that.'

The girl stopped cutting and looked at her in the mirror.

'You mean you've never done it?'

'Not on my own.'

'You're not on your own. You meet people.'

Annie didn't speak and she could see what the kid was thinking: you're no good at that, are you?

'Can't beat it,' she said, suddenly animated. 'Out every night, the drink's so cheap. Late as you like and no one moans. Boys if you're bothered. And the best thing is . . . a week later they're gone. Don't ever need to see them again.'

She had dark hair shaved on one side. Tattoos and piercings. At that moment Annie Schrijver felt old, could see the gap between them.

'No one minds?' Annie asked. 'What about your mum and dad?'

The answer came automatically.

'Glad to see the back of me. Living at home. On top of each other. I do what I like. Nobody owns me. Back here in April. In this . . .' She looked around to make sure no one heard. 'This dump if I can't find somewhere better. Wouldn't mind the money to get a place of my own though.'

'Freedom,' Annie whispered.

The scissors clipped, the girl nodded at her.

'You bet. Nobody's putting any chains on me.'

No need, Annie thought, not when you put them on yourself so easily. You could run halfway across the world if you liked. But if the thing you were fleeing still lived inside . . .

'Be careful,' was all she said and something seemed to change then. The kid just got on with her hair. Not another word until a simple thanks when Annie paid. It was a conversation in a hair salon. Words by rote. No one was listening on either side.

Back in the street, without the golden locks that had defined her as the flower girl of the Albert Cuyp, she could feel a stiff breeze swirling round as she wandered back towards the market. In a travel agency along the way there were escape routes everywhere: cheap tickets to Spain and Italy, Florida and the Caribbean. She had enough money in the bank to get her there, keep her for a few weeks while she searched for work and company.

There was a shade of winter in the sky, the wind, her heart. Soon the city would be cold and grey, the days so short you sometimes wondered where they'd gone. It would be so easy to take flight and chase the sun hoping that somewhere different she'd find the elusive thing called peace.

Annie Schrijver looked at all the photos in the window and wondered.

Marly Kloosterman knew doctors made the worst patients. She understood her condition only too well after demanding to see the charts. GHB was only dangerous if the dose was massive, which was not the case. The wounds were minor. The few stitches she could handle herself.

The registrar in the long white coat looked no more than twenty-five. If anyone was going to give lectures here it wouldn't be him.

'We're not in the habit of allowing patients to decide their own treatment,' he said quietly. 'Whoever they are.'

We.

In that one word, the quiet and faint-hearted decision not to place the decision on himself, he'd lost the battle before it had even begun.

She smiled at him and thought he softened a little with that.

'You're busy. I'm not. I've probably dealt with a lot more stitches than you have. The things you see in prison . . .'

'Same blood. Same bone. Same skin.'

She tapped a finger on her hospital gown.

'My blood, my bone, my skin.' The smile weakened. 'My choice if I want to discharge myself. Which I do. In an hour or so after I've made some phone calls. Send in someone with the waivers and I'll sign them. But thanks for thinking of me all the same.'

He didn't move.

'What difference would one more night here make? You've got your own room. The food's not so bad—'

'I want to go home. I need to be surrounded by the things . . . the things I own.'

He stood there in silence as if his presence alone was enough to change her mind.

Then finally he muttered, 'On your head be it.'

That morning she'd asked one of the uniform officers in the wing to go to her houseboat and get some new clothes. They'd found her mobile in the Artis pump room where it had skittered across the floor after she hit Vos's number. Lucas Kramer's blood still stained the screen. It came off easily with a medical wipe.

The director at Bijlmerbajes had been briefed already. He was all sympathy and readily cleared her for two weeks' leave.

More calls then. Practical ones. A taxi home. People who needed to know.

One more task she couldn't avoid.

He'd still be busy, she was sure. And more . . . she didn't want to talk to him at that moment. It would be easier, kinder, though somewhat craven, to say what was needed in a more impersonal way.

Jillian Chandra checked her watch again, brushed the sleeve of her jacket, looked at Vos and said, 'I need someone's head for all this. Bakker's too junior and besides she shows some promise. So I'll make it yours.'

'Commissaris . . .' Vos began.

Before he could get any further Bakker leapt in.

'What the hell are you talking about? If it wasn't for Pieter this case would still be open. You'd have Annie Schrijver's lawyer at your throat as well.'

'Loyalty,' Chandra said with a sigh. 'So much of it around here. Like dust in the corridors nobody's swept up. Touching in a nostalgic way. Unnecessary and unwanted too. We live in different times.'

Bakker was starting to fume.

'Laura . . .' Vos said. 'Best you go back to the office.'

She sat upright like a headstrong child.

'Screw that. I want to hear this.'

'Very well,' Chandra agreed. 'Let's keep it short. Grateful as I am that the mess you failed to clear up four years ago now appears over, the time has come for some frank speaking. You've persistently disobeyed my orders, Vos. Wilfully so. Time and again you listen to what I say then do the very opposite.'

'Only when the case demanded it,' he pointed out.

She didn't take that well.

'I'm going to give you till tomorrow to decide what happens next. There are two choices. I can bump you down to uniform somewhere a long way from Marnixstraat. Community relations perhaps. I can imagine you in a customer-facing role. People do seem to find you engaging.' She took a long breath. 'Alternatively

I can start disciplinary proceedings. Take your pick. You've got tonight to think about it. I'd recommend you stay sober to do that. Tomorrow—'

Bakker jabbed a finger in Chandra's direction.

'You're just trying to keep the flak away from here.'

'Not at all. I have all the evidence I need.'

Chandra asked Van der Berg to read out the list of infractions she could put before a panel. He reached for his notebook, flipped idly through the pages and detailed them one by one. It took a while.

'That's enough for me to suspend you with immediate effect,' she said when the litany of transgressions was over. 'They'll dismiss you in short order not long afterwards. Trust me. I know how these things work.'

Vos didn't doubt that last part. Then Van der Berg leaned forward and said, 'There is more.'

'Thanks, Dirk,' Bakker hissed at him. 'Good to know who your friends are.'

Chandra appeared thrown by this.

'What do you mean, there's more?'

He fumbled in the pocket of his old grey jacket and retrieved the phone.

'Well, you told me to keep track of everything.'

He pressed the screen and then did something to the volume. A voice, Chandra's, came out of the speaker, loud and angry.

'I want Vos brought into line. I want you to help me put him there. If you don't . . .'

Van der Berg brandished the phone and said, 'I've got the answer to that too. It wasn't nice. How about this one?'

The recorded voice returned.

'Cut it out, Schuurman. I've got Vos's name on the list already. Don't make me add yours.'

'That I recorded on Friday,' he explained. 'Along with the time and place of course.'

'You have a *list*?' Vos wondered, half-amused.

'Lists are very fashionable in management circles,' Van der Berg explained. 'Or so I gather.'

Another press on the screen.

'Yesterday . . .'

Again the tinny voice.

'How many chances does he need? So he's popular. All the better. Don't worry. I won't sack him unless he really asks for it. A job somewhere else. In uniform. Out of my hair. Out of your way.'

Van der Berg leaned forward and said, 'That is you, Commissaris. We both know it. I was there. I believe we have policies on bullying and victimization. Perhaps you wrote them in Zoetermeer for all I know.' He scowled. 'Personally I can't stand all that bullshit. I'd rather be getting on with the job. But as you said . . . these are different times.'

Chandra stared at him, stony-faced.

'There are others,' he added. 'Quite a few considering I haven't been following you around this place very long. But I can see it's your day off and you must have an appointment somewhere.'

'You had the temerity to tape me? Without my knowledge?'

'My instructions were to keep a thorough record. So I did. If you want to make this official, I'll have to hand over all the material I've got. Notes.' He held up the phone. 'Recordings.' A brief smile. 'Personal observations from an officer who's worked here a very long time. So long you gave me that nice medal only last week.'

Vos looked at his watch and said he needed to get back to the office.

'I assume,' he added, 'I can have Detective Van der Berg back on my team now?'

'He was never off it, was he?' Chandra snapped.

She leaned back in her chair and looked out of the window at the street beyond, an officious, insecure, lonely woman, Vos thought. No less dangerous for that. More so in all probability.

Then she began to shake with slow, quiet laughter.

It didn't last long and perhaps it was forced. They weren't sure and Vos wondered if Jillian Chandra knew herself.

'Very well,' she said with a sudden clap of her hands. 'You caught me in a good mood. The status quo rules for now. We carry on as we are. I am learning, you know.' The smile vanished in an instant. 'Lots of things. You can go. All of you.'

Relieved, the three of them got up.

'Oh,' she added. 'Send Den Hartog in here. I need a word.'

Back in the office Van der Berg went to his old desk and told the young detective there to beat it. A brief complaint followed about how tidy everything looked and then he sat down.

Bakker came over and gave him a hug and a quick kiss on his bristly cheek.

'Sneaky bastard. Do you think she has a date? She looks nice when she wants—'

'The private life of Jillian Chandra is a mystery I do not wish to contemplate,' he answered. 'And if I ever hear the phrase customer-facing in this place again . . .' He opened up his inbox and swore at the mountain of messages there. 'Sometimes I think the world's just going backwards.'

One of the junior officers had started unpinning the photos of De Graaf's victims from the walls. Vos told her to leave them for now.

'This is a ceasefire, Pieter,' Van der Berg told him. 'Not a sudden and unexpected outbreak of peace. You do know that?'

'So be it.' He couldn't stop staring the photos. 'Peace can be very boring.'

There was one obvious gap in the story. Nola van Veen, it seemed, had slipped out of the station before anyone had taken her statement. When the night team chased later they found that the VU had no record of any student of that name. The address she'd provided was fake. It was all an act. A performance. A very good one. Whoever the panda called Li Li was in real life . . . she was gone.

'Something's bothering you,' Van der Berg added. 'And I don't think it's just seeing our beloved leader in all her finery.'

'Lots of things.'

'Such as?' Bakker asked.

He did his best to tell them. Most of the story appeared straightforward. Lucas Kramer may well have wanted to murder the upstart American Greg Launceston and his old sidekick Jef Braat for trying to revive the Sleeping Beauty game. Self-interest came into play there. Kramer had escaped the notice of the police four years before. If Braat began putting himself about again perhaps he'd expose others.

'But then . . .'

Vos fell silent.

'Why come for you?' Van der Berg asked.

'For starters.'

Bakker slapped her forehead and let out a low wail.

'God, you two drive me nuts. We know it was him with De Graaf. We know what kind of bastard he was. He tried to kill Marly, for pity's sake. What else do you need?'

'Reasons? Motives?' Vos said. 'Why kidnap Sam? Send me out to Zorgvlied to find them? Why taunt me with those messages?'

She thought about it.

'Because you put Vincent de Graaf away in the first place. He was . . . pissed off with you.' An idea. 'Maybe De Graaf told him you and Marly were close.'

The two men waited for more.

'All right,' Bakker cried. 'Because he wanted to leave that hat Jef Braat had nicked for him. So if we ruled out Braat we'd think Rob Sanders arranged it all.'

'There had to be two hats,' Vos pointed out.

'Why?'

Van der Berg rolled his eyes and said, 'Laura, Laura. Think about it. Kramer knows Jef Braat hates Sanders. So he tells Braat to get him something that belongs to the guy. Jordi Hoogland obliges with the hat out of nothing but spite. Braat can leave it with a victim and send us chasing after Sanders. He doesn't know he's the next one for the chop.'

She nodded.

'And?'

'If Kramer had the thing on outside the Drie Vaten his DNA would be there too. Can't fool a hat band. So he must have worn his own and dropped the Sanders one when he left. Kept it in a bag maybe. Wake up please.'

'Dirk. You've no idea how much I've missed you.'

'And,' Vos added, 'we didn't find a hat like it in Kramer's house.'

'Well, I don't know! You tell me.'

'Can't,' he admitted. 'I'm buying beers later. The usual place. Attendance is mandatory. It may well run into unpaid overtime.'

A door slammed. Down the corridor Den Hartog, the PR man recently imported from Zoetermeer, was stomping towards the lift, face red and furious, his hands full of filing boxes, a black bag over his arm. Chandra was watching him go, amused. One wave in his direction and then she checked her watch and went for the stairs.

'I think the commissaris has found her sacrificial victim,' Bakker said.

'PR men,' Van der Berg grumbled. 'How will we ever manage without them?'

The junior asked if she could remove the pictures of the secret basement in the Zuidas. Vos walked over and took another look.

They joined him by the close-ups of De Graaf's right arm. All the stab marks from a cannula needle. On some of the pictures the morgue had outlined the wounds and bruises with blue ink. Seventeen in all.

'There's that too,' Vos said. 'You'd think a man who can pin butterflies to a piece of card might have a more delicate touch.'

Along the wall were pictures of the tattoos on the shoulders of the American Launceston and Jef Braat. The same words Braat and his accomplices had left inked roughly into the skin of their female victims: *Sleep Baby Sleep.*

Now on two men.

Back at the computer the message notification was blinking.

'It's from Marly,' Vos murmured. 'Looks like she's discharged herself. And . . .'

He stopped. Puzzled. The subject line of the latest read, 'Sorry to break it this way but . . .'

Van der Berg caught the mood, coughed then said maybe he and Laura could go to the canteen for a coffee.

'Do that,' Vos told him, barely listening.

There was a crowd around the market stall. It had been a long time since she'd seen that. Her father had done what he'd promised: split the business in two. On one side the Syrian was busily selling flowers and bouquets. On the other his wife stood behind a wooden table brought out from the courtyard. Pastries and sauces were arrayed in front of her, soup and stews were bubbling away in urns.

Lia, the little girl, was perched on the counter behind, taking money while her mother bagged up food in takeaway containers. Good idea to have the kid there, Annie thought. Great marketing. But the authorities would be along at some stage and she'd surely have to go to school. Which, when she thought of it, was doubtless what Adnan and Mariam wanted.

Unnoticed by the throng around the stall Annie Schrijver walked into the shop and found herself next to her old bedroom.

The door was open. A brightly coloured plastic trike was parked by some cardboard boxes full of clothes. Annie's old toys were strewn on the threadbare carpet beside it. She couldn't forget that last time she'd lured Rob Sanders here. The desperate passion. The fight with Jordi Hoogland afterwards. She'd never come back to this place. It belonged to a family who needed it more.

Back in the hallway her mother was standing in front of a portable gas hob, stirring pots bubbling away over low blue flames.

'Mum,' she said and kissed her on the cheek.

Nina looked up and pulled a face.

'Oh, my God. Annie! What have you done?'

'This smells great.'

She got a spoon and dipped it into one of the pots. Nina jokily pretended to slap her hand, the way she did when Annie was tiny, begging for food in the kitchen.

They both laughed at that. It was lamb, she guessed, in a thick brown sauce that tasted of pomegranates.

'Had a haircut, that's all. I decided I was sick of Goldilocks. She kept running into too many bears. That tastes great.'

'It does,' Nina agreed and still couldn't stop staring. 'We're going to run out. Didn't make enough. Your hair looks . . . good. Different.' A pause and then, 'Older.'

'Where's Dad?'

A nod towards the courtyard.

'Out back dealing with some estate agent who wanted to sell the place. Had an offer too apparently. But . . .' She turned down the heat. A long day ahead. 'Where would we go? What would we do? We can make a go of it with Adnan and Mariam's help. Well, maybe. At least we've got to try.'

Then, very carefully, she added, 'It's OK. We know you don't want to be a part of it. We understand. Maybe over the years we got too close to one another. Like your dad says. We forgot to look outside.'

319

Annie nodded and walked to the storeroom. Her father was waving goodbye to a smartly dressed woman who was carrying a couple of plastic food containers.

'There,' Schrijver said, when she was gone. 'Decisions made. I sent her off with some of the food. Free sample. You're never going to get an estate agent turning down something they don't have to pay for. I reckon we could drum up a bit of business that way. Word of mouth.'

He looked at her finally and started to say something.

'I just had a haircut, Dad. Don't start.'

'I wasn't going to. It's your hair. Besides . . . it looks good.'

'Thanks.'

'You've heard the news? About that man from the zoo?'

'Yeah.'

He frowned. She wondered if he was going to start up about Sanders but instead he said, 'I guess that means it's done with, then. Thank God for that.'

Done with. Once she'd have got mad at the easy way he dismissed it all. Not now. He was a man. Not bright, not stupid. Somewhere in between like most.

'Anyway.' He looked at his watch. 'I'm sorry, love. I can't talk. Now Jordi Hoogland's gone I've got Adnan out there shifting flowers faster than your granddad managed in the old days. I need to fetch some more for tomorrow and do the deliveries. Haven't had time to catch up with the orders on the computer. Got to take the van—'

'I'll do it,' she said.

'That's nice. But you don't have to. Not after—'

'I want to. I can stay with Mum for a while longer. Help out here. Do what you want.'

She looked around the grubby storeroom. When winter came it was freezing and she'd be tapping on the computer in the same woolly half-finger gloves she used on the stall. There were worse things.

'This place has got a buzz about it again. Can't go now. I want to see.'

'Well.' He scratched his cheek. A habit, a tic of his. One of those things the people you loved did so often you never noticed usually. 'If you want.'

'You can give me the van keys and the delivery run. Or let me loose on the computer. You choose.'

He took her in his arms and kissed her, stroked the short, spiky hair, a colour that was new.

'I'll do the van,' Bert Schrijver said. 'You stay here. As long as you want. We'll make this right.'

We'll try, she thought.

Pieter.

This is the way of the faint of heart. In the circumstances I hope you'll forgive me.

By the time you read this I'll be home. I should be thinking of that creature from the zoo. I should be cursing my own stupidity for falling for such a stupid trick. And full of guilt for what happened. I've never hurt anyone before. Never dreamed it possible. The fact I can barely remember it as anything more than a bad dream should make a difference. Should . . .

Mostly though I'm not thinking of any of that. I'm thinking of you. A kind and gentle man who's doubtless wondering what you can do to help.

This: nothing. We need room to breathe. I cannot, must not see you now. For shame, for fear, for . . . whatever stupid reason I can invent. It doesn't matter. If there are police conversations to be had I'll speak to Laura. Anyone you choose. Except you.

Maybe we're cowards, dithering at the threshold. I don't know. This I do. We're damaged, both of us, with broken lives that have left deeper scars than either of us appreciate.

321

Shattered pieces do not mend each other. Now, through no fault but my own, I've fresh wounds to heal.

I need time to do that, back with my family, away from the city. Away from you. I need your understanding and one final kindness: to let me seek this on my own.

One day, if you still wish it, I'll call. But I don't know when and if I do I'll understand completely if you feel no need to listen. I owe you so much. You owe me nothing. Remember that.

With all my fondest love.

Marly

'One day,' he whispered and wondered how he felt.

Surprised. Disappointed. Hurt. Bemused. They hadn't dithered on the threshold entirely. A year or so before, the two of them a little foolish and full of drink, she'd crossed the gangplank of his houseboat, Sam on the other side wagging his tail. Looking back, he realized they'd gone through the preliminary confessions: shattered relationships they blamed so easily on work. Then, as if these two agonies cancelled each other out, spent a single night together with an awkward parting afterwards.

It was the resurrection of the Sleeping Beauty case that had brought her back. Living on a houseboat just like him, not far from Artis, a decision that might have cost her everything.

The earlier message she'd sent him, the one with the pictures of her boat from the article in the paper, was above this strangely lyrical farewell. Uncomfortable that he wanted to know more, to peer inside her life and appreciate what seemed lost, he opened it again. Before he'd only seen the photos on the tiny screen of his phone. On the computer he could appreciate why *Het Parool* had wanted to splash her in colour on its weekend pages. Relaxed, ready for the camera, on her own territory, dressed for the shoot, she was elegant, composed, certain of herself. Everything he wasn't.

The boat seemed more like a modern and elegant apartment. Tasteful furniture, abstract paintings on the freshly painted timber walls. A view out to the canal from the French windows he'd seen but never entered. And then, one tantalizing last picture, a shot the photographer must have coaxed out of her.

She was sitting cross-legged on the double bed, laughing, blue eyes shining, arms around the knees of her silk pyjamas, short fair hair ruffled and spiky as if straight from sleep. There was a soft toy on the pillow. A lion it looked like. And a line of photos on the bedside cabinet.

Family. They'd never talked about that in any detail. Vos zoomed in to see her face more clearly. She had crow's feet around her eyes, perhaps from the smile. Perhaps from something else. An air of melancholy seemed to hang around her and she'd doubtless say the same for him. Perhaps that had drawn them together, like attracting like.

He shifted his attention to the pictures by the neat silk pillow, aware that this was prurient even if half of Amsterdam must have seen the glossy spread.

In a silver frame stood a posed shot of a young woman in university graduation robes: a long black cloak, white collar. She was holding her mortar-board cap, grinning, looking ready to launch it into the air. A torn-off yellow note was stuck to the glass. He could just make out the writing there: *We will always love you, Hanna. Always.*

Next to that . . .

Vos looked, blinked, tried to clear his thoughts.

A long minute later he called down to forensic. Aisha Refai was on duty. He asked if they'd run a detailed check on the half-full bottle of spritz found in Lucas Kramer's costume pocket. They'd already established it contained GHB, she said. More than that . . . she'd need to check.

Then he got the number for the Amstelpark administration office. The woman on the other end didn't sound helpful to begin

323

with and turned even more surly when he said he was from the police.

'I need some information on the driver who was working the kid's train on Thursday afternoon,' he said.

'Why?'

'It's just routine. He's worked with you a long time, hasn't he?'

'What makes you say that?'

'He said he saw me there with my daughter years ago.'

'You got that wrong. Toine Brouwer's a volunteer. Does the odd afternoon. Maybe started here a month or so ago. A nice man.'

'Is he working now?'

'This isn't an odd afternoon.'

'I need his address.'

She growled down the line.

'I don't know who you are, friend. Anyone can say they're from the police. I've no idea where he lives and even if I did I wouldn't tell you.'

'A phone number then.'

The line went dead.

Two quick searches and the fog was starting to clear.

Aisha Refai rang back with the analysis report of the drinks bottle.

'Absolutely dripping with GHB. Would have knocked out an elephant. Is that what you wanted to know?'

'Kind of.' He kept thinking. 'You mean it was more than normal?'

'I'm not sure how you'd define normal for something like this. Wait a moment.'

He heard the phone go down and then a distant but clear curse.

'Yuk,' she said when she came back. He could hear her spitting. 'You can't even taste the Campari and that's saying something.'

'I didn't ask you to try it, Aisha.'

'I know. It was just a drop. Sometimes it's easier to take the direct route. You'd need to be seriously drunk not to notice the junk in that. I guess they are usually. Can I go and find some mouthwash now please?'

Van der Berg was still in the canteen with Bakker.

'Is it early beer time?' he asked when Vos called.

'No. I need you back here. Both of you.'

The two of them listened as Vos told them what he wanted.

'There's a man called Toine Brouwer who drives the train part-time at the Amstelpark. I think he killed Launceston and Braat, not Lucas Kramer. Abducted Annie Schrijver too, did his best to make sure she didn't die.'

Van der Berg started clattering the keys of his computer straight away. Bakker, always the one to ask questions, tugged her red hair and didn't move.

'I'm being slow here. It was Kramer working with De Graaf. He spiked Marly's drink and attacked her, for God's sake.'

'It was Kramer with De Graaf,' Vos agreed. He got up and picked the photo off the wall. A young woman in her late twenties, eyes closed, mouth open, saliva dripping from the corner. One of the sleepers. 'I think this is Toine Brouwer's daughter. Hanna. She survived Vincent de Graaf and his friends. For a while.'

He showed them the cutting he'd found online. It was from the *Leidsch Dagblad*, the local newspaper in Leiden. The suicide of a postgraduate student at the university there. Two portraits ran alongside the piece, next to a shot of the tower block from which she'd jumped. The first must have been from the graduation ceremony. She looked young, happy, elated as she looked into the lens. The second, taken a week before her death, was very different. Face haggard, eyes staring, cheeks hollow, a shaky, insecure grin. The picture was a mug shot taken after she was arrested following a hysterical outburst at Leiden police headquarters.

'According to the paper she was a bright postgrad student. Won prizes. Then went to pieces on hard drugs.'

Van der Berg came off the computer.

'There's nothing in criminal records for that name. I can try the news archives. Just out of interest how did you . . . ?'

'Let's find him first. Explanations later.'

'Leiden, Leiden, Leiden,' Bakker muttered, dashing to her desk.

Vos wasn't listening. Something Marly had said off the cuff when he'd called her on Saturday came back to him. Perhaps with her guard down.

I've got a bit of police blood in me too. But that's a story for another time.

'Maybe he's a police officer. Let's try the internal directories. I'll take the present. You . . .'

Van der Berg didn't need to be told. He set about accessing the historic records.

Ten minutes later Bakker was still on the phone and Vos was getting nowhere. Then there was a groan from Van der Berg's direction.

'Looks like you're right. Toine Brouwer's one of us. Or was. This has to be him.'

On his screen was an article from the internal police news magazine the year before. It was brief and recorded the award of a bravery medal to an undercover officer referred to as AB. Antoine Brouwer, he guessed.

'They kept his full name out of it but I cross-referenced with the force retirement records from that quarter. He was undercover drugs squad in Rotterdam. According to the papers there was a shootout during a raid down the docks. He got a bullet in him. Lucky to get out alive. Had to take retirement.'

He scrolled through some more pages.

'You need some balls to work that beat. I wouldn't want to mess with a guy like that. The only address on the system is old, in Rotterdam. Not much use. Sorry.'

Bakker came back clutching her notebook.

'How do we know all this?' she asked. 'How does a man from Rotterdam we've never heard of suddenly become prime suspect?'

Laura Bakker to a T, Vos thought. Come straight out and ask.

'Because Marly Kloosterman's his daughter. Hanna Brouwer's sister. That's her married name.'

They stared at him in silence.

'This has been about revenge from the start. Lucas Kramer was the last man standing. She must have offered herself as bait. When he lured her into the zoo—'

'Pieter,' Bakker interrupted. 'Are you going daft? He doped Marly. We found that bottle in his pocket. There was that date rape drug in there. The hospital—'

'She took it herself. Timed it before she killed him. Then she added more to his bottle. Marly didn't know whether he was going to try to dope her or not. So she had to make sure. Turns out he had it in there too. So it was a double dose. Undrinkable. Aisha tried.'

She placed her notes on the table and said, 'Where did Commissaris Chandra go, Dirk?'

He peered at her, baffled.

'What kind of question is that? I don't know. A date maybe. You saw how she was dressed.'

'We really need to find her,' Bakker told them.

She'd been on the phone to Leiden about the dead girl. The case was well known in the station. Hanna Brouwer had been coming into the station, distressed, for weeks trying to complain about a sexual assault. But she was so out of it on drugs the acting commissaris refused to take her seriously.

'That was when Jillian Chandra was there on secondment

from Zoetermeer. Acting commissaris,' Bakker went on. 'It was her decision. Wasn't hard getting the story out of the locals. They wanted to take up the case. Chandra refused to let them. She said they weren't there to waste their time on delusional dope heads.'

'So,' Van der Berg said, reaching for his phone, 'we didn't just get that poor bastard shot on duty. We ignored his little girl when she was going off the rails too. Wonderful.'

Chandra's number came back with a personal voicemail: *leave a message.*

'Do we have any idea where she's gone?' Vos asked.

Van der Berg grimaced.

'If she's not at home? Single woman. Stranger in Amsterdam. No friends. Needle, meet haystack.'

'Get on it,' Vos ordered. 'We're going looking.'

They'd arranged to meet in a restaurant called Klein Kalfje on a sleepy stretch of the river beyond the Amstelpark. The place was empty on this quiet weekday. It was just about warm enough to sit at an outside table by the water's edge. Jillian Chandra knew central Amsterdam well enough but this part of the city was new to her: remote, rural, deserted. Lush fields stretched away from the Amstel, cattle and sheep grazing on thick meadow. The occasional jogger puffed and panted up the quiet lane by the river. A fisherman was bent over his rod, watched by bored wildfowl and dozing cows. Marnixstraat with its traffic and its worries was just four kilometres away. But here she might have been in the countryside, away from all those cares.

His name, he said, was Pieter. That was all. Nothing like the awkward, slippery Vos she had to work with, or so she hoped. When she'd answered his message on the dating app – a middle-aged, recently retired police officer looking for company – they had, she felt, hit it off from the very beginning.

She didn't even mind when he asked for a photo. They all did and often that was the end of things. But not this one. He'd come back keen and said she looked . . . nice. After that they'd chatted and he'd offered to send her his picture too. Something about the shy way he'd said it made her say no. They were adults, surely able to meet one another, have a congenial lunch and decide afterwards whether it was worth pursuing the matter further.

Chandra had started using dating apps in Zoetermeer and knew her way around them. It was like a game, a tease, hide and seek, kiss but never tell. Most of the men – she assumed they *were* men – she corresponded with were time wasters. Only a few she met, occasionally checking them out surreptitiously against criminal records first. Very rarely she'd gone back to his apartment or hotel, slept with someone there and then. Got it over with, knowing she'd never see him again.

This one sounded different. So easy-going she'd never asked for enough details to check him out at all.

He wasn't there when she turned up in a taxi from Marnixstraat. She didn't want to take the unmarked saloon that came with the job. There were footprints that way. If things worked out . . . if there was the possibility of a permanent relationship, who knew?

That was always the distant promise, not that she was sure she wanted it at all. Brief intimacy was easy. A longer closeness required commitment, dedication, patience. A selflessness she found difficult, a distraction from the greater prize: work, promotion, the challenges that lay ahead. From impoverished immigrant's daughter to commissaris in Amsterdam was a leap beyond her imagination even five years before. Who knew where the next decade might take her?

The waiter came and made small talk about how slow the day was, how lovely the river. There were boats here, some for pleasure, a few residential. The place wasn't far from the point where, the previous Thursday, they'd swung Jef Braat's van from the water and his corpse had sent her screaming into the dark. An unpleasant memory she'd already begun to thrust aside. The Sleeping Beauty case was closed at last. She would take the lion's share of the credit. Vos could be contained until he stepped out of line once more. Which would happen, she was sure of that. It was in the man's nature to go his own way, hoping the results would excuse him in the end.

A time would come . . .

'Your order?' the waiter asked.

A glass of water, she said. For now.

Ten minutes later she saw him loping along the path. A tall, muscular man, late fifties she guessed, older than she'd hoped. He was wearing a tweed sports jacket, grey trousers and brown shoes, the colours clashing somewhat. A bachelor's outfit. He had a broad, handsome face, short silver hair, very closely shaven as if he'd taken a razor to it only minutes before. The fact he'd walked here suggested he lived nearby. Perhaps an invitation would be forthcoming. And perhaps she'd accept it readily. She was a stranger in Amsterdam, and days off could be long and empty.

'Jillian,' he said, taking her hand.

He had a firm, warm touch and an astute, fixed gaze.

'I am very bad at these assignations,' he confessed. 'In fact.' A comical grimace. 'This is my very first.' He took a seat and looked at the river as he spoke. 'I'm nervous, you see. A complete virgin in these things. What must you think of me?'

'I don't know. That's why we're here.'

He grimaced and clutched at his right leg.

'You're hurt.'

'Just an old wound. A physical thing. There are worse.'

In their brief exchanges she'd never asked much. Divorced. A bachelor. Widowed. The last, she guessed. He seemed a strong, fit man, active probably, but he had that worn-down look about him. As if there were cares that never went away.

'First of all . . .' He took out his phone and made a show of turning it off. 'Enough of this. You don't know a person through one of these things.'

'No,' she agreed. 'You meet them.'

His eyes were incisive and on her then. She got the message, took out her own phone and turned that off too.

Still no sign of the waiter. He asked her if she knew what she wanted.

Something light. Shrimp croquettes with mayonnaise and fried parsley.

He nodded.

'A glass of white wine, I suggest. They have a Marsanne. Wonderful. Normally it only comes by the bottle. But . . .' He tapped his nose and winked. 'I have my ways. If you like it there's always more . . .'

'That would be good,' she said, amused by this man, touched by the air of sadness about him too. It would be an interesting lunch.

'I'll go inside and get it,' he said. 'Easier that way.'

Vos drove. As they crossed the river Van der Berg called. Chandra was still untraceable, phone off, apartment empty, car still in the garage, not a soul who knew her in Amsterdam, no one to talk to, no one to ask. Brouwer's old colleagues in Rotterdam said he'd retired to a place in the country after he got out of hospital. No one knew where. Divorced years before. His wife couldn't take the strain of being married to an undercover officer incapable of leading a normal life. No one had a mobile. The man had had few friends to speak of inside the police, none after he left injured and bitter.

'They say he was quite a guy. Got inside one of the Rotterdam rings. As far as most people down there knew he *was* a criminal. Deep cover. You know what I'm saying, don't you?'

'We'll be careful. Don't worry.'

A long pause then, 'I think you should have armed backup. I can send one. If—'

'I'll deal with it,' Vos said and ended the call.

Bakker was listening as always.

'Maybe Dirk's got a point,' she said and checked her own weapon. As usual Vos was unarmed.

'Let's find him first,' he said and parked a little way along from the tidy green houseboat in the placid waters of the canal.

They could just make out someone beyond the French windows.

Vos strode up and called for one uniform patrol car to wait outside until they were summoned. Then he stepped across the gangplank, remembering the pleasant, awkward conversation they'd enjoyed here only the day before.

She was inside with her back to him. Jeans and a jacket, packing a small suitcase on the table by the kitchen range.

Vos slid open the doors and walked straight in. She turned then, looked surprised. Offended. Her face was swollen, the cuts and bruises obvious.

'Pieter. I'm sorry. I thought I said—'

'Going somewhere, Marly?' Bakker asked, gun out low, checking the cabin to her right. 'And you just out of hospital?'

'Paris,' she answered, watching her wide-eyed. 'My cousin lives there. She's in one of the theatre companies. I thought I'd spend some time with her. I don't understand—'

'Is she good at playing pandas by any chance?' Vos wondered.

She shook her head.

'What on earth are you talking about?'

From her face he could see: she knew.

'I'm talking about timing. About how a young woman sent me out to Zorgvlied. And yesterday dispatched me to Artis, to you.'

No answer.

He walked into the bedroom, found the photos, brought them back. A man in a striped train driver's hat. Close up now he looked as if he was pretending to be happy, hiding something, forcing the smile. And the other photo of the happy young woman.

Vos threw the pictures on the table in front of her.

'I'm talking about your sister, Hanna. Your father. When we went to the Amstelpark he was there, driving the train. Convenient place to be, I guess. He said he saw me there with my daughter when she was little.'

'Pieter . . .'

He held up a hand as she approached.

'Hear me out. I know that was a lie. Ten, fifteen years ago he was in the police. He didn't come to Amsterdam until a few weeks ago. When he was getting ready to find the people he blamed for Hanna. To kill them. With you.'

She sat down. Bakker returned and declared the boat empty apart from the three of them, no sign of another visitor at all.

'You saw that picture in my place,' he added. 'You told him about it.'

She picked up the photo of him and peered at it.

'What a clever man you are. When it comes to catching people like me.'

Vos couldn't think of a thing to say.

'My dad lost a daughter. I lost a sister. A husband too.' She scowled. 'He couldn't take it when I went . . . off the rails for a while. Hanna was my blood. He wasn't.'

'Where's your father?' Vos asked. 'This is important. Before he does any more harm.'

'Harm?' She was on her feet again. All the small cuts and bruises on her neck, her arms, her fingers, the short line of stitches at her neck seemed to grow larger with her anger. It must have been a fierce struggle though not the one they'd been led to believe. Lucas Kramer was the one fighting for his life, not her, and a doctor surely knew where to find that fatal artery. 'It was justice. The thing you were supposed to deliver and didn't.'

'Which is why you picked me—'

'I'm sorry I screwed with your feelings. Honestly.'

The patrol car had turned up outside, two uniform officers were climbing out. He asked Bakker to tell them to wait there until he called.

They were alone together in a place he'd been thinking about a lot, not that he belonged here.

'How did you know?' she wondered.

He held up his phone and showed her the email, the photo from *Het Parool*. A bed. A line of family pictures.

She rolled back her head and sighed.

'God, it's always your emotions that kill you in the end, isn't it? I'm a fool. I so . . . want . . .' Her eyes were on him. 'Well. No point now . . .'

The words drifted away. He found the message she'd sent that morning and read from it, 'Shattered pieces do not mend each other.'

'Nothing ever puts us back together, does it?' she said. 'It's just a forlorn hope.'

She walked to a black lacquer set of drawers by the TV. Bakker slipped in to listen, got there first, checked it.

Letters, bills, magazines. Marly Kloosterman waited until she was allowed to touch things. Then she retrieved a plastic folder with what looked like a handwritten letter inside.

'There's something you need to see.'

He was funny. He was wry. An engaging man, more interested in her own opinions than his. As for the police . . . he shrugged, frowned and said he'd been a humble traffic officer, handing out speeding fines, clearing up after accidents, never seeking advancement or anything different. When she pressed him for a reason the smile vanished and he said, simply, there were reasons.

A divorce perhaps. A death. She didn't want to ask and believed that there'd have been no quick answer if she had. With some of the others she'd have thought straight off: he's married. Then, depending on the circumstances, decided what to do. Not now. Pieter – she'd yet to ask his second name – was surely what he seemed, a solitary, contented lowly former officer looking for amenable companionship. Older than she'd hoped for but no less interesting for that.

Then he'd said with a smile, 'But I know you, don't I? From somewhere . . .'

Perhaps, she agreed, and told him who she was. He'd probably seen her on the TV. The newspapers had made quite a fuss when she arrived too.

'Commissaris?' he asked, pretending he was scared. 'I'm having drinks with the big boss? Oh dear . . .'

'Not your boss. We're equals here.'

He shook his head.

'I was never equal to that kind of job. It requires someone . . . special. Not a man with big boots and . . .' He tapped his forehead. 'A tiny brain.'

After that he asked the questions no one ever did. About how she'd struggled up the police ladder. The personal costs of private ambition. The ways she'd deflected the occasional obstacles of prejudice and sexism and turned them to her advantage. She couldn't remember talking so freely since she arrived in Amsterdam. Two glasses of the Marsanne, a wine not as good as he thought perhaps, helped.

Then the inevitable. The invitation. He lived in a boat a short walk along the river. Would she care to see it? No strings attached. No expectations. Just a pleasant cup of coffee and then he'd call a taxi home.

'I wondered when you'd ask,' she told him, though when she walked it was a little unsteadily. Wine at lunchtime. Never a good idea.

A thought as they left and he paid the bill in cash. She looked at him and asked, 'You are discreet? A woman in my position—'

'Must be careful.' He gestured with his arms. 'I believe I am discreet. A decent man. But you must judge for yourself.'

'I'm good at that. Assessing people,' she told him and linked her arm in his, for support as much as anything. They walked along the path, away from the city, talking idly of the weather and the news, of politics and the state of the world. There was only a jogger or two down the narrow shingle track by the sluggish green water. On the right the fields were interspersed with bungalows and houses, vast gardens, swings and benches, fields with animals behind. It was hard to believe she was in Amsterdam at all. Then a cyclist tore towards them, shiny athletics gear, face and burly arms gleaming with sweat, yelling at them to get out of the way.

She did. He stood there, hand up, stopped the man and the briefest argument occurred. Curt, sure of himself, a big fist in the biker's face he read out a lesson about politeness and courtesy then let the mortified cyclist go on his way.

'I apologize,' he said. 'The modern world forgets itself at times and an old fool feels it falls to him to remedy matters. I'm very bad at looking the other way. You should know this. One of my many faults.'

'A fault?' She laughed. 'We need more like you. And me. People who care. Say what needs to be said when others won't. Do you know . . . ?'

She was about to say something about Marnixstraat and the officers there. Words that were somewhat unfair, she realized. She was a stranger in that place. They had been allowed to become set in their ways. Turning round a staid ship set in its ways was never going to be easy. The job had to be done by an outsider and there would always be casualties during the change. Not now. But soon.

'Do I know what?'

'I forgot what I was about to say. Where are we going?'

There was a ramshackle barge in front of them, scruffy and old. Beyond it sat two rowing boats, one old and fading white, the other more recent and bright yellow. A scruffy chap in ragged blue overalls stepped out of the barge, doffed his cap and said, 'Good day to the two of you.' He had a fishing rod in his hand. 'You will wish me luck I trust, Toine.'

The man with her saluted him and said, 'Tight lines.'

A smart cruiser was moored on the opposite bank in front of some rough ground covered in low scrub. There wasn't a soul on the footpath next to it.

'Mine,' he said proudly. 'I hope you'll like it.'

They walked to the yellow rowing boat. He held out his arm to help her. Jillian Chandra sat on the narrow bench seat. As he unhooked the rope from the bank she said, 'He called you Toine, didn't he?'

'Crazy,' he said, rolling a finger round his ear. 'A nice chap but truly, he's not with it most of the time. You must excuse me.' He pulled out his phone and turned it on. 'My daughter sometimes calls round now.'

He whistled a short refrain, an old song she dimly recognized but couldn't name. Then dipped the oars into the water and began to propel them to the other side.

Half the story Vos had guessed already. But not the letter. A suicide note from her younger sister, posted the day she threw herself off a tower block in Leiden.

The week before their father had been shot in an abortive police raid in Rotterdam, so badly wounded the doctors wondered if he'd survive. A final twist of the screw. The handwriting told a tale itself: careful, feminine. But there was a slant to it that spoke of anger and desperation, a need to get the details down before they vanished forever.

Hanna had been in Amsterdam with friends from Leiden for the weekend. A bar somewhere. Too many drinks. Separated from her group and then someone offered to help. A cocktail too along the way.

The next part he could barely read. She was half-awake for some of the time they assaulted her, desperately trying to pretend otherwise for fear of what they might do. Then the blackness fell and the next morning she woke cold and hurt in bushes in the Vondelpark, too ashamed to tell anyone, to do anything except make her way back to Leiden and a life that was forever changed.

There were names she'd heard when they were talking about what to do with her. De Graaf was one she'd recognized when he went to jail, Sanders another. And then a third who'd found his way to prison too: Braat. But there was a fourth, a man who'd hurt her more than the rest. He was quieter, more violent, even though he hadn't been there long. She never caught who he was, not that it mattered anyway because by the time she'd plucked up the courage to approach the Leiden police the woman in charge had rebuffed her. By then the drugs were taking hold. It had been more than two years since she was attacked. Why wait? Why would anyone believe her now? Who was really talking? Her? Or the drugs?

'She could have come to us,' Vos said.

Marly Kloosterman glared at him.

'Hanna was too scared to set foot in Amsterdam. She didn't dare. If the police wouldn't listen to her in Leiden . . . why would it be any different here?'

He thought of their brief relationship the year before.

'You might have told me.'

'I thought so too for a while,' she said wistfully. 'But you never called. Never phoned me back when I left a message. We needed someone we could trust.' She reached for a bottle of mineral water and took a swig. 'Then one day Jef Braat got free.'

Vos mumbled an apology, unable to find the right words. She listened, nodded, shrugged.

'Dad was pissed off with you. But really . . . what could you have done? Vincent wasn't talking. Braat was too scared. So Dad did what he'd learned. What he knew best. Hung around in De Pijp until he found Jef Braat. And his new friend. Made out he had the same kind of . . . interests. Worked his way inside.'

She picked up both photos, captivated by them, smiling to herself.

'The American . . . ?' he asked.

The smile vanished.

'Greg Launceston was a lunatic. Braat was a loose cannon. We should have guessed when he got that job in Artis. Kramer must have found it for him. Then regretted it. We weren't going to get a last name from either of them. Only Vincent and he was dying. I left him that phone. Dad fixed the messages. Made him think his friend of old was going to set him free for one last trip. No mention of a name, of course. He wouldn't expect it.'

She closed her eyes, rolled her head around as if it was stiff and painful.

'Vincent was all we had left. I lied when he said he didn't feel pain by the way. He did. A lot.'

The photos went back on the table.

'Sadly I couldn't be there when Dad got Lucas Kramer's name out of him. If only. I'd have stuck that cannula in him gladly. But I was owed. When it came to it Lucas Kramer was mine. It was so easy too. A creature like that would have swum that damned canal if he thought a woman was waiting for him on the other side.' She looked at him and smiled very deliberately. 'Just for the record he didn't attack me. Didn't get the chance. He thought it was all just sweet and fine. One more trophy for his list. This . . .' Her hands went to the wound on her neck. 'This was me.'

She clapped her hands.

'There you have it. I won't give you my father. Even if I had any idea where he is. Dad was always very strict about that. If you don't know you can't tell.'

'You phone him though,' Vos said.

'No. He always calls me. Withholds the number. I don't have one for him. Again . . . he learned it from you.'

'Oh, that's right,' Laura Bakker retorted. 'Blame us. Blame anybody but yourself. What about Annie Schrijver? She did nothing to hurt you. She was a victim too. She nearly died.'

Kloosterman laughed at that.

'Oh, please. I'm a doctor. Braat and the American had dragged her off to the boat by the time Dad turned up. He dealt with those two. I kept her sedated for a day. That was all. We didn't want her harmed. We saved her. Why do you think Dad got Pieter out to Zorgvlied to find her in the first place?'

Bakker punched the air.

'I'm sure she's going to feel really grateful.'

'Are you serious? One more idiot hanging round bars, messing with strangers, thinking the sky never falls. That kid needed a lesson. I hope she got it.' A thought then. 'I wish my kid sister had been that lucky. Anyway. It's finished now.'

'It's not finished,' Vos said.

'But it is. And you're out of time. Take me to Marnixstraat. Find me a lawyer. I'm done talking.'

Bakker shook her head and said, 'She really doesn't know.'

'Know what?'

Vos checked his phone. Nothing new from Van der Berg.

'The acting commissaris your sister talked to in Leiden was Jillian Chandra. The locals wanted to take the case. She was the one who told Hanna to get lost. Chandra's gone missing. We can't trace her.'

Marly Kloosterman thought about that.

'Is this some kind of joke? Chandra's been in the papers. On the TV. If she was the one Dad would have mentioned it.'

Vos waited, let it sink in.

'It's true. She kicked your sister out of the building in Leiden. It was no great secret the other officers there were appalled. Your father could have found that out easily. And he never told you. Why do you think that was?'

Marly Kloosterman glanced around the cabin.

'I've nothing more to say.'

Laura Bakker got close to her.

'He's out there. With the police officer he blames for Hanna's death. Why do you think he's hunted her down just like the others? For a friendly chat?'

There was a trill from the phone on the table. Marly picked it up, looked at the number, looked at them.

'Vos knows, Dad. Run and keep running. I love you.'

Before he could snatch the handset she lobbed the thing through the open windows. It turned round in the bright afternoon then fell with a splash into the grey-green waters of the canal.

'I'm sorry,' she said, staring at the ripples it left behind. 'For some things anyway.'

'Dry cleaning,' he said and pocketed the phone as they reached the bank. 'I'll pick it up later.' The cruiser looked just about big enough for one. The rear deck had a single chair and an umbrella on it. Thick grey curtains covered the windows. The yellow rowing boat he tied up next to a gangplank near the prow.

She felt giddy and had to hold on to his arm to stay upright when he helped her onto the bank.

'That wine . . .' It was funny. She never drank much usually. 'I shouldn't at lunchtime.'

'Come inside. Sit down. I'll make you a coffee.' A thought then. 'Do you fish? I mean, angling. Rod and line and hook. Like my crazy friend on the other bank.'

The question made her laugh.

'Of course not. Do you?'

He held her arm as she stepped unsteadily onto the boat.

'Oh yes. Ever since I was a child. In the sea. On the river. Lakes. Anywhere there are fish.' The door to the cabin had a heavy padlock on it. He unlocked the thing and placed it in his pocket. 'No point in throwing your bait into a stretch of water without them, is there?'

'A man needs a hobby,' she said, leaning against the handrail.

The river here was deserted. Only the scruffy boat opposite to see them. The odd man she'd spotted there was gone.

'It's not a hobby. It's a calling.'

Carefully, making sure she didn't trip, he led her inside. The cabin was small and cramped and poorly lit. Instead of opening the curtains he turned on a dim yellow overhead light. She sat down heavily on a low bench seat beneath the far window by the sort of small table she associated with caravans. There was a newspaper there, a small laptop, a cardboard box full of mobile phones.

'A calling?'

'One must prepare, organize, devise strategies. Understand the tides if it's the sea, the currents if it's . . .' He waved at the closed curtains. 'A stretch of water such as the Amstel. Then you prepare your weapons according to the prey. No point in trying to catch a perch on a pike rig, is there?'

'The coffee. I feel a little—'

'Once you identify your target you choose your line, your hook. Then position yourself on the bank or . . .' He nodded at the stern. 'The boat. And choose your bait.'

Chandra found it hard to keep her eyes open. She didn't feel sick. Didn't feel drunk. Just hopelessly incapacitated. If this turned wrong somehow, if he wasn't the man he appeared, there'd be no way she could fight back. At that moment she doubted she could even reach the door.

'The bait,' he repeated, leaning down to look at her very carefully, 'is important. It must be appropriate, right for the thing you want to catch. Without it your prey will never come near.'

His right hand, so strong, so gentle it had seemed to her, took her by the chin. Then with his left he opened her failing eyelids and stared at her, much as a doctor might.

'Jillian. Do you remember a young woman in Leiden?'

'What . . . ?'

He sat down next to her, so close his arm touched hers.

'She needed help.' His face was different, stern and disapproving. 'Her father was unable to offer that, you see. He was engaged in other matters. The call of duty. Not to his family but to others. To a badge. A cause that cared little for him. So he didn't know his own flesh and blood was in agony.'

'What are you . . . ?'

Even the words were hard.

'Lie down.' She couldn't stop him as he pushed her down on the hard bench seat then pulled out the cushion from beneath. 'It'll be easier that way.'

She did, had no alternative really, and found herself staring at the cream plastic ceiling, head spinning round and round so relentlessly she thought she could feel its whirling motion.

'Let me ask again. Do you remember that young woman?'

'No . . . I . . . what are you talking about?'

'A life.' His voice had risen. 'That's what. A young life lost. Discarded as if it had no value. By a thoughtless bureaucrat whose only thought was for her own career. Who believed . . .'

He pulled up a chair and moved to that, sitting beside her. Then he retrieved a plastic box from the floor, placed it on the table and opened the lid. A leaping fish was etched on the side, smiling at the line that had seized it from the water, oblivious to the sharp hook caught in its cheek.

'Believed what?' he wondered. He raised a finger in the too-hot humid, river-heavy air. 'Ah. I know.'

His eyes were on her then and they were cruel, judgemental.

'That there's no profit in the damaged and needy. No promotion or advantage to be found in a sorry and lost young woman pleading for help, begging for someone to listen to her. Aching to be believed.'

A rag came out of the box. Something from fishing, she thought, since it bore greasy brown marks and filthy organic stains. As easily as if he was wrapping a wound he tied it round her head, slipping the stinking gag between her teeth.

Her breath caught. Her gorge rose.

Then he reached down and grabbed the long gold necklace she'd picked out carefully, wondering where the day might lead. Raised it in his hand until she could see and ripped it from her neck. It didn't hurt much.

I am a bloody fool. I drank the wine he brought knowing it should have tasted better. Thinking these things happen to others, never me.

Jillian Chandra started to moan, tried to shape a pitiful plea for help, for mercy, for anything. But the drug and the gag and the fear meant all she could do was utter a low and pitiful whimper that no one heard but him, a man who was not called Pieter, a creature who didn't care.

The red silk shirt he ripped off next. By then she was barely conscious at all.

The uniforms cuffed Marly Kloosterman and put her in the back seat, pushing her head down the way they always did.

Bakker was still on the call. When she finished she watched the patrol car drive off and said, 'Nothing. Dirk's come up with nothing. How the hell are we going to find her?'

Vos pulled a number out of his phone and called. A voice so bright it took him aback said, '*Ja?*'

'Is that Annie Schrijver?'

'It was the last time I checked. Who is this?'

'Brigadier Vos. I really don't want to bother you—'

'Then don't,' she said and the line went dead.

Bakker watched as he hit redial.

'We need to talk, Annie. It's not about you. I know it's painful all the same . . .'

'Don't you get it, Vos? I'm out of all this.'

'We let Rob Sanders go. I thought you ought to know.'

A pause and then she said, 'That was on the news last night. What's this really about?'

'The man who woke you at Zorgvlied—'

'Do you never give up?'

'Not till it's done. Do you remember anything—?'

'Yes. He slapped me awake. Made me mumble something to my dad. And straight after that I blacked out again.'

'It wasn't the one we thought. He's still loose.'

She hesitated then said, 'Can't help. Your problem. Not mine. Bye.'

Bakker had been following every word.

'We need someone he dealt with, Pieter. Normally. Not pretending to be someone else.'

The Zuidas. Zorgvlied. Amstelpark. Everything happened around there. Brouwer surely couldn't be far away.

Again he called the park office. The same surly woman answered the phone.

'This is Brigadier Vos from the police. We spoke earlier. You didn't help me then. If you don't now I'll go to your superior and tell them you're obstructing a murder inquiry—'

'What murder inquiry?' she demanded. 'You were asking about Toine. He wouldn't hurt a fly. You should see him with the kids.'

'I need his address.'

'I told you! He's a volunteer. We don't—'

'The man has to be insured, for God's sake,' Vos barked. 'He's driving that train.'

Silence, then he heard the clattering of keys.

'Well,' she said eventually. 'There's an insurance address. Of course.'

'Where?'

'I'll be damned. Bovensluis in Willemstad. We've been there. It's a holiday camp. Nearly bought a chalet once but they were a bit pricey. There's a coincidence. Toine never mentioned it—'

A good hour and a half south of the city. A long commute.

'He didn't drive all that way, surely.'

'No,' she agreed. 'He didn't.'

It was like pulling teeth.

'So how did he turn up to work? By bike?'

'Now that's the funny thing.' She sounded very satisfied with herself. 'Most people do cycle here. I do. I'd say—'

'Please,' Vos begged. 'How?'

'I saw him sometimes. Toine walked. Came in the back way, the little footpath from Amsteldijk. No bike. Just him on foot.' She thought about that. 'He must have a place down by the water. More money than me . . .'

Like a winding artery, the river ran south into the open countryside that began beyond Zorgvlied. There was just a single crossing close to the park: the triple bridges that carried the busy ring road and the train tracks into the centre. Vos ordered a second team to take the area around the opposing bank. Bakker at the wheel, scanning the low, calm water, he headed for the eastern side.

Five minutes, light flashing, and a funeral procession blocked the single track road at the cemetery. A hearse bedecked with flowers, black saloons filled with grim, dark-suited mourners.

There was a logical reason Brouwer would have picked this area and he cursed himself for not seeing it. A base here would be close to Braat, make it easy to pounce when he and Launceston found their prey, started a new cycle. Before they'd even started assaulting Annie Schrijver in all probability. Maybe they'd invited him round.

They left the Volvo on the verge and headed for the nearest boats. One empty. On the deck of the other a young woman was busy with yoga on a mat next to a small altar burning incense. She didn't like being disturbed, didn't recognize Brouwer from the park photo or Chandra from the picture he had on his phone.

The funeral crawled slowly through the cemetery gates. The track ahead was clear until they reached a restaurant by the water next to a lane leading back into the Zuidas.

There was a waiter clearing up. Vos flashed the photos and his face lit up.

'They had lunch here.' He smiled. 'A friendly one.'

'Do you know where he lives?'

A frown.

'No. Somewhere close. He's been here quite a bit. Picky about his wine.' The waiter pointed down the river. 'They went off that way. She looked a bit worse for wear. Two glasses of white. I ask you.'

The next boat was a wreck. Vos was about to climb on board when someone shouted, 'Hi!'

Across the water, on the other bank, a tall man sat on a canvas chair in the stern of a cruiser. He had a fishing rod in one hand and a can of beer in the other. The hat he wore was familiar: floppy, broad, dark.

'What kept you, Vos?' he cried.

A bleary-looking individual of around sixty, bearded, probably half drunk, emerged from the barge in front of them.

'Who the hell are you two?' he asked.

'Police. I want your rowing boat.'

'Didn't say the magic word.'

'No, mate,' Bakker said, untying the battered dinghy from the bank. 'We didn't.'

Vos hadn't rowed since the days when he used to take his

daughter out on the lake at the park. He sculled across the grey-green water, watching Toine Brouwer sit idly on the back of his boat, casting, recasting, sending his line out into the depths.

'Call in backup,' Vos told Bakker. 'Medics too.'

When they got there she was first off, gun out, heading for the cruiser.

The cabin was empty. There were clothes strewn across the timber floor. A navy jacket. A torn silk shirt. Underwear.

Vos got past her and went to the back. An open cooler box stood next to the door, cans of beer poking out from ice.

Brouwer reeled in the line then swung something onto the boat: a stiff perch, spines, slime and blood, entangled in a set of fierce triple hooks. Dead bait, he said, unpicking it from the sharp metal, then threw the fish over the side, stood up and cast the empty rig very deliberately towards a patch of water close to mid-stream.

Bakker walked round him, weapon out, tense.

Toine Brouwer scowled at her, disappointed.

'Put that thing away, young lady. I'd rather not break your arm.' He nodded at the beers. 'Help yourself.'

'Where is she?' Vos asked.

He had bright eyes, the ghost of a smile, blood on his thick fingers as he reeled in his line.

'I knew I should have quit this place earlier. But the fishing. It's too good to waste.'

He eyed Bakker's gun again.

'Put it away, Laura,' Vos ordered.

With a grunt she holstered the weapon. There was nothing else near the boat. Just fields behind with a ragged line of bushes, shrubs and weeds. And the river. Vos couldn't stop thinking about the river.

Brouwer nodded and said, 'Thanks. You found me how exactly?'

'We looked,' Bakker told him.

The smile turned grim.

'Time you started, wasn't it?'

He heaved his rod up hard, striking at something beneath the water, trying to find purchase for those sharp triple hooks.

'Oh!' Brouwer's eyes lit up as the tip bent double. 'See. I said it was a good day for fishing.'

Something was getting dragged from the depths.

Bakker was on the phone, talking to control.

'Jillian Chandra?' Vos began.

He wasn't answering that question.

'As I said . . . you miss things. A pity. Everyone says you're a good man. My daughter especially and she's no fool. How's your dog? I'd never have hurt him. Not willingly.'

Vos walked over and sat on the side of the boat. The line ran taut into the water, forty-five degrees. Brouwer was having to work hard to bring in whatever was on the end.

'I'm sorry we didn't do better. Didn't find Lucas Kramer. Jillian Chandra isn't responsible for your daughter's death. She doesn't deserve—'

A scowl and he saw the violence in the man.

'Please. Don't demean yourself. Life's not about what you deserve. It's about what you take. What you get.' A shrug and another hard heave at the line. 'Still. Thanks for not saying it.'

'Saying what?'

'That my girl was beyond saving anyway. The damage was done. I was invisible. Her mother had given up. Had we been paying attention . . . Still, you should have done better.'

'It's not easy. Trying to stitch the world back together as fast as people manage to break it.'

Brouwer glared at him for that.

'Are you talking about me? Surely not. I spent most of my adult life working for the same people as you. What did I get in return?' He raised the rod again and reeled in more tight line. 'A bullet in the hip. A funeral I never hoped to see. One daughter dead. The other, her life ruined. A bastard for a husband who walked out just when she needed him. Night after night of agony wondering why I didn't see any of it coming. Why?'

Bakker was off the phone, scanning the area round the boat.

'Because I was being you. Caring about what others wanted when I should have been thinking about my own.'

'It's the job,' Laura Bakker cut in. 'You can't blame yourself for that.'

Puzzled, he said, 'Mostly I don't.'

Ten metres away a swirl of dark green weed appeared, writhing in the current like a long, sleek serpent.

A powerful draw on the rod, so bent it seemed about to break, then the thing broke the sluggish green surface just beyond the boat.

It was a blue tarpaulin bundle a couple of metres long. Black tape round the sides.

'Shit,' Bakker cried and grabbed the rod from him.

Toine Brouwer let her, stood up, wiped his hands, went to the cool box and picked out another beer. While he popped it Vos found a grubby cloth among the fishing gear, took hold of the line, tugged hard. The two of them hauled in the blue bundle, hand over hand.

When it was close enough Vos reached out and took hold of the edge, pulling it into the boat. A minute and more effort and then they had the thing on the deck.

'That's the delight of fishing,' Brouwer declared, raising his beer to them. 'The serendipity. The surprise. You never really know what's down there. You never see what's coming up next.'

She had her knife out, was sawing at the black tape, band by band. Vos tore at the plastic from the top as soon as he could. The tarpaulin opened. Dark green and slimy weed came pouring out.

Then a hand, bloodless and limp, two fingers clearly broken, flesh and bone showing through.

Vos ripped away the remaining ties. The rank stink of the river hit them and they saw a face streaked with weed, covered in bruises, a ragged cut above the eyes, a grimace halfway to a dead smile, neck to one side at a crazy angle.

Brouwer came and looked. Rob Sanders lay a stiff, drenched and bloodied corpse on the cruiser's shiny white deck.

'You should know . . . I'm a tidy man. I hate loose ends. When the news said you'd let him free, well . . .' He shrugged. 'It seems to be my lot in life to do the jobs that others deem beneath them.'

Vos took the corner of the plastic shroud and covered the dead man's face.

'Where's Commissaris Chandra?' Bakker demanded.

Brouwer sat down in the canvas chair, cut the fishing line with scissors and started to tidy away the gear, whistling to himself all the while. She lost it then, was yelling at him, too close. A trick.

'Laura . . .' Vos began, starting for them.

Brouwer moved. Arms up, one quick punch, he reached round, seized the Walther from her holster. Stood behind her, one hand round her neck, the other jabbing the barrel of the gun to her skull.

'You heard me, girl?' he asked, holding her tight as she struggled in his arms. 'Choose your time. Else the time chooses you and there's a world of hurt.'

'Let her go,' Vos said, measuring the moment, wondering how and when to strike.

He didn't need to. The barrel of the gun came away from Bakker's temple and Brouwer shoved her back towards the cabin.

'We're supposed to teach them lessons, Vos. This one needs them.'

There was the sound of a vehicle coming from the direction of the bridge. A blue light. A patrol car. Then another racing along the single track from the opposite direction.

Vos took a step towards him, held out his hand.

'Give me the gun. I want to know where Jillian Chandra is.'

'Don't want much, do you?' He shook his head. A shadow of despair darkened his face, a sign of a moment approaching.

The nose of the weapon nudged through Brouwer's close-clipped grey hair.

'Can you begin to imagine what memories, what sights I've got in here?'

Vos shrugged.

'You put them there. No one else.'

'I did. And I don't regret it. But if you think a man like me's going to fester in jail . . .'

Vos looked surprised.

'So you really want your daughter to stand in the dock alone? No one else to blame. No one by her side. No one to share the guilt. Not very brave. Or loving. The action of a caring parent. Is that what this is? Toine? Just an act? You're nothing but a common murderer?'

The man's hard grey eyes were on him.

'I made Marly do it.' He glanced at Bakker. 'I threatened her. You're my witnesses. You tell them that.'

The patrols were stopping in the lane. Two officers in each. The first pair saw them, came over, guns out. Vos waved them back, told them to start searching the river bank.

'All I ever wanted was for what happened to Hanna to be remembered. By you. By kids who walk out into the night and think there's nothing there but pleasure.'

'Won't be like that,' Vos told him. 'They won't even know her name.'

The gun came away. The barrel waved towards them.

'The only thing they'll remember is a police officer who turned as bad as the men he hated. It's Marly who'll pay. How many years do you think she'll spend inside? What—'

'This was me! All of it. You're my witnesses. I forced her . . .'

Vos shook his head.

'I didn't hear that. I'll say you told us it was her idea. She brought you here. Made you feel so guilty you had no choice. She arranged for De Graaf's release. Found Braat. Helped you kill the others and kept Lucas Kramer for herself. You were just the means. The plans were hers.'

'I heard that too,' Bakker added. 'How the pair of you let a damaged young woman be a victim twice over . . .'

'I saved that girl! Marly didn't even know until I called her. Tell them . . .'

Bakker reached for her plastic cuffs.

'You tell them, mate. We won't.'

'There's blood enough already,' Vos said, holding out his hand. 'Where's Chandra?'

Toine Brouwer looked at the crooked corpse by his feet. He turned the gun on Vos, then Bakker, mouthed one word for each: bang.

Then pulled the trigger, fired into thin air. Ducks and geese flew up from the rushes, squawking, terrified. He watched their anxious wings flap into the pale blue September sky, lobbed the weapon out over the river, turned his back, held his hands behind him, waiting.

'Deal with it,' Vos said and before the words were out she was clasping the cuffs round Toine Brouwer's wrists.

From the river bank came a shout.

They were young. Inexperienced. Wary. Scared. Two young men in uniform who'd blundered into the bushes by the gravel track that ran beside the Amstel. Standing there wide-eyed, waiting to be told what to do when Vos pushed through.

A shape lay at the bottom of a rough gulley half filled with water.

'Medics?' Vos said. 'The ambulance?'

On the way, one muttered. Things didn't happen in an instant. Mistakes weren't remedied in a heartbeat. Blunders went unnoticed until all you could do was mourn too late their making.

You're a clumsy man, Vos.

You miss things.

There was a shroud in the mud. A bed sheet by the looks of it, soiled and bloody, swaddled round something that didn't move.

Laura Bakker came to stand by him, hand to her mouth, eyes glistening. Behind was the sound of argument as the other uniforms crammed Toine Brouwer's big frame into their car.

Vos scrambled down the greasy bank, tripping, stumbling into the pit. Cold sludge came up to his ankles then his knees as he struggled towards the sad bundle.

'Get the damned ambulance!' Vos yelled, not taking his eyes away.

A clumsy man.

It wasn't that. Sometimes you didn't see enough. Sometimes the burden was so heavy it was easier to give up and look the other way. Not that it made the thing you were supposed to look at invisible. All it did was wait.

Head to toe the dirty fabric covered her. At one end there was blood leaking through the cotton.

Gingerly, with shaking fingers, he began to unroll the sheet.

Jillian Chandra was naked underneath, dirt on her brown skin, mucky gag around her mouth.

He reached for her wrist. Breath held tight, trying to hear the commotion growing behind him, he waited.

Cold flesh met his fingers as they reached for the soft hollow of her throat, felt for something there, the seconds ticking away in his head.

Vos eased the gag free. After what felt like an age the gentlest beat came back.

'Jillian . . .'

The first time he'd ever called her by that name.

Maybe that made a difference. Her olive eyes opened and she looked at him, half-doped, half-stupid, baffled, scared. Just the slightest flash of anger too and he was glad to see it.

'We're here. You're safe. It'll be fine.'

A klaxon sounded somewhere. The medics turning up at last.

She started coughing then sobbing, a deep, hurt sound, someone waking from a foul and unimaginable dream.

He tugged the cotton sheet round her. Then saw it. The thing that made the stain.

Three words scrawled on her shoulder, black ink, red blood and shredded skin. The tattoo, a last gift from an angry father determined to leave his mark upon the world.

Sleep Baby Sleep.

'You'll be fine,' Vos lied again.

The House of Dolls
by
DAVID HEWSON

Where dark secrets lurk behind every door . . .

Anneliese Vos, sixteen-year-old daughter of Amsterdam detective Pieter Vos, disappeared three years ago in mysterious circumstances. Her distraught father's desperate search reveals nothing and results in his departure from the police force.

Pieter now lives in a broken-down houseboat in the colourful Amsterdam neighbourhood of the Jordaan. One day, while Vos is wasting time at the Rijksmuseum staring at a doll's house that seems to be connected in some way to the case, Laura Bakker, a misfit trainee detective from the provinces, visits him. She's come to tell him that Katja Prins, daughter of an important local politician, has gone missing in circumstances similar to Anneliese's.

In the company of the intriguing and awkward Bakker, Vos finds himself drawn back into the life of a detective. A life which he thought he had left behind. Hoping against hope that somewhere will lie a clue to the fate of Anneliese, the daughter he blames himself for losing . . .

The Wrong Girl
by
DAVID HEWSON

She knew they would come for her. How long can she wait?

The arrival of Sinterklaas is an annual event which marks a high point in Amsterdam's calendar. The city is full of children trying to get a glimpse of their hero, and the police are out in force to manage the crowded streets and waterways.

Detective Pieter Vos is on duty with his young assistant, Laura Bakker, when the alarm is raised. A young girl wearing a pink jacket seems to have been kidnapped, but the ransom is not as expected, and it seems there could be a case of mistaken identity.

In the city of vice, tension runs high with opposing gangs protecting their individual patches and the security forces and the police frequently clashing over responsibility. When the perpetrator's horrifying demands become clear, the investigation is stepped up. What the police uncover is an operation so sinister, with such far-reaching implications internationally, that they have to work around the clock to find the true heart of evil – before it's too late.

Little Sister
by
DAVID HEWSON

Their family was killed. The price must be paid.

The Timmers sisters, Kim and Mia, were just eleven years old when they were accused of murdering the lead singer of a world-famous pop band in the Dutch fishing village of Volendam. They believed he was responsible for the death of their family, including their sister known as Little Jo.

Ten years have passed and it is now time for their release from Marken, the local psychiatric institution.

Pieter Vos, a detective with the Amsterdam police, is given cause to re-open the case when the girls disappear along with the nurse responsible for escorting them to a halfway house. The investigation uncovers a shocking cover-up which leaves one of Vos's closest colleagues under scrutiny.